of love & life

ISBN 978-0-276-44275-9

www.readersdigest.co.uk

The Reader's Digest Association Limited, 11 Westferry Circus, Canary Wharf, London E14 4HE

# of love & life

Three novels selected and condensed
by Reader's Digest

The Reader's Digest Association Limited, London

CONTENTS

Chance

More than twenty years ago, teenagers Holly,

Saffron, Olivia, Paul and Tom became firm

friends. Since then, their loves and lifestyles have

scattered them far and wide, and they would

probably have lost touch were it not for Tom

keeping them up-to-date with each other's news.

Then, tragically, Tom is killed and, as the group

gather to mourn him, they rediscover the true

power of friendship just when they need it most.

Prologue

THE WINE HAS BEEN DRUNK, the pasta demolished, three-quarters of the tiramisu polished off. Were you to peer through the window you might think you were looking at a group of old friends, laughing, catching up, and having a wonderful time, never seeing the gossamer-thin threads of grief that are woven between them, that have brought them together.

Look a little more closely and you'll see the way the brunette—Holly—has a tendency to gaze into her wineglass, lost in a memory as a tear wells up in the corner of one eye; how the blonde—Saffron—will lean over and ask gently if she's OK, lay a hand softly on her arm; how Holly will nod her head with a smile as she blinks the tears away and gets up to clear a dish that doesn't yet need clearing.

Observe how the thin girl with the short, dark bob watches them both with concern, her eyes softening as she sees how, even after all this time apart, Saffron doesn't feel the slightest bit awkward about reaching out to make Holly feel better. There is a part of Olivia that wants to be able to do this, too, but she has spent years trying to find comfort in her skin, in who she is, in being someone who has not followed the paths expected of her, not being a lawyer, or a doctor, or a super-successful, high-flying businesswoman, and while she thought she was happy, finding herself surrounded by her school friends has brought back those insecure feelings of old.

His name is not mentioned; they are too busy focusing on catching up. They go round the table, haltingly at first, as they fill one another in on where their lives have taken them.

'Short summaries please,' Paul requests with a grin. 'No more than two sentences to start off with, I think.'

Saffron looks at him in amazement. 'It's over twenty years since we left school and you haven't changed a bit. Still trying to be the boss.'

'Fine, I'll start,' he says. 'Freelance journalist for various newspapers. Quite successful, quite enjoy it. Evenings and some mornings spent writing the great British novel. Small house in Crouch End but fast car to make up for—'

'Small penis?' Olivia remarks.

'Not small—average I think but no complaints from Anna.'

'Tell us all about Anna.' Saffron raises an eyebrow.

'Swedish, thirty-nine, gorgeous. Also highly tolerant, given she puts up with me. As you know, founder of Fashionista.co.uk. As a result, she is frighteningly trendy, which is stunning given she's married to me. Desperate for children, have been trying for two years, and currently undergoing yet another bloody round of IVF, after which I think we may have to resign ourselves to having cats. Anna is the best thing that ever happened to me, but starting another cycle will turn her into the hormonal horror from hell, so not particularly looking forward to it.

'Hopefully'—he looks round the room and attempts a smile—'this time will be the last time; hopefully this will be successful. Keep everything crossed for us . . . Saffron? Your turn.'

'That was more than three sentences,' Saffron says softly. 'But I will keep everything crossed for you. So . . . me. Actress, a bit of theatre, hopefully big role coming in major film with Heath Ledger. Split time mostly between LA and New York. Am very happy with someone, but complicated so can't talk about it. No children, animals or other dependents, but good circle of friends. Although have to say, nothing like being with people you've known almost your entire life.' She looks at each person sitting around the table and smiles. 'Having a shared history is something you just can't create with the new friends. No matter how much you like them, it just isn't the same.'

'And . . . time's up,' says Paul, looking at his watch.

'My turn?' Olivia sighs. 'Where do I start?'

'At the beginning?' Paul offers helpfully.

'OK. Did drama at university, which was ridiculous really as nowhere near confident enough to be an actress.' She looks nervously at Saffron, who gives her an encouraging smile. 'Played around for a few years doing various jobs—worked at health food store, ran bookshop for a while, then asked to volunteer at animal sanctuary. Seven years later, run the place and love it. Gorgeous flat in Kensal Rise, and'—she takes a deep breath—'still single. Was in relationship with George for seven years, but he upped and left six months ago and is about to marry ghastly American girl called Cindy. I am now planning on turning into the crazy old woman with a million cats and dogs.'

'No one else on the horizon?' Paul is surprised.

'Well . . . oddly enough Tom put me in touch with someone from his American office. We've been emailing for a few weeks, and he's coming over here soon, but what was fun and sweet seems just awful now, since . . . since everything. I feel really weird about even meeting him now.'

'Bollocks,' Saffron says. 'You have to meet him, especially if Tom set it up.'

'You're probably right. I just feel completely unready for a relationship,' Olivia confesses.

'Darling.' Saffron shrugs dramatically. 'Who's talking relationship? I bet you haven't been laid for six months.'

Olivia blushes and looks over to Holly for help.

'OK,' Holly laughs as she interjects. 'My turn. That fine arts degree wasn't a complete waste of time as I've managed to make a somewhat decent living over the years. I'm an illustrator for a card company, although my dream is to work on children's books. Met Marcus in Australia at twenty-five; he seemed, on paper, to be everything I was supposed to be looking for in a husband, now rather think no one should get married before the age of thirty.'

Olivia raises an eyebrow as Saffron's eyes widen.

'Whoops,' Holly says, knowing that she has drunk too much. 'Did I say that out loud? Oh well. Two gorgeous children, Oliver and Daisy, and truthfully Marcus is a pillar of strength. Really. So strong. Harbour secret fantasies of running away with kids, but know that's just typical of an old married woman thinking the grass is always greener. Have to say, in all, life's pretty good.' Holly takes a deep breath. 'I sent Tom an email because I hadn't spoken to him in ages, but I never heard back. What about you lot? When did you last speak to him?' She looks up at each of them, and the tension, almost undetectable but nevertheless present all evening, dissipates.

Finally, it is safe to talk about Tom. They had spent the evening talking about themselves, reminiscing about school days, but none of them wanting to bring up Tom, none of them knowing the appropriate way to talk about him, knowing what to say. None of them ready to face the reason they were all sitting in this room.

Friends reunited. After twenty long years.

Chapter One

TOM WAKES UP FIRST. Lies in the blackness and sighs as he reaches over to turn off the alarm clock. Five thirty. He turns his head to see if Sarah has woken, but no. She is still soundly asleep.

He had packed the night before, so accustomed now to these business trips, to getting up in the middle of the night, looking out of the window to check that the car is waiting in the driveway, the driver killing time by reading the *New York Post*.

The payoff, as he and Sarah both know, is that these business trips and his life as the chief executive officer for a large software company won't go on for ever. He's thirty-nine now. Another two or three years and hopefully the kids will be set for life—some money already having been put aside for their college accounts—and he'll be able to retire, do something that doesn't involve travel time away from the family.

In the bathroom, he trips over Tickle Me Elmo and smiles at the memory of Dustin, two years old, giggling uncontrollably alongside Elmo until his older sister, Violet, grabs it away.

A hot shower, the last of the packing, and he's ready to go. Back into the bedroom to kiss Sarah on the cheek. 'Love you, Bunks,' he whispers, using their pet name for each other, a name they've been using for so long they don't even remember how it came to be. Sarah stirs and opens her eyes. 'Love you,' she murmurs. 'What time is it?'

'Just after six. The car's here. Are you going to get up?'

'Yup. Have to get the kids ready for the first day of school.'

'Promise me you'll take pictures of Dustin, OK?'

'OK, sweetie. Promise. Have a safe train journey.'

'I will. I'll call before I get on the train.'

''kay.' And Sarah smiles and sinks back into the pillows and falls asleep again before Tom has even made it to the front door.

Across the Atlantic Ocean, just as Tom's driver pulls out of the driveway, Holly Macintosh also wakes up. One a.m. She stumbles through her bedroom, hits the light switch just outside the doorway of her tiny bathroom, and sinks her head in her hands as she sits on the loo. This has started happening every night. At more or less the same time, Holly wakes up needing to pee, and by the time she climbs back into bed her mind is up and racing and she finds she is still awake when the sun comes up.

Yesterday she had just managed to fall back into a deep sleep when four-year-old Daisy came in, clad in mismatched socks, her younger brother Oliver's oversized Spiderman pyjamas and Holly's favourite cashmere scarf wrapped round her neck. Daisy demanded Weetabix and Holly stumbled out of bed, shooting daggers at Marcus, who, she was convinced, was merely pretending to be fast asleep.

Again, tonight, she lies in bed, her eyes closed, trying to ignore the occasional snore or grunt from her husband, too deep in sleep to notice her. When his snoring becomes too irritating to bear, she sits up and turns on the light, waiting as her husband stirs, then rolls over again, still sleeping. She gathers up a magazine from the pile on the floor next to their bed, resigning herself to yet another of those nights that render her almost senseless in the mornings.

Yesterday morning, Holly just about managed to get the children up and dressed. Frauke the au pair had stumbled down at the end of breakfast, and Holly had smiled gratefully as Frauke had bent down to get the children buttoned up, slapping some ham and cheese on pumpernickel bread for herself and holding it in her teeth as she took Daisy and Oliver by the hand.

Holly finds herself describing Frauke to friends as 'my grown-up daughter from my first marriage'. She feels endlessly thankful that Frauke, who is organised, strict, loving and happy, has come into her life. When Marcus goes to work and it is just Holly and Frauke alone with the kids, the house always feels lighter, happier, the energy changing entirely.

So tonight, awake again at 1 a.m., Holly gets up and makes herself a cup of tea, loving how quiet the house is in the middle of the night. This is the house she and Marcus lived in together before the children were born. It is in Brondesbury, north London, and when they had moved in, Holly knew that she would never leave. A house we can grow into, she thought. A house that will truly be a home. Five bedrooms for all the children she was convinced they would have, a large garden for barbeques and a huge, dilapidated kitchen that Holly started mentally reorganising as soon as they first saw it. Holly has bought every piece of furniture herself, has trawled through dusty, fusty antique shops. She still gets pleasure every time she comes home, and still, at least four times a week, she finds herself wandering around her house, leaning in doorways and looking at rooms, smiling at the home she has created.

In so many ways, Holly has exactly the life she always wanted. She has her gorgeous, adorable children—Daisy, who is like a mini-me of Holly, and Oliver, who is more serious, pensive, more like her husband. She has a career she loves—she is a freelance illustrator—and a husband who would appear to be the perfect husband. He is successful—a lawyer in one of the top family law firms, he has become the divorce lawyer of choice for several celebrities of late; he is tall and distinguished-looking in his bespoke suits and natty silk ties, the salt and pepper of his hair giving him a gravitas he only aspired to when he and Holly met. He has changed enormously, but Holly tries not to think about it, or at least tries not to dwell upon it.

Holly remembers a time when they used to go out with friends and she would wipe the tears of laughter away from her cheeks. She doesn't seem to have laughed with him for a long time, Marcus working longer and longer hours as his career has continued to shoot upwards.

They haven't seen friends either, for that matter, not for a while. Holly, who loves cooking, would regularly host dinner parties in the old days. She would actually have preferred casual kitchen suppers, but Marcus insisted on the best crystal being out, the silver cutlery. He insisted on eating in the dining room at the mahogany pedestal table with the Chippendale chairs.

Marcus has an awful lot of theories, particularly about what is *right* and what is *wrong;* how one is supposed to act; how children are supposed to behave; what is *common* and what is not. Holly thinks that people take Marcus at face value. She thinks that he has perfected his image as someone who comes from a good family, from old money, from aristocratic intelligentsia, and has managed to pull it off. Admittedly, the few friends from university who remember his parents, his childhood home, know that it is all an act, but they are still in his life because they have learned the art of discretion.

So Marcus has acquired manners and tact and graciousness and charm from Holly, but because none of it comes naturally to him, the charm has a habit of falling off, the manners have a tendency to disappear. He tries desperately to keep his mother, Joanie, down in Bristol, terrified that she will give his past away. And poor Joanie Carter, who longs to spend time with her grandchildren, doesn't know what to make of this son who speaks with more marbles in his mouth than the Queen. She's desperately proud of what he's achieved—the only mother in the town who has a son who's a lawyer and working his way towards becoming a partner. A partner! Who would have thought! But on a personal level, she has to admit she doesn't like him very much.

Joanie feels awful saying that about her son. How could she possibly feel that about her own flesh and blood? Joanie can see her son growing more and more self-important, more and more puffed up with pride, and she hopes, has always hoped, Holly will knock it out of him. She loves Holly and doesn't know how she puts up with Marcus. Marcus. Joanie sniffs every time she thinks of the name. He's not Marcus to her. Will only ever be Mark. Still, she loves those children and is thrilled when she talks to Holly. But she can't help but wonder what Mark and Holly are doing together, can't help but think that this may be the most peculiar match she's ever seen.

Holly could judge Marcus, could find the faults his mother finds unbearable but, on the whole, she doesn't. She knows that there is a different Marcus, wouldn't be with him still, surely, if there wasn't a different Marcus hiding behind the pomposity and grandness?

Holly knows that deep down, there is a frightened little boy who doesn't feel good enough; and in order to feel good enough, he has to surround himself with people he deems worthy.

It was one of the reasons he fell in love with Holly. She was everything he wanted to be, came from the background he wished he had, was the ultimate trophy wife. Except once he had her, he had to make sure she never thought she was better than he was, make sure that he was still able to feel superior.

Despite all this, Marcus has good points. For starters, he loves her or, at least, Holly believes he loves her. He is, when home, great with the children. Not for very long, and only when the children are behaving as he thinks appropriate, i.e., no screaming, whining, crying or hitting—all the behaviours, incidentally, that Holly has to put up with all the time—however, the children are too terrified to behave in ways anything other than exemplary, and, on those occasions, Holly's friends will watch him approvingly and murmur what a wonderful father he is.

And he is a wonderful husband, too, Holly tells herself during those moments in the middle of the night when she wakes up, gripped by panic, panic that she has nothing in common with him, that they are growing further and further apart.

Marcus wouldn't see this. Why would he when Holly, like most women, is a consummate chameleon? During the day when Marcus isn't around, she can be herself, can have girlfriends and their children round for lunch round the kitchen table.

And when Marcus comes home, she can slip into what he likes: crisp, dark jeans and a cashmere sweater, small diamond studs in her ears, or, if they're going out to supper, smart woollen trousers, high-heeled boots, a velvet jacket.

Holly finds herself running through the house every night before Marcus comes home, checking that all is exactly the way he likes it. The children are not allowed to build forts out of the sofa cushions in the living room, so Frauke is in charge of making sure Marcus doesn't know that almost every afternoon every cushion in the house is piled up in the centre of the room.

Holly's own father had stopped showing interest in her soon after the divorce. She remembers being fourteen years old and her father taking her to the soda fountain at Fortnum & Mason for tea. Over a huge chocolate sundae, he told her that he would always be there for her, and that he was going to see her every week and every other weekend.

For six months, he kept his word about seeing Holly. But then he met Celia Benson, and suddenly he was jetting off to Paris or Florence, or St Tropez with her, and soon he had a new family and Holly was largely ignored. Celia Benson didn't want the child from his first marriage around and her father acquiesced.

Is Holly happy? Happiness is not something Holly thinks about very often. She certainly has everything a woman could want in order to be happy, so how could she be anything but? The fact that they rarely have sex any more doesn't mean she's unhappy, surely? The fact that Holly finds herself withdrawing more and more from life, having already given up several friends Marcus deemed 'unsuitable', doesn't mean she's unhappy. Surely?

Her life is not quite what she expected it to be, but there are her children, for starters; her house and, of course, her work. As a freelance illustrator for Jubilation, a greetings-card company, Holly can lock herself away in her studio at the top of the house and lose herself in a delicate watercolour of a little girl and a puppy for hours. A couple of days a week she goes to the studio at the card company, mostly to remove herself from the isolation of working alone.

She hasn't been in that much recently, not least because of her exhaustion. Sleep is a growing problem, and Holly's defences are nowhere in sight when she wakes up in the night, her heart pounding with fears she refuses to acknowledge.

Now, sitting at the kitchen counter drinking her tea, Holly finds herself thinking about when she had last been truly happy. School? Well, no. She hadn't been happy at school, but outside school when she,

Olivia, Saffron, Paul and Tom had been together, then she'd been happy.

And at university—she and Tom, best friends, in love with one another since the day they'd met at fifteen, but somehow never managing to make it happen . . . those had been happy times.

Holly smiles as she remembers. She hasn't spoken to Tom for weeks. They kept in touch for ages with phone calls, then dwindling emails; but once Tom had met Sarah, who had been working in his London office, and then moved to her home town in America to marry her, their friendship never seemed quite the same.

Every now and then Holly will spend an afternoon Googling friends from a previous life, hence her discovery, some years ago, of a picture of a smiling Olivia holding a kitten at a fund-raising event. Olivia, Holly had discovered, worked for an animal refuge. She looked much the same as she did when they'd last met by chance shortly after finishing university. Holly had sent her an email after seeing the item on Google, to which Olivia had responded warmly, but somehow they had never managed to follow through.

Saffron is now a semi-famous actress trying to become a movie star in Los Angeles. She has been in several low-budget British films, has had small parts in major films and is often recognised in the streets. She is regularly profiled in British magazines and newspapers as the next big thing.

Holly hasn't seen Paul for years, although he and Tom have kept in touch. Now and then Tom'd send Holly an email, making her laugh with stories of what Paul, the eternal womaniser, was up to.

Holly remembers sitting at the hairdresser's, flicking through *Vogue,* when she turned the page and came across Paul, lounging across a sofa, dressed head to toe in Prada, with a gorgeous blonde draped between his legs, a Chloé dress on her spectacular figure.

Her mouth had dropped open as she started reading about Paul Eddison, journalist and man-about-town, and his marriage to Anna Johanssen, founder and CEO of Fashionista.uk.net.

Of course Tom had told her that Paul was getting married, but she had no idea it was such a big deal. She was stunned by how trendy he had become, but when she'd phoned Tom to squeal about it, Tom had just laughed.

'It's not what he looks like,' Tom said. 'Paul's still exactly the same. He's still happiest in his scruffy old jeans and T-shirts with holes in them.'

'I don't know,' Holly had said dubiously. 'It sure as hell looks as if he's changed. What's she like, anyway? She looks terrifying.'

Tom had shaken his head in sorrow. 'Don't be jealous, Holly. She's lovely. She's incredibly sweet, and she adores him.'

'You're right. I was making assumptions because she is stunning. Lucky Paul. Lucky couple,' she sighed. 'Looks like they have a completely glamorous, perfect life.'

'*Vogue* made it look like that,' Tom said, serious now, 'but trust me, their life isn't as glamorous as it looks. Nobody's life is perfect.'

'Mine is,' Holly said wryly, and Tom had snorted.

With these memories Holly gets up from the kitchen counter and switches on her computer. Why not email Tom now? It's been ages since their last contact and she misses him. He and Marcus had never seemed to gel, and Sarah wasn't exactly Holly's cup of tea, hence their drifting apart.

She had first met Sarah after she got back from the trip to Australia, during which she had met Marcus, whom she'd married a year later. She hadn't spoken to Tom the entire six months she'd been away, and soon after she got home and got back in touch, Tom had started talking about this cute American girl who was working in their London office.

'How's the Yank?' Holly would tease, secure once again in their friendship now she had Marcus, unable to believe that she had ever thought of Tom as anything other than her best friend, even after that night . . .

'She's pretty amazing actually,' Tom would say hesitantly, going on to tell Holly how much she would love this Sarah, how he couldn't wait for them to meet, how they should get together as a foursome.

And so they did. The four of them going to a pizza place in Notting Hill one night, Holly excited about meeting this girl that Tom had been talking about for so long, who had now become his girlfriend, who was soon to move in with him.

Holly wanted to love her. Was convinced she would love her, but she found Sarah to be prim, proper and cold.

'God, she's awful,' she'd hissed to Marcus when they were safely in their car on the way home. 'What does he see in her?'

'She's quite sexy in a standoffish kind of way,' Marcus said, instantly regretting it as he watched Holly's eyes narrow.

'Sexy? What's sexy about her? What? Because she's addicted to the gym? Is that why she's sexy? She's had a complete sense of humour bypass as far as I'm concerned plus she's intense beyond anything I've ever known. Does this woman even know the meaning of the word "relax"?'

'You liked her then?' Marcus had said with a grin.

'**D**id you like her?' Tom had phoned first thing from the office.

'I thought she was great,' Holly lied smoothly.

'Isn't she? I knew you'd think so.'

'She's quite serious though,' Holly had ventured.

'Is she? It's probably because she doesn't know you that well. You'll get to know her better once she's moved in.'

'What about us?' Holly's curiosity got the better of her. 'Did she like us?'

'Oh yes,' Tom lied smoothly. 'Very much. She thought you were both great.'

And that was the start of the wedge that lodged itself into the heart of Tom and Holly's relationship. At first just a splinter, but the more the four of them endured one another, attempting to find a way of turning Holly and Tom's friendship into an equal friendship among the four of them, the larger the splinter grew.

Holly always thought of Sarah as Scary Sarah. It had slipped out once, by accident, when she and Tom were having lunch. It was still a shared private joke between them, something that indicated the intimacy they had had before.

Hey stranger! Holly taps into the computer, as sleep continues to elude her. As usual I just woke up in the middle of the night . . . and I've been thinking about my past and realise it's been ages since we spoke. How are you? How's Sarah? And those little munchkins? How's Paul? Any little ones yet? Would love to hear from you. Actually, would love to see you—can't you do a business trip over here? Anyway, thinking of you and sending you much love. Send my love to Scary Sarah. Big kiss, Holly xxxxx

Much later, Holly found out where Sarah was at the precise moment Holly hit the SEND button on her computer.

Sarah was shouting up the stairs to Violet to hurry up or they would be late for school. Violet is four, in her last year of preschool before starting kindergarten, and as slow as molasses, particularly when her mother is in a hurry.

'Come on, honey!' Sarah had shouted. 'It's your first day, we don't want to be late. Oh, Violet!' she had said, as Violet appeared in the doorway of her bedroom, naked, clutching her threadbare pet elephant. 'I asked you to get dressed!' Sarah had snapped as Violet started to cry.

'Oh God,' Sarah had muttered. 'Please give me patience.' She took a deep breath. I will not shout at the kids this morning, she told herself. So what if we're a bit late? It doesn't matter. Feeling more calm, she grabbed her bag and took the kids down to the car.

An hour later—so many mothers to catch up with in the car park—Sarah had been about to get in the car when Judy, another mother, raced up, her face stricken.

'Have you heard?' she said, her eyes wide with horror.

'What, what?' The mothers gathered around her, some turning as cellphones started to ring simultaneously.

'Another terrorist attack! They bombed the Acela!'

Sarah's focus shifted as everything became fuzzy. The Acela Express. That can't be right. Tom was on the Acela.

'No!' came the clamour of voices. 'What happened? Is it bad?'

'I don't know,' Judy said. 'Happened just outside New York. Oh God, we're bound to know someone.'

And all eyes suddenly turned to Sarah, who found herself sitting on the floor of the car park, her legs having given way.

Holly Macintosh wakes up, as she has woken up every morning since she heard the news, and feels the weight of grief settle upon her chest.

It is all she can do these days to get out of bed, to go to the kitchen and pour herself a coffee with shaking hand, to sit at the kitchen table lost in a cloud of memories, of things unsaid, of might-have-beens and of missing Tom—the Tom she grew up with and the Tom she will never see again—so very, very much.

She shakes it by breakfast, has to for the sake of the children. Marcus has been wonderful. When he got home on the day she'd found out, Holly had collapsed in tears and Marcus had wrapped his arms round her as the children had looked on, fear etched in their eyes.

'Why is Mummy crying?' Oliver asked.

'Mummy's sad because she's lost one of her friends,' Marcus said softly over the top of Holly's head.

'Shall I help you find them?' Daisy said after a pause, and Holly was able to smile through her tears.

Just three days earlier, Holly had watched the footage on the news with Marcus. One hundred and forty-seven people dead. Since then she had shaken her head with her friends and they had spoken about how unbelievable it was, how they lived in a different world, how they wondered whether it could ever end.

And then one afternoon, while on the Internet, she had found a list of names on the BBC News web site. I wonder if I know anyone? came the thought. Unlikely, she knew, but she clicked on the page and started to read.

Names. Brief biographies. A banker from Islington, in New York for a business trip; a mother and daughter from Derbyshire, there on a brief holiday; Tom Fitzgerald, a software chief . . .

Holly kept reading, then her eyes went back to his name and she reread it a few times. *Tom Fitzgerald. A software chief* . . . Tom Fitzgerald . . . *Tom!*

But it couldn't be. This happened outside New York. Tom is in Boston. Confusion swept over her as she picked up the phone to call Tom at work, but it was now night-time, and she dialled the home number.

'Hi, this is Tom, Sarah, Dustin and Violet,' Sarah's voice singsongs down the phone, lending this phone call a normality that makes Holly think perhaps she is imagining all this. How could the message still be the same if something terrible has happened to Tom?

'Oh, hi. Sarah, Tom, it's Holly.' She spoke haltingly, unsure, Googling Tom's name as she spoke, looking for more information. 'Um, I just . . . I was reading . . . God. *Sorry.* But can you call me? Please? I . . .'

There was nothing else to say. She finds another article. *Tom Fitzgerald, chief executive officer for Synopac, was on the doomed Acela Express on his way to a business meeting . . .*

The phone was placed back in the receiver in slow motion.

'Holly?' Frauke had come into the room. 'Is everything OK?'

And Holly had turned to her, stricken. 'It's Tom,' she had managed to whisper eventually. 'He's my oldest friend. On the train . . .' and she had stopped speaking as the sobs took over and Frauke had rushed over to comfort her.

At thirty-nine years old, perhaps it is not surprising that Holly had not fully known grief. She had had a passing acquaintance—various elderly relatives had died over the years—and Holly had naturally been upset at the time, but you could accept that this was their time or, if not their time, they had at least managed to live a full and fulfilling life.

But this was something entirely different. This was a deep, searing, tearing, raw grief. This was with Holly all the time. It woke her up in the morning by settling itself on her chest, sank down on the floor with her as she collapsed in sobs next to her desk.

She had taken a week off working altogether, going back into the studio at Jubilation feeling numb, but thinking she would be better off being surrounded by people, having to make conversation.

'I heard you knew someone who died on the Acela Express,' a man who worked in Marketing had said nonchalantly in a meeting. 'Awful thing, wasn't it?' He'd shaken his head, preparing to move on to the business at hand—Holly presenting her drawings of elephants for their new line of belated birthday cards. 'I just can't believe what's happening in the world today.'

And Holly, who was replaying the tape in her head of the train blowing up in flames, had looked up at the man and the tears had started falling again.

'I'm sorry,' she said. 'I don't understand how this could happen to Tom. This just doesn't make sense to me . . .' and her shoulders had started heaving, her body wracked with sobs as her colleagues looked on nervously, none of them knowing quite what to say, all of them wanting to climb back into their comfort zone, to have the old Holly back.

'I'll take her out,' mouthed Simone, leading Holly out of the door and into the small kitchenette, gathering her in her arms, and letting Holly sob.

'You need to take a break,' Simone said when Holly had finished. 'Grief is a process you have to work through, and you certainly shouldn't be in here. Take some time, a month, at least.' Holly nodded mutely and looked down at her hands, unable to meet Simone's eyes.

Things like this aren't supposed to happen to people like me and Tom, she thought, as she gathered her things and allowed herself to be put in a radiocab back home. *This was not supposed to happen.*

But she can't sit there doing nothing, replaying all the memories, all the horror stories in her head of how Tom might have died, how it must have felt.

Do the others know? Their gang from school, people she hasn't spoken to for years, but who suddenly seem as close as the day they finished their A-levels, old friends she is now compelled to see.

She phones Paul first. Given his high-profile wife, he is easy to track down. A phone call to Anna Johanssen at Fashionista.co.uk, an urgent message left with the assistant for Paul to call.

'Holly Mac!' he said later that day when he phoned. 'How lovely to hear from you, what a tremendous surprise!'

'Well actually . . .' Holly pauses. She hadn't worked out what she was going to say, the right words to use.

But of course there are no right words to say that someone you both love has died. Holly has cried more tears these last few days than she thought possible. Her head feels woollen, she is exhausted with the constant thump of a headache from too much crying. And now that she has Paul on the phone, Paul with whom she knows Tom was still in touch, Holly cannot believe that she must be the one to tell him the news. She had half hoped he would know.

'I'm not phoning up with good news, I'm afraid,' Holly says, her voice dropping. 'It's Tom.'

'Tom?'

'Yes. You know he and Sarah live in Boston. He was on a business trip to New York, and he was on the train that was bombed . . .'

There is a gasp and a long silence.

'You mean he's dead?' Paul's shock comes down the phone.

'Yes. Tom's dead.'

A long silence. Then a whisper. 'I don't believe it.' There are a few muffled moments as Paul turns away from the phone. When he comes back, his voice is already starting to break. 'Give me your number. I'll have to call you back.' And as his voice cracks he puts down the phone.

An hour later he calls back.

'I've spoken to Tom's dad,' Paul says. 'The funeral is family only. He said they know how many people would want to come, so they've decided to have two memorial services. There's one in America, I think, and then one in England at the family church on the thirtieth. I thought maybe we could all go to that together. I've spoken to Saffron and she's going to fly over here. Will you speak to Olivia? I know this is crazy, that none of us have seen each other in years, but I thought maybe we could all have dinner the night before . . .'

'Yes.' Holly says quietly. 'That's a wonderful idea. I'd love you all to come here.'

'Then we will,' Paul says. 'October 29th?'

'October 29th,' Holly repeats quietly. 'I'll see you then.'

Paul puts the phone down in the cradle, not noticing how much it is clattering, how his hand is shaking uncontrollably.

He makes his way from the desk to the sofa, numb. His thoughts are a jumble. The phone rings and he can't move, can't pick it up. It was all he could do to call the others, but he had to, had to do something before he could call Holly back. But then he hears Anna's voice on the answering machine and he rushes over, the safety and familiarity of hearing the woman he loves bringing him back just for a moment.

'Hey!' Anna says as he picks up. 'Where were you? I thought you were going to be stuck to your desk for the whole afternoon. I got your message. Is everything OK?'

'I . . .' He doesn't know how to say it, how to fit his mouth round the words.

There is a silence and Anna takes a sharp intake of breath, knowing suddenly that there is something terribly wrong.

'What is it, Paul? What's happened?'

'It's Tom,' he says, his voice flatter and darker than Anna has ever heard it. 'He was on that New York train. He's dead.'

Another sharp intake from Anna, and then her business side takes over. 'Stay where you are,' she commands. 'I am coming home now.'

Chapter Two

THE GIRLS' SCHOOL where Holly, Saffron and Olivia met sits high up on a hill in one of London's leafier suburbs.

ST CATHERINE'S PRIVATE SCHOOL FOR GIRLS says the sign outside. Although if you drive past at 3.20 p.m. on a weekday, you won't see the sign for the swarms of girls, large and small, identically dressed in burgundy pleated skirts and white shirts.

Nestled in the valley of the leafy suburbs a few streets away is St Joseph's Private School, yang to St Catherine's yin, home of St Catherine's male counterparts, recipients of thousands of schoolgirl crushes over the years.

Holly had been a late starter when it came to boys. The other girls in her class had seemed to discover them around twelve, but apart from a crush on Donny Osmond when she was a little girl, Holly had not really understood what all the fuss was about. Olivia, her best friend since they had started senior school, was exactly the same. Both of them were slightly worried about Saffron, who had always been just like them but in the last six months had started getting in with a crowd that already wore make-up, already had boyfriends, met up after school every day with a gang from St Joseph's, usually going to someone's house to listen to LPs—Madness, Police, David Bowie—in someone's bedroom, while an unconcerned mother sat chatting on the phone to a friend, unaware and probably not caring what a group of eight teenage boys and girls were doing behind a locked bedroom door.

And then came Saffron's birthday. Her fifteenth. Her parents had let her rent out a youth club, and she was determined to have the best party anyone had ever seen. Someone's older brother was doing the music, friends of said older brother were going to be bouncers because there had already been three parties this year at the youth club and teenagers from all over the area had come, whether invited or not.

Holly and Olivia were in almost matching outfits of grey rah-rah skirts, pink off-the-shoulder sweatshirts and striped leg warmers with—oh thank you, Mum!—*jazz shoes*. Real, proper jazz shoes that everyone wanted but nobody had.

The hall of the youth club was so dark it was almost impossible to see anything. As promised, Saffron had rigged up the disco ball, which spun round slowly—small squares of light rotating round the room, lighting up the groups of people who had gathered in corners.

The bouncers turned out to be ineffective. It seemed the entire year of lower fifth from St Joseph's had got in, whether invited or not. They stood at the side of the room, eyeing up the girls, putting on macho displays, a group of male peacocks strutting around showing their feathers as the girls giggled and played along.

'Do you want to dance?' Holly had been sitting with Olivia and she looked up into sweet, eager brown eyes.

'Sure,' Holly said awkwardly, turning to Olivia with a grin and a shrug as if to ask, 'What could I say?' Self-consciously, she followed the boy onto the dance floor, relieved the room was as dark as it was, knowing that every eye was upon them, that she would be the centre of attention tomorrow, and finally having a slight understanding of what it is to be a girl, what it is to attract boys, and how addictive that feeling of power is.

'I'm Tom,' he said, bopping in front of her with a grin.

'I'm Holly,' she said, switching feet, hoping she looked cool.

'I know.' He grinned. 'I've seen you before.'

'Oh. OK.' Pause for a few seconds. 'Where?'

'Just around.'

They danced to Adam Ant, Michael Jackson, and Human League. And then 'Every Breath You Take' by The Police came on, and Tom opened his arms, and Holly wrapped herself around him.

Together they stood, barely moving, rocking gently from side to side, and Holly had never felt so safe before, her head resting on someone else's shoulder, wrapped tightly in someone's arms.

Through Culture Club, then Lionel Richie and Christopher Cross, Holly and Tom didn't move. Holly felt as if she had been waiting her whole entire life for this moment, and, in a flash of light, she knew what everyone was talking about. She understood about boys. She understood about love. And by the end of the night, she knew that Tom Fitzgerald was her soul mate.

When Tom asked for her phone number, she thought she would burst with happiness. He phoned the next day and they talked for an hour and a half. She gleefully reported every sentence of their conversation to Olivia, who felt slightly left out and didn't quite understand what all the fuss was about. And so Holly turned to Saffron, and soon Holly and Saffron were sitting on the phone every night talking either about Tom or his best friend, Paul, who Saffron fancied.

It didn't strike Holly as odd that Tom and she never kissed. She knew it was only a matter of time. What they did was talk.

And laugh. They, and soon a large group of them, would go out every weekend. They'd meet up at the park and just sit on the swings for hours, a curious mix of adult and child, trying to act older than their years, yet still young enough to shriek with laughter as they squeezed down a slide.

Soon, Holly's crush on Tom dissipated. Daniel joined the group—taller, louder, funnier than Tom—and within weeks Holly and Daniel were propped up against every available wall, snogging for hours, Holly feeling so grown up, so sophisticated.

Tom became her best friend. When Daniel dumped Holly for Lisa, Tom was the one who comforted Holly, who confessed that he had fancied her when they first met but that now he was glad they were just friends, especially since he'd now started going out with Isabelle.

And of course Holly, who had got over Tom completely, found herself developing a major crush on him again. Except by the time Tom and Isabelle split up, she was going out with Dom Parks. By the time Holly and Tom rediscovered their friendship, A-levels were looming and surely they both knew one another far too well by now for there to be anything between them other than friendship?

Olivia found animals more interesting than boys, but eventually, as they were preparing for their 0-levels, she developed a crush on her maths tutor. Ben was a first-year student at Durham University, only three years older than Olivia, but a maths genius whose mother was a friend of Olivia's mother, hence the tutoring arrangement that Olivia was initially furious about.

Furious until Ben walked in. Quiet. Studious. Gentle. Olivia finally realised what everyone else had been talking about, and for the next two years she carried the weight of her crush in her heart, fantasising about Ben admitting he'd fallen in love with her.

The day finally came in the upper sixth, when she had passed her Maths 0-level with a B and had run out of excuses to see Ben. Her mother mentioned one day she had to go over to see Ben's mother and that Ben was down from university. Olivia had jumped in the car, desperate to show him how grown-up she was and how perfect she would be for him.

And he had noticed. He had noticed and he had liked; he had been surprised at how easy she was to talk to, how sweet she seemed.

Ben had taken her to a film that weekend and then out to the Queen's Arms for a drink a couple of nights later. Olivia had invited him to a party the next weekend, slightly apprehensive about Ben meeting her friends, worried he would find them too young, but after he'd told her how much he liked them, he'd kissed her, and Olivia had floated up to her A-levels on a cloud of joy.

They all studied together for their A-levels. At the local library, Holly, Olivia, Saffron, Tom, Paul, and sometimes a couple of others, would grab a table upstairs, throw their books open and whisper to one another as they worked.

Over twenty years ago and Holly remembers it as if it were yesterday. She remembers when Holly loved Tom, and knew that there would never be another Tom. How Tom and Paul had the same jacket in different colours. They had, in fact, bought them together one Sunday morning down at Camden Market, the five of them weaving their way through the crowds on Chalk Farm Road, cool, confident, indestructible.

Tom's jacket was navy. Paul's was green. Holly's heart used to lift when she saw Tom's jacket. Just a glimpse of navy in those early days would send her heart soaring, stick a smile on her face that seemed to last for weeks.

Holly remembers how Tom used to smile at her across the desk as they worked in the library. Sometimes she'd be buried in revision and she'd look up and catch his eye and he'd grin. Even when she was over her crush, knew that Tom probably wasn't the one for her, no longer spent nights crying in her bed as she listened over and over again to the soundtrack of *Endless Love*. Even then she knew that whatever she and Tom had, it was special.

And that maybe at some point in the future they would find one another again.

Holly spreads photos out on the floor and starts to move them around, sifting through for the photos from school, photos of Tom, needing to see him again if only in a photograph.

She pulls one from the pile. It's Tom and some girl. Holly had been at Tom's flat when she had seen the photo, in one of her phases when she had been in love with Tom, but gently, one of the resigned phases where she didn't expect anything to happen. She had seen the photo and had demanded to have it because Tom looked so handsome.

Tom had cracked up laughing when Holly had said she was taking it. 'I'm going to cut her out and stick me in instead,' she had said with an evil glint, and Tom had shaken his head as if he didn't know what to do with Holly, which he didn't. She was, in turn, funny, delightful, warm, wise and insufferable, jealous, insecure and impossible. He loved her but didn't know how he could live with her. He loved her but wasn't in love with her. Not today, at least. She was just Holly Mac. Someone that would always be a part of him. As he would always be a part of her.

Holly gathers all the photos of Tom and stares at them, one by one, thinking back, emerging from her reverie only to answer a ringing phone.

'Hello?'

'Holly?' It's a familiar voice from a long time ago.

There's a pause as Holly nods, the voice trying to place itself, stopping her from speaking.

'It's Saffron.'

'Oh, Saff.' Holly starts to cry. 'Tom.'

There are tears on the other end of the line. 'I know,' Saffron says, her voice uneven and small. 'Tom.'

Olivia steps through the door of her basement flat and flicks the light switch on as her three cats and two dogs come running over to greet her excitedly. She bends down to cuddle them, folding her lips inwards as the dogs lick her all over her face, then walking through her flat turning on all the lights and all the table lamps until there is a warm glow throughout.

Grabbing the leads from the pegs by the front door, she clips them onto the dogs as they whirl around in joyous delight. She allows them to drag her up the front steps, turning once at the top to look back at her flat, which looks warm and welcoming even from the busy street.

Olivia never used to keep all the lights on, but since she and George split up, coming home to a dark flat makes her feel far more alone than is altogether necessary, and her routine now involves whisking the dogs out for a walk and returning to a flat that could almost, *almost,* have a husband lying on the sofa reading the papers.

Except it doesn't. Not any more.

Not that George was her husband, but since she was with him for seven years, he might as well have been, and frankly she wouldn't have stayed with him all that time if she didn't think that at some point they would be walking down the aisle.

Olivia was thirty-two when she'd met George. Fantastically happy with her job as deputy director of the animal refuge, oblivious to the dating world unless one of her well-meaning friends set her up on a blind date—most of whom, Tom always said, would fall madly in love with her, and none of whom she was particularly interested in.

She had never wanted children—her animals were her babies, she always said, and she was close to Ruby and Oscar, her niece and nephew, as close as she ever wanted to be—so didn't feel the pressing ticking of the biological clock and was quite happy with everything in her life. Then George turned up one day to find a dog, and her life turned upside down.

It was his sweetness that did it for her. That, and the fact that he was as lovely with his three-year-old as he was with the animals. She leaned in the doorway and watched him play with one of her favourite dogs, Lady, a dog that no one would adopt because she was eleven years old and deeply terrified of people.

George had taken his daughter, Jessica, into the meet-and-greet room, and Olivia had brought Lady in, crouching down with her and soothing her.

And George hadn't done what most people in this situation would do. He hadn't advanced on Lady, crooning in an attempt to make her feel comfortable, overwhelming and crowding her, he had just sat at the other end of the room, Jessica sitting next to him, and he had watched Lady as he talked to Olivia.

'We have an open house next Sunday,' Olivia had volunteered. 'It's our big annual fund-raiser. We have stalls and games and pony rides. And the kids get to play with some of the animals.'

'Oh, we'd love that,' George said. 'Next weekend you're with Mummy though, but I'm sure she'd let you come with me.'

Ah, Olivia thought, her heart fluttering in a way she'd almost forgotten. Divorced. But he couldn't be single, not this kind, lovely, gentle man. Surely he had a girlfriend, someone.

George and Jessica came for the entire day. He bought twenty-four raffle tickets and won a course of pony rides for Jessica (I think you may have to wait until she's a little older, Olivia said with a smile), a giant bag of dog food, and dinner for two at Chez Vincent in the high street.

'As the deputy director of the refuge,' George said, having collected his prizes, 'I hope you'll be my guest at Chez Vincent.'

'Oh . . . um . . .' Olivia flushed. 'Well, yes. I'd love to.'

One dinner became many, which became a relationship, which became months, then a year.

After a year Olivia's mother sat her down and asked whether George was planning on marrying her. Olivia's mother had divorced her father five years ago, and Olivia was surprised that, given this unexpected turn of events, her mother still seemed to think that marriage was the very pinnacle of achievement for a woman.

Olivia's mother continued to ask, on a regular basis, whether they were planning a wedding soon, inevitably sniffing and stating, to end the conversation, 'Of course he's never going to do it. Why buy the cow when you can get the milk for free?'

'Mum!' Olivia had reprimanded her sharply. 'I don't know when we're getting married. Or even *if* we're getting married. We're quite happy as we are.'

Which was true. There was no doubt in Olivia's mind that she and George were utterly committed to each other. They had Jessie every other weekend, which was easy for Olivia since Jessie loved animals. And Ruby and Oscar adored Jessica. Olivia's sister, Jen, would drop the kids at Olivia's almost every weekend they had Jessie, and when she and George went out with all of them, everyone would tell her what gorgeous children they had.

One year became two, then three, and after seven years, Olivia knew that she was going to be spending the rest of her life with George, ring or no ring.

Until the night they went out for dinner and George announced that he was one of the people going out to New York to get the American office of his advertising firm up and running.

'New York?' Olivia felt as if the air had been knocked out of her. What could she possibly do in New York? What about the refuge?

'I'm going alone,' George said gently.

'What do you mean?' Olivia hadn't understood. 'What about Jessica?'

George sighed. 'This has been the hardest thing. I get her for the entire holidays, every school holiday, and I'm going to try to come back a couple of times a month, so hopefully it won't be so different. But when I say alone . . .' He sighed. 'God, this is so hard . . . I'm not taking you with me, Olivia. I love you, but I think this has happened for a reason, that it's time for us both to go our separate ways, to move on.'

'But I don't want to move on,' Olivia said, tears welling in her eyes. 'I want us to be together. I thought we were happy.'

'We were,' George said sadly. 'But I'm not any more.'

Six months on it was supposed to have become easier, but the truth was, it hadn't much. Tom checked in on Olivia regularly, other friends dragged her out, and although she threw herself into her work, often the last one to leave the refuge, she still came home and lay on the sofa for hours, completely numb.

Bed offered no respite. She would wake up in the middle of the night and replay their relationship, wonder how it went wrong, think about the reasons why she wasn't good enough for him to stay.

'It's not you, Olivia,' Tom would say, his voice tinny on the line as he sat at his desk at the office in Boston. 'Don't ever think it's you. He's obviously got some issues he needs to work out, but don't ever think it's because you weren't good enough for him.'

And then George had phoned one night with some news. He had sounded happy, as high as a kite, and Olivia was waiting for those words she had been waiting for for months: *I've made a mistake. I miss you. I love you and I'm coming home.*

But instead George had told her he was getting married. Oblivious to the pain that would cause, he told her that Cindy was someone Olivia would love, that he hoped Olivia would come to the wedding.

'Cindy!' she had spat to Tom later that night on the phone. 'How could he? How could he do this? Why didn't he want to marry *me*? What's wrong with me?'

Tom listened, and then, a couple of weeks later, phoned and said he thought the best thing for Olivia to do would be to have a fling and he had just the person in mind.

'I'm not trying to fix you up with the love of your life, but what harm could it do to go out and have some fun, at least recognise that George isn't the only man in the world. There's a guy in the office—Fred—who's really great, and he mentioned he's got a trip to London in the New Year. You'd like him and it could be a fun few days.'

'So tell me about him,' Olivia had said reluctantly.

'He's thirty-three, single, freakishly fit—he does these Iron Man competitions that are all the rage in our office, which are completely mad, and horribly addictive.'

Olivia burst into laughter. 'I suppose your idea of exercise is still ambling around a cricket field?'

'Yes, well. Quite. It was before I worked here. Have a look at his picture. It's on our web site.' And Olivia had looked while talking to Tom. Fred was rather dishy, and even though she wasn't looking for anything at all, maybe Tom was right.

'Go on, then,' Olivia said. 'You can give him my email address.'

Fred had emailed her the next day, and the two of them had embarked on a fun, and rather more flirtatious than she had expected, email exchange.

He sounded boyish and relaxed, and there was something about Fred's youth that filled her with delicious anticipation.

'I wish I was coming over sooner,' Fred had written. 'January seems so long to wait to meet you. I am thinking maybe I could orchestrate a London meeting in November. What do you think?'

'I think that's a wonderful idea,' Olivia had written back.

Olivia walks back into her flat, unclips the dogs and feeds the animals before starting to think about feeding herself. She can barely think about food. She keeps a stock of sliced turkey breast in the fridge, and usually eats it with half a bag of carrots and a couple of spoons of hummus. As a consequence, she has lost a stunning amount of weight. She knows she will have to buy new clothes soon, but the thought of shopping for clothes has always filled her with horror.

Still. There are times when she feels like eating, and tonight is one of them. Sod's law: when she opens the fridge door, she is confronted with a nearly clear expanse of white. The cupboard doesn't offer much more. A couple of crackers rattling around in the box, a full box of cornflakes, which doesn't hold much appeal without milk, and some tea bags.

There is only one thing to do. She grabs her keys, heads out the door, and drives up the road to Maida Vale. To her sister's house and, more specifically, her sister's fridge, which is always stuffed with delicious leftovers.

'Jen!' she calls out, throwing her coat on the chair in the hallway. 'Jen?'

She knows her sister's home, because her car is in the driveway, so Olivia heads through to the kitchen.

As she opens the door, she sees Jen sitting at the kitchen table, and immediately she knows something is wrong. Her sister is just putting down the phone and she is as white as a sheet.

'Jen?' Olivia feels fear grip her chest. 'Jen? What is it? What's the matter? Is it Mum?'

'Oh, Olivia,' Jen says, her eyes filled with sadness. 'That was a friend, Elizabeth Gregory. She knows . . . well, her husband knows your friend Tom. I don't know how to say this. I don't know how to tell you, but Tom was on that train.'

'What train? What are you talking about?'

'He was on the Acela. In America. He didn't make it.'

'What do you mean, Tom was on the Acela? What are you talking about?' And then slowly it starts to dawn. 'Tom? You mean *my* Tom? He's *dead?*' And without realising it, Olivia sinks down to the floor, her body trembling like a leaf.

Chapter Three

MARCUS IS GOING BACK to the office to work now the kids are in bed, leaving Holly to get dinner ready for the people she once felt she knew better than anyone else in the world, people she hasn't seen for years.

Saffron has flown in from New York where she had been meeting with a film producer. She had been staying at the Soho Grand, had been right there when the train exploded. She, like many New Yorkers, who were instantly transported back to 9/11, was stunned that the city had been a target yet again.

Olivia had been at home, leafing through the *Guardian* as the dogs begged for food at her feet, mindlessly flicking pages as she tried to comprehend the tragedy, when Holly had phoned her.

As soon as Olivia heard Holly's voice she had known it was Holly. She had seldom thought about her over the years. The two friends had bumped into each other once after leaving university, and both of them had laughed at how different they looked. Olivia's waist-length hair had become a short, dark bob, and Holly's curly, mouse-brown locks were a sweep of straightened gloss with mahogany lights.

Olivia would have stayed longer, wanted, if not to become friends again, at least to find out more about Holly, but she had just started seeing Andrew, jealous, insecure Andrew, and he had hovered behind Olivia, creating an atmosphere so tense that Olivia had allowed herself to be pulled away from Holly at the earliest opportunity. More recently they'd exchanged a few emails, after Holly had found a picture of her on the Internet, but they hadn't arranged to meet up.

'Holly?' Olivia finds herself saying now, incredulously.

'It *is* you!' Holly says. 'I wasn't sure I had the right number.'

'Oh, Holly,' Olivia says, as the tears start. 'Isn't the news about Tom just awful?'

'I wasn't sure if you would have heard.' Holly is relieved that she is not the one to break the news to Olivia.

'Have you spoken to anyone else? Have you been in touch with Saffron? And Paul?'

'I've spoken to Paul,' Holly says, finding her voice suddenly choking up. 'He phoned Saffron and she's flying over from New York for Tom's memorial service on October 30th. We thought we could all meet up here at my house for supper the night before.'

And Holly gives Olivia her address.

Since Tom's death, Marcus's behaviour has reminded Holly of all that is good about him, and during those few moments when her grief subsides, she is grateful for that. He was, she thought one day as she looked up at him, her pillar of strength, and she knew immediately that that was why she had married him.

Everything about Marcus spells strength. From the set of his jaw to his quiet but firm insistence that his way is the right way. The first time Holly saw Marcus she'd known she had never met anyone like him before. And it helped that he was the diametric opposite of her father. She'd known he wasn't the sort of man who would have an affair, wasn't the sort of man who would leave his wife and daughter.

She was at a friend's house in Sydney, having a cookout, when she met Marcus. Sitting on the grass in frayed denim shorts and a T-shirt, she was as brown as a berry from travelling. There were tons of people there. Surfers mostly, and neighbours and friends, everyone arriving cheerfully bearing more food, more beer. Marcus had looked like a stuffy English lawyer in his Ralph Lauren polo shirt tucked into chino shorts, belted with a plaited brown belt. Holly had watched him sipping his beer, not bothering to make small talk, and she had felt sorry for him as the only other English person there and a man who so clearly did not fit in.

'I'm Holly,' she had said, clambering up and going over to him, extending a hand. 'You must be Marcus.' She had heard one of the neighbours had a stuffy English lawyer by that name staying with them.

His face had lit up. 'You're English!' It was a statement, not a question, and his gratitude at having been rescued was endearing, and Holly found she didn't mind spending the evening talking to him, and she didn't mind when he phoned the next day to ask her for lunch, and she didn't mind a couple of nights later when he kissed her as he was saying goodbye and dropping her off at her house.

He wasn't really her type, but perhaps, she thought then, that wasn't such a bad thing. And where had her type got her, anyway? A series of destructive, disappointing relationships in which Holly always seemed to be the one who got hurt. Marcus was tallish, not bad looking, clearly successful, and he seemed to adore her. Frankly it was bloody nice having a bit of adoration in her life.

I'll just enjoy it, Holly thought to herself. I know he's not the man of my dreams, but he's so different from everyone else I've been involved with, maybe this is better for me, maybe this is what a real relationship feels like. Maybe I shouldn't have looked for a soul mate, a perfect partner, maybe this is what I am supposed to be looking for.

Holly was looking for security. Her heart had been broken one too many times. She told herself that happy endings only existed in Hollywood films, that friendship and security were far more likely to result in a long and happy marriage. She told herself that it was OK to settle, that it would be enough.

During her marriage, when Holly's thoughts turned to Tom, he was always there as the symbol of what might have been. He wasn't just the one that got away, the road not taken, the love she didn't choose. Tom was the one Holly knew deep down she should have been with.

And so the loss is double. Holly is grieving for her best friend, a man she loves, and she is grieving for the life she was never able to have.

Tonight, at this pre-service dinner, Holly is hoping that somehow the four of them will be able to share their grief and move beyond it onto a path of healing.

She is nervous about seeing the others. Is excited but apprehensive. She remembers one night with Tom, many years ago, when they were sitting in a small Greek restaurant in Bayswater shortly after she had bumped into Olivia. 'All these years of not seeing each other, and you'd think we'd have a fantastic reunion, but her awful boyfriend dragged her away. You ought to say something to her about her taste in men.'

Tom laughed. 'She likes him, Holly. Isn't that all that matters?'

Holly sighed. 'I suppose so, it's just that Olivia was always so naive around men. What's Saffron up to? Have you spoken to her recently?'

'You should ask her yourself. She'd love to hear from you.'

'It's been too many years. I love hearing about her, but we've all drifted apart, and I doubt she'd want to hear from me.'

'I think she would,' Tom said. 'You all ask about each other but none of you will actually pick up the phone.'

'It's because I don't think any of us have anything in common any more,' Holly said. 'Other than a shared history.'

'Of course you would. There was a reason we were all good friends.'

'I don't know,' Holly said doubtfully. 'I think it was just being forced together for so long. You are funny, though,' Holly said. 'I can't believe that you're still in touch with everyone. How do you do it? I barely have time to respond to the calls on my answerphone, let alone make time to phone a ton of people from my past. You're amazing, you know.'

'I know. Isn't that why you love me?'

'Speaking of love . . .' Holly felt a familiar flutter. Here it was again. She was sitting across the table, aged twenty-five, looking at the face of her best friend, and all she could think of was what it would feel like to kiss him. 'Are you . . . seeing anyone?' She fidgeted on her seat.

'Why? Do you fancy me again?'

It had become a standing joke between them, this falling in and out of love with each other, but to Holly's embarrassment she found herself blushing deeply.

'Oh God.' Tom was mortified. 'If you'd have told me two months ago, Holly—'

'Well, why didn't you say something?'

'Because you were with Jake. What difference would it have made?'

'I might have dumped him for you.'

'Holly, Holly, Holly'—Tom shook his head—'we're not destined to be together, you know that.'

'I know.' Holly sighed. 'But what about if we're both still single at thirty-five? How about we make a pact that we get married then?'

Holly extended her hand across the table and Tom shook it firmly. 'OK. Thirty-five and we get married.'

'Done.'

Holly has made a salad, has picked up a gourmet pasta dish, a couple of baguettes and a tiramisu from the Italian deli down the road. Several bottles of wine are chilling in the fridge.

She finishes getting the table ready, then goes to the bathroom in an attempt to mask the pain her face has been carrying the last few weeks. Eyedrops to wash the redness from her eyes, tinted moisturiser to even out her skin, now blotchy from the streams of tears. Eye shadow to make her eyes bigger, blusher to bring colour to her face, recently an unbecoming shade of grey.

Holly has often thought about a school reunion, but never thought it would be under circumstances such as these. The doorbell rings and she sighs and walks downstairs.

Olivia is the first to arrive. Standing awkwardly on the doorstep proffering a bottle of wine, she is surprised at how naturally she and Holly fall into each other's arms, and then pull apart, shaking their heads, too overcome with emotion to speak.

A Saab crawls slowly up the road, and they turn, Holly squinting at the car, a man and a woman peering out of the window. She waves furiously as they pull into a space, and Paul and Saffron make their way up the path. All of them smile sorrowfully at one another, before wrapping each other up in huge tear-filled hugs, unable to believe they are all together again after all these years, unable to believe what has brought them back together.

Holly is enormously relieved that the clattering group has made its way into her kitchen.

'How are you?'

'You look fantastic!'

'Look at you!'

'Our friend the film star!'

'How long has it been?'

Their voices echo around the kitchen as they smile at one another, Olivia grinning at Saffron, Paul squeezing Holly's shoulders, Saffron feeling that here she doesn't have to be Saffron Armitage, movie star, here she can be just Saff.

Paul sinks into a kitchen chair, gulping from a glass of wine. 'These are horrible, awful circumstances but, Christ, it's good to see all of you.'

'Forgive the movie cliché,' says Saffron, emotion choking her voice, 'but I feel like I've come home.'

Olivia breaks the silence by prodding Paul. 'You've obviously eaten well all these years,' she says with a grin.

'Oh charming,' Paul says. 'I don't see you for, what? Twenty years? And the first thing to come out of your mouth is an insult. I see you haven't changed a bit.'

Olivia puts her arm round Paul's shoulders and squeezes, leaning down to kiss him on the cheek. 'I'm just teasing.'

Saffron wanders into the living room looking at the photographs dotted around. She picks one up—Holly and Marcus grinning at the camera as they perch on a gate in the country.

'Holly,' Saffron calls out. 'Is this your husband?' She holds up the photograph.

'Yup.' Holly peers round the door. 'And those are my kids over there.'

'I can't believe it.' Saffron shakes her head. 'Holly Mac married. With children no less.'

Holly comes back in from the kitchen with a smile. 'Hey, Paul.

Speaking of married, I saw some spread you did in *Vogue* when you got married. Mr bloody Prada.'

Paul dips his head sheepishly. 'Ah, yes. I did feel a bit of a *poseur*. Only did it because Anna thought it would be great publicity for Fashionista.'

'Was it?'

'Yup.'

'God, I love that web site!' Holly says. 'It's amazing. Tell your wife I'm a huge fan and she's doing an incredible job.'

'I don't suppose your wife would give us mates' rates?' Saffron attempts.

'Sure. You'd have to meet her first, and she'd have to like you, which is obviously a problem but I'll work on it.' Paul smiles.

As the evening wears on, inhibitions are loosened and connections are being made again. Whatever it was that kept them from one another all these years has now disappeared without a trace.

Olivia, so nervous about seeing these people beside whom she always felt so inadequate, doesn't feel inadequate any more, is surprised to find that she no longer feels Saffron is prettier or that Holly is cleverer and, although it may still be true, it doesn't bother her any more.

Saffron is calmer. The Saffron of old was a shrieker, but the Saffron sitting here today seems, even through her sadness, to be at peace. She is comfortable in her skin and far more beautiful because of it.

Paul is the same. He hasn't changed at all. Tom was right; Holly thinks back with pain, remembering her conversation with him when she first saw Paul pictured with Anna in *Vogue*. Paul is still a scruff, just one with the ability to scrub up incredibly well.

And Holly? Holly is the one whom you might perhaps worry about the most. She is the one who seems lost. Even here, among people who have known her longer than anyone else, even though she appears comfortable, her feet tucked under her at one end of the long, squishy sofa, even here she looks lost.

'Tom was probably the most consistent thing in my life.' Olivia reaches over to the coffee table and pours herself more wine. 'Whatever was going on, whoever might have left me, Tom was always there. Not that I saw him that often, but he was so fiercely loyal in his friendships. I tried to get rid of him in my twenties, but he just wouldn't disappear . . .'

The others laugh and Saffron takes over.

'You know what I loved best about Tom? That he didn't change. He was never impressed by people or things. He knew me for so long that he refused to be impressed by my acting or the films I was in. Used to piss me off enormously,' she admitted with a shrug. 'After I was in that film with Dennis Quaid, I thought he'd treat me with a bit more respect, but he didn't.'

'I know this sounds terrible,' Holly says quietly, 'but don't they always say you never appreciate what you had until it's gone? I spent years falling in and out of love with Tom, and then I met Marcus, and then obviously Tom and I were just friends, but I wish I'd shown him how much I loved him.'

'He would have known,' Saffron said. 'He knew how much we all loved him. That's why he insisted on staying in all our lives.'

'More coffee?' Holly sighs as she pulls her legs out from under her and hoists herself up from the sofa, knowing that there was a difference in her relationship with Tom but not wanting to share it with the others. Not yet.

'I think more wine,' Paul says, draining the dregs of his fourth glass.

It was not long after her dinner with Tom in Bayswater, and before her trip to Australia, where she would meet Marcus. Before a time when Holly would look at Tom and see nothing more than a best friend.

Another dinner. This time in Holland Park. Not for any reason other than to catch up with each other. Holly had been to the huge Ghost warehouse sale that morning—had pushed her way through hundreds of desperate west London women to grab anything that looked vaguely her size—and had found a beautiful diaphanous lilac coat. Sheer, flowing, it wafted out behind her as she walked. It was tied around the neck with a delicate beaded string, and worn with sheer flared lilac trousers and a camisole vest.

The afternoon had been a hot one. She'd met a group of girlfriends on Primrose Hill. One had brought an oversized rug, another baguettes, another cheese. Holly had brought wine and they'd all taken off their T-shirts, rolled their peasant skirts up as far as they dared, and basked in the sun.

Holly had the kind of skin that looked at the sun and bronzed. That evening she tipped her head upside down and shook her hair out to achieve that slightly wild, sexy look, swept Ultraglow on her cheeks and popped silver hoops into her ears. She looked beautiful. She wasn't doing it for Tom but for herself, although she knew that Tom would appreciate it.

He pulled up outside her flat at seven, beeped the horn, and she ran downstairs and tumbled into his car.

'You look *gorgeous!*' he said in surprise as she leaned over and kissed him on the cheek.

'I know!' she said. 'Ghost sale. Dirt cheap. Isn't it fantastic?'

'Yes, and how come you're so brown?'

'Mixture of Primrose Hill and make-up. You like?'

'You look the very picture of health. Come on. I've booked Julie's.'

'Oh, I say'—Holly settled back in the car seat—'how romantic.'

'I know. I was hoping I might get lucky.'

Holly raised an eyebrow. 'Play your cards right . . .'

They had a quiet, candlelit table in the corner. For anyone other than Holly and Tom it would have been absurdly romantic, but instead of murmuring sweet nothings across the table, they chatted nineteen to the dozen and kept bursting into splutters of laughter over shared jokes.

They ordered one crème brulée between them, clashing spoons like swords as they each battled to get more, and when Tom pulled up outside Holly's flat, he did as he usually did, walking upstairs with her for one last coffee.

It was a perfect evening. Neither one had fallen in love with the other, both of them just enjoying one another's company, no false expectations leading to disappointment.

Holly sank into the sofa next to Tom and threw her legs over his.

'Careful,' Tom said with a grin. 'You wouldn't be leading me on, would you?'

'Not bloody likely,' she said, sipping her coffee. 'I've learned my lesson too many times before, thank you very much.'

'I've often wondered,' Tom said, not looking at Holly but focusing on her lilac Ghost-clad legs instead, 'what it would be like to kiss you.'

'Oh, stop it!' Holly burst out laughing. 'Don't tell me you're actually going to make a pass at me?'

Tom shrugged and grinned. 'I was thinking about it.'

'Go on then.' She raised an eyebrow, knowing this wasn't going to happen—there was no sexual tension, no heat, no admissions of sexual attraction. 'I dare you.'

For a few seconds neither of them moved, Holly about to burst into laughter with an 'I knew you were just faking', and then Tom put down his coffee and turned back to face her, and all of a sudden she wasn't laughing any more.

It was the slowest, most tentative, most thrilling kiss she had ever had. Even as his lips first met hers she didn't think it was happening, was still sitting there with a smile, not expecting Tom to really go through with it.

Soft, gentle, just the feeling of his lips on hers, and her smile disappeared. Then again, the kisses on her upper lip, her lower, until she dared lick his upper lip, ever so gently, and there they were. Kissing. Arms reaching up to stroke a face, trace a cheek, fingers run smoothly down the nape of a neck.

'Holly.' A whispered sigh from Tom.

'Sssh.' Holly dissolved into him, then pulled back to look at him. Tom. Her Tom. Gazing up at her through half-closed eyes, glazed with lust. She didn't say anything, didn't want to spoil the moment, and leaned down again to kiss him more, clever fingers swiftly undoing the buttons on his shirt.

'Tom.' A whispered sigh from Holly as she plants kisses on his chest, moves back up to reach his lips.

So familiar. So safe.

So this is what it's like. Like coming home.

Tom left before morning. What felt so right and so natural under the cover of darkness started to feel increasingly unnatural as daylight approached. He left Holly sleeping. He stood next to the bed and watched her as she slept. And he felt an enormous sadness. He never truly thought this would happen with Holly. He loved her more than he'd ever loved anyone. However attracted he was to her, he couldn't sleep with his best friend and then expect everything to be normal.

You can't sleep with your best friend and then start dating, going out for dinner, sharing your stories, seeing how it goes.

You can't sleep with your best friend and be anything other than an immediate couple. There is no halfway measure. You sleep with your best friend and you have one of two consequences. Either way the friendship is over.

Tom didn't plan this, isn't ready for this. He's only twenty-five, not nearly ready to settle down with anyone, not even Holly. He still has wild oats to sow. What on earth had he been thinking? But Holly, so lovely in her lilac, so much lovelier later in bed, how could he not? How could any man resist? But what does he do now?

Holly called Tom that afternoon, whereupon they had an awkward, stilted conversation. The most awkward conversation Holly had ever had with anyone. These are the conversations you have with men who feel you are putting pressure on them, she realised. These are the conversations you have when you are about to be dumped, when you are clearly feeling so much more than they.

But how can this be? This isn't just anyone. This is Tom. *Tom!*

They said goodbye and Tom put down the phone and dropped his head in his hands. He hated this. The last person in the world he wanted to hurt was Holly, but what choice did he have?

He'd take some space, he decided. Not phone her for a while. Not abandon her, never abandon her, but they would both take a little space until they could pick up the friendship where they left off. Prior to last night, that is.

For several weeks Holly was devastated. She had had enough relationships over the years to know, with pain and shock, that Tom was no different from any of the others, that their years of friendship stood for nothing, and that things would never be the same between them.

Leafing through the back of *Time Out* one afternoon, she saw an ad for a three-month expedition in Australia. Life in England had never been bleaker, and the constant entreaties from friends to just get out and get on with life fell on deaf ears. She needed a change, needed to get away from the memories, needed to replace the videotape in her head with something other than that one night with Tom. That whispered 'Holly', which she had thought meant that he loved her, would never leave her.

Tom tried, at last, to get in touch with Holly when she was in Australia. He missed her. Ultimately all roads led to Holly, all other girls were not what Holly was, and mostly he remembered the longing, the feeling of having come home.

'Tom? It's Holly!'

'Holly? Where are you? Where the hell have you been? I've missed you!'

Holly laughed. 'Australia. I was meant to go for three months but ended up staying for six. I've had the greatest time of my life and I've met someone! Can you believe it? This is it, Tom, this is the man I'm going to marry. I can't wait for you to meet him.'

Sweet Tom, Holly thought, having made a date for him to meet Marcus. How I've missed him, she thought, too caught up in the rebound to hear Tom's confusion, to think that she might have broken Tom's heart in much the same way he had broken hers a few months earlier.

'I loved him,' she wants to shout, to tell Paul and Olivia and Saffron, but she doesn't because she knows what they will say. That they loved him, too.

Chapter Four

'CHRIST, THERE ARE A LOT of people,' Marcus mutters, turning the wheel hard as he circles the block for the third time.

Holly is scouring the line of people walking up towards the church to try to find someone she knows. 'Oh look!' she says. 'There's Saffron. Saffi! Saffron!' She sticks her head out of the window as Saffron turns and waves, hurrying gratefully over to the car.

'Oh, thank God,' she says breathily. 'I didn't want to go in on my own.'

'Can I get out and go with Saffron?' Holly turns to Marcus, only to see he is completely starstruck, and she suppresses a giggle. 'You two haven't met, have you? Saffron, this is my husband, Marcus. Marcus, this is Saffron.'

'How lovely to meet you.' Saffron shines her most luminous smile.

Holly uses the opportunity to hop out of the car. 'I'll see you in there,' she says as Marcus regains his senses thanks to a car behind them honking. He drives slowly down the road, leaving the two girls standing facing each other.

'Was it just me or was Marcus a little bit starstruck?' Saffron giggles.

'Yes, well. It seems Marcus isn't quite the cool and collected man he thinks he is when faced with genuine celebrity.' Holly rolls her eyes.

'I thought your husband was supposed to be an arrogant wanker,' Saffron says, linking her arm through Holly's.

Holly should be upset, but has long suspected that people secretly think this and so it has ceased to bother her. 'Most of the time he is but he can also be devastatingly charming. Anyway, who told you he was an arrogant wanker?'

'Am I allowed to drop Tom in it at his own memorial service?'

'Figures.' Holly snorts.

'So did Marcus see *Lady Chatterley*? He probably fancied me rotten when I played the leading role. I can't seem to meet a man these days without his tongue hanging out.'

'Sounds good to me.' Holly laughs. 'Seriously though, Saff. If you want Marcus you can have him.'

'Thanks.' Saff peals with laughter. 'But my hands are perfectly full dealing with P.'

'Is that what you call your luvvver whom you refuse to talk about? P?'

'Easier than his full name, and no one would guess if they overheard anything. I . . . you can keep a secret can't you, Holly?'

'Of course.'

'He's famous. Incredibly famous.' Saffron leans forward and whispers a name into Holly's ear.

'But . . . isn't he married to—?'

'Exactly. That's why it's so secret. Sssh.' Saffron puts her fingers to her lips as they approach the door of the church. 'I'll tell you more later.'

They step into the cool porch and follow the crowds into the building. The church is packed and it's standing room only.

'Excuse me. Excuse me. Sorry.' Holly and Saffron shuffle past huddles of people until they can just get a glimpse of the pulpit.

'Let's stay here,' Saff says. 'At least I can breathe. Do you think your husband will be able to find us?'

'I hope not.' Holly sighs.

Saffron frowns at her. 'Is everything OK with the two of you?'

Holly's laugh is hollow. 'I'm just being silly,' she says. 'Ignore me.'

Holly and Saffron stand silently as Linda Ronstadt's voice flows aas clear as a bell from the speakers, and reverberates around the church.

> So goodbye my friend
> I know I'll never see you again
> But the love you gave me through all the years
> Will take away these tears
> I'm okay now
> Goodbye my friend

And the grief that had been waiting at the door is welcomed in as finally people start to cry.

Laughter and tears. Pleasure and pain. The range of emotions throughout the service is so great that at times Holly thinks she can't stand it.

They are all so dignified, she thinks. His dad able to smile through his speech, his mum looking pale but strong beside him. Will, his brother, telling funny stories of things they got up to when young, ridiculous pranks they had played on each other, and how they were so close people would think they were twins ('Will being,' he said, 'the better looking, more charming, more successful one,' which cracked up all Will's friends who knew him to have a somewhat unreliable career).

One more friend, and then Sarah. Still and quiet, there is something mesmerising about her lone American voice. She talks about why she fell in love with Tom. About what a wonderful father he was. And as she is talking a little girl runs over and tugs on her sleeve.

'Mommy?' she says loudly. 'Why are you talking about Daddy? Can we see him now? Is this heaven?' And Sarah picks Violet up to comfort her as the church fills with tears yet again.

Finally, Chopin's Prelude No. 6 eases through the speakers, allowing people to hug one another and break down, file slowly outside, blinking in the glare of the sunlight.

Holly takes deep breaths to regain her composure, then turns to see Marcus joining them.

'Where were you?' he says sternly. 'I was looking . . .' and he notices Holly's tear-stained face and stops, holding his arms out to hug her instead.

'Thank you,' Holly says, disengaging herself after a few moments. 'Wasn't it heartbreaking?'

'It was tough,' Marcus agreed. 'I thought Sarah was wonderful though. So strong and stoic.' Ah yes, thinks Holly. How typical of Marcus to admire those qualities.

'I don't think it's necessary to go back to the house,' Marcus says. 'Far too many people, plus I've got to prepare for a court hearing tomorrow. We have to leave.'

How very different we are, she thinks again, and then, as so often happens these days when she thinks about Marcus, a word flits into her head, announces its presence, then disappears.

Arse, she thinks but forces a smile. 'I have to find Tom's parents,' Holly says. 'And Paul and Olivia are here somewhere. And I think it's wrong not to go back to the house. Work can wait, surely? I mean, this is more important.'

'I'll bring Holly home,' Saffron says brightly. 'You go off and do your work, Marcus. Don't worry about Holly.'

'Oh, thank you, Saffron, that's incredibly gracious of you.' Marcus smiles, giving Holly a perfunctory kiss, and then Saffron the standard double-cheek air kiss. They stand watching him stride off towards wherever his car is parked.

Arse, she thinks again as she turns to Saffron. 'Gawd. I'm surprised he didn't try and stick his tongue in your mouth.' Holly rolls her eyes.

'Oh behave,' Saffron says. 'He'll get over it. Frankly it's bloody nice to be appreciated though, particularly at a memorial service.'

'Yes, nothing like a spot of inappropriate flirting at a memorial service,' Holly says.

'Speaking of which, horribly and entirely inappropriate to even mention this, but did you see Will?'

'You mean, cute and cuddly little baby brother, Will, who we used to occasionally let in to watch us being horrible teenagers and play spin the bottle?'

'That'd be the one. But did you see him?'

'Big brown eyes, messy longish hair, gorgeous smile with dimples and an undoubted six pack under the suit? That one?'

'That'd be the one.'

'Nope.' Holly shrugs. 'Can't say I noticed him.'

'Who would have thought he'd grow up to look like that!' Saffron says.

'Actually I think he looks just like Tom,' Holly muses. 'A messier, more laid back, younger version of Tom. Imagine him with a short back and sides in a polo shirt and jeans, and he's basically Tom.'

'Maybe, but I never fancied Tom and I do quite fancy Will.'

'Saffron!' Holly glares at her. 'That's just sick. This is his brother's memorial service.'

'I know, I know,' she grumbles. 'And I'm not actually interested, just observing, that's all. Oh, come on Miss Holier Than Thou, just because you're married doesn't mean you can't look.'

'Well, ask me again when today is over. Right now I just want to find Tom's mum and dad.'

Holly hovers a few feet away from where Maggie and Peter are greeting a line of people. Maggie looks up and catches her eye, turning back to the people who are giving their condolences, and then she looks back at Holly.

'Holly?' she says, as Holly nods shyly, and Maggie opens her arms for Holly to go running up for a huge hug. 'Oh, Holly!' she says. 'It's been too long. Years and years. Look at you, Holly! Peter! Look!' she calls over to her husband. 'It's Holly Mac!'

After Holly's parents divorced when she was fourteen, her mother had moped for the year after the divorce, then had got out of bed, got a job in the trendiest interior design shop, and suddenly turned into the mother from hell.

She started to wear tons of make-up, all the clothes that Holly and her friends wanted to wear but couldn't afford, and went out clubbing every night, staying with a series of friends, each one seemingly younger and funkier than the last. In short, she'd had enough of being a mother, and even though Holly at fifteen was more or less old enough to take care of herself, she didn't want to.

Holly's friends adored coming over to her house because, save for a Spanish au pair who didn't seem to want to have anything at all to do with Holly or her friends, there were no adults to tell them what to do.

At Holly's house, they didn't have to sneak cigarettes on balconies or stick their heads outside open windows in the middle of a freezing winter. Hell, at Holly's house, they could sit around the kitchen table and get high as kites or drunk as skunks, whatever the substance of choice happened to be that day. It was not dissimilar to life at Saffron's, except Saffron's parents were around. Liberal enough to let Saffron do whatever she wanted, at least they were there.

Everyone was jealous of Holly, and all Holly wanted was to be normal. She wanted a mother who would tell her she couldn't wear make-up to school and a father who said she had to be in by eleven.

What she wanted was a family.

And what she got through her friendship with Tom was Tom's family. Their kitchen was always filled with delicious smells from Maggie's cooking, the kettle seemed to have just boiled no matter when you walked in, and every cushion was plastered with hair from the labrador, Boris, or one of the cats. It was messy, noisy and fun.

'I always wanted a daughter,' Maggie would say, and Holly felt as much part of the family as Tom and Will.

They even gave her a bedroom. Actually it was the junk room, but they cleared the stuff off the bed so Holly always had a place to sleep, and Peter bought an old turntable at a car-boot sale so that Holly could listen to her beloved Police albums.

Holly and Tom would lie on the floor in his room (Tom had a much better turntable and stereo system) and make compilation cassettes. Some were love songs, others dance songs, but they spent hours painstakingly recording their LPs and writing in all the songs on the tiny lines. 'Tom, Will, Holly . . . supper!' would come up the stairs, and they would yell down 'in a minute', as Tom would complain and Holly would pretend to complain when, in fact, she was overjoyed to be treated as just one of the kids.

She stayed close to Maggie and Peter until she got married. Even after her marriage she saw them a bit, but then Tom had moved to America, and it was true she hadn't seen them for years.

Peter's mouth falls open when he sees Holly. 'My goodness, Holly Mac! You're all grown up,' he says, and as he hugs her Holly feels her eyes well up.

'I'm so sorry,' she says, looking from Maggie to Peter. 'I wrote to you and I tried to call but I couldn't get through. I just wanted you to know how terribly sorry I am, how much I miss Tom.'

'Thank you,' Maggie says, squeezing her arm. 'It's the most terrible thing that's ever happened to us but you know he would have loved the service. He wouldn't have wanted everyone to stand around and be sad, he would have wanted to be remembered for all the good things.'

'I know,' Holly says, smiling; and then, out of nowhere, her face crumples and she starts to sob.

'Oh, love,' Maggie says and, putting her arms round Holly, she finds that the stoicism she has faked so well for today—this day she had been dreading—disappears, and the pain of losing her son is so great she leans on Holly and dissolves into tears.

They stand there for a long time, crying silently, and then they break away and wipe the tears.

'Oh, Holly, I'm sorry,' Maggie says. 'I didn't mean to collapse on you like that.'

'Oh, Maggie, it was me. I had no right to cry on you after everything you've been through. I'm so embarrassed.'

'Don't be embarrassed. Come back to the house and have a cup of tea. That should make us all feel better.'

It smells the same. Despite all the people crowding into the hallway, the living room, the first thing Holly notices as she walks through the door is that Maggie and Peter's house still smells the same.

Like home.

The same dhurrie rugs thrown down haphazardly in the entrance hall, the same huge squishy sofa now covered with various throws under the giant mirror against the back wall.

Paintings Holly recognises, new ones filling every square inch on the walls, all thrown together and all working perfectly.

And then, above a console table, a framed line drawing of the Fitzgerald family—Maggie and Peter grinning with their arms wrapped round each other, and Tom, Will and Holly lying on their tummies in front. *Happy Anniversary 1984! Lots of Love, Holly,* written at the bottom. Holly had copied a photograph with her Rotring pen, then had added herself as part of the family.

Maggie is, as always, in the kitchen. Unwrapping cakes and platters of sandwiches on the kitchen table as friends of hers bustle around refilling the kettle and making sure there are enough cups.

The kitchen table is still the same, the kitchen cupboards updated—

no more seventies pine and melamine counters. The cupboards are now a pretty antique white with thick butcher-block counters, but the dresser holding all the plates is still there, and the old church pew serving as a bench on one side of the scrubbed refectory table is the same.

'What do you think of the old place?' Maggie asks, looking up and seeing Holly. 'Hasn't changed much, has it?'

Holly shakes her head with a smile. 'Apart from the cupboards in here, it looks exactly the same. I keep expecting to see Boris leaping about the kitchen.'

'Oh, Boris.' Maggie smiles. 'What a good dog he was. A maniac, but a good one. Nowadays we have Pippa. We think she's spaniel crossed with retriever.'

'Where is she?'

'Olivia has taken her out for a walk. Thank goodness I was able to say we'd rescued Pippa—I think it put us in her good books immediately.'

'As if you would ever be anywhere else.' Holly laughs. 'Do you need help?'

'No, love. I'm almost done. Anyway, keeping myself busy seems to be the best thing for me at the moment.' Maggie's eyes glaze over for a second, then she shakes her head to dislodge the thoughts and reaches behind her for some plates.

Holly leaves the kitchen and pushes her way through the people standing around with cups of tea in hand, sharing their stories of Tom as she walks upstairs, knowing she has to see Tom's room. Pushing the door open, she expects to see little changed. But, bizarrely, this is the one room that is entirely different. The walls are a fresh yellow and there are pretty twin beds with teddy bears sitting atop the pillows.

Holly smiles. Of course. This is now Dustin and Violet's bedroom, where they stay when they come over here. She walks over to the window seat and sits down, leaning her head on the window pane as she looks out on this familiar view.

The door creaks and Holly turns round with a start.

'I thought I saw you at the service, and I had a feeling I might find you up here.' Will stands in the doorway with a huge grin, then holds out his arms for Holly to run in.

'Oh, Will,' Holly says, leaning her head on his shoulder as she squeezes him tight. She steps back to look up at him. 'It's so good to see you. Look at you—you're a long-haired version of Tom. Oh God, Will.' She feels her eyes well up. 'It's so awful. I'm so so sorry.'

'I know,' Will says, rubbing her arm. 'I still feel a bit numb, really, and it's so completely weird seeing Tom's old friends here, most of whom I haven't seen for years.'

They both move towards the window seat, grinning at each other.

'You look great,' Will says. 'It's so good to see you. What happened to you? You got married, we all came to the wedding, had a couple of Christmas cards, and then you dropped off the face of the earth.'

'I know. I can't believe I lost touch. I suppose life just got in the way. Husband, children, work.'

'Ah yes. Those things that normal people do. I can't say I have much experience in those things.'

'No? Why? Are you still the reprobate son?' Holly laughs.

'According to my parents the answer would be yes.' Will shrugs. 'I've been accused, several times, of being a commitaphobe, but I think I just haven't met anyone I've wanted to commit to.'

'So how old are you now? Thirty-five?'

'Yup. Exactly.'

Holly smiles. 'You have plenty of time. I got married in my twenties and frankly I think it ought to be illegal to be married before thirty.'

'Because?'

'Because you change so much in your thirties. How can you possibly predict whether you'll grow together or apart?'

'So'—Will studies her face for a second—'have you and . . . is it Marcus?' Holly nods. 'Have you grown together or apart?'

'Oh God, Will! Isn't this a bit heavy for today?' Holly won't answer the question. Can't answer the question. 'Enough about me. What about you? Are you hugely successful at something? A millionaire with gorgeous models hanging off his arm?'

Will laughs. 'Hardly. Well, I have had a few gorgeous models, and I'm relatively good at what I do when I do it.'

'What is it?'

'I'm a carpenter, I suppose. Or cabinet-maker. I mean, I do everything, but I do it to fund travelling. I try to do six months here to make enough money to spend six months travelling abroad.'

Holly raises her eyebrows. 'Isn't that opting out of real life a bit? I mean, I could understand you doing this at twenty-five, but thirty-five?'

Will laughs. 'I'm living the life that makes me happy. I can honestly say I love my life, and how many people do you know who can say that?' There's a pause and he grins. 'Can you?'

'I have wonderful children,' Holly says. 'I adore my work, and the life I've created.' But even as she says it she knows it's not true, particularly after walking back into this house today.

For Holly always wanted *this*. She wanted crazy and chaotic, wanted the house filled with laughter and fun. And it is just starting to dawn on Holly that she may never have this with Marcus.

'But are you happy?' Will persists.

'I think most of the time I'm just getting on with life.' Holly tries to shrug it off. 'But happy all the time? I think that's unrealistic.'

Will tilts his head. 'That's the point. While I can't say I'm happy all the time, I can say I'm happy *most* of the time. I wake up in the morning and I enjoy every day. That's why I live like I do. If I wake up one day and decide that now's the time to settle down and buy a house, have two point four children and everything that comes with it, I'm sure I'll do it. But right now this is what makes me feel good.'

Holly shakes her head with a resigned smile. 'If it works for you, that's great. Really. I always think we can't question another person's choices—how can we judge unless we've walked in their shoes?'

'My philosophy exactly. So . . . have you seen Scary Sarah yet?'

Holly's mouth falls open. 'How do you know I called her that?'

'Tom told me.' Will's eyes sparkle with amusement. 'He thought it was hysterical.'

'Oh God, I'm so embarrassed,' Holly groans, sinking her head in her hands. 'And, no, I haven't seen her yet. How is she?'

Will looks sad. 'The truth is she's a complete mess. I would have expected her to be incredibly cool and stoic and to act as if she were handling it perfectly, but she keeps breaking down in tears. I was amazed she managed to pull it together for the service.'

'Is she downstairs?'

'Probably. Or maybe in the guest room. I have to say I've warmed to her enormously these last days. I always called her the Ice Queen, but I think I'm seeing the real Sarah now.'

'Come on.' Holly stands. 'I have to find her.'

As they head out of the door they turn to one other spontaneously and give each other a hug.

'It's so good to see you,' Holly says into his ear. 'Like rediscovering my long-lost little brother.'

'Ouch.' Will pulls away then smiles. 'Did you know I used to have the most enormous crush on you?'

'You did?' Holly is stunned.

'I did. You were the first great love of my life.'

'I was?' Holly's hand flies up to her heart that just fluttered in an unexpected way. 'I never knew!'

'I never told you. Come on. Let's go and find Sarah.'

'Come back tomorrow,' Maggie says as she hugs Holly goodbye. 'Everyone will have gone and I'd love to spend some real time with you. How does the morning sound?'

'It sounds wonderful,' Holly says. 'Will Sarah be around, do you think? I'd love to talk to her.'

'I hope so,' Maggie says. 'She couldn't face talking to people after the service. All so draining for her, plus her doctor's got her on all these pills. Still, hopefully she'll be up tomorrow. I'm sure she'd love to see you.'

At three in the morning, as usual, Holly finds herself wide awake. She tries lying in bed for a while listening to Marcus snore, and eventually gets up, throws on a dressing gown and goes upstairs to her studio. Sitting down at her desk she switches on her computer, then slides the scrap of paper that Will had scribbled his details on from under her notebook and studies his email address.

Opening her email, she taps his address in and is smiling as she types. A few sentences about how lovely it was to see him, how much she misses Tom, then she erases and starts again.

A few sentences about how good it was to be able to really talk to someone, how rare to reconnect so strongly with someone from your childhood, then she erases and starts again.

If I was the first, she taps, a smile playing on her lips, *who was the second? From Curious Insomniac in Brondesbury*. Then she switches off her computer and goes downstairs to make herself some tea.

Marcus leans over to kiss her goodbye, as he always does at 5.30 in the morning before he leaves the house to drive to the tube station. Today Holly lies in bed listening until she hears his car start up and pull out of the driveway. When she can no longer hear it she leaps out of bed and runs up to her studio, turning her computer back on, going straight to her inbox and smiling as she sees a reply from Will. Wow, she thinks. Sent at 4 a.m. He doesn't sleep either.

Dear Curious Insomniac in Brondesbury,
    Interesting question. Am thinking that perhaps there has only been one great love of my life, however had a lesser love at Durham for Cynthia Fawley. Have had several loves, unsurprisingly for a thirty-five-year-old, over the years, but none quite as innocent or pain-searingly sweet as my prepubescent dreams. Do you remember we almost snogged once? You and Tom let me join in spin the bottle and I spun that thing, praying to God and promising that I'd never do anything bad again if I got you, and I did. And we went into the cupboard and

you kissed me on the lips, and I was desperate to kiss you properly but I didn't know how. That kiss kept me going for years (may still even be keeping me going today) . . .

Is he flirting with me? Am I flirting with him? What is this? What am I *doing*? Isn't this how affairs start? Haven't I always said I would never have an affair, not after my father? Haven't I always said infidelity is the greatest betrayal a human being can commit? Oh, for heaven's sake, Holly, this isn't flirting. This is just having some fun. Who said anything about an affair?

And it *can't* be flirting. This is Tom's brother, and Tom's not even cold in his grave. How entirely inappropriate would flirting be? There. Settled. This isn't flirting. This is friendship.

Odd perhaps that these questions are even there, albeit not in the forefront of Holly Mac's mind, so Holly tells herself that she has rediscovered an old friend and that the reason she is sitting in front of her computer at 5.30 a.m., checking emails, is because she is excited at finding the Fitzgeralds again, excited at seeing Will again after all these years.

And so what if there is a touch of innocent flirting going on? How lovely, actually, to be flirted with after so many years of having no one look at her.

Holly used to feel gorgeous, but lately she feels harassed. In her running-around-with-kids clothes she feels like a stressed mum, and in her cashmere sweaters and pearls, out with Marcus in the evening, she feels like a fraud.

Rarely does she feel like Holly, the real Holly. The Holly that Will had known. Perhaps this is why she feels so comfortable, she muses, as she thinks about what to write back. And if he is flirting gently, so what? Holly would never do anything, and how invigorating to have a gorgeous, single man pay you attention. They will just be friends, she decides. And how lucky to have a male friend; how much she has missed male friendship since she and Tom drifted so far apart.

Paul rings later that morning. 'Maggie said you were going to their house today and I'd love to go, too. I barely saw you yesterday, and Saffron disappeared early to take a call from P. I'm picking Olivia up at eleven, then heading over there. Want me to come and get you?'

'Thanks, Paul, I'd love it,' Holly says, replacing the phone and wondering how it is that you can go for twenty years not seeing people, and when you do, nothing has changed.

She takes extra-special care today before going to Maggie and Peter's.

A little more make-up than usual, a little more blow-drying to ensure her hair is smooth. A sexy shirt and navy trousers, high-heeled boots.

'Wow! Look at you!' Olivia grins as she gets in the car. 'Are you off for a job interview later?'

Holly blushes, instantly self-conscious. She has sent an email back to Will telling him she is coming over today. She'd found herself thinking, If he likes me, he'll be there, and then instantly reprimanded herself for being so childish.

'No, but a meeting at work,' Holly lies. 'I usually try to dress up a bit when I go in.'

'You look great,' Paul says. 'Hey, both of you, if either of you want anything from Fashionista just let me know. You should look at the web site because Anna says she'll give you anything wholesale.'

'I'm not sure Fashionista is my thing,' Olivia laughs, gesturing at her old jeans and workman's boots. 'I think my fashion days are long gone.'

I wouldn't mind looking, Holly thinks. Although she'd said she bought from the web site all the time, it wasn't strictly true. She *had* bought from there, but Marcus never seemed to like anything. 'Too trendy,' he always said. 'Inappropriate.' So it had been a while since Holly had browsed Fashionista.co.uk.

Before Marcus, Holly had loved expressing herself through her clothes. She had spent hours at Portobello looking for the perfect vintage dress, had always known exactly what was in and what was out that season, even though she couldn't afford it.

And when she could afford it, when Marcus started to make serious money, she found that he hated the clothes she would bring home: gorgeous shift dresses from Egg in Knightsbridge, beaded kaftans from little boutiques in Notting Hill, tumbling chandelier earrings of amethyst and quartz.

Holly had learned to dress in clothes that Marcus approved of: conservative, luxurious. Her jewellery was classic and unobtrusive, her hair pulled back because Marcus didn't like it down.

Today she had put on the hoops that he hated and that she loved and had slipped on the high-heeled boots that Marcus deemed cheap. She had looked in the mirror before leaving and had felt sexy, something she hadn't felt for years. And now, sitting in the car, Holly thinks she's fed up with the cashmere jumpers and the loafers. She will go to Fashionista.co.uk, and she will see if they have anything she likes. She's too young to dress like a sixty-year-old, and so what if Marcus doesn't like it. She doesn't like his monogrammed Turnbull & Asser shirts, but that doesn't stop him from wearing them.

Sarah is sitting at the kitchen table as they walk in. Today her face is puffy, her eyes red-rimmed, deep shadows underneath. She is in an oversized sweatshirt that Holly knows must have been Tom's.

Had you been at the service yesterday, you would not credit that you were looking at the same person. Will was right. Sarah had managed to pull it together yesterday.

'Oh, Sarah,' Holly says, sympathy and sorrow washing over her. 'I'm so sorry.' And she puts her arms round her.

'I just miss him,' Sarah sobs. 'I just miss him so much.'

'I know,' Holly whispers. 'I know.'

'He loved you, Holly,' Sarah says suddenly. Unexpectedly. 'You always had a special place in his heart, and I was always jealous of you. I'm so sorry.' And this time it is Holly's turn to cry, her carefully applied make-up running down her face.

'No Will today?' Holly has waited, hoping, each time the door opens, that Will will walk through, but no.

Maggie shakes her head. 'Darling Will,' she says. 'We love him but he's hopeless. Responsibility has never been his strong point, and he's never been good at timekeeping. He'll probably show up some time this evening. Isn't he something? Can you believe our little Will has grown up?'

'Unbelievable,' Holly agrees, wondering why her heart is sinking. So much for 'if he likes me, he'll come,' she thinks, and when Paul walks over and asks her if she's ready to leave, she nods, amazed at how you can go from such a high to such a low in such a short space of time.

Chapter Five

'Mummy, can you give me some cereal?' Daisy's plaintive voice is inches away from Holly's face, as the sun streams through the wooden blinds on this bright Saturday morning.

'Yes, darling.' Holly groans, opening one eye and squinting at the alarm clock. Six fourteen. Oh God. What she would give to have children who sleep in late. 'Just give me a minute.'

Holly finds herself drifting back to sleep, when Daisy's voice intrudes again. 'Mummy? When are you going to get out of bed? Are you stuck?' Holly has occasionally got away with Daisy believing she is stuck in bed, running into Frauke's room instead, allowing Holly to get back to sleep.

'No. Coming,' she says, throwing the covers back and looking at the lump on the other side of the bed that is Marcus. In all their years together, Holly doesn't remember a time when Marcus got up to give the children breakfast. He is busy working all week, he says, and the weekends are the only time he gets to sleep. What about me? Holly had once tried to argue. I work, too, and I raise the children and I run the house and I pay the bills and I cook. When do *I* get a lie-in?

You have Frauke during the week, Marcus had argued back. And then had inferred that Holly's job was largely irrelevant. An indulgence, she thinks he had called it, whereas his job was very important and he was tired and he *deserved* to sleep.

There are times when Holly looks at Marcus and hates him.

Oliver is already curled up on the sofa at the far end of the kitchen, glued to some inappropriately violent cartoon, which he shouldn't be watching, but it stops him and Daisy from fighting, and it is Saturday morning after all.

'Morning, Olly,' Holly calls, but no response. She tries again, and is rewarded with a flicker of eyes in her direction.·

'Who wants French toast?' she calls brightly, checking she has enough eggs, and Oliver rouses himself enough to say he does.

'Can I help, Mummy?' Daisy drags a chair across the kitchen and hauls herself up next to Holly. 'I'll do the eggs,' she says, and Holly smiles and watches as Daisy cracks both eggs and eggshells into the bowl.

'Watch me,' Holly says, taking an egg and separating the shell carefully with her thumbs as the egg plops into the bowl. 'See? Now you try.' Daisy does the next egg perfectly, her little chest puffing up with pride.

Holly changes the radio from Radio Four—Marcus's choice—to Radio One, and makes a strong cup of coffee for herself, opening the local paper on the counter to see if there is anything to do with the kids this weekend. Saturdays and Sundays have started to crawl by, and these last couple of years she has dreaded the weekends.

Holly can't organise the playdates she organises during the week because weekends are family time, and Marcus isn't usually up until lunchtime, so every weekend morning is now spent trying to find things for the children to do. She would be perfectly happy to stay at home with them, but at some point a fight usually breaks out and the couple of times they have woken Marcus he has emerged in a fury. It's easier just to take them out.

Olivia had left a message last night, saying she had her nephew Oscar for the day and did Holly want to get together? Her nephew and niece are older than Oliver and Daisy, but they're happy to play with younger ones occasionally, and she'd love to spend some time with Holly again.

Holly calls her back and a few minutes later their date is set.

The park round the corner is Holly's favourite Saturday morning destination, especially on a crisp autumn day like today. The children can go leaf jumping, there's a great playground, both of them love seeing the dogs out on walks—several of whom they have come to know—and there's a sweet little café where Holly can get a cup of tea and occasionally a croissant or a pain au chocolat as a treat.

Oliver and Daisy both love the playground, although Oliver is professing to be slightly bored with it now that he's nearly seven, therefore nearly grown up and it's really for children, but there are always other mothers for Holly to talk to and she had found most of her friends in the neighbourhood here in the park.

'Yay!' Oliver's face lights up as they walk through the park towards the playground, and he breaks into a run, tearing in front of them as he pushes the gate open. 'They fixed the pirate ship!' And he roars into the playground, closely followed by Daisy.

Holly sees Olivia sitting on a bench, and realises that the only other boy in the playground must be Oscar; she sits down next to Olivia, who grins widely as she finishes her phone call.

'Gotta go,' she says on the phone. 'I'll call you back later. *Holly!*' She stands up and the two women hug. 'It's so ridiculous how years can go by without seeing each other, and now I haven't seen you in a couple of weeks it feels like it's been years! How are you?'

'I'm great. It's good to see you. It was a complete godsend when you called.' Holly sticks her hands in her pockets and shivers at the November sky. 'I thought I'd die of boredom sitting in the park again by myself.'

'I know how you feel.' Olivia laughs. 'Why do you think my cellphone is surgically attached to my right ear?'

'Where's your niece?'

'My sister's taken her to a girly birthday party. Hence Oscar's day with me. So where's Marcus today?'

Holly looks away.

'Uh-oh. If he's anything like my sister's husband I'd have to take a guess that he's either working or sleeping. Hmm. I'll go with working.'

'Nope, sleeping. Why is it that they think they work harder than anything and deserve all this time off, when they have no idea what we do. Christ, if Marcus had to look after the children and run the house it would be a disaster. It would be like bloody boot camp.' She starts doing an impression of Marcus: 'Oliver! Get your shoes off the sofa now! Daisy, put those cushions back. Oliver! Upstairs to your homework now! Holly! Stop breathing! Now!' Holly sighs.

'Oh well.' Olivia rubs Holly's arm, surprised at how much Holly is sharing. 'These things are sent to try us. It's really great to see you, you know. You and I ought to do lunch sometimes. Or a girls' night out. I could do with a few laughs now and then.'

'I'd love to,' Holly says truthfully.

Suddenly, Olivia's face lights up with inspiration. 'What are you doing tonight? Why don't you and Marcus come over for supper? I always feel horrible about not doing anything on a Saturday night.'

'No baby sitter,' Holly says. 'Frauke's going to Brighton for the weekend. But why don't you come over to us?'

'Are you sure? I feel like I've just invited myself.'

'That's OK. We weren't doing anything. It will be lovely.'

By the time Holly and the children get back home, Marcus is sitting at the kitchen table with a cafetière full of coffee, classical music wafting softly from the speakers in the wall and the papers spread out in front of him.

'Hello, my darling children,' he smiles, putting the paper down and opening his arms wide for his giggling, excited children to run into. 'I've missed you this week. Oh my goodness, Daisy, have you grown two inches since Tuesday?'

'No!' she giggles. 'Maybe just one inch.'

'Well, you look much much taller. And, Oliver, where did those muscles come from?' He squeezes Oliver's forearm gently.

'I've been practising my push-ups,' Oliver says proudly. 'And my gym teacher says I'm the best in class.'

'Well, that is good news, isn't it? I can tell!' And Marcus looks over the children's heads at Holly and winks at her, and Holly can't help but smile.

At times like these, when Marcus is loving, kind and gentle, Holly knows that it will be fine. That she didn't make a wrong decision, that perhaps it is possible that she will spend the rest of her life with him. There are things missing, undoubtedly, but perhaps what they have is enough. Marcus is a good man. He may want a different lifestyle than Holly, but it is not a huge hardship for her to step into the role he expects, and surely the payoff is worth it. He is a good husband, a good father, a good provider.

He is steady and reliable, the very opposite of her own parents. Everything about Holly's life is safe and stable, exactly what she had grown up vowing she would have when she was married and had children. So there's no passion, no excitement, no spark. So what? Doesn't that inevitably disappear after a while anyway? There are other things that make up for that.

'Oh, I met Olivia at the park,' Holly says. 'An old friend from school, remember? I've invited her over for supper.' A pause, as she remembers how much he dislikes impromptu invitations. 'Is that OK?' she says hopefully.

'It's fine!' Marcus says, cheerfully.

Holly feels her shoulders sink with relief.

'I could do with a good evening,' he says. 'Anyone else we should invite?' This is when Marcus throws her, when he is unexpectedly generous and warm. 'It might be fun to have a dinner party. I could see if Richard and Caroline are around.' Holly's heart sinks. Richard was a boring old colleague of Marcus's. 'You'll like his wife,' Marcus says. 'She's a fashion journalist, very fun.'

'It's just that I don't think Olivia's expecting a proper dinner party,' Holly says cautiously. 'I think more of a kitchen supper, and it's very last minute, I doubt anyone will be around. But we could try . . . how about inviting Paul and his wife Anna, as well, if your friend's wife is a fashion journalist?'

Marcus looks confused.

'Paul is another old school friend,' she reminds him, 'married to Anna, who runs Fashionista.co.uk, so she'll probably have tons in common with Caroline. I haven't even met Anna yet—she was on a business trip, so couldn't make Tom's memorial service—and I'd love to know what she's like. Paul's so easy he gets on with everyone. They may not even be able to come, but I'd love to ask them.'

'Great idea!' Marcus says, having read a profile of Anna just last week.

Holly picks up the phone to call Paul.

By six o'clock the children are bathed, fed and mesmerised by *The Incredibles* on the DVD player in Holly and Marcus's bedroom. The braised lamb shanks are bubbling merrily in the Le Creuset in the oven, and the tarte tatin is cooling off next to the stove. The table in the kitchen has been set with pretty Provençal-style blue and yellow linens, and Holly has only checked her email eight times since waking up this morning.

I am being ridiculous, she tells herself. Of course Will isn't going to send me an email. This isn't dating, for heaven's sake. I am a married mother of two, and just because he confessed he had a crush on me twenty years ago, it means nothing today. Will is lovely, but he's Tom's brother, which is probably what this whole thing is about. Less about Will than about having a connection to Tom. This isn't a real feeling and I know, I absolutely know, that this will pass.

These thoughts fly around Holly's head and, with a sigh of relief— now she understands—she turns her computer off and walks downstairs to get ready for supper.

'She's gorgeous!' Holly whispers to Olivia as they emerge from the basement—or, as Marcus would call it, the wine cellar—with another couple of bottles. 'I feel so dowdy next to her.'

Holly colours immediately as they walk into Caroline, standing at the foot of the stairs. She is surprised when Caroline leans forward with a conspiratorial whisper. 'Did you see her Chloe bag? That thing's impossible to get—waiting lists for months—unless you run Fashionista.co.uk.'

'I'm so sorry.' Holly tries to get her foot out of her mouth. 'You've never even met me before and here I am, gossiping.'

'Don't worry about it,' Caroline says as Holly relaxes. 'Fashion's all about gossip. What a boring world it would be without it.'

'Well, then . . . I know this is a terrible thing to say, but I feel slightly embarrassed about my house.' Holly winces. 'I feel Anna ought to be sitting on a Conran sofa in a beautiful house in Regent's Park, not on my shabby old sofa, which used to be my mum's, in my Edwardian house in Brondesbury.'

'Don't be silly,' Olivia chides her firmly. 'First of all your house is gorgeous and second of all they live in Crouch End. That's hardly Regents Park. Anyway, everything Tom ever said about her was good..Caroline, you'll know Anna's reputation. What have you heard?'

'That she's delightful. One of the most down-to-earth people in the business. Come on, let's go and talk to her properly.'

Holly groans. 'Oh, do I have to?'

'Stop it,' Olivia grins. 'I'll start and you can join in.'

But she doesn't have to. As soon as they walk back upstairs and into the kitchen, they find Anna with her shoes kicked off, sleeves rolled up, chopping the salad that Holly had abandoned to go and gossip with Olivia in the basement.

'Oh, Anna, you don't have to do that!' Holly is horrified.

'I do not mind in the slightest,' Anna smiles. 'I grew up in Sweden where the whole family always mucked in to help out with the meals.'

'But . . . I don't want you to get your clothes dirty.'

Anna leans towards her with a smile. 'The beauty of having a fashion company is that you can always get a replacement for the clothes. Anyway, where are the kids? Paul told me you had two. I would love to meet them.'

'Upstairs watching a DVD. Would you like to come up? I ought to put them to bed now anyway.'

'I would love to,' Anna says. 'Let us go and find those munchkins. Can I read the stories? I have three nieces who let me read the stories. I'm particularly good at the scary monsters.'

Holly laughs. 'The kids would love it. Although Daisy's current favourite is *The Tiger Who Came to Tea*. Not sure your monster voice would work.'

'You have created a real home,' Anna says, as she steps onto the upstairs landing and stops to admire the antique games table, piled with books, and knick-knacks. 'I always remember something I read somewhere once that said, "Houses are made of sticks and stone, but homes are made of love alone." This is definitely a home. I am envious.'

'Isn't your house a home then?'

'It is beautiful but quiet. Too perfect. We need children running around to mess it up a bit, bring it to life.'

Ah, yes. There it is. The sensitive subject of children.

'Oh, don't worry.' Anna puts a hand on Holly's arm. 'It is no secret that I am having IVF. We keep telling ourselves that this will be the last time we try, but then I keep thinking that perhaps the next time is the magic time.'

'I hope it works for you,' Holly says. 'I really do.'

'Thank you,' Anna smiles, as they walk through the door and find Daisy and Oliver sprawled out on Holly's bed, all the pillows scattered around them on the floor.

'She's amazing!' Holly whispers to Olivia, back downstairs.

'Told you!' Olivia smiles. 'So it's true what they say.'

'What are you two talking about?' Paul wanders over to the cupboard to get a refill of wine.

'Actually we were just saying how much we like your wife.' Holly grins. 'How did you end up snagging a gem like her?'

'God only knows.' Paul laughs. 'I ask myself the same question pretty much every day.'

'How did you meet?' Caroline asks.

'I interviewed her for the *Sunday Times*. I knew I had found someone special and kept calling her on the pretext of having forgotten questions. Then, of course, I had to meet her for coffee to fact-check, and in the end, she said she'd really just prefer it if I came clean and took her out for dinner.'

'I hope you took her somewhere smart and trendy.'

'Actually no.' Paul grins. 'I took her to Nando's.'

'What!' Caroline is horrified. 'You took her to a fast-food chicken place? Please tell me you're joking.'

Paul shakes his head. 'Whatever for? I wanted to see if she was really as down-to-earth as she seemed. It was great. She picked up that chicken with her fingers and ate as if she hadn't eaten in months.'

'I knew there was a reason I liked her,' Holly chuckles.

Marcus raises his glass. 'Here's to Anna. Holly would have been livid if I'd taken her somewhere like that on our first date.' The others laugh, but Holly grits her teeth at the lie—she wouldn't have cared; it was Marcus who cared about things like that.

'Where is Anna anyway?' Paul frowns.

'Reading stories to Daisy, who's got her reading *Cinderella*, which goes on for ever. Not stupid, my daughter.'

'Clearly,' Paul says, smiling, but there is sadness in his eyes.

'I'll go and rescue her in a minute,' Holly says.

'No, don't. She'll be having a wonderful time,' Paul says, and sure enough, when Anna walks back in the kitchen, half an hour later, her eyes are shining and she is beaming from ear to ear.

The meal is a huge success, and by the time the tarte tatin is brought to the table, with vanilla ice cream, talk has turned to Tom.

'I can't imagine losing a son,' Caroline says, shivering with horror. 'There just can't be anything worse than losing a child.'

'What about losing your partner?' Paul says. 'Obviously I can't speak about losing children, not yet, but I can't think of anything worse than losing Anna.'

For a moment they all lapse into silence as they think about losing the person they love most in the world.

And Holly starts to cry. Not because she's thinking about Marcus. Because she's thinking about Tom.

Saffron wheels her bag through LAX and waves hello to Samuel, P's driver. He's standing where he always stands, as reliable and discreet as ever, and Saffron has long got over the discomfort of Samuel knowing that she is the mistress.

Heads turn as she strides behind Samuel to the car park. A few Brits recognise her, but it is more likely that they are looking because she is beautiful. Beautiful and clever but not so clever that she knew not to get involved with a married man. Not so clever that she was able to resist the demons that even now are hovering just above her shoulder.

Saffron was six years old when she met Holly. She was the new girl in school—a tiny, pretty blonde thing who walked into Miss Simpson's classroom with confidence and assurance. They didn't become friends. Saffron fell in with one of the cool kids—how ridiculous it is now to think that even at that age there were cool kids, and that they all knew exactly who they were—and Holly sat with the clever kids on the other side of the classroom. Saffron, it turned out, was clever as well. She crossed the bridge between the groups and, as they grew older, she gravitated towards Holly and Olivia and the threesome worked.

Saffron's home was in Hampstead. Her mother was an architect and her father was a magazine editor, and they lived in a house that was so ultra-modern that Holly and Olivia begged to go over there on a daily basis. Her bedroom was the converted attic. Enormous and surrounded by huge windows, there were no curtains, and in the middle of the room was a see-through acrylic tube, which was actually a shower. At one end was a sunken living area, complete with fuschia cushions.

Saffron's parents were the unlikeliest parents Holly and Olivia had ever seen. They were, well, *exotic* is the only word that comes to mind. They were also hardly ever there. Saffron and Holly bonded over their shared freedom although Saffron handled it differently. Where Holly was desperate for parents to be around, Saffron thrived on the freedom and was enough of a free spirit to recognise that conventional parents would have suffocated her.

Conventional parents might also have stopped her drinking.

It seemed to be normal for all of them as teenagers. Most of them would get drunk or stoned when they went to parties. The difference with Saffron was that she would drink on her own. Not to get drunk, just because it felt good.

And then, at university, she didn't drink very much at all. Unlike her friends, most of whom were away from home for the first time and took advantage of the freedom by getting drunk every night.

Back in London, having got a first in English and drama, she started working: one of the lucky few to get immediate castings in TV ads. Drinking seemed to become easier in London but, still, never enough to get drunk, just enough to unwind.

She didn't eat much during these years. She liked being thin. Liked not eating. She felt clean and in control when she climbed into bed knowing she had eaten just fruit and vegetables all day, and the less of them she ate, the better she felt.

Her career took off. A part in a TV series, and a cleverly concocted fake romance with one of the hot young stars in film pushed her into the public eye, and soon she was one of the bright young things in London. She was also drinking more and more.

When Saffron moved to LA for a movie her agent insisted she go to rehab. She didn't want to, but nor did she want to lose the part. Rehab was followed by intensive twelve-step meetings. AA was her life saver. If ever she felt lonely or insecure, or just needed some company, she could turn up at one of the hundreds of meetings on her doorstep and instantly feel at home.

But it was more than just the company. She really lived the programme. She was doing what she was told to do: taking it a day at a time, learning that she couldn't do it alone.

One day, Saffron had been sitting in the corner, absent-mindedly doodling on the tiny notepad she always brought to the meetings, when she heard a rich and warm voice. It was familiar but she couldn't place it. When she looked up, she recognised him instantly. Three times voted Hollywood's sexiest man by *People* magazine, in one of those fairy-tale marriages with an equally famous film-star wife, he was one of the biggest earners in the business.

But an alcoholic? She never knew. He shared that day about humility. About how, when he was drinking, he was pompous, thought he knew the answers to everything. He was a nightmare on film sets, he said, but this programme had changed his life, had given him a second chance.

He had learned the gift of humility, had learned that he was one of God's children, no better and no worse than anyone else. Now, he said, he treated everyone with kindness and respect.

Saffron went up to him at the coffee break. He was standing at the literature table looking at some leaflets.

'I just want to tell you,' she said, her heart beating faster because, even though she wasn't intimidated by celebrity, there was something about him that was different. 'I just want to tell you that I loved everything you said. It is exactly what my experience has been, and I love that you were able to be so honest in these rooms, that despite your fame, you trust this programme enough to be able to do that.'

He'd turned and really looked at her then. Intrigued by her English accent and the force behind her words. 'Thank you.' He'd held out his hand. 'I'm Pearce.'

Their friendship took a while. Initially they'd see each other at meetings, smile hello, occasionally have a brief chat during the coffee break.

Her sharing was always startlingly honest and usually peppered with swear words, which made him smile. He always found himself commenting on something she had shared—whatever she said always seemed to speak directly to him, and he found that on the rare occasions she didn't turn up at a meeting, he missed her, would wonder where she was.

He had been married for seven years. Ah, the seven-year itch, people would joke, but in truth the itch had started at one. The marriage had become a business arrangement. They didn't have children and would have divorced, but both their agents said their careers needed them to stay together—so much mileage out of being Hollywood's golden couple.

Both of them had had flings on movie sets, but both had learned to be discreet, and the truth was they were friends, they still liked each other. They accepted that this was the way it had to be for now.

It took about a year for him and Saffron to start having coffee after meetings. And then coffee became an occasional lunch, and soon they were chatting on the phone every day. Saffron had the glow of a woman in love, and P felt as if he were eighteen again—full of hope and excitement about the future.

He kissed her in her living room. Far too recognisable to take a chance on kissing her in public, he had come into her house one day instead of dropping her off and, as soon as they walked in, they both knew things were different.

Saffron had stopped worrying about his being married, stopped worrying about his desire not to fall in love. All she could think about was him. Not because he was a movie star, not because of the fame or the money, but because she adored him. Because he made her laugh. Because he understood her like no one else in the world and because she understood him. Perhaps because of the intimacy fostered in the safe confines of their meetings, they revealed things to each other that neither had ever told anyone else.

Their affair had progressed, always in private, often with other people around to throw the press off the scent. He even got her a part in his movie to legitimise their being seen together.

She, in turn, had manufactured a romance with her costar, a lesser, but rising star, and they were regularly photographed kissing on beaches. The costar was grateful that his lover—a male model—remained a secret and, of course, Saffron couldn't be linked to anyone else while so clearly in love with her costar.

Saffron had learned to put her life on hold for P. He would phone her whenever he could, but when he was away filming, it was so hard. Saffron tried to bury herself in yoga, in seeing friends, but her friends had fallen away somewhat—it was hard to maintain a friendship with someone who cancelled whenever her lover called—and even her meetings were suffering.

When P was there, they would sit next to each other and surreptitiously touch—she cross-legged on the sofa, her knee gently touching his thigh. She would tune out for most of the meeting, closing her eyes and thinking about him, opening them only to catch him looking at her, both of them smiling and looking away.

She wasn't focusing on the lessons of the programme at all. Her sponsor—the only person who knew—was trying to be firm, trying to point out all the dangers that came with her behaviour, how ultimately it would be Saffron who was at risk by not working the principles of the programme.

And it is true that Saffron hadn't found being around alcohol quite as easy as she used to. Just lately, walking into her little house at the end of the day, she found herself thinking, Wouldn't it be nice to have one drink? Just one. And last week, when she had finished her grocery shopping, she had found herself passing the liquor store and had hesitated for longer than was comfortable. She knew what this was called. She was white-knuckling it. She hadn't even told her sponsor she'd had these feelings, convinced that she could do it on her own.

'You need to start working the steps,' her sponsor would say. 'You haven't done any step work for ages.'

'I know, I know,' Saffron would groan. 'It works if you work it.' But she didn't seem to have the will to do anything other than turn up to meetings as an excuse to see P.

Sarah groans and rolls over in bed as the sound of tapping on her door continues.

'Sarah love.' Her mother-in-law's voice is soft as the door gently pushes open. 'Paul and his wife, Anna, are here to see you. They're playing with the kids downstairs, and Paul's brought some school photographs of Tom that he thought you'd like.'

Sarah sits up and throws the duvet back. 'Tell them I'll be down in a sec,' she says, as she runs her fingers through her hair and sighs. Why do people keep coming? Why do they keep arriving proferring photographs, stories? Do they think it's going to make her feel better? Is it going to bring Tom back? All Sarah wants to do is crawl under the covers and sleep for ever.

It is easier to hide here in this house. Despite being surrounded by photographs and constant reminders of Tom, this is his childhood home, not the home she and Tom created together.

Paul hovers in the doorway of the living room and watches Anna tickling Violet, whose peals of laughter ring through the house.

'I'm guessing it won't be long before you have children of your own,' Maggie says, placing a hand on Paul's arm and smiling up at him.

'Fingers crossed,' Paul says, and as Anna looks up and catches his eye, he feels a wave of sadness wash over him. Life never turns out to be the way you expect. How could Tom possibly be taken from them at such a young age? And how is it that he and Anna, Anna who would make the most wonderful mother, have not been able to have children?

This morning they had been back to the hospital for egg collection. When Anna came out of sedation, the specialist told her they had released six eggs from the follicles. Better than last time, and they had both left feeling a surge of optimism and hope.

Tomorrow, as had always happened, they would receive a phone call to tell them how many of the eggs had been fertilised, or if, as before, no eggs had been fertilised, there are no embryos to potentially carry your hopes and dreams into the future.

That had been the case so many times already, and Anna didn't know if she had the emotional fortitude to go through it again, not to mention the financial ability. She didn't mind that the money which kept their joint account afloat was almost exclusively hers. Paul would put the money he earned from freelancing into the same account, but it seemed to be a drop in the ocean towards funding their lifestyle.

Not that it was particularly extravagant, but they travelled well and often, went to the best restaurants, and a couple of years ago, just before finally deciding to go forward with IVF, they had bought a barn in Gloucestershire. It hadn't been touched since the early seventies. They had taken their friend Philip, an architect, to view it; and Phil's enthusiasm for the project was so infectious they had found themselves, shortly afterwards, the proud but slightly apprehensive owners of White Barn Fields.

The barn was a bargain and they had paid cash for the entire thing, planning on starting the work immediately.

It was Anna's idea of heaven: what a wonderful place for children, how perfect to spend summers out here with the kids or come down on winter weekends for leaf stomping and hot chocolate in front of a roaring fire in the huge stone fireplace at one end of the enormous great room. Even Paul, who had mostly thought of himself as an urban creature, had to admit that Phil's plans were remarkable, and they would end up with an idyllic getaway. Anna had made sure to include a study for Paul—at the top of the barn, up a hidden staircase. 'If you can't write the great British novel here,' Philip had joked when he had shown the plans to Paul and Anna, 'I don't know where you can.'

Nearly a year later, they can hardly bear to think about it. Almost all of the money they had intended for the barn has been eaten up by back-to-back IVF treatments. So far they've spent about £50,000 on IVF, a huge chunk of their savings.

The work on the barn has started. The rotten walls have been replaced with reclaimed barn siding and the roof has been done. But the kitchen and bathrooms were ordered and then cancelled.

The last time they went up to have a look, Anna burst into tears. 'This was our dream,' she said to Paul. 'And now we cannot afford to finish it.'

'We will one day,' Paul said, so sorry that he wasn't able to pull a magic wand out and make it happen, so sorry that his work didn't provide him enough money to take over when the going got tough. 'I promise you one day this will be finished.'

They left that night and stayed at a local B & B—a few hundred paces down the road from the Relais & Chateaux hotel where they used to stay before.

'If they could see me now,' Anna sang, picking her way gingerly down the hallway, having run a lukewarm bath in a cracked bath in the bathroom at the other end, and Paul shrugged. 'We have to stop the treatment, you know,' he attempted carefully. 'It is ridiculous that we can't afford anything any more. We can't keep going like this.'

'Hopefully we will not have to.' Anna had squeezed his arm. 'I have a feeling this one is going to work.' Paul had sighed. She had said that every time.

You would never guess any of this. Looking at Anna right now, sitting cross-legged on the floor as Violet, who, like all children who come into contact with Anna, has fallen completely in love with her, you would think that Anna is beautiful, poised and perfect. You would think that nothing in her life could ever go wrong.

'**H**i,' Sarah's voice is listless as she comes into the room and sits on the sofa, dark shadows under her eyes, her hair still mussed.

'We brought some photos of Tom.' Paul thinks about going across the room to hug her, but something about her is so shut down, he knows he'll be rejected, so stays where he is.

'I know. Maggie said.'

'Would you like to see them?'

'Sure,' she says, and Paul hands them to her.

Sarah starts to sift through the photographs and a ghost of a smile hovers over her lips as she stops at a picture of Paul, Holly and Tom, all of them with braces on their teeth, at Paul's fifteenth birthday party.

'God, look at that hair!' Sarah says. 'I never knew Tom had long hair. He looks awful!'

'We all looked awful,' Paul says, grateful that Sarah finally seems to be engaged. 'Look at Holly's shocking-pink lipstick.'

'Tom was so skinny,' Sarah muses. 'You'd never think he'd become so buff.'

'Buff?' Paul asks.

'Fit. He was forever in the gym. He got this thing about Iron Man contests. Crazy stuff where you bike 12 miles, swim 2.4 miles, then run 26.2 miles. He did one in Florida and was training for another.' She shakes her head. 'He was so fit. So strong. That's what I find so hard to believe. I mean, I could understand almost anyone else not surviving, but Tom? How could Tom not have got himself out of there?'

There's an awkward silence, neither Paul nor Anna knowing what to say, and after a while, Sarah turns to the next picture and bursts out laughing. 'Tom was in the army?' she sputters.

'TA,' Paul says sheepishly, 'was the thing to do at the time.'

In the kitchen, getting a tray of tea ready, Maggie sits down heavily at the kitchen table.

'Thank you.' She looks up at a concerned Anna. 'This is the first time Sarah has sounded anything like herself. Those photos are just what she needed right now.'

'What about you?' Anna asks gently. 'What do you need right now?'

'Oh, I'll be fine,' Maggie says with a false brightness. 'I'll just finish making this tea and if you could just take Pippa outside to pee that would be wonderful.'

Anna leaves, but she turns just as she reaches the doorway to see Maggie lean her head on her arms on the kitchen table and groan softly as she rocks back and forth.

Chapter Six

'WHAT'S THE MATTER with you today?' Yvonne, the receptionist at the animal refuge, walks into the sitting room with a lunchtime sandwich and collapses on the sofa.

Olivia looks up in surprise. 'What do you mean? Nothing's the matter.'

'You're acting like you've got ants in your pants,' Yvonne says. 'We think it must be a man.'

'What?' Olivia attempts a laugh. 'Haven't you got anything better to do than gossip about my love life?'

Yvonne purses her lips. 'Actually we all wish you had a love life for us to gossip about. You deserve someone much better than that awful George.'

Olivia's mouth falls open. 'But you all said you loved George.'

'Yes, well. That was before he dumped you.'

'I'm not going to talk about that,' Olivia says, standing up and walking to the door. 'But just for info, I do have a date tonight.'

As Yvonne's face lights up and she prepares to shower Olivia with questions, Olivia shuts the door and walks back to her office, giggling.

She is meeting Fred tonight. He is finally here. She shouldn't be excited, particularly given that this is a five-day business trip, but this is the first time for a long time that she has felt there is something to look forward to. She has arranged to meet him at the Dorchester Hotel at seven o'clock.

At three, she does something she never does. Pulls on her coat, picks up her bag, and announces to Sophie, her assistant, that if there's anything urgent, she'll be on her mobile. And Sophie, who has inadvertently seen a couple of emails from Fred, winks her approval and shoos Olivia away, knowing that nothing, bar the refuge burning down, would cause her to phone her.

Olivia's first stop is the hairdresser's. 'I need to cover the grey,' she tells Rob the colourist, 'and then I need a trim. I'm in your hands. Knock yourself out.'

Two hours later, Olivia stares in awe at her reflection in the mirror.

Chestnut and copper streak her hair; and Kim, the junior stylist, has cut long layers into her bob that sweep her cheeks and make her look years younger.

Kim and Rob stand behind her, waiting for Olivia's reaction.

'I love it,' she squeals. 'I love, love, love it,' and Kim hands her a mirror to see the back, both of them laughing as she stares with obvious delight at herself and her new swinging, shiny hair.

'Now just remember,' Rob says as he walks her to reception to pay. 'Lipstick and blush, little black dress and a lot of confidence.'

Olivia turns to him. 'Thank you so much,' she says, spontaneously reaching out and giving him a hug. 'Wish me luck!'

There are pools of men huddled at the bar, and Olivia's first instinct is to turn and run. She can't do this. Has never been any good at this.

Some of the men turn and look at her, a couple of them approvingly, and she takes a deep breath and looks around, hoping to see Fred, hoping to know instantly which one he is. Sitting at a table in the corner is a man reading the *Financial Times*. He looks up and catches her eye, his face breaking into a huge grin.

Please, God. She whispers a silent prayer in her mind as this tall, broad-shouldered athlete of a man comes over, a perfect American smile—huge white teeth and boy-next-door good looks. Please God, she whispers, let this be him.

'Olivia!' There's no question in his voice but, of course, she had sent him a picture of herself.

'Hi!' she says shyly, gratitude and delight in her eyes as he stands up and envelops her in a bear hug, making her feel very small and delicate and feminine. Fred steps back to grin at her, then ushers her over to where he was sitting, a large, strong hand resting in the small of her back.

'Wow!' he says, holding out a chair for her to sit down. 'You look great.' And as he looks around for a waiter to take their order for drinks, Olivia finds herself smiling.

'Tom was right,' Fred says, as the waiter places one Cosmopolitan and one vodka martini on the table.

'Right about what?'

'Right that I should meet you.' He smiles, raising his glass for a toast. 'To new friendships, and to Tom.'

Olivia smiles even as the tears well up in her eyes. 'To Tom,' she echoes, and Fred passes her a napkin, which she dabs against her eyes, blinking until the tears go away.

'I'm so sorry.' She smiles then. 'It still gets me at the most unexpected times.'

'Of course it does,' Fred says. 'It gets me, too, and I was just a work colleague. When it happened, it was all I could think about for days. I became, like, addicted to the news. I was watching everything, reading everything about the survivors, the families of those who had been lost, and I still think about it every day, but not all day, not the way I did.'

'That's true,' Olivia says. 'I do think about it, too, but not all day, not any more. Still, Tom wouldn't want us to sit here and cry over him. Let's talk about dinner. Where do you feel like eating?'

'Apparently there's a great noodle place round the corner.'

Olivia grins. 'Wagamama. It's one of my favourites.' And with that they drink up and leave.

As soon as they walk in Olivia feels at home. All dressed up in the bar of the Dorchester Hotel was about as far removed from Olivia's life as you could get. She realised, as she sank down on the bench opposite Fred, squeezed between strangers busy slurping noodles, that she had been playing a role tonight, something she was never comfortable doing.

'You know what?' Fred looks around the restaurant. 'I wish I wasn't in this damn suit. I'd much rather be in jeans and sneakers.'

Olivia starts to laugh. 'Thank you for saying that. I was just thinking I wish I was in my jeans and boots. When I'm all dressed up, I feel like I act differently.'

Fred grins at her. 'Same here. Tell you what.' He looks at his watch. 'How long would it take you to run home and throw on jeans, then get back here?'

'About half an hour if I rush,' Olivia says, smiling.

'OK. Done. I'll run back to the hotel and I'll see you back here in twenty minutes.'

'Are you sure you're not going to do a runner on me?' Olivia asks quickly. 'This isn't a way of saying you think this is going to be an awful evening so let's end it now?'

Fred looks shocked. 'Are you kidding me? This is going to be a great evening. Let's just get it started on the right foot.'

'That's the best idea I've heard all week.' Olivia laughs, and when they stand up and thread their way through the restaurant to the door, she doesn't mind in the slightest that Fred again places a hand gently on her back to guide her through.

In fact, if she had to be honest, she'd have to say the shiver that ran up and down her spine was something she hadn't felt in a long time.

Olivia wakes up early as she always does and lies in bed for a while replaying the events of last night. She turns her head slightly to see Fred, face squashed into the pillow, snoring gently, still sound asleep. Yes. It was real. Yes. She did bring him home to her flat. Yes. She had sex for the first time since George. And yes. It was fanfuckingtastic.

She had been making coffee when Fred kissed her. He had come up behind her and put his arms round her—such strong arms—and she had tensed slightly, unsure of what to do, when he had taken the decision out of her hands by turning her to face him and leaning down to kiss her.

What a wonderful night it had been. And now . . . what? Morning. Isn't this when it is supposed to be awkward, difficult? Isn't he supposed to wake up and be cold, regret what happened, get out of the flat as quickly as possible?

Olivia gets up and goes to make coffee in the kitchen. Under normal circumstances it would be instant, but—a clue that this outcome isn't altogether unexpected—she has fresh ground coffee to put in the cafetière and huge buttery croissants in the fridge.

'Morning.' Olivia jumps, turning to see a dishevelled Fred padding sleepily through the kitchen in his boxer shorts. God, she thinks, taking in his chest, the muscles in his legs. He is just so delicious.

'Morning,' she says, a touch frostily, but only because she is not sure where this is going and doesn't want to be humiliated by coming on too strong when he may be getting ready to cold shoulder her and walk out of the door.

'So, Saturday morning, huh? What do we have planned today?' And he comes up to her and wraps her in his arms, bending down to kiss her on the lips, and Olivia folds into him feeling warm and secure and oh so very, very good.

'Thank you, God,' she whispers, as she hands Fred a towel for his shower. 'And thank you, Tom,' she grins at the ceiling. 'He's pretty great. You did good.' And when Fred hollers at her to join him, she slips her dressing gown off and opens the steamed-up door.

'Helloooo?' Olivia pushes open the front door as her niece and nephew trip in behind her. 'Holly? Anyone here?' She follows the sound of a television and walks through to the living room where Daisy and Oliver are comatose in front of a cartoon.

'Hey, guys,' Olivia says, as her niece and nephew move like zombies towards the sofa, planting themselves next to the other kids without taking their eyes off the screen for a second, without even saying hello.

'Where's Mum?'

No answer.

'Where's Mum? Oliver?'

'Upstairs.' He gestures feebly with a hand.

Holly hears the footsteps on the stairs and quickly minimises the email she was writing, so what is left on the screen is an innocuous picture of a ladybug.

'Hey you!' Olivia walks over and gives her a hug. 'What are you doing?'

'Oh, I just had some bills to pay online,' Holly says. 'I know, I'm a horrible mother sticking my kids in front of the TV, but it's the only way I can get anything done.'

'Do you not think my sister Jen does that about a million times a day?' Olivia laughs. 'Still, do you want to turn it off now that we're here? Probably best that they all play, don't you think?'

Holly flushes a bright, guilty red. 'Oh, yes, of course. You should have just switched it off. Come on, let's go downstairs.'

Twenty minutes later Oscar and Oliver are racing round the house shouting, waving swords, and Ruby and Daisy are behind closed doors in Daisy's bedroom, Ruby helping Daisy to draw pictures, much to Daisy's delight.

Olivia sips her tea and recounts the events of her glorious few days with Fred.

'He sounds completely delicious.'

'He is.' Olivia blushes. 'He's practically perfect in every way.'

'So . . . how are you going to navigate it?'

'Navigate what?'

'A long-distance relationship.'

'I'm not.' Olivia frowns at Holly. 'The truth is he was, he is, gorgeous, but he's in his early thirties, and not someone I could see myself with.'

'Really? So it was just mad sex?'

'Pretty much.'

'Oh God.' Holly sighs heavily as gets up from the table. 'How I miss those days of mad sex.'

Olivia laughs, thinks nothing of it as Holly bends over to get the carrot sticks and hummus out of the fridge for the kids.

'OK, so come on then, confess,' Olivia says at last. 'What have you been doing?'

Holly straightens up and looks at Olivia in confusion, and ever such a tiny touch of guilt. 'What are you talking about?'

'You look fantastic, that's what. You look like you've lost about a stone since I last saw you. And you're all glowy and gorgeous. Hang on, let me guess . . . Pilates? No, it's probably Bikram yoga.'

Holly starts laughing. 'I'm far too lazy to do exercise, are you mad? Running around after the kids is more than enough exercise for me.'

'So . . .' Olivia muses, refusing to let it go. 'Are you and Marcus having lots of fantastic sex all of a sudden? Is that what it is?'

'Christ, no.' Holly swallows quickly. 'I just haven't been very hungry. You know how it is, sometimes you're hungry and sometimes you just seem to have no appetite.'

'Well, whatever it is you're doing, don't stop. You look completely fantastic,' Olivia says, reaching for a chocolate digestive.

'**D**on't stop,' is what she said. Does that mean I have permission to carry on doing what I'm doing? But what am I doing? I'm not doing anything. We're just friends. That's all.

Holly had forgotten all about Will. She had written him off as one of those silly crushes you have when there has been an emotional turmoil in your life. She has been to Maggie and Peter's house several times since the day after the service and is grateful to have them back in her life. She knows that if she had run into Will there, she would have been polite but cool.

One morning she had just got back from taking the kids to school and had dashed upstairs to get her portfolio before running into the office for a meeting about next year's line of Christmas cards—the theme was going to be angels, and Holly had spent a week researching and putting together a presentation of her ideas. She had been completely consumed by this for the past few days, and turned back just to check her email before she left, just to be sure there wasn't a last-minute message from work saying the meeting had been cancelled.

And there it was. An email from Will. Holly was in a hurry, but she leaned over her chair and clicked it open.

To: Holly
From: Will
26/11/06 4:56:09
Subject: Apology

Dear Holly,

I meant to write earlier but life suddenly seemed to become very difficult. Losing Tom felt like I was living in a dream sequence for a while. A part of me kept expecting that the next time the phone rang it would be Tom at the other end.

But after the service, it hit me. He's dead. And I just couldn't handle speaking to anyone at all. I think it hit Mum and Dad at the same time. It's almost as if having a house full of visitors, people dropping in all day and night to pay their respects, allows you to not think about the terrible thing that's happened to you.

I've been going over to see Mum and Dad every day, and they're fantastic when people call in—they can sit and chat about nothing and everything and listen to stories about Tom without falling apart, but then as soon as everyone leaves, as soon as the house is quiet, I hear Mum sobbing in the bathroom, or Dad goes out to his greenhouse and I see him there, shoulders heaving as he buries his head in his hands. So I have to be the strong one, particularly now. It's strange to find yourself taking care of your parents. I didn't expect to be doing this until they were old, although even then I suppose I had thought Tom would be the caretaker. It's a role I've never played. Tom was the strong, responsible one.

We'd grown apart the last couple of years. Mostly because I always sensed Sarah didn't approve of me. Of course, now I feel so guilty. So much I wish I'd said, so many things I wish I'd told him. I imagine he knew that I loved him, but I'm not sure I ever told him, and I wish I had.

I think one of the biggest surprises is how alone I feel. Even though Tom lived in America, and I barely saw him, I feel completely alone in the world, and the grief sometimes does seem harder than I can bear, after all. And I suppose with that loneliness comes fear—not an emotion I'm used to, and I still can't figure out exactly what it is I'm fearful of—my own mortality, perhaps?

So, I digress. The point of this is twofold: somehow I feel that I can talk to you and not be judged. I want to apologise for not being in touch sooner. I just couldn't talk to anyone for a while. I hope you understand and hope you're still willing to play the role of big sister— God knows I could do with someone like that now.

Thinking of you and sending my love,
Will

To: Will
From: Holly
27/11/06 9:56:24
Subject: Apology

Will

What an amazing email. Thank you for being so honest and so brave. I feel honoured that you've chosen to reveal yourself to me.

I think I do know what it feels like to be that alone. In many ways, I feel like I've been alone for years. I'm not sure whether you'll understand, but when I was younger, I suppose when Tom and I were closest, I never did feel alone. Tom was always my best friend, my ally, but since I've been married I haven't really felt like I've had an ally. Of course Marcus is my partner, but he is at work so much. (God, big step for me even writing this down . . . and I apologise if I'm gabbling.)

Tom's death has forced all of us who loved him to re-examine our lives, and perhaps with you, you are having to step into a role that you weren't prepared for. BUT—and so important for you to hear this, Will—it's a role I know you can do. I have such wonderful memories of you when we were younger—you were always so sweet and so caring even when you were, as usual, getting into trouble (of course, I didn't know then you had a crush on me . . .). This is a difficult time for all of us, but we can get through it. Tom wouldn't have wanted us all to give up our lives.

I'm also so glad you felt able to write as honestly as you did, and so eloquently as well—who knew the annoying little brother would grow up to be so emotionally aware? Seriously though, if there is any outlet at all for the kind of grief you must be feeling, the kind of grief we are all feeling, writing is probably one of the best.

And I'm sure I don't have to tell you this, but you can absolutely trust me. I would love to become friends, and mostly would love to be there for you if ever you need to talk.

Holly x

Friends. They could be friends, couldn't they? Naturally she can't deny a slight hint of attraction, but weren't all her old friendships with men based on a hint of attraction? And aside from Olivia, Saffron and Paul, who better to be friends with now than Will? Not a replacement for Tom, but someone else who loved Tom as much as she did, someone else who has a shared history with her.

For Holly has missed having a man to talk to. For the last year, she has tried very hard to talk to Marcus. She stores up stories about the children and about her work, but she tails off when she realises Marcus isn't paying much attention. So unlike her dinners with Tom, the two of them talking so quickly because there never seemed to be enough time to say everything they wanted to say.

'One person can't give you everything,' she'd said to Saffron just the other night when Saffron had phoned her from LA to bemoan the fact that P, who was supposed to be coming over, had just cancelled, and she wished he'd just hurry up and realise they were soul mates, made for each other, perfect together.

So odd, Holly thought in the beginning, to have fallen straight back into these friendships as if no time had gone by at all.

'I know that,' Saffron had said. 'I do, really, but I love this man. I just never expected life to be this hard.'

Me neither, Holly had thought, but she didn't say anything.

To: Holly
From: Will
30/11/06 22:23:38
Subject: Friends

Dear Holly,

I liked getting your email. It made me smile, and it made me think. All the things you said about questioning your life are absolutely right and I have begun to think, If I were to die tomorrow (more apologies for the morbidity), what would I leave behind?

Tom had created so much. There is no doubt in my mind that he and Scary Sarah, who, as you know, is not entirely my cup of tea either, loved each other, and although I couldn't ever imagine myself with anyone that rigid, I know it worked for Tom and that they had an exceptionally strong marriage.

And of course the children. Dustin and Violet, Dustin like a little Tom, serious and gentle, always preferring to hang out with the grown ups just as Tom did when he was little. But both of them so incredible—little people that will take Tom's spirit into their world.

Not that I ever wanted what Tom had . . . the conventional life, which always fills me with horror, but Tom always seemed to know where he was going, and I have less than no idea what I am doing from one day to the next, let alone for the rest of my life.

So the answer is I wouldn't leave much. All of a sudden that bothers me. Not that I'm going to do anything stupid like get married to the first girl who captures my heart (although if you're interested in divorcing Marcus and making an honest man out of me, do let me know!), but Tom's death has made me think, for the first time, that maybe I should settle down a bit. Get a mortgage. Find a girl I could love. Maybe have a couple of kids.

Hope you are having a peaceful day and that you have got your little monkeys to bed. I'd love to see photos of them—do they look like you? I'm imagining Daisy as, naturally, a mini-Holly—I know she's much younger than you were when I first met you, but I still remember you as this exotic bohemian creature. Unfairly I see Oliver as being a mini-Marcus, and I only say 'unfairly' because I hope he isn't as serious or as stuffy as I've heard Marcus is.

Love,
Will

To: Will
From: Holly
01/12/06 04:09:28
Subject: Friends

Will

I ought to be fast asleep, but find, like most nights these days, I wake up in the middle of the night and I'm done for. But how lovely to have your email and lovelier still to have some peace and quiet to send back a proper response.

My day yesterday was quite peaceful, since you asked. The monkeys went to bed early, and I was able to sink into a hot bath with a glass of wine, then crawl into bed. As far as I'm concerned, a good night is going to bed by nine, and a great night is going to bed by eight. Tonight was a great night. I have to say I do love it when Marcus travels around the country for trials—I can do whatever I want whenever I want.

You made me laugh saying I was exotic and bohemian. I never saw myself like that at all. I'm thinking it was those cheap Camden Lock Indian fringed skirts with little mirrors all over them that must have made me look bohemian. I have a very hard time picturing myself as anything other than a mum and wife these days.

I am enormously happy that you said such sweet things and I feel I have rediscovered a friend I didn't know I had.

Holly goes back to reread his previous emails. She's not sure why she does this, but she has reread them every day. They make her feel happy. Free. Young. She even stole away one night when Marcus was asleep just to check to see if another email had arrived. It had. It seems Will is as curious as she. For the first time in years, Holly has something to look forward to. She is fun and playful with the children but far too distracted to give them her full attention, and her distraction is affecting her relationship with Marcus.

Just the other night he came up behind Holly in the bathroom and put his arms round her. She turned round and kissed him and fifteen minutes later, when he rolled off her on their king-sized bed with a kiss and a smile, he said, 'Holly, that was fantastic.'

'It was rather, wasn't it?' She shot him a smile before getting up and disappearing back into the bathroom. What she didn't tell him was that she had closed her eyes—just twice, and only for seconds at a time—and imagined he was Will. Not that she was planning an affair—God, no!—but she just wanted to see what would happen if she did it. Isn't everyone entitled to a little fantasy now and then?

Across the Pond Saffron is indulging in a little fantasy of her own. P's wife is away filming, and he's staying with Saffron while she's away, at least for tonight.

Her legs are newly waxed, her nails newly painted, and her hair newly highlighted. She hasn't seen P for two weeks and, as always, is almost dizzy with excitement at the prospect of seeing him, and not just for the evening but for the whole night.

No make-up though. P loves her natural. He tells her frequently he loves her best first thing in the morning when her hair is messed up and her face scrubbed clean. He loves her in old sweats, baseball caps, and his oversized sweatshirts. That's how she looked when he fell in love with her, he tells her, seeing her at meetings looking as if she had just fallen out of bed.

Her fantasy tonight is much the same as it is every night. That he realises the futility of staying in a marriage just for the sake of his career and finally decides to leave. That he moves into this little house and that they fall asleep every night, wrapped around one another.

The fire is lit, the food warming gently in the oven, the setting is perfect. When P rings the doorbell, Saffron runs downstairs like an overexcited teenager, flings her arms round him in the hallway and kisses him for hours.

And Saffron is not the only one with fantasies. P has fantasies of family life. He has fantasies of a wife who loves him, who sleeps cuddled up to him at night. He has dreams of children—a pack of kids running around laughing—of his wife showering them all with kisses and fun. He dreams of wide-open spaces, horses, and owning land. And he still can't quite believe he made the choice he made when he married his wife.

In the beginning, he vaguely recalls, they would talk about their vision for their lives. He remembers her saying she wanted a production company, but she also said she wanted kids. He told her of his vision of the ranch, and she said it sounded wonderful. She said a lot of things in those days he realises now. A lot of things he wanted to hear, very few of them true.

When he first walked into AA, he resented her for trapping him in a loveless marriage, hated her for lying to him, could barely bring himself to talk to her. They would sit in limos on the way to premières, arguing fiercely, then step into the flash of light bulbs to demonstrate how much they loved one another. They gave interviews about the strength of their marriage, the things that they loved about each other, and with every one he believed he was giving the performance of his life.

The 12-step programme gave him the gift of acceptance. He learned to accept her rather than hate her because she wasn't who he wanted her to be. And just as he had learned to accept that his marriage was a great friendship and a wonderful working arrangement, Saffron had appeared at a meeting and captured his heart.

There is no doubt in his mind that he and Saffron were in that particular meeting that particular day for a reason, and however much he tells his manager he is committed to perpetuating the lie of the golden couple that is his marriage, he knows that there is only so long that he can live while not being true to himself, and the longer he stays in AA, this programme that demands nothing less than rigorous honesty, the harder it becomes.

And so much harder on nights such as these when Saffron is so clearly everything his wife is not.

Chapter Seven

HOLLY IS FIRST TO ARRIVE. She hates being first. She had deliberately timed it so she would be five minutes late, but when she walks into Nicole's, she doesn't see him.

'How many?' The maître d' asks politely and leads her to a table at the back for two. Holly resists the temptation to run to the loo to check her make-up. She knows it's fine—she checked it at every red light on the way here and several times while driving somewhat erratically along the winding London streets.

She taps her boot impatiently on the floor and catches sight of herself in the mirror on the other side of the room. God, if she didn't know better she'd never recognise herself. Skinny jeans tucked into knee-high, buttery leather boots, high enough to be sexy as hell, not so high she can't walk.

A cotton shirt, classic, but slim and long, and a chunky wide belt. She realises as she gazes around at the rest of the clientèle, she looks as if she belongs. She looks no different from the other young mothers sipping cappuccinos as they park their buggies next to the tables. Even though she is childless and buggyless today, she is what she is and, how funny, she thinks; her uniform of cashmere and pearls, so befitting for a lawyer's wife, has been swapped for a uniform of Notting Hill trendiness and Holly feels so much better in what she is wearing today.

'You look amazing!' Will's eyes widen in surprise and, she hopes, delight. No. She doesn't hope that. No point in hoping that. Or is there? Isn't it fine to enjoy someone appreciating you?

'Oh this? Wow. Thanks.' Holly blushes as she stands up to step into his hug, receive Will's air kisses on either cheek. Except his lips land softly on each cheek, even as hers skim the air on either side of his. Stop it! she tells herself as her heart flutters and she sits down quickly.

'Now you look like the Holly I remember.' Will grins, and as he does, she thinks with a jolt how much like Tom he looks.

'This is a bit weird, isn't it?' Holly finds herself saying.

'What? You and I having lunch? Frankly I think it's about time we took our email correspondence forward to a proper friendship, and you can't be friends if you never see one another. As the dating service says, it's only lunch.'

'No, not that. You just looked exactly like Tom when you smiled.' Holly picks up the napkin and holds it to her eyes. 'I'm so sorry, Will. So stupid that I'm the one sitting here with tears in my eyes when he's your brother. I don't feel I have a right to this display of emotion in front of you.'

Will leans over and places a hand on Holly's, squeezing it ever so gently. 'Holly, you loved him, too. Just for the record, you do have a right to display any emotion you want. I know how it reaches up and grabs you at the most unexpected times.'

'I'm sorry,' Holly says as a tear slides its way down her nose.

'It's OK,' Will says, and he keeps holding her hand.

'I'm pathetic,' Holly says through her sniffs. 'I'm sorry.'

'The only thing that's pathetic is that you keep apologising. Will you stop? Please?'

'OK.' She smiles. 'Sor . . . oh fuck off!'

'That's better!' Will grins. 'When was the last time you told a friend to fuck off?'

'Probably yesterday,' Holly says. 'I think I told Saffron to fuck off over the phone.'

'That's nice,' Will says in mock horror. 'Can't imagine why she's friends with you.'

'Because I'm kind and funny and loyal.'

'And pretty damn sexy with that hair if I may say so.'

'I . . .' Holly flushes bright red and Will starts to laugh.

'Are you going to turn scarlet every time I compliment you? Because if you are that's fantastic. I can start piling them on. Those jeans and boots make your arse . . .'

'Will!' Holly stops him, even as she's laughing.

'What? Can't I say arse?'

'No, you bloody can't. You don't know me nearly well enough.'

Will leans back in his chair, studying Holly with a smile. 'Well, well, well,' he says. 'Holly Mac, a prude.'

'I am not a prude,' she says indignantly.

'Tell me you have a great arse then.'

'No! I absolutely do not have to tell you I have a great arse to prove to you that I'm not a prude.'

'Go on. I won't believe you unless you tell me.'

'Fine. I have a great arse. Happy now?'

'Very. And yes, I agree. So. Shall we get menus?' The waiter appears, and Holly hides her embarrassment—her secret thrill—behind choosing what to have.

You're not used to being complimented are you?' Will muses, gazing at Holly over the rim of his cappuccino at the end of the meal, each of them reluctant to end what has been a lunch filled with laughter and teasing.

'No,' Holly says cautiously. 'Although I can't imagine being in a situation where I would be complimented these days. My life as a mother and freelance illustrator is very dull.'

'Holly?' Will's face is serious. 'May I ask you something?'

'Yes, but I'm not altogether sure I'll answer.'

'In one of your emails you said something about a good night being in bed by nine and a great night meant being in bed by eight. You didn't really mean that, did you?'

Holly smiles and leans forward. 'Will, my darling, one day hopefully you will have small children, and then you will understand exactly what I mean, and why sadly, it is the truth.'

'But I have tons of friends with kids and I don't know anyone besides you who actually goes to bed that early.'

Holly shrugs. 'I just get tired.'

'Are you sure you're not just checking out of life?'

'What?' Holly sits up straight, shocked.

'I'm sorry, Holly. I don't meant to say anything to offend you. It's just that you're so vibrant, you always were, but today, sitting here now, is

the first time I've seen the old Holly. When I saw you after the memorial service I couldn't believe how, well, how old you seemed. Obviously
it wasn't ideal circumstances, but even the way you were dressed was so
staid and proper. Like a shadow of who you used to be, who I always
dreamed you'd become.

'And I'm not saying this to upset you, but I think it's heartbreaking
that you're in bed every night by eight or nine. That's not living. That's
running away from life. That sounds to me like you're burying your
head under the covers, literally, and checking out of your life.'

Holly doesn't say anything for a while. When she looks up and meets
Will's eyes, she just shrugs sadly. 'Maybe you're right. A little,' she says.
'Maybe going to bed keeps me from examining my life more closely,
and maybe things would be different if Marcus were around more.
There is nothing else for me to do. Admittedly, I could stay up and
watch TV, but I'd rather climb into bed with a good book.'

'It's ridiculous that there's nothing else for you to do . . . OK,' Will
says. 'I'm throwing down the gauntlet. I'm going out on Friday night
with some friends to see a band. It's very casual, just live music at a bar.
If Marcus is working, I want you to come. Just do it. Say yes. Get a baby
sitter and come.'

'I can't.' Holly shakes her head, but even as she shakes her head she
knows she can. She knows she will.

'I have tons of married friends,' Will continues. 'And what they all
have in common is that they still go out drinking, still have fun, still
retain enough of their identity that they never feel as if a part of them
died when they walked down the aisle.'

'God.' Holly sucks in a breath. 'That's how I felt when I walked down
the aisle. I've never realised it before.'

'See? And here's your chance to change. Go on. Say you'll come. I'd
love you to meet my friends and I think you'll enjoy them. Will you?'

'Yes.' Holly leans back and relaxes. 'I'll come.' And as the words What
am I doing? enter her head, she shouts it back down. I'm not going to
think about this, she tells herself. I'm just going to be in the moment
and see what happens.

In a quiet restaurant in Highgate Village, Paul and Anna sit in a corner,
nursing their wine, trying to find the words.

'I'm so sorry, Anna,' Paul says again as he puts his arm round her and
pulls her close for a hug. 'I'm just sorry.'

'We can try again, no?' Anna looks up at Paul hopefully, but she
already knows the answer.

'I just don't see how we can,' Paul says. 'I know we both want this more than anything, but I think that physically and emotionally this is going to destroy us. I don't know how many more times we can go through it. And the financial burden is just so big. We need to start building our savings again, putting aside money for a rainy day, not to mention the barn that we're not even using because we haven't put a penny into it. I think . . .' He pauses. 'I don't know if you're ready to find out about this yet, but I think that now might be the time for us to start investigating adoption.'

Anna sighs as a tear drips onto the table. 'I did not honestly believe this would happen,' she whispers. 'I just kept thinking that the next time it would happen, the next time I would get pregnant. I still cannot believe it. I know we've always said we would look at adoption, but it's so final. Adoption means I have failed. We have failed. Why me?' Anna leans her head into Paul's shoulder as he cradles her gently. 'Why us?'

'I know,' Paul says. 'I feel the same way. But even if you're not ready to actually start whatever the adoption process is, I feel like we've reached a time when we have to explore it.'

He continues to rock her, kissing the top of her head and shushing her like a baby until she stops crying.

'Shall we go away this weekend?' Paul says as they gather their coats and thread their way through the tightly packed tables.

'White Barn Fields?' Anna smiles grimly. 'Go and see all the work we have not been able to afford to do?'

'We could always do it ourselves.' Paul shrugs. 'On some level I'm sure it would be a hell of a lot of fun.'

'Do you think they have *The Idiot's Guide to Renovating Houses*?' Anna smiles, the first genuine smile of the evening.

'If not, I could always write it and make ourselves a fortune.'

'Now that is the best idea of the night.' Anna smiles up at him. 'I do love you, you know.'

'Even though I can't afford to keep you in IVF?' Paul is joking, but Anna sees the doubt in his eyes.

'Yes, even though you cannot afford to keep me in IVF. At least they will never say I married you for your money. Actually I think you hypnotised me some time during that newspaper interview. The good news is I am still waiting to wake up.'

'I love you, too,' Paul says, kissing her on the forehead as he closes his arms around her for a hug, both of them swaying gently on the pavement outside the restaurant. 'Really, I feel so lucky to have you, to have us.'

'So are we going to White Barn Fields this weekend with our toolbox in the back of the car?'

'Let's do it,' Paul nods as they start walking towards the car. 'Let's go down there and get busy.'

'**W**hat do you think?' Will leans over and whispers in Holly's ear so she can hear him, and Holly grins at him.

'I think your friends are great. The music's great. I'm having a great time.'

'So it's all great?' Will laughs.

'It's all great,' Holly says, as Will orders some more beers.

They are sitting in the Jazz Café in Camden. The band is a jazz trio. Not too soft, not too loud. The music is wonderful, and Holly is stunned at how much she is enjoying this: sitting at the bar listening to music, a beer in hand, surrounded by good people. Easy people. People who don't need to impress, who aren't judging her but are just happy to be where they are.

She told Marcus she was going out. She had mentioned Will, couldn't lie completely, but had told him that Paul and Anna, Olivia, a couple of others would be there as well. 'It's such a shame you're not here,' she lied to Marcus on the phone.

'Have fun,' he'd said distractedly.

Hugs all round at the end of the evening and Will turns to Holly. 'I'm going to pop in to Mum and Dad's tomorrow, and I'm planning on staying for lunch. Do you want to come? They'd love to see you.'

'Tomorrow?' Holly looks at her watch, stalling for time. Tomorrow. Marcus is still in Manchester and not expected home before late afternoon. 'I have the kids,' Holly says, not sure what Will is saying.

'So bring them.' Will grins. 'I'd love to meet them.'

'Do you want to check with your mum and dad? Make sure it's OK?'

'Oh, come on, Holly, you know Mum will have cooked enough to feed an army and, as far as she's concerned, you're family anyway.'

'Will you tell them we're coming? Make sure it's OK?'

'If it makes you happier, I'll tell her you're coming.'

And with that they have one last hug goodbye and Holly climbs into her car. She turns the music up and smiles all the way home.

'**O**h, look at her!' Maggie stands back and watches Daisy with a delighted smile on her face. 'She's a little you, Holly! She's gorgeous!'

'And this is Oliver. Oliver, say how do you do to Mrs Fitzgerald.'

'Mrs Fitzgerald? Don't be ridiculous, Holly. Mrs Fitzgerald is my mother-in-law. I'm Maggie to everyone, children included.'

Of course she's Maggie, Holly thinks. How could she possibly be anything else? Holly had never been comfortable instructing her children to call her friends Mr and Mrs, but Marcus had insisted.

It was, she realised, part of Marcus's pomposity, part of his behaving how he thought he was supposed to behave if people were to believe that he was from the upper-crust background he so desperately wanted to come from. In line with his behaviour, Marcus had very clear rules about how the children ought to behave.

They were to shake adults by the hand, look them in the eye and say how do you do. They were to sit at the table and not speak unless they were spoken to. They were not to watch television during the week and only an hour on each day of the weekend. Daisy was to wear smocked dresses and patent leather shoes and Oliver was to wear corduroy trousers and woollen sweaters.

'They're children,' Holly had moaned to Marcus's mother when she was visiting her at her home just outside Bristol.

'They're only little.' Joanie had agreed with Holly. 'And we're living in 2006, not 1886.' Holly had burst into laughter. 'You just keep on doing what you're doing and they'll turn out great.' Joanie had nodded. 'I think you're a wonderful mother.'

Holly stands at the kitchen sink, peeling potatoes, and stops for a few seconds, smiling as she gazes across the garden to the large old oak tree at the bottom where Peter and Oliver are looking very industrious as Peter—rather bravely, Holly thinks—holds a nail and Oliver hammers it very carefully.

Peter came into the kitchen when they arrived and squatted down on his haunches so he was the same height as the kids.

'You look like you're very strong,' he says to Oliver. 'Do you have big muscles?'

Oliver nods cautiously.

'Oh good, because I need some help building a treehouse. Do you think you'd be any good at building a treehouse?'

Oliver almost squeals his answer, jiggling with excitement.

'Well, actually it is built, but the ladder is broken, and there's no point in having a treehouse if you can't climb up to it, is there? How are you with a hammer and nails?'

'I'm really good with a hammer,' Oliver says, although as far as Holly knows, he's never picked up a hammer in his life.

'Come on, then. I'll be the builder and you can be my second-in-command. Sound good?' He extended a hand to Oliver who immediately slipped his hand in Peter's and nodded as he walked out to the garden.

'He's lovely with kids, isn't he?' Maggie slides up next to Holly and smiles as she watches them. 'He misses Dustin and Violet so very much. We both do. It's so difficult when they live so far away.'

'Have you spoken to them? How are they? How's Sarah?'

Maggie lets out a long sigh. 'Mostly distraught. I expected her to be fabulously stoic, to get on with her life and keep her grief contained, but it seems grief gets us in unexpected ways. Her sister is living with her for a while, helping out enormously with the kids. We offered to have the kids for Christmas, give her a break, time to grieve properly, but of course she rightly pointed out that the kids are the only thing keeping her going at the moment.'

'And the kids?'

'I think a lot of it is over their heads, particularly Dustin, the little one. Violet is struggling with it. She understands that her daddy isn't coming back and just misses him hugely. She draws him pictures every day . . .' Maggie's voice tails off and she wipes a tear away, biting her lip to suppress the tears.

Holly puts her arm around Maggie, and together they stand at the window until Daisy, sitting at the kitchen table making dolls' houses out of cereal boxes, demands some help.

At one fifteen, there's still no sign of Will. The roast lamb is 'relaxing' on the counter, the fresh garden mint has been chopped into a sauce with vinegar and sugar, the vegetables are steaming, and the potatoes are crisping up in the oven.

Holly has been surreptitiously looking at her watch for the last hour. She is dying to ask when he is coming—whether he is, in fact, coming—but she does not want to give Maggie any indication of what she might be feeling.

Hell, she doesn't even know herself what she might be feeling.

She does know that she got home last night on a high, which continued this morning when she woke up knowing that she had something to look forward to today. But with every minute that passes, the high is starting to fade, and Holly is moments away from sinking into a depression. Stop it, she tries to tell herself. You are here with your children, here for Peter and Maggie, not here to see Will. So what if he doesn't come, you'll still have a lovely time. You're having a lovely time.

But she knows it's not true.

Maggie calls everyone to the table, and Holly promises herself she will not ask about the empty place at the table.

She doesn't have to.

'Where's Will?' Peter says.

Maggie shrugs. 'You know our Will. Saying he'll come at twelve means he could come any time between ten in the morning and ten at night, if he comes at all.'

Peter shakes his head. 'Sometimes that boy is so infuriating.'

'We've learned not to rely on Will very much. Although'—she shoots a cautious look at Daisy and Oliver, both engaged in teasing Pippa—'he has been fantastic through all . . . this.'

'Yes, he has.' Peter nods sombrely. 'And now I suppose it's back to business.'

'Well, I don't know about you, but I'm starving,' Maggie says, even though she has eaten almost nothing since the day she heard about Tom and has dropped over a stone. 'Let me serve the kiddies first.'

Holly clears up the dishes then excuses herself to go to the loo. She feels like crying. From the heights of exhilaration to the depths of depression in the space of an hour. Grow up, she hisses at her reflection in the mirror. You are a married woman, she tells herself. Stop behaving like a teenager.

But that is exactly how she feels. Like a teenager who has no control of her emotions. Whose emotions and mood can be changed in a heart-beat by external influences.

She still has no idea where this is leading, still thinks of herself as someone who would never have an affair, and the truth is she hasn't contemplated anything happening between her and Will, hasn't thought about what the end result of all this . . . friendship . . . might be.

She knows she is attracted to him, but he's gorgeous, how could anyone not be attracted to him? And yes, so there have been a couple of times when she has closed her eyes while having sex with Marcus and has pictured Will there in his place, but only out of curiosity, only to spice up their sex life a bit, and God knows it worked.

What is clear is how much she has missed having a man in her life who is a friend. Marcus has never been her friend, she realises now. Has never been her partner. Where Marcus puts her down—subtly, always so subtly—Will listens. Their emails are still fun, still funny, but now Holly finds she is revealing more about herself, letting him into how she really feels.

The one subject they haven't discussed, not in any great depth, is her marriage and why she feels the need to seek out a male confidant, someone to offer her a man's point of view, someone to make her feel beautiful again when she has a perfectly good husband at home.

Or not, as the case may be.

The front door slams shut and Holly tenses as she hears the familiar jangling of keys. She can picture exactly what Marcus is doing. He is fishing his BlackBerry out of his pocket, scrolling down quickly to see if any emails have come in during the last ten seconds that absolutely must be taken care of now. He's putting his keys in the ashtray, emptying the coins from his pocket into the same ashtray, and will shout a quick hello before taking his briefcase into his office on the ground floor and unpacking it quickly.

While unpacking his briefcase, he will pick up the post that arrived yesterday and skim through just to check there's nothing that cannot wait, and, at the same time, he will listen to the messages on his office answering phone. Inevitably, there will be issues that cannot wait and he will spend the next hour tapping out emails and making calls.

As usual, Holly gets a perfunctory kiss on the way to his office, and the kids get a perfunctory ruffle of the hair.

'Off Daddy now,' he says sternly to Daisy, who has entwined herself round his legs. 'Daddy needs to work.' He looks up at Holly, gesturing impatiently at Daisy, and Holly attempts to disentangle Daisy, who starts crying. 'Will you just keep them away from the office while I check messages,' he says. 'I'll be out in a sec.'

'Fine,' Holly says, carrying a now-screaming Daisy into the kitchen and shutting the door behind her. She sits down at the kitchen counter and sinks her head in her hands. 'Jesus Christ,' she whispers. 'Is this all there is?'

An hour later Marcus is still locked in his office, the kids are bathed and happily playing in the playroom.

She runs up to her studio and clicks on her inbox. Just to see. If he loves me, he'll have sent me a message, she finds herself thinking, reprimanding herself sharply. But she can't help the flutter when she sees the email waiting for her.

In another room, a few miles away, Olivia is also checking her email. Stupid, stupid me, she thinks, battling the hope that there will be an email from Fred. Stupid, stupid me for jumping into bed with him, for allowing myself to feel that this might be something special, that he would have got back home to America and felt that he missed me. That perhaps there was enough here for us both to want to work at it.

But the truth is, deep in her heart Olivia knows that Fred was, exactly as Tom had said, just a fling. For a couple of days there, as she and Fred had the most blissful time, she had allowed herself to think, what if . . .? But even then she knew that 'what ifs' were unrealistic.

And yet every night before she goes to bed, she checks her email to see if he's written. There were a couple of exchanges when he first got back, a thank-you for the most wonderful time in London, for being such a special friend, and wishes of luck and happiness in the future. She wished him the same and then all email correspondence had stopped. Was that it? She had let the grey start poking its roots back into her hair and sadly relegated the black dress back to the corner of the wardrobe.

It had been, she decided, a lovely experience, but not one to be repeated. The confusion and uncertainty of relationships or flings, or whatever it was you called it, was something that Olivia was quite certain she could do without.

To: Holly
From: Will
23/01/07 19:52:32
Subject: No-shows and apology

Holly, Holly, Holly. Am SO very sorry I wasn't there today. Had far too much to drink last night, it seems, and was horribly hung over this morning. Didn't wake up until lunchtime and just blanked about going to Mum and Dad's until Mum phoned after you'd gone. I feel awful about letting you down. Not to mention what a treat it would have been to meet your kids. Please, please say you'll forgive me . . . would like to buy you lunch this week to apologise properly.

On another note, fantastic night last night. Do remember you looking rather sexy (am I allowed to say that now that we're becoming friends?), good music, good people. Hoping you're not furious with me, Will x

Holly reads the email five times until Daisy starts screaming at Oliver. She walks downstairs smiling, every disappointment forgotten, back on the cloud of exhilaration.

He thinks I'm sexy! He thinks I'm sexy! I'm seeing him this week!

And floating into the playroom, she dives on the children and covers them with kisses, both of them so shocked they dissolve into uncontrollable giggles.

'I have a friendship,' Holly says awkwardly, unable to look Olivia in the eye, but knowing she needs to say something, knowing that Olivia is the right person to be talking to about this. They are sitting at the counter in Holly's kitchen, having each eaten two tiny fruit tarts and two chocolate éclairs.

'Great,' Olivia says nonchalantly, alerted to something else when Holly finally looks up and meets her eyes. '*Oh!* You mean, *a friendship.*'

Holly nods.

Olivia's eyes widen. 'Are you having an *affair?*' Her voice drops to a whisper on the last word.

'No!' Holly says loudly. 'Sssh. Frauke's upstairs, I don't want her to hear any of this. But, no, I swear to you, I'm not having an affair. I am having a friendship with a man, and I just feel . . . incredibly confused.'

'Confused because you want to be having an affair?'

'No! Well . . . maybe. No, I don't think so.' Holly sighs deeply. 'Oh God, Olivia, I don't even know. I just know that my marriage feels . . . I don't know. Just nothing. And this awful thought just keeps coming back to me: What if I married the wrong man?'

'Wow!' Olivia exhales. 'That's pretty bloody huge.'

'I know.' Holly looks at her sadly. 'It's awful, and hearing the words out loud makes it more awful because it makes it real. I'm not going to have an affair, but the fact is I have this friend who, yes, I'll admit it, I am attracted to, but more than that, he's interested in what I have to say; he thinks I'm funny and clever; and he makes me feel important.'

'And Marcus doesn't?'

Holly snorts. 'What do you think?'

'Well, yes, OK. I see your point.'

'What do *you* think of Marcus?' Holly asks suddenly. 'I mean, I know you hardly know him, but what impression did he make on you? Do you think he's the right man for me?'

'No way, Holly.' Olivia laughs and shakes her head. 'That's one road I won't be going down. All I'll say is that you just seem like very different personalities; but hey, opposites attract and all that, and I've certainly come across other couples who seem like chalk and cheese. But what about this other man? Does he have a name? Could he, in fact, be someone I might know?'

Holly turns bright red.

'I know,' Olivia sighs. 'I knew there was something with you and Will. Every time you mention him, which by the way you do an awful lot, just in case you haven't realised and are doing it when you're with Marcus, you go all sort of dreamy.'

'So what do you think about it?'

'I think we lost one of our best friends, and you're obviously unhappy or unfulfilled by other things in your life, so I wonder if you might be projecting it, or whatever the hell it's called, onto his brother.'

'If it's just that, how come *you're* not feeling anything for him?'

Olivia burst out laughing. 'Your logic seems a little off-kilter, Holly. Will's not my type in the slightest. I'm just worried that this is a crush that has emerged because of losing Tom, and I wonder whether it's actually something that should be causing you to question your marriage. Do you think you'd be happier with someone like him?'

'Well . . . no. He'd probably drive me mad. He's thirty-five years old and doesn't have a proper job—he's a carpenter slash beach bum. He travels abroad for six months, sleeping on beaches, or camping out on friends' sofas. He's clever and funny and amazingly sexy, but you couldn't find a worse proposition for a husband if you tried.'

'So what makes you think you might be happier with him?'

Holly is quiet for a while as she thinks. Then eventually she looks up at Olivia, her voice almost breaking. 'I just miss having a friend. I miss having a partner. I feel like Marcus and I are two ships that pass in the night. And more than that, I worry that we are just so completely incompatible and that I've spent my married life trying to be this . . . this *wife* he wants me to be, but that it isn't me; it's not how I want to spend the rest of my life.

'The only time this house comes alive, the only time the children and I can laugh and be free is when Marcus isn't here, because these days when he is here all he does is bark at everyone to behave differently, to do something differently. I feel like I'm trapped in a prison when he's around. Tiptoeing about, walking on eggshells in case something displeases him. And all he cares about is work. All he thinks about is work. Even when I try to have a conversation with him, I can see that he's not even listening, he's thinking about some bloody case.'

'Couldn't you tell him?' Olivia says gently. 'Couldn't you sit down with him and tell him all that? Surely he'd understand, surely the two of you could work it out?'

'Maybe.' Holly shrugs, but what she doesn't say is that she no longer has the will to work it out.

'Would you ever leave him?' Olivia asks after a while.

'I think I'd be too frightened to.' Holly sighs. 'I mean, he's a divorce lawyer for God's sake. I think it would be a nightmare.'

'Well, then, you'll have to find a way to make it work. Talk to him, Holly. It's not too late, you just have to communicate.'

Chapter Eight

SAFFRON OPENS THE DOOR as everyone looks up to see who is coming in. She waves at the handful of people she has grown to know and love during the years she has been coming to this room, and pulls a folding chair from a cupboard in the corner of the room, sitting down as quietly as possible at the back. She is thirty minutes late but knows it is better to hear thirty minutes of a meeting than not to come at all.

As she sits down someone hands her a notebook and she scribbles her name and number, the best time to call, and thinks for a second about what to write under the heading 'feeling'. *Irritated*, she finally writes, leaning forward to put the book on the table.

No P today. He's flown to New York for a preproduction meeting of his new movie, and although he wanted her to come, she has a meeting of her own tomorrow. The producers of the biggest hit of last year have shortlisted her as the love interest for their new film. If she gets it, it will be the biggest break of her career.

P sent flowers and a 'good luck' card this morning, phoned to tell her he was missing her, then made her laugh by describing quite how much she was missing in his suite at the Carlyle.

She needed a meeting today, and a meeting in which she wasn't distracted by P's presence was always welcome.

'Hi, I'm Saffron and I'm a grateful recovering alcoholic.' Funny how smoothly those words roll from her lips, even though, of late, she has been doubting their veracity. 'I'm sorry I'm late,' she continues, 'but I'm so happy to be here. I missed the reading of the step, obviously, and I skimmed the Big Book a bit, but I really need to talk about where I am today.' She takes a deep breath. 'You know, for years I've had good, clean sobriety. I swore I'd never go back to the place I came from when I first came into these rooms and, for so long, it's been so easy for me to be surrounded by alcohol without giving it a second thought. I think that recently I've been trying to do it by myself, and it's not working.

'I find myself sitting in meetings fairly regularly, talking about what I'm *not* doing—no stepwork, barely calling my sponsor, occasionally reading literature when I'm desperate—but I don't seem to have the will to do anything more. And even though I'm not drinking, recently I've found myself watching people in restaurants with, say, a glass of wine, and thinking, I could do that. Why couldn't I just have one glass of wine with dinner in a restaurant? I'm sure I could do that.' The group laughs in recognition. 'And even though on some level I know I can't, on another I think I can, and I have to tell you, I'm completely white-knuckling it.'

She takes a breath. 'And then there's my relationship.' She doesn't say his name, remembers her sponsor's advice from a long time ago: 'Don't talk about him unless it's in very general terms. Despite the principle of anonymity,' she had said, 'everyone loves to talk, loves to gossip, and this is too big a secret for people to keep to themselves. Be careful. Very careful.'

Still. There were people who knew, or thought they knew. No one had proof, but a few had seen the way he and Saffron looked at each other; a few noticed the closeness between them, even when they were sitting on opposite sides of the room and even when they took great pains to avoid each other during the coffee break and after the meeting.

'I'm struggling with it at the moment. I know that I have to learn acceptance. That it is what it is, and I have to accept that he can't be with me all the time, but it's just so bloody hard. And then I've got this huge audition tomorrow that I feel a bit sick about, and'—she heaves a big sigh—'you see? This is what happens to me when I don't work my programme. I just get completely overwhelmed with my life. But I'm here, and I'm making a commitment to the group today to go home and start working on my step one again. I've been promising my sponsor for ages that I will do it, and this is my commitment to you. Anyway'—she glances down at the timer in her hand—'time's up. Thank you everyone for sharing, and I'm just so grateful I have a place where people listen and understand.'

Afterwards, a girl Saffron has only seen a couple of times comes up to her. She's pretty, dressed like every other actress in LA and something in her eyes gives the impression that she may not be entirely trustworthy.

'Hi, I'm Alex,' she says, putting her arms round Saffron and giving her a hug, which is something Saffron is not entirely comfortable with although she thinks perhaps this is her English reserve.

'I just wanted to thank you.' Alex pulls back, but keeps hold of her hands, looking Saffron in the eye. 'Everything you said spoke to me. It was like hearing my story and I got so much out of your share.'

'Thank you,' Saffron says, willing herself not to judge, to find the part of Alex she could love or, at the very least, like.

'So you have an audition tomorrow? That's so exciting. What's it for?'

Saffron's heart sinks. Of course. As if she expected anything different. 'A movie,' she says.

'I have an audition tomorrow for a movie,' Alex lies smoothly. 'I bet it's the same one. Which one are you auditioning for?'

As if I'm stupid, Saffron thinks, but she smiles pleasantly. 'It's the remake of *The Wizard of Oz*,' she says. 'Spielberg's producing it and I'm up for Dorothy.'

'Me too! Well, good luck; maybe I'll see you there,' Alex says and practically runs out of the door, clearly about to phone her agent to find a way of getting in on the audition.

Saffron smiles to herself as she picks up her bag. Shame there is no remake of *The Wizard of Oz*. She imagines Alex phoning Dreamworks, demanding to be seen.

At home Saffron finds a message from Paul. Nothing much, he says, just caught a rerun of one of her movies on cable TV and he is thinking about her and wondering how she is. She smiles as she hears his voice and calls him back, leaving a message on his machine; then she dials Holly, and leaves a message on hers.

She loves LA. Loves the life she has built out here, but meeting up with this huge chunk of her past has made her homesick in a way she didn't expect. Homesick for friends. For real friends. She is homesick for the people who knew her when it all began, who loved her when she was a gangly teenager with railway tracks on her teeth. Friends like Paul, Holly and Olivia.

Ringing Olivia, Saffron readies herself to leave another message when Olivia picks up.

'Hello?'

'Olive Oil? Saffron here.'

Olivia starts laughing. 'God, I'd completely forgotten you ever called me Olive Oil. That's hysterical. Where are you?'

'LA. Bored. Missing my old friends. What are you up to?'

'Actually it's not very pleasant. I've picked up a stomach bug and I've been throwing up for days.'

'Food poisoning or a bug?'

'I think a bug. Doesn't food poisoning end after about a day?'

'I think it depends on how severe it is. You should go and see a doctor. Unless of course . . .' Saffron allows a dramatic pause, 'you could be pregnant.'

'Hardly,' Olivia laughs, but then the colour drains from her face.

Just such a treat.' Maggie smiles over at Holly and covers Holly's hand lightly with her own. 'All these years of not seeing you, and now it's just like you're my daughter again, back in the family, and seeing you with your own children, a mother yourself.' She laughs. 'It's just lovely, Holly, and thank you for inviting me out for lunch. I haven't been out anywhere since we lost Tom.'

Holly's smile is tinged with sadness. 'It is so lovely to see you and to be with you. You've always felt more like my mother than my own mother did. I hadn't realised, all these years, how much I had missed talking to you. Do you remember how you would sit with me at the kitchen table for hours, talking through my problems, giving me advice while Tom rolled his eyes and went upstairs in a huff?'

Maggie nods and closes her eyes as she remembers, the pleasure and pain burning a tear down her cheek. 'I think he was always a bit jealous of how easy it was for you to turn to me,' she says. 'Tom was never much good at asking for help.'

'That's because he never needed any,' Holly says, and they laugh.

'My heart always went out to you, Holly,' Maggie says, her face now serious. 'You always seemed so lost in those days. So unhappy.'

'I did?' Holly is shocked.

'Peter always used to say that you would grow up to be a great beauty.' Maggie's eyes grow distant as she reminisces. 'And although I could see the possibility, I was never certain you were going to be able to sit in your skin and be proud of who you are.' There is a long pause as Maggie enfolds Holly in the warmth of her smile. 'But,' she continues, 'look at you. So beautiful and lovely and very sure of who you are.'

'Oh, Maggie. How can you say that? How can you have so much faith in me? There are times when I have no idea who I am or what I want.'

Maggie leans back in her chair. 'Aaah.' She smiles. 'This sounds like a midlife crisis.'

And Holly leans towards her, her face now alert. A midlife crisis. Something about this sounds right. And if it is, in fact, a midlife crisis, then there are ways to get beyond it, surely? Ways to move on without blowing your life up and watching the pieces land where they may.

'Do you really think that's what it might be?'

'I had one when I was thirty-nine.' Maggie smiles. 'Just where you are now. You and Tom were fifteen. It was soon after you came into the family. An awful time. The things I put poor Peter through . . .'

'How so?'

'Remember, I married Peter when I was twenty-three. I married him because I was desperate to be a grown-up, to have a house of my own, children of my own, and it was the only way I could see to do it.'

'So you weren't in love with him?'

'Oh, darling, of course I was in love with him.' Maggie frowns. 'I was madly, hopelessly in love with him. But I married him too young. He was my first serious boyfriend. We married a year after we met; and I thought I'd never look at another man again for the rest of my life.'

Holly has a sharp intake of breath. 'You mean you did?' Her voice drops to a whisper. 'Did you have an affair?'

Maggie smiles. 'No, my sweet girl. I didn't. It wasn't about someone else. It was about wanting to be young again. I had joined a life-drawing class at the local art school, and all my friends were young and hip. Even the ones who were the same age as I was had carved out very different lives for themselves, lives that didn't involve boisterous teenagers and entertaining the husband's boss at home. I didn't want to be me, I wanted to be one of them.'

'So what happened?'

'I was going to leave, not because I didn't love Peter any more, but because I needed some space to figure out what I wanted.'

'How did Peter react?' As she speaks, she is thinking about Marcus. How would he react? Would he care? Did he even love her any more?

'He put his foot down and said no. Absolutely not. He wasn't having it. He said it simply wasn't acceptable. He said he wouldn't tolerate the damage it would do to Tom, Will and him, and that if I thought he didn't sometimes think about going off and spending night after night at the Playboy Club chasing after blonde models, I'd better think again.

'He said that marriage was for life and that this was what commitment meant. It meant weathering the storms and emerging stronger as a result.'

Holly's eyes are wide as she takes it all in. 'So you stayed.'

'Of course I stayed.' Maggie smiles. 'Reluctantly at first, but honestly, that bit about him seducing models gave me a bit of a start. It was one thing for me to fantasise about being single, but quite another to think of Peter going off with some blonde floozie. Also'—she leans forward with a conspiratorial smile—'I actually fancied him when he got all stern.'

Holly breaks into peals of laughter.

'It's true.'

'And you've never regretted it?' The laughter disappears as Holly grows pensive.

'No, my darling. I never have. We've been married over forty years, and it is exactly as he said.' She smiles gently at Holly. 'If my experience can help you in any way, Holly, so be it, but whatever journey awaits you, it will be yours alone and no one can tell you what to do.'

Holly sighs. 'That doesn't help, Maggie.'

'I know, darling. It's not supposed to. Your answers will come. Time and experience will tell you what you need to do.'

'You really are my other mother, aren't you?' Holly smiles. 'My real mother would sit here and tell me exactly what I have to do to fix things.'

'It's not my job to judge you, Holly.'

'Now you sound like Tom.'

'That's what Will always says.'

At the mention of Will's name, Holly feels herself flush ever so slightly. Would Maggie feel differently about Holly's impending journey and the outcome if she knew that Will was the catalyst for this storm of emotions and doubts?

Maggie watches Holly colour, and she is not sure what to say, whether to say anything at all. For just as Tom was the caretaker, her reliable, wonderful, consistent son, Will has always been her irresponsible, frustrating, but oh-so-beloved baby of the family.

As a mother you are not supposed to have favourites. If anyone ever asked Maggie—before this, of course, before Tom—whether she had a favourite, she would shake her head and say she loved them the same, loved them differently, but not one more or less than the other.

But that is not quite true. Tom had a special place in her heart as her firstborn, a bond that could never be replicated; but something in her heart shifted the moment Will was born, a love that was so overwhelming, so overpowering in its purity that she didn't actually know before that moment that love that strong could exist.

Even now, at thirty-five, and allegedly independent, when he should be getting on with his life, Maggie knows she would do anything for Will. The son who leaves a trail of broken hearts wherever he goes, who she prays will find happiness eventually, who is so clearly, frustratingly, the force behind whatever crisis dear, lovely Holly imagines herself to be going through in her marriage.

Oh Lord, she thinks. What am I supposed to say? But the words come out without her even thinking about them, for she has sat here too many times with other women who have been heartsick over Will, heartsick over his lack of commitment and his inability to love them in the way they love him.

'Be careful, Holly,' Maggie says.

Holly's faint flush deepens to a rich burgundy. 'What do you mean?'

'I mean Will, my darling.'

Holly attempts a laugh. 'Maggie, Will and I are just friends. He's certainly not the reason for this . . . midlife crisis.'

'Darling girl, if I am mistaken, then I do so hope you will forgive me.' She takes a deep breath. 'If Will has anything to do with whatever you are going through, please don't make any changes, don't do anything in the belief that Will is the man for you.'

Holly is mortified. Humiliated. Wishing a hole could open beneath them and swallow her up.

'I haven't . . .' she starts. 'I wouldn't . . . I mean . . .'

Maggie leans forward, holds Holly's chin in her hand, and forces Holly to meet her eyes. 'My darling girl, I love you and I want you to be happy. And I love my one remaining son more than anything else in the world . . . and yet I, as his mother, can vouch that he is a bad bet. He is handsome and funny and exciting, but a worse possible proposition for a relationship you couldn't find. If you leave your marriage because you think there will be a future with Will, it will not end well.'

'So I shouldn't leave Marcus and run away to the Bahamas or wherever Will is going next winter?' Holly is attempting humour.

'I'd say by all means leave Marcus if that is the right thing for you to do, but do it for the right reasons. Not because of Will or anyone else for that matter. Do it, if indeed you end up doing it, because you are certain that you are not happy, that you will never be happy if you stay. That, to me, seems the only justifiable reason.'

'So when you were ready to leave Peter, how did you know you could be happy again?'

Maggie shrugs. 'I think because I'd been so happy before. I still loved him, I just needed to make myself fall in love with him again.'

There is a long silence as the waiter brings them cappuccinos. Holly raises hers to her lips and sips thoughtfully. 'What if . . .' she begins. 'What if you were never in love in the first place?'

Have I ever loved you? Holly thinks later that evening as they sit having dinner in a restaurant with a couple from Daisy's school.

Holly talks to the mother, Jo, about nannies and other mothers in the class, and where they might consider sending the children for junior school. Marcus and Edward talk about work—Edward is a barrister—and when their main courses are served, the four of them finally talk in a group. Jo keeps them amused with funny stories about how she and Edward met, and Marcus offers his own version of events back when he and Holly first got together.

She watches him talk, is aware that when she tries to interject to correct him or add something of her own, he subtly puts her down or ridicules her, or waves her comments aside as if they are irrelevant. And eventually she finds herself doing what she always does—withdrawing.

What is love anyway? she finds herself thinking. Maggie talked today of loving Peter, of being in love with him, of losing it temporarily and then being able to fall in love again.

Holly knows she wasn't in love with Marcus, not even in the beginning, although she thought she would grow to love him. But there is nothing about Marcus that she loves, little that she even likes. They are not partners. They are not friends.

And if they are not partners, if they are not friends, if they are not lovers—even if she does have sex with Marcus when she has to—then what are they?

Olivia stands in line at Boots and clutches the pregnancy test to her chest. She's convinced someone she knows is going to walk in and catch her in this miserable, awful situation. She knows this test is merely a formality. She didn't use protection. She forgot the rules, forgot how to play them. Somehow bringing up condoms hadn't seemed quite, well, appropriate. And it had been straight after her period ended so she was pretty sure it would be fine.

But she now knows that it probably wasn't. Back at home, she pees on the stick and waits for the test to take hold. Already, as she stares, she sees the beginning of a blue line.

She rips the other packet open, pees on the stick, and again, there it is. No doubt about it. Olivia, who is single and who has never wanted children, is pregnant. There it is in blue and white. Undeniable.

Saffron reaches for the phone, bleary-eyed. 'Hello?' She is still half asleep, and half opens one eye to see the time flickering on the digital clock on her bedside table. Five thirty-six. Who in the hell is calling at this ungodly hour of the morning?

'Saffron Armitage?'

'Yes?'

'I'm calling from the *National Enquirer*. We're running a story in the next edition about your affair with Pearce Webster and wondered if you'd like to make a comment?'

'What?' Saffron sits bolt upright in bed and shrieks, then slams down the phone, shaking.

The phone rings again seconds later.

'Hello, this is Jonathan Baker from *E! Online*. We'll be running a story in this morning's edition about your relationship with Pearce Webster. Would you give us a—' Saffron slams down the phone and huddles in bed under the covers as the phone rings. And rings. And rings.

Each time she hears the machine pick up. Journalists leaving messages, and then, horrifyingly, ten minutes later her doorbell rings. Gingerly, she opens one wooden slat of her blinds and gasps in horror as she sees news crews parked all the way up her street. Journalists huddled together drinking Starbucks with microphones tucked under their arms, waiting for her to emerge.

'Oh fuck,' she whispers, sinking into a corner of the room and rocking back and forth. She grabs her cellphone and dials the only person she can think of to get her out of this mess.

P.

'**D**o you know how lucky I am to have a husband like you?' Anna opens her arms as Paul carefully sets her tea down on the bedside table, then sinks into her, planting a great, squashy kiss on her lips.

'And do you know how lucky I am to have you?' he says.

'So, oh lucky man of mine, how do you feel about White Barn Fields?' Anna has been lying in bed waiting for Paul to come home with fresh croissants and the Sunday papers, entertaining thoughts of how they could do up the house.

'You're thinking it's a project, aren't you?' Paul smiles at her.

'I am thinking, my darling, that I want to take a break from thinking about babies. I just want to live for a little while without thinking about how incomplete our lives are when they are not really so incomplete at all, so yes, in that respect, I am thinking it would be a great project.'

'I'm glad,' Paul says. 'And I think you're right. I feel like everything in our lives has revolved around possible pregnancies for months, and we both need a break. The question is, can we do it ourselves?'

Anna props herself up on the pillows and spreads butter and marmalade thickly on a croissant. 'Here is the thing,' she says, chewing slowly. 'As lovely as Phil's plans are, we haven't got the money to spare now after the treatments. But,' she pauses, 'it would not take that much to make it livable.'

'What do you think it would take?'

Anna counts off the list on her fingers. 'The one thing that we do need to spend money on is the bathroom.'

Paul grins. 'You mean you don't want to use the outhouse?'

'Exactly. So if we could find a plumber to do the plumbing in that useless bedroom next to the master bedroom, we could have a bath-room; and we could also put one in downstairs. If a plumber does the work and installs the stuff, we could tile and paint it and do the floors.

'The kitchen just needs a face-lift. We could paint the kitchen cabi-nets and replace that horrible Formica work top with butcher block, then put simple white subway tiles on the splashback. And I found this place online that sells industrial stainless steel worktables for next to nothing. After that,' she continues, almost breathless with excitement, 'we could get away with painting the place and sanding the floors.'

'What "we" is this?' Paul looks at her in amazement. 'When have you ever tiled or sanded anything in your life?'

'Since before I started Fashionista, my darling. I used to do every-thing myself. I have just never had the time since starting Fashionista. Plus there has never really been anything here that needs doing.'

'So given that time has always been a problem, when could we do it?'

'That is what I have been thinking about. I think a plumber could do the bathrooms in a flash, then I could go down for a couple of weeks and get most of the rest done, I think. The biggest key is having the materials ordered and waiting there.'

'I know you,' Paul says slowly. 'You've already ordered everything, haven't you?'

'Well . . . not *all* of it. But I did get a plumber in, and the bathroom has been done, well, the big stuff anyway. Not the tiling, which means we could go and stay there now and do the rest of the work.' She pouts. 'I thought you would be pleased.'

Paul shakes his head. 'I'm just surprised that you'd make such a big decision without talking to me.'

'Are you angry at me?' A little girl voice.

Paul shakes his head. 'No. Not angry. I'm just upset you didn't dis-cuss it all with me. It feels dishonest.'

Anna looks aghast, then hangs her head. 'You are right. I am so sorry. I did not mean to deceive you, I just got carried away.'

'It's OK,' Paul says. 'I suppose it's good that we can use the barn now. So where *is* all the stuff?'

'Hopefully sitting in the barn, waiting for me to confess so we can plan a trip down there to start the work.' She reaches into the drawer of her bedside table and pulls out a stack of catalogues.

Half an hour later Paul is having a shower while Anna lazily flicks through what she jokingly refers to as her 'secret shame'—the *News of the World*. As she turns to the centre pages, she gasps in disbelief. 'Paul! Quick! Come here . . . it's *Saffron!*'

The story is everywhere. First broken in America, every news channel has picked up on it; everybody is talking about it; everyone wants to know everything they possibly can about Saffron Armitage, Pearce Webster, and how the two of them got together.

Saffron spent a horrified couple of days holed up in a hotel—whisked there by P's manager until they got wind that she was staying there—flicking through every TV station, feeling more and more sick as she heard what they were saying.

A lot of it was false. She froze in horror when one of the entertainment shows had as their guest that bitch Alex from the AA meeting. Introduced as a 'close friend' of the couple, the more Saffron listened to Alex, the more she suspected that she was the one who gave the story away.

But enough of it was true. Enough of it made her shrink with horror at the people coming out of the closet to talk about her, to give their opinions, to share some minor piece of information.

Her parents offered her refuge at their house, but given that they, too, were surrounded by the press, as was her flat, there seemed to be little point. Nowhere felt safe. Never had she felt so exposed.

'I love you,' Pearce said earlier that morning on the phone. 'And it will all be fine. This will blow over.'

'Are you saying anything?'

'Nope. My managers have advised me to keep quiet. Marjie and I are doing this ridiculous fake romantic dinner tonight to try to calm things down.' Saffron feels her heart sink as he says this—the last thing she expected was for him to pretend to the world that his marriage was far stronger than the public now believed.

'Are you OK?' Pearce can tell from her silence that she is not.

Saffron takes a deep breath. This is what she's learned in recovery. Not to say 'I'm fine, I'm fine', but to explain how she feels. It's still hard though. Even after all these years, it's still so hard to tell someone how she really feels, especially someone she loves. The fear has always been, still is, that she will end up being abandoned for expressing her needs.

'To be honest,' she says quietly, 'I'm hurt that you're telling the world that you and Marjie are fine. I feel . . . I feel completely irrelevant in your eyes.'

Pearce sighs. 'I'm so sorry, Saff. I never want you to feel that way, and it has never been my intention to hurt you. You know I want to be with you, but I also have my career to think about.'

Saffron forces her voice to stay calm, light, unemotional. 'So where does that leave us?'

'The same place we've always been, but the one thing I'm certain of is that we can't be seen together until this all blows over.'

Saffron pouts in silence. He's right. Of course he's right. It's just not what she wants to hear.

'So how is Marjie taking it?' she asks finally, curiosity getting the better of her.

'She couldn't care less about you and me, but she feels she's been publicly humiliated and she's pretty damn furious about that.'

'I'm sorry,' Saffron says sadly.

'So am I. But I'm most sorry I can't be with you now, making you feel better. Did someone from my management team talk to you about England?'

'Yes. They're putting me on a plane in the morning and I'm going to hole up there for a bit until it dies down. Mum and Dad have been besieged by the press, but I've left messages for old friends. Hopefully one of them will come through.'

'Just make sure you stay in touch and let me know where you are. I'll call you later, my darling, and remember, I love you.'

'Saffron? Are you OK? We've called and left messages. We just read . . . well, we were worried about you.' Anna bites her tongue, stunned to have picked up the phone to find Saffron on the other end.

'I'm sort of OK if being holed up at the Beverly Hills Hotel with bodyguards outside the door counts as OK.'

'Oh, you poor thing. And you must want to speak to Paul, since this is his phone, but he has gone out for a while and left it here. I can get him to call you as soon as he is back.'

'So are there no press outside your house?'

Anna snorts with laughter. 'No! Should there be?'

'They've managed to land on pretty much everyone else. Look, Anna, I know you and I don't know each other very well, but I'm desperate for somewhere quiet to stay until this blows over. Is there any chance I could come and stay with you and Paul? I know it's a huge imposition, and I promise I wouldn't ask unless I was desperate.'

'Of course you can come and stay. As it happens, you could even stay in the country if you wanted some serious peace and quiet. We have got an old barn in the middle of nowhere in Gloucestershire, which would be much better for you; although at the moment it is a bit of a dump. We are just starting to do it up, but there's a nice new bathroom. If you stayed with us here in north London, the press would find you very quickly, but Gloucestershire would be perfect.'

'Oh, Anna! I love you already. Thank you, thank you, thank you!'

'So when are you coming?'

Now it's Saffron's turn to sound sheepish. 'Actually, I'm hiding in the first-class lounge at LAX about to get on a flight.'

'You mean you were flying over here with nowhere to stay?'

'I didn't know what else to do.'

'Do you need anyone to pick you up from the airport?'

'No. Pearce has organised a driver. Should I go straight down to the country? I just feel a bit weird about going somewhere I've never been before by myself.'

'You know, you will be fine.' Anna gives Saffron instructions about how to find their London house. 'We'll drive you down to the barn. I am sure long walks in the country and a roaring log fire will do you the world of good.'

The first-class lounge is quiet, but even with few people there, Saffron is aware that everyone is staring at her. The staff have been whispering behind the bar, shooting glances over at her, and free newspapers are scattered around for everyone to read the latest instalment.

This sort of publicity is not what she has ever wanted although she knows there are many—Alex for one—who would kill for this kind of attention, however badly they may come across.

For that is what is so hard. They are painting Saffron as a marriage wrecker who set her sights on Pearce and is determined to break him up with his wife. Ghastly men she has dated once or twice have emerged to say that Saffron is the most ambitious woman they have ever met, that nothing could stand in the way of her drive.

None of it is true.

An hour to go before her flight is called, Saffron finds herself walking past the bar. A wall of free drinks. In the old days, she would have perched on a stool and ordered one after another.

God grant me the serenity . . . she starts to recite in her mind, but the serenity prayer is drowned out by a buzz that seems to drown out all sane thoughts, any mechanisms she may have used to stop herself.

She should call her sponsor. Call someone in the programme. Anyone who could talk her down from this, but the buzz has now propelled her back to the bar.

Fuck it, she thinks. After what I've been through, I deserve a drink. Just one, just to calm me down, and who wouldn't deserve a drink after this? What normal person wouldn't be entitled to one drink after this?

And what harm could it do? What harm could it possibly do?

Chapter Nine

HOLLY PHONED MARCUS and asked if they could go out for dinner that night. There are some things Holly wants to talk about.

And this time Holly really does want to talk. Her conversation with Maggie has stayed with her. Although as time progresses, she is becoming more and more unhappy and she knows that she can't just let it slide without involving Marcus. They never talk about what each of them wants, where they are going, or whether they are continuing to grow in the same direction. This, particularly given her growing friendship with Will, bothers Holly the most.

Their emails and occasional lunches have progressed to phone calls. When things happen to Holly during the day, if the children make her laugh, or she reads something interesting, or she is thrilled with herself because of a new card design, the only person she calls is Will. They are able to tease each other, she is able to reveal things to him she has never told anyone else, and certainly not Marcus.

Holly still doesn't talk much about Marcus with Will. They touch upon Holly's unhappiness, but she doesn't go into the details, doesn't share the intimacies of their life. And she hasn't told Will that tonight she's asked to go out for dinner with Marcus. She's going to take a deep breath and tell him that she's not happy. She's going to ask him to spend more time at home, to pay more attention to the kids. To pay more attention to her. She doesn't particularly want him at home more, but perhaps, she thinks, it would all be better if they were together more, if they had more of a partnership.

He is coming home at seven and they have a table at E&O for eight.

At a quarter to seven, just as Holly is stepping out of the shower, Marcus phones. 'I'm sorry, darling,' he says. 'I've just had a client call who needs me to do some urgent case-history research on child support. It won't take too long, but can I meet you at the restaurant?'

Holly shakes her head in dismay. What can she say?

An hour later, she is sitting at the table at E&O, nursing a Cosmopolitan and smiling broadly as she reads a text from Will. These days, Holly goes nowhere without her phone. Even when she is out shopping or picking the kids up from school or on her way to the studio, she can text Will. Not as good as email, but not far behind.

'Hello.' Marcus swoops down and pecks her on the cheek. 'I'm so sorry I'm late. What are you drinking?'

'A Cosmopolitan,' she says, leaning back and watching him as if watching a stranger. Dutch courage, is what she thinks. This is her second drink. She was early, Marcus was late, and she has been sitting here for twenty-three minutes. The first Cosmopolitan took the edge off her nerves; the second is making tonight's mission—the business of telling Marcus she is unhappy—almost ridiculously easy.

'How was your day?' Marcus smiles across the table at her as he accepts a menu, his thin fingers opening it up, and as he glances down, Holly thinks about Will's fingers. She loves his thick fingers. Loves his large hands. Marcus's fingers are elegant and expressive but not sexy.

Holly can see the muscles move under Will's skin when he moves his wrists. His skin is dark, almost olive. How different from Marcus. Holly thinks of Marcus's lanky, pale body, the hair on his arms black against the whiteness of his skin, and suppresses a slight shiver. She moves her gaze away from Marcus's fingers to meet his eyes.

'Everything all right, darling?' he says, but he is not asking because he suspects anything; it is just one of his stock phrases.

'Let's order.' Holly forces a smile and swigs another gulp of her drink as the waiter comes over. She takes a deep breath when he leaves.

'Marcus,' she starts. 'We need to talk. I . . .' She pauses. 'I feel so disconnected from you,' she says slowly, barely able to look him in the eye. 'You seem to be at work all the time and uninterested in us and I'm not happy.' She raises her eyes to meet his, almost scared of his reaction. 'This just isn't what I expected marriage to be.' There. She'd said it.

'What?' Marcus looks dumbstruck. 'What on earth are you talking about? I don't understand. What are you trying to say?' He looks hurt and angry, exactly the reaction Holly had expected. Exactly the reaction she didn't want, because Marcus's anger scares her. It is why she has never confronted him before. His temper is not something she sees often, but when it emerges it is explosive. He shouts and stamps, much like a little boy, and he can be both cutting and cruel.

He has said many things in anger that have wounded Holly deeply, and she has retreated from him for a few days to lick her wounds and attempt to heal. He is always contrite eventually and she has always forgiven him and has tried hard not to do or say anything that will set him off again.

She has thought many times of what her life would be like if she were to leave Marcus and raise her children herself. She has lain in bed and planned it, but the plan always starts with her telling Marcus she is leaving and she can almost predict what he would say. He would shout, his voice fierce with anger: 'Right! You're the one who wants to leave. So leave. I'm staying in the house with the kids.' And he is a divorce lawyer after all and knows what he's entitled to. He knows how to fight the dirty fight, and Holly has always been just too scared.

'I'm not saying anything.' Holly speaks calmly, trying to smooth things over, and she reaches out to take his hand. 'I'm just telling you that I'm not happy. I'm sure this is a phase in our marriage, but that something needs to change. I can't go on like this.'

'Like what?' His voice is icy cold.

'Like this!' Her voice rises with anger, and she consciously takes a deep breath. 'Like you being late for everything. Like you being away all the time, cancelling our plans, not seeing the children. When I do see you, we barely even talk. I don't feel married, Marcus.'

'So what are you saying?' Marcus leans forward, his voice dangerously soft. 'You want me to leave work so you can see me more? You want me to leave my job so I can spend more time with the children? Fine.' His voice starts to rise. 'You want me to be a stay-at-home husband or dad, fine. But who's going to pay the mortgage? Who's going to put food on the table? Who's going to put the children through school? Your illustrating work doesn't exactly contribute anything. But, fine, if that's what you want, I'll give my notice in tomorrow.'

'For God's sake,' Holly whispers, rolling her eyes. 'I'm not saying that. I'm trying to talk to you, to tell you how I feel. I'm not attacking you. I don't know why you're jumping on the defensive.'

'I'll tell you why,' Marcus hisses. 'Because I work like a dog to keep you happy. Do you think I'm doing it for me? I'm doing this so you and the children can live in your beautiful house in Brondesbury. I'm doing this so you can wear your cashmere sweaters and not worry about anything. You can't have it both ways, Holly. That's not how it works.'

Holly sits back and looks at him, four words going through her head.

You big fucking liar.

He's not doing this for her. Or the children. And Holly doesn't give a damn about the beautiful house or the cashmere fucking sweaters. She never has. She doesn't give a damn about any of the stuff that Marcus deems so necessary in order for people to look at him and think he is someone important, someone special. A big shot.

Their hors d'oeuvres arrive. Holly looks miserably at her parsnip and apple soup—her appetite long since disappeared—and back at Marcus, who has now fished his buzzing BlackBerry out of his pocket and is punching an email into the phone.

'So what do you want me to do?' Marcus says, when he finishes his correspondence, placing the BlackBerry on the table next to his plate.

'I don't know.' Holly shrugs. 'I wanted you to know how unhappy I am. I wanted you to care.'

'I do care, Holly.' His voice is gentle now, now that he no longer feels attacked. 'And maybe you should go to see a doctor. It could be depression. Perhaps you could look at medication. I do understand you're unhappy, Holly, but I also know it's nothing to do with me.'

Holly shrugs. She tried, she thinks. At least she tried.

The phone shrills, waking Holly out of the most bizarre dream. She and Will are at the theatre. The actress on stage is supposed to be Saffron but, in fact, it is Olivia.

'Holly? Are you awake? It's Paul.'

'Hey Paul, how are you?'

'Well, I'm fine. But the thing is, you've seen the gossip about Saffron in the papers, right?'

'Yes, I know! Isn't it awful? I've left her messages but we haven't managed to catch up. Have you spoken to her?'

'Well, that's the thing. You know we've got this place in the country? Well, we offered it to her as a hideout because it's in the middle of nowhere and . . . basically her driver just called us from Heathrow, asking for help because she's arrived and . . . well . . . she's shit-faced.'

Holly sits bolt upright. 'What do you mean "shit-faced"?'

Paul starts laughing. 'What do you think I mean? Here, I'll pass you over. She wants to talk.'

'Holly Mac? Is that my darling Holly Mac?'

And, of course, Holly hears instantly that Saffron is drunk. And she knows instantly what this means. She knows about her long-standing sobriety since walking into AA. She isn't supposed to know but Tom told her, swore her to secrecy. Paul thinks Saffron is just drunk. A one-off. An amusing incident.

'Where are you, Saff?'

'About to get in a car, darling. Where are you? Why aren't you here? I want us to be all together again.'

'Let me talk to Paul a sec, Saff. I'll talk to you in a minute . . . where are you, Paul?'

'Driving down to Gloucestershire to deposit her. Except she can't be on her own. I think we'll stay with her just until she sobers up.'

'Paul,' Holly whispers, 'do you know she's in AA?'

'What? You're not serious!'

'Desperately. This is huge, Paul, she's fallen off the wagon.'

'Oh shit,' he mutters. 'I had no idea. I thought it was just funny she was . . . Oh God, Holly. Now what do we do? I'm completely out of my depth here. Can you come? Please?'

'Come where? Gloucestershire?'

'Yes. Bring the kids. Bring Marcus. Whatever. But please come.'

Holly takes a deep breath. 'OK,' she says. 'I'll need to rearrange some stuff but I'll come. Ring me later and I'll tell you the plan.'

'**W**here are we going, Mum?' Oliver asks again as Holly hauls their suitcases downstairs and throws them in the back of the car.

'To my friends Paul and Anna, darling. Our friend Saffron is here and she hasn't been very well, so she needs all of us to go and look after her.'

'What's the matter with her?' Daisy asks. 'Does she have flu?'

'Sort of.' Holly smiles, hoping they won't arrive to find Saffron drunk.

Earlier in the day, Paul had phoned Holly and provided her with an update. 'Saffron fell asleep in the car and now she's awake and pretty hung over,' he'd told her. 'She says she'll never drink again.'

'Do you think she means it?' Holly had asked dubiously.

'I think so. She seemed pretty low key and said she had a splitting headache. I think she feels awful about what happened, but God only knows whether she'll drink again. I suppose we'll just keep an eye on her. What time are you thinking of leaving?'

'After school. The au pair will get the kids, then I'll pack them up and come down.'

'Great. Saffron's put in a request for sushi. Any chance you could stop somewhere and bring some down?'

Holly had laughed and rolled her eyes. 'God, you can take the girl out of LA, but you can't take LA out of the girl. Sushi indeed. Where does she think she is?'

'Not Gloucestershire, that's for sure.' Paul had laughed. 'Oh, and one more thing. It's bloody freezing. The plumber's supposed to be coming tomorrow morning, and we're waiting for the chimney guy, but bring tons of clothes. We may have to sleep in our coats tonight.'

'Oh terrific.' Holly had affected a dramatic sigh. 'Anything else I ought to know before I climb in the car?'

'Yes! Can you pick Olivia up? I know it's a bit out of the way for you, but Saffron insisted Olivia come too. Is that OK?'

'Sounds great. A proper reunion. I imagine we'll be there around five or six. See you later, and thanks for the directions.' And Holly had taken her cup of coffee up to her studio to phone Marcus.

'What? You're what?' Marcus spat with anger. 'Taking the children and going where? Just a little bit of a coincidence, isn't it? You tell me you're unhappy and now you're leaving with no notice? Do you really think I believe this is about Saffron? Christ, Holly, you haven't seen these people in, what? Twenty years? And now all of a sudden you're dropping everything for them?' And then his voice dipped to a familiar calm. 'No,' he said. 'I will not tolerate this. You're not going.'

'I am, Marcus,' Holly says quietly. 'I'm sorry, but I have to.'

'If you go . . .' Marcus is still eerily calm. 'If you go and take the children, Holly, don't bother coming back. I will not have my wife deliberately defy me in this way. It's me or these people you think are your friends. Your choice, Holly. Your choice.'

Here it is. As if God has reached down and opened up a window of opportunity for her. One that, till now, she has only fantasised about.

Here it is.

And there is no doubt in her heart, no second thoughts. Freedom is being offered to her on a plate.

'I'm sorry you feel that way, Marcus. I'm sorry you're making me choose, but I can't let my friends down. I'm going.'

'Fine,' he shouts. 'I'll get your stuff packed while you're away because let me tell you this, you're not getting the house and you're not getting a penny out of me.'

'Fine,' Holly echoes, and she hangs up the phone and calls Will.

She leaves him a message on his cellphone, a message at home, and sends him a brief email explaining what just happened. She isn't sure how she feels, and part of her knows she should be scared, but why does she skip down the hallway to pack?

Already, a few minutes in, she knows there is no going back. Think. Think. She has to take everything that is important to her, she realises. She checks her watch. There isn't that much time. She goes from room to room, picking up the things she really wants. She takes some smaller paintings, stacking them in the car, and her collection of antique porcelain pill boxes. The books she leaves, aside from a few she has had since she was a little girl, a few she was hoping to pass on to Daisy. Her mother's pearls, her grandmother's ring, some favourite scarves.

The children's rooms are harder. How is she going to explain this to them? How will they take it? Particularly Oliver, who adores his father even though he hardly ever sees him. She shakes her head and gets on with the business of picking the important things for the children.

A necklace Daisy had been given by her great-grandmother. Her teddies and favourite dresses. Her colouring pads and crayons. Oliver's Star Wars transformers collection. Uppy, the threadbare stuffed dog, once brown and white, now mostly grey with his fur loved off that Oliver sleeps with every night.

Holly gathers them all up and crams them into the boot of the car.

'You look good!' Olivia climbs in the car and wedges her rucksack under Daisy's feet on the floor of the back seat.

'Thanks!' Holly smiles. 'I think my marriage is over.' She keeps her voice low so the kids don't hear.

'What?' Olivia's mouth drops open. 'What do you mean? I thought you weren't going to do anything?'

'I mean I just had the mother of all arguments with Marcus, and he told me that if I went to Gloucestershire, my marriage would be over.' Holly feels completely stupid because she can't stop smiling. Hasn't been able to stop smiling.

'Well, he obviously doesn't mean it.' Olivia is confused. How can Holly be giving her such terrible news with such a huge grin?

'No, no. I think he does.'

'So how do you feel, or is that a stupid question?'

'Honestly?' Holly turns her head to look at Olivia. 'I feel free. For the last three hours I haven't been able to stop smiling.'

'God, Holly, I had no idea you'd be so impulsive . . . Oh no. Stop the car!'

Holly pulls over and watches, concerned, as Olivia jumps out the car and reaches over to vomit into the gutter. She leaps out and rubs Olivia's back. When Olivia has finished and is wiping the tears from her eyes, Holly asks gently if she's OK.

'Yes, I'm OK,' Olivia says, suddenly leaning over again and vomiting violently into the gutter.

'No, you're not,' Holly says. 'We ought to get you to the doctor.'

'Really, I don't need the doctor,' Olivia says flatly. 'But I could do with some crackers.'

Holly looks at her carefully as it dawns on her. 'Are you . . . ?'

Olivia nods.

'But . . . who? The American guy? I mean, congratulations . . . no?'

'No.' Olivia shakes her head. 'I don't think I'm going to keep it. The father is Fred, the American, but he's no longer in the picture.'

'Look, you get back in the car if you're feeling up to it, and I'll run into that shop and get you some ginger ale and crackers. I know all about morning sickness.'

Half an hour later, Olivia starts laughing. The two women haven't stopped talking since Holly got back in the car with the ginger ale, crackers and snacks for the kids.

'What are you laughing at?' Holly sneaks a sideways glance as she zips across to the fast lane to overtake a white van.

'I'm laughing at how much of a mess we all are. You may have just left your husband; I'm pregnant; Saffron's been exposed. What else could possibly happen? I feel like Tom's death has propelled all of us into these huge midlife crises.'

Holly snorts and peers through the windscreen at the grey sky. 'Thanks a lot, Tom, interesting way to keep us all together.'

'Isn't that weird though?' Olivia shifts in her seat so she's looking at Holly. 'It is keeping us all together. It does feel that this is Tom's doing,' and with that she peers up at the sky herself. 'Nice one, Tom.'

'Do you do that too?' Holly asks quietly.

'What? Talk to Tom?'

'Yes, but look up at the sky when you do it. I do that a lot. Still. I have little chats with him.'

'I know. It feels, a lot of the time, like he is watching and, corny as it sounds, I feel like he's become a sort of guardian angel.'

'It's not corny.' Holly can feel the tears well up. 'It's exactly how I feel.'

'Oh God.' Olivia reaches into her bag for a tissue. 'Don't set me off. I cry at everything these days.'

'You're supposed to.' Holly smiles through her tears as Olivia hands her a tissue. 'Your hormones are all out of whack.'

The phone starts ringing and Holly picks it up, plugging the earpiece in as she looks at the screen to see who it is.

Will.

'Hey,' she says softly. 'Did you get my message?'

'Oh, Holls,' he says. 'I was so shocked. I can't believe he did that. I can't believe you left. How do you feel? Are you OK?'

'Yes. Better than, actually. But I can't really talk. I'm on my way down to the country. Long story. I'll tell you another time. Is everything OK?'

'Everything's great. I'm just worried about you.'

'Don't be. I'll call you when I can.'

She hangs up to find Olivia looking at her with raised eyebrows.

'What?' Holly says although she is flushing with guilt.

'Sounds like there's more to the story.'

'What? The phone call?' Holly attempts to laugh it off. 'That was just a friend . . . oh God. OK, it was Will.'

Olivia tilts her head. 'Oh, I didn't realise. Thought it might have been some other dangerously sexy, single, completely gorgeous man.'

Holly laughs. 'I thought he wasn't your type?'

'Only because men that perfect terrify me.'

'There's nothing going on. I promise you. We're not having an affair.'

'You don't have to explain anything to me. Anyway, Will is lovely, and Tom was never very keen on Marcus so I know he'd approve.'

Holly is stunned. Tom not keen on Marcus? He never said anything.

'What did Tom say about Marcus?'

Olivia groans. 'Oh, here I go again, putting my foot in it.' She sighs. 'Ah well, in for a penny, in for a pound . . . he just never understood why you two got together, what you saw in him. He said that Marcus was pompous beyond belief and he couldn't understand how you put up with him. So, bottom line is, I would think Tom would be delighted if there was something going on with you and Will.'

At that they both lean forward and look up at the sky, then look back at one another and burst out laughing.

It's dark by the time they bump over the old gravel driveway that leads up to the barn. The children are fast asleep in the back, and Holly and Olivia haven't stopped talking for a second.

'Hello!' Paul comes out of the house and tramps over the driveway to help them in.

'Good God, Holly. Are you moving here permanently?' He peers nervously into the back, where the bags and possessions reach the roof.

Holly starts to laugh and then finds herself suddenly, unexpectedly, sobbing.

'I didn't mean anything,' Paul says nervously. 'I'm really sorry.'

Olivia walks over to Holly and puts her arms round her, and Holly leans her head on her shoulder and lets the sobs come.

'Mum?' comes a small voice from the back of the car. 'Mum? Are we there yet? Why are you crying?' And Holly gently disengages and plants a bright smile on her face as she tries to think of an excuse to tell Oliver, before she helps the children inside the barn.

'Wow . . . this place is . . . unfinished.'

They are standing in the living room, looking at the piles of paint tins in one corner, the dust sheets in another, and the lack of furniture.

'I warned you we were doing it up.' Paul grins.

'I thought . . . well, I didn't think you were *building* it,' Olivia says. 'Is this part of your evil plan?'

Anna walks in from the kitchen. 'You mean get you down here and get you working? Absolutely. Do you think we are idiots or something like that? What is that expression . . . there's no such thing as a free lunch?' And with a laugh she comes over and gives them both hugs.

'So where is she?' Holly says. 'Where's Saffron?'

'She couldn't get any reception on her phone,' Anna explains. 'She went to the top of the driveway to make a call. Didn't you pass her?'

'Probably,' Paul says. 'It's pitch-black out there, though. Which reminds me, can we see if we can rig up some sort of outside light?'

'I'll add it to the list.' Anna rolls her eyes. 'I have to warn you the beds are a bit funky.'

'Beds? I thought we were on the floor with sleeping-bags?'

'We were, but we found this company that makes wild and wonderful blow-up beds in seventies retro patterns and we bought a load.'

'I have to say I wasn't looking forward to a sleeping-bag. Lots of fun approaching twenty, not so much approaching forty,' Holly says.

'**S**aff!' they all chorus as they walk up the driveway half an hour later, cutting through the darkness with torchlight. 'Saff? Saff!'

'I don't suppose there's a pub nearby, is there?' Holly shines her torch on Paul.

'Funny you mention it. I'll go.'

'I'll come with you,' Anna says. 'God, you don't really think she's drinking? She said this morning that she wouldn't drink again.'

'Coming from an alcoholic in relapse,' Holly reflects sadly, 'I'd guess that doesn't mean a lot.'

Chapter Ten

SAFFRON HAS PASSED OUT on a pink and orange inflatable bed in one of the bedrooms off the gallery upstairs. The children are fast asleep, Anna and Holly are in the kitchen making coffee, and Olivia is helping Paul bring logs in from the shed to keep the fire going.

It is almost as cold inside the house as it is outside. Holly leans back on the counter as Anna puts the kettle on the stove.

'I am really sorry,' Anna mutters, rubbing her hands together over the gas flame. 'I think the pipes must have frozen or burst or something.'

'I think we're probably all much hardier than we look,' Holly says. 'Anyway, this feels sort of like getting back to basics. This barn is gorgeous, and it just makes you realise that you only need a few things to make it perfect—a sofa, a table . . .'

'. . . beds.' Anna laughs.

'Well, yes, but not all the stuff that we all tend to collect.'

'Paul said you'd brought a lot of things with you . . .' Anna turns to give Holly a suspicious look. 'Is everything OK?'

'Well, I feel like saying it's a long story, but it really isn't.' She takes a deep breath. 'I think I've left Marcus.'

'I should say I'm surprised, but I am not.' Anna frowns.

'I have a feeling that nobody is. The truth is, Anna, I haven't been happy for ages. Years, I think. Obviously I've got my wonderful children, but I think it just dawned on me that the thing that's making me so unhappy is the one thing I haven't been able to face.'

'Your marriage.'

'My marriage. For so many reasons. I never see Marcus, I don't feel that we have a partnership of any kind.' Holly sighs deeply. 'I think he loves who he wants me to be, which isn't who I am. I don't think he's the slightest bit interested in any parts of Holly that don't fit the picture he has of me, so I've become someone else, a Holly I don't recognise.'

'To thine own self be true,' Anna says.

Holly nods. 'I haven't been true to myself at all. I understand the reasons why I married Marcus. On paper he seemed to be everything I thought I should want, and I was completely on the rebound and he seemed to offer such a steady, secure life. I thought . . . well . . . I suppose I knew I wasn't in love with him, but I thought we'd have a different kind of love. I thought it would grow, and I kept telling myself that passion always dies, so it doesn't matter if you don't have it there in the beginning. The important thing is that you're best friends.'

Anna tilts her head. 'It sounds like you never thought it was possible to have passion and a best friend.'

Tears fill Holly's eyes. 'I didn't. I didn't think I could do better than Marcus, he seemed to adore me and I thought that was enough.'

'I hope you do not take this the wrong way,' Anna says carefully, 'but that night we all came over for dinner . . . when Paul and I left, Paul asked me if I thought the marriage was OK.'

'He did? But how could he have known anything when I didn't even know myself?'

'For exactly the reasons you just gave to me. There did not seem to be any kindness between you. You were funny together and obviously something worked, but Marcus seemed to take every opportunity to put you down, pretending to be funny except it was not funny. I was horribly uncomfortable. I think he put down everyone. It would seem to be a habit of his.'

'I know.' Holly winces. 'He's just incredibly insecure with an enormous superiority complex that disguises an even bigger inferiority complex. He thinks he's being funny, but it's a way of subtly keeping everyone beneath him.'

'That's exactly what we saw that night. And he controlled you so much, Holly. Every time you opened your mouth he would stop talking to hear what you were saying, and you became quieter and quieter until you seemed to have disappeared. I was not the one who noticed, for I would not have known you to be any different, but Paul was surprised. He said it felt like Marcus was the puppeteer, pulling your strings until you were absolutely under his control.'

Holly shakes her head in amazement. 'Not exactly a healthy relationship, right?'

Anna laughs. 'Would not seem so.'

Holly wipes her tears away. 'So . . . do you and Paul have both? Do you have passion and friendship?'

'After as much IVF as we've had, let me tell you, there is not a lot of passion left.' Anna rolls her eyes. 'But even now, even after all this, I still look at him and want to rip his clothes off and jump him in the bed.'

Holly laughs at Anna's English. 'Are you serious?'

'Yup. And he is my best friend. Most of the time, quite honestly, I am in bed by nine and the last thing I want to do is even think about sex, much less do it, but there are those times when I remember, when I feel exactly the same way about him as I did in the beginning. But you must have fancied Marcus at some point . . . No? . . . not even a bit?'

Holly continues to shake her head sadly.

'But you were married for, what, thirteen . . .? Fourteen years? You had two children. Why would you stay with a man for that long, given everything you've said?'

Holly shrugs as she tips coffee into the cafetière. 'I think fear,' she says slowly. 'I think I was just too frightened to leave. And then of course the children. I feel horrible about them. How could I have done this to Daisy and Oliver?'

'They will be happy if the mother is happy,' Anna says gently. 'There is nothing worse for children than to grow up in an unhappy marriage. Are you sure it is over though? Would you give it another chance?'

'I don't know,' Holly says. 'I do feel sure it's over, but it's only been a few hours. God knows how I'll feel in the morning.'

'I think you are very brave,' Anna says, setting the coffee on a tray. 'And I believe that whatever decision you make will be the right one. Come on, let's try to warm ourselves up.'

'Is Saffron asleep?' Paul says, prodding the logs so the flames shoot up.

'Asleep? Unconscious I think would be a better term,' Holly laughs, coming down from checking on the children and Saffron.

'How are the kids?'

'Cold. I piled everything I could find on top of them, but they're fast asleep so presumably they're OK. I'm a bit worried though.'

'Why don't we all sleep in here by the fire tonight?' Anna says suddenly. 'The plumber's coming tomorrow so we should have heat then, but tonight this is the warmest room. We can carry the kids down.'

'And Saffron?'

'I think we should leave her,' Paul says. 'The cold will probably help her hangover. Anyway, speaking of cold—' he reaches into his jacket pocket to pull out a small bottle—'does anyone want some brandy in their coffee?'

A muted cheer goes up as three mugs approach Paul, who pours copious amounts into each. 'Probably better to finish it, given we have Saffron here,' he muses, tipping the last drops in.

'I have to say I was stunned at how drunk she was,' Olivia says.

'I think what stunned me most was how drunk she was in so short a time,' Holly says. 'Wasn't she only gone about forty minutes? How much do you have to drink in forty minutes to get that drunk?'

'The barman said she was drinking vodka martinis like they were water. And through a straw.'

'I do feel a little out of my depth here,' Anna says quietly. 'I had no idea she is an alcoholic. I'm really worried about how she's going to cope. I for one certainly don't know what to do or how to help her.'

'I looked up interventions on the internet,' Holly says. 'That's when you tell the alcoholic what it's like living with them and what they're like when they're drunk. The thing is none of us are present in her life to see the difference. I feel a bit helpless, too.'

The fire starts to give off some serious heat and Paul unbuttons his jacket. 'I think there's probably nothing we can do to stop her drinking, but perhaps she'll want to stop herself. She's done it before so she can do it again. We should all do our best to keep her away from alcohol, but I also think we shouldn't judge her if she slips.'

'What about keeping her busy?' Anna pipes up. 'I think we should get her working on the house.'

Olivia bursts out laughing. 'What? "Saffron? Just climb up and retile the roof while you're here?" "Saffron, I see you sitting around with nothing to do, would you mind just building some kitchen cabinets?"'

They all laugh, but Holly says, 'Actually, I think it's a brilliant idea. I know we were joking about your evil plan to recruit your friends for slave labour, but I would think the best thing we could do for Saffron is to keep her busy, and I wouldn't mind keeping busy myself.'

Paul looks at her quizzically.

'Long story, Paul. Short version is I think my marriage is over, which is probably a huge blessing in disguise. Anna can give you the details later. I'm a bit talked out for today if that's OK.'

'That's OK,' Paul says, sympathy in his eyes. 'I'm sorry if you're in pain.'

'I'm very much not in pain, and don't be sorry. Right now I still feel liberated. Ask me again in the morning.'

'Speaking of morning.' Olivia says, stretching. 'I'm completely exhausted. Would anyone mind if we brought the beds down now? I don't think I can keep my eyes open for another second.'

At five in the morning Holly is wide awake. It takes her a while to orientate herself—too many people breathing, too cold, where is she? She slips out of bed, bundles the sleeping-bag around her and puts some more logs on the fire, poking and blowing until the flames catch.

Holly sits for a while staring into the fire, thinking about her life. For the first time in years, she feels at peace.

She takes her cellphone and a deep breath as she braves the outside to stomp up to the top of the driveway. Frost is on the ground and the grass crunches under her boots as she makes her way to the road.

She can't call Will, not at five thirty in the morning, but she is hoping there will be a text from him, and turning on her phone she walks around until she gets the briefest of signals. One line, but enough.

Miss talking. Am thinking of u & worrying. R u ok? Where r u? lunch? Wxx

She smiles. Why do his messages, his texts, his emails, or phone calls make her instantly happy?

am v. ok. In country. Miss u 2. can't do lunch. Will try 2 talk later.
Me XX

A minute later, shockingly, her phone rings.

'What are you doing awake?' Her smile stretches from ear to ear.

'Couldn't sleep,' Will says. 'I was up at my computer reading some of your emails, when boom! your text arrived. Where are you?'

'What a gorgeous surprise,' Holly says. 'I'm in Gloucestershire. At Paul and Anna's place.'

'How come?'

'We've got Saffron,' she says. She trusts him. After all, she's been trusting him with her private thoughts for weeks now. 'We're hiding her. You've seen the papers, right?'

'Seen them? I was reading all about it yesterday online. It seems they're obsessed. Brad and Angelina have been relegated to page four thanks to Saffron and Pearce Webster. Have to say it's pretty damn impressive though. Pearce Webster!'

'God, you're shallow.' Holly starts to laugh. 'You're impressed, aren't you?'

'Well, have to say I *am* slightly. Not bad for a girl from northwest London.'

'More LA-influenced now I'd say,' Holly snorts. 'I had to do a sushi run on the way up here to keep her happy.'

'You're not serious?' Will laughs. 'You can take the girl out of LA . . .'

'That's exactly what I said!' and they both laugh. 'I'm so glad you called,' Holly says. 'It's really good to hear your voice.'

'It's really good to hear yours,' Will says, his smile audible.

'Don't you think it's odd,' Holly starts haltingly, 'that we've become such good friends after such a short space of time? I . . . well, I don't want to embarrass you or anything, but I missed having a male friend. I really don't know what I would do without you.' She stops, flushing. Has she gone too far? She didn't mean to get sentimental, serious.

'I feel the same way,' Will says. 'Sometimes I find it hard to believe that we didn't really know each other four months ago. I feel like I've become so reliant on our friendship, on filling you in on everything that's happening in my life. I do feel that I finally have a best friend.'

A pang. Pleasure or pain? Holly doesn't know whether she wants to hear this or not. Does being a best friend preclude anything else? And why did that thought suddenly make its way into her head? Hadn't she accepted that they were friends?

'But I want to hear about you.' Will moves swiftly on. 'In your message it sounded like Marcus took it really badly. Are you OK?'

'I am,' Holly says, sitting carefully on a large stone as she checks her signal, desperate not to lose Will. 'I know this sounds bizarre, but I feel at peace. I mean, obviously, a bit scared and apprehensive about the future, but I feel . . . free. Like me.'

'Do you think this is it, though?'

'I think so,' Holly says. 'The thing that scares me most is that I'll go back because I'm too scared to do it on my own. Marcus hissed that I wouldn't get the house or a penny out of him.'

'Sounds like he's just reacting because, as far as he's concerned, you've just destroyed his life and humiliated him royally.'

'You know what's weird?' Holly says. 'I was sitting in front of the fire just before thinking about him, and I suddenly had this really strong feeling that he will look back and know that this marriage was wrong. I don't love him, and everybody deserves to be loved.'

'You're right,' Will says quietly. 'Everyone does deserve to be loved. Including you. Haven't you always said that you felt that Marcus didn't love you, but that he loved who he wanted you to be? Don't you deserve to be loved for who you are, not for dressing up and entertaining and being a perfect trophy wife?'

'Yes. Thank you for saying that.'

'My pleasure. So how long are you up there for?'

'I have no idea. Saffron will be here until it all blows over I suppose, and the rest of us will just have to see.'

'Is Saffron not capable of being alone?' Will laughs. 'Has she turned into that much of a diva?'

'God no. Not what you think. She's just . . . fragile right now. She needs her friends.'

'I was joking,' Will says. 'I think you're all amazing being there for her. It's exactly what Tom would have done.'

Holly shivers, standing up and pacing in the cold. 'I'm freezing, Will. I have to get inside but there's no reception there.'

'Can I call you out there?'

'You probably won't get me, but text or leave a message and I'll call you back. Thanks for phoning, Will. It means so much to me.'

'Bacon, eggs, bread, orange juice . . .' Paul turns to Olivia. 'Was there anything else?'

Olivia looks at her list. 'Milk. Papers.'

'OK. I'll get the papers, you get the milk.' Paul grabs a handful and stops in his tracks as he looks at the front page of the *Mirror*.

'Got the milk!' Olivia calls as she comes back down the aisle, weighed down by a giant carton of semi-skimmed milk. 'What's the matter?' And she sidles next to him, her hand flying up to her mouth as she sees the front page.

'"Saffy Daffy and Drunk,"' Olivia whispers, reciting the headline. '"Brit actress bonking Pearce flies into Heathrow, smashed! Do you know her mystery new man? Call this number and tell us who he is!"'

'Oh shit!' she whispers. 'It's you. I mean, you're carrying Saffron.'

'Let's just hope nobody phones them. The last thing we need is for the press to bring Anna into it and then find out where we are.'

'What a bloody nightmare.' Olivia sighs. 'Don't bring it home, let's check the rest for Saffron-free papers, and we'll bring those instead.'

Saffron has never done anything by halves. When she smoked, she smoked two packs a day. When she quit, she never looked at a cigarette again . . . until she started again. When she exercises, she does so obsessively, two hours a day with a personal trainer, every day, lying in bed exercising in her mind, thinking of little else until she misses a day or two and then does nothing at all for months.

So when she falls off the wagon, she does it in the way she does everything in her life. Spectacularly. At great speed and to great excess.

She hadn't meant to lose her sobriety. When she was sitting in the airport bar, her intention truly was to have one drink. Other people were able to have one drink, why not her? she told herself.

Then there was the plane. First class champagne on tap. Why not, she told herself. Just this once. Such a warm, familiar feeling. So lovely to relax as the buzz started up. She felt loose and giggly and happy. Happy again for the first time in days. She wasn't a noisy drunk, just snuggled up quietly under her blanket downing glass after glass.

She doesn't remember much about arriving. Stewards and stewardesses seemed to be muttering in their walkie talkies, and she was able to cover her head with a scarf and huge Jackie-O-style sunglasses onto her face. She remembers being hustled through noise, her name being called, and then—bliss—being picked up and falling asleep on someone's shoulder as she was carried out to a car.

Again, last night, she hadn't meant to drink. Had absolutely meant every word when she told Anna and Paul, who had come to her rescue, that she would never drink again. She felt horrible now she'd finally woken up. Her head was pounding, waves of nausea kept coming over her, and she knew she never wanted to feel this way again, the way she felt for so many years before coming into AA.

'Saff!' Holly looks up from whisking some eggs and grimaces at the sight of Saffron, who's standing in the kitchen doorway, bleary-eyed, hung over, skin an odd shade of grey, long glossy locks held back messily in a clip.

'Oh,' Saffron groans, coming over to give Holly a kiss. 'I feel horrible. If the press could see me now they'd have a field day.' Paul and Olivia exchange a glance—thank God they didn't bring that paper home.

'Oh, look at your chickens, Holly!' Saffron says, seeing Daisy and Oliver, bundled up in hats and gloves, playing outside the kitchen window. 'Aren't they gorgeous!'

'I'm surprised you can see them under all those layers.' Holly smiles. 'But, thank you. I think they're pretty gorgeous, too.'

'Coffee?' Paul says brightly, placing a mug in front of a grateful Saffron and a plate piled high with bacon in the middle of the table.

'Mmm.' She takes a sip, looking sheepishly around the table. 'I think I owe you all an apology,' she says quietly. 'I'm so sorry about last night. I didn't mean to . . .' She stops, sighing. 'It won't happen again.'

'In actual fact'—Anna starts setting the plates around the table as Paul brings the eggs over—'you'll probably be too busy to think about sneaking off to the pub again.'

'Busy? How?'

'We've decided to try to get this house finished.' Paul sits down and helps himself to bacon. 'We've assigned everyone jobs, and you and Anna are starting with tiling the bathroom.'

Saffron starts to laugh. 'Ow,' she groans, holding her head. 'Shit, that hurts. You have to be kidding . . . me? Tiling a bathroom? I've never tiled a thing in my life.'

'You'll be fine,' Anna brushes her off. 'I'm doing it with you and I'll show you what to do. It's easy. Of course, you could do the floor sanding instead, if you wanted.'

Saffron shakes her head, looking through the kitchen floor at the vast expanse of rough, stained wood in the living room. 'Tiling's fine.' She starts to laugh.

'What's so funny?' Paul looks up.

'Just that I never expected to be here tiling a bathroom. It's just so bizarre how everything in life can change in a heartbeat.'

'Tell me about it.' Holly snorts. 'Just so you know . . . I've left Marcus.'

'You have? Good girl!' Saffron exclaims.

'Why good girl?' Although it's not as if Holly doesn't know.

'Because he's a pompous, stuck-up arse, that's why.'

'Saffron!' Olivia admonishes her.

'What? It's true, isn't it?'

'You haven't changed at all, Saffron,' Holly laughs. 'You still say exactly what's on your mind.'

Saffron shrugs. 'I'd rather be honest, although I apologise if I upset you. I could have been less mean.'

'Don't worry,' Holly says. 'He is a pompous arse. Do me a favour, though, don't say anything in front of the children.'

'Of course I won't. If breakfast is ready, shall we get them in now?'

'**M**ummy.' Daisy has put down her fork and is staring at Saffron. 'I thought you said your friend was a beautiful famous actress.'

Paul shouts with laughter as Saffron gives him an exaggerated evil eye.

'Daisy!' Oliver says loudly. 'That's very rude.'

'No it's not!' she says, her voice rising towards tears. 'It's not rude, it's true.'

'It *is* rude, isn't it, Mummy? To make comments about people when they're sitting in front of you?'

'It wasn't making comments.' Daisy pouts. 'I was just saying she's not beautiful.'

'It's OK, Oliver.' Saffron smiles. 'I don't mind. Usually I am beautiful and famous, but today I'm just ordinary. I change, a bit like Cinderella.'

'You forgot to say modest.' Paul grins.

'Ah, yes. That too.'

Anna suddenly looks over at Olivia. 'Are you OK, Olivia?'

'Back in a sec,' Olivia gulps, standing up and rushing from the table, hand over her mouth.

Seconds later the unmistakable sound of retching and heaving comes from the upstairs bathroom.

'Oh God.' Paul stops chewing and lays his knife and fork down. 'Just what I need to hear in the middle of breakfast.'

Saffron reaches over and steals a piece of bacon off his plate, chewing on it thoughtfully. 'Doesn't bother me. Is she ill or is she pregnant?'

Paul starts to laugh. 'Olivia, pregnant? Hardly.' And then he sees Holly's face. 'Oh God. Is she?'

Holly tries to feign ignorance. 'Don't ask me,' she says. 'It's got nothing to do with me.'

Olivia comes back into the room, breathing newly brushed minty breath, looking more than a little uncomfortable.

'So . . . are you preg?' Saffron looks straight at her.

'God, Saff.' Paul rolls his eyes. 'Subtlety would take you a long way, you know.'

Olivia shoots a look at Holly, who shakes her head vigorously. *It wasn't me,* she wants to say.

'What does preg mean?' Oliver pipes up loudly.

'Sssh, Oliver,' Holly says. 'I'll tell you later.'

'It's OK, Oliver.' Olivia sinks down at the table. 'It means I'm having a baby. It also means it's a bloody nightmare. Whoops, excuse my language. But, yes. It would seem that despite being resolutely single and having never wanted children my entire life, I am now pregnant.'

'So who's the lucky man?' Saffron says.

'Nice guy, American, we're no longer in touch.'

'Not the man Tom introduced you to?' Saffron asks.

Olivia nods.

'Does he know?' Anna asks.

Olivia shakes her head. 'I can't see the point,' she says quietly. 'I haven't decided whether or not I'll keep it.'

'You would have an abortion?' Anna asks softly, attempting to keep the emotion out of her voice, attempting not to judge.

Olivia, now remembering Paul and Anna talking about IVF, looks directly at Anna. 'I'm so sorry. I didn't want to say anything.'

'It's fine,' Paul says as a tear rolls slowly down Anna's face. 'Don't worry. What's important is how you feel.'

'Mum?' Oliver again, looking confused. 'What's a bortion?'

Holly rolls her eyes and leans towards him. 'Ask your father,' she says with a sigh, reaching over to pour herself more coffee.

How are you?' Paul crunches over the field to an old tree stump where Anna is sitting. Her eyes are red-rimmed, and, at the sight of Paul, a few more tears squeeze their way out.

'It just does not seem fair.' Anna's words come out as sobs. 'We have tried so hard and for so long, and then Olivia just falls pregnant at the drop of a hat, and she is going to have an abortion. I . . . I just do not understand how someone could do that when there are so many people who are desperate to have children and who cannot have them.'

Paul puts his arm round Anna and hugs her as she settles in, leaning her head on his chest. Safe. Loved. Exhausted. No more sobs for now, just a blankness as she whispers over and over again, 'It's just not fair.'

They keep to their separate corners of the house for the morning, waiting for the emotions to die down.

Anna and Saffron in the bathroom, Paul sanding the floors of the living room, Olivia painting the window frames. Holly and the children are sanding down the kitchen cupboards, the children delighted to be taking part in grown-up work.

'Paul!' Holly walks into the living room, yelling over the noise of the industrial sander, coughing as a cloud of dust settles over her.

'Hang on.' He switches the machine off and pulls the mask off his face. 'Yup?'

'You need to come look at the kitchen cupboards. I think all the wood might be rotten.'

'Oh God,' he groans. 'Get Anna down here, she'll know more than me.'

Anna crouches down, stroking a finger down the wood, then looks up at Paul with a frown. 'Yes. They are rotten all right.'

Paul sighs. 'That's the problem with these bloody renovations. You think you know exactly what has to be done, but the more work you do, the more you uncover that needs doing. It will probably cost a small fortune to get this done. Just what we need.'

Holly's face lights up. 'We could ask Will!' she says as Olivia suppresses a smile, raising an eyebrow instead as she turns to look at Holly. 'Will. Tom's brother. He's a cabinet-maker. He'd come in a heartbeat.'

'Oh my God!' Anna starts leaping in delight. 'What an excellent idea! I did not know Tom's brother is a carpenter.'

This time, Holly avoids catching Olivia's knowing eye. 'I've got his number,' she says, happiness lifting her up and floating her towards the door. 'I'll go outside to get a signal and call him.'

A beaming Holly comes back twenty minutes later.

'What took you so long?' still-disgruntled Paul asks, convinced Will won't come, convinced Holly won't even have his number.

Holly blushes. 'It took me a while to get through,' she lies unconvincingly. 'But Will's coming. He's taking the train this afternoon. I'll take the kids and go and pick him up at the station.'

'Yay!' Anna shouts with joy, turning to Paul. 'See? I told you everything would be all right.'

'We don't know how much he's going to charge us,' Paul grumbles. 'It might still be more money than we can afford to spend. Even this plumber to fix the heating is yet another unexpected expense.'

'Will said he'd do it for cost,' Holly says, unable to wipe the smile off her face—and not because he's doing it for cost. 'He's bringing all his tools. Apparently wood is much cheaper out here, and he's not going to charge anything for his time.'

Anna plants her hands on her hips and shoots Paul an I-told-you-so look as Paul shrugs his shoulders. 'If that is true, that is amazing.'

'Of course, it's true,' Holly says. 'Remember, he's Tom's brother. Tom would never have promised something he wasn't going to deliver. Think his brother's going to be any different?'

'Let's just hope you're right,' Paul says, and donning his face mask he goes back into the living room to finish sanding the floor.

Marcus has left two messages on Holly's phone. The first furious, the second sad, asking if they could talk.

She has responded by phoning Frauke. She has left details of where she is with her, in case of emergency only.

Holly is burying her head in the sand, just as she did throughout her marriage. If she doesn't think about it, it isn't happening.

There is only one thought filling her head today.

Will.

Saffron, when sober, is as perceptive as she is direct. As an actress, she has learned to become an expert people-watcher, and as soon as Holly mentioned Will, Saffron saw how her eyes lit up, saw how she couldn't stop smiling when she came back from having phoned him.

Hmmm, she thinks. Interesting. Not that she could see Holly and Will together—Will, though sexy and charming, is definitely not ready to settle down, but doesn't Holly deserve a bit of fun after being married to that awful Marcus? And maybe it's a good thing there's someone else around to help Holly see she's made the right decision.

Maybe it's a very good thing indeed.

Chapter Eleven

H OLLY PULLS IN to one of the parking spaces next to the little station. She is nervous, jittery, so lost in her own world she's tuned out of the constant questions from Daisy in the back seat.

'I'll be back in a second.' She turns to the kids as she sees the distant lights of the train, and she jumps out of the car and up the steps onto the platform, feeling dizzy with excitement.

She paces nervously as the train doors sigh their way open and squints as she sees him—one of three to get off the train—walking up towards her from the far end of the platform, waving.

There is no mistaking Will, and Holly's heart leaps as she takes in his familiar face, his familiar stride. In old Levis, leather boots and a beaten-up old jacket that can't possibly be keeping out the chill, Will looks, as far as Holly is concerned, perfect.

His tousled brown hair seems to have grown longer, his green eyes are sparkling as he gets closer, his grin widening. He is quite simply the most gorgeous man Holly has ever seen—the most perfect specimen of maleness Holly could possibly imagine. His legs are long and strong, his shoulders broad, his neck thick, and that smile—oh that smile! It is a smile that could launch a thousand love songs.

Holly grins. Cannot stop grinning. She starts walking towards him, and as he gets closer, she sees he is grinning too. The force of mutual attraction pulls them together with the speed and intensity of magnets. Holly's arms automatically wind themselves round Will's back, and his round hers, as they squeeze one another tight and he rests his cheek on the top of her head, pulling away after what feels like hours to reach down and plant a kiss on her cheek.

Holly is shaking. She has been fighting these feelings for so long now, so guilty at feeling this way about a man other than her husband. It is overwhelming now that she can no longer hide her feelings.

'God, it's good to see you.' Will grins down at her as he picks up his bag and toolbox and they start walking towards the car. 'I was sort of hoping I might get an invitation down here, and then there you were on the phone, my damsel in distress.'

Holly blushes. 'Not quite. If anyone's the damsel in distress, it's Paul. He's being a bit of an old woman about the kitchen cupboards. He really seemed to panic when Anna said they needed replacing.'

'Glad to be the knight in shining armour,' Will says as they reach the car. 'Hi, you two.' He taps the back window before climbing into the front seat and leaning into the back to shake Oliver by the hand. 'Hi, I'm Will. You must be Oliver. And this cute little thing must be Daisy.' Daisy smiles flirtatiously up at him and Will laughs, turning to Holly. 'Good lord, Holly. She's exactly like you. She's gorgeous.'

'Thank you.' Holly turns the ignition on.

'So'—Will turns in his seat so he's leaning back against the door— 'how's everyone getting on? Any exciting bits of gossip?'

Holly barks with laughter. 'God, Will. This is about the most dramatic gathering you could ever imagine. First, you have to swear not to tell anyone. If you're staying, I think I should fill you in on everything.'

'I swear,' he says solemnly, placing his hand over his heart, and Holly tells him the whole story.

'Tea?' Will hollers from the kitchen as the gang lay down their tools and come gratefully, one by one, into the kitchen, to be met by a tray of steaming mugs and a plate of chocolate digestives.

Anna looks at the tea, then admiringly at Will. 'You are good,' she says. 'Any chance you would be interested in being a second husband?'

'Not the slightest bit interested in being your first husband, thank you.' Will looks aghast, as Paul barks with laughter. 'Sorry.' He back-tracks furiously. 'I didn't mean that to come out the way it sounded. Not because of you, it's just that marriage isn't my bag.'

Holly hears this and turns away quickly, busying herself with getting more milk from the fridge. She feels uncomfortable hearing him say marriage isn't his bag, which is absurd. What was she expecting? That he would say he's desperate to get married, and his idea of the perfect woman is Holly? And more to the point, why is she even thinking about it? She shudders at the stupidity of it all, at how this obsession is turning her into a teenager.

There is no doubt about it being an obsession. There is no doubt that she has allowed herself to give in to it, to focus on Will, to think only of him, to dream the dreams that have been lingering on the outer edges of her subconscious for months now.

The handful of times that she had allowed herself to close her eyes and picture Will when Marcus was pounding away on top of her had led to yet more guilt, and she had promised herself she wouldn't do it again. But last night, lying in bed upstairs—the plumber had come and the defective pipe had been replaced so the barn was finally warm—Holly had allowed herself to give in to the fantasies she had always been too frightened to invite before.

She had lain in bed and thought of undressing Will. Imagined stroking his forearms, his chest. Imagined him kissing her, moving slowly down her body.

Could he in fact be the right man for her? Could Will be her soul mate? Could he be the one that she is destined to be with?

Holly had never particularly believed in soul mates. Until now.

'So come on, be honest with us,' Anna ribs Will. 'You must get millions of passes made at you by bored horny housewives.'

Will looks slightly sheepish. 'Not millions, but I've had a few.'

'A few what? Passes made or horny housewives?' Saffron laughs.

'Both,' Will says. 'In all seriousness, though, I haven't taken anyone up on those particular kinds of offers for a while. I had the misfortune to get caught by a husband who was supposed to be away on a business trip. His flight got cancelled so he came home.'

'Could it be more clichéd?' Saffron rolls her eyes.

'I know.' Will laughs. 'Wasn't funny at the time though. I fell down the stairs, pulling up my trousers, with this madman roaring he was going to kill me. I was lucky to get out of that one alive. I retired from the business of mixing work with pleasure about a second later.'

'Doesn't that make you think of Tom?' Paul looks around the table with a grin.

'What do you mean?' Olivia looks confused.

'Don't you remember that time he was upstairs in a bedroom with that girl, oh God, what was her name . . . pretty, blonde, year above you. Kate something . . .'

'Oh *God!*' Saffron barks. 'Kate Barrowman! I'd completely forgotten that!'

Holly and Olivia start to laugh as Paul continues telling the story to Will. 'He was getting up to no good.'

'Almost to fourth base from what I remember,' Holly adds, rolling her eyes.

'Yes, well, everyone was supposed to be out of the house but her dad apparently had his workshop or something in the attic, and he came down and caught Tom and Kate, half-naked, writhing around on the parents' bed. I think Tom had a similar thing—falling down the stairs as the father threatened to kill him.'

There's a silence as they all sit, remembering Tom, remembering being sixteen, snuggled under coats in dark bedrooms on the top floors of strange houses.

'This is very weird.' Saffron breaks the silence, softly, her voice in a half whisper.

'What?' The others look at her questioningly.

'*This.* That we're sitting here talking about Tom with Tom's brother, and Tom's not here. It's just . . .' She blinks hard two or three times, willing the tears that have suddenly welled up not to fall.

'It's just that Will looks exactly like Tom used to look, and I keep catching myself wanting to call him Tom, or about to remind him of something he did or something we all did, and then I remember that it's not Tom because Tom is dead, and I just feel this enormous sense of loss.' Saffron wipes a tear from her eye.

Nobody feels differently. They have all been sitting there thinking exactly the same thoughts, but no one has dared say it, no one has dared to admit their own grief or their own loss when Tom's brother is sitting in the room. *Tom's brother.* How could they possibly have a right to feel this way when his own brother seems to be managing fine?

'I'm so sorry I'm not Tom,' Will says quietly, his voice breaking. 'I'm sorry for all of you that it's not Tom sitting here, and mostly I'm sorry for me. I'm sorry that it wasn't me that was on that train. Tom was so good. Just all good, through and through. He was loved by everyone. He had a wife and children. He never deserved to be blown apart. I keep thinking that his absence has left such a gaping hole in so many people's lives when it could have been me, and I wouldn't have been missed. It should have been me,' he says, as his own tears start to fall.

'That's not true, Will.' Saffron turns to him. 'It shouldn't have been you. You would be missed by a tremendous number of people and I'm so sorry, Will. I never meant to upset you or to make you feel unwanted.'

Will stands up and allows Saffron to give him a hug before he walks quietly out of the back door. They all watch through the window as he walks across the field to the tree stump, where he sits down and buries his face in his hands.

'I feel horrible,' Saffron says. 'I didn't mean to make him feel bad.'

'I have a sense this may have been . . . cathartic . . . for Will,' Anna says. 'I imagine he has just been able to say the thing he has been carrying around with him for months. Can't you just see it all over his face? Poor man, the guilt he is carrying must be terrible.'

Holly stands up with a start. 'Keep an eye on the kids,' she says quickly. 'I'm just going to see if he's OK.' And she disappears out of the door. She hadn't been able to take her eyes off Will, and knowing he was sitting there crying was tearing her heart apart. How could she let him feel these terrible feelings all by himself?

She tramples over the grass and stands behind him, resting a hand on his shoulder to let him know she's there, and when he turns, his eyes red, his face streaked with tears, she sinks down and wraps her arms tightly around him as she rocks him gently and whispers in his ear, 'It's OK. It's OK.'

When they come back in, everyone is still drinking tea around the table. Saffron goes straight up to Will.

'I owe you an apology, Will,' she says. 'I want to tell you that I'm glad you're here. That I'm not expecting you to replace Tom, but that I'm glad you're with us. In a funny way, as odd as it feels, it also feels very right that you're here.'

'Hear, hear!' Paul raises his empty mug in a silent toast.

'Not a replacement for Tom,' Olivia says, munching her way slowly through one of the biscuits. 'You fit in in your own right. It's lovely having you here.'

'And to Tom.' Holly raises her mug and looks up at the ceiling. 'For in his own twisted way, he's brought us all back together again.'

The others look up and raise their own mugs. 'To Tom,' they say, and as they sip their tea there are tears in all of their eyes.

'Mum?' Daisy and Oliver come in, their hands and faces covered with purple felt-tip. 'We've finished colouring and now we don't know what to do.' They scan the table, spy the biscuits, and both their faces light up.

'Go on.' Holly laughs and pushes the plate towards them. 'Just one. How would you like to watch a DVD?'

'Yay!' Both kids jump up and down. 'Can we watch *Ice Age 2*?' Oliver asks.

'No!' Daisy squeals. 'I want to watch *The Little Mermaid*.'

'No way,' Oliver says. 'I'm not watching a girl film. *Ice Age 2*, Mum.'

Daisy starts to cry.

'Enough!' Holly looks at both of them sternly. 'I'm choosing the film.' And she goes out to the car, bringing back *Shrek*.

'Oh, not again.' Oliver groans, but he follows quietly as Holly sets the computer up in their room and puts the DVD on.

'You know what we should do?' Anna breaks the silence that descends. 'We should cook a wonderful dinner tonight. Fancy clothes. Candlelight. Delicious food.'

Paul bursts out laughing. 'There's just one problem, my darling wife, we haven't got a table big enough for all of us to fit at the same time.'

'Not yet, but there's a filthy old trestle table outside. We could grab a tablecloth from the supermarket in Gloucester.'

'Chairs?' Paul persists.

'Don't be such a killjoy. We could drag the benches in from the garden,' Anna suggests.

'Great idea!' Holly echoes. 'Let's do it. God knows all of us could do with a bit of fun, and God knows I could do with a few drinks. Oh shit . . .' Her face falls and she looks nervously at Saffron. 'I forgot. Obviously no drinks.' She tries hard to hide her disappointment.

'I'll be fine.' Saffron lays a hand on her arm. 'I know I've had a couple of slips, but remember, guys, I've spent years surrounded by alcohol without wanting to have any. I don't mind if you have alcohol. Especially if it's red wine.' She grimaces. 'I've always hated red wine.'

'Done!' Anna says, excitement sweeping her up, sweeping all of them up, removing all sensible thought. 'Why don't we pack up and hit the shops now? We should make it there and back by six.'

The iPod is plugged into Paul's speakers as K T Tunstall's sweet voice fills the room. Holly has made a deliciously retro coq au vin, Olivia is tackling the salad and Anna is finishing off a gingerbread trifle. Saffron is whipping up some disgusting-looking fat-free, sugar-free concoction that is masquerading as some sort of butterscotch pudding.

Paul walks past and swipes a finger round the top of her mixing bowl. 'Mmm.' He looks at Saffron in surprise. 'That's pretty good. Sugar-free, fat-free, eh? What's in it?'

Saffron looks at him coolly. 'Chemicals,' she says as he recoils in horror and Anna starts to laugh.

'At least you'll die thin.' Olivia doesn't get this whole obsession with supposedly 'healthy' eating.

'Exactly.' Saffron laughs, licking the spoon with put-on joy.

Holly laughs and walks into the living room to finish setting the table. She's delighted with how cosy it looks. The fire is blazing; there are candles filling the room with a warm glow; and the table, complete with place settings designed and executed by the kids, looks gorgeous.

'Come on, you two.' Holly holds her hands out for Daisy and Oliver. 'Bedtime.'

'But Mum . . .' Oliver starts to whine.

'No buts.' She smiles. 'It's already half an hour later than your usual bedtime. Come on. Up we go.'

Holly kisses Daisy on the top of her head, standing back and watching her for a few seconds. 'Good night,' she whispers, 'I love you,' and as she tiptoes out of the room, she bumps into Will, who leans back on the wall, arms crossed, smiling down at her.

'It's really weird, seeing you as a mother,' he says softly.

'Weird, how? Weird bad?'

'No, no. God, no. You seem to have a really warm, loving relationship with the kids. But weird because I've never thought of you as a mother. I just always think of you as being young and, well, like me.'

Holly raises an eyebrow. 'You mean young and irresponsible?'

He shrugs. 'I'm afraid so. I think I just never thought about the responsibilities you actually have. I mean, you're a grown up.'

'So . . . does that mean you think of me differently now you've seen me with my kids?'

'A bit,' he says.

'Uh oh. Different good or different bad?'

'I could never think of you as anything bad,' he says softly. Neither of them is smiling any more, and Holly's heart is beating very fast.

'So what are you thinking?' she whispers, her voice almost catching with apprehension.

'I'm thinking'—he leans forward ever so slightly—'I'm thinking about what it would be like to kiss you.'

Holly had forgotten the sweetness of a first kiss. Had forgotten how you lean your foreheads on each other's, looking into each other's eyes with a sweet smile when it is over, cupping each other's faces with your hands, wanting to drink the other in.

She had forgotten.

Now she remembers.

It has been a wonderful meal. A meal filled with laughter. It is almost as if the mantle of grief they have carried since arriving, with Tom's absence being so very noticeable, has been shed—perhaps temporarily, perhaps not.

But not for Anna. Anna who never really knew Tom. Anna is carrying her grief for a different reason. She is trying so hard not to resent Olivia, but as the evening wears on, with Olivia rushing off to the bathroom all the time, she is finding the sadness that perhaps she and Paul are not destined to have children settling on her shoulders once again.

Anna goes into the kitchen to bring out the salad. She leans her hands on the counter for a second, breathing deeply. The bathroom is directly above the kitchen, and she hears Olivia retch into the toilet bowl, then a soft knocking as Saffron walks in. She can picture Saffron rubbing Olivia's back and hears her gently asking if she's OK.

'Why do they call it morning sickness?' She hears Olivia groan. 'It lasts *all* bloody day.'

'I had a friend who had this during the entire pregnancy,' Saffron says. 'Can you imagine? Her gynaecologist told her it would be over at three months, but it went on for nine. Ghastly. They had her on all sorts of drugs, but nothing worked.'

'That's horrific,' Olivia says. 'Thank God this is going to be over soon.'

'You're definitely not having it?'

There's a silence. 'I can't,' Olivia says in a soft voice. 'What would I do with a baby? There's no room in my life, and, frankly, I've never been one of those women whose biological clock started ticking. Either mine wasn't working or I didn't have one.'

'What about adoption?' Saffron asks. 'Would you ever consider that?'

'I don't know. I've never thought about it.'

Everyone looks up as Anna rushes back into the living room. 'Paul,' she blurts out urgently. 'I have an idea! We could adopt Olivia's baby!'

'*What?*' Paul shakes his head. Did he understand her correctly?

'She does not want a baby and we do? Doesn't it make perfect sense?'

'Oh, Anna,' Paul says sadly. 'I don't think she wants to have a baby at all. Listen to her, she's been throwing up for days. The last thing she wants is to go through the whole pregnancy. It's a wonderful idea, but I don't think it's ever going to happen.'

'Why not ask?' Holly interrupts. 'It is a wonderful idea, and you won't know unless you ask.'

'Do you think?' Paul says doubtfully. 'I think it's presumptuous.'

'It's not!' Anna insists. 'Imagine if she said yes? This could be the answer to everything. I swear Paul, do you not think it is too much of a coincidence that Olivia is pregnant and does not want a child? And here she is, staying with us, when we have been trying for a baby for two years and now we are talking about adoption? I think God brought us all together for a reason, and I think this is it. I swear to you, I really do.'

'God brought us together for what reason?' Olivia asks. She has come downstairs with Saffron.

Paul looks down at his plate, not wanting to be the one to ask.

Anna waits until Olivia sits down, then looks straight at her.

'Olivia . . .' She is suddenly nervous. 'You know Paul and I have been trying IVF and it hasn't worked? Well, we were thinking that . . . we were thinking that if you would consider having the baby, perhaps we could adopt it.'

'God . . . I . . . I don't know what to say.' Olivia is shocked. Has never truly considered adoption as an option. For it's not simply that she doesn't want a baby, it's that she doesn't want to be pregnant, doesn't want to be any place other than where she was a few short weeks ago. 'I don't know,' she repeats, thinking for the first time about carrying a baby to term, what that would mean, giving birth and then giving a child away. 'I didn't seriously think . . . hadn't thought . . .'

'We don't want you to feel any pressure or to do anything you don't want to do,' Paul interjects, 'but if you did decide to go through with the pregnancy and put the baby up for adoption, we would love to adopt your child.'

'And think'—Anna knows she is too eager, too excited, but she can't help herself—'you would still be around, still be part of the child's life.'

'I need some time.' Olivia looks first at Paul, then at Anna. 'I think it's an incredible offer, but I need to think about it.'

'Of course,' Anna says. 'Take as much time as you need.'

Will lays down his knife and reaches down to where no one can see, resting his hand on Holly's leg, then running a finger round her wrist, sending shivers of electricity up and down her spine, an electricity she hasn't felt in years. An electricity she never expected to feel again.

The others may not see, but they know. The air around Holly and Will is fizzy with electricity. Holly may think she is being subtle by not giving any indication that anything has happened, but there is now a thread joining them, a thread that may not be visible but can be felt.

Saffron clears the plates, and on the way back from the kitchen her eyes are drawn to Will's hand pulling quickly back from Holly's lap. But she is too caught up in her own troubles to give it much thought.

For Saffron did think she could handle the alcohol. She thought tonight would be like all those other nights when she could happily sip her water or her juice and not feel the taste of alcohol on her tongue. But as the evening progresses it is becoming harder and harder. Her mind is barely focused on the conversation and she loses herself in a fantasy of everybody leaving the room so she can grab the bottles of wine, tip her head back and pour the contents down.

She can't sit still. She keeps jumping up from the table, her body suffused with an itch for which there seems to be only one cure.

'I'm Saffron. A grateful recovering alcoholic,' she had got used to saying. Yet at some time over the last few months, she had stopped thinking of herself as recovering and started thinking of herself as recovered. Which is when the problems started.

And now, just like those days of old, Saffron finds herself wishing the evening was over so she could run down to that lovely cosy pub and settle in a corner, drinking herself into oblivion.

She misses Pearce. Misses him so very much. And as lovely as it should be here in the country with the friends who have known her for ever, she'd rather be somewhere else.

She'd rather be drinking.

They get to bed by midnight. Saffron kisses everyone good night, distracted as she plans her return to the kitchen for a drink. She goes upstairs and listens to the sounds of the house, waiting until she can sneak downstairs in secrecy and drink the bottle of wine she surreptitiously hid behind the cleaning stuff under the kitchen sink.

Every time she hears a footstep, a door creak, a toilet flushing, she wants to scream with irritation, cast a spell to send everyone into a dreamless sleep.

Eventually, she is certain the house is quiet. She pads out and downstairs to the kitchen, opening the cupboard doors under the kitchen sink, reaching towards the back.

'Fuck!' she hisses as a bottle of bleach falls over, the crash shockingly loud in the stillness.

'What are you doing?' Saffron jumps as Olivia stands in the doorway, rubbing the back of her neck with a cold, wet flannel.

'I'm . . .' Saffron, so good at excuses, has nothing to say. She shuts the cupboard door quickly, but Olivia moves her out of the way and sinks down herself, reaching behind the bleach to pull the wine bottle out.

She shakes her head, disappointed, and uncorks the bottle, both of them watching in silence as the wine glugs its way down the drain.

'Why?' Olivia turns to look at Saffron.

'Why do you think?' Saffron snaps, anger getting the better of her. 'Because I needed a drink, for God's sake. I'm an alcoholic, aren't I? What a stupid bloody question.' She snorts derisively.

'Saffron!' Olivia is shocked. 'I'm trying to help you. We're all trying to help you. Do you think any of us would be here if it weren't for you? We've all bent over backward trying to keep the press away from you, trying to keep you away from alcohol. How are we supposed to help you if you're not willing to help yourself?'

'But don't you see?' Saffron hisses. 'I'm *not* willing to help myself. That's exactly the problem. I wish I was. All I want to do is drink.'

'Sssh!' Olivia is suddenly distracted. 'What's that?'

'What?'

'Listen. That . . . oh my God, is that groaning?'

Saffron stops in her tracks as both of them move towards the door, listening to the unmistakable sound of a couple making love.

'Is that Paul and Anna?' Olivia is confused.

Saffron starts to laugh and, for a minute, her urge to drink recedes. 'No!' she whispers. 'It's Holly and Will.'

'No!' Olivia starts to smile.

'I know.' Saffron rolls her eyes. 'Come on. Let's go back in the kitchen. I feel like a voyeur.'

They walk back and Saffron sits down at the table, sinking her head on her arms as Olivia fills the kettle, then turns to look at Saffron. 'I don't suppose a cup of tea is enough to stop you wanting to drink?'

'Hardly. But it's better than nothing. Oh God, Olivia.' Saffron looks up at her pleadingly. 'What am I going to do?'

Holly lies snuggled up against Will, his arm wrapped tightly around her shoulders as he lies on his back, snoring gently.

She turns her head to look at him, wanting to trace his profile with her fingers, but she doesn't, too scared she'll wake him. What she wants to do is exactly what she's doing right now—to drink him in, watch him breathing, marvel at the feeling of wanting to snuggle up with someone, wanting to stroke her fingers over his chest.

She had known, from the second Will had kissed her, that something more would happen. She had wanted to have sex, wanted to make love, but she had found that she couldn't go further than foreplay. It was a bridge she wasn't prepared to cross yet. But oh how lovely the rest of it was. This was intimacy. This was what she had missed.

Perhaps tomorrow they will be able to make love. Perhaps tomorrow she will not feel guilty. She plans on getting out of bed, going back to her own room but before she knows it, she has fallen into a peaceful sleep.

At five in the morning, Holly wakes up. She swims into consciousness, aware that she is squeezed up against Will in the middle of the bed. She can feel his body the length of hers, and she lies for a minute trying to get used to the sensation. Then she slips out of bed, grateful that the children haven't woken, haven't found her with Will—how stupid; she shakes her head. She never meant to fall asleep in his bed. She pads down the hallway to her own bed and lies there smiling.

When Daisy wakes up and climbs into bed with her for a snuggle, Holly strokes Daisy's face and gazes into her eyes with love. How lucky I am, she thinks, to have my children, to have all these people I love right here with me. And lying in her bed with Daisy's arms wrapped round her neck, Holly feels, for the first time in years, entirely happy.

Chapter Twelve

'I'M EXHAUSTED,' Olivia announces over breakfast. 'We've all been working like dogs, and I haven't seen anything of the area. Would it be awful if we took the afternoon off?'

'I think that is a great idea,' Anna says. 'God knows you all deserve it.

I'll stay to help Paul to finish the floors, I think, but you could go into Gloucester, do some shopping. And Holly, if you want to leave those yummy children with me, I would love to baby-sit.'

'You would?' Holly's face lights up. 'That would be amazing!'

'So you'll come?' Olivia turns to Holly. 'And Saff? Will?' They all nod.

'I wouldn't mind seeing what the shops are like.' Saffron gets up and pours herself some more coffee. 'I want to get some presents for friends back home.'

'Home as in LA?' Holly asks.

Saffron nods.

'Friends as in Pearce?' she asks again. Saffron shrugs.

'I would like to get something for Pearce. Not that I even know if I'll see him any more.'

'Have you been in touch?' Olivia says gently.

'He's been texting me, but it's not the same as talking to him.'

'What is he like?' Anna ventures curiously, the question all of them have been dying to ask but none of them wanted to bring up.

So Saffron tells them. She tells them first about most of the actors in Hollywood. She tells them of people who have struggled from humble beginnings, who have then made it big, have not known how to deal with the sudden fame and fortune.

She tells them of young starlets, featured in every gossip magazine, every week, who get swept up in the Hollywood party life of drink, drugs, sex with a small coterie of wealthy playboys, who seem to shuffle the women among them. She tells them of huge Hollywood names leading secret double lives, some involving substance abuse; most involving affairs with partners of the same sex, who sign secret contracts with naive young actors and actresses to date them and sometimes marry them while carrying on the front for years.

She tells them of how lost she felt when she first got there. That she thought she was a good judge of people, knew how people worked.

But she learned that in Los Angeles nothing and no one is quite what they seem. She found out that lying through their teeth came as naturally to most people as waking up in the morning.

She was taught never to get excited about a movie until the contracts arrived at her agent's office and were signed. She learned not to trust anyone—not the actress friends she thought she had, who would have dropped her friendship in a second for a part, and not the good-looking producers and directors—who subtly, oh so subtly, offered to make her huge if she would just do something for *them*.

She tells them that integrity is something she has found to be in short supply and that when she first went to that AA meeting, it wasn't just that it stopped her from drinking and saved her life, it was that for the first time in LA she found *real* people. People who may have been in the same business as she was, but were living honestly.

Not everyone, she said. AA meetings were filled with wannabe actors and actresses who had heard that this was the place to get work, the place to make contacts, to see and be seen, but you quickly found out who was real and who was not.

She tells them about Pearce. About how honest he is in the meetings and how brave she thinks he is when everyone knows him, anyone could go to the press.

'But it's Alcoholics *Anonymous*,' Anna says. 'Who would go to the press?'

It happens, Saffron says. There are breaches all the time.

She tells them that Pearce is a kind man, that he treats others as he himself wants to be treated. She describes him as funny. Gentle. Sweet. She says he is the wisest man she has ever known, that above all else, she considers him her best friend. That whatever he is doing or wherever he may be, he has always been there for her when she needs him.

And finally there is his marriage. A business arrangement, Saffron explains. He has too much to lose if he leaves. They have been waiting for the right time.

'Wouldn't now be the right time?' Paul ventures.

'One would think so, right?' Saffron snorts to hide her fear. Because, of course, that is exactly what a secret part of her has fantasised about.

If their relationship were to come out in the press, what reason could there possibly be for him to stay in his marriage?

Holly, Will, Olivia and Saffron are standing at the edge of the pedestrian precinct in Gloucester, cobbled streets beckoning invitingly. Will needs to find new headphones for his iPod, and Saffron wants to look at the touristy shops on the other side.

'Let's split up,' Saffron suggests, a smile twitching at the corners of her mouth. 'Holly, why don't you go with Will and Olivia can come with me?'

'Great!' Will says. 'Let's meet back here in an hour.'

'That was very nice of you,' Olivia says as they walk off.

'I figure a young couple in lurrve need a little time together.' Saffron laughs.

'Do you think they're in love?'

'They're definitely in lust. Does that count? Did you see in the car she kept touching him when she thought no one was looking? Oh God,' says Saffron with a sigh. 'I miss that. I miss Pearce.'

'It sounds like you have something very special.'

Saffron stops and turns to look at Olivia. 'Thank you.' She smiles as she blinks back tears. 'Thank you for saying that. I think we do.' She links her arm through Olivia's as they walk. 'And what about you, Olivia? So far you've said nothing about the mystery father.'

'There really isn't anything to tell, except that, oddly enough, this is Tom's doing.'

'What?' Saffron's mouth drops open as she stops in her tracks. 'You mean . . .'

Olivia bursts out laughing. 'No! Tom's not the father. He was trying to set me up with a guy in his office: Fred. We were emailing each other for a while, and then, after Tom died, he came to London, and I guess we fancied one another and one thing led to another.'

'No protection, huh?'

Olivia shakes her head, almost in disbelief at her stupidity. 'I know. In this day and age I can't believe it either.'

'Hmmm . . . but tell me more about this Fred. And more to the point, *where is* he?'

'He's back home in Boston. He's gorgeous, Saffron. Exactly the kind of man I would have fallen in love with when I was younger, but he's only thirty-three, and it really was just a fling. There's no reason for him to know.'

'You don't think he has a right to know, given that it is his child?'

'Saffron, I'm never going to see him again. Why bother giving him the heartache? My child, my body.' She sighs deeply. 'My decision.'

'So . . . you haven't thought about Paul and Anna's offer, then?'

'I have. It's about all I have been thinking about. I just don't know. One minute, I feel I have to do what's right for me, however selfish, and then the next minute, I think about how desperately Paul and Anna want a baby, and how the most wonderful thing in the world would be for me to give them mine. I honestly don't know what I'm going to do.'

Saffron puts an arm round her shoulders and squeezes for a second. 'Whatever decision you make it has to be the right one for you.'

They walk for a while in silence until they reach a gift shop that is obviously doing a brisk trade in catering to American tourists. The window is filled with a miniature village, tiny thatched Cotswold cottages, some of which light up, a couple of which play music.

Saffron yelps with laughter. 'Oh joy!' She stands outside the shop, smiling with delight. 'My American friends will love these!'

They go inside the shop and Saffron sweeps almost a dozen assorted houses onto the counter. The young girl smiling shyly and serving them keeps stealing looks at Saffron. There was something so familiar about the woman buying all these cottages, and as she watched the two friends walking round the shop, she realised who it was.

Saffron Armitage! The film star! For the publicity has served to elevate Saffron's status enormously in the eyes of the world at large, particularly naive shop girls in the Cotswolds.

'You'll never guess what!' she whispered on the phone to her best friend when they had gone. 'You'll never guess who just came into the shop! Saffron Armitage!'

'You're joking!' her friend had said. 'You should call the papers! The *Sun* is printing a number asking for her whereabouts! Go on! You could make yourself some money.'

The girl had laughed. 'Nah,' she'd said. 'I'm too shy. Anyway, she was nice. I don't want to mess up her life. Still, not too often we get a film star in the shop. I wish I'd asked for her autograph.'

On the other side of town, Holly and Will sit in a tea shop. They are surrounded by elderly women sipping English breakfast tea out of delicate, floral-printed china cups, slightly tarnished silver trays on each table, piled high with tea sandwiches, tiny cakes and lopsided scones.

Will ordered the tea, but neither of them is eating anything, neither of them having the slightest appetite today, too high on each other to do anything other than gaze, kiss and touch.

Even now, tucked away at a table in the corner, they are kissing, oblivious to the rest of the people in the tea shop, some of whom are openly staring at them with envy, others trying not to look.

'I can't believe this has happened to me,' Holly says, unable to stop taking Will's face in her hands and planting soft kisses all over it.

Will is adoring being adored. As the apple of his mother's eye, he has always adored being adored. But he'd be lying if he said he wasn't a little apprehensive about this. Holly isn't just anyone, she's *Holly*. Holly Mac! Almost family, not to mention the fact that she's married.

He got seriously involved with a married woman once before. He had thought she was on the verge of finalising a divorce but, in fact, she had only recently separated.

Will found himself named in the petition and had to deal with a woman who wasn't, as he had thought, fun and clever and independent, but who coped with the stress of the divorce by crying and clinging. He wanted to leave, but he didn't know how to extricate himself.

He swore he'd never go down that road again.

Yet here he is with Holly. Object of his teenage fantasies. As much as he adores her, loves the friendship they have built, he is unprepared for the floodgates of adoration that seem to have opened up in Holly.

Maggie didn't tell Holly to be careful with Will because Maggie doesn't love her son, but because Maggie knows that the one thing guaranteed to send Will running for the hills, quite literally for that matter—Thailand, New Zealand, Vietnam—is adoration.

Maggie is the one person who knows about the night that Tom and Holly slept together. She had always hoped that Tom and Holly would get together, had always thought they had the ability to bring out the best in each other.

Tom was too young then. Maggie always hoped that time would work its magic, that they would find their way back to being lovers again through their friendship, but then Marcus had come along, then Sarah, and she knew that was one wish she would have to set aside.

And now Will. *That* she had never imagined. But her fear is, once he has unleashed a passion in Holly, he will not be able to deal with it.

If Maggie were to walk past the tea shop today, look inside and see Holly and Will, Holly gazing adoringly up at Will, resting her head on his shoulder as she strokes his hand, Maggie would groan. Other people might look at Will and think he feels the same way, but not Maggie. And she is, after all, his mother. She is the woman who knows him better than anyone else in the whole world.

The car bumps over the driveway as Holly, Saffron, Olivia, and Will head back home with the boot filled with food for tonight's dinner and, of course, Saffron's prized Cotswold cottages.

There is another car in the driveway as they pull up to the house. From afar, Holly catches her breath; it couldn't be . . . could it? A black Mercedes, a recognisable number plate.

'Whose car is that?' Saffron wonders out loud. 'Doesn't look like the plumber.'

'No.' Holly's heart sinks to her knees. 'It's Marcus.'

Her first instinct is to hide. Childish, she knows, but she doesn't want to see him, doesn't want to face him, wants to continue to pretend that she has no husband, that she is as free and single as Will.

Oh God. *Will.* How difficult this will be. How uncomfortable. Is it possible that Marcus will be able to see the guilt in her eyes? She turns her head, aware that Will is looking at her.

You OK? he mouths, and she nods, swallowing hard.

These last few days have been the happiest days she's had in fourteen years. She has barely given Marcus a thought, and now . . . memories flood into her head as they pull closer. She is shocked but not surprised that he is here. Marcus is a man who must get what he wants.

Holly climbs reluctantly out of the car.

Marcus is sitting at the kitchen table with Daisy on his lap. She has a huge grin on her face as she says over and over again, 'Daddy! I love my Daddy! I love my Daddy!' Oliver is running excitedly around the kitchen table, holding the bag of things he collected on the nature walk, explaining what each thing is as Marcus tries to divide his attention between the two.

Holly stands in the doorway watching for a while, everybody too immersed in what they are doing to notice her, when Daisy looks up and sees her.

'Mummy!' she squeals, wriggling off Marcus's lap and running over to her, wrapping her arms round Holly's legs.

'Hi, darling.' Holly bends down to give her a kiss, grateful she can busy herself with Daisy, win just a few more seconds before she has to confront the inevitable.

'Holly?' She hears something—anger? hurt? dismay?—in his voice and looks up to meet his eyes.

'Hi, Marcus.'

'Holly, we need to talk. Anna has said she will look after the children. I thought maybe we could go for a walk.'

Holly nods. She knew this moment would come. She just wishes she was a little more prepared for it.

They don't say anything for a while. Holly is hunched up, hands tucked firmly in her pockets, shoulders raised to protect her from the wind. And Marcus.

The sun is dipping slowly behind the bare branches of the trees lining the edge of the field. Holly looks over at the sky, thinking that under different circumstances the peace and beauty of this scene would redeem her soul.

Now, though, strolling across the field with Marcus, Holly thinks about how different they are. How different they have always been. And she wonders why she never admitted it to herself sooner.

'We have to talk,' Marcus says eventually, his voice gruff and tough. The Marcus she has always known.

'OK,' Holly says slowly. She doesn't want to be the one to talk. She wants to listen first, to hear what he has to say.

Marcus takes a deep breath. 'I didn't mean what I said,' he says quickly. 'I thought I meant it at the time, but I . . .' He tails off, then looks over at her for a second. 'I never thought you would go.'

Holly knows this. Knows that Marcus was employing the same bullying tactics he always has, fully expecting Holly to back down.

There is a long silence as Marcus waits for Holly to respond. She doesn't. She doesn't yet know what to say.

'Holly,' he says again, and this time he places a hand on her arm to stop her, to force her to look up at him. 'I love you,' he says pleadingly. 'I don't understand what's happening to us. I don't understand why you came here when you knew how important it was to me that you didn't.'

I know, thinks Holly. I have always known how important it is that I obey you.

'But that doesn't matter now,' Marcus says. 'I've forgiven you. And I want you to come home now. I want us to be together again.'

'You don't get it, do you, Marcus?' Holly is incredulous. 'This isn't about my coming down here or disobeying you. This is what I was trying to tell you that night we went for dinner.'

'What night we went for dinner?' Marcus genuinely doesn't remember. He doesn't know what she is talking about.

'When I told you how unhappy I am!' Holly whirls on him. 'When I said I didn't feel that I had a marriage or a partnership. I told you I never see you any more and that I'm not happy. I just'—her voice lowers as she almost whispers the next words—'I just don't think I want this any more.'

'How can you say that?' Marcus says, and she thinks he has finally heard. 'How can you seriously say that? I love you, Holly, we have two beautiful children and a wonderful life together. It just doesn't make sense to me, how you can even think of throwing all this away.'

'It doesn't make sense to you because you never listen, Marcus,' Holly says softly. 'You refuse to hear anything you don't want to hear. I'm tired of trying to explain to you why I'm not happy in this marriage and why I need some space. I just . . .' Fear dwindles her voice away to almost nothing. 'I just don't think I can do it any more,' she whispers.

And Marcus starts to cry. Holly stands awkwardly, watching him. It feels wrong to reach out to him to try to comfort him when she is the cause of this pain, yet it feels more wrong and more awkward to stand here doing nothing.

She reaches up and puts her arms round him. He buries his head in her shoulder sobbing, and she strokes his back, feeling his pain, suddenly realising how hard this is going to be, knowing she is not able to do anything about it. Not if she is to be true to herself.

Marcus has let go. His defences are down. So rarely has Holly seen this side of him, seen him vulnerable. No more arrogance and pretence, just a scared little boy, terrified of the future, of his life being turned upside down, of not being the one in control.

And even as Holly attempts to comfort him, she knows there is no going back. If she has ever thought of staying married to Marcus for the sake of the children, perhaps until they go to college, standing here with him right now, she knows she cannot.

'Please think about it,' Marcus sobs, pulling away to look her in the eye. 'Please come back. I miss you. I miss us. We have so much to look forward to, you'd be throwing away so much.' He stops, unable to go on, and takes a few deep breaths before continuing. 'I'm a divorce lawyer.' He tries again, a different tack. 'I see what this does to children and I see what it does to families. Our children don't deserve this. I don't deserve this. Whatever the problems are in our marriage, none of them are insurmountable. I can be home more, maybe work from home on Fridays. We can do marriage guidance counselling. I mean it, Holly. I'll do whatever you ask me to do. I'll do whatever it takes.'

'OK,' Holly whispers, nodding, not knowing what else to say. 'I need to think about it.' Not true, but she is buying time.

'I've booked a room,' Marcus says. 'I'm staying in a hotel if that's OK with you. Can I take you all out tomorrow morning? With the kids?'

Holly shakes her head. 'I . . . can't, Marcus. But if you want to come and take the kids out that's fine. They'd love it. They've missed you.'

He gulps and swallows hard. 'OK,' he says. 'I'll come and get the children early. Maybe I could take them out for supper tonight, too?'

'Sure.'

'There's a film on in town, *Night at the Museum*. I know they'd love it, but it's a bit late. Would it be OK if I brought them back around nine?'

Holly doesn't remember Marcus taking the children to the cinema before. She doesn't remember him spending any time with them unless she was present. But she can't dwell on that.

'That sounds lovely,' she says. 'Hopefully they'll sleep in in the morning, and Daisy can always have a nap tomorrow if she needs it. They need to spend time with you. Thank you.'

Holly turns her head, gesturing back towards the house, and Marcus turns and falls into step beside her as they cross the field, the sun now streaking the sky with pink and orange.

'Where are you staying?' Holly asks, not because she wants to know, but because she's struggling to make small talk.

'Le Manoir.' He grins and, in a flash, his humility disappears. 'It's fantastic!' he enthuses, back on familiar territory at last. 'I've got the Lavande suite, which you'd love.'

In her mind's eye, Holly rolls her eyes. Here is the Marcus she has known. As he describes Le Manoir—the food, the service, the expense, and luxury of it all—Holly knows that, without question, she is doing the right thing. He may think she would love it because she has always accompanied him to the best hotels in the world, but Holly couldn't care less. It just isn't what she's about, and she's finally realising that their worlds are so different, there isn't a way to meet in the middle.

Chapter Thirteen

THE THRILL AND EXCITEMENT of communal living is beginning to pall somewhat. No arguments, not yet, but Olivia is starting to miss her flat, miss her animals. Saffron seems . . . fine. Certainly not fragile enough to need to be surrounded by five people to look after her.

Saffron always was strong, Olivia realises. Stronger perhaps than all of them. They ought to have changed so much, she thinks, since school. Ought to, as they approach forty, feel grown up, surely, but Olivia certainly doesn't. Just more tired, and with this pregnancy, sicker.

Holly *feels* different, which is not to say she is. But, in fact, Holly, like all of them, has barely changed. Look just slightly below the surface and they are all exactly the same.

Holly lost herself for a while this evening. The kids had just left with Marcus, Will was finishing off the kitchen cupboards, and Paul and Anna, Olivia and Saffron were reading the papers in front of the fire. Holly poured herself a vodka and went to sit outside.

It was cold. Too cold really to be outside, but she kept her hat and gloves on, and snuggled down in one of the beaten-up wooden chairs that Anna had found in a local junk shop.

After a few minutes, as the vodka warmed her up and her body started relaxing, her mind started wandering. She no longer has a home to go back to, no longer has the safety and familiarity of her old life. Will she feel grief? Holly swishes the vodka gently in her glass as she shivers, the cold starting to seep in through her coat. No, she thinks, she has done enough grieving during her marriage. And she couldn't feel any lonelier than she has felt the last few years. There is no denying that at her very core she feels just one thing: relief.

Even Will doesn't seem quite as relevant as he did. It is as if, by finally giving in to this attraction, her eyes have cleared again, she is able to see him for who he is, rather than as her saviour.

And who is he? Handsome, wonderful, sweet brother of Tom. The man who, she realises, gave her the strength to get out; for in her obsession, she didn't stop to think of the fear or stop to consider how frightened she was to live life on her own.

Marcus stopped having power over Holly because she was too distracted to give in to him. And in detaching from her fear, she was able to detach from her marriage.

But these months of thinking that Will might be the man for her now seem unrealistic. He's already talking about his next trip. He can't wait for the sun, for Thai beaches, for joints at sunset. It's a world she left behind many years ago, not a world she wants to be in now. While it might be tempting to pretend to be a teenager again, the fact is she has children of her own, she is now a grown-up.

Holly sighs and tips the dregs of the vodka back, standing up and going inside to see what's happening for dinner.

'So what can I do to help?' Saffron walks into the kitchen and leans over Olivia's shoulder, reaching down to steal a carrot.

'Are you . . . ?' Olivia turns round and looks at Saffron, then, with panic in her eyes, at Anna.

'Oh God.' Holly shakes her head. 'You're drunk, aren't you?'

'I am not!' Saffron says, and were it not for the tiny weave as she sat down, the slight misfocus of her eyes, you might not notice.

'You bloody are,' Holly says. 'How much have you had?'

Saffron sighs and leans her head on her arms. 'Not much,' she mumbles into her arms. 'Just a tiny bit.'

'I'll go,' Olivia says, leaving to hunt for the source of the alcohol. She comes back with a nearly empty bottle of vodka in hand.

'But we still *have* the vodka.' Holly opens the cupboard and, sure enough, the bottle of vodka that she and Will bought in town is there.

Olivia groans. 'I can't believe how sneaky she is. I've just remembered that when we got back to the car, she said she'd left her purse in that gift shop and ran back to get it. She must have bought it—'

'Oh, stop being such a killjoy,' Saffron snaps. 'Yes, that's exactly when I got the vodka. So what? I'll start my sobriety again in the morning.'

'I just do not know what to do,' Anna says helplessly, looking to Olivia and Holly for help. 'I am completely out of my depth here.'

'Me too,' they say in unison.

'Good!' Saffron laughs, getting up to pour herself a glass of wine. 'Cheers!' And oblivious to the worried looks of everyone around her, she takes a large sip. 'Oh relax.' She puts the glass on the table with a laugh. 'At least I'm a fun drunk. You should just enjoy me while it lasts.'

It's true. Saffron is fun while she's drunk. Still the centre of attention, perhaps more so.

'Who is that?' Anna frowns at the headlights shining brightly through the window. 'Oh, Marcus, I forgot.'

'Ah, my number one fan, Marcus.' Saffron grins. 'I'll go,' and before anyone can stop her she is up and out of the door to greet Marcus.

'Guess what?' She reappears in the doorway. 'He's staying for a drink!' Holly's heart plummets and she scoops the children up and upstairs to bed, not wanting to spend a minute in his company, furious with Saffron for inviting him in. What the hell was she thinking?

Marcus is staying because he wants to spend time with Holly. He is convinced that given a chance he will prove to her how much he loves her, how much she needs him. He doesn't think for a moment that this hiccup will end in divorce.

And he should know. He has seen exactly how these stories play out, has heard about every trick in the book, and he will not let that happen to his marriage. He will not let Holly throw this all away.

So he is not comfortable, but he is here. He is here with Holly and there is no doubt in his mind that he will win.

But as they sit down at the table, this is not a Holly he is used to. This is not a quiet, pliant Holly. A Holly he has always been able to control. This Holly is stiff and uncomfortable and he sits and gazes at her across the table, wanting her to be normal, wanting everything to be as it was.

'More wine?' Paul is passing the bottle to Holly, and Holly doesn't look at Marcus for permission as she always has, and he finds himself biting his tongue as she pours herself yet another glass.

He can see she is drinking her discomfort away. Oh hell. Perhaps this will work in his favour. Perhaps she will soften as she drinks. Who knows, perhaps the left side of the bed in his suite at Le Manoir will stay uncreased tonight. Perhaps he will be back in Holly's bed.

'So, Marcus.' Paul is desperate to dissolve the tension. 'How's the hotel? I hear you're staying at Le Manoir. Meant to be amazing.'

'Very nice,' Marcus says, on familiar territory at last. 'I was telling Raymond this morning that he's done a really wonderful job.'

Anna exchanges a look with Olivia and quickly looks down, suppressing a small smile.

'Who's Raymond?' Olivia asks.

'Raymond Blanc.' Paul fills in the blank. 'The owner and chef.'

'He must be thrilled you're staying with him,' Will pipes up as Holly looks at him in amazement—is he joking? Is he serious?

Marcus chooses to take Will's words at face value. 'I think he's just thrilled to have anyone staying there,' he says. 'It's apparently one of the quietest times of the year.'

'You obviously know him well, socialising in London,' Will persists.

'Oh, you know.' Marcus shifts around in his chair. 'We know some of the same people, go to the same parties, that kind of thing.'

'Who do we know?' Holly asks, no longer willing to play his pretentious game.

'Sally and Greg in my office. I don't think you know them. They're great friends; they stay at Le Manoir all the time.'

Holly catches Will's eye and he winks at her. She looks down.

'So . . . Marcus.' Saffron drags her chair over to Marcus and gives him her most killer smile. 'I'm playing a lawyer in a new film. Tell me some of your best tricks for winning clients.'

Marcus loves it. A famous beautiful actress is sitting next to him, hanging on to his every word. Right now he is not Marcus Carter, potential divorced father. He is Marcus Carter, world-renowned lawyer, omnipotent and omniscient. Master of his universe.

'Oh this must be so boring for the rest of you.' Saffron looks up after a few minutes. 'Marcus, I'm dying to hear more. Let's you and I sit in the kitchen,' and a mesmerised Marcus follows her out to the kitchen.

'Shit,' Olivia says. 'She grabbed a bottle of wine. Did you see that?'

'There's nothing we can do,' Paul says. 'I'm telling you. If she chooses to drink, we can't stop her.'

'I can't believe we brought alcohol into the house with an alcoholic who's fallen off the wagon,' Holly says. 'I just can't believe how stupid we've been in believing her when she said she wouldn't drink again.'

'Me especially,' Olivia agrees. 'I was the one who managed to talk her out of it the other night, and I thought . . . I suppose I just hoped that every day it might get easier.'

'Actually, what's so scary is how normal she seems,' Paul says. 'She's been drinking like a fish all evening, and now she seems sober.'

'She's not,' Olivia says. 'Trust me.'

'Do you think I should maybe go and grab the wine or something?' Anna says. 'It just feels wrong to leave it with her in there.'

Holly sighs. 'Don't worry. I'll get it. I'm going to try to get rid of Marcus, too.' She pushes her chair back and walks into the kitchen.

Saffron is sitting on Marcus's lap, with her arms wrapped round his neck, kissing him passionately. Marcus's hands are running up and down Saffron's back, and were it not for Holly's sharp intake of breath, they would have continued.

'Oh God,' Marcus groans, standing up and pushing Saffron, who lands in a heap on the floor.

'Get out,' Holly says coldly.

'It's not what . . . it wasn't . . .' but he can't quite find the words.

'Out!' Holly fumes. 'Just go. Now.'

The others come in, unaware of what happened, aware only that Holly's voice has carried, that she is furious, and that Marcus has gone. They gather Saffron up and take her upstairs to bed, and Will sits downstairs with a fuming, shocked, disgusted Holly.

'How could he?' she keeps saying, more upset by the betrayal than the actual fact of what happened. 'And how could *she*? What was Saffron thinking?'

'Holly.' Will puts his hand gently on hers. 'Saffron was drunk, she probably didn't even know what she was doing, and as for how he could . . . think of where you were last night.'

'But that's different,' she explodes.

'How?' he says softly. 'Because we're friends? How is Marcus kissing Saffron different from you kissing me? Oh, Holly,' he sighs, looking intently at her, sorrow in his eyes as he shakes his head sadly. 'I don't think you're ready for this. I don't think you know what you want.'

As she raises her eyes to look at Will, she knows that he is right. She is not ready for this. She's not ready for a relationship. She's not ready for Will. For anyone.

She is furious, but not with Marcus. With Saffron. Saffron who is supposed to be her friend, who has no reason to seduce Marcus. She knows it's time to go, to leave this house and get on to whatever her new life will be.

Upstairs, Anna gently pulls Saffron's cellphone out of her bag and tip-toes downstairs and outside to the end of the driveway. She scrolls through the address book until she finds it. P.

The phone is picked up on the first ring.

'Pearce? I am so very sorry to bother you. This is Anna Johanssen, I am a friend of Saffron's in England. I would not be calling if this were not urgent, but she is drinking again, big time, and none of us know what to do. We need your help.'

'Give me your number, Anna,' says a voice that Anna knows well. The voice of one of the most famous men in the world. 'I'll get back to you in twenty minutes.' Anna clicks off the phone and goes back to the house. She doesn't know if she's done the right thing, but she knows that calling Pearce seemed the only thing left to do.

Holly goes upstairs slowly, her feet feeling almost as heavy as her heart. She checks on the children, then gets undressed, switching off the light and climbing gratefully into bed, longing to forget everything in her sleep, even for a while, when her door creaks open.

'I can't, Will,' she whispers, irritated that even after their chat earlier he presumes she still wants him in her bed. 'I'm sorry but I just can't.'

'It's not Will,' slurs Saffron, sliding over to the bed and half sitting, half falling onto the pillows.

Holly groans. Saffron is the very last person she wants to see. 'Go to bed, Saffron.' She sighs. 'I've got nothing to say to you.'

'Oh, Holly,' Saffron pouts, still clearly drunk as a skunk. 'Don't you see, darling? I did it on purpose. Your pompous awful husband can't accuse you of anything now. You caught him kissing another woman! How could you ever trust him again? Never mind what Marcus comes up with, *you* caught him with someone else—what's the judge going to think about that?' There is a drunken, triumphant smile on her face.

'What?' Holly sits up and switches on the light. 'You mean you did this for me?'

'Course!' Saffron giggles. 'You don't seriously think I fancied him do you? Yuck yuck yuck.' She starts sputtering all over the duvet.

'You're crazy,' Holly says, not knowing what else to say. 'I can't believe you seduced him.'

'Yup.' Saffron grins in delight. 'I've known men like Marcus before and he would wipe the floor with you. Can't do much now though. I know it was only a kiss, but how could you possibly stay married to a man who does this?'

'But, Saffron, if this went to court I'd have to name you.'

'As if my reputation could get any worse? Fuck it.' Saff flings her arms in the air. 'If you believe everything you read in the papers, I'm Scarlet Saffron, superslut and destroyer of marriages.'

Holly shakes her head, unable to resist a smile. 'You're amazing . . . I don't know whether to thank you or never talk to you again.'

'Trust me.' Saffron falls into Holly's hug. 'I had to be shit-faced to do what I just did,' and she snorts with laughter, knowing she will be forgiven, before snuggling down next to Holly.

Holly leaves the house early, doesn't want to talk to anyone this morning. Marcus has cancelled seeing the children—an urgent work thing—so she takes them down to a horse-riding stables down the road, and spends an hour there, pretending to be normal, pretending to be happy as they feed the ponies polo mints and let them nuzzle in their pockets.

She doesn't want to see anyone. What she really wants to do is climb back into bed, pull the covers over her head and not come out again.

'Mum?' Oliver asks on the way back to the house via the bakery for cinnamon rolls and hot chocolate. Holly would have driven away this morning, she knows it's time to get back to London, but she is taking Olivia back with them in the car and Olivia's morning sickness tends to abate somewhat by mid-afternoon, hence this wait.

'Yes, darling?'

'Are you and Dad going to be in divorce?'

Holly almost jumps with shock. 'What do you mean, Oliver?'

'Well, there's a girl in my class, Jessica, and her parents are in divorce, and if we're here with you and Dad's not here, then I was thinking that maybe you'll be in a divorce.'

Holly crouches down so she's on eye level with Oliver. 'Did Daddy say something to you?'

Oliver shrugs and looks away.

'It's OK, darling. You can tell me anything.' Holly tries to keep the anger out of her voice.

'Well . . . Dad did say that he wanted to be here with us but you wouldn't let him and that it was up to you if we went home. So is it, Mum? Will you let Dad stay?'

'Oliver.' She looks him straight in the eye. 'Sometimes mummies and daddies need to have a little time apart. But the most important thing is that Daddy and I both love you very much, OK?'

Oliver nods, not really understanding. Holly wraps him in a tight hug, opening her arms to include Daisy.

Her phone rings on the way back to the barn. It's Marcus.

'Yes?' Her voice is terse.

'Holly. I need to explain. I didn't do anything last night, Saffron just jumped on me and started kissing me . . .'

'You think I believe that?' Holly hisses softly so the children don't hear. Trying not to smile for she believes Saffron, and she can see how this works to her advantage. 'You think I didn't see your arms around her? How many other women have there been?'

'None!' Marcus almost shouts. 'I swear.'

'Right. And I'm supposed to believe you. And another thing, Marcus, don't you dare tell the children this is my fault. I've never said a word against you, even after last night, and I expect the same of you. I'm going now. I don't want to talk to you any more.' And she puts the phone down just as she turns into the driveway of the barn.

The house seems empty when they get back.

'Where is everyone?' Holly asks, finding Will on his own in the kitchen.

Will puts the hammer down and comes over to help Holly unbutton the kids' coats.

'It's Olivia,' he says gently. 'She was bleeding. They've taken her to the hospital.'

Holly has a sharp intake of breath. 'The baby! Is she losing it?'

'I don't know. She was having some cramping as well, and they just bundled her into the car and took her to the Gloucestershire Royal Hospital. Paul said they'd phone when they knew something.'

'When did they leave?'

'About an hour ago.'

Olivia is scared. She has never liked hospitals and wishes that she could turn the clock back to when everything was fine.

Anna sits on a chair in the corner of the room. Paul and Saffron are outside in the waiting room as the sonographer places icy cold gel all over Olivia's bare stomach.

'I'm sorry,' she says. 'I know it's cold but it won't last long.'

Olivia is transfixed by the television screen. Her head is turned uncomfortably, eyes glued to the screen, wanting to see. Not wanting to see. This is a blessing, she keeps trying to tell herself. This is a blessing in disguise. I don't want this baby.

She steals a glance at Anna who looks far more terrified than her.

There is silence in the room as the screen lights up with a greyish triangle. In the middle of the screen, there is something pulsing and Olivia squints at the screen, trying to make it out.

'What do you see?' she says after several minutes of silence as the sonographer scans and clicks and types numbers into the screen. 'Is it dead?' she whispers.

'Very much alive, I'd say,' the sonographer says. 'Look, can you see?' She moves the scanner on her stomach, and Olivia and Anna gasp, for there, quite clearly, legs furled up, is a baby.

'So the bleeding? The cramping? What was all that about?' Paul looks at Olivia, who walked into the waiting room with such a huge smile on her face he assumed she had lost the baby and was thrilled.

'I've got a tiny subchorionic haematoma. It's basically a collection of blood between the placenta and the uterine wall. They said that given the size, it's probably going to be fine.'

'You're keeping the baby?' Saffron is the only one who dares to ask.

'I have to.' Tears well up in Olivia's eyes. 'I mean, I don't know about adoption, or Paul and Anna.' She turns to look at them as the tears spill out. 'I'm so sorry, I know you want me to make a decision but I just can't do that, not yet. The only thing I do know is that I can't have an abortion. Not now.'

Paul looks at Anna, then back at Olivia. 'We understand,' he says, walking over to Anna and putting his arm round her. 'It's your baby and your choice. Just know that we're here if that's what you decide.'

'What the hell is going on?' They are about to turn into the driveway when they see cars lining either side of it, men running around, stepladders everywhere.

'Oh fuck,' Saffron whispers, just as someone turns and shouts, pointing at the car. 'They've found me.'

'Saffron! Saffron!' Dozens of paparazzi swarm the car, light bulbs flashing in the windows as Saffron buries her head down.

'What the hell do I do?' Paul, in his panic, has frozen, not knowing whether to try to reverse out of there or whether to keep going.

'Let's just get inside,' Saffron says. 'They're not going anywhere.'

'Olivia! Are you OK?'

They get inside, slamming the door in the face of what feels like a pack of wolves, and Holly gives Olivia a huge hug as Will explains he's covered the windows with sheets, that they somehow managed to get reception on the cellphone and the police are on their way.

Paul's face is grim as he directs everybody into the kitchen, then goes to the front door, opening it wide as he waits for the photographers to stop yelling for Saffron, quieting down enough to hear him speak.

'You are standing on private property,' he says calmly and clearly. 'The police are on their way and I would suggest you all get off my property immediately or you will be arrested for trespassing.'

'Where is she?' someone shouts. 'We just want one shot,' another says. 'A quick comment,' says someone else.

'You have two minutes to get off my property,' Paul says, and grumbling and swearing, the paparazzi start moving their equipment to the top of the driveway.

'It's just like a movie,' Olivia says. 'Now we're all prisoners inside.'

'Saff,' Holly says quietly, pulling her aside and taking her hand. 'There's someone upstairs to see you.'

'*What?* Who?' Saffron is immediately suspicious.

'You need to go,' Holly says. 'Your room.'

Saffron walks upstairs, shooting quizzical looks at the others. When she has disappeared Olivia looks at Holly and raises an eyebrow.

'Who?'

Holly starts to smile. She was sitting at the kitchen table with Will, both of them sharing their concern for Olivia, when they heard the noise of the first cars arriving. She was stunned when she looked out of the window and saw all the commotion. As she watched she saw a black Jaguar with tinted windows pull up, and Pearce Webster climbed out, striding quickly and purposefully towards the front door, ignoring the shrieks and shouts and the frenzy that his arrival inspired.

'Look.' Holly had pulled Will over to see. He immediately ran to the front door and opened it, pulling Pearce inside.

'I'm Pearce.' He extended a hand.

'Hello.' Holly had blushed like an idiot. 'I'm Holly. These are my children, Daisy and Oliver.'

Pearce came into the kitchen and sat down while she made tea. Finally, he asked about Saffron.

'She's not good,' Holly said. 'I mean, she's great, but she's drinking.'

'Out-of-control drinking?'

Holly nodded. 'We all feel lost. None of us know what to do.'

'It's OK,' Pearce said. 'That's why I'm here.'

Saffron doesn't say a word. She walks in as Pearce rises from the bed he was sitting on in the darkened room and flies into his arms.

They stand there, hugging each other tightly for a long time as the photographers' shouts recede. Nothing else matters except for these two people, locked together in this darkened room.

'You've got *some* friends,' Pearce whispers, kissing her hair, her cheeks, her nose, her mouth. 'They're worried about you. They called.'

'You're here!' Saffron wipes the tears off her cheeks as she pulls back to look at him. 'I can't believe you're here. Oh God. The press. Everyone will know.'

Pearce shrugs. 'They already know. They got me on the highway and now they have pictures of me walking into the house. Fuck it.'

'What about Marjie?'

'I just had to be here,' Pearce says. 'I couldn't bear hearing that you were struggling. We'll figure it out.'

'A day at a time, right?' She smiles up at him.

'Exactly.' He pulls her into him. 'A day at a time. Would you be willing to have a meeting? Right now? With me?'

Saffron looks up at him, feeling for the first time in days that everything will be all right. 'Yes.' She exhales loudly. 'It's exactly what I need.'

Chapter Fourteen

THE FIRST FLAKES come quickly, swirling slowly over the Connecticut countryside, twirling around trees, floating softly down to the grass. They are warning drivers that this March snowstorm will be a big one, that people should stay inside.

However, there is a small contingent of cars crawling along the highways, slowly and carefully, on their way to the Mayflower Inn for a birthday party. They are gathering in Washington, Connecticut, for Saffron's fortieth birthday party. People she hasn't seen for years. Some not since a gathering in a yet-to-be-renovated barn in deepest Gloucestershire.

'Holly!' Saffron squeals as she walks out of the Tap Room, turning into the lobby and seeing her friends. She rushes over, feet flying noiselessly over the carpet, flinging her arms round Holly. 'It's so good to see you.' She turns and hugs the others.

'I cannot believe we are here,' Anna says. 'I mean, I cannot believe you sent us tickets for your birthday.' She turns back to Saffron. 'Organised a plane . . . This place is gorgeous, and I just—'

'She feels guilty.' Paul grins. 'She doesn't think you ought to be paying for everything. I think she wants to pay for the room.'

'Darling girl.' Saffron links her arm through Anna's as she walks her through the lobby to a small, cosy living room. 'Between Pearce and me, we get paid a fortune, and I can't think of anything I'd rather do than gather my friends together for my thirty-seventh birthday.'

'Don't you mean fortieth?' Anna is confused.

'Sssh.' Saffron holds a finger to her lips. 'As far as everyone here is concerned, I'm thirty-seven.'

'*Everyone?*' Holly raises an eyebrow 'It's not just us then?'

'God, no!' Saffron says. 'It's all the people we love. Close friends and family. We've flown people in from England, LA, Australia.'

'I take it things are great with you and Pearce?' Anna grins. 'I just keep thinking of that whole fiasco when it first came out and you came to stay in the country. You did not expect, well, *this*, did you?'

Saffron laughs. 'I didn't expect anything. But no, I didn't think he'd leave Marjie and even if he did, I didn't expect us to be together.'

'You look so happy.' Holly looks at her and sighs.

'OK.' She leans forward and whispers. 'We're not supposed to be saying anything until tonight, but you're not here for my birthday . . .'

Anna squeals and gasps, knowing what she's going to say.

'. . . we're getting married!'

Shouts of delight and hugs all around, only interrupted by the sound of footsteps approaching and a baby crying.

'That is Tommy!' Anna leaps up and goes out into the lobby to get him as Olivia appears in the doorway.

'I'm sorry,' she says. 'He needs a nap but he won't go down.'

'Do you want me to take him for a walk?' Anna says, rocking the baby up and down on her hip.

'Would you?' An exhausted and grateful Olivia sinks into the sofa and reaches for a cup of tea from the tray that has just appeared with a silent, smiling waitress. 'This place feels like Buckingham Palace.'

'I know!' Saffron smiles. 'And the whole place is ours for the weekend. Now that you're here, I've got some news.' And soon the only sound in the room is the excited chatter of a group of old friends.

It is a road Saffron never expected to walk. How long ago was it, those days when she fell apart, hit rock bottom when she had vowed never to hit rock bottom again? Nights of drinking and blacking out, days of vomiting, Pearce staying with her, promising he'd never leave her.

Then rehab. Three months. AA meetings all day, therapy, group therapy. Her family and friends coming in and telling her what she was like when she was drunk, the shame of being in that dark, lonely hole again. So lonely that nothing and no one could fill her up.

She finished rehab and walked out with head held high. A new sponsor, a new resolve. For the past year she has been to a meeting every day and Pearce has been right by her side.

He finally stood up to his manager and said he wasn't going to stay in a marriage that was dead any more. He moved into his beach house in Malibu and Saffron joined him a month later. The press drove them crazy. There were times Saffron didn't think she could cope with the loss of normality.

She couldn't run to the corner store for a pint of milk, couldn't dash out in the evenings to grab a movie and a burger with Pearce. They tried, but even if they managed to escape the press, they'd be sitting in a restaurant trying to pretend that the buzz wasn't singing in their ears, that they didn't know that all eyes were upon them. There was no such thing as privacy any more.

Saffron has worked constantly this past year. Between recovery, Pearce and work, she hasn't had time for much else. She hasn't seen her friends since that time in Gloucestershire, but knew she couldn't get married and not have them here.

It has taken months of planning to keep this secret, to keep the press away. They have taken over the inn for the weekend, have managed, thus far, to keep it private, largely by gathering their friends and family here under false pretences.

Pearce comes into the living room to greet everyone, and Holly watches Pearce and Saffron together with a smile on her face for their joy is infectious; and, as she watches, her mind wanders over the ocean to her little Georgian house in Maida Vale.

She isn't divorced, and it has not been easy, largely because Marcus has made it as difficult as he possibly can. He is, just as she suspected, unwilling to pay alimony, unwilling to pay a decent amount of child support, unwilling to do anything because, as he puts it, 'you wanted this divorce, why should I have to pay?'

The only times when she has felt really low and wondered if she has the ability to do this on her own are when she is ill, but thankfully those early days of staying in bed all weekend when the children were at their dad's, those days when her headaches were so blinding she thought her head was going to split open, have passed.

Marcus has kept the house. She thought she would mind, but, in fact, she found she just wanted to close the chapter and move on. They went through the inventory of furniture in the house and there was little she wanted.

The best thing she ever did was spend the afternoon wandering around Dream Beds superstore to choose her own mattress, her own bed.

Of course, the worst thing she did, she now realises, was buy a king-sized bed. When she was married, she couldn't think of having anything smaller than a king, just in case she should wake up in the middle of the night and become aware of Marcus. Now, though, she wishes the bed was smaller, wishes she could cuddle up to Jonathan, finds herself frequently waking up squeezed against him in the middle of the bed, his arm across her chest, her legs across his.

Jonathan. Ah, Jonathan. Just thinking about him, she smiles. *I love him*, she whispers to herself over and over as she goes about her day, delighting in the joy of loving, of having found someone who not only adores her, but who she adores in return.

He is her neighbour, three doors up. Such a cliché, she smiles to herself, too good to be true. He came and introduced himself on the day she moved in, returning later with his toolbox to put up shelves, pictures, Ikea flat-pack furniture for the kids' rooms.

She thought he was lovely, but nothing else . . . He has two children, the same ages as Daisy and Oliver, who are with him every other weekend and one night during the week. They started doing things together at the weekends and the kids liked one another.

Holly didn't think about him other than to think how much she liked seeing him when she did, and soon she would look for his car as she returned home. When she heard his voice on her answering machine, she would smile—there was something about him that made her feel good. Happy.

It has been five months since they kissed. They had both been in to kiss Daisy and Abigail good night. Abigail was having her first sleep-over, and as they stood outside the door in the darkened corridor, smiling at each other as they listened to their girls happily chatting away, Jonathan kissed her.

Five months on, five months of the happiest, healthiest relationship Holly has ever had—a relationship that surpasses anything she might have dreamed of. She is constantly astounded by their kindness to each other, the sense that each of them values the other, and the appreciation they have for each other.

This, she finally realises, after all these years, is love.

She has never felt so peaceful as she does these days. And so safe. And watching Saffron with Pearce, Holly can see echoes of her own relationship with Jonathan.

'I am so happy for you.' She reaches over and whispers into Saffron's ear. 'You deserve this, my darling.' And Saffron squeezes her hand and nods. For the first time in her life, she thinks she is good enough. She deserves to be in this wonderful relationship with this wonderful man.

'So how do you find single motherhood?' Saffron turns to Olivia who rolls her eyes at the question, then laughs it off.

'It's amazing,' she says. 'Exhausting. But amazing. I never thought I could love anyone as much as I love Tommy. I never thought I could do the mothering thing, but it's working. He's the light of my life.'

'And how is Fred doing?'

'He's actually been fantastic. After I told him, he wanted to get involved. We've made a decision to co-parent and to raise Tommy together even though we're not together. Fred's really come through.'

'I guess Tom didn't do so badly with his choice after all.' Saffron smiles.

'He obviously saw things I couldn't,' Olivia says as Anna walks back in and parks a buggy containing a sleeping baby by the door.

It is difficult for Anna to remember that there was a time when she wouldn't have been able to take a friend's baby for a walk without feeling inadequate or being eaten up with jealousy. Without thinking of everything in life she was missing, instead of everything in life she is lucky to have.

There is indeed something large missing from her life since we last saw her. Fashionista.co.uk was sold several months ago to a huge public company, Anna retaining a role as consultant and getting paid far more money than she could ever have dreamed of.

She didn't do it for the money. She did it because she realised that Fashionista had been her baby for too long and that the stress of running it was probably contributing to her problems in getting pregnant. She wanted to stop, to jump off the conveyor belt to see what it was like to be a real person again.

She has taken up Pilates and yoga. Has learned to cook wonderful meals for herself and Paul and has taken seriously her role as Tommy's godmother.

The whole room is crying tears of joy, the joy that comes when you know that two people who are supposed to have found each other have found each other and are not about to let the other go.

Pearce stands and clears his throat, so handsome in his dinner jacket, better looking than even he has a right to be, and he speaks of the reasons he loves Saffron. He speaks of being the best man he can possibly be when he is with her, of the serenity he feels every day when he wakes up and knows she is by his side.

'I feel so blessed to have found Saffron, to have found the woman who graces me every day with her strength and her beauty and her joy. She is the greatest gift I have ever known, and I want each of you to witness our bond and know that I will love her and look after her for ever.'

Paul turns to see Holly wiping a tear from her eye, and he nudges her and rolls his eyes. 'Couldn't he have been a bit less Hollywood?'

'Nah,' Holly laughs. 'His whole life probably feels like a movie. I think it's sweet.'

'Do you really? Where's my cynical old Holly gone?'

'Gone for good. This new improved Holly's madly in lurrve and thrilled by oversensitive film stars waxing lyrical about how wonderful women are.'

'I can't believe we haven't met Jonathan yet,' Paul whispers as the applause dies down. 'Why don't you bring him down to the barn?'

Holly raises an eyebrow. 'I take it you've got a bathroom that needs tiling? Or a roof that needs replacing then?'

'Thankfully not. Anna's windfall took care of everything. We've even got heating under the floors now. Go on. Come down. Let's get everyone down and start fresh. A new beginning, and this time the beginning of the best times. Isn't it all supposed to start after forty anyway?'

'Only for women, I've heard.' Olivia leans forward with a grin and raises her glass. 'But here's to new beginnings and second chances!'

One by one, they all raise their glasses as the band begins to play.

Jane Green

Jane Green worked as a journalist in London for various national newspapers and magazines before making the difficult decision, at twenty-seven, to give up her job on the *Daily Express* and concentrate on writing a novel. Luckily it paid off and three months later she signed a publishing deal for *Straight Talking*.

Just after the release of that first novel, Jane met her American husband, and the couple soon moved across the Atlantic to Connecticut. Recently divorced, Jane now has four children, including a set of twins, yet still loves to write. Here are some more insights into this exciting, best-selling author's character.

Who or what always puts a smile on your face?

My children laughing uncontrollably, usually at something completely ridiculous, and inevitably when they're either in the car, or just before bed when it's supposed to be 'quiet time'.

Which author do you most admire?

JK Rowling, for obvious reasons.

What's your earliest memory?

I remember clearly lying in bed when I must have been about three, looking at the window at night time and being terrified the big bad wolf would appear there. Around the same time I also remember watching my mother bathe my brother in the bathroom sink, although that may be a memory created from a photograph—so hard to distinguish.

What is your greatest fear?

Disloyalty.

How would you like to be remembered?

As being a great mother and friend. Oh, and of course as being spectacularly beautiful, gracious, stylish and kind. In fact, if people could remember me as Jackie Kennedy that would help enormously.

Have you ever done something you've really regretted?

I once behaved appallingly with a friend of mine, way back in my early twenties. We had an odd relationship that once crossed the line into something more, then settled into friendship, but always with a frisson. He once came to stay with me in Manchester and I realised as soon as he arrived that I didn't want him there, and I practically ignored him the entire time. We spoke once when I phoned to apologise and he expressed his disappointment, and I've always felt terrible about it because he was a lovely man and deserved better.

How do you spoil yourself?

By shopping compulsively, usually for bags, and usually horribly expensive ones.

Who do you turn to in a crisis?

I am very lucky to have three great girlfriends, and lucky because I found them all after I'd moved to America, at a time when I think it is hugely easy to make acquaintances, and incredibly difficult to make real and lasting friendships. I tend to go to Heidi because she has wisdom and great common sense, and Stacy and Dina to pick over all the emotional elements.

What makes you angry?

Rudeness, and being taken advantage of.

Are you in love?

With my family. I am blissfully happy and content, in a way that I never thought I would be.

What's your worst vice?

Not remembering people.

What are you proudest of?

Clichéd though it may be, my four children.

Where do you write?

I used to work at home but now find I spend far more time messing around on the internet or playing spider solitaire, so I take my computer to the library, find my spot which overlooks the river, and work from there.

Where's your favourite city?

Probably New York—I still find it so energising and exciting.

One wish; what would it be?

To keep my family safe from harm.

What do you believe in most?

Do as you would be done by: treating others with kindness and respect.

Taken from: www.janegreen.com

Carmen Reid

The
Personal
Shopper

Annie Valentine, high-fashion, personal shopping expert, knows everything there is to know about designer labels and the new season's trends. She can restyle and reinvent her clients from top to toe and fix the gaps in any wardrobe. But when the glitz and glamour of the day is over, what she doesn't know is how to fill the empty space in her heart...

The first of Svetlana's new outfits for spring:

Dress in vibrant purple, green and white (Pucci)
Wide green suede belt (Pucci)
Purple boots with rapier heels (Manolo)
White cashmere coat (MaxMara)
Green handbag (Chloé)
Total est. cost: £2,800

'Sexy but ladylike.'

ANNIE VALENTINE, senior personal shopper at the five floors of London retail heaven, called The Store (because less is oh-so-much-much-more), watched Svetlana Wisneski emerge from behind the fuchsia velvet curtain of the changing room. The silk jersey dress clung to the curves of the billionaire's wife and, in three-inch heels, she towered like a blonde superhuman.

The effect was breathtaking, but Annie, who always exceeded her monthly commission targets and almost always scooped the 10 per cent bonus for highest sales figures, immediately read the look on her VIP client's high-cheekboned, high-maintenance face.

'Not working for you, darlin'?' Annie asked. 'Not channelling spring, lambs frolicking, Easter bonnets or April in Paris?'

Svetlana shook her head gravely.

'Never mind . . . have no fear . . . we will find it for you here . . .' Annie singsonged, flicking through a rail packed with sensational dresses—Chloé, Missoni, Temperley, Gucci, Versace. She pulled out another stunning day dress and offered, 'Mmmm . . . how about Pucci?'

'We trrrry,' came Svetlana's deep-voiced reply.

No one left Annie's two hours of personal attention in anything less than the perfect outfit—more usually perfect outfits—blowing three, four, even five times as much as they'd planned to spend because her advice, delivered in a down-to-earth, no-nonsense, London-born-and-bred accent, was so persuasively excellent. Annie shopped for her customers, for her friends and for herself with the ruthless zeal of a Wall Street stockbroker on her last day of probation. Nothing was too much trouble for this professional: she scoured every white, down-lit corner of The Store for the exactly right item and she knew every department's designer collections right down to its 'diffusion' thongs.

'*Just for you, mind!*' This bustling, tireless, working wonder could track down a coat direct from the atelier, charm grumpy Italian boot-makers into parting with the last size 41 available in that style. She could even, in a wardrobe emergency, cut a deal with the tiny Brighton boutique that had the only other one of *those* dresses in a size 12.

This afternoon's client, the statuesque Svetlana, was a cherished customer. Married to the richest, potbellied, lumpy-looking Russian in London, Svetlana was one of a select handful of shoppers entitled to a free limousine ride home with the boot full of purchases.

Today, early in February, the everlasting winter sales were almost over and the bright new Spring collections were finally breaking through in shades of palest lemon, baby pink, green, green and more green. Svetlana was in to shop for the new season as early as possible because she liked to be first and to have the pick of the new.

For close to an hour, Annie had walked this elite customer and her dumpy personal assistant Olga round every one of The Store's glittering floors. They'd begun in the dazzling cosmetics hall where assistants trilled the delights of spring's 'fresh new palette'.

While Svetlana had let herself be lavishly made up and manicured, Olga had scathingly pronounced the shimmery nude polish 'almost invisible' and 'far too expensive'.

'She works for him,' Svetlana had whispered in explanation to Annie when Olga was out of earshot.

'Who?' Annie had asked, suspecting the answer.

'Potato-face,' came Svetlana's low voice as she examined her Ocean Spray eyelids and Blossom no.5 lips in the magnifying mirror. 'He thinks I spend too much money and *she* is spying on me.'

'No!' Annie assured her, although, much to her continued disappointment, she knew nothing of life as a trophy wife, whereas Svetlana was on her third and most wealthy husband. She'd traded up spouses the way other women trade up houses. It was obvious to Annie that if she wanted advice on finding a rich husband (and boy, could she do with one; her eye-watering credit card bills had come in this morning), this was the woman to ask. Surely it was just a matter of the right question at the right moment to get the conversation started?

Up the glass escalators they'd sailed, into white marble-floored designer heaven where clothes were hung and lit as preciously as works of art . . . and cost as much too. Should a customer be so foolish as to display any shock at the astronomical price tags, the best sales staff would gush, '*But it's such a unique piece. Fabulous quality. You'll wear it for years.*' The condescending ones would cock an eyebrow and ask: '*Oh? Too expensive for Madam?*' in a way that made Annie want to shriek, *As if you could afford it!*

But then the girls here did buy the clothes. They used their staff discount, maxed their plastic and shared cramped studio flats to wear McQueen and Jimmy Choo on their nights out. It made no sense but was unmistakably glamorous.

Once Svetlana had toured the new collections of the designers she regularly chose—Yves Saint Laurent and Givenchy for dressing up, Donna Karan for casual—Annie had tried to entice her into some more colourful directions: Missoni, Pucci, Matthew Williamson.

The billionaire's wife had looked mournfully through the rails. 'No, no . . . well . . . maybe . . . I don't know if Igor will like it,' she'd declared. 'He likes sexy but ladylike, always ladylike.'

Annie was not usually a fan of the lazy, self-indulgent and spoilt wealthy wives she regularly dressed, but she was beginning to understand that Svetlana was an exception. Svetlana's marriage was her career. She hosted bi-weekly dinners and monthly cocktail parties, she attended endless business receptions, made charming small talk for hours, always looked impeccably elegant, and all for the benefit of Igor and his empire. Svetlana had staff to organise: cooks, housekeepers, cleaners and maids. She had five houses in three countries to furnish, refurbish and decorate. Clearly, it was a demanding, full-time job being Mrs Igor Wisneski. But as she'd confided to Annie—when Olga was once again out of earshot—she was approaching thirty-five, and although she was tall, ice blonde and breathtaking, not to mention the mother of the gas baron's two sons and heirs, her place as drop-dead-gorgeous status wife was never taken for granted. She'd once pointed out the faint creases on her cheeks as 'blow job lines' with a telling roll of the eyes.

Now she stood before Annie, with a far more satisfied expression because she could see she was a knockout in the tight, belted Pucci. 'I don't know why I'm ever unsure about your ideas, Ahnnah'—she'd never got the hang of 'Annie'—'You are always, always correct.'

'You need a pale coat for that dress,' Annie assured her. 'I have a white cashmere, knee-length, beautiful cut. I'll have it brought up.'

'Erm . . . sorry to interrupt.' Paula, the other personal shopper on today, put her head round the curtain.

Annie shook her head and raised her eyebrows. 'Urgent?' she asked.

'Your bid's been exceeded on the vintage Miss Selfridge . . .' Paula began.

Although she had primed Paula to keep an eye on the items she was bidding for on the internet today, this news wasn't important enough to justify abandoning Svetlana. 'Thanks, but don't worry about it,' Annie instructed, and with a swish of eighteen inches of genuine Asian hair extension, Paula was gone.

Svetlana had firmly decided on three evening gowns, five day dresses, two trouser suits, a coat, four pairs of shoes and two handbags. She was turning from side to side in front of the mirror trying to decide whether the handbag in her left hand was a better match with the coat than the handbag in her right hand when Paula appeared at the curtain again.

'Help!' she mouthed at Annie, who gave a little sigh. She suspected this was about Paula's next client. Paula wasn't exactly bad at her job, she was just young (twenty-four), inexperienced, and so obsessed with fashion that she couldn't translate what was hot into what would really suit and work for someone. She would quite happily stuff a chunky fifty-four-year-old barrister into Juicy Couture and studded gold mules because 'Wow, that is so now! So happening!'

Usually Annie tried to make sure Paula's clients were of the rake-thin, fashion police variety who wanted to be talked through combining a baby doll with a tulip skirt, gaucho belt and cork wedges by an expert, but this afternoon Annie had Svetlana, so Paula had to look after Martha Cooper, a new client.

'Can you excuse me for just a few minutes?' Annie asked Svetlana.

'Of courrrrse.'

'Definitely the green,' Annie pronounced and turned to follow Paula into the cream-carpeted reception area.

There she saw Martha, a very tall, slouchy late thirties, in the universal uniform of busy stay-at-home mum: washed-out jeans, washed-out T-shirt, washed-out face, long hair with four inches of root, green gym shoes and Martha's own personal touch, a truly diabolical grey parka. No wonder Paula had panicked.

For a split second, it struck Annie that such a lack of care about appearance, fashion and what people thought of you was almost enviable. Then she imagined how she would look without heels, red lipstick, foundation and blonde highlights . . . and the moment passed.

'Hi, Martha, I'm Annie Valentine, lovely to meet you.' Annie held out a hand and treated Martha to her most reassuring smile. 'Have you been looking around?'

'Er . . . yes . . . . And now I'm even more worried,' came Martha's reply.

Annie was used to dressing all kinds of women but she hadn't had such a bad case in her suite for some time. Poor Martha, she'd wandered the floors, clocked the price tags, and now here she was, faced with one of the most glamorous shop assistants she'd ever encountered: Paula, as lithe and elegant as a young Naomi Campbell, complete with nutcracker buns and ultraviolet talons. Although Annie was a little more real-looking, she was still extremely groomed and elegant: a shimmering (originally mouse-brown) blonde, expertly made up with perfect brows, French manicure and light tan, tastefully dressed, high-heeled and utterly convincing in her role of persuading endless women and occasional men to part with extraordinary amounts of money in an effort to look more stylish and attractive.

Martha was probably now convinced she did not belong here, but in an episode of *What Not To Wear*.

'You are going to have such fun with us today,' Annie told her, still keeping hold of Martha's hand, so that she couldn't bolt.

In fact, Annie loved clients like Martha. You had to start slowly with the most sober clothes The Store had to offer, but these clients were always the most grateful and the most enduringly loyal because Annie helped them to work out all the things a woman needed to know about her look.

By thirty, according to Annie, every woman should have put in the hours in the fitting room to work out the colours, the shapes and the cuts that flattered. By thirty, every woman should also have grasped the power of one great accessory and have the fundamentals of a personal style in place. Great dressers also understood the importance of trademark items, such as Princess Diana's blue blazer; Mrs Thatcher's pussycat bow; Posh's bustier; Liz Hurley's white jeans. These were the secrets, the dressing lessons, which Annie could reveal.

'Great height,' Annie told Martha straight away.

'Pros and cons . . .' was Martha's reply. 'Sleeves . . .' She made a chopping motion close to her elbow. 'Dress waistbands come in under my armpits,' she gestured.

'Don't worry, we'll work with it. Please follow me into my boudoir.' She finally let go of Martha's hand, trusting her to follow.

In the airy, opaque-windowed room at the heart of the Personal Shopping suite, Annie and Martha sat down together on the fuchsia velvet sofa for a preliminary chat, while Paula hovered close by.

'So, how old are your children?' Annie wondered, not needing to ask if Martha had any.

'Oh . . . Six, five and just turned two.'

'You must be busy,' Annie sympathised. 'And are you going back to work?' This was usually the reason harassed mothers of toddlers appeared in her suite in a panic.

'Yes. First job in seven years. Three days a week in Personnel . . . nothing from Life Before Children fits . . . and I've no idea what people wear in offices any more. Help!'

'OK. Well . . .' Annie was almost rubbing her hands. This was going to be easy. With the right clothes and a bit of care and attention, Martha would scrub up nicely. She wouldn't recognise herself.

'Paula is your guide for today, so'—Annie shot Paula her 'pay atten-tion' look—'she is going to help you buy *not* a trouser suit. No, no! Sooo over! But trousers that fit and flatter. I'd recommend grey, straight legs—not too narrow, not too wide—then a short, *toning*, but not matching, swingy jacket with a single button. OK?

'You need to find day shoes that fit well and that you love in a colour to go with the suit. Now, Martha, you are not allowed brown, black or navy.' She winked at Martha, so it wasn't too bossy. 'Go for gold, green, purple, red, orange, yellow . . . Something lovely. Who needs black?'

'So, once you have the shoes,' Annie went on, 'you're to find three knockout tops that go with the trousers, jacket and the footwear. Three is the minimum. Then, your final mission for today, should you choose to accept, is to find a colourful skirt that goes with all three tops, the shoes and the short jacket. OK? Got me?'

Martha and Paula nodded obediently.

'This way, I promise you'll be beautifully dressed for the office every single day. Obviously, if you want to look at raincoats, umbrellas, boots, cardigans . . . or *make-up*,' there was a noticeable stress on this final item, 'Paula can advise, but get the basics in place first. You can always come back to us. In fact we'd love you to come back.

'Now . . . just one last thing, darlin', then I really have to shoot back to my other client, how are you planning to . . . er . . . . style your hair for work?' Annie had decided this was the most tactful way to frame: *For God's sake, woman, get a decent cut and colour!*

'Style my hair? Style . . .' Martha gave a deep sigh then blurted out, 'All I'd like is to be free of headlice just long enough to remember to make an appointment and actually get to the hairdresser's.'

'Oh! Oh no!' Annie, who'd once had to deal with an 'outbreak' on her son's head, at least had some sympathy, but Paula had taken several steps backwards.

'Oh, I'm clear at the moment,' Martha added quickly.

'I'd forgotten about headlice,' Annie said, trying to resist the urge to scratch her head at the thought. 'My children are older now. So . . . well . . . better get the haircut as soon as you can, before they pop up again. Right! Off you go, you two.'

'**N**ow what?' Annie wanted to know when, twenty minutes later, Paula was back. 'I can't do your job for you!' she hissed, losing patience.

'Donna! In your office,' Paula said huffily.

'What!' This was not good news. Annie tried to see as little of her witch of a boss as possible.

'She's logged on to your computer,' Paula warned.

No doubt about it, Annie would have to go, and just as she'd finally begun to hit Svetlana for some priceless new-husband advice.

'I am so, so sorry,' Annie told the Russians. 'There's a tiny problem I have to sort out.'

'No matter,' Svetlana assured her. 'We are finished here. Everything is decided. We get ready to go now.'

'OK, I'll see you in a minute,' Annie said as she rushed out of the changing room towards the windowless matchbox of an office that housed her desk, files, company computer and, most importantly, personal laptop, which right now was plugged into The Store's internet connection and up and running on her eBay homepage.

Personal shopping at The Store was Annie's day job. Around it, she crammed in private home make-overs via her Dress to Express service; then there was the Annie V Trading Station on eBay, which did great business selling designer items: BNWT (brand new with tags), new, nearly new, secondhand and vintage. Where did Annie source these items? Her own staff-discounted wardrobe, The Store's sale rail, the bargain bins of other shops, junk shops, charity shops, other eBay auctions and sites. Annie had a saleswoman's eye for a great bargain and a profitable resale.

Personally, she never bought anything at full price: not a haircut (her hairdresser came to all her sale pre-previews), not a bottle of shampoo (bulk buy on the internet), not a tin of beans (she knew what was on offer at every supermarket and cash-and-carry within a twenty-mile radius), not a car (secondhand, Christmas Eve, fantastic deal). And she was generous: family and friends all benefited from her bargains.

'Donna! Hi there! Can I help you with anything?'

Donna, who'd been retail manager, Women's Fashion, for five months now, did not take her short 'squoval' orange nails from the keyboard. She carried on typing, eyes in narrow black Prada frames fixed to the screen in front of her.

Despite the charming floral Issa dress wrapped round her lithe body, Donna, with her long dark hair scraped back from her face, still looked ready for the kill.

'Annie V Trading Station,' she snarled. 'My goodness, what a lot of items I recognise. Isn't that one of our latest Mulberry bags? And look, it's about to be sold for a hundred and fifty pounds more than its recommended retail price.'

'It's come from a client who's fed up with it already,' Annie explained. 'You know how fickle some of them are. Look, this is all totally above board, Donna. I can even show you my Trading Station tax returns.'

'Of course, I'm sure it is. There's just one slight problem, Annie.' Donna turned to glare at her, her Botoxed brow doing its best to scrunch into a stern warning, while Annie tried not to wonder yet again why Donna didn't wax the noticeable moustache from her upper lip. Was it a lesbian thing?

'You're doing this at work,' Donna snapped. 'And you've already had two verbal warnings from me about this.'

Verbal warnings? Was Snakewoman trying to insinuate that previous conversations about Annie's internet activity counted as official warnings? 'We've had several *discussions* about this, yes,' Annie agreed, 'and I've explained to you that I am not doing this at work. My computer is on, open at the web page. When I have the odd moment, you know, tea break . . . nipping out for lunch . . . I have a quick look. I'm not causing my work a problem in any way whatsoever. Why don't you look over my sales figures for this month, Donna?' Annie dared her.

'It's not just about sales figures,' Donna countered. 'You're setting other members of staff a bad example. So I'm giving you this.' She picked up a white envelope and handed it to Annie. 'It's a written warning, so we're both clear.'

'What!!!'

The devious, scheming cow!

It had been obvious to Annie from Donna's first week that she was the kind of manager who actually felt threatened by a really good member of staff, rather than supported. But much as she suspected Donna would love to be rid of her, Annie had always thought her awe-inspiring sales power would protect her. Now she wasn't so sure.

'And what about Paula?' Donna launched straight into a new line of attack. 'She's not pulling her weight. You have another month to train her up properly for this job or we'll have to find someone else.'

Considering Paula had been chosen for the position by Donna, and Donna alone, this was somewhat unfair, but Annie had come to expect nothing less from her.

The mobile beside the computer began to ring. Annie had two mobiles and as this was her business phone, her heart sank as Donna snatched it up and barked 'Hello?' into the receiver.

'Yes . . . aha . . . oh really? . . . Well, that's very interesting . . . No. I'll get her to call you back.' Donna clicked off the phone and glared at Annie. 'That was your estate agent. He wants to talk to you about a "very exciting new investment opportunity". I suggest you call him back when you've read your warning and finished for the day.' There was no mistaking the withering look that came with this.

Just then, Svetlana appeared at the office door. 'Ahnnah, we are ready to leave,' she said, demanding immediate attention. 'If you have arranged for everything to be taken to the back door, Olga and I will go and meet the car.'

Annie kissed Svetlana and then Olga and thanked them profusely for their visit. She was thanked profusely in return.

Svetlana, as if noticing Donna for the first time, asked her, 'Are you Ahnnah's boss?'

When Donna gave a curt nod in reply, Svetlana enthused, 'She is wonderful. The best stylist in London. Rrrreally. Be nice to her, because if she ever leaves The Store, I will leave with her.'

Donna's expression darkened, but she did her best to force a smile.

Then, in a small, carefree gesture of thanks, Svetlana handed last season's Chloé handbag to Annie with the words, 'You have it. For your business. I am very admiring of your enterprise.'

'No, no, darlin', I really couldn't . . .' Annie began.

'Yes, of courrrrrrse,' Svetlana insisted, 'and there's something inside for you. Special information, Ahnnah, because it is time for you to find New Husband. It's not good to be alone for long time.'

Before Annie could even say thank you, Svetlana had swept out of the suite towards her packed limousine and her luxury life in Mayfair.

The look of genuine pain on Donna's face was a joy to behold, but it didn't stop her from snapping, 'What a walking cliché the woman is.'

Becca Wolstonecroft at Parents' Evening:

Grey T-shirt (M&S)
Pink fleece (M&S)
Grey (formerly black) chinos (Gap)
Grey (formerly white) underwear (M&S)
Short black socks (husband's)
In misguided attempt to disguise the above:
Cream fake fur coat (Xmas gift six years ago)
Total est. cost: £220

'*Good God!* How much!?'

SHORTLY BEFORE CLOSING time, Annie left The Store with two luxurious handbags over one shoulder: her own pumpkin-coloured Chloé, which now held Svetlana's, slipped into a protective cloth inside. She hadn't decided yet whether she was going to keep it or sell it. On her other shoulder was an enormous tote bag filled with the day's other treasures: three Tupperware boxes crammed with leftovers from the staff canteen for supper, twelve (last season's) Estée Lauder lipsticks, one pair of (damaged) trousers, bought at a snip. She'd fix them and sell BNWT.

Donna's warning letter had been read then scrunched up in fury. It was now buried underneath all the other items because Annie was doing her best not to think about life without her job at The Store. She was her family's sole provider. Yes, she worked very hard to supplement her main income, but if Donna pushed her off the tightrope, there was no safety net.

Her personal mobile began to ring in a rap version of the *Star Wars* theme, because her nine-year-old son, Owen, had doctored it again. On the line was her fourteen- nearly fifteen-year-old daughter Lana (what you get at thirty-five if you think babies are soooo cute when you're twenty and madly in love). 'Hi, Lana. I haven't forgotten, honest. I will be sitting down with your form teacher at seven fifteen. I will not be late, promise.'

'And you're to get me out of the charity thing, OK?' Lana was using her whiny voice. 'Speak to Owen's teacher about that.'

'I'll think about it,' Annie told her, not promising anything further.

Annie was heading for Highgate, one of the nicest and oldest parts of north London, where she lived. There were still flagstone pavements and listed Georgian houses with lumpy glass windows and sagging oak beams. Although it was now bisected by a main road, Highgate still felt 'villagey'. The high street had real shops as well as a Tesco Metro, banks and estate agents. People moved there, fell in love with the place and tended to stay, making it slightly more neighbourly than many other parts of London.

Annie had always wanted to live in Highgate, despite the outrageous prices, and she'd achieved the cramped three-bedroomed flat she shared with her two children through her personal property-development programme. It was testament to her unflagging energy, not to mention her dislike of settling down or staying still, that she'd moved home eight times in the past ten years, always buying run-down, junky places and using cheap tradesmen, her own DIY skills and, above all, her unerringly great taste to turn in a profit and move on to something just a little bit better and a little bit closer to her dream destination.

Rotten carpets, dodgy roofs, rattling windows, rodent infestations, dry rot: none of these things could frighten Annie any longer, she'd lived through them all and come out the other side with equity.

In her current flat, she'd just had a fabulous (heavily discounted) limestone bathroom installed; now she was preparing to sell for maximum profit in the spring and move on, even though she'd be really sorry to say goodbye to the steam sauna shower. Well . . . in fact, she'd be really sorry to say goodbye to this flat, for many reasons, and she suspected it was going to be hard to convince the children it was a good idea . . . but, like it or not, she needed the money.

Heels clacking on the pavement, she headed from Highgate underground station, not in the direction of her home, but towards St Vincent's, the excellent, although totally exclusive and smug, private day school her two children attended.

Sending her children to St Vincent's at a cost of over £2,000 a month was what kept Annie focused and motivated through her long days of wheeling, dealing, advising and selling. She'd been brought up, the oldest of three girls, in a much less inviting corner of London by a single, non-stop-working mother who had sent her girls to the local primary and then the local comprehensive until one by one they'd hit the critical age of fourteen. Then, chiropodist (although she preferred 'podiatrist') Fern had used her overtime, her savings and their natural intelligence to secure them places at the extraordinarily upmarket Francis Holland School for Girls to 'get their exams' and 'a bit of polish'.

For Annie, Francis Holland had been the Promised Land. Yes, she'd suffered a degree of taunting for living in the wrong part of town and having an accent more gravel than cut glass. But mainly she'd attracted a big friend-and-fan base because she was street-smart, savvy and cool and because she knew so many, many boys.

Annie had left four years later with several defining attributes: the qualifications necessary for art school, the firm conviction that if she ever had children they'd go to a school like that from day one, no matter what the cost, and finally, perhaps most importantly, she'd learned that even if you didn't fit in, you had to be yourself, because people responded so much better to down-to-earth reality than to nervous, put-on airs and graces.

'**A**h, Mrs Valentine, lovely to see you. And how are we doing?' The headmaster, Mr Ketteringham-Smith, severely smart in his light grey meet-the-parents suit, was greeting at the main door in person.

'Top form, Headmaster,' she assured him with her best smile. 'And how about you? You're looking fit.'

'Oh, well . . . am I?' He was flustered by the compliment.

'Definitely. You look like you've been coaching the First XV single-handed.' This, admittedly, was going a tad far.

'Well . . . erm . . . like to keep my hand in,' came his reply.

She restrained herself from the cheeky answer to this because although there were many, many interesting men to be found wandering the corridors of St Vincent's on a parents' evening, slightly balding Mr Ketteringham-Smith was not one of them.

Annie, perhaps understandably, had a thing about dads. Well, first of all, she'd never had much of one. Who had Fern chosen to give her heart to? Fern had picked a cargo-ship captain. What an obvious mistake! Mick Mitchell was always away, on the other side of the world away: places like Hong Kong and Rio de Janeiro. The brief times he was home, he still liked to be captain, which infuriated Fern, who was used to doing everything for herself and by herself. But it was the all-too-regular medical evidence (requiring hefty doses of antibiotics) of the other women in the other ports that finally sank his boat.

Owen and Lana's dad, Roddy Valentine—mischievous and funny, a Celtic blue-black-haired heart-throb—had been so much better at family life at first. But then he was an actor, away a lot, and, despite his assurances, Annie had not been able to stop herself from wondering about the possibility of other women. However, nothing had prepared her for the abrupt and shocking end to her marriage. The total and irrevocable breakdown and break-up. The full stop. Overnight, Roddy had become history and she'd had to deal with it, somehow get over it, pick herself and her two devastated children up and carry on.

How had this happened? It was a story that she didn't like to tell. It was a story that somewhere in her head she didn't really believe. She still didn't like to hear his name unexpectedly, as it made her jump. Although Roddy had left over two and a half years ago now, she still woke up most mornings and looked across the bed for her handsome husband, momentarily convinced that it had all been a terrible dream.

A schoolboy handed her an information sheet and she scanned it over, checking the order of events and the rooms she should be heading towards. An hour and a half had been allocated for form teacher talks, then it was into the hall for the headmaster's speech and the performances. Would anyone notice if she skipped the main event?

'Annie! Hello! How are you?' Becca Wolstonecroft was bounding over, a plump, curly-blonde-haired mother of four. 'You're looking wonderful—as usual,' she said, kissing her on the cheek.

'Oh, that's sweet of you,' was Annie's response.

'I'm going to have to get you to make me over one of these days. Look at me!' Becca gestured with her arms. 'I look like a bloody Lab.'

Annie choked back the laugh this deserved. Blonde knee-length fake fur wasn't perhaps the best look for Becca's short, stocky physique. 'Right, OK. Do you do anything on a Tuesday evening?' Annie asked.

'No,' Becca said hesitantly.

'Next Tuesday evening, then.'

'Hmmm?' Becca sounded confused.

'Next Tuesday evening,' Annie began. 'Me in your wardrobe sorting you out, telling you what to keep and what to bin. Explaining in detail, with pictures, what and where you need to buy to make sure you always look amazing from now on.'

Becca was looking doubtful. 'Erm . . . What do you charge?'

'Just a bit more than the value of your current outfit,' Annie teased.

'And what do you think that is?' Becca looked down at her furry coat.

'Hmmm . . . two hundred and twenty pounds?' came the guess.

'Good God! *How much!?*' Becca seemed genuinely horrified.

'It'll be mates' rates,' Annie assured her. 'Look, I'll pencil you in. What's your telephone number? I'll phone to confirm.'

'OK, great.' Becca brightened up, obviously under the delusion that when the call came, she'd be able to play for time. But Annie knew perfectly well that, on the phone, she would win.

'C'mon.' After scribbling the number down, Becca dived for a change of subject. 'I want to get Eric's teacher out of the way first. Shall we go up to Godzilla's room together?'

'Don't,' Annie warned her. 'I'll probably call her that.'

Lana's, and therefore Eric's, current form teacher was the school battle-axe: the kind of dragon who roared just for the sake of roaring.

Upstairs in the corridors and in the classrooms, parents were milling, looking at the artwork on the walls ('*Gosh, Jessamy's showing so much talent. We should take her to Florence for the summer holidays.*'); leafing through jotters and textbooks ('*Isaac's just brilliant at maths. The Kumon classes after school were worth every penny.*'); waiting for their turn to speak to the form teachers ('*George already thinks she's Oxbridge material . . . that's right, she's ten in April . . . but she already reads Dickens. Oh? Henry's on to James Joyce?*') At St Vincent's, parents were very, very interested in how their children were doing.

'Jill!' Annie tapped the shoulder of one of the mothers, who had recently become a client of hers. 'Look at you! Lovely.' She smiled, appreciating Jill from head to toe, taking in the caramel mac they'd bought together and the confident Bobbi Brown glow on Jill's face.

Smiling back, Jill said, 'Thank you,' just as Annie had taught her: '*Thank you is enough, no more "oh this old thing?" or "I just threw this on" . . . or whatever else you used to say in response to compliments.*'

After several minutes of chat, Jill whispered to Annie, 'There's Tor! Tor Fleming. She's been completely shafted in the divorce; I think she's going to fall apart. No one needs you more than her, Annie.'

Annie followed the discreetly pointed finger to the mother of one of Lana's classmates. Poor Tor. Her bare, exhausted face hovered above a shapeless pale blue anorak and beneath a scruffy mid-brown bob with a tragic grey parting. Annie bustled forward. 'Tor! How are you? I haven't seen you for ages, you've got to come round . . .'

Soon enough, it was Annie's turn to pull up the chair opposite Lana's form teacher, the fifty-something, super-strict Miss Gordanza.

'Well, Mrs Valentine, there were certainly some difficulties with Lana in the run-up to Christmas,' Miss Gordanza began, adjusting purple cat's-eye spectacles on her over-powdered, pointed nose.

'Difficulties' was putting it mildly. Lana and her gang of friends had egged each other on to play a series of increasingly daring and dodgy pranks throughout the Christmas term: raw fish hidden in classrooms over a holiday weekend and then the spectacular treacle-based sabotage of the school orchestra's brass instruments. The Christmas concert had come to a very sticky end.

An MI5-scale investigation had followed. Lana and five of her friends had been punished and had left for the holidays in disgrace. Back at school in January, a clever penance had been devised: Lana and the others involved were now in charge of the school's charity fund-raising group, although Lana was still trying to weasel out.

'She's enjoying school a lot more,' Annie was telling Miss Gordanza. 'She promised me a fresh new start this term and she seems to be keeping to that. She's really into her GCSE course . . .' she gushed.

'I'll be keeping a close eye on her,' Miss Gordanza said.

'Yes, so will I,' Annie assured her.

'There are . . . I mean . . . Lana is bound to have issues because of her father's . . . ah . . . situation,' Miss Gordanza went on awkwardly. 'But I'm sure they're not beyond the control of this school.'

'Yes, well . . .' Annie told her gently, 'I'm sure we all have issues, Miss Godzil— zanza.' She thought she'd saved herself.

'So many people call me that, I'm considering a name change,' the teacher added testily.

'Sorry.' Annie suddenly felt mortified and about ten years old.

'No matter. Shall we turn to Lana's subject choices?'

Owen's new form teacher, in the Junior School, was the head of music, Mr Leon. He was a recent addition to the school staff and already very popular. Not just with the pupils, it seemed. Certain mothers had even been seen to blush in his presence. But Annie, who'd met him several times now, failed to see the attraction. To her, Mr Leon was undoubtedly nice and a terribly committed teacher, but he was just a little too English-eccentric-stroke-tramp for her.

Waiting in the corridor for her turn to speak to him, Annie could overhear the anxious parents ahead of her. 'Marcus is astonishingly bright,' the mother was informing Mr Leon. 'We want to make sure he's being stretched.'

'Well, unfortunately we don't keep a rack on the premises any more, Mrs Gillingham, but I'll see what other ideas I can come up with,' Mr Leon replied, provoking at first silence, then a confused titter from Mr and Mrs Gillingham.

When her turn arrived, Annie went in to find Mr Leon seated on the corner of his desk, humming cheerfully.

'Mrs Valentine! Come on in.' He unfolded his arms, stood up, tried to sweep a hand through his hair but got stuck in the tangle, so pulled out and waved at the two chairs set out for parents. St Vincent's School parents tended to come in pairs, it occurred to Annie with a pang.

'What about the violin?' Mr Leon asked, sitting down. He looked strained and uncomfortable in the clothes he'd chosen for this evening in an effort to be smart. Not a big effort, it had to be said. Tonight he'd taken the eccentric tramp look and run with it: worn-out cords paired, unhappily, with clumpy brown hiking boots and a tight tweed jacket, so hairy, Annie wondered when it was going to bark.

His top shirt button was undone and his tie had been pulled into a tiny scrunched knot, at odds with his broad shoulders, tanned face and spectacular mop of hair. He looked as if he'd come down a mountain and stepped into the first clothes to hand. There was a funny smell wafting about him as well: damp, slightly smoky, even boggy.

'What *about* the violin?' Annie repeated, wondering if she'd missed the start of this conversation.

'We should get Owen playing the violin. He can play just about every instrument he picks up in my class; he's nine, great age to start, very good ear, really very good. Plus,' he rushed on, 'we're desperate for new violins. Three will be leaving at the end of this year.'

She had to assume he was talking about members of the school orchestra. 'Mr Leon—' she began.

'Ed,' he interrupted. 'Please call me Ed.' He turned away, catching a violent sneeze just in time with his crumpled cotton handkerchief.

'Well, bless you, Ed. Where did you catch that cold?'

'Fifth form orienteering in Snowdonia; just got back.' He blew his nose vigorously. 'Brilliant time.'

'Bit cold for camping, wasn't it?' She understood the damp boggy smell now.

'The kids were in the youth hostel, but it wasn't any problem for me. I've got Arctic kit.'

'Right. Well . . .' *Sleeping outdoors in February?! See? Mad, eccentric tramp.* 'Believe me, Ed, there is no way that either of us is going to persuade Owen to take up the violin. No way! You may not have been able to discuss this fully with him'—this was her way of gently introducing Owen's acute and, at times, crippling shyness—'but I can assure you the super-cool-skateboarding, science-kit blasting-rapper boy that I know won't want to play something as poncy and nerdy as the violin.'

'I play the violin,' Ed told her.

'Oh . . . well . . .'

'It's not just about concertos,' he assured her. 'Although they are lovely. There's folk music, Irish jigs, even rock 'n' roll.'

'No, I don't think he'll go for it and I don't want to force him.'

'I just think of the violin as such a personal voice . . .' Ed began.

'Owen has a perfectly good voice of his own. He uses it beautifully at home and when he's really comfortable with people. It's our job, everyone's job, to help him feel just as comfortable at school.'

'I totally agree,' Ed said quickly, 'but he's very good at music and we should be encouraging that. All creative outlets are a good thing for children. Did you know that Owen speaks about five words a day to me, which is great progress and I'm trying, just as gently as I can, to increase that. What about guitar then?' he suggested. 'Guitars are cool.'

'I suppose so,' she said carefully, worried she was going to agree to something by mistake.

'Well, that's it then,' Ed said enthusiastically. 'Guitar lessons!'

See.

She worried about shy Owen having to cope with one-to-one lessons from a stranger. 'I don't know if he'd want to have . . .'

'I'd be happy to give him guitar lessons,' Ed cut in. 'At home, even, if that would make him feel more comfortable. Don't you think that would be a good idea? Seeing me, his class teacher, in a less threatening setting? It might really help him to relax at school.'

'Erm, well . . .' Annie was reluctant. Aside from what Owen might think of this, she didn't know if she wanted this big, hairy man in her home, clumping about in hiking boots, wafting bog.

'Ask him what he thinks,' Ed urged her, 'then I'll give you a call to discuss when might be a good time.'

Once numbers had been exchanged, Ed asked, 'Right, so, and my favourite member of the Syrup Six is coming on nicely, isn't she?'

Annie had no idea what he was talking about.

'There weren't enough for a Treacle Ten, so ever since the sabotaged concert I've thought of them as the Syrup Six . . . Lana,' he explained.

'Oh, Lana! Yes, she's fine. She's really not enjoying the fund-raising thing, though,' Annie began. Why Ed Leon was the teacher in charge of fund-raising remained a mystery to Annie. He obviously couldn't even raise enough funds for new trousers.

'No?' he lifted an eyebrow. 'Well, she'll have to stick with it. This was her punishment and anyway, I think it's good for her to get involved with the school again; she was starting to tune out on us.'

'Yes . . . hmm . . . well, you could be right.'

'I've had an idea for the fund-raising that might make it more interesting for her,' he added. 'We might try to run a charity auction web site. The Syrup Six will have to track down all sorts of things to flog off and there'll be a little group competition to see who can raise the most money. She'd enjoy that, wouldn't she?'

Annie couldn't help smiling. As Lana was already a budding eBay trader, this would be right up her street. 'She'll love it. But keep a sharp eye on her. She's likely to get naughty just as soon as she gets bored. Keep making it very hard and very interesting or watch out.'

'Will do. Now, how would Thursdays suit you for guitar lessons?' Ed wasn't going to let the subject drop.

'I'll have to see what Owen thinks first.'

'Oh yes, fair enough. Now, I suppose we should talk about his school work too—shouldn't we?'

'**M**rs Valentine?'

Annie felt the tap on her shoulder. Turning, she saw the tall, lean figure of the school bursar behind her.

'Just a very quick word, Mrs Valentine, I was hoping to catch you.' He lowered his voice. 'Well, in a nutshell . . .'

With a lurch, Annie knew what was coming next.

'Your cheque for this term's school fees has bounced, Mrs Valentine,' Mr Cartledge informed her.

She'd taken a risk buying the limestone bathroom and steam sauna shower so soon after Christmas. Looked like she was going to have to sell up sooner than expected.

'You do take credit cards, don't you?' Annie asked. She knew perfectly well that five of her cards were dangerously close to their limits, but there was the sixth, emergency-use-only card.

'We make a one per cent charge for credit card payments.'

'Never mind, I think that's what I'll do, just this once!'

She'd put it on the card and just—well—just work harder. It wasn't as if she hadn't juggled overdrafts and debts about like this before.

For most of the time Annie had been managing on her own, it felt fine. Most of the time she could cope. But there were moments when she hated it, resented it, felt she couldn't stand it for even one more day.

At times like this, she was certain that having anyone, any partner at all, would be better than being alone. A back-up, a supporter, that was all she was asking for, even if he was just someone to go home to, someone to give the kind of neck rub Roddy had been so good at. Someone who could soothingly remind her, just as Roddy would have done: '*Hey, it's only money. They print more of it every day.*'

Once she was outside, Annie squeezed her eyes shut and then wiped carefully beneath her lower lashes. Only someone looking very, very closely would have seen the slightest of smudges there.

She tied the belt of her raincoat tightly round her, pulled up the collar, then straightened her shoulders and held up her head. OK, she resolved, she'd put Svetlana's handbag up for auction tonight and maybe she'd look into the intriguing information the billionaire's wife had left inside.

Dress-down Dinah:

Swirly blue and green above-the-knee dress (Topshop)
Dark straight jeans (Topshop)
Soft leather rubber-tread boots (Camper)
Green necklace, green sparkly hairclips (Claire's Accessories)
Pea-green leather knee-length coat (Oxfam)
Total est. cost: £185

'*So, ask me where I got my coat?*'

'It could be worse,' Annie's younger sister Dinah told her as they surveyed a slimy, slightly mildewed shower curtain.

'It could,' Annie agreed. 'If there was a large, black, plague-carrying rat sitting on the kitchen floor, for instance, that would be worse.'

This was the 'exclusive investment opportunity' she'd got out of bed early on a Sunday to view? What a joke.

She was exploring the possibility of swapping her beautiful, fully renovated home for both a doer-upper and a little buy-to-let, but if this was the quality of the doer-upper she could afford: forget it.

This was a gloomy basement prison, inhabited by three, probably more, New Zealand travellers who clearly had better things to do than keep house. Every available surface was covered with their clobber: wet towels, unemptied ashtrays, clothes and empty beer cans.

'Their landlord must be insane, trying to sell it while they're still all here,' Dinah whispered to her.

'As you can see,' the estate agent continued, 'the lounge could benefit from a little freshening up, but there's a lot of potential.'

Ha! Yes, with some effort, the room could be transformed from a filthy, north-facing gloomy dungeon, to a clean, nicely painted north-facing gloomy dungeon. On the plus side, the little kitchen faced south and even had a minuscule strip of lawn outside it.

'It could look just so completely different all white, Annie,' said Dinah in her usual, touchingly positive way.

The estate agent was nodding agreement.

Were they joking?

In the kitchen, one of the tenants was making a fried-egg sandwich.

'What do you think of the flat?' Dinah asked him.

'Great!' came his brief reply.

Annie caught herself staring at his bare bronzed pecs a moment too long. She couldn't think when she'd last been so close to tanned nipples. This really was a small kitchen.

'Shall we go and take a look outside then?' Dinah asked.

'Oh . . . yeah.' Annie tore her eyes from the pecs.

Out in the tiny garden, Dinah's three-year-old daughter Billie skipped in a circle. Her straight, shoulder-length hair, the same light brown as Mummy's, bounced on her shoulders.

She came to a stop before her beloved Aunty Annie (the adoration was mutual), made an attempt at crossing her chubby arms and asked, 'You can still be a fisher lady if you're a princess, can't you?'

'Yes, definitely.' Annie didn't know what a fisher lady was, but she wasn't capable of denying this soft round face, bright eyes and perfect pink mouth anything at all. No one else was either, which was probably something of a problem for Billie's long-term development.

'Well, I'm going to be a princess fisher lady when I grow up, then.'

'What does a princess fisher lady do, babes?'

'Well . . .' Billie began, putting her hands on her hips and leaning forward in a theatrically conspiratorial kind of way, 'it's a princess, so she wears a pink dress and eats pink cakes all the time, but she also fishes, you know, with a fishing rod.'

'Perfect. Now, I think we should go to my house and eat croissants. How does that sound?'

'Yesssss!' Billie began to skip in her circle again.

'So, ask me where I got my coat,' Dinah challenged Annie on the walk back to her flat.

'That's no use!' Annie laughed. 'Now I know you got it in Cancer Research or the PDSA. What did you pay?'

'Oxfam, thirty pounds,' came Dinah's completely honest reply.

'Could have got it for you for less,' Annie told her, but this wasn't true today, it was just a knee-jerk reaction, something she always liked to say to Dinah when they were talking about shopping.

Annie and her sister Dinah—three years younger—had always understood each other almost perfectly. They weren't alike. They appreciated each other's differences and clicked. Always had done.

Although Dinah spent far less on clothes than Annie, she still maintained a lively, edgy style all her own and never shied away from a fashion challenge: tank top and Bermudas? Mini kilt and woolly tights? Sweater dress and kinky boots? Bubble coat? Dinah was game.

'How's Bryan?' Annie asked next, aware that she'd been with Dinah for almost an hour and not enquired once after her brother-in-law. But then it was a badly kept secret between the sisters that although Annie was crazy about Billie and couldn't imagine life without weekly get-togethers with Dinah, she wasn't quite so smitten with Bryan.

'He's fine.' Dinah smiled. 'Still waiting to hear about that project over in Hammersmith. He's pitching for work all the time, but you know how competitive it is.'

One of life's true romantics, Dinah, in Annie's opinion. She was dreamy and sweet and softly pretty: pale skin, rosy cheeks, dark brown hair. After an unexpectedly druggie youth and many disastrous relationships, she'd finally found Bryan, a 'soul mate' (supposedly) just as kind and gentle as she was. Bryan was an architect, who only ever seemed to secure work on the smallest of projects like rearranging kitchen units, and as Dinah was an *occasional* children's book illustrator, they lived in a tiny flat, not far from Annie's, in a state they liked to describe as 'impoverished bliss'. It drove Annie slightly wild. She was always nagging them to be more proactive and ambitious . . . not that it made the slightest difference.

Annie would ask things like, 'But don't you want to do up the kitchen at some point?'

Dinah, oiling some ancient French casserole dish she'd bought at Brick Lane market for twenty pence, would answer, 'Oh, but at least this is a real wooden cupboard.' (Cue cupboard door falling off hinge.)

Or, 'Have you thought about where you're going to send Billie to school?' Annie, ever practical, would ask.

'Oh, her nursery's so *lovely* and most of her friends there are going to the local primary, so we'll probably send her there and . . .'

'But you can't! It's a sink! It came bottom of the entire league table!'

'Did it?' Genuine surprise, followed by, 'Well, apparently they've got a *lovely* new head.'

Annie, preoccupied with earning enough money for her family, couldn't help suggesting moneymaking schemes for Dinah and Bryan: 'If you put together a web site, Bryan, showcased your best ideas . . .' 'Dinah, have you tried contacting other publishers?'

But she suspected Dinah and Bryan quite liked things the way they were: they liked not having to work too hard, they liked being at home with each other and their precious little girl.

'Aunty Annie,' Billie piped up now, 'is it true that Lana and Owen's daddy lives on a hill with other ladies?'

Startled by this question, Annie turned to look at Dinah for some guidance on how to reply. Dinah just shrugged her shoulders and looked as if she was trying not to laugh.

'Well, er . . .' Annie began, but to her relief, Billie had moved on.

'Mummy?' she asked next. 'You know the pink fish we eat . . . is that a real fish? The same as the ones you catch? Do we eat *real* fish?'

'I'm leaving that answer to you,' Annie smiled, suddenly recalling Owen's devoutly vegetarian phase, at the age of four.

Back at Annie's flat, there was an overwhelming smell of nail polish. Lana and her friends Greta and Suzie were giving each other lavish, diamanté-studded manicures and trying to eat toast at the same time.

Annie made the girls and Billie sit down at the kitchen table, where she spread butter and jam and cut toast into manageable pieces for the manicurists, while Dinah went in search of Owen, who was in his room reading and hiding from the teen excitement in the kitchen.

Annie's children had managed to jumble up their parents' looks and features so thoroughly that they looked very like both their mother and father, but completely unlike each other. Lana had Roddy's thick, straight black hair, blue eyes and pale skin, as well as Annie's fine mouth, nose and long limbs. Owen had Roddy's face but coloured with Annie's brown eyes, rumpled mousy hair and a tawnier skin.

'Ask him to come through, will you?' Annie had said to Dinah. 'At least for a croissant.'

Owen eventually sloped in and blushed deepest pink at the sight of Lana's two teen invaders. Greta and Suzie, being two of Lana's closest friends, knew not to speak to Owen or even look in his direction, which was easy enough as he was far too young to be of any interest.

After a while, he would usually calm down and chip into conversations with a few words of his own, but direct questions from non-family members were too stressful. When Annie brought his croissant over on a plate, she didn't say anything to cajole him into talking, but just massaged his slight shoulders for a few minutes, hoping to help him relax.

Sunday mornings were a constant problem in the Valentine household. There had once been lavish Sunday brunches with the most astonishing, homemade, thick and fluffy pancakes.

To Annie, it wasn't so long ago that brunch had never begun before 9.30 a.m. because she and Roddy had always insisted on a Sunday morning lie-in after Saturday's weekly 'date night', when a rota of three baby sitters took charge of Lana and Owen while their parents went out. Didn't matter where they went out, the important thing was being out and having time together: for dinner somewhere smart if they were feeling flush, to see friends or to the cinema, or even for fish and chips on a park bench if they were skint, Roddy whispering in her ear, 'Can we go home yet? I want to do filthy things with you.'

Back at home, the ideal end to the evening was to lock the bedroom door and get close in the way only people who've been happily together for a long time can: 'I know just what you want and I'm so going to make you wait . . . and wait. . . before I finally give it to you.'

She had loved him, through and through and inside out, every completely thoroughly explored square inch of him. 'We'll always have each other,' he'd told her so many times.

The liar.

Sunday brunch had once meant happy, sleepy parents in pyjamas and Roddy making pancakes with banana and maple syrup, or blueberries, or bacon and syrup, or even, not so successfully, Smarties.

For a while after Roddy had gone, Annie had tried to keep the Sunday morning pancake tradition going on her own. But she couldn't get it right. The pancakes came out black on the outside, raw in the middle. Or the batter went runny and they came out like crêpes.

But then, when Dinah came round and made them wonderful pancakes, Annie and her children understood that even perfect pancakes wouldn't work. What was missing, all too obviously, was Roddy and his huge, sunny presence in their lives.

So Sundays were now a careful exercise in avoidance. There was a different routine going. Lana usually invited friends round, Owen and Annie often went out for a long, early-morning walk, although more recently Annie had spent Sunday mornings viewing flats.

Today, Annie had brought back the new Sunday-morning delicacy: butter croissants from the deli. She put them into the oven to warm, filling the room with a toasty comforting smell. There was lovely cherry jam and Lana's music on the stereo, pots of tea and the busy chatter of seven people in the kitchen. This way, Annie, Lana and Owen were able to not think about pancakes.

Once the meal was over, Annie lured Dinah to the sitting room with the words, 'I've got something very interesting to show you.'

The south-facing, windows-on-two-sides, third-floor sitting room was an Annie make-over triumph. Now the room was a delicate shade of lemon-green with fresh yellow blinds (sale), luxurious green and lemon curtains (secondhand), a slouchy biscuit-coloured sofa (small ads) and all the little touches—antique mirror, rugs, beautifully framed photographs—that ensured her flats always sold for a bomb.

'I have a new plan,' Annie told her, taking a seat.

'You always have a plan, Annie. Does this one involve going round another dodgy flat at nine thirty on a Sunday morning?'

'No, no, no,' Annie assured her. 'Although I will have to move. No, this plan is about giving up the Lonely Hearts columns.'

'Oh, thank God!' was Dinah's reaction. 'I know you tried very hard, Annie, but I didn't think it was ever going to work.'

Last summer, Annie had decided that the best cure for the aching loneliness her absent husband had left in her life was maybe not to pretend that everything was fine, but to find someone new.

She'd approached the project as she'd approach a shopping quest: she'd looked in all the places she could think of where available men were on offer and she'd tried out many, many different styles. Unfortunately, finding a replacement partner was turning out to be much more difficult than finding a new pair of shoes.

She had been out with twenty-two men. She'd kept count. Eighteen of those men had been complete losers of the tragicomic variety: badly divorced, depressed, dumped, dysfunctional or defective—truly the very end-of-sale rail in the romance department.

Three had been a little more promising. Well . . . they'd been worth a second, even once a third date for closer inspection, but nothing had come of them. And then there had been the One Night Wonder. Oscar, the man in a crumpled linen suit, incredibly good-looking for the dating circuit, funny, attentive and so persuasive that she had taken advantage of the children being away and invited him home.

There was no hanging around waiting for Oscar to make a move, oh no. No sooner had she brought him in through the front door than he'd caught her wrist and pulled her in close saying, 'We have to kiss, right now. It can't wait,' in a voice not unlike Cary Grant's.

He was a fabulous kisser: his tongue moving against hers had felt breathtaking; she'd wanted to eat him up, right there in the hallway.

Of course they'd gone to bed together. She'd found herself running up the stairs and throwing herself on top of him.

Kissing her busily, but still talking to her, joking, charming her all the way, 'Hello, I think I love you, what's your name again?' he'd sung in a giggly whisper against her ear, running a finger teasingly round the rim of her belly button. Then two fingers had begun to walk from her knee upwards, taking the hem of her skirt with them.

'No, no,' she'd giggled back, pushing his hand away.

'You so want to. You do,' he'd told her, moving his hand slowly up her leg again, taking big wolfish bites and licks at her mouth and neck.

He'd smelt spicy, sweaty, grassy and delicious. She'd been unable to recall wanting anyone more, was ravenously hungry . . . starving.

It had got much more heated, deliciously desperate . . . frantically probing fingers and mouths until they were naked and sweating, gasping together, Annie determined to have him, make up for all the time she'd lost, cram in every sensation she'd been so deprived of.

Finally they'd fallen asleep in the not-so-small hours, they'd kept each other awake so long. He'd been unbelievably tender and she had so, so fallen for him. But in the cool light of the morning, he'd already seemed detached—had to hurry off—left a number that, when three days later she finally ventured to call, turned out to be *wrong*!

'I'm emotionally scarred and vulnerable!' she'd shouted at the receiver once she'd hung up. 'It's against the rules to treat me like this!'

Her best friend, Connor, had christened Oscar the One Night Wonder and tried to make a joke of him ever afterwards, to ease Annie's pain as quickly as possible. Now, she tried to remember just the very good bits (not so hard) and hey, Oscar had broken the ice, hadn't he? He'd been the first person she'd ever slept with since her husband. Not that he deserved the honour.

'You're going to meet your next Mr Right one of these days; you're going to bump smack bang into him when you're not even looking,' Dinah soothed her. 'You've just got to give yourself time.'

Annie gave her a sympathetic look. Her sister was touchingly sweet and naive in so many ways. Did she really think something this important could be left to chance? To fate? That she should rely on Mr Perfecto waltzing into The Store one day, setting eyes on her and declaring that she was the one?

In Annie's experience, men were nothing like that. Even when they were madly in love with you, they rarely did anything about it. They had to be seduced, cajoled, reassured: in short, hunted down.

Even securing Roddy, hardly one of life's shy and retiring types, had been hard work. Nineteen-year-old Annie, wildly in love, convinced this was the man for whom she was destined, had had to keep a constant track of his nightlife via a friend to make sure she turned up at all the right places, *accidentally*, looking as sensational as possible for the early nineties when everything came from Gap, was black or grey or plaid, and the highest heels were kitten. (See the first series of *Friends* for details and try to imagine: the hair-straightener hadn't even been invented!) But the plaid miniskirts had worked and finally she had landed the prize. And there's nothing, nothing in the world as wonderful as the one you've longed for, dreamed of, ached over, suddenly turning all his dazzling attention on you. Full beam.

The very depressing thing about blind dating was that she'd not yet met anyone who even came close. Instead of bringing Annie a sexy new life full of glamorous, hot men and sizzling romance, the hopeless encounters made her miss Roddy and every moment of comfortable, intimate married life even more.

But never mind. New plan. 'Dinah, I haven't given up the chase, babes, I've just discovered a much, much better hunting ground,' Annie informed her sister. 'I've been trawling the bargain basements for a man, when I should be looking for a really class label.' With a flourish Annie brought out the glossy brochure she'd found inside Svetlana's cast-off handbag. 'One of the wealthiest wives in London gave this to me,' she explained, 'so it's got to be a very good idea.'

'*Discerning Diners?*' Dinah read aloud in a tone of disbelief. '*London's most exclusive dinner-dating experience* . . . Oh, Annie, I don't know.'

But Annie brushed her sister's reservations aside and eagerly spread out the profile pages of the 'dynamic, single, hand-selected guests' who would be coming to next week's five-star 'dining experience'. This agency came with Svetlana's recommendation ('*I meet my second husband there*'). If Svetlana was now with a billionaire gas baron, surely Annie could manage a man with nice clothes and a six-figure salary?

'Isn't this going to be very expensive?' Dinah worried.

'That's the point!' Annie exclaimed. 'I could meet not just the man of my dreams, but the very wealthy man of my dreams.'

Dinah rolled her eyes. 'Annie! What you're telling me is you are now looking for a rich man.' There was no hiding the irritation in her voice. 'You know, not a nice man, or the right man, or someone you could fall in love with again, but Mr Moneybags.'

'No, no. Of course I want to fall in love again. I just think I should be looking for the right, really nice Mr Moneybags,' came Annie's reply. But when she saw the sceptical look on Dinah's face she added, 'Would it really hurt to look? The world's available men aren't divided into "Nice" and "Rich", you know. There's overlap. Would that be so bad?'

'But the money issue is just going to colour your judgment, Annie,' Dinah insisted. 'You'll pick a creep because he's loaded and supposedly going to solve all your problems.'

'Thanks for the vote of confidence, Dinah,' Annie snapped.

'Why do you have to do this anyway? You will meet someone, when the time is right.'

'I need someone else. You have no idea. I want someone to share some of the pressure. I want to live somewhere nice—'

'You do live somewhere nice,' Dinah broke in.

'But I want to be able to afford to stay!' There. Annie hadn't meant to spell it out quite so clearly to her sister.

'Oh, Annie!' Anxiety was already crossing Dinah's face.

'I want someone . . .' Annie's voice was quieter now. She wanted to explain it to her sister properly, but she didn't like to admit all this need. 'I want to find someone soon because I really, really want to get over Roddy and I think someone else would help. I mean, it's going to be three years soon. I think it's going to take another five before it even begins to feel less . . . raw. And I'm thirty-five; I can't let all that time pass me by while I just wallow.'

Dinah's expression softened now, to one of great sympathy.

'And I'm so pissed off Roddy left us just after he'd landed the soap part!' Annie exclaimed. 'Just as things were about to get so good for us. A year into that job and we'd have been minted! Absolutely minted and all these problems wouldn't exist. I wouldn't even need to work. Can't you understand how cheated I feel?'

'I know,' Dinah soothed. 'It was very unfair. Of course you deserve someone else. I want you to find someone great, Annie, and not settle for anything less. Maybe you should go to this dinner thing and I should just shut up.'

'Oh, babes, I don't know what I'd do without you.' Annie sat up and wiped her eyes.

'No, don't be silly. What would I do without you? Come on, what have you got there? Details of your fellow Discerning Diners? Show!'

'Bet you I get a great date on my first dinner,' Annie challenged.

'Bet you don't.'

Discerning Diner Annie:

Rose-pink strappy cocktail dress (Monsoon sale)
Sequinned evening bag (Accessorize sale)
Purple suede Manolo heels (The Store's sale preview day)
Yellow cropped swing jacket (Valentino, eBay, used but flawless)
Total est. cost: £380

'I thought we were supposed to dress up?'

'OPEN THE DOOR!' Annie shouted to her children from her bedroom at the top of the stairs. 'That'll be Mr Leon.'

It was 6.45 p.m. and she was having a last-minute fret about her hair. She'd decided not to scrape her blonde locks into the usual slick ponytail for her first Discerning Diner dinner but to wear them loose.

Now that the hair was falling down about her face she didn't know if she liked it. She looked so different. Maybe too pretty. Curly blonde locks and a pink dress. Maybe it was too much.

But this was dating. High-level, designer dating. And wasn't she always, always telling clients that they had to dress for the occasion?

She pressed her pink glossed lips together, slung her yolk-yellow Valentino over her shoulders and picked up her evening bag. Heels trip-trapping, she headed down to say hello to the music teacher.

Ed Leon with his hefty woollen overcoat and bright red guitar case was filling up the entire hallway as he chatted to Lana and Owen.

'Yeah, basic chords,' he was telling them. 'Easy once you've got the guitar tuned. But tuning the guitar, that's the difficult bit . . . Lana, why don't you join us?'

Ha! Good luck trying, Annie couldn't help thinking. Lana had moaned and scowled from the moment Annie had come through the front door about 'that geek Mr Leon' coming round.

'D'you know what he's called at school?' Lana had said.

'Ed the Shed,' Owen had butted in. 'Because he smells a bit parky,' and when Annie had rattled with laughter, he'd added, 'You have to admit, it's funny.'

'We're going to do some chords,' Ed the Shed was telling Lana down in the hallway. 'We might break into a bit of 1980s retro guitar . . . hey, Owen? Have a little Billy Bragg moment. C'mon, Lana, just listen in.'

'Who?' was Lana's response, but to Annie's surprise her daughter seemed to be showing some signs of interest.

Then Annie was in the middle of the stairs when she caught Ed looking up at her and doing an obvious double-take at the heels, the hair and the dress, definitely the dress.

'Hello, Mr Leon, great of you to come.' She smiled a welcome. 'I'm leaving the three of you in peace and going out to a dinner party,' she explained over his insistent 'Please call me Ed'.

'Into the sitting room,' Annie directed her children. 'Ed, can I have a tiny word?' She came down the last of the stairs and said in a low voice, 'We've not talked about payment for these lessons.'

'No, no . . .' He was waving his hand.

'But don't be silly,' she insisted. 'You've come over here, you're giving up your time to do this. You need to be paid.'

'I want to do this for Owen and . . . I do have the interests of the school orchestra at heart as well.' He held up a small brown violin case.

She looked at him for a moment; he had a kind face, slightly too kind. He was definitely the sort of well-meaning twinky who would get himself into a situation where giving music lessons was *costing* him.

'Now look, Ed,' she told him a little firmly, 'I can understand if you don't want to be paid for the lessons, but I'm giving you something, OK? Are you a wine man or a beer drinker?'

'Erm . . .' Ed seemed unsure and slightly taken aback at the question. 'Well both, really—but red wine probably has the edge.'

'Well then, that's easy,' she told him. 'One lesson equals two bottles of red. Do we have a deal?' She held out her hand.

They shook on it, his face creasing into a smile. 'If you insist,' he said.

'Yes, I bloody do . . . and don't be too impressed. They'll be cheap bottles. Come on in, then,' she said and opened the sitting-room door. Ed followed her into the room and began to take off his coat.

Annie took it from him, noting that he wasn't in his usual tweedy schoolwear, but in very well-worn jeans and an ancient dark blue Guernsey jumper, fraying at the cuffs. A desperately unironed shirt was peeking out at the collar and hem. This was obviously Ed doing casual. He looked like a refugee from a badly dressed war.

'So you're heading out?' he asked.

'Yes. Yeah. A party . . . dinner . . . thing.' She didn't want to be specific about the dating scene she was venturing into.

But Lana's acutely perceptive teen antenna flicked on and she didn't hesitate to inform Ed, 'Mum's going on another blind date.'

'Well, it's not quite like that . . . Lana!' Annie warned her daughter with a look, but no . . .

'What do you mean "not quite like that"?' came Lana's testy response. 'Forty single strangers are getting together for dinner tonight and you're going to be one of them.'

'Well! What can I say?' Annie forced a smile onto her face and gritted her teeth. 'There's a first time for everything,' she managed.

'Right,' said Ed. He looked astonished, which made Annie feel slightly ridiculous and irritated. 'Best of luck,' he added.

'I'll tell you how it goes.' She tried not to snap, giving Lana a pointed glare. 'Anyway, a friend of mine, Connor, will be round later on. He's baby-sitting because I don't like to leave them alone at night. Do I, babies?'

Owen made vomiting noises while Lana crossed her arms and scowled at her mother.

Annie climbed the hotel's thickly carpeted staircase with unbridled optimism. This was a classy place. Nothing cheesy about it. Well, OK, maybe booking the 'Anne Boleyn' Function Room hadn't been the organisers' best decision . . . but red-carpet dinner dating was the way to go. Yes, it was expensive, at a moment in her financial life when she really couldn't afford it. But she was looking on it as an investment. Finding not just Mr Right, but Mr Wealthy-and-Right was going to be money so well spent.

How Dinah had rolled her eyes as Annie had read to her from the brochure: '"A gourmet dining experience with forty hand-selected singles . . ." Look through the guest list,' Annie had urged her, handing over the profile pages studded with grainy passport-sized photos. 'There's a property developer, a Czech businessman, a computer entrepreneur, someone interesting from the West Country . . .'

But Dinah had labelled each photo in her own way: 'Man who does DIY, Eastern European gangster, mono-browed Welsh werewolf . . .'

'Stop it!' Annie had ticked her off. 'What about him then?'—she'd ringed one profile—'Dominic runs a garden design consultancy. He loves French wine and Cuban music . . . Ooh!' Her eyebrows had perked up with interest. 'Half French. Now *he* is very, very promising.'

Smoothing down her dress, Annie opened the Anne Boleyn Room door and stepped inside. At a reception table directly in front of her an overenthusiastic girl with a stack of name badges was gushing, 'Hello and welcome to Discerning Diners.'

Name badges? Annie hadn't expected something as functional and conferencey as name badges, but far, far worse than that was the fact that everyone she could see milling around in the drinks area was dressed in regulation office clothes: the men were all in grey and navy suits, the women likewise. She was going to look like a divorced and desperate housewife amid all the high-flying, executive girls.

'So, what's your name?' the super-smiley blonde behind the desk wanted to know.

'It's Annie Valentine and . . . I thought we were supposed to dress up?' she added in dismay.

'We do ask everyone to make an effort, but I'm afraid so many people come straight from work, they don't have time. Can I take your jacket?'

'No . . . ummm . . . well . . .'

It was warm in the Anne Boleyn Room, too warm for yellow wool gabardine, especially now that she was feeling the added heat of embarrassment. She could either hover round the drinks reception quietly sweating her jacket up and her make-up off, or she could be brave and breezy and take it off. 'Yes, I suppose so,' she relented, slipping off the Valentino and exposing slim shoulder straps, bare arms and a lot more cleavage than the event required.

'I'm going on to another party afterwards.' Suddenly the perfect excuse, not to mention fib, sprang to mind. She would tell everyone this. Oh and it meant she could leave early *if*—surely no chance of this—the evening was a horror.

'OK, Annie. Hi! Welcome! I'll take you over to Hillary, who's going to introduce you to everyone.'

With Hillary at her side, Annie was whisked through a blur of faces, smiles and introductions. She recognised some names from her list: the Czech turned out to be a rather meek-looking salesman; Idris was indeed a mono-browed Welshman, though probably not a werewolf; most disappointing of all was 'very, very, promising' Dominic, the garden designer, who was handsome, but came in at about five foot three. So, Annie, in heels, was a clear eight inches or so taller than him.

When they were ushered through to dinner, she felt a little disheartened to see that the name tag on the place next to hers was Dominic's.

A rather shy, bland man called Will was seated on her left opposite a pale, nondescript woman called Maisie. But some sort of salvation seemed to loom in the form of Lloyd, the greying but nonetheless debonair-looking fifty-something opposite her. When he smiled, introduced himself and complimented Annie on her 'ravishing' dress, she found that her will to live seemed to be returning.

But over the starter Annie discovered that Lucinda, the woman seated on Lloyd's left, was also very taken with him.

Within minutes, it also became clear that Lucinda was very, very chatty and was imagining that she was helping everyone to mingle by going round the table asking all those excruciating personal questions Annie did not want to answer: 'Are you divorced?' 'What do you do for a living?'

As her turn to be asked approached, Annie made the mature decision to bolt for the loo. When she came back, she felt she should leave off Lloyd and devote some attention to Dominic, so as not to be rude.

'The wine's nice, isn't it?' she asked him, remembering his interest from the profile pages.

'Not bad at all,' he replied, turning the bottle to read the label.

'I've taken the decision not to drink plonk any more,' she explained. 'Life's just too short.'

He held up the bottle and said, 'Indeed,' as he refilled her glass.

Was it her imagination or had he given a little wince? What had she done? Maybe it was her use of the word 'short'. Subconsciously, she'd drawn attention to his height, or lack of it. Mental note not to use the word short again.

She asked him about his journey to the hotel and got an almost funny anecdote in reply. Half French, Cuban-music-loving Dominic should have been very promising date material. But eight inches . . . eight inches was quite a gap to overcome. Even sitting down, his head was tilted up to meet her eye level.

'Your nephew's at St Vincent's!' she exclaimed, because they had just made this discovery. 'Small world.'

He gave the little wince again. Ooops.

As the first course had arrived, they began to talk about favourite foods: vegetables, to be precise.

'Aubergine in a tomato ragout,' he was telling her.

'Dwarf beans, steamed with butter, delicious,' Annie said.

Dwarf?? Why did she have to say dwarf?

Lloyd shot her a wink. Was he just being friendly or had he noticed her unfortunate choice of words? By the way, that was Lloyd, property developer, divorced, no children—Lucinda had her uses.

After a few moments of attempting to make chit-chat with taciturn Will, Annie turned back to Dominic as it was hard to wrestle Lloyd from Lucinda's focused attention for more than a moment or two.

'I love her, she's adorable . . .' Dominic was telling Maisie about his long-standing admiration for the French actress Audrey Tatou.

'Oh, I feel the same way about Billy Crystal,' Annie chipped in. 'Although he's obviously tiny.' It was out of her mouth before she could even think about it.

Dominic's smile was definitely too tight at the edges.

'So, tell me about your gardening work?' she asked, deciding any sort of apology would just make things worse.

This turned out to be a good question. Dominic was very enthusiastic about his job and talked with animation about the Modern Garden.

Annie and several other diners listened closely, chipping in with questions about their own little plots, wondering if he could offer a few tips. This was one of the many sad things about getting older, Roddy always used to joke; suddenly everyone's as interested in gardens and where to score the best bedding plants as they used to be in drugs.

'It's not growing, it's just so . . . stumpy.' Aaargh! Wasn't there another word she could have used to describe a hedge that was failing to thrive?

Dominic glared at her but fortunately a little bell rang, which turned out to mean that the first course was finished and all the women had to stand up and move three places to their right. To Annie's relief, this put her in Lucinda's seat, right next to Lloyd.

Lloyd was a honey. He asked her about where she lived, he listened to her job description and property empire expansion plans with interest, he topped up her wineglass. She asked where he'd got his tan and he muttered modestly about business in Argentina and how a trip to the Caribbean made February so much more bearable.

Annie felt a warm wave of happiness wash over her. A warm, sun-kissed Caribbean wave of happiness. He was lovely. Perfect.

'So you have children, do you?' he asked.

'A gorgeous almost-fifteen-year-old, Lana, and Owen, who's nine.'

'Fifteen?!' Lloyd was trying to restrain himself from a splutter.

'Well, she's my love child,' Annie explained, always pleased with the 'you look so much younger' effect that mentioning her daughter had on people. 'I had her when I was twenty.'

'You're thirty-five?!!' Lloyd asked. 'But you look so much younger!' Unfortunately, this sounded almost angry, unlike the usual compliment that revealing her age brought her.

'Well, thank you.' She smiled at Lloyd, but he didn't look happy. 'What's the matter?' She decided it would be best to know.

'My cut-off point is thirty-three,' he said coldly.

'Thirty-three what?' she asked, not sure what he meant.

'Thirty-three years old,' he retorted. 'My ex-wife is thirty-four, so I'm going younger. *Much* younger.'

'Oh!' For a moment Annie was too taken aback to say anything. Then plenty of pithy responses came to mind like, 'You sad old goat', or 'Is dating a teenager so much fun?'

But she reined them in and settled on a dignified 'Well, Lloyd, that's your loss. Women get so much more interesting in their thirties. Not to mention *expert*.' Unfortunately, she followed this with a snarled, 'But why are you here when there are so many dodgy Thai agencies that could help you?'

There was nothing for it now. Time to execute plan A and claim she had to leave early to get to her 'other' fictional party.

With a quick glance round at everyone within earshot, she announced that she would have to leave and exited the table head high in what she hoped was a dignified manner. She buttoned her jacket up, fled to the first pub she could find and gulped down a Bailey's while waiting for her minicab to turn up, more thoroughly humiliated than she could ever remember feeling after any school disco.

As Annie walked to her front door, her phone beeped with a text from Dinah. DID I WIN THE BET? it read.

As she opened the door, she could hear the very, very welcome sound of Connor McCabe—the six-foot-three, dark-haired, devastatingly handsome actor that every woman deserved to have as a best friend—calling to her from the sitting room.

'Hello, sex bomb!' he greeted her. 'How did it go?'

Connor was sprawled right across her sofa, effortlessly gorgeous as always. Two empty beer cans and a family pack of cheese-and-onion crisps were on the table beside him. He had the remote in one hand, a late-night chat show murmuring on low volume on the telly.

'Snog!' he said, holding out his arms.

Annie leaned over and kissed him on the lips, feeling his arms hug her in tightly. He pulled her down onto the sofa on top of him.

'With or without tongues?' he joked, pecking at her lips again.

'I think without, what with the cheese and onion, but thanks for the offer,' Annie said, coming up for air. 'Nice to see you.' She tucked her head against his chest and smelt comforting manly scents of shaving cream, beer and well-worn jumper.

'So did you meet Mr Perfect?' he wanted to know.

'Yeah, right.' She rolled off and budged Connor over a bit so she was snugly sandwiched between the back of the sofa and his warm body. Ah, the comfort of a gay man. You could use their body for all the huggy, snugly stuff without risking any misunderstanding.

Then she gave him the story of the evening, blow by blow, leaving in as many stupid details and silly moments as she could.

'Anyway, how were the children?' she asked.

'They were fabulous,' he assured her. 'Lana's still awake in her room I think, listening to her iPod. Owen is probably playing the guitar under his covers to impress his music guru.'

'You met Ed?'

'Yes. I'm nearly as impressed with Edible Ed as your children are.'

'Ha. Edible Ed?' She wondered how anyone could find Ed remotely edible, unless they were a dust mite.

'C'mon,' Connor insisted. 'You've got to admit, he exudes a certain old-school charm . . . but the "gaydar" says he's not one for the boys.'

'No . . . school rumour is he's something of a ladies' man, but I find it hard to believe. How's your love life anyway?'

'Oh, absolutely nothing to report,' Connor assured her.

'So The Manor's policeman remains "the most eligible bachelor in showbiz" then?' she teased. 'I dunno, Connor. You're gorgeous, you're on TV, you're loaded—maybe people don't want to wake up and find themselves being interviewed by Grazia magazine?'

'Oh, very funny.'

She looked at his handsome chin. She'd inherited Connor. He'd been Roddy's best friend, but when Roddy exited stage left, he'd come over to her side. Connor and Roddy had met on some low-budget film set in Romania. They'd hatched a plan to leave their noble, badly paid film and theatre careers and break into soaps, Roddy as a sexy baddie and Connor as handsome, hunky boy-next-door.

After extensive restyling by Annie, Roddy had emerged as crew-cut, leather-jacketed, slightly stubbly and wicked, and had progressed from thug in *The Bill* to a bad, newly returned brother of somebody in *EastEnders*. Meanwhile, a scrubbed-clean, rosy-cheeked, knitwear-clad Connor had landed the starring role in the Sunday teatime-slot nostalgic series *The Manor*. On the back of this, stage roles in the West End came rolling in.

'How's work?' Annie asked.

'Oh daaaling, it's wonderful,' Connor said at first, then added grumpily, 'I'm never agreeing to go on stage again, it's bloody drudgery. When are you coming to see me anyway?'

'Oh, well . . . very soon,' she assured him, secretly thinking that musicals, even those by Noël Coward, weren't really her thing. 'Now, Connor,' she began, 'my gorgeous one?' She linked fingers with him.

'Uh-oh,' he replied. 'This sounds as if it's going to be dangerous— expensive—or possibly both.'

'I've got a favour to ask. Actually, two favours.'

'You'll definitely have to grovel. Preferably on your knees.'

'How do you feel about camping? The tent kind?' she added quickly.

Connor pulled a face. 'I know everything about camping and nothing about tents.'

'There's this male-bonding, man-and-boy, orienteering event—men and their sons, or their nephews, or their friends' sons even.' She caught his eye, to make sure he understood. 'And Owen has shown me a leaflet for it, has been saying, about fifteen times a day, "Wouldn't that be really good fun? Doesn't that sound like a great place?" and so on. You know how much camping he used to do with Roddy . . . and I can't think of anyone else who could take him.'

'I don't know anything about camping, Annie,' Connor moaned.

Annie gave a sigh, 'OK, OK, I'll let you off camping. But now you have to say yes to my next request. You know it's my mum's retirement party next month?'

'Would I be correct in thinking you're about to utter the oh-so-flattering words, "plus one"?'

'Connor?' Annie snuggled up against him. 'You could ask for favours in return for this. It's worth at least two, maybe even three extra discount purchases from the Annie V Trading Station.'

'Oh, thanks a lot!' he said huffily. 'I want free designer knickers or I don't cooperate.'

'I may be able to arrange that,' she said, recalling a pyramid of Calvin Kleins on three for two at TK Maxx.

'Big family gathering for the retirement?' he wondered.

Annie nodded. 'I don't want to go on my own. I mean, obviously Lana and Owen are coming, but I want someone there just for me.'

He stroked her hair, then let a smile break over his impressive features. 'Will there be ageing aunties?' he asked.

'At least three. Maybe four.'

'Ooh, I do like a tipsy ageing aunty, that's my core fan base, you know . . . Wild drunken dancing?'

'Definitely. A live band apparently because it's a Scottish-themed ceilidh evening. In fact'—she sat up and grinned at him: she had just had one of her best ideas of the day—'I'm going to hire you a kilt.'

'A kiltie?' Connor grinned back, revealing perfect—and laser-treated—teeth. 'Oh, yes, Annie, yes! One of those black leather ones?'

'Whatever turns you on, darlin'.'

Paula on parade:

Genuine Asian hair extensions, braided (Blaxx salon)
Spray-on black Gucci dress (The Store's sale preview)
Fuchsia thong (Brick Lane market, three for £1)
A 'Hollywood' wax (Blaxx)
Orange and fuchsia striped false nails (Blaxx)
Orange suede Jimmy Choo stilettos (mates' rates
at Annie V Trading Station)
Total est. cost: £805

'What's on special offer at Asda?'

'DELIA, GIRL, you're in early, aren't you?' On spotting the bustling, well-upholstered figure of the floor's cleaning lady, Annie had checked her watch and noted that it was still an hour and a half till closing time.

'I'm tidying out my cupboard,' Delia explained. Annie found this hard to understand as Delia kept the neatest cleaning cupboard in the Western world. The frayed mops were carefully rinsed out, squeezed and hung to dry; the cloths were pegged up on their own little washing line and the bottles of industrial cleansers and polishes were always wiped down and lined up on the shelves with all the labels facing out.

'Then I'm planning a little shop for myself.' Delia's gleaming dark face split with a giggle. Stepping close to Annie, she asked, 'I take it we're still OK with our little arrangement?'

'We certainly are,' Annie assured her, trying not to imagine what Donna would think of it.

On the very rare occasion when Delia bought something from The Store, Annie put it through the till under her name because she was entitled to a 20 per cent staff discount, whereas Delia, employed by a subcontracted cleaning company, was not—an injustice Annie was delighted to subvert. 'What are you buying?' she couldn't help asking.

'Oh, I'm going to enjoy myself looking for a while, then I'll come to you with my extravagances,' Delia chuckled and gave Annie's arm a squeeze, her chubby, dark brown hand adorned with five short, but beautifully lacquered plum fingernails. 'First off, I'm walking my butt to lingerie.'

'Oooh!' Annie teased. 'Something fancy?'

Delia gave her great rattling, throaty, chest-clearing laugh at this. 'Oh yeah . . . I'm gonna make some lucky man's day,' she chuckled.

Annie watched Delia walk off in the direction of the underwear department, still chuckling and swishing her substantial derrière from side to side just for Annie's benefit.

Delia had three jobs, four children and one cramped council flat on the very outer reaches of Isleworth. Considering her personal circumstances, she was allowed to be the most grouchy, bitchy, irritable person in the world, but Delia remained stubbornly happy and upbeat. Maybe it was her devout religion. Delia was always busy on Annie's behalf. 'I'm praying for you, baby. Don't even try telling me not to.'

But Annie, almost as much as Delia, understood that when life handed you a bum deal you either had to get up, put on your face, pull back your shoulders and make the best of it, or else go under.

The phone in the Personal Shopping suite began to ring, so Annie answered.

'Annie? Hi, it's Dale. You busy?'

'No one in at the moment,' she told him.

'I'm going to send someone up to you, then. Check yourself over in the mirror, girlfriend.'

Click. He hung up. She suspected this might have something to do with her coffee break chit-chat about how she was on the lookout for a *very* wealthy husband and couldn't you boys down there in Menswear do something to help me out?

Annie didn't trust Dale's judgment on a tie, let alone potential husband material, but nevertheless she redid her ponytail, applied a fresh dab of lip gloss, spritz of perfume and waited.

No sooner did she clap eyes on Mr Spencer Moore, as he was grandly introduced by Dale—weighed down by a selection of suits, shirts, jackets and ties—than her suspicions about the menswear assistant's judgement were confirmed. Spencer was gay. Definitely. Why hadn't Dale been able to tell? Weren't the round, red-rimmed glasses perched in the middle of his face clue enough?

'Mr Moore, hello, I'm Annie,' she gushed in the direction of the new arrival. 'Come in, come on in. I'm here to help, so . . . Take the lovely big changing room on the right here. We'll hang everything up for you.'

'He's gay!' she hissed at Dale as soon as she got the chance.

'Na-ah.' Dale raised his eyebrows at her teasingly. 'He's a divorced, straight man who dresses gay. I know. It's weird, he's an urban subspecies . . . I thought he needed a woman's touch, plus, you might get a date out of it. He's loaded,' he added in a whisper.

It turned out Spencer, late forties, fit and freshly divorced, obviously took the fashion section of the Sunday supplements far too seriously for a man of his age and status. Hence the confusing signals.

'Are you dating again, or is it too soon?' Annie asked, quickly defusing the rather bald question with, 'I'm just wondering if you'll need some more casual outfits?'

'Oh, definitely ready to date again,' Spencer confided as she paired a pale grey pinstriped suit with a pastel-coloured shirt and tie and urged him to try them on.

'So, we have to make a babe magnet of you,' she smiled.

'Er, well . . .'

She had to tone it down, she told herself. Clearly, he was a reserved kind of guy. 'Where do you live?' she asked him from the other side of the drawn curtain as he tried on the outfit she'd suggested.

'Kensington,' he told her. And didn't return the question, she noticed. Some customers always assumed that shop staff were so beneath them. It was up to her to put herself in a very different light.

'Oh, lovely,' she told him. 'I was at school there. Francis Holland.' There, that would put him straight. Everyone had heard of Francis Holland, one of the smartest all-girl schools in London.

'Really?!' It was a little too surprised.

'Yes. I loved it. I discovered art there.' Now she was sounding posher than the Queen. 'Yeah, then did art school afterwards: theatre costume and design. I worked in films for a bit and now I'm a consultant here.' Consultant sounded great. As if she didn't work here all the time. As if she had another high-flying career elsewhere, away from The Store. It seemed to do the trick. Spencer asked which art school she'd gone to and told her where he'd studied.

Then he pulled open the curtain, stepped out and asked, 'What do you think?' making eye contact now, appreciating that he was dealing with a high-calibre 'consultant'.

He looked good. The suit was a great cut but roomier and so a little more macho than the one he'd come in wearing. The pale pink suited his complexion. She couldn't get past those awful glasses though.

'Nice.' She stroked down the lapels, then made him turn round so she could run her hands over his shoulders and back, all in the name of smoothing out the suit, obviously. 'Very nice. We'll put that on the "definitely maybe" rail and then I want you to try this on.'

She held out a cashmere blend Nicole Farhi. Super-hetero wear. 'This is real quality, Mr Moore. I don't waste my money on anything inferior.'

He took the suit from her, meeting her eyes and brushing past her hand in the process, which she took to be an excellent sign. She pulled the curtain shut and grinned.

'"*Nowt as expensive as cheap*," as my dad used to say.' When Spencer made no response to this, she explained: 'Because cheap things wear out so quickly and have to be replaced.'

But then Paula breezed in and asked in a loud voice, 'Hey, Annie, what's on special offer at Asda this week?'

Annie pulled a face and pointed at the curtain.

'All right,' Paula said, more quietly, 'but I've got loads of birthdays coming up, no money and I need to know where to get cheap presents.'

'Later!' Annie hissed.

Joy of joys, their boss Donna was now striding into the suite looking as if she'd bitten on a bee, 'Paula! Annie's office, now!' she barked, acknowledging Annie only with a quick raise of the eyebrow.

'Yes, that will be fine, Donna,' Annie told her with mock politeness. 'Please make yourself at home in my office.' Clearly a major telling-off was about to rain down on Paula's pretty, plaited head.

Oblivious to the latest developments in in-store politics, Spencer pulled back the curtain to have his second outfit appraised.

'Hmm . . .' Annie wasn't as happy with this one. Together, they sorted through Dale's selections for the next possible ensemble.

Once Spencer was safely back behind the curtain, Annie decided that she couldn't leave Paula in there to face the witch alone.

She tapped on the door of her office and opened it without waiting for a reply. 'Is everything OK in here?' she asked.

One glance at Paula's tear-stained face told her that it was not.

'Can I help with anything at all, Donna?' she went on. 'Would you like me to explain anything? I do oversee Paula after all.'

Donna spat out, 'We've had the suite's sales figures in for the month and Paula's are way down on January.'

'But February is always lower than January,' Annie reminded her, trying to keep the indignation out of her voice.

'I'm aware of the general pattern of annual sales, thank you, Annie,' Donna snapped, 'but Paula's figures are much lower than they should be. There's a job on the shop floor open, so I'm pulling Paula out of here. People come to the Personal Shopping suite desperate to buy new clothes. If Paula can't sell to them, then who the hell can she sell to?'

Despite her written warning, Annie couldn't help mentioning 'the difficult new collections' in Paula's defence. What she would have loved to say was that if Donna hadn't gone to the trade shows right after she'd been dumped by her girlfriend, then maybe the collections wouldn't be quite so *difficult*. The sales team were now flat out trying to shift 'tulip' skirts (i.e. universally unflattering sacks) in shades of 'mushroom' and 'taupe' (otherwise known as hessian), not to mention cashmere trapeze tops in screaming orange and lime.

'Don't ever, ever complain about my collections!' Donna looked poised to gouge out an eye now. 'The Store is proud to showcase some of the most cutting-edge fashion in London . . . in the world!'

Annie was bursting to say, 'I rest my case.' But she had her own interests to look after, as well as Paula's. She heard Spencer opening the changing-room curtain, so knew she had to get back, but before she did Donna managed to issue another threat: 'And don't you dare abuse your staff discount. If I find anyone has used it apart from you . . .'

Vicious cow.

Spencer was happily admiring himself in the mirror. 'This is fantastic! You're a genius!' he enthused, which cheered her up immediately. 'I'd never have thought of Romeo Gigli. I thought he was for girls.'

'Italian,' she told him. 'You can't go wrong with a good Italian. Mr Moore . . .' she began.

'Please, call me Spencer.' He straightened the heavy silk tie.

'OK, Spencer . . . we have to talk about your glasses.'

'Do we?'

'Yes, we do.' Annie leaned in to tell him gently, as if breaking seriously bad news. 'I'm sorry, this may come as a terrible shock, but those are gay glasses.'

'Oh? The glasses? The glasses are gay?' He sounded completely taken aback.

'Yup. Definitely,' she assured him. 'Your shoes too. Too pointed and with top-stitching. I'd even say the belt as well. Women pick up on these things and you are giving off a gay vibe. Which is obviously great, if you're gay. But you're not. Right?'

'Well, no.'

'You need something smaller, maybe with a silver frame . . .' She stared quite unapologetically at his face. Not bad, she was thinking, in need of some general upgrading but some excellent period features.

'You'd look very handsome with contacts,' she told him. 'We definitely need a moss green tie for you. With those distracting red frames, I hadn't noticed your eyes were green. We need to find you ties in exactly the same shade. But don't wear them with the pink shirt . . . obviously.'

Spencer had the decency to blush slightly. He was really quite nice; she was warming to him by the moment.

'Try on the Paul Smith,' she told him. 'I'll go in search of ties.'

As she stepped out of the suite, she ran right into Delia.

'Annie, I'm back . . . laden down!' An even happier Delia was carrying one of The Store's pink rubber shopping baskets. Annie ushered her to a till well away from the Personal Shopping suite. Donna would be out of there like an angry wasp any moment, but there was no question of letting Delia down.

Annie tapped her code into the computer and rang up Delia's treats: four pairs of Sloggi super-comfort thongs, size 22, Chanel No. 5 bath soap and a Mac nail varnish in brightest orange. All good choices. Every woman, no matter how hard pressed, needed box-new, comfortable thongs in the knicker drawer, a perfectly indulgent bar of soap and a flash of designer colour, even if it was just on the nails.

Delia was just bustling out of sight when Donna stormed out, spotted Annie at the till and for one long, eerie moment stared straight at her. But then she carried on.

With a selection of ties in her hand, Annie headed back to the suite, taking a moment to pep talk Paula, before she returned to Spencer.

'C'mon, girl,' she said and passed Paula a tissue. 'Don't let the Queen of Spleen get you down. Do a stint on the sales floor and then I'll wangle you back in here again. Honest. You just need practice. C'mon.' Annie worried about the proximity of Paula's nails to her tearful eyes.

'We're supposed to go out tonight, aren't we?' Annie reminded her. 'So glad rags on. Touch up the face. I'll be with you in'—she checked her watch—'twenty or so.'

Spencer was tiring of trying new things on. Men's shopping tolerance was so tragically low, she'd noted before. It was time to close the deal with him . . . on all fronts. Two suits, four shirts, two green ties (he must have liked the eye compliments), a pale suede blazer, two T-shirts and six pairs of new boxers, because 'You never know,' she'd said, as she winked at him cheekily.

'I've never, ever bought this much all at once before.' He looked concerned at the packed rail they'd amassed.

'You're going to get total value for money from these clothes and wear them to bits,' she assured him. 'You've got to start going out straight away. This week! Tonight!' Was that hint enough?

But nothing came, so she prompted, 'What's your idea of a good night out?'

He thought for a moment before telling her. 'You know what I like? A really well-made gin and tonic in a great bar. Somewhere with atmosphere, not too noisy, not too quiet. Somewhere . . .'

'Classy.' She finished his sentence.

'I can't stand cocktails and girlie drinks, happy hour, all that sort of thing,' he added.

'No, no. Me neither,' she nodded, but these words just served to summon up Paula, in a spray-on black dress and neon heels.

'Annie, are you ready yet?! We're going to miss happy hour at Freddy's and we're sharing a jug of margaritas after the day I've had.'

Classy. Oh yes.

'Theatre? I bet you like the theatre?' Annie made one last attempt at somehow connecting with Spencer, as she rang up his purchases.

'Oh, yes. I'm going to the Noël Coward thing that's just opened; what's it called again?'

'*After the Ball*? When?' Annie could barely contain her grin.

'Thursday night, I think.'

'No! Really?' she gushed. 'My friend is in one of the lead roles and that's the night he's invited me along. He says Thursday night is the real theatre buff's night.' She was making this up as she went along.

'Really!' Spencer didn't sound quite as pleased as she'd hoped.

'I might see you there then, in your fabulous new clothes.'

'Well, yes . . . That would be nice . . .'

It was hard to judge whether Spencer was pleased at this turn of events, or worried that he now had a stalker on his hands.

Megan's outfit for her ex-husband's wedding:

Missoni dress (The Store)
Manolo boots (The Store)
Gucci bag (Gucci)
Philip Treacy hat (The Store)
3.5-carat emerald engagement ring (ex-husband)
Cartier diamond watch (ex-husband)
Asprey gold and diamond bracelet (ex-husband)
Total est. cost £220,000

'I want to look everything his cheap little girlfriend is not.'

'Nooooooooooooo!' shrieked Taylor. She yanked the four-figure Matthew Williamson creation up over her head and tossed it onto the floor. 'No more empire lines! They make me look fucking pregnant!'

'Taylor!' Megan warned in knee-jerk reaction to the swearing.

Annie was so exhausted, she was going to have to mainline Red Bull when this ordeal was finally over. She'd already been with Taylor and her terrifying mother, Megan, here to choose outfits for Taylor's father's remarriage, for one and a half hours. The hour spent finding Megan's perfect outfit had passed satisfyingly well. She had come in with a wonderfully clear idea: 'I want a severely smart dress. I want to look everything his . . .'—dramatic pause to deliver these words as witheringly as possible—'cheap, little girlfriend is not: sophisticated, complicated, intelligent, elegant and grown-up.' It hadn't taken long to find the dress: cream with an olive-coloured leaf print, Missoni, comfortingly extortionate.

But Taylor was, like every precocious sixteen-year-old, a special shopping challenge. She was extraordinarily pretty, with long flicky blonde hair and the lean, perfectly proportioned body and dewy complexion born of great genes and lashings of money.

Megan wanted Taylor to wear something sweet and girly, whereas Taylor wanted the kind of dress a thirty-year-old vamp would consider daring. It didn't look as if they were ever going to agree.

Taylor had dismissed all suits as 'bo-oh-ring', including a gorgeous pale pink Miu Miu.

'I want the black wrap! Pleeeeease,' Taylor whined, sounding more and more like the spoilt princess she was.

Megan drew herself up to full height, formidable in head to toe Dior, before explaining once again. 'Taylor, you cannot wear black to your father's wedding. Absolutely no! Look,' she added bitchily, 'I don't think he should be marrying a twenty-two-year-old Romanian gymnast either, but we can't go in mourning and that's final.'

Annie had to turn her mind to very sad and lonely thoughts, to prevent herself from snorting with laughter at this. Megan was far, far from over the biggest disappointment of her life. Her marriage to Mr Fabulously Wealthy Bigwig had ended and she was still devastated by her loss of status. Although—Annie couldn't help thinking—surely the jewels and the annual allowance, generous enough to make small African nations weep, must be of some comfort?

'I think we need a little break,' Annie suggested in UN-style peace-keeping mode as Taylor flung another dress on the floor. 'Why don't we go down to the vintage boutique in the basement?' she risked.

Taylor's response to this looked reasonable, but Megan's eyebrows were arched and twitching.

'Don't worry,' Annie soothed, 'it's The Store's version of vintage: exclusive one-offs and collector's items worth more now than when they were bought.'

Down in the glamorous basement floor, a section had been made over as an antique clothes shop, complete with picturesque, worn wooden shelves crammed with dainty crocodile handbags, long leather gloves, feathered and furred hats. The rails were adorned with silks, lace, taffeta, chiffon. Dresses with history. Ghosts from parties that had been held all over the city since the 1920s.

Annie had always liked secondhand; these were not dresses that whispered 'you shall go to the ball'; these gowns had been to the ball, danced till they dropped, sipped champagne, met the man of their dreams, sneaked a cigarette or two, kissed, maybe more, and come back to tell the tale.

Taylor was already flicking through the size eights and tens with a keen eye and, as Annie stood outside the fitting room, she tried dresses on with a serious intent than she had before.

She looked dangerously close to declaring, 'This is the one,' in a boat-necked slim taffeta dress, turquoise with big silver buttons, which made her look like an old-time Hollywood starlet.

'Oh, that is pretty,' was Megan's verdict. 'With silver shoes maybe . . .'

'Hmmm . . .' Taylor was not quite 100 per cent happy.

'We've still got a few more.' Annie handed over a deep-sea-blue satin Chinese-style dress, with a high mandarin collar, a row of tiny satin-covered buttons that led all the way down to the knee and unusually modern sleeves that stopped just past the elbow. Annie thought it was very promising.

Taylor took it into the fitting room and after several minutes of wriggling and wrestling with hooks and eyes, she opened the curtain with something of a flourish.

'What do you think?' She looked at Annie first then her mum. Annie suspected Taylor loved it, but wanted to sound them out first.

How could she not love it? She looked incredible.

Megan seemed quite mesmerised by the effect too. To her, the dress still looked girlish and charming. To Taylor it was dangerously sophisticated. So it was perfect for the wedding, and yet, of course, quite devastatingly sexy.

Taylor declared, 'I love it. I don't care if I never get another penny of pocket money this year . . . I have to have it . . . oh and a bag and shoes to go with it, *obviously*.' She peeped up at her mama with a wheedling little smile.

Megan gave a nod. 'OK, back upstairs, we'll go and look at shoes.'

Annie made an excuse to go back to her office for a few minutes where she hoovered up her entire stash of emergency chocolate. And she'd thought choosing outfits with Lana was hard work.

'**S**he didn't want a *Matthew Williamson*?!' Lana wanted to make sure she'd heard that bit right.

'Balled it up and chucked it on the floor!' Annie elaborated, passing thirds of garlic bread over to Owen, who'd already ravenously polished off everything else on his plate.

'No!' Lana sounded quite thrilled by this sacrilege. 'On the floor!'

'Miu Miu was rejected, Marc Jacobs she wouldn't even try on, Chloé was "so over"—God, she was a nightmare. Imagine being able to afford any designer dress you could imagine, plus the bag, the shoes and real jewels to go with it, and being so miserable! Such a waste.' Annie forked up the last rubbery mouthful of Spanish omelette and chewed . . . for quite a long time. Her omelettes were never 'fluffy' like Dinah's; they were tough. Why was that?

'So, have you had a chance to think about what you'd like to wear to Grandma's retirement party?' she asked Lana, while they were on the subject of teen dress traumas.

Something about Lana's smile made Annie slightly anxious.

Lana didn't shop with her mother any more. All day long Annie styled others while the one person she'd always loved to dress found it 'too much pressure' to go shopping with her. Since Annie and Lana's last changing-room tantrum over a five-inch-long miniskirt for school, Lana now only shopped with other members of the Syrup Six—Annie liked that nickname, it had stuck in her mind ever since Mr Leon, no, must-remember-to-call-him-Ed, had told her about it.

'Have you bought something?' Annie tried to sound pleased. 'Come on then, show me.'

She didn't really feel she'd been adequately prepared for the sheer, backless, slashed-to-the-upper-thigh frothy black lace creation hanging on the front of Lana's wardrobe, still with its Primark price tag proudly attached. Scratchy black nylon lace . . . nice . . . if Lana went anywhere near a candle in that thing, she'd be toast.

'Oh! Well! Yes!' Annie began, trying to muster as much calm as she could from the torrent of maternal negativity pulsing through her brain. No use, she couldn't help blurting out, 'You're fourteen, Lana! But you've gone straight from velvet with bows to see-through lace. Weren't we meant to have the taffeta years in between?' Even as Annie said it, she knew it sounded unlikely.

But she'd love to see Lana shine in bright blue: an iridescent silk that exactly matched the colour of her astonishing eyes. Annie—who had brown eyes, who had coveted Roddy from the moment he'd set his swimming-pool-blue eyes on her—could be overwhelmed by Lana's eyes. Lana had sensed this weakness, of course, and in an argument she did everything she could to make eye contact with her mother.

'This is the dress I want to wear,' she said fiercely.

'But why?' Annie asked.

'Because it's cool . . . and I think I look good in it.'

'Does it make you look a lot older?'

'Maybe.'

'Do you want boys to think you're older?'

'Maybe.' Her arms crossed and she huffed.

Annie was now tempted to shout all sorts of unhelpful, bossy mum warnings: *'Haven't you heard of date rape?' 'You'll look so tarty in this!' 'This is your granny's party!'* and so on, but she restrained herself.

'I know this isn't what you want to hear, Lana,' she began, 'but there's no need to be in such a rush to grow up. Honestly. Take your time.'

Lana just gave an exasperated sigh. Again, Annie bit her tongue. 'Why don't you put the dress on for me?' she asked.

'No!'

'Oh, please . . . I'll be totally constructive. On my best behaviour.'

Once Lana was standing in front of her, hands on lace-clad hips, face in a defiant pout, Annie knew she had to proceed with caution, utmost caution, or she would never, ever be allowed to shop with Lana again.

The dress looked . . . well . . . being totally honest . . . looking as neutrally as possible . . .

'Turn round, baby . . .' she instructed. 'I like the back. Your back looks lovely. You'll have to wear one of those backless bra contraptions . . .'

'I've already bought one,' Lana said grumpily.

'And what about shoes?'

Lana slipped on wine-coloured suede slingbacks. They looked fine.

'Hmmm.' Annie tried to keep her professional eye on this. Not her maternal eye ,which was, just like Megan's earlier today, finding it hard to move past the cleavage on display, the acre of creamy teen thigh. Lana had a good figure, Annie couldn't help but proudly notice.

'Did it come in any other colours?' Annie wondered.

'Muuuum!' Lana warned, but then volunteered the information, 'Navy blue and purple.'

'And you wouldn't consider maybe . . .'

Lana just glared.

'Just a second, I have something that could . . .' Annie went out of the room, took deep breaths and counted to ten. After a few minutes, she came back in with a large, overblown fake rose, almost the exact shade of Lana's shoes. 'Can we try it pinned to the front?' she asked. 'It's just . . . I'm not sure you'll want Granny's boyfriends talking to your boobs all night long, will you?'

A smile almost threatened to break over Lana's face now.

Annie pinned the flower in place.

'A little sparkly, wine-coloured shrug . . . would you let me treat you to something like that?' Annie asked.

'Maybe.' Lana didn't sound convinced.

'A little bag?' Annie added.

'Maybe.'

'And just maybe, maybe, maybe . . .' she wheedled, 'we could just pop back to the shop and try . . . just *try* . . . the navy blue?'

'Maybe.' But this came with the teensiest smile, which gave Annie the hope that her foot was in the door. She would broach the subject of stitching the split to a more modest knee-high another day.

That night, in front of her computer, watching the latest Trading Station deals close, Annie let her mind wander to her own outfit for the retirement party. There were things in the wardrobe, obviously, but she wasn't sure if she wanted to wear them. She'd tried on a four-year-old party dress in front of the full-length mirror in her bedroom, but it had brought tears to her eyes. The dress, sky blue slippy satin with vivid red poppies printed all over it, was a Roddy dress. She'd bought it for a first proper celebby event. Red-carpet, cameras flashing . . . Roddy's reaction to her dress had been a frank, succinct Roddy special: 'Fucking brilliant! Take it off, immediately!'

Alone, in front of the mirror, Annie unzipped it, let it fall to the floor, wondering if she would ever be able to wear it again.

Never mind, she told herself, blowing her nose firmly when the tears were over. There was the rose-pink velvet dress she'd seen on eBay; she knew the label; it would definitely fit. It would be perfect, in fact. It was probably going to go for too much . . . but it wouldn't hurt to look, would it? Just a teensy peek?

Dress-up Dinah:

Gold Grecian goddess dress (Miss Selfridge)
White fake fur coat (Cancer Research)
Gold tap shoes (Dancewear shop)
Gold and ruby earrings (Portobello market)
Liberal amount of Fake Bake
Total est. cost: £95

'I've overdone it. I'm the Fake Bake sheikh.'

'HE'S THERE! I've just spotted him, down at the front. Best seats!' Annie couldn't keep the glee from her voice as she told Dinah.

'Thank God for that,' was Dinah's response. It was obvious from the outset that Annie's outing to *After the Ball* was not purely in the interest of theatrical pleasure or even Connor support. She'd insisted Dinah 'dress up', then she'd confided there was 'someone' she was hoping to 'bump into' in the audience.

Annie had turned up at the theatre looking her very best. She'd come straight from work, but this hadn't stopped her devoting twenty-five minutes to her outfit, hair and make-up in the changing room.

'Oooh, very . . . Mediterranean,' Annie had greeted her sister.

'Shut up!' an extremely tanned Dinah had told her through gritted teeth. 'I know, I know, I've overdone it. I'm the Fake Bake sheikh.'

The first fake tan of the season (March had just arrived) was always an initiation. Dinah had forgotten how little of the stuff was needed.

'Do I look different?' Annie had asked her sister.

'You look great,' Dinah had assured her. 'I always love you in that dress.' She had surveyed the black crêpe Diane von Furstenberg wrap approvingly.

'Yeah, but look closely, babes,' Annie instructed, fluttering her eyelashes. 'Clue,' she said.

When Dinah had just stared back blankly, Annie had explained, 'I've had eyelash extensions. Aren't they gorgeous?'

'Eyelash extensions?' Dinah had never even heard of such a thing.

'I went with Connor,' Annie had explained. She had scanned the foyer like a twitchy bird of prey, as they went in.

'Connor?'

'He needs them for his close-ups, apparently. It makes all the grannies swoon when McCabe bats his lovely long lashes in soft focus.'

'Ha. Will you stop looking round like that?' Dinah had hissed. 'You look like you're wanted by the Mafia or something.'

'I can't see him.' Maybe she'd scared him off.

Although they were among the last to take their seats, she still hadn't spotted him; no sign of him in the interval either. It was distracting her immensely from Connor's clever, comic performance. But just as the lights were starting to dim for the third act, Annie's eyes alighted on a promising-looking head of grey hair and she watched as Spencer— minus the glasses—glanced over his shoulder.

'Bingo!' she told Dinah and began to plan for the 'accidental' meeting at the end of the show.

'Spencer, hi!' she called, frantically treading on toes in her rush to get out of her row and greet him.

'Oh, er . . . hello,' he managed once he had got her into focus. Maybe he hadn't sorted out the contacts yet.

'Did you enjoy the show? Wasn't Connor great?'

'Oh, Connor McCabe, is he the actor you . . . ?'

'Yes, yes . . .' And who was this woman by his side, so obviously with him? This attractive, raven-haired sophisticate in an elegant grey pashmina?

'This is my sister Dinah,' Annie offered as Dinah came up behind her. 'She's been on holiday.' Well, it seemed necessary to offer some sort of explanation, although the urge to add *in her bathroom* was strong.

'Oh, really, where've you been?' Spencer asked politely.

'Dubai!' Annie answered for her, inspired by the sheikh comment.

The elegant one cleared her throat slightly.

'Oh, Louisa, this is Annie. I met her just the other day, we were . . . um . . . introduced by a friend. This is Louisa, my date.' He smiled shyly at grey pashmina girl. 'You don't mind if I call you that, do you?'

Louisa beamed.

Annie's hopes were dashed.

'Why don't you come backstage with us and meet Connor?' was Annie's fresh new idea. 'He'd love it.'

Connor was slightly taken aback by the rapturous 'Darling, you were wonderful' and full-on mouth kiss that Annie treated him to. 'You were brilliant, honestly! Connor, this is Spencer, and his lovely date Louisa.'

At these words, Connor understood his role completely. 'Pleased to meet you! Very nice of you to come backstage to say hello.' He shook their hands and casually folded Annie in under his arm, hugging her tightly round the waist. 'You really did enjoy it, did you?'

'Oh, yes,' they both gushed.

'I think Noël Coward has so much to say to twenty-first century audiences and he always says it so wittily . . .' Connor began.

And so it went on, getting luvvier and luvvier by the minute, until Spencer warned that they would have to make a move or else they'd be too late for the table he'd reserved at the Ivy.

Ha! The Ivy for dinner, huh? Annie couldn't help feeling a stab of jealousy. 'How lovely,' she said.

'What on earth were you two playing at?' Dinah wanted to know when Spencer and his date had left.

'Oh, Dinah! You are just so sweet!' Annie teased her. 'Luckily Connor understands. It's just the same with handbags.'

'What is?'

'You only want a handbag if somebody else has it or if it's hard to get hold of, a limited edition, or collector's item. I'm expecting a message from Spencer on the Personal Shopping suite's answering machine tomorrow morning, guaranteed,' Annie told her.

'Hmmm.' Dinah couldn't help feeling this was a tad optimistic.

'Woooo hooo! We're so hot, we're smokin'! Every single one of us is going to pull tonight . . . Especially Owen,' was Connor's verdict as the party of four got out of the car and launched themselves—arm in arm, as he'd insisted—across the gravelled courtyard towards the country-house hotel Annie's mother had chosen for her retirement party.

Annie smiled proudly at her children. Lana, negotiating heels, bag, fluffy bolero, way too much purple eye shadow and the lace dress (in navy), returned the smile a little nervously, but Owen grinned. He'd gone for a hired mini dinner suit with wing collar and red satin bow tie.

Connor in black leather kilt, ruffled shirt and black leather waistcoat looked unforgettable: 100 per cent Highland hunk.

'Now remember, Owen, the fact that you are a man of few words is going to stand you in great stead tonight,' Connor was confiding to his youngest friend. 'The ladies love a bit of mystery. I am always saying far too much, shooting my mouth off, and that's why I am sooo single.'

Owen giggled at this.

'Lana, you are a knockout,' Connor assured her. 'I'll have to be your bodyguard for the evening to keep the swarms of suitors at bay.'

'Oh, ha ha,' she told him, but a smile was breaking at the corners of her mouth and threatening to run away across her face.

The sweetheart, Annie thought.

With her hair piled up glamorously, bright lipstick and highest heels, Annie felt the soft pink velvet of her breathtaking dress stroke comfortingly against her. There were going to be many people at this party that she hadn't seen since her sudden, devastating transformation from happily married to single, and she wanted to show them how together she was now. The dress was her suit of shining armour, although she would be selling it on . . . tonight, hopefully.

And anyway, while Annie awaited Spencer's phone call—two weeks had passed and still nothing!—and her next Discerning Dinner, what harm could there be in checking out the party talent?

'I've invited someone very interesting, just for you,' Fern had told her, when they'd met up three days ago for a pre-party nerve-calming afternoon. Fern had had to put her outfit on yet again just to make sure she was totally happy with it. Annie had been on hand to soothe and recommend make-up.

'Uh-oh!' was Annie's reaction to 'someone very interesting'. 'I've told you, Mum, our tastes in men are a little different. Is your fancy boy coming? Mr Lubkin and his Zimmer frame?' she'd asked, which had caused her mother to hoot with laughter.

'Walking stick, Annie!' Fern had corrected. 'He broke his leg hang-gliding and now walks with a stick. And he's a *friend*.'

'Ooooh, fancy. Mum . . .' Annie had asked her next, 'do you ever mind that you're still on your own?'

'No, no,' Fern had insisted with a smile. 'I was far too busy to find someone else when you were growing up, and then I was too bossy and now I'm too old. Past it.'

'Sixty is not the same as dead, Mum,' Annie had told her.

'To most men it is,' Fern had replied.

Annie had considered telling her mother, 'I think you've missed out. You never got all the really good stuff about being a couple.' She was even tempted to blurt out: 'I'm not fine like this. Some days I feel like

I'm missing an arm . . . like I'm hardly even alive!' Instead, she'd kept quiet, but Fern had seemed to read her feelings and had said gently, 'You've had a very hard time, sweetheart. It'll take a long time to begin to feel normal again. But you'll get there. I know you will.'

'I've brought you a present.' Annie had surprised Fern, handing over a wrapped, pink-ribboned box. 'I'm treating you . . . and I want you to know I paid full price, you old moo, because you're worth it.' Then, in a much more serious voice she'd added, 'Thank you, you know, for everything. You've been such a help to me . . .' and they'd both had to hug very tightly and squeeze back their tears.

Her mother's reaction to the pale cappuccino-coloured suede heels inside the box seemed to be very positive. She'd tried them on underneath her pink skirt, oooohed and aaaahed, had said many, many thank-yous. But Annie still wasn't convinced her mother *really* liked them.

Fern had always been a grade A dresser. She lived in wool trousers, silk blouses and little cashmere cardigans. A fabulous coat or jacket completed the classic look.

Now that the days of scraping together school fees were long behind her, Fern had a little more money to herself. She lived in a modest bungalow but bought top-quality clothes, drove a classic Jag and had never, ever been seen with her legs in need of a wax or with one single grey millimetre of root emerging from her blonde bob. 'If I'm not wearing lipstick, you'll know I'm dead,' she'd once told her daughters.

But Fern did have one fatal dressing flaw, which Annie was constantly trying to correct. Because Fern was a podiatrist, she dealt with so much footwear-inflicted misery that she would never, ever wear pretty shoes. Even her most delicate of outfits was finished off with duck feet: sensible pumps, low squared heels, or worst of all, those white comfy slingbacks that were a great favourite with H.M. The Queen, a woman Fern greatly admired, by the way.

Annie, shocked by the beige, orthopaedic-looking things her mother was intending to wear with her party outfit, had decided the only way to persuade her otherwise was to buy the alternative footwear herself.

With Connor on one arm and Owen linked to Lana on the other, Annie went through the foyer of the swanky hotel and into the tasteful drawing room, already swarming with guests.

Dinah spotted them before anyone else. 'Hey, Annie and the gang are here! Annie Valentine, you are wearing a sensational *new* dress . . . you bad girl!'

'Yeah, but I'm going to sell it tonight, so it's OK. Watch and learn,' Annie said with a wink. 'Is that Nic, our lawyer, over there?'

Nic was their middle sister, the lawyer, who they hardly ever saw because she lived in Cornwall and was extremely busy, being a lawyer. Oh, and by the way, had she mentioned Nic was a lawyer?

'C'mon, I'll take you over. She's brought her new man, Rick,' Dinah whispered. 'And guess what, he's a lawyer.'

'No! That's amazing, because you'll never guess? Nic's a lawyer too!'

They did their hugs, hellos, how are yous, how are the children . . . then Annie was properly introduced to Nic's new man and immediately asked how they'd met.

'Oh, through work,' came the reply.

'Aha . . . maybe I should retrain. Do you think I'd make a good lawyer?' Annie joked.

'No,' Nic told her, 'but you're a wonderful shopper. Tell me about this dress. I love it. Love it! Much better than this disaster.' She gestured at her long-sleeved navy and silver matronly frock—there wasn't a better word to describe it. Good grief, unless Annie was actually in the shop with Nic, telling her what to buy, she got it wrong every time.

'Feel.' Annie held out her arm. 'Feel the sleeve, go on. Silk velvet. Mmmmm. And isn't this just the perfect shade of salmon pink for our skin colouring, babes?'

Nic's fingers were rubbing against the material. 'That is gorgeous. Where is it from? It looks like one of our favourite labels.'

'No, no, no, you don't, Nicky. Look at her.' Annie winked at Nic's really very impressive Rick. 'She'd have the clothes off my back. She was always like this. Stealing stuff out of my cupboard.'

'Did not!' Nic protested. 'But I do like that dress. It's a Dries, isn't it? What do you think, Rick? Would I look good in that or not?'

Rick looked slightly uncomfortable at having to scrutinise a woman he'd only just met and imagine her dress on his girlfriend.

'This is not for sale,' Annie insisted.

'Of course it is, Annie,' Nic countered. 'Everything you own is for sale. Always has been. And we're exactly the same size . . .'

'Speak to me later,' Annie whispered. 'You might be able to persuade me once I've had a drink or two.

'Mum!' Annie took in the pink and white vision that was their mother making a beeline for them. 'Belle of the ball!' She hugged her, but then she pulled back, looked down and saw not the suede creations she'd parted with £250 of her hard-earned cash to buy, but the bloody beige orthopaedic sandals! 'Muuuum!' she scolded.

'Oh, I can't drive the Jag in those heels, sweetheart,' was her mother's practical explanation.

'I thought we'd agreed you were getting a taxi!' Annie exclaimed.

'I hate taxis. Such a waste of money,' her mother replied, but before she could be told off further, she was swept away by a tide of new guests.

Owen and Lana were still hovering not far from Annie's side, Owen very shy in the presence of so many friends and relations. 'You're going to be fine,' Annie reassured him.

'Annie Valentine!'

They pulled to a stop in front of Aunty Hilda, the old crone.

She was Fern's aunt, Annie's great-aunt. She was acidic, rude and wealthy so she felt entitled to be judgmental and critical. She was also family, so was tolerated and invited.

'Aunty Hilda, how are you doing?'

'You're looking nice, dear,' was Hilda's verdict after a lengthy up-and-down, but it came with the rider, 'for a change.' She was so hard of hearing now that she spoke in harsh silence-slicing sentences. 'Oh, and Owen here'—she pulled him in with her meaty arm for a sadistically close hug—'You're so tall and handsome, but still the deaf mute?'

'No! He's not that at all—' Annie began but Hilda chose not to hear and carried on. 'Lana? Ah, well . . .'

Annie wanted to put her arm up to defend her daughter and issue a stern, *Oh no you don't, you evil old bag, fragile teenage ego in development.*

'Hmmm . . . feathers?' Hilda remarked of Lana's bolero, in a way that conveyed her deepest disregard for plumage.

Annie hoped Lana wasn't going to say anything regrettable.

'Well now.' Hilda met Annie's gaze with cool blue eyes, misting with age. 'And where's your husband Roddy? You haven't gone and got your-self divorced as well, have you, like your mother and your sister?'

As if this was some kind of witty conversational gambit.

Where's Roddy? Annie turned the question over in her mind. She and Aunty Hilda weren't exactly close. Hilda was in her eighties, her memory was bound to be failing, but still . . .

The booming voice had carried Hilda's inappropriate question across the room and turned down the volume as people waited to see how she'd answer. From the corner of her eye, Annie—momentarily too stunned to reply—could see Fern powering down the room towards them, cushioned orthopaedic soles assisting her naturally vigorous stride, as she came to rescue them. Suddenly Annie was grateful her mother had chosen not to wear the two-inch suedes.

'Aunty Hilda!' Fern pretended to trill with delight. 'No one's even found you a glass of champagne yet, Aunty. Follow me!'

Terrifying tongue boy:

Black skinny trousers (Topshop)
Ruffled white shirt (Camden Market)
Selection of silver pirate earrings (Camden Market)
Nose piercing (his one-before-last girlfriend)
Tongue piercing (someone slightly more professional)
Total est. cost: £75

'Whatever.'

'SO, THANK YOU ALL for coming tonight. There's going to be dancing, the bar's open 'till two a.m. . . . so don't even think about going home early!' Fern was closing the little speech she'd made and the relief on her face was obvious. 'Before I go, I just want to say thank you to my three wonderful, fabulous girls. I'm so . . .'—then came the crack in the voice—'proud of you all,' she managed before sitting down abruptly.

There was warm applause and Annie might even have let a tear or two well up in the corner of her eye, except Connor touched her elbow and directed her to look towards a window in the corner of the room. Tucked in behind a tall green chintz curtain was a couple snogging frantically. A white-shirted teen boy was kneading his hand vigorously on a—yikes!—lacy navy breast.

It was several moments before Annie could tear her gaze from them. Who is he? she wondered. It was hard to tell from the back of his head.

She mouthed the word 'Help!' to Connor, but his response was to whisper back, 'Like you never!'

Annie turned her attention to the pudding in front of her: chocolate profiteroles. Suddenly a bowlful of toxins had never looked so irresistible. She sunk in her spoon.

Connor, catching sight of the choux pastry demolition, took her firmly by her spoon hand. 'Duty calls, Annie,' he said. 'They're playing our song.'

'Since when is "The Dashing White Sergeant" our song?'

'C'mon. The kiltie wants to dance. The kiltie wants to twirl. I'm fully in touch with my inner Highlander tonight and he wants to boogie.'

'We need a third person for this dance,' Annie warned him.

'A threesome? Excellent. Who shall we have? Spotted any handsome single men yet?'

'Not a one,' she smiled, greatly cheered at the prospect of swinging it with Connor. She'd always loved to dance at parties with Roddy. Disco, of course, but properly, with all the moves. Or salsa. The Roddy and Annie floorshow had been semi-practised and crowd-pleasing. Wrapped up tightly together, snaking across the dance floor, Roddy's warm hand on her bare back . . .

'Aha, just the man.' Connor had spotted Lana's tongue boy walking past. 'Hello, there,' he said, catching the boy by his wrist. 'We need a threesome for this dance. This is Annie Valentine, Lana Valentine's mother. We noticed that you'd met Lana.'

'Oh, ermmm . . . hi there,' tongue boy mumbled. He had shoulder-length brown-blond hair and three earrings in one ear, not to mention his nose. He was way too cool for school and looked frighteningly like a seventeen- or even eighteen-year-old.

'I can't dance to this stuff,' the boy said dismissively. Annie noticed the metal stud gleaming on his tongue and shuddered.

'Hey, c'mon, give us a chance. It'll be fun. What's your name anyway?' Connor persisted.

'Seth.'

'Ooh, like the baddies in *Star Wars*,' Annie jumped in.

'No, that's the Sith Lords,' came the cool response.

Could he have been more huffy?

'Well, never mind, this is "The Dashing White Sergeant". You'll love it. It's easy,' she said and took hold of one of his hands.

It was a memorable dance for Annie, what with Connor on one side whooping, yeehahing, and twirling enough to give alarming flashes of dark hair—yes, under *there*; he'd gone with the traditional Scottish no pants thing—while the Seth Lord barely raised a shuffle on her other.

Annie spotted Lana at the edge of the dance floor; arms crossed, glaring. Lana was clearly convinced that a CIA-style interrogation was under way, with Connor on hand to administer torture.

So, Seth, what grades did you get in your last round of exams? Do you have a serious profession in mind? Teenage sexuality—your prevailing ethics, attitude, morality and most recent experiences: please, discuss.

Much as Annie might have liked to ask all these questions, she managed to confine herself to a polite, 'So, how do you know my mum?' But got only a mumbled, 'She plays golf with my dad,' in reply before Seth broke away and headed off in the direction of Lana's wildly enthusiastic smile.

'Big trouble,' Annie muttered at Connor.

'Oh, c'mon, it's a snog,' he reassured her. 'No teenage relationship is going to survive the vast distance between north London and Essex.'

'Hmm.' Annie headed back to her seat to see if there was a pudding bowl around to lick.

Nic, still at the table, greeted her with the words, 'OK, how much do you want for it? But I'll have to go to the toilets with you first and try it on.' So there was one reason to be cheerful. She wouldn't make a profit from Nic, that would be entirely unethical. But she'd break even.

As Annie stood up, she saw 'nice Mr Wilkinson' approaching.

Mr Wilkinson was forty-five but, due to severe asthma and a limp, more like seventy-five, and she'd once been set up with him by her mother. The dinner hadn't been a great success; nice Mr Wilkinson had got so nervous, he'd inhaled his entire inhaler, then had a wheezing fit and she'd ended up driving him to A&E. It was never a good sign when a date ended with medical intervention.

Ah, the kilted one was in sight. He had already told her he was there to do her bidding all night long.

'I need to go outside, now, straight away,' she hissed at both Connor and Nic. 'Disastrous date approaching, due north.'

Connor peeked over her head. 'Ooh, nasty. Take my arm.'

Outside, in the chilly darkness, looking through the windows at the brightly lit fun, Annie felt an unwelcome gloom descending on her. With her arm still through Connor's, she confided, 'You know, there are still so many times when I really, really miss Roddy.'

Connor nodded slowly. 'I still miss him too,' he said.

'The bugger!' she added, forcing a smile.

'Bastard!' Connor agreed.

'Do you think he has any idea how furious I am with him?'

'Still?' Connor wondered.

'I get angrier,' she confessed. 'As the time goes by and the kids get older, I'm much more angry with him. Bloody, flaming furious.'

Connor paused before beginning, 'I think there's a lot more I could do for you and the children . . .'

'No, no, I don't know what we'd do without you . . . Well obviously, there's taking Owen camping,' she reminded him, hoping both to lighten this conversation and tweak at his conscience once again.

'For goodness' sake, woman, there are limits!' He flashed one of his bright white smiles. 'But I did have one idea . . .'

'Yeah?'

'What do you think about me moving in with you?'

'What?' Annie couldn't have been more surprised.

'Give it some thought, Annie,' he insisted. 'You wouldn't be so lonely. You'd have me around all the time. I really love Owen and Lana. And

I'd be a father figure—a man about the house. We could even get married,' he added.

The kilt was obviously having a very strange effect on him.

'Connor, aren't you overlooking something? I love you, I really do, and I'm sure you love us all too. But we're not *in* love and the way you're made means we never will be,' she reminded him.

'Oh, but . . . you know . . . how important is all that other stuff in the long run?'

'Don't say that!' She smacked his shoulder. 'If we moved in together'—Why were they even talking about this? It was ridiculous—'it would put other people off.'

'Off what?' he asked.

'Off falling in love with us.'

'Oh God, I've given up on that.'

'Well, you mustn't. And I haven't, thank you very much.'

'Ah, yes, your prince in shining armour.' He sounded a little scornful. 'Or should that be shining Armani?'

'C'mon.' She yanked at Connor's arm. 'You're my best, best friend, Connor,' she told him. 'And that's enough.'

'Am I interrupting something? I do hope so.' A disembodied voice came from the doorway, then a tall man stepped out into the darkness.

'No! No!' Annie replied.

'I take it this is the smoking section.' The man held out a broad red packet of Dunhill cigarettes with one hand and a proper gold lighter—Cartier, she suspected—with the other.

Both Connor and Annie shook their heads.

'No thanks,' she told him, 'but I won't hold it against you.'

'That's very kind, I only smoke at parties, they make me nervous.'

Maybe he was another of her mother's golfing pals. Whoever he was, he was much more handsome than Spencer. Lean and smart in his soft, well-fitting dinner suit with starchy white cuffs, gold links flashing at the buttonholes.

He was very upright, with a handsome tanned face and the kind of swept-back sandy grey hair that put him anywhere from forty to sixty.

'I'm Gray Holden'—he held out his hand—'and I'm guessing that you must be Annie Valentine. I've heard so much about you.'

'That's right.' She took his hand and felt his warm, firm touch.

'Your mother told me to look out for you.'

'Oh, she did, did she?' Annie smiled, but immediately felt slightly on guard; this could be another 'Nice Mr Wilkinson' in disguise.

'Connor McCabe,' Connor introduced himself.

'I know,' Gray told him, shaking his hand. 'I've seen you on TV.'

Annie gave Connor the kind of raised-eyebrow look that warned him to make his excuses. 'I just have to go back inside for a moment, check on my . . .' with a little wink at Annie, 'Armani.'

'His what?' Gray wondered once Connor had left them.

'Oh, nothing, nothing, just his idea of a joke. So . . . you must know my mother through the golf club?' was Annie's starter for ten.

'No, no. Too busy for golf.' He smiled at her, flashing teeth even whiter and straighter than Connor's. 'I'm her new dentist.'

'Oh, right . . .' This had to be the 'interesting man' her mother had lined up for her tonight. He wasn't bad, not bad at all.

Annie had just finished an extended shopping session with her two favourite Kuwaiti princesses—never before life in The Store had she realised what sometimes went on under a modest, Muslim jilbab: YSL, Chanel, Pucci, short tight skirts with stockings and killer heels.

Now she was taking a moment of 'rest' in her office before her next appointment. Annie's idea of a rest meant placing eBay bids as she listened to messages on her business phone. She regularly collected unwanted clothes, shoes and bags from many of her clients to sell on for them, taking a little slice of commission. Tonight, she'd have to take her jeep on a London circuit of pick-ups.

'Annie!' Her office door opened and one of the floor assistants, Samantha, was there looking anxious. Annie suspected she knew what was coming next. 'We think we've got a lifter. She's been down in Handbags, there's something missing and she's on our level now.'

'What did she take?'

'A Marc Jacobs; it's the second to go this week.'

Annie stood up. No one else on the floor was as awesome in the presence of shoplifters as her, which is why she usually got called in. This occasion was no different.

When the lifter had emptied out all her bags and pockets, as instructed by Annie, and sloped out of The Store, ears ringing with the telling-off she'd been given, Annie winked at Samantha. 'I *hate* thieves.'

'Annie Valentine!! You're keeping me waiting, you should know better than that. I won't have time to spend as much money with you!' a familiar voice rang out from the suite.

'Got to go,' Annie told Samantha. 'Mrs B-P—one of my favourites.'

'You always say that!'

But Mrs Tilly Brosnan-Pilditch was not just one of Annie's favourite clients, she was a favourite creation. Mrs B-P, as Annie liked to call her, had arrived in The Store's Personal Shopping suite on Annie's third day in the job. She'd wandered in looking for help, because 'It's *terrifying* out there,' she'd confided. Mrs B-P wasn't even Mrs B-P back then, she was Tilly Cathcart, an art lecturer in her early fifties. She'd been dressed in self-conscious bohemian head-to-toe black: a retro astrakhan coat, flat boots and long skirt.

'I have a problem,' she'd said, once Annie had settled her down on the suite sofa with a cup of tea. 'I'm about to get married.'

'Oh, congratulations,' Annie had offered. 'Lucky man.'

'Yes, a lovely man who is unfortunately'—she'd lowered her voice to a whisper—'quite wealthy.'

'Oh dear!' Annie had winked.

'Everyone has a fault, don't they?' Tilly had winked back, and they'd felt themselves warming to each other. 'I'm trying my best to overlook it.'

'Good for you,' Annie had encouraged.

'This lovely, unfortunately quite wealthy man understands many of my anxieties about becoming his new wife, about taking part in his public life,' she'd sighed, 'and he thinks they'll be helped by a great big shopping trip . . . by dressing expensively for the part.'

'But you're not so sure?' Annie had suggested.

'No. I've been independent for so long—and I want to stay independent within our marriage. I don't want to be dressed suddenly from head to toe in his money, in status symbol clothes. I can't mutate into a Nancy Reagan lookalike,' she'd insisted. 'I need to remain me.'

As Annie was to learn time and time again in her new job, it was rarely simple. Dressing was always fraught with all sorts of issues, meanings and hang-ups.

After Annie had heard all the concerns of Mrs B-P-to-be, she'd taken her on a tour of all three floors of women's clothing and accessories.

'At which college do you teach?' Annie had asked. On hearing the answer, she'd nodded and mentioned her own time at art school. 'The fashion school. Ever visited there?' she'd asked.

'Oh, yes, I've been to the end-of-term shows and marvelled at the creations, just like everyone else.'

'You know, there are some amazing hats you should see.' Annie had steered her in their direction. 'We've taken a chance and bought them directly from a student who graduated this summer . . .'

And thus had begun Tilly Cathcart's transformation, not into status-laden trophy wife, but into generous patron of the arts, supporter of creative students.

Mrs B-P stood before Annie today in a funky Vivienne Westwood green and red checked skirt-suit they'd bought together, a magnificently arty, embroidered bag and wonderful red shoes that exactly matched her red lipstick.

'You're an art expert, you can be painterly about the way you dress,' Annie had encouraged her. Definitely not Nancy Reagan. Still the intelligent, creative, thoughtful art teacher Mr B-P had fallen in love with.

'This is going to be a long session,' Mrs B-P warned Annie as they sat down together and drew up a list of her requirements. Mrs B-P was no longer quite so uncomfortable about spending her clothing allowance. 'I'm giving up suits,' was the first instruction. 'I want very soft, comfortable clothing: sensational pyjamas, loads of cashmere, but in lovely colours, wraps, shawls, your best slippers.'

'Are you going into hibernation?' Annie wondered.

'Yes, that's exactly it—a spring hibernation. A rebirth, a renewal.'

'Aha! Spa visit?'

'Something like that . . . Come on, take me out there.'

Palest pink silk pyjamas and embroidered sheepskin house-boots met with Mrs B-P's approval. Teal-blue cashmere jogging trousers joined the pile of possibilities, a pale yellow cashmere dress. Mrs B-P couldn't get enough cashmere; she kept putting the woollens against her cheek. 'Oh, delicious, so cosy and soothing.'

During the trying-on session, it didn't escape Annie's notice that Mrs B-P had lost weight. Her slim figure was now verging on the slight.

'You're the only person who needs to go to a spa to fatten up,' she told her. 'Get a little meat on your bones.'

Mrs B-P wasn't just shopping for herself either; she wanted birthday presents for her two stepdaughters.

'What's happening in your life anyway?' she asked Annie as they made their way down to the Accessories department. 'Any news from the love life front, or is it still a no-man's-land?' she teased.

'Now funny you should ask about that,' Annie confided. 'As a matter of fact, I've met someone quite interesting.' She then proceeded to give an intrigued Mrs B-P the rundown on Gray.

'We talked and talked for the rest of the evening. He's promised to call and take me out to dinner . . . He is charming, good-looking . . . I've got high hopes for this one,' Annie enthused, 'because I'm definitely ready to meet someone else . . . have someone there for me again.'

'Of course you are.' Mrs B-P smiled at her. 'I can't think of anything better that could happen to you.'

They were standing in front of a display of the most exquisite velvet devoré scarves. 'These are beautiful . . .' Mrs B-P ran her fingers slowly over the pile. 'This is just what I want for Georgina and Ellie. Then I'm going to Cartier to buy them something . . . solid.'

Annie took the two scarves and folded them carefully. 'Are you all right?' she asked finally, putting a hand on Mrs B-P's arm.

'I'm fine, I'm fine. I just have to spend some time in the damn hospital.' Mrs B-P turned to look her directly in the face with her sharp, blue eyes. 'Oh, it's so boring, Annie, totally dull . . . I need a mastectomy, chemotherapy and all that *dreary* stuff. I'm going to need a lot of interesting hats and scarves, I can tell you.'

She brushed away Annie's shocked look of concern with, 'It's very, very early stages. And I'm going to recover, my dear. Not a single question about that. I'm not even entertaining the possibility of not recovering. You think I'm exiting now? Just when it's got this good?!'

'I know.' She acknowledged Annie's slightly tearful eyes. 'Bummer. Now come on.' She took up Annie's arm again. 'There's a time for weeping and wailing but now is not that time. Now is the time to buy a wonderful new handbag. I'm leaving it entirely up to you. When I'm shuffling from home to hospital and back, I want to have Archie on one arm, and something just as fabulous on the other.'

Tor in recovery:

White blouse (M&S)
Deep-red cardigan (M&S)
Jeans (no recollection)
Black boots (back of wardrobe)
Black fake fur (ditto)
Total est. cost: £360

'. . . *to new men and new scarves.*'

TOR, THE ST VINCENT'S MOTHER Annie was making over for free, had met Annie at the door of the family home she was about to be kicked out of and shown her into the kitchen for tea.

'No, I think we better make it red wine, babes,' Annie had insisted, taking a bottle from her bag.

'I've made a rule never to drink by myself though,' Tor had told her, taking two water glasses out of the cupboard, already stripped of almost all its contents.

'Good thing I came round then,' was Annie's response, before she assured Tor, 'I think a little drinking on your own might be OK right now—for a few weeks anyway—until you've got the move behind you. You better not have packed up any of your wardrobe yet, otherwise how am I going to do my job?'

Annie slipped off her leather coat to reveal a patterned dress elegantly set off with high brown boots.

'No, no,' Tor insisted, taking in the many details of Annie's outfit. She looked so together, so carefully considered. 'It's still three weeks away,' she continued. 'I've just put away kitchen stuff . . . books . . . Things that are definitely mine.'

After a bit of talk about Tor's new flat and her daughter Angela and how the divorce was affecting them (badly to say the least), Tor suddenly put her glass down on the table and blurted out, 'I don't know why you're here, Annie! I don't know why I've agreed to this. I don't want to think about clothes. I don't care! I've got no money . . . showing me some clever things to do with scarves is just not going to help!'

'Tor, calm down,' Annie soothed, reaching out to pat her arm. 'I am so sorry about what you're going through. I am so, so sorry. I really do understand how you feel, honestly. I have been there.'

Tor looked up and met Annie's eyes.

'Yes, of course you have,' she said. 'I'm sorry.'

'I'm not a therapist,' Annie continued gently, 'and it could be that you should see someone like that, to get you through the worst of it. But there is something I can do, I promise. I'm here to make you feel just a tiny bit better about yourself, and what's so wrong with that? C'mon, drink up,' she instructed, 'then we're treating ourselves to a refill and heading to your wardrobe.'

In the bedroom, Annie took two bin bags out of her make-over kitbag.

Tor looked at them anxiously. 'I wasn't planning on throwing much away,' she said.

'I know.' Annie sounded brisk. 'No one ever does, but don't worry, you will. There's a lot of dead wood in a divorce wardrobe, believe me. For starters, we're going to get rid of all the unsuitable presents *he* gave you. You know, the expensive things that didn't fit but you didn't have the heart to exchange? Open your underwear drawer,' Annie instructed. 'C'mon, pass it on out. I wish I could think of a good home for all the expensive underwear I have to get rid of . . . Charity shops don't want it, no one will buy it on eBay . . . Maybe I should be donating it to schools for their arts and craft boxes . . .'

Tor was almost threatening to smile at this; she was also opening a drawer, stuffed full of all the usual suspects: a tiny corset, dainty peach-coloured feathery things, quarter-cup bras for breasts the size of raisins, not Tor's ample cleavage. 'What was he thinking?' she said, picking up the wincy bra and gazing at it in bewilderment. 'Not of me, anyway . . .' She tossed it into Annie's bin bag.

The emptied drawer seemed to have just the galvanising effect on Tor that Annie had hoped for. Soon she was ferreting about for anything suspect dumped on her by her soon-to-be-ex.

A revolting primrose-yellow cashmere cardigan: 'Yup, put it in the sale bag,' Annie instructed. 'I'll put it on my web site for you and you'll get eighty-five per cent of the price paid. Sound fair?'

'Sounds bloody marvellous,' Tor told her.

Paisley scarves, a tweedy jacket and a scary loud pink cocktail dress with matching bolero followed on quickly. Tor rooted deeper. 'Oh God!' She took out a beaded, pastel-coloured wrap of sorts.

'eBay, eBay . . .' Annie instructed. 'We don't want anything hanging about that is going to make you think of Richard and weep. Obviously, I'll make an exception for very expensive jewellery and handbags.'

'Hah!' Tor snorted and took another gulp of wine. 'My engagement ring was the one and only decent bit of jewellery I got from him.'

'Ah well,' Annie said, 'I never even got an engagement ring. We were young and couldn't afford it.'

'Do you think I should still wear it?' Tor wondered, holding out the triple-stone ring for inspection. 'On my other hand, maybe?'

'If you love it, why not? Or you could have the stones reset . . . or sell it off and buy something just for you.'

'Hmmm.' Tor turned back to her wardrobe. 'Everything in here is utter crap,' she announced, the wine now loosening up any inhibitions about this task. 'I sort of rummage around in here every day and bring something out and just plonk it on.'

Now this was just so heartbreakingly sad, it made Annie want to cry.

Today, Tor was wearing washed-out jeans, a T-shirt with a sagging neck and a bobbly grey fleece cardigan. 'Babes, if I gave that cardigan to Gisele Bundchen, she'd struggle to make it look good,' Annie told her gently. 'You've got to stop with the lucky dip and find some things that are a little easier to work with.'

'I'm not going shopping,' Tor said firmly. 'I can't afford it.'

'I know, I know. But c'mon, let's get it all out and see what's hiding in there . . . and by the way, what is this nice little collection hanging up here on the rail?' She made a quick rifle through the smart black skirts and jackets, sparkly tops and silky summer dresses.

'Oh, work clothes. Then dress-up things. I never wear any of those; I never go out any more.'

Annie tutted and shook her head. She brought down a lovely knee-length dress and held it up against Tor. 'You know, once a week, babes, you've got to dress up: hair, make-up, shoes—the full monty—and get out there.'

When Tor scoffed at this, Annie insisted, 'Not on the pull. Just nicely turned out for a special occasion. And then you make the occasion happen. You take your daughter out for coffee at a nice hotel . . . you go to the cinema in town . . . you ask your friends out for a drink. Once a week, girl, you have to dress up and remember how great you can look when you want to. Otherwise, all these beautiful things, they're just hanging here with nowhere to go.'

Tor's shoulders seemed to droop at the thought of having to make this effort.

'OK, work with me,' Annie encouraged her. 'Let's get rid of the unwearables and see what's left, shall we?'

They spent the next ten minutes or so sifting through Tor's daily lucky-dip outfits. Everything worn, saggy and baggy hit the bin bag.

'You do not need me to tell you that you need new underwear, Tor. You can afford new pants, OK? Everyone can afford new pants.'

Annie looked carefully through the clothes that remained and could see that there was going to be enough . . . just.

'You don't want to think about outfits every morning yet, so what we need is an easy uniform . . .' Annie began to lay the remaining clothes out on the bed. 'I'm looking at your nice white shirts, and this little red cardigan here and the two woollen V-necks and these jeans, and your nifty black trousers . . . But please, Tor, a skirt at least twice a week, not just for work. Anyway, I'm thinking, here is the beginning of a chic French mama uniform. White shirts, *ironed*,' she warned, 'are very morale boosting, so c'mon, into the first outfit.'

Tor put on the white shirt, jeans and red cardigan.

'Right.' Annie turned her in the direction of the mirror. 'Feeling a little bit more together?'

When Tor nodded, Annie moved in and undid the shirt one button lower. 'You're not teaching at Sunday school. Now, show me your jewellery box.'

Annie clipped a red and silver necklace round Tor's neck, instructed her to put on earrings, then brushed out her scrappy bob before securing it with an elaborate silver clip she'd found in the jewellery box.

Then she went into her handbag and brought out blusher and lip gloss.

Once this was applied, they both looked at the effect in the mirror.

'Better?' Annie asked.

Tor nodded slowly. But she didn't seem convinced.

'I really do understand why you don't want to care about how you look, babes,' Annie began. 'Sometimes when everything's turned to crap, we want it to show on the outside too. But the problem is . . . if you hide inside a baggy grey fleece every day, believe me, it's much harder for things to get better again. Great things do not happen to people hidden inside grey fleeces . . . They don't land exciting new jobs, or meet brilliant new friends, or have amazing ideas, or get invited out spontaneously. They just get greyer and fleecier. Maybe the best piece of advice I can give you is to dress for how you want to feel again. Because then it will happen more quickly.'

Annie squeezed Tor's shoulders because she could see her eyes welling up. 'You're going to be fine, Tor,' she assured her.

Annie let Tor blow her nose while she turned her eyes in the direction of the wardrobe again. 'And what is this lovely coat doing hiding in here?' she asked, taking out a cosy, black fake fur. 'And these boots!' Her hand reached for the black suede mid-heels, almost unworn.

'Well, they're special occasion . . .' Tor began.

Annie shook her head vigorously. 'No, no, no! You need all your special things around you right now. For support,' she insisted.

Tor put them both on. And now Annie could see she was more convinced. The boots gave her an extra inch or so and forced her to straighten up, her hands were sunk into the coat pockets and she was actually admiring herself, if only slightly.

'Oh, yes!' Annie raved. 'Now you're good to go!'

Tor's smile suddenly appeared and she gave a relieved giggle.

'More wine for the lady!' Annie teased.

'No, no, I need to concentrate or I'm going to forget everything you've told me,' Tor replied.

Together they wrote down all the outfits Annie had put together for her and lots of Annie's top tips including, 'Lip gloss, tinted moisturiser and blusher, it's not rocket science' . . . 'Smile more—laugh, even' . . . 'Cheap but glamorous sunglasses for bad eye days' . . . 'Always, *always*, jewellery to make you sparkle.'

'Clever ways with scarves,' Annie scribbled down in the notebook. 'Let your sexy new boyfriends teach you these.'

'Oh, ha ha,' Tor responded.

'It's true though,' Annie insisted. 'There will be new men—and think how exciting that's going to be. But you do need new scarves, honestly, babes; you need the colour and the comfort, something to snuggle up in, a buffer between you and your coats, you and the world. A sprinkle of colour when you're feeling totally monochrome.'

'Well, then'—Tor met her eye and smiled broadly, as if she was finally enjoying herself—'here's to new men and new scarves.' She held up her tumbler of wine.

'I'll drink to that.' Annie clinked glasses with her.

When Tor's session was over, Annie buttoned herself back into her leather coat. She ran a hairbrush through her locks, applied lipstick, a little spritz of perfume and set her shoulders back. This meant that when she was out of the front door, she was ready to face her mobile.

She switched it on and looked for the voicemail symbol. Nothing there. She checked her inbox just in case.

No. Nine days had passed and Gray had not called her. What a total, utter bummer. She couldn't understand it. He'd seemed so keen. He'd promised! He'd even put her number directly into his mobile. She wasn't sure what she was going to do now. Going back to Tor's house to rescue the grey fleece from the bin bag for herself was tempting.

Annie's 'accidental' date outfit:

Pink cardigan (Whistles sale)
Flowered pink and camel skirt (same)
Camel trenchcoat (the trusty eBay Valentino)
Pink pashmina (so out of fashion, but still so good)
Flower necklace (Topshop)
New high-heeled camel T-bars (Chanel, but with a staff discount, and consider the Trading Station resale value)
Cloud of Chanel's Cristalle
Total est. cost: £490

'Gray! What are you doing here?!'

'SO WHEN IS YOUR DATE with Gray?' Dinah had been introduced to Gray at the party, then she'd pulled Annie off to the loos to tell her that Gray was 'very promising' and that Annie was to 'go, go, go for it, girl!'

The pause that followed told Dinah all she needed to know. 'He hasn't called?' she asked, outraged. 'Oh, Annie! Have you got his number? Aren't you going to call him? It's not like you to—'

'I thought about it,' Annie cut in, 'and I decided it wasn't cool.'

'So you're not going to see him?' Dinah sounded very disappointed.

'No. I didn't say that. I have a plan,' Annie confided. 'He's going to a conference and I've found out it's at Claridge's. I'm going to think up a very good, very glamorous reason for me to be at the hotel at the same time. So we'll meet by accident . . . me looking fabulous. He'll be really, really sorry he didn't call me and the rest will be easy!'

'Hmmm . . . It sounds a bit obvious.'

'It won't be obvious. You forget what a brilliant actress I am. Haven't I learned from the masters, Roddy and Connor?'

Annie had never set foot in Claridge's before. Although she'd left work early in a fresh, painstakingly chosen camel and pink outfit with new (Chanel!) shoes, as soon as she entered the marbled, chandeliered lobby, she felt a little unequal to the occasion.

This was true early twentieth-century splendour. This was a hotel where women should still be wearing veiled cocktail hats and lizard-skin heels, toting alligator handbags and silver cigarette cases.

After asking directions as casually as she could, Annie made her way to one of the most elegant bars she'd ever encountered. It was dark and snug, but the mahogany table tops, brass lamps, glittering mirrors and glasses meant it sparkled with very expensive glamour. She approached the handsome dark-haired barman and smiled winningly.

'Hello, how are you? Quiet afternoon?'

Once he'd made his reply, she asked for a gin and tonic.

'A double, madam?' he wanted to know, because this was, of course, the kind of place where everything came with a possible upgrade.

'No, thanks. And can I have a mineral water too, please?'

Once further clarification had been made as to which of the five available mineral waters she wished to drink, Annie had another question: 'I just wondered if I could ask a little favour?'

'No problem, madam,' he assured her, when she'd explained what she wanted. 'Please, take a seat, make yourself comfortable and I'll bring your drinks.'

The drinks were beautiful: they sparkled and fizzed from real crystal tumblers. But Annie wasn't so lost in her admiration that she didn't notice the small stream of people heading from the direction she'd carefully positioned her chair to observe.

OK—she took a steadying sip of her G&T—time to be cool.

She watched as Gray came into the lobby. He looked good: dark navy suit, crisp white shirt, navy tie with subtle polka dots. He had that proud, upright posture of a confident man. A good profile, she noted once again, nice nose, strong chin. Yes, he would do.

Annie turned her head slightly to the side and willed him to look over. Several long seconds went by. She took another sip of her drink.

'Annie?' came his voice finally. 'Annie? Is that you?'

She turned to see him striding purposefully towards her.

'Gray! What are you doing here?!'

'Annie, what are *you* doing here?' he countered, adding quickly, 'I mean, my God, that's fantastic'—he looked almost flustered—'I've been trying to call you for days but I must have got your number wrong and I haven't been able to get hold of your mother to—'

'You could easily have got me through The Store,' she reminded him.

'The Store!' He smacked his forehead. 'I've been phoning Selfridges!'

Ah! Now he was forgiven. Annie smiled broadly at him. 'That's very sweet of you. Is this where your conference is being held?' she asked.

He nodded. 'Why are *you* here?' he asked.

'Well, obviously, I'm stalking you,' she said, an eyebrow arched.

When he just smiled in response to this, she quickly corrected him. 'No! Don't flatter yourself! I've got a job on here.' Her voice dropping low, she elaborated: 'An American actress, far too famous to actually come into The Store, is upstairs in the honeymoon suite trying on a load of our clothes and any moment now I'm going to be summoned up to help her and her stylist with the final decisions. That's why I need a quick drink, believe me.' She winked at him.

'Who?' He was desperate to know.

'I can't tell you!' she teased. 'Goodness me, we've only just met.'

'But we're going to meet again, aren't we?' he asked. 'I'm a bit tied up right now . . . but could we get together for dinner later? You are look-ing fabulous, by the way.'

See? He was delighted to see her. Dinner?! No. It was time to be cool. He had not phoned, so she was not available. Basic dating rules.

'Oh! I'm going out tonight . . . What a shame.' She didn't explain fur-ther. Let him think she was on a scorching hot date.

At that moment, bang on cue, as previously arranged, the barman approached the table. 'Madam, I'm so sorry to interrupt, but there's a call for you from suite number one. You're to make your way up.'

'Thanks,' she told him with a smile. A great tip really did buy you fabulous service here.

'I have to go,' she told Gray. 'Wish me luck!'

'At least let me make sure I've got the right number for you, so we can set something up soon.' He was almost pleading. Excellent.

'Hmmm . . . My evenings are a bit tied up for the next week or two,' she told him, just to dangle the carrot a little longer. 'But . . . how about Sunday? Would you like to meet for lunch?'

'I'd love to,' he told her.

'Well, let's meet on Tower Bridge at one p.m., Sunday then; I know a nice place round there. And here'—she reached into her handbag—'this is my card. You can phone me if you're going to be late.'

'I won't be late!' he assured her. Then, as she stood up to leave for her phantom appointment at suite number one, he leaned over and kissed her on both sides of the face, giving her a hit of sexy citrus aftershave.

'Is there something . . . ? Umm, on your cheek? What is that?' He brushed at her face. On the tip of his little finger was a frazzled clump of eyelash extension, which he was examining with great curiosity. The acrylic debris looked like a squashed spider.

'Ah! It's my new mascara,' she managed. 'I think I'm allergic to it or something. Anyway, I'd better head off.'

On reflection, her sashay through the lobby would have been so much more elegant and effective if her brand-new, staggeringly high heels hadn't caused her a vicious ankle twist and her mobile hadn't been trilling with the latest Crazy Frog anthem. Thank you, Owen.

'Dinah!' she hissed into the phone, once she was safely at the top of the stairs, into a corridor and out of sight. 'I said I'd phone you!'

Silver fox Gray's date wear:

Black lightweight wool suit (Armani)
White T-shirt (Paul Smith)
Thick white shirt (Gant)
Black socks (Paul Smith)
Boxers (Paul Smith)
Black lace-up ankle boots (Oliver Sweeney)
Aviator shades (Ray-Ban)
Total est. cost: £890

'And how would you make me over?'

ANNIE LEANED on the metal railing of Tower Bridge and marvelled at the great swollen 'gherkin' building which rose up and swaggered high above all the other office blocks surrounding it. The gherkin? Really? Why not just name it 'the willy' and be done with it?

She turned to take in the view on the other side, just in time to see Gray walking along on the opposite pavement. He was early too.

'Gray!' she called out. For late forties, he looked fit. Worked out, she thought, watching the wind push his T-shirt against his flat stomach.

'Annie! Hello there!' He pushed his shades up into his hair and walked over, moving straight in to give her a kiss—not on each cheek, but on the lips—as he put a bunch of flowers into her hands.

The brush of lip, hit of mint breath and spicy aftershave was a very pleasant experience Annie thought she'd definitely like to repeat soon.

'Flowers! Thank you. You really shouldn't have!' she gushed with a big smile, although the waxy white lilies and green garlanding were so funereal that she would have quite liked to throw the bouquet off the bridge. She liked colourful, cheerful flowers. Nothing poncy.

'So,' she began. 'We meet on the bridge. The master of bridgework and me.'

'Oh ho! Very good. How are your children? What are they up to today?'

'Oh, they're busy,' she told him. 'Hectic schedule . . .'

Annie had arranged for Dinah to take them for lunch, then Lana had agreed to walk Owen up to his karate lesson and wait for him there. This meant her home was empty . . . So, if lunch went well, she was going to invite Gray back for coffee and a little light canoodling.

Annie held his arm as they crossed Tower Bridge and made their way down to Butler's Wharf, where she'd booked a table at the Chop House.

Gray kept up a pleasantly steady flow of chat and, with the anxious butterflies in her stomach settling, Annie began to enjoy herself.

Their table came with the riverside view she'd requested.

'I love it down here on the river,' she said once they had ordered. 'It doesn't feel like London, it feels European. Yet this is one of the oldest parts of the city. This is where ships once set sail hoping to return laden down with goodies from all over the world. I like to think that this'— she gestured to the stretch of river—'is where shopping began.'

It made him laugh.

When the wine was poured, they clinked glasses and he asked her to tell him more about her work. 'It sounds very intriguing. Basically, you help people to shop?' He sounded a little incredulous.

'Think of me as a super-enhanced sales assistant,' she told him. 'Customers book an appointment with me, we discuss what clothes they're looking for, what lifestyle, what budget they have, then I make suggestions until we find all the outfits they want. I help people make great wardrobe investments, not expensive mistakes.'

'And you do this on a freelance basis as well?'

'I have fingers in many pies. I do home consultations, because they pay well and because they're such great fun. I also buy and sell used designer clothes and accessories on the internet and I'm a trained stylist, believe it or not.'

'Oh, yes! You told me when we met that you'd worked on films.'

'Aha . . . the film days . . .' She smiled, carefully picking a large cooked prawn out of its shell. 'My globetrotting twenties. Roddy, me and our surprise baby Lana. We were always happy to go wherever the work was: France, Romania, Poland, Morocco . . . wherever.'

'Sounds incredibly glamorous,' Gray said.

'It was,' she agreed. 'But babies grow up, they get baby brothers, everyone has to go to school; suddenly you need a bigger home and a regular income. Roddy landed a string of good theatre jobs based in London, so we stopped travelling so much. Finally he got his soap role, I had my nice job at The Store and we got grounded, just like everyone else I suppose . . .' But this came with a cheerful smile. 'I don't regret it,' she told him truthfully. 'I've done my wandering and it's nice to be home again. And I'll tell you one thing, it's much more fun making the not-so-beautiful look wonderful than dealing with leading ladies.'

'So how would you make *me* over?' he challenged her, giving her a look that made her suspect the intensely green eyes leaping from his tanned face were created by tinted contact lenses.

'I don't think *you* need a stylist,' she told him, hearing the flirty little purr in her voice.

'Oh, well . . . that's very nice, but we could all improve, couldn't we?'

'You've got very good taste, Gray.'

'Hmmm,' he nodded in agreement. 'And not just in clothes.' He kept his gaze trained directly at Annie, until she couldn't help giggling.

'So,' he said unfolding his hands, 'you should venture out, start your own big business. How about a shop?'

'So very last century,' she teased. 'You should look up my virtual store some time, Annie V Trading Station. Who wants to pay staff and overheads when you can create your own cyber shopfront?'

'You're very good,' he told her with a smile. 'Maybe I should get you to look over my business, see if you can think of any improvements.'

'I'd be delighted. So are you into cosmetic dentistry as well as fillings, extractions and root canals?'

'Oh yes,' he assured her, as their plates were cleared away. 'Teeth straightening, veneers, dental implants, all the high-end stuff. I'm hoping to add Botox to our range of treatments very soon.'

'Really? But my ladies tell me Botox is over and everyone's doing Restylane now,' she informed him.

'Yes, well, possibly. I'm looking into that. But you've not had anything done, have you?' He was scrutinising her just a little too closely for comfort.

'No! I'm not ruling it out though. If I wake up one morning looking like a haggard old witch, then I might just come to you.'

'Well . . .'

She'd meant this as a cheeky, flirty comment, but now his scrutiny of her face was too professional for her liking.

'Not everyone looks as fantastic in their thirties as you do, but a tiny hit, just in there between your brows,' he said, pointing, 'would work wonders. What I'd really love to make over is your mouth.'

No, no, no! This wasn't sexy. What was wrong with her teeth?

'The overcrowding on the bottom could be cured with wisdom tooth extraction and a gentle brace. On the top, I'd put in two or three veneers to smooth out those slightly crooked angles, then whiten everything. You'd be stunning. I'd give you a great rate,' he offered.

'Erm, well . . . that's very kind of you . . . ' Lying back in a dental chair with her tonsils and all her fillings on display didn't strike Annie as the best of wooing techniques.

As their coffees arrived he turned the conversation from teeth to ask, 'So you like it down here on the river? I'm thinking of buying a flat down here to rent out.'

Aha, a budding property mogul. Her ears perked with interest.

'I've got a viewing at about three p.m. Would you like to come along? I'd value your opinion.'

The flat was smart if a little boxy: maple flooring, recessed lighting, two small bedrooms, two high-tech bathrooms of dark greenish slate, a glitzy open-plan kitchen and living area with big floor-to-ceiling windows offering views of . . . well, another development.

It was obvious that Gray was not impressed.

'It's very small,' he told the estate agent. 'The kitchen's part of the living room and it's hardly a view, is it? I wasn't expecting this.'

'This is a very prestigious address,' the estate agent argued. 'Excellent area for shopping, eating out, you're so close to the City—only a ten-minute walk over the bridge to the tube . . .'

Clearly wherever Gray lived, he was getting a much better deal than this. But he lived out of town. He was a 'burbs man, probably the proud owner of a driveway, a front lawn and French windows out onto his own back garden. This was city living—more luxury, less square feet.

'What did you think?' He canvassed Annie's opinion once they were out of the flat and had bid the agent farewell.

'Complete rip-off,' she informed him confidently.

'And what makes you so knowledgeable?' he asked, draping an arm over her shoulders, where it sat comfortably, if a little self-consciously.

'Well, Gray, if you offer to drive me home, I might tell you all about my successful scramble up the London property ladder,' she said, imagining the two of them cosied up together on her big white sofa.

'It's a deal,' he agreed. 'But only if you invite me in.'

Result!

As he opened the passenger door, so she could climb aboard his sleek silver Mercedes convertible, Annie surveyed the black leather seats, high-tech dashboard, and the suave gentleman who would be getting into the driver's seat, and she thought, I could get used to this.

As Annie pushed open her flat door, she wasn't exactly thrilled to hear the noise of the kettle coming to the boil in the kitchen.

'Lana?' she called. 'I thought you were at karate with Owen?'

Lana in head-to-toe clinging black appeared in the kitchen doorway. 'He didn't want to go,' she said grumpily. 'I couldn't make him.'

'No? No . . . well . . . right.' She tried to keep her annoyance under control. The meeting of children with prospective boyfriends was something that had to be carefully managed, not just sprung on them. 'Well, now you'll get a chance to say hello to my friend Gray.'

'Hello there, Lana.' Gray offered a hand for her to shake. 'I remember seeing you at your grandmother's party—but you were a little busy . . .'

Lana blushed, shook Gray's hand and managed a mumbled hello.

'Come into the sitting room,' Annie offered. 'I'll just go and dig Owen out of his room, but he's a little shy,' she reminded Gray in a quiet voice.

Owen waved at Gray from the doorway then fled back to his room. Annie left it at that. 'Shall we go into the kitchen and have some coffee?' she asked.

'Yes, definitely . . .' Gray got up from the sofa arm he'd perched on. Annie was still thinking she'd like to push him back onto the cushions and rumple him quite a lot, but the presence of the children made that impossible.

At the kitchen table, Lana was texting frantically.

'Everything OK?' Annie wondered.

'Yeah, fine, everything's fine,' she answered, not breaking eye contact with the screen.

'Does the Seth Lord still rule?' Annie couldn't help herself.

But she shouldn't have; she just got a black look and deepest scowl in reply. 'At least he doesn't use hair dye and fake tan,' Lana snapped.

'Hopefully it won't *kill* you to be nice,' Annie whispered at her, just before Gray was in earshot.

'D'uhhh,' came the great grudging sigh.

Once the kettle was on for the coffee, Annie felt an unusual desire to play domestic goddess. She set out cups, saucers and cake plates and shook almond biscuits out of the packet. She warmed the rarely used cafetière before adding the ground coffee she'd unearthed in a cupboard.

Then, using the typical parental combination of threats and bribes, she made Owen and Lana sit up at the table properly to meet Gray.

'I hear you're both at St Vincent's?' was Gray's ice-breaker, once he was settled into his chair. But the question didn't go down so well.

Lana scowled. 'Godawful place, I absolutely hate it.'

'No, you don't,' Annie said with her nicest smile. 'Tell Gray about the charity web site. They're hoping to make ten thousand pounds.'

Lana pulled a face, but then her phone bleeped with a reply text and she pounced on it, snatching it up, eyes lighting.

Gray and Annie watched as Owen picked up four biscuits and crammed them all into his mouth.

'Of course we won't be at St Vincent's for long,' Lana fired out, taking Annie completely by surprise. 'Mum's totally broke and we'll either have to sell the flat or leave school.'

'Or both,' Owen added for emphasis, spraying crumbs across the tablecloth. Despite her embarrassment, for a moment Annie managed to feel proud that Owen had actually spoken two words despite the presence of a stranger.

'Er . . . well.' She smiled at Gray and twisted the coffee cup round in her hands. Maybe last night hadn't been such great timing for the earnest little conversation she'd had with the children about the hole in the family finances. 'It's hardly as bad as that.'

'But you said—' Lana began.

'I may have to free up a little equity,' she breezed, seeing what she read as concern in Gray's face, 'but St Vincent's is a great school. They're both going to be there for many years to come.' She shot a look at Lana, who slumped melodramatically over her phone.

Then the landline began to ring and to Annie's surprise, Owen stood up and ran out of the room to answer it. He picked up, said, 'Hello,' in a very calm-sounding voice and then carried on something resembling a normal conversation. This was very unusual.

'Oh yeah . . . hi . . . aha . . . that's really cool,' she overheard. Then came, 'Hmmm . . . Wednesday? This Wednesday? Muuum!' came the shout. 'Are we doing anything on Wednesday evening?'

Annie flicked mentally through the following week's family schedule. 'No,' she said finally, 'I don't think we're doing anything—but why? Who?'

Owen didn't answer her, he was back on the phone. 'Wednesday's fine. Great . . . So about seven p.m.? OK cool. Yup.'

'Who was that?' Annie asked as soon as Owen came back.

'Ed,' Owen replied. There was a pause and Annie thought the presence of Gray was going to silence Owen once again, but instead he took a breath or two to calm himself, as he'd been taught to do but rarely remembered, then he continued, 'There's this singer, Rufus Wainwright, and he's doing an acoustic thing at the National Theatre. Ed said he'd look into getting tickets for us. It's going to be cool!'

'All of us?' Annie wondered.

'You, me, Lana.'

'Oh no,' came the groan from Lana.

Rufus Wainwright wasn't registering on Annie's radar. She looked at Lana, to see if she could spot any signs of recognition there.

'He's gay, took crystal meth . . . folk-type god,' was Lana's biog.

'Don't you want to go?' Annie asked.

'Oh yeah . . . Well, Ed the Shed is so not cool, but Rufus is crack!'

Annie worried for about the tenth time that day if her children were watching too much American TV.

Gray's contribution to this new turn in the conversation was to ask what crystal meth was, which earned him the kind of scowls and shrugs Lana usually reserved for *total losers* such as children's TV presenters, people in cagoules or the Royal Family.

This caused Gray to look at his watch (stainless steel TAG Heuer) and announce his departure. Annie suspected he still wasn't over the 'Mum's totally broke' comment. She would have to do something to remedy the situation or she wasn't going to see him for dust.

As he got up, she ushered him through into the sitting room. 'Take a look at that building over there.' She pointed it out from her window. 'Now that is really worth investing in.' Her tone was cosy and confidential now. 'Lovely part of town, great views, good school catchment, right on the tube. It will rent like a dream. I happen to know that the developer desperately needs money coming in to finish the project off. I'm absolutely certain that he'd take a very low bid on a two-bedroom flat. I would be investing in that right now . . . except, as my children have so helpfully explained,' she said, trying to make light of it, 'I'm not exactly so flexibly . . . liquid at the moment.'

'Great tip.' To her relief, Gray was purring again. 'I'll look into it,' he added. 'And by the way, what are you doing next weekend?'

Yes! 'Well, let me see . . . There's the shopping trip to buy gags for Lana and Owen . . . but otherwise . . .'

Ed dressing for the occasion:

Yellow polo shirt (drawer)
Red polo shirt (drawer)
Green tweed jacket (can't remember)
Baggy khakis (Army and Navy stores)
Heavy boots (same)
Total est. cost: £45

'Music always gives me an appetite!'

'THERE YOU ARE!' were Ed's opening words as Annie, Lana and Owen arrived wet and slightly bedraggled at the doors to the theatre. They were twenty minutes late and now there was barely time to say hello because the performance was just about to begin.

'Sorry, Ed,' Annie began. 'It's taken us ages . . . We got totally lost out there.'

This wasn't untrue, there had been some confusion about directions, but she decided she'd bypass an explanation about the enormous Lana row that had really held them up. Just your standard mother–teenage daughter 'you're not going out like that' argument, which had of course escalated to great, hurtful insults being tossed around at random.

Lana: 'You're such a cow! I hate you!'

Annie: 'You're just a spoilt brat; I'm not buying you anything, ever again! This time I mean it!' And so on.

Owen had quietly put on his shoes and anorak, then he'd gone to stand by the door, headphones in, iPod cranked up, foot tapping to the rhythm, as he'd waited for the storm to finally blow over. The sight of him had taken the wind out of Annie's sails.

'Right, Lana, that's it, I'm done,' she'd announced in the coolest voice she could summon. 'Just put on the sparkly boob tube, skinny jeans and platform boots if you want. I'm not saying another word about it. Just make sure . . .' See? She was already saying another word about it, but she couldn't resist. 'Make sure you've got something waterproof on top because it's definitely going to rain.'

In the concert hall, they had to squeeze past twenty people or so to get into their seats, Ed leading the way, then Lana, Owen and finally Annie.

During the performance Annie kept catching sight of Ed's face appearing over the top of teen boobs hoicked up in a padded bra underneath a boob tube. They were listening to a song about a teenager being in love with an art teacher. Another time Annie might have loved this song, all haunting and melodic, but instead, she felt her world view shift a little uncomfortably. Was Lana attracted to Ed? Despite her cool disdain, maybe she had a little crush? That wouldn't be so surprising, any teacher slightly more attractive than Frankenstein could usually be guaranteed a decent pupil fan base.

But . . . did Ed have any sort of thing for Lana?! Just the thought of this made little prickles of anxiety stand up on the back of her neck. Lana was at that tricky teen age; she looked older than she was and tonight she looked lovely, sexy even. Annie turned her head and watched the two of them to see if there was any sort of . . . well . . . what? A look? Nudge? Communication between them?

Ed was leaning forward, totally wrapped up in the performance. Lana was scratching at her bare arm in a slightly distracted way.

There was nothing obvious.

The next time she looked, Ed turned his head and looked not at Lana and her overexposed teen boobies, but at Annie.

She felt caught out and gave an automatic little smile, which he returned with something much broader and kinder. He tilted his head in the direction of the music and raised his eyebrows as if to ask her, Is this OK? Are you enjoying it? And she nodded enthusiastically back.

'You've got to come to the café with me,' he insisted when the performance was over. 'It's fantastic! And I bet you've not had time to eat.'

This was true.

Then he gave one of his spectacular sneezes and took a big cotton handkerchief from a pocket to blow his nose.

'Still not over your cold?' Annie asked.

'Doh, dot really,' came from the depths of the hankie. 'Think I'm allergic to London,' he added when the hankie was out of the way.

It was a self-service café, so they got their plastic trays and stood in the queue. Despite Ed's rave review, Annie didn't feel tempted by any of the main courses on offer, so decided to go for lentil soup with a roll. She watched Lana make the same choice, while Owen plumped for an open sandwich with prawns, lettuce and pink mayonnaise.

While Ed got caught up in the ordering process for a hot meal, Annie paid for her family's food and drinks and went to find a table for four.

As they sat down, she wondered if, like her, the children were registering the empty fourth seat. The fourth chair was usually something she would quickly move away to another table, so that it wasn't staring at them, glaring with emptiness as they ate. But tonight there would be a fourth person. The fourth chair would be filled.

When Ed joined them, his tray was laden. He had a steaming plate of steak and kidney pie with mashed potatoes, vegetables, an orange juice, a glass of red wine, a side dish of bread and butter.

'God! I love the food here,' he announced, settling himself into the seat. 'I'm absolutely starving. Music always gives me an appetite!'

If Ed had noticed that no one else had such a big meal in front of them, he certainly didn't feel shy about it. He was tucking in with an enthusiasm bordering on the alarming.

Annie, on his left, felt a touch on her hand and realised it was a splash of Ed's gravy. 'Steady on!' she warned him.

When his plate was a little emptier and he could turn his attention to the business of conversation he focused on the children, very interested to know what they thought of the music. Owen gave it a rave review and Ed even managed to coax some words of enthusiasm from Lana. Annie could see he was a natural at his job.

'Yes, that was very clever,' he was telling Lana, 'and you know, I don't think it was based on any more than three different piano chords. You could probably teach yourself that in ten minutes.'

'Really?!' Lana was close to sounding impressed.

'But obviously I'm not sure if it's going to be appropriate for me to teach you a song about falling in love with your teacher!'

When Lana made a groaning sound, both Ed and Owen laughed and Annie felt herself relax. If he was just going to come out and joke about it like this, then there couldn't be anything to worry about, could there?

He was chewing vigorously again, loading up the next forkful.

'Do you go to many concerts?' Annie asked him, then wished she'd left it a few moments. Ed's mouth was full. Annie wondered where he put it all. He had a squarish build with broad shoulders, but he didn't give the impression of being at all chubby, although under the monumentally baggy khaki trousers and hairy tweed jacket chosen for tonight, it was hard to tell. And why had green tweed been paired with a double layer of red and yellow polo shirts? Annie wondered. Was he in some sort of competition for worst-dressed man in London?

'I try to do two a week,' came Ed's answer finally. 'No preference, all types of things.' He waved his knife and fork expansively and she saw Lana dodge slightly to avoid being sprayed. 'The cheap seats at the big operas, folk and classical here and at the Barbican, jazz nights, dodgy gigs in pubs. I just like to see the action. What about you people? What kind of things do you like to go to?'

Before Annie could consider her answer, Owen shook his head. 'We never go to anything like this. It's the first time I've been out in ages.'

'That's not true, Owen!' Annie was quick to deny, but she couldn't help smiling because she'd never seen Owen so at home with someone from outside the immediate family-and-friends circle. Her son had been seven when his dad had left and the debilitating shyness had set in almost immediately. Despite all sorts of expert advice and opinion, there had been little real improvement until Ed had become his teacher. Now, Owen seemed to be coming on in leaps and bounds, flourishing. She would have to take Ed aside and thank him for his help.

'Yes it is!' Owen retorted.

'We go out!' Annie insisted, but the more she tried to think of an example to prove Owen wrong, the more she couldn't. Plenty of memorable family outings with Roddy were filling her mind, but her and the children at a concert . . . at a play . . . 'Help me out, Lana!' she said.

'We go to the cinema a lot,' Lana reminded Owen. 'We go to Dinah's, Connor's, we visit friends and relatives . . . so we go out. But we don't do the concert, theatre, art gallery thing hardly at all.'

'Well, you have to,' Ed told them. 'You have to get out there. Rub shoulders with the world, find out what's goin' down.'

This was met with smiles from both Lana and Owen, even though they always rolled their eyes if Annie dared to use this phrase.

'So you're more a cinema person?' He directed this at Annie, as he used a thickly buttered roll to mop up the last of the gravy.

'I suppose so,' Annie replied.

'And what kind of films do you like?'

'Oh . . . stylish films,' she told him, 'with lovely clothes, beautiful people and beautiful settings, a touch of romance and there always, always has to be something to make me laugh.'

Ed was nodding vigorously. 'I love comedies,' he confided. 'Love them! And I love good music in films . . . but films of musicals, well, unless they were made before 1960, forget it. Pudding!' He smiled at Owen and Lana in turn, while Annie struggled with the connection between musicals and pudding.

'The pudding is sensational here,' Ed enthused, 'and it's my treat.'

He returned to the table, tray loaded with four bowls. Some sort of crumble dripping with cream: a calorific disaster. 'Ah!' was Ed's benediction over the plateful before he sank his spoon in. 'Like it?' he asked Owen, who was already wolfing down his third or fourth spoonful.

'Oh, yeah!' came Owen's answer through a full mouth. 'This is the best crumble I've ever had. What's in it?'

The small spoonful Annie had taken was just hitting her taste buds, so she was too late to save Owen.

'Rhubarb,' came Ed's reply.

Annie could only watch, hoping he'd be fine. Hadn't he just declared this the best crumble he'd ever eaten? Which, yes, had dented her pride slightly, although she'd be the first to admit she wasn't exactly gifted in the kitchen department.

Owen stopped chewing and began to change colour. Pink first, then red, then a deep purple-tinged scarlet.

'He's not allergic?' Ed asked anxiously, dropping his spoon.

Annie shook her head and explained. 'Only in his mind. Owen, you're going to be fine,' she soothed, reaching to pat Owen's hand.

But Lana couldn't resist. 'I don't think so,' she teased. 'Rhubarb, Owen, rhoooooo-barb.'

'Lana!' Annie hissed.

Scarlet, Owen made choky, gagging noises before a soggy lump of the offending crumble landed unceremoniously back in his plate.

Now it was Annie's turn to blush, but Ed, entirely unruffled, sprang into action. 'No need to panic. I'm so sorry, Owen, I didn't know anything about your dislike of this fruit . . . or is it in fact a vegetable? Anyway . . . let me take that away.' He stood up and whisked the offending plateful out of sight as quickly as possible.

When he got back to the table, Ed was determined to put the abashed Owen back at ease. 'Did you know there is a great long list of foods that have exactly the same effect on the Queen?' he asked Owen. 'Oh, yes,' he added, without waiting for an answer, 'if she's eating away from home, the list gets sent out in advance, just to make sure she doesn't barf at a state banquet, while she's sitting between the President of Russia and the King of Swaziland or something.'

A teacher talking about the Queen barfing was enough to make Owen grin despite the unfortunate rhubarb incident.

When Owen had exited to the loo, Ed told Annie, 'I've been a teacher for nine years. If there's any regurgitating, losing control of bladder or any other bodily functions to be done in public, I'm your man.'

'Well, that's very reassuring,' Annie told him. 'You know, I have to thank you for all your help with Owen. He's coming on so well . . . And you handled that . . . well. Better than I would have.'

'No problem, honestly . . .' Ed was threatening to blush. 'Now'—he went quickly for a change of subject—'shall I get the tube back to Highgate with you charming people? See you safely to your door?'

Then, just as Annie had thought she was beginning to warm to Ed, he plucked a yellow cagoule from his backpack, pulled it over his head and—although they were still indoors—put the hood up and pulled the toggles tight so that his face was framed with scrunched nylon.

This gave Annie something close to a rhubarb moment of her own.

She quickly looked away. Owen's admiration for Ed had given her an idea. She'd ask the teacher in and sound him out over coffee.

Ed lived in Highgate too ('I must show you my grimy little abode . . . maybe next time, when I've arranged for the industrial cleaners to come round'), so he insisted on walking them home and Annie, in turn, insisted he come in for a coffee.

Even if she hadn't had something she wanted to ask him, she wouldn't have liked the thought of sending him straight back to a grimy little abode without something in the way of thanks, so she guided him into the kitchen, while her children splintered off to their rooms.

'I need to make a call,' Lana explained.

Yes, I know, darlin', you've not spoken to Seth for at least two hours now, was what Annie wanted to say, but didn't.

'There's something I want to show you; just give me a minute,' Owen told Ed.

Annie put the kettle on and made a quick check on her emails and her eBays at the kitchen table while she chatted to Ed.

'So, how long have you lived round here then?' she asked, able to meet his eyes again now that the cagoule was off.

'Oh, ages,' Ed replied. 'But on and off. My mum bought her place here years and years ago and I used it as a base whenever I needed to. I've only been here full-time for a year and a half. Mum got ill. I took the job at St Vincent's so I could move in and look after her.'

'Oh . . . and how's she getting on?' was Annie's next question.

With a sad little smile, Ed told her, 'I'm afraid she died. Six months ago now.'

'Oh! I'm ever so sorry, Ed. I'm sorry,' she repeated, trying for one horrible moment to imagine life without Fern. 'I didn't know. How are you coping?' she asked, full of concern for him now.

'Well, I'm . . . you know . . . just getting on with things.' He ruffled his hair before continuing. 'Hannah, that's my sister, and I . . . we were looking after Mum full-time at the end, which was what we all wanted, but it was pretty hard going . . . My Italian girlfriend left me and went back to Italy, my rubbish car got nicked, the usual triple whammy stuff.'

'Oh dear, oh dear,' Annie sympathised.

'Obviously we miss her . . . miss her a lot.' Annie heard the involuntary swallow. 'But,' he went on, 'I'm trying to focus on how great it is to be back out here again. Back teaching, getting out again . . . meeting new people.' He nodded, as if in her direction. 'It's very nice to be taking part in life again.'

'How old was she?' Annie wondered.

Owen's head popped round the corner of the kitchen door and he asked, 'Can Ed come to my room for a minute?'

'Hang on a minute, Owen,' Annie told him. The head disappeared.

She turned her attention back to Ed and he replied, 'Mum was fifty-nine, four weeks from her sixtieth birthday. It was such a bugger. It was all a bugger.' He let out a sigh and turned his attention to his coffee cup.

'I'm really, really sorry,' Annie said once again.

'Anyway'—he looked up at her and gave a smile—'I have a favour I want to ask you. It is a bit bizarre, though.'

It was her turn to smile. 'Now that's funny,' she told him, 'because I have a favour I want to ask you . . . and it's really bizarre.'

'You first, then,' he said.

'No, no, definitely you.'

'Well, I was just wondering, if you'd consider . . . I mean, if it's not too much . . .' The request was turning him slightly pink.

Owen's head popped in again. 'Ed? Could you come and see—'

'Just a minute!' Annie cut him off and he skulked back out again.

'Ed,' she reassured the teacher, 'it's OK, just spit it out.'

'Boston, USA. Job interview. Well, not job, exactly . . . a term's paid research into the roots of rhythm and blues. I was supposed to go last year, but because of poor old Mum . . . well . . . you see?'

No, she did not see at all. Boston? His mother? What?!

'I need a suit,' he clarified. 'A proper, decent suit that will stand up to an interview with American academics.'

Ah! The fog was clearing.

'I need not just the suit, I need the whole outfit, you know, quite the thing. I think Americans take all that pretty seriously, don't they? And anyway, I have no clue. But you, you're always so wonderfully'— he waved his hand in her direction, taking in the happy pairing of red lipstick, red Topshop jacket, black ankle boots and Dries Van Noten skirt—'wonderful. And you work in that scary place. So I thought, you'll be just the right person to help me. There.' He looked really very embarrassed about it. 'Bizarre request. What's yours?'

Wonderfully wonderful? He was a case this man, no doubt about it.

'I'd be happy to help you find a suit, Ed,' she assured him. 'You tell me when and I'll book you in an appointment. Now . . .' she hesitated. 'I know you like to camp . . . Have you heard of the Man and Boy Orienteering weekend by any chance?'

'Heard of it? My friend Clyde runs it! It's brilliant. Does Owen want to go?' Ed guessed straight away. 'Are you looking for someone to go with him? I am definitely your man. So long as you're OK with that . . .' He backed down quickly. 'And obviously so long as Owen . . .'

She waved away his reservations and told him that she would of course check Owen was happy with the idea, but he was certain to be delighted. Such was Ed's enthusiasm for the project, she began to think he wasn't just a case; he was, in fact, bonkers.

'What tog rating is his sleeping-bag?' Ed asked, along with other incomprehensible questions. 'It's just, if he has a thick one, we could bivouac. We could do without the tent altogether. Spend the night under the stars. Bivvy down with nature.'

Annie had been thinking campsite, with hot showers, a restaurant, possibly even Tourist Board stars. She was now feeling nervous.

'Owen's got all the details. Maps, plans and projects. He'll love talking to someone else about it who can make out one end of a compass from another. What is Owen up to anyway? Owen!' Annie called.

'How's your dentist?' Ed asked, taking her by surprise. In response to her raised eyebrows, he explained, 'Owen told me about him.'

'Oh! Well, he's not "my" dentist. It's early days. Very early. I'd forgotten how stressful the whole dating, getting-to-know-someone thing is . . . trying to say and do the right thing all the time. God, it's exhausting! Tonight has been great fun. So relaxing.'

Ed held up his coffee mug to her in a toast-salute. 'To relaxing fun.'

Lana slouched into the kitchen and crumpled melodramatically into a chair, head slumping to the table.

'You can only get voicemail?' Annie guessed.

'Why won't he answer his phone?' Lana wailed, obviously so stricken that she wasn't embarrassed to mention this in front of a teacher.

'I'm sure there's a perfectly good reason,' Annie soothed. 'The battery's probably flat. Please, stop worrying about it.' Although secretly, she suspected Seth was not phoning as often as he had before. She wasn't sure whether to be relieved about this, or worried.

Gray, on the other hand, was phoning very regularly and had already lined up several intriguing meetings.

'Er . . . I think there's a slight problem in here!' came the sound of Owen's voice.

With a lurch, Annie thought she detected a note of fear in those words. As she got up from her chair, there was a bang. Not a loud, startling bang, but a whoosh that climaxed in a surprising pop.

She rushed for Owen's room, Ed on her heels.

Pulling his door ajar, she registered the smell: smoky, of bitter burnt toast. 'Owen!' she called out. 'Are you OK?'

'Well, erm, I had a little problem,' he said shakily. 'I mean it's fine now . . . fine . . . but . . . a bit messy.'

Annie stepped inside. It looked as if he had built a bonfire on his desk. Even more alarming was the big sooty black scorch mark that covered the white wall from desk to ceiling, three feet wide. 'Oh. My. God,' was Annie's first reaction. 'What on earth?!' But then she saw the science kit box upturned. 'Owen! You're not supposed to get that out when Connor's not around,' she snapped.

'I know. But I wanted to show . . .' He tailed off, but it was obvious he'd wanted to show Ed some experiment from the kit.

'What were you trying to do? Build the indoor atomic bomb?'

'I went a little bit off plan,' Owen shrugged, looking annoyingly unapologetic.

'You're lucky you didn't take out an eye, Owen, or burn down the house.' There was a big glass of water, full to the brim, standing in the middle of the floor. Annie pointed at it questioningly.

'Yeah, I thought I should have that on stand-by. But then I worried I'd make it worse.'

Knowing the chemical mixture would be wasted on his mother, he lobbed an explanation over to Ed, who had come to the door too and was looking on wordlessly.

Ed gave a whistle. 'You took a risk there, Owen,' he said. 'That could have been very nasty. And the water! Water would have . . . well, never mind,' he decided to say, seeing the look on Annie's face.

'We'll have to speak about this later,' she told Owen. 'Anyway, you should be in bed.' She flicked a glance at her watch. 'It's almost eleven o'clock! You should definitely be in bed.'

She headed back to the kitchen. Ed followed.

She had her back turned to him and Ed was surprised to see she was shaking slightly. He hadn't realised how much the incident had upset her. 'Don't worry about it,' he began, coming up behind her. 'I'm sure he won't do that again.'

'Oh.' She turned and wiped her eyes. 'I bloody hope not!' she said just as Ed realised she was shaking with silent laughter.

His arm, which had been raised slightly to offer her a comforting touch on the shoulder, fell back to his side and he gave something of a laugh himself: 'At least he didn't add the water . . .' Ed said. 'I think you could have been looking at . . . well . . .' He didn't want to frighten her. '. . . A fairly extensive bit of redecoration.'

After the Tower Bridge date, Gray had taken Annie out for lunch again and then came a big, swanky dinner.

That night, she had found Gray quite irresistibly attractive. Ordering the wine, sweeping up the bill with his platinum card, he'd been the suave, witty grown-up she was certain she wanted. Strolling along the streets of Knightsbridge afterwards, Annie had felt a wave of happiness wash over her. At last, she was beginning to allow herself to think that she had found a person she could share her life with once again.

They'd looked in furniture-shop windows and he'd wanted to know her opinion about everything. Each time they agreed on something, she'd felt a little internal 'yes!' and in her mind the domestic fantasy of being Gray's stay-at-home wife had cranked up again.

La-la-la, she would wear dresses all the time, because he'd complimented her on her legs. She would learn to cook, beautifully, and be able to lavish her undivided attention on Gray and her children. She would housekeep to perfection: ironing sheets with lavender water, folding fluffy towels, baking bread. La-la-la. There would be no more house renovating, no more moving, no more dealing with Donna the total bitch. Life would just be so peachy and perfect . . . wouldn't it?

Having just agreed with her that the sofa in the window of the Conran Shop was far superior to anything else they'd seen the length of the street, Gray had wrapped both arms around her and said, 'Annie, I think I'm going to have to kiss you. I hope that's OK?'

The formality of the request had caused her to tease, 'Well . . . depends what your kissing's like. Shall we see?'

Very minty breath, moist, but the moves needed a little practice, was Annie's first thought. The kiss didn't go on for long and she was aware of the carefulness of it. For instance, a full six inches apart at the hip had been maintained at all times.

Maybe Gray, being fourteen years older than her, was going to be very formal and measured about wooing her. There would be no getting swept away with your passions here. He was too grown-up. They were both testing the waters and cautious about the decisions ahead.

'So what are you doing tomorrow?' he'd asked after a second, slightly more intimate kiss.

'Nothing I can't get out of—if it's for a very good reason,' she'd decided to answer.

'Why don't you come and have lunch at my house?'

'I'd love to,' she told him, wondering how to bribe Lana to look after Owen . . . and Dinah to supervise Lana. They would finally be alone and undisturbed in a private place tomorrow. She hoped he had a lot more than lunch on his mind, because she certainly did.

She looked at his face closely as he drove her home. He must have been gorgeous when he was younger. Maybe it was hard for him to grow middle-aged. That might explain the green contact lenses, perfect teeth and just slightly odd-looking hair; it was a little too coppery and too smooth. But she had run her hands through it several times and was certain that Owen and Lana were wrong. He didn't deserve the nickname 'rug boy'.

Just before noon the next day, Sunday, Annie climbed into her jeep, fully briefed with directions from Gray, and set off to find his home in a bijou Essex village.

She was depilated, exfoliated, moisturised and fragrant from top to toe. All twenty nails were manicured and painted, she was wearing stockings and her teeth were flossed. She even had condoms. She was as ready for seduction as she was ever going to be.

After forty minutes of driving, the scrappy retail parks gave way to countryside. The sky was cloudless, the landscape a fresh, spring green, and Annie felt her mood lift and soar.

As she drew nearer to Gray's village, she called him up on the in-car mobile. 'Hello, Sexy Suburban Man,' she greeted him, 'I'm on the out-skirts of your village, so you'll have to talk me though the final turns.'

'This is not a suburb!' he insisted. 'Upper Ploxley is the most expensive village in Essex.'

'Gray, I'm driving through a housing estate!' she countered. 'Anyway, I hope you've got the wine on ice.'

'Champagne, my dear. Champagne. Have you brought your swim-suit?' he asked. He hadn't explained why she needed a swimsuit. She suspected a small kidney-, maybe heart-shaped, outdoor pool. But it better be heated; it was only April.

'That must be you now, coming down the road in your small

armoured tank,' he joked. 'I'm the white house, third on your left.'

She slid the jeep into a short driveway before an impressive 1970s boxy glass and concrete construction, painted bright white.

It was so neat, was her first impression. Every piece of gravel was raked into place on a driveway that bordered a smooth, green crewcut of lawn. Even the plants inside the window-boxes were standing to attention against a background of flawless brown earth.

Gray was already at the front door.

'What a lovely house,' she said immediately, as she climbed out of the jeep. 'Your garden is so immaculate, you must be at it all the time.'

'I use a weekly gardening service.' He batted the compliment away. 'They're really good.'

Of course he did.

He waited until she'd stepped inside to give her one of his careful kisses. 'Come on in,' he said, breaking off, 'I want to show you round.'

She was desperate to look round too. To glean all the clues she could, not just about Gray but also about his estranged wife. Annie felt sure that the taste stamped all over this expensive 1970s home would not in fact be Gray's but, much more intriguingly, Marilyn's.

Gray did not like to talk about Marilyn. All Annie had been able to find out had come from her own, fairly blunt questioning.

The ongoing divorce was not exactly a happy one.

'Marilyn had made my life miserable by the end,' Gray had told Annie as he drove her home the previous night. 'Now we're fighting over every little detail. Sometimes, I would just like to let her have what she wants and be done with it. Start again, start over. But then I remind myself that she never *did* anything. She never had a job, we didn't have children, all she did was spend my money and now she wants to be left with half of all the things she spent my money on and half of the home she didn't contribute one penny towards.'

Staying at home to bake for Gray with the crisp and shiny oven gloves had suddenly not looked quite so rosy to Annie.

'My lawyer has prepared a more than generous "clean break" settlement for her and still she's refusing to take it,' Gray had added angrily.

They'd been married for five years. Marilyn—originally called Tracey, she'd changed it by deed poll, he'd told her just a little cattily—had been with him from the age of thirty-four until she was forty. Apparently the neurotic dread with which she'd approached her fortieth birthday had been the final straw that tipped their marriage into irretrievable breakdown.

'She acted as if she was going to die on the day, not reach her fifth decade. You seem so much more relaxed,' Gray had told her. 'Marilyn was in a frenzy about everything, from which colour to paint her fingernails to how to arrange the plant pots. It was totally exhausting.'

'I'm not forty yet,' Annie had warned him. 'It could all change.'

But to Annie's slight disappointment, there didn't seem to be any clue to Marilyn left in Gray's home now. It looked as if he'd completely redecorated since she'd gone.

There was a huge dark brown leather sofa in the bright sitting room. Floor-to-ceiling windows overlooked the neat front garden, and a wide opening in the back wall led through to a dazzling slate and stainless steel kitchen, divided from the back garden by another huge window.

'Wow,' she kept telling him. 'This is amazing.'

'Now, let me show you the roof terrace,' was the way Gray framed his invitation to upstairs.

Out on the terrace, surrounded by dark decking, tall shrubs in pots and ornamental marble balls, was a generous, two-metre-wide Jacuzzi.

'It's a bit of fun, isn't it?' Gray said, unlocking the glass windows so they could go out. 'It's heated, obviously . . . I worried it was a bit too James Bond, but now I'm a total convert. Sitting out here, glass of champagne in one hand . . . Maybe we'll do that later,' he added gently.

'Oh, bollocks to later!' she announced, only partly because staying here too late was going to cause her a baby-sitting headache. 'Let's get into the water and build up an appetite for lunch!'

She reached for him and, as they kissed, began to unbutton his shirt . . . but, to her disappointment, he broke off. 'There's a big dressing gown and towels for you in here.' Then he opened the door to his spare room and ushered her in. 'I'll see you in a few minutes.'

Well, it wasn't the giggly stripping off and jumping in stark naked she'd envisaged, but then this was Gray's old-fashioned charm, wasn't it? The reserve she'd seen in him and found so likable?

Annie took her clothes off in the neutral hotel-like room. There was even a cushion on the bed that matched the fabric of the curtains. She *hated* that. Bet that was a Tracey-turned-Marilyn touch.

She pulled on her red with white polka-dots swimsuit. It was a glamorous 1950s style with a hefty 40 per cent Lycra. With its eye-distracting dots and elastic cling, this baby did almost as much for her as a corset. Now, if she'd just thought to buy the matching Joan Collins sarong and wide-brimmed straw hat . . . But then, it was April. The thick dressing gown was probably completely necessary.

She looked herself over in the mirror and reapplied the red lipstick chosen to match the swimsuit. What a dish—even if she had to say it herself. Stepping out into the hall, Annie saw that the roof-terrace door was open, the Jacuzzi was bubbling fiercely, but Gray was not there. Never mind, she would get in first. A toe-test assured her that the water was bathtub warm, so she slipped into the pool.

Oh! Delicious! There was a curved comfortable bench beneath the surface so she could sit and look up at the sky as her body was pummelled with surprisingly vigorous jets of water.

She threw her head back, tits out, and waited for Gray to catch her looking utterly irresistible. But long minutes passed and there was still no sign of him. Her neck was stiffening, so she relaxed the pose and her eyes fell on the stacked pyramid of large black marble balls between the potted palms. Surely this was another Tracey-Marilyn thing? No man went into a shop and came out with marble balls.

What was keeping Gray? She must have been in the water on her own for at least ten minutes now. Maybe he was showering?

And what would he look like naked? she couldn't help wondering. He would be muscular, but as he was almost at the fifty mark, there would probably be those tell-tale age signs: slightly shrunken buttocks, little baggy wrinkles at the armpit, elbow and knees. *OK, no need to panic!*

On a whim, she reached over to pick up one of the marble balls: it was much heavier than she'd expected. She felt it slip just slightly and panicked that she was about to drop it to the bottom of the pool and cause thousands of pounds' worth of damage. She tightened her grip on it and quickly turned to put it back into the pile.

But the marble ornaments had been stacked with far more skill than she'd appreciated and the ball she returned was still for only a moment before it rolled off, taking down another five balls with it in a loud, cracking tumble. For solid marble, they rolled away at a surprising rate in three different directions—which didn't say much for the skills of the joiner who'd done the decking.

Annie leapt out of the pool to herd them.

She had three balls under control and was bending over trying to reassemble the pile when she heard Gray asking, 'How's the water?'

Peering over her shoulder, she saw him swathed in a dressing gown at the terrace door, balancing a small tray with a bottle of champagne and two delicate glasses. Instead of finding her in the pool looking fabulous with a come-hither smile upon her face, he was subjected to a full-on rear-end view as she wrestled with the slippery ornaments.

'Oh dear, what's happened?' he asked.

'Nothing, nothing . . . no damage done.' She turned to get her bum out of the spotlight. 'The marbles . . . They've rolled about a bit.' She spotted the fourth and kneeled gracefully this time to pick it up.

'Here, let me help you,' Gray insisted, setting the tray down on the floor. He put his hands out to take the ball from her, but misjudged and made contact with her cleavage. He jerked his hands back again, which was a mistake, as Annie had now let go of the ball, thinking Gray had it. It crashed down, landing squarely on Gray's foot.

'Aaaargh!' he cried out, and instinctively brought his knee up so that, hopping slightly, he could clutch at the mashed toes. Another error, as he slipped on the now wet decking and lost his balance.

He wobbled for a moment, arms flailing, Annie reading the shock in his look, and then with a resounding *crash!!!* he went down, falling backwards into the champagne tray and knocking himself out cold.

'Gray! Crap! Bloody *crap*! *Gray*!' was Annie's cool, collected response. Her rearranging of the ornaments had killed him: it was Ms Scarlett on the decking with the marble ball.

She crouched down beside him. His head had crunched into one of the glasses, the overturned bottle had rolled away and was now glugging its contents into the Jacuzzi.

Gray's lips were white, which didn't strike her as a good sign, but there was definitely breath coming from his nose, so she let her panic subside slightly.

What was she supposed to do? Maybe she should splash him with a little water? She leaned over to the pool, scooped up a handful of water and dripped it over his temple. It ran off his forehead and into his hair.

She couldn't help taking just a nanosecond to scrutinise his hair, now that she had the opportunity. Leaning in, she satisfied herself once and for all that Gray didn't wear a toupée, but he did use hair dye: there was just the tiniest millimetre or so of grey root visible on inspection. Fair enough, he liked to look good.

But anyway . . . She had to get on and do something to help him. She decided to roll him gently onto his side, into the recovery position, then phone for an ambulance.

Once he was in position, a fold of his dressing gown fell open to reveal a fresh surprise. Was that a . . . ? Could that really be . . . ?

One part fascinated, one part horrified, Annie examined this new development. There was no mistaking it: poking up from the thick white cloth of the dressing gown was a rigid, pink erection.

You couldn't be unconscious and have a boner like that, could you? No. Gray must have taken something. One of those products everyone with an email address opened up to every morning.

Gray gave just the slightest of groans and Annie quickly got to her feet. It wouldn't do to get caught examining a man's penis while he was unconscious. His eyes were still closed, so she ran to find her mobile, snatching it from her handbag to dial 999.

She was back on the roof terrace, trying to put her folded gown underneath Gray's head, when he came round. Annie was trying to explain what had happened, but it was taking some time to sink in.

'What do you mean, hit my head?' he asked in a slurred voice.

'You've had a fall . . . Just stay still, there's an ambulance on its way.'

'An ambulance! Oh God,' he groaned. 'This wasn't supposed to happen.'

There was no ignoring the Bone. It was still there, poking well clear of his dressing gown.

Annie was just about to throw her towel over his middle to stop him from realising about the very embarrassing little situation going on down there, but then came a much deeper groan and the pulling up of his knees as he noticed. 'Oh Jesus!' he exclaimed.

'Hey, don't worry about that . . . I'm flattered,' Annie joked, trying to put him at ease. 'Would you like a drink of water?'

He just closed his eyes and groaned again.

The ambulance crew of three arrived and included Brenda, a visual feast from Tasmania. Deeply tanned, tomboyish and gorgeous, she at least perked Gray up slightly.

'A romantic moment gone wrong here, then,' she summed up, surveying the bubbling Jacuzzi, Annie still in glamourpuss swimsuit and pole-axed, tent-pole Gray.

One crew member spoke into his radio: 'Middle-aged male: glass injuries to the scalp, injury by a spherical marble ornament to the left foot, suspected concussion and a possible Viagra reaction. Yes, I am in Upper Ploxley . . . How did you guess?' He did at least try to keep the chuckle from his voice.

Gray was finally carried out on a stretcher with the weight of three towels over his middle in an attempt to keep the Bone at bay.

Once they'd all left, Annie switched off the Jacuzzi, swept the broken glass from the decking, drank down the mouthful or so of champagne left in the bottle, locked the terrace doors, changed out of her swimsuit and exited the house, pulling the front door shut behind her.

Back in her jeep, she wondered if she should have accompanied Gray to hospital, but he'd told her not to. She wondered if she would ever hear from him again . . . Finally she had to give in and allow herself to do the one thing she hadn't been able to do ever since the marble boulder had slipped from Gray's grip: she began to rock with laughter.

New, improved Martha:

Orange, red and white dress (Issa)
Slouchy brown boots (Miu Miu)
Caramel tote (Chloé)
Total est. cost: £1,400

'Don't you think I'm transvestite tall?'

PAULA, NOW BACK on the shop floor, was the assistant who led Martha Cooper into the Personal Shopping suite for her second visit with the words, 'Wow! I can't believe it's really you!'

Annie, who was trying to arrange a delivery of flowers to Gray at his hospital bed, took her feet off her desk and began to clap.

'Oh, very good!' she told Martha, who was smiling from ear to ear.

The mum who'd turned up in old jeans and a parka now stood before them in the sharp trousers and swing jacket she'd bought on her first visit, nicely grunged down with a pair of green gymmies. But the biggest change was the healthy, make-up-assisted glow on her face and the hair. The lank mop was now a tonged, caramel-coloured mane.

'Grrrrrrr,' Annie purred. 'Look at you. And are you back at work now?'

Martha nodded.

'So you've returned to spend lots of your new lolly?'

'Oh, yes. I want a raincoat . . . and a dress . . . maybe some boots . . . and *possibly* a bag.'

'Oh, you are so in the right place, babes.'

After a speed search of the collections, they were back in the suite. A vibrant orange and red Issa dress with high-heeled boots and a fab bag were the choices Annie was nudging Martha towards. The dress was beautiful on. Unfortunately the high-heeled brown slouchy boots that went so brilliantly with it seemed to be the problem for Martha.

'I know everything looks better with heels,' she began, 'but don't you think I'm transvestite tall?'

'No,' Annie assured her, but, well . . . She was about six foot four in those boots, which was a little scary.

'There's no use telling me how tall Cindy, Lindy, Elle etc. are, I just don't want to be the tallest thing in a room bar the column holding up the ceiling. And I just don't think this—'

'Is really you?' Annie jumped in. 'Too smart, too dressy . . . too much, too soon! Sorry, I'm rushing you in there. OK. We like the dress? Agreed? So maybe we need to style it down. And we need to bring you down too, don't we?'

She disappeared off into the store and came back with several accessories. The dress was tried on again, but this time with a white vest underneath, brown footless tights and flat gold pumps.

'Oh yes! Yes. So much better!' was Martha's verdict.

Then Annie handed over the killer accessory: a Chloé tote bag—big, astronomically expensive in a go-with-everything tan leather.

'No, no!' Martha didn't even want to hold it.

'Just try it, girl, get it onto your arm,' Annie wheedled.

Annie handed it over and was too fascinated to see what Martha would think to notice Donna stalking into the suite.

Martha was staring at her reflection. 'I have a handbag morality,' she explained. 'I draw the line at two hundred pounds. You should be able to get a fantastic bag for no more than two hundred pounds. I can't walk about with a month's salary slung from my shoulder. I certainly can't carry my packed lunch in it, or baby wipes, or beakers.'

'OK . . . well, then, you know where you have to shop?'

'Where?' Martha wondered.

'eBay! You could probably get this bag for two hundred pounds on eBay, but you have to accept that it's a fake. Or then again, downstairs we have wipedown PVC Orla Kiely bags, very, very popular with the Yummy Mummy. But I love you in that bag!' she added.

Annie also did not see Donna stalking out of the suite with an expression on her face that was hard to read: part sour, part satisfied.

'The bag is absolutely stunning, baby. A real investment . . . But no pressure. I've got three lovely raincoats here for you to try on while you think about the bag. Orange? Great with that dress. Or classic light beige? Or maybe both?'

'Annie, *stop*! You are so good, you are very, very bad. I'm going for a strong, sobering coffee before I decide about the bag. I'll buy the dress, the tights, the flats, probably a raincoat too . . . but I need coffee for the bag decision!'

'OK, OK.' Annie smiled at her. 'You know where we are!'

She heard the curtains at the entrance to the suite parting, then Ed Leon was standing there, looking sheepish. 'Sorry, am I a bit . . . erm . . . early?'

'No, no. Take a seat,' Annie instructed. 'I just have to sell this nice lady here a raincoat, then I'm all yours,' she told him.

When Martha had paid for the purchases she was certain about and gone for her bag-decider coffee, Annie was able to turn her attention to the dweeby teacher. 'So,' she said, settling onto the sofa beside him, 'tell me all about your tailoring requirements.'

'Top-to-toe overhaul,' was Ed's verdict.

'Where do you usually shop?' she wondered.

'Oh well, er, Burtons . . . and what's that place? Mister Byrite. There's the Highgate Cancer Research once in a while, it's pretty good . . .' Watching her melodramatic eye-roll, he didn't like to continue. 'You're not impressed, are you?'

'It's OK, you're here now,' she told him, teasing slightly. 'This is where I begin to convince you of the merits of investment dressing. I have an investment dressing lecture, if you'd like to hear it.'

Ed said, 'I'd like to hear any lecture of yours very much.'

Annie assembled suits, shirts and ties for Ed, while he was held hostage, stripped to his underwear in the changing room. He kept appearing at the door in a slightly alarming pair of crinkled purple boxer shorts and short red socks to ask how it was going.

Annie couldn't help catching a glimpse of his unexpectedly muscular stomach. 'Do you work out?' She tried to keep the incredulity from her voice.

'No!' He was equally incredulous.

'You look . . . fit,' she said to justify her remark.

'Rugby coaching . . . keeps the gut at bay,' was his reply.

In every one of the suit, shirt and tie ensembles, Ed would step out and Annie would give a businesslike appraisal: shoulders too broad, jacket too long, trousers too tight. He was proving a difficult figure to fit.

Finally, a navy-blue suit, matched with pale pink shirt and blue tie, ticked every box in Annie's checklist.

'Goodness!' was Ed's verdict as he walked around the shop floor a little, then surveyed himself in the full-length mirror. 'Look at that! I hardly recognise myself! Just wait till I get my hair cut, then all traces of the old Ed Leon will be erased.'

Annie was looking at him closely, professionally. There was no denying that the jacket shoulders were a perfect fit; that pink and blue were a great colour combination for him. He had bright blue eyes, summer-sky blue, and she'd not noticed that until she'd held shirts up to his face to check for colour matching. He also had rosy cheeks and very pink lips. These details hadn't come into such sharp focus before. No. Before the blue suit and pink shirt effect, she'd seen only Ed's woolly hair, bushy eyebrows and tweed.

'Haircut?' she asked, not sounding convinced.

'Yup, short back and sides. I'm taking this very seriously.'

She tried to imagine how his hair would look short. He'd be certain to go to a £5-a-pop barber who'd massacre it, so she told him firmly, 'No. Definitely no haircut—and you know what?' This wasn't exactly good business, but she felt she had to say it: 'I don't think you should buy this suit either, Ed, because it's just not you.'

Just as Martha had looked great in the high-heeled boots, so Ed looked good in the suit. Really, she'd been quite taken aback by how good he looked. But it was as if she'd extinguished everything that was Ed. Everything that was sparky and quirky about Ed was buried now that she'd put him into this regulation dark blue suit.

How was anyone going to know the slightest thing about him in this outfit? How were they going to know that he could play ten different stringed instruments? Or that he had a folk and blues LP collection to rival any New Orleans DJ's? Worst of all, he looked uncomfortable. He kept tugging his cuffs and smoothing his lapels. The stiff black shoes he had on his feet weren't helping, either. They seemed to weigh him down; he'd had a funny, lolloping spring to his step before, a bounciness that went with his mad hair.

She checked her watch: ten past five. She could slip out early, there were other places . . . 'I think we need to try somewhere else. C'mon. Put your things back on and we'll head out.'

He raised his eyebrows questioningly. He quite liked this blue suit. He thought he looked like, well . . . someone with an office job, someone with means . . . someone who could be seen with a woman as gloriously elegant as Annie.

But she was frowning and the frown, which made a captivating little 'v' between her eyebrows, was not directed at him. No, her eyes were firmly on the suit and she wasn't happy with it at all, so he began to undress and re-dress all over again.

From one of The Store's exits, which happened to be overlooked by Donna's office, they set off in the direction of Jermyn Street to an enormous corner building entirely devoted to the fitting out of 'gentlemen'. 'We'll just wander for a little,' Annie instructed him. 'Tell me if anything catches your eye.' She loved this shop. It was living, breathing proof of the very different way men and women approached clothes. Whereas women wanted to know what was new and what was now and didn't care what it was made of, how tight or ill-fitting it was, men wanted the traditional, the familiar, the long-lasting and the practical.

The difference always struck Annie most at black-tie events when men wore beautiful suits they could put on year after year, which made them look fantastic but kept them warm and allowed them to enjoy the food to the full, whereas women flitted like butterflies in wonderful chilly creations they couldn't sit in, let alone eat in.

In this shop there were socks available in three leg lengths, eight different sizes and twenty different colours. There were racks filled with the kind of suits and overcoats that would last for the next fifteen years and beyond. The ties came in different widths, different silks, different weaves. There were scarves, gloves and hats, waistcoats, shirts. Only the sober, quietly spoken male assistants could possibly know the full range of collars available here.

'If sir requires any assistance, he should not hesitate to ask,' came the gentle instruction from one of the impeccably dressed staff.

'Yes, erm . . . right,' was Ed's slightly tense reply.

Sensing he was out of his depth now, Annie stepped in and directed him towards the long rails packed with tweed jackets. 'Have a look through . . .' There was a small check in beige and brown with an accent of maroon, which she homed in on, pulling the jacket out with its hanger. 'This, maybe?' she wondered.

'Nice,' he agreed. 'Very nice,' then put his hands on something way too yellowy with a bold black check.

'I dunno,' she warned him. 'Rupert Bear?'

Together they picked out jackets and toning checked shirts and moleskin trousers. In and out of the changing room Ed went, as Annie checked everything over for fit, for colour, for proportion.

The tills were being closed down, but their salesman insisted, 'No trouble, sir, take your time. One must have the right apparel.'

Finally Ed and his stylist were finished. Their work was done, their creation was complete. Even the salesman, George, as they'd come to know him, admired the effect: 'A little eccentric, but very pleasing, sir.'

Ed stood before them smartly and appropriately dressed but also still totally Ed. 'Brilliant!' Annie allowed herself to grin at the outfit; no more frowning and letting the furrows form between her eyebrows.

Ed was in the beige, brown and maroon tweed jacket, the very first one Annie had picked out, a white with a pale brown check country shirt underneath. A very thin, finest spun-silk golden tie with ducks flying upside down was tied into his trademark tight knot at his neck. Most striking of all were the close-cut bright maroon moleskin trousers. Very rock and roll star retires to country estate, Annie had thought.

The long trouser legs rested and rumpled against softest caramel suede punched brogue boots. And on top of all this was a swinging short beige mac with a bright green padded lining and a scarf.

Ed was going to buy two more checked shirts, a maroon tie and a pair of beige moleskins, on Annie's instruction, to make sure he had plenty of different ways to wear the jacket.

He was also going to be getting another pair of glasses—small gold rims—and a 'really funky bag', she had informed him.

Turning to look at himself in the mirror, he told her, 'You're really good at this, you know. Have you ever thought about doing it for a living?! I look just like myself . . . but much better.'

He'd wow them, he'd definitely get the post, she knew.

'Ed.' She made eye contact with his reflection. 'You're hot, baby.'

Ed began to blush, then didn't seem to be able to stop. He turned a deep burgundy red.

Annie's phone began to ring.

When she answered, she heard Gray's voice on the other end of the line. 'Annie, what beautiful flowers,' he began in a low purr. 'You shouldn't have. You really shouldn't have . . . Now, how am I going to make up to you for that *fiasco* the other day?'

'Oh, Gray, hello. I'm sure I can think of a few ways.'

Ed was obviously tired of the shopping session. As she made arrangements to meet Gray, he went back into the changing room and pulled the curtain shut behind him.

'**N**ow, we know all about your first attempt and the trip to A&E with the tent pole . . .' Connor was talking quietly as Annie and Dinah moved their heads closer to catch what he was saying. 'But what Dinah and I are gagging to know is, have you and the dirty dentist done the deed yet? We know you went to his place again last weekend, Annie, so time to confess. How was he? Does he have an impressive instrument?'

Annie just smiled as Dinah ticked him off with the words, 'Hey! This is an old-fashioned romance. It's progressing nicely, slowly, in a ladylike and gentlemanly way. Keep your overactive sex drive out of it.'

Connor just snorted.

Their first courses arrived, delivered by a waiter with splendid buttocks and a quite Parisian level of rudeness. 'The soup?' he snapped and dumped the dish in front of Connor, so that the liquid slopped.

Annie was not sure about this restaurant. It was in its first week and had been opened by Henrik, a friend of Connor's, who'd had the novel idea of combining a hairdressing salon with a restaurant. As you walked in there were smart white-linen-covered tables ready for diners, but on a raised platform beyond were all the accoutrements of a hair salon. It didn't make for a happy combination. Annie could not imagine wanting to be spotted in a headful of highlight foils by people eating their lunch. Nor would she want to eat in a place filled with the smell of hair dye, with hair clippings on the loose.

'Do you dare me to tell the waiter there's a hair in my soup?' Connor whispered at them.

But this plan was thwarted by the appearance at their table of the owners. 'Hey, Connor, my man, you've made my day!' came the greeting from a tall, very blond, tight-pink-T-shirted man.

'Henrik!' Connor greeted him. 'This place is great!' he gushed.

All three told Henrik as many complimentary and flattering things as possible until finally he went away, promising the chef would be out to meet them later.

Connor tried to look as thrilled as he could at the prospect of this.

'So, c'mon,' Connor urged Annie, 'cough! It's Sunday afternoon, you arrive at Gray's house for lunch and . . . ? Take us from there.'

'OK, OK . . . Gray was looking good,' she relented. 'He'd obviously made a full recovery from . . . the Jacuzzi moment.'

'Excellent!' Connor noted. 'So did you get down to it straight away or was there alcohol involved first?'

'You don't have to tell him!' Dinah insisted.

'Yes, you do!' Connor insisted. 'We're family. We deserve to know about Annie's first shag since . . . he who shall not be named.'

'We had lunch,' Annie continued, ignoring Connor. 'Gray made seafood risotto with champagne. He *cooked* with the Taittinger!'

Connor looked impressed.

'Then we ate, and talked and drank the rest of the bottle.'

'Aha . . .' Connor prompted. 'And then?'

Dinah dug her elbow into his ribs sharply.

'We went to the sofa . . . And it got . . . nicely steamy,' she decided on.

She'd liked Gray's kisses. His mouth was very clean and probing. The brown leather sofa had been too slippery though. She'd kept having to put an arm down on the floor to keep them both from sliding right off and this had been distracting.

His careful questioning—'Can I undo this? Would that be OK with you?'—had been a mixture of charming and annoying.

But the prospect of undoing his perfectly ironed black Hugo Boss shirt had begun to make her feel pleasantly hot and bothered.

Opening one button at a time, she'd discovered that his nipples were small and his chest hairless.

'And did ya?' Connor asked.

'Kinda,' Annie replied.

'Oh, no, the Viagra didn't let him down again, did it?'

'No!' Annie insisted. Lowering her voice, she added, 'They've worked out a new dose for him at the hospital, one that won't make him dizzy . . . and believe me, it's quite impressive.'

'Oh yeah!' Connor encouraged.

'Like a ramrod,' Annie added.

There was a pause and even Dinah had to admit to herself she was quite interested in hearing the rest now.

'Well . . . were you ramrodded?' Connor asked with a wicked grin. 'Brace yourself, Annie, I'm a dentist. Brace yourself . . . geddit?'

'Oh ha ha,' came from Dinah.

'Er . . . no. It was all a bit too much, too soon. I ducked out,' Annie confessed. Did she want Connor to know the nitty-gritty? That making use of the shiny sofa surface, she'd slid herself away from Gray's heated kissing and easily down towards his navel.

'You went oral on the dentist, didn't you?' came Connor's merciless question.

'I'm not answering,' she told him.

'Did he ask you to open wide? And try not to swallow?' he teased. 'No. Let me guess, he made you rinse and spit?' Connor couldn't help laughing at his own joke.

'I'm *not* answering!' she told him.

'Stop it, Connor,' Dinah warned.

'It's been a little confusing,' Annie confided. 'There I was, convinced I was desperate to have sex with the guy. And when it came down to it . . . well . . . it was too big a step to take all at once.'

'How did he react?' Dinah asked.

'He was fine. Charming . . . very grateful,' Annie told them.

'I bet he was,' said Connor, and Annie's cheeky smile returned. 'And afterwards?' he prompted.

'It was very comfortable. We snuggled on the sofa, cuddled up and we were able to talk about things. He's really nice, you know. I wish you two would give him a break. He said he really missed having a wife.'

'His wife?' Dinah checked.

'No. A wife. Someone to come home to, someone to share even the very small things with.'

'I miss that too,' she'd told him. 'Obviously I have the children, and they're fantastic, but being part of a couple . . . it's very special,' she'd said, feeling slightly nervous that she'd overexposed herself.

But Gray had just nodded and squeezed her hand.

'We got into his rooftop jacuzzi,' she told Connor and Dinah.

'Nice. Very nice,' said Dinah. 'Left the ornaments in peace this time.'

'Then he drove me home, but we made a bit of a detour via the shops. He bought me a very nice pair of shoes.' Annie lifted a foot up into the air. All her waking hours since Sunday had been spent with her feet in these adorable pointy pumps, palest biscuity gold leather with just a hint of glitter to them.

'Nice. Marc Jacobs?' Dinah guessed.

'Miu Miu.' She gazed at them fondly. They were just so pretty: girlish, ready to party, light-hearted, and Gray had been very good at shoe-shopping. Seemed to understand why shoes were such a tonic: because you were never too fat for shoes . . . you'd never crept up a size without noticing. They were the perfect present to yourself.

'Look and be jealous, Dinah,' said Connor, stroking the shoe. 'Bryan could really learn from this man.'

'How?' Dinah asked a little sharply.

'He'd get so much more sex if he took you out shopping afterwards, wouldn't he? For Miu Miu, you'd probably do some very filthy things.'

'Bryan doesn't need to buy me anything,' Dinah huffed, but quickly followed it with, 'but if Gray wants to treat Annie, that's lovely. Now we're asking you about your sex life,' she told him, because for three whole weeks now (surely a record?) Connor had had a lover he was crazily excited about. 'And you will not be spared,' she added.

Connor looked at them in a seriously unusual, blissed-out kind of way, then tugged up his white T-shirt. There were deep red pinch marks on either side of his rosy nipples and a brand-new raw-looking metal stud in his navel. 'It's love, definitely love,' Connor said. 'Where would you like me to start?'

Dinah let out a little scream before saying, 'It's OK, we're fine. Really.'

Connor got hold of his wineglass and held it up, Dinah did likewise, then Annie too. 'To falling in love,' Connor offered.

Annie was sitting, feet up, on the big sofa holding a vast bowl of popcorn, with Owen curled up on one side of her and Lana on the other. It was Tuesday night, DVD night. Whenever possible on Tuesdays, the three of them snuggled up together for a pizza and an evening of giggling through the most hilarious film Blockbuster had to offer.

When the phone began to ring, Annie leaned forward.

'Muuuum,' Lana complained. 'Leave it! I'll have to move my feet.'

'Lana!' Annie stood up, pushing Lana's legs away from her lap. 'I won't be long.' Annie hurried out of the room to take the call in her bedroom before it was too late.

'Hello there, lovely to hear your voice . . .' It was Gray calling. She lay back on her bed to enjoy the chat.

'I'd like to see a lot more of you,' Gray purred. 'A lot, lot more.'

Annie's attention was distracted by Lana coming into the room.

'Are you on your own?' Gray was asking.

'No, not any more.'

'Now that is a shame,' came his reply. 'I was wanting to have a private chat with you . . . very private.'

No mistaking the sauciness in his voice. 'Sounds very interesting,' she told him. 'I think I'm definitely going to phone you back later. Bye for now.'

'How's your auction website going?' Annie asked Lana, who was still hovering. Neutral questions were best when Lana was sulky.

'Great. Check it out some time, there's stuff even you'd consider buying,' came the offhand reply. 'That was the dentist, wasn't it?'

'It was *Gray*, yes, Lana,' Annie said pointedly.

Lana gave a deep sigh and told her, 'I don't like your boyfriend. But I'm trying to give him the benefit of the doubt.'

'Well, that's very kind of you. I'm trying to do the same for your boyfriend.' Annie tried to leave it there, but then several moments later felt the irritated need to ask, 'What don't you like about Gray?'

'Well, his name for a start,' Lana told her. 'You do know he's called Gary really, don't you?'

'Oh.' *No!* 'How do you know?' Annie wondered.

'Gran told me.'

Hmmm. Annie would check with Fern. Maybe it was a guess.

'Gary is just a bit full of himself, don't you think?' Lana added.

'He's a successful man and he has a certain confidence,' Annie told her. '"Full of himself" sounds nasty and really, I think he's pretty nice.'

Lana's sulky response was the inevitable, 'He's not the same as Dad though, is he?'

'No,' Annie told her gently. 'But your dad isn't exactly here right now, is he? So you've got to give someone else a bit of a chance. I think we could all be happy with someone who is nice and caring, and who could look after us all. Someone who'd make me feel a lot less worried.'

'Someone rich,' Lana interpreted.

Annie turned to her daughter so she could speak to her eye to eye. 'You know, that's another nasty thing to say, Lana. Do you honestly think the only thing that interests me about Gray is his money?'

'I can't see what else there is.' Lana was definitely sulking now, her arms crossed tightly over her black vest top.

'He's handsome, he's caring, he's interesting. I like to talk to him. He's got really good taste. We have lots of things in common.' None of this was convincing Lana. 'I don't know . . . He makes me feel interesting too . . . appreciated . . .' Annie said with some exasperation.

'He's so *old*!' came Lana's scornful response. 'And it doesn't exactly sound like mad passionate love.'

'No. It's not!' Annie was trying not to raise her voice. 'I'm not expecting that. I'd be happy with something a bit more companionable.'

'You still have to sleep with him though,' came Lana's retort. 'Wonder if he'll take his wig off. Have you had sex with him yet?'

Annie felt a surprisingly powerful flash of anger. 'He doesn't have a wig! And how would you feel if I asked about your sex life like that?'

She regretted it immediately. This wasn't the way she'd rehearsed the close and confiding mother and daughter chat she'd been mentally preparing for, ever since Seth had come onto the scene.

Lana offered a scornful scowl in response to this.

'Look,' Annie began, 'I haven't slept with Gray. But if I do, it will be for all the right reasons.'

'Ditto,' Lana said.

'Fourteen is too young for sex, Lana.' Annie tried to keep her tone friendly and encouraging. She couldn't believe that she was already discussing the very real possibility of her little girl . . .

'Did I ask you for advice?' The pale little face was pointy, facing away and closed off from her for the moment.

'I'd be so happy if you came to me for advice, Lana. And I will try to be as open-minded about it as I can be,' Annie told her as calmly as she could. She felt as if she'd just aged about five years.

After a burning silence, Lana decided to air a different sore point: 'Why do we have to sell this flat, Mum? I don't want to move again. I don't want to be living in some grotty dump all over again with rotten carpets and a hideous toilet and a horrible bedroom. And this isn't just any old flat! This was our home with Dad!' she burst out. 'Doesn't that mean anything to you?! Don't you think me and Owen might like to stay in our family home? All you can think about is yourself and how to earn more money for yourself.'

'I don't think that's very fair, Lana,' Annie warned. 'I have to look after you both on my own and that's very expensive.'

'Yeah well, but you're very expensive too.' With that Lana got up, flung open the white door of Annie's fitted wardrobe and began flicking through the hangers one by one. 'Gucci!' she read from the label of the first top. 'Valentino, Nicole Farhi, Paul Smith, Westwood, Diane Von Furstenberg, McQueen, Karen Millen—you were slumming it that week—and back to Gucci. My God, this one's Chanel! Do I have to go on or do you get my point?'

'Lana!' Annie could barely contain her fury at this little lecture. 'You know perfectly well I get a great deal on all the clothes I buy and that I have to dress really smartly for The Store. Yes, we might have to sell the flat, just to make sure there's plenty of money in the bank to pay for the great school I send you to, which you are so determined to run down all the time. You know what? Maybe one of these days you should try working hard too. No one's going to give you great exam results because you're cool, Lana! You get out what you put in, Lana, and maybe it's about time you understood that!'

A furious 'Huh!' came back from Lana. 'And I suppose you're planning to solve all your problems by marrying Mr Rich Dentist, are you?'

'Shut up, Lana!' Annie shot back. 'I've been on some dates with Gray and I like him. Who said anything about marriage?'

'I'm not moving out of here!' Lana shouted at her. 'You can't make me. I am not leaving this flat and that is final. I'd rather leave school!'

'Oh, you would, would you? Fine, tomorrow morning I'll take you along to . . .' Annie shoved in the name of the worst comprehensive in the area she could think of and watched for her daughter's reaction.

'Suzie's boyfriend goes there and he says it's cool.'

'Enough about *cool*,' Annie practically shrieked.

But with that Lana stormed to the bedroom door, slammed it shut behind her and shouted, 'I'm getting out of here!'

Annie stayed on her bed, heart pounding. Twenty minutes or so later, when a bit of vigorous nail filing had calmed her down slightly, she decided to go out of the bedroom to see what was happening.

In the sitting room, Owen had turned off the TV, tidied away the pizza and popcorn debris and was reading on the sofa.

'Hey, Owen.' She ran her fingers over his hair. 'You're a star for clearing up. I'm really sorry about all that. We spoilt the film, we spoilt the evening . . . Is Lana in her room?'

'No. She went out,' came the reply.

'What . . .? Out of the flat? When?'

'Not long after the fight.'

'Why didn't you tell me?'

'You sounded scary,' was Owen's answer to this and now Annie felt like the worst parent in the world.

She hurried to the telephone, dialled Lana's number and got straight through to voicemail: 'Lana, don't be so stupid, phone me up and let me know where you are.' Clunk. She put the phone down and began the ring-round of all the home numbers of Lana's friends.

An hour later, Annie was almost in tears. Despite the soothing words of the six parents she'd spoken to, she was panicking about her daughter. 'She'll be fine,' Lana's friend Greta's mother had assured her. 'Greta did this a few weeks ago, stormed off to someone's house and didn't come back for hours. Could she have gone to her boyfriend's?'

'He lives in Essex. She'd have to go to the station, catch a train . . . I don't know. I don't have his number, his mobile . . . I don't even know his surname.'

'I'll see if I can find out. And if Greta hears anything at all, I'll phone you, OK? Try not to worry too much.'

But when Annie put the phone down, after leaving another message on Lana's mobile, she realised she was scared and flooded with guilt.

It was 11.40 p.m. when the phone rang. Annie snatched it up.

'You're alone now, aren't you?' came the husky voice. 'I'm alone too and I can't stop thinking about you and all the things I'd like to do . . .'

'Gray, now's not a good time,' she told him briskly. 'Sorry. Lana's gone out . . . without permission and I'm waiting for her to phone.'

'Oh.' There was a pause.

'Sorry,' she repeated. 'Can I speak to you tomorrow?'

'Yeah, no problem.' He hung up abruptly.

If Gray never called her again, it would be Lana's fault.

It was almost 12.30 a.m. when the phone rang again.

'Lana! For God's sake—' she began.

'Ermm,' came a male voice.

'Gray! Not now!' she snapped.

'My name's Matthew Laurence,' the voice informed her. 'I'm sorry to phone you so late at night. It's about Lana.'

'Oh . . .' Annie, mind racing, felt nothing but blind fear.

'I'm Seth's dad and she's here with us,' Matthew continued calmly.

'Oh, thank God for that.'

'Umm, I'm sorry this is so late. I didn't know she was here because I've been out. She was upstairs with Seth and they've fallen asleep . . . in front of the TV,' he added, although this didn't allay Annie's fears about underage teen sex one little bit.

'I've woken her up and told her to give you a call but . . . erm . . . she doesn't want to.' There was no denying the embarrassment in his voice. 'Anyway, I told her I would phone to let you know she's safe. She can spend the night here, if that's OK with you . . . She can sleep in my daughter Libby's room,' he added quickly.

'I'm so sorry about this,' Annie began. There was no mistaking the loud sniffle she now made down the phone.

'It'll all blow over. Seth's our third and we've seen it all before,' Seth's father assured her. 'I can give her a lift into London early tomorrow morning; she should make it to school in time.'

'She's only fourteen,' Annie heard herself blurting out. 'I don't even know if Seth knows that.'

'Well, I'll make sure he does and don't worry, we'll look after her.'

When the call was over, she turned her face into her pillow and let out the long, hard sobs which had been building all night. How did anyone manage to parent on their own? How did anyone do it?

Annie goes yachting:

White cropped jeans (Tesco)
Red boatneck top (Joseph)
Red and white plimsolls (La Redoute)
Red, white and black scarf tied into ponytail (Tie Rack)
Thin black raincoat (Miss Selfridge)
Total est. cost: £110

'Does anyone have a plastic bag? Quickly!!'

GRAY CAME TO PICK the three of them up in his car. His beautiful, new £45,000-plus red Mercedes with steel fold-down roof, bright red upholstery and a jet-black dashboard studded with dials. Annie wasn't sure what was wrong with the silver one he'd traded in, but apparently every year for the last decade, he'd upgraded his car.

Since Lana's runaway stunt, Gray and Annie had decided he should make a concerted effort to get to know her children better and as the attempts to go out for cosy lunches and little excursions round town hadn't gone so well—Owen silent and Lana sullen—Gray had made a bold new plan for a day trip.

'A friend of mine has a yacht,' he'd announced. 'He's offered to take us all out for a day, as soon as the weather's good. It's fantastic. Blasts the cobwebs away . . .'

Now that April was well under way, the better weather had arrived and along with it, Gray's yachting day trip.

His car swept into their Highgate street early one morning and he came up to the flat laden with flowers for Annie and Lana and an over-sized slab of chocolate for Owen. 'You mustn't always think you have to bring us presents,' Annie said, ticking him off.

'Shhh!' he told her. 'There are many things you can tell me off for, but this isn't one of them.'

'Owen,' she warned, 'don't even think about eating any of that before we get into the car. Go and put it in your room.'

Once the car was packed, she was buckled into the passenger seat and Lana and Owen were installed comfortably in the back.

Gray, in a gesture of child-friendliness, had decided to take the option of the built-in back-seat DVD player and screens, so they just needed to agree on a film to watch (Annie's UN-level negotiator skills were required), put their headphones on and enjoy. Gray had insisted the children take their shoes off, however, so as not to dirty the carpet or the backs of the front seats, which Annie found a bit over the top.

'Erm . . . Lana?' he was now asking awkwardly. 'I don't want any eating in the car, if that's OK.'

'It's just gum,' Lana snapped.

'Well, I'm sorry, I hope you don't mind, but could you take it out? Just in case it somehow by accident lands on the carpet?' He did ask very nicely, but the sigh it provoked showed how annoyed Lana was.

For a moment, Annie couldn't decide who she should ask to back down . . . but the thought that he'd installed back-seat DVD players *just for her children* clinched it. 'Lana!' she growled.

Once the offending gum had been deposited, they set off.

'Shame about the drizzle,' Gray told her. 'Otherwise we could have had the roof down and fresh air.'

'Don't know how much fresh air there is in north London, matey,' she reminded him.

'You should think about moving to the country,' was his reply. 'Fresh air, greenery, much more space . . .' A light-hearted debate broke out between them as they batted about the pros and cons. Annie felt an undercurrent of excitement because she wondered if he was sounding her out—if he had in mind asking her to move out to Essex with him. What would she do if he asked her?

The M25 was clogged with traffic, even this early on a Saturday morning, so their progress was slow and jerky, but finally they got onto the M11 and Gray was able to nose his red beauty into the fast lane.

'Mum, I'm feeling a bit dizzy,' was the first warning from Owen.

'Oh dear.' Annie looked over at him. He looked fine. Perhaps the back-seat DVD wasn't such a great idea. 'Maybe you should switch your screen off and just lean back in the seat for a while,' she suggested.

Ten minutes later, when Owen told her he *really* wasn't feeling great, his face was white with an unmistakable green tinge to the edges. He was going to puke, no doubt about it.

Annie instructed Gray to pull over. 'Just as soon as you can!' but they were on a three-lane motorway, in the fast lane; she could see it would take time.

'Does anyone have a plastic bag? Quickly!! Lana? Anything at all?!'

Annie, and of course Roddy, had learned how to drive in a travel-sickness crisis: as smoothly as possible. But Gray swooped the car into the middle lane, which made Owen puke down his T-shirt. Gray then made a panicky lunge for the slow lane, causing Owen to vomit harder, all the way down to his knees. The abrupt ABS-induced halt on the hard shoulder . . . well, Owen bravely tried to cup his hands to contain it, but it overflowed, splatting all over the crisp red seat beside him.

Defeated, Owen let his hands drop and two puddles of vomit dripped to the seat then down his trouser legs and onto the carpet.

'Oh sh-sugar!' Annie managed to restrain herself.

A strained expression was pulled tight across Gray's face.

'Don't worry,' she said, aiming it at both Owen and Gray, 'I'll deal with this, it'll be fine. We'll get as much off here as we can, but we might have to stop at the service station ahead.'

Annie opened Owen's door and surveyed the damage. He'd obviously made serious inroads into the chocolate slab. The vomit wasn't just chocolate coloured, it smelt sweet and sticky too.

'Owen!' Seeing his pale damp face, it was hard to be angry with him. But with just a small packet of pocket tissues in her handbag it was difficult to know what she could do. She helped Owen change into his spare clothes and dabbed hopelessly at the enormous brown stains on the back seat with her tissues. Vomit staining was bad . . . Chocolate-flavoured vomit staining? Oh boy.

The next forty minutes of the drive were a tad tense. The car stank of spew; Owen still felt bad; Lana's attempts to giggle-stifle would fail every so often in a snotty explosion. 'I'm sorry to be just a little ticked off.' Gray tried to justify his barely contained fury. 'I was just looking forward to showing the car to John.' Ah, the man with the thirty-foot, interior-designed yacht . . . Ah. Annie understood now. A bit of man-to-man size-comparing had been in the offing.

The drizzle cleared, the sea sparkled, the yacht bobbed up and down on the water, desperate to play. John appeared in top-to-toe white with a sailor's cap and a sunburnt face, but still Owen felt horrible.

'I think Owen and I will have to sit this one out,' Annie, almost sick herself—but with regret—told a dumbfounded Gray and Lana.

Gray and Lana looked at each other in undisguised confusion. Neither felt they could say, 'I'm not going with you—without her!'

Annie managed to persuade Gray that she should take the keys to the car and find a valeting service, once Owen had recovered.

With hindsight, the day went extremely well: Annie and Owen spent hours walking along the beach, talking, throwing stones, finding shells, enjoying each other's company; Lana and Gray came back from the yacht trip glowing with excitement and finally comfortable together. Jim of the Washaway Valet had not flinched from the stains on the Mercedes back seat; he'd managed to turn the deep brown marks into something much more biscuity and used a fine internal 'cleansing' mist to reduce the nostril-clogging stink.

That evening, Owen went to bed very early, worn out. Lana left before dinner in a great full-of-the-joys-of-yachting mood, for her friend Suzie's house for a prearranged sleepover, so Annie and Gray ate alone together: a gourmet curry meal for two, bought specially from M&S. There was a scented candle burning in her room. Annie had a sleepover of her own in mind.

Kissing in the kitchen led to kissing in the bedroom.

As she licked his neck and began to unbutton his shirt, Gray excused himself and in the moments he was gone, Annie whipped off her clothes and brought out the brand-new lilac satin knickers and bra she'd selected for this little scene, then tied a silky, matching kimono on top. She applied lip gloss and arranged herself attractively across her bed. And waited . . . And waited . . .

Once a full fifteen minutes had passed, she got up. 'Gray?' she asked, tapping lightly on the bathroom door. 'Is everything all right?'

'Yes, well . . .' came a hesitant, slightly strained reply, 'not really.'

There was deep sigh, then she heard Gray's footsteps coming towards her. He undid the lock and put his head round the door. 'Well . . . I forgot my medication, you know, the love drug.'

Oh God, he meant his Viagra. He'd obviously been searching his overnight bag and maybe trying to kick things off naturally on his own.

They'd had a little chat about the Viagra recently, and he'd assured her it was more of a psychological prop than a physical necessity.

'You're fine,' she told him, reaching out to take hold of his hand. 'Just come into the bedroom with me and we'll . . . play.'

There was a strange moment when Annie found herself lying on her back, with her head hanging from the bed and an extremely willing, able and raring to go Gray on top of her, looking very pleased with himself and definitely wanting to put the nonmedically enhanced Bone to good use. But . . . but . . . looking up at her very own familiar ceiling, headboard and pink lights, she knew she definitely didn't want to do this here, on her marital bed.

No, no, definitely not.

She began to pull slightly against him, down towards the floor. Her bed had a satin bedspread, so it was easy. Already her head was touching the carpet, now her neck and shoulders were following.

'Whoaaaa . . . where are you going?' Gray asked, still holding on.

Her elbows took her weight and as she giggled at him, her hips and legs followed a little too quickly as she brought both herself and her would-be lover down onto the floor with a thud.

The angle of Gray's bodysurf to the floor was much steeper than hers and as his hands were behind her back, he couldn't put them out to save himself. He hit the carpet, chin first, and gave a cry of pain.

'Are you OK?' she asked him, slight flicker of worry now. Were all her romantic encounters with Gray going to end with a 999 call?

He raised a hand and put it gingerly onto the small of his back. 'My sacroiliac!' he gasped. 'It's popped out before . . . I'm going to have to get you to roll me over.'

Once he was on his back, he raised his right knee slowly and painfully, finally managing to pull it to his chest, where he held it tight and began to rock from side to side, going 'Aaaah'. Whatever ardour Annie may have had for Gray, it was a little quenched at the sight.

He made the 'Aaaah!' sound again. Then, finally, there was a look of relief on his face. He stood up and walked gingerly, not to mention butt-naked, in a semicircle. He was limping slightly, but declared, 'Don't worry, it'll settle down.'

Annie put on her kimono and went in search of wine. She didn't want to risk killing him with a further lovemaking attempt.

Later, snuggled up under the covers together and relaxed by the wine, Annie began to touch him again. She played with his nipples then began to watch the changing expression on his face.

Suddenly, she found she was more than interested herself, wanted him to make her just as breathlessly ready as he was now.

Then they were making love, properly . . . and it was OK, she was telling herself. It really was OK. Not amazing, but not disastrous. She was optimistic that from here on in, it would get a lot better.

Afterwards, when they were both almost ready to fall asleep, Gray startled her with the words, 'I don't really like doing this.'

'What? Sex?' she asked.

'No, no . . . Are you joking? That was great. No,' he went on, 'I mean coming here, sleeping over . . . you visiting my home every now and then. Your children must be wondering what's going on.'

'Oh, I think they know,' Annie responded.

'Annie, I'm taking a risk. I know we've only been seeing each other for six weeks or so, but we're grown-ups . . . I think we both know what we want.' He paused, then came right out and asked, 'Why don't you rent out your flat for a bit and move in with me? The three of you. Give me a trial period. Properly. Nothing ventured, nothing gained.'

She was glad he was cuddled in behind her, talking into her neck, so that he couldn't see the look of astonishment cross her face.

There was a long, long pause, as all sorts of arguments, thoughts and emotions raced through her mind. Finally, she told him, 'That is a very kind, very generous offer, Gray. Really. You're just going to have to give me some time to think about this.'

Footballer's wife in spring:

Black tight top (D&G)
Boyfriend cut jeans (Sass & Bide)
Black strappy wedges (Gucci)
Black raincoat (Burberry Prorsum)
Gold bag (Balenciaga)
Huge black shades (Chanel)
Total est. cost: £2,700

'Black's so slimming, innit?'

'I KNOW SPRING IS unpredictable here,' Annie said. 'One minute it's blazing hot, the next it's chucking it down and there's a wind from Siberia howling round your ankles. But your spring/summer wardrobe plan cannot be black. It just can't!' she insisted. 'You've got to blossom, Dannii. You've got to be in tune with the seasons.'

Dannii (yes, with a double 'i') was twenty, the luscious (obviously), blonde (predictably) girlfriend of a Chelsea Football Club midfielder with—according to WAG bible, *Heat*—£4,000 of 'pocket money' a week to spend on herself, although at the rate Dannii was burning her cash, £4,000 a week wouldn't be enough and she'd soon be asking her twenty-one-year-old lover-boy for a raise. 'So long as I keep him very happy, he pays up and keeps me very happy,' she'd cheerfully confided.

This was the third week in a row she'd been in for a personal shopping session and although she spent lashings of money, Annie's enthusiasm for her was waning. A big part of the problem was that the magazines Dannii had been so keen to appear in had now started to poke fun at her. *Dannii shows off another new £3,000 outfit, but don't be jealous, girls, on her it still looks cheap!*

Despite Dannii's pleas to Annie that she wanted to look 'a bit classy, right?', she'd so far turned all Annie's suggestions down and was drawn like a moth to the gold, the glittering, the sequinned and the spangly and, well, even in Diane Von Furstenburg, with her surgically enhanced breasts, she looked like the wrong kind of working girl.

Dannii had recently taken to squeezing her voluptuous self into tight black in an effort to counteract the 'cheap' accusations and, in her words, 'Black's so slimming, innit?' But Annie's pet hate was clients who dressed in monochrome. It was so draining on the complexion and as Annie was trying to explain . . . it *was* spring!

'I've brought a beautiful pale green raincoat down for you, white jeans, pale blue jeans, pink jeans, violet jeans. I've got really sweet, demure little blouses—Missoni, Paul & Joe—which are sexy, but not quite so . . . in your face. And I think platform-heeled loafer-style shoes for you, my darlin', for daywear at least. The thing about always having your pedicure on display is that it's just not elegant. I know you have a driver to take you everywhere, Dannii love, but you're always getting photographed with your tits and your toes hanging out.'

'Come on then, pass me the coat,' Dannii relented.

'Ooh, that is very pale,' was her verdict. 'God! Look at my tan now! I look like a blooming *Efiopian*; wish I was as skinny as one an' all.'

Annie cringed slightly. Clearly an invitation to fund-raise for Oxfam wasn't going to be heading Dannii's way too soon.

'Nobody wants to lighten and brighten up for spring, babes, because we think it's never going to happen. Then the first hot days are a fashion disaster: sparkly sandals and raincoats, wool trousers with vests, summer skirts with black boots . . . It's horrible.'

As Annie finished her lecture, she began to wonder if she was just talking about clothes. It was beginning to occur to her that she could be caught in the 20+ degrees of Gray's sunshine in her emotional equivalent of thick jeans and a black jumper. Was she ready to go to the next stage with Gray? Should she be ready? She hadn't been with him for long, but they knew what they wanted, they didn't need to play games.

It took another hour of concerted effort, but Dannii finally headed tillwards with two tasteful dresses, two blouses, three pairs of coloured jeans, new shoes, a new bag and the raincoat. A fortnight's worth of pocket money, at least. Annie hoped she'd stay away that long and wondered whether she should risk giving this lucrative new client the advice to slash her daily dose of St Tropez bronzing gel.

'I am so sorry, can you just give me five?' she asked her next customer. In front of her computer, Annie made her quick email and website checks. Three great offers were in on Trading Station items. Buoyed by this, she clicked over to Lana's school charity website to see what her daughter's fund-raising gang had managed to get hold of this week.

Just as Ed had suspected, Lana and her friends loved running the website and had hustled all sorts of goodies to flog on it.

Meanwhile, Annie opened her mobile and speed-dialled Gray.

'Hello there, girlfriend,' he answered. 'I'm in the car. You're on hands-free.'

'I'm a bloody hands-full, babes, you should be warned . . .' She took a deep breath and then began, 'I've been thinking about what you said . . . you know . . . the *big* question . . .' She paused and so did Gray.

'Have you talked to Owen and Lana about it?' he wondered, which was the right thing to ask. Annie felt a surge of affection that he'd thought to ask about her children's opinion before he heard her own.

'I've not had a big discussion with them, to be honest,' she told him, 'but I've mentioned it, as a possibility. They're . . . well . . . I think "curious" is the best word. They'll have a long commute to school . . . but they might want to give it a go.'

'My offer stands, Annie,' was Gray's response to this.

Annie took another steadying breath before telling him, 'OK, I'll have to talk to Lana and Owen, but I'm thinking we should give it a whirl.'

When the call was over, Annie put her phone down, then her professional eye took over, directing her attention to the item on the screen in front of her: yes, it really was this season's BNWT Marc Jacobs handbag with serial number for sale on Lana's charity website. The top bid was £120 and the deal was closing at the end of the day.

She speed-dialled Lana and left a message on her phone: 'Babes, I've just put in two hundred pounds for your handbag, but tell me if I need more to get it; I'll sell it for you on my site and give your charity the extra money. You should get four hundred and fifty for that bag at the very least, if it's genuine. Call me.'

Then her phone rang and she saw it was Owen, who did have his own mobile but it was for emergency use only.

'Everything OK, Owen?' she asked before he'd even said hello.

'*Yes!* I just wanted to tell you . . .' He was breathless.

'My God! What's the matter? Are you OK?'

'*Yes!* It's just I've been picked . . . I auditioned . . . it was so scary . . . but I've been picked for the school show. A guitar solo . . . and a song!'

He didn't need to say another thing, the happiness that beamed from those words was so radiant, she could feel the warmth of it down the line. 'That's just fantastic,' she told him. 'A solo! I can't believe it!' This was how far he'd come, her little boy, the boy who'd once only spoken six words at school in an entire term. 'I am so proud of you.'

Arriving home just after 7.30 p.m., Annie saw a notice warning that the lift was out of order, so with the last burst of physical energy she had left for the day, she took the stairs up to the third floor. Just as she approached the top of the last flight of stairs, the stairwell door burst open and Ed Leon was at the top of the steps.

'Owen!' they exclaimed together.

'It's fantastic news about him,' Ed said next. 'I waited to speak to you about it but I thought you must have been held up.'

'I know. I'm later than usual.' There was a slight breathlessness to her voice because she'd taken the stairs at a brisk trot. 'Anyway, he phoned to tell me. Singing with the guitar, solo?' She wanted to check she'd understood it right.

'Yes. Not a whole song. He does the first verse, then the group join in.' Ed smiled at her. 'I worried it might be too much too soon, but his reaction is so positive that I think he'll be fine. And he did the audition brilliantly, put himself in for it. Nothing to do with me.'

'Thank you, Ed.' Annie had made it up to his level now. 'But don't be so modest: it is all down to you. You've been the best thing that's happened to Owen for a long time and I'm thrilled for him.'

She gave him a broad smile and wondered how she could show her gratitude to this nerdy but very kind man, who had taken her shy and wobbly son under his wing for no reason other than he seemed to really like Owen. Quite spontaneously, Annie opened her arms and threw Ed a generous hug and a kiss on the cheek.

The effect of this on Ed was unexpected. He kissed her back, first on the cheek and then, turning his head slightly, he sought her mouth. Their lips brushed together and they *seemed* to be kissing.

Her lips were pressed against his, his arms were round her back, her mouth was feeling for more and yes, they did definitely seem to be kissing. She felt the prickle of stubble at the corner of his mouth . . . Her hands moved underneath his jacket and down to the small of his back. Her tongue quite of its own accord ventured past his teeth. There she had found a reassuringly warm tinged-with-coffee taste.

His tongue responded and she found it interestingly mobile and very, very satisfyingly kissable. Yes, this was definitely kissing.

Annie would have quite liked to have stopped for a moment to assess the situation. The kissing of Ed. This was a situation fraught with problems. It could even have something to do with telling Gray this afternoon that she was going to move in with him. Surely this was a reaction? A strange and unexpected reaction . . .

But there was no chance of stopping to think for even a moment because she was enjoying this so much. Ed was squeezing at her bottom in a particularly tickly and quite fascinating way. She did not want him to stop. But he really should stop . . .

Her fingers wound themselves into his tangly hair. His hands behind her back pulled her closer towards him. When she realised her hand was on the smooth leather of his belt, sliding along towards the buckle with intent, with a purpose all of its own, she opened her eyes.

She pulled back from the kiss and took a small step backwards. His eyes were very dark blue now, his lips not just full and pink but also damp. He was much, much better looking than she'd noticed before. Now she got a glimpse of what all the fuss was with the St Vincent's mothers and Ed. He was genuinely cute . . . when he didn't have a yellow cagoule tied around his head, obviously.

'Ed,' she said, trying to keep her voice level. 'I think we may have overstepped the parent–teacher relationship here.'

'Completely,' was his reply. He gave a little smile.

'I'm sorry, I have to go,' she said abruptly. For goodness' sake, she'd just agreed to move in with Gray . . . what was she playing at?

As quickly as she could, she hurried past him, out of the stairwell door, pulling it firmly shut behind her. Because really, anything else would have been far too complicated.

With great care, Gray reversed his still smelly Merc into the slightly too small parking space in front of Annie's block. He would not miss visiting this cramped corner of London for one moment. Thank God she'd agreed to move.

On the passenger seat beside him was the enormous bunch of flowers he'd ordered as soon as she'd phoned him with her decision. He'd considered having them delivered, but then he'd decided it would be far, far more romantic to take the flowers in person.

He locked the car, then, flowers in one hand, bottle of champagne in the other, he strode along the pavement to her door. There was a guy ahead of him who was approaching the block as well. A scruffy-looking bloke: washed-out jeans, baggy shirt and an awful green cord jacket, and he needed a haircut. This man too was carrying flowers but it was the sorriest, scrappiest bunch Gray had ever seen. Limp weeds from the back of the garden.

'You after the Valentines?' Gray asked, noticing the man's finger head towards Annie's buzzer.

'Yes, I am. You too?' The man turned to face him for the first time.

'Oh! Are you the music teacher? Ed the Shed?' Gray was trying to remember what Annie had told him about this character: one of those slightly nutty professor types by the look of him.

'I'm Owen's teacher . . . yes,' Ed replied. 'Ed Leon. I've not heard the other name before,' he added with some irritation.

'Have you got a lesson on?' Gray asked.

'No. No. That was earlier in the evening. I was just . . . ermm . . .' He lifted his bunch of flowers slightly.

'Those aren't for Lana, are they, mate?' A note of concern had entered Gray's voice now. 'Annie's very protective of Lana and you wouldn't want to give either of them the wrong idea.'

There was a cool tone to Ed's pointed 'These aren't for Lana.' *Who was this arrogant shit who'd just got out of the flashy Merc?* 'They're for Annie.'

Gray managed to check a laugh and, lifting his own extravagant bouquet and champagne bottle up, said, 'These are for Annie, too. She's agreed to move in with me, with her children. I've brought these to celebrate.'

There was a pause as Ed seemed to struggle slightly with his response to this. He put his hand to his head and scratched.

'Tell you what.' Gray leaned in chummily. 'Would you like me to take yours up too? Save you the journey?'

Ed looked up at him; the guy was tall, his aftershave expensive but just a touch too noticeable. 'No, no. It's just a bunch from the garden. No big deal. I was just passing. If you two are celebrating, I'll leave you to it . . . Congratulations. She's a . . .' Once again he found himself struggling for the words. 'They're a . . . lovely family.'

'Thank you.'

If Gray had followed Ed round the corner, he'd have seen him throw the flowers, with a bowler's overarm, into a neighbouring garden.

Donna on the warpath:

Red and white tunic (Anna Sui)
Linen trousers (Whistles)
White heels (Gucci)
Gold tassel necklace (Erickson Beamon)
Total est. cost: £730

'Flouncing round here like you own the place.'

FERN HAD A WEDDING to go to. Annie's mother always had weddings to go to: a busy schedule of remarriages and the weddings of her children's friends, at least three, sometimes even five or six a year.

Fern was that woman of a certain age in a wonderful hat who could be counted on to give an expensive gift from the gift list (not something radical and alternative), who would look good in the church and good in the photographs without in any way upstaging the bride, bridesmaids or, more likely, the bride's and groom's mothers.

'I'm not shopping in your shop,' she'd informed Annie on the phone. 'Even with your discount, the prices are absolutely ridiculous. Jaeger, Annie. I want something beige . . .' Before Annie could groan in response, Fern added, 'I've got this sensational hat, cocoa straw with a wonderful cream gardenia; it's so lifelike. A beige jacket will be just the thing.'

Jaeger was a disaster, though. 'Just office clothes.' Fern had sniffed at the selection. 'Black and white, white and black, black stripes, so brutal on the complexion.'

Fern had an enviable understanding of which colours suited her. Most of the people Annie dressed had never got to grips with colour and wondered why they always looked so washed out or so flushed . . .

As Annie shopped with her mother, she enjoyed another admirable trait: her mother never once uttered the words, 'I look so'—insert derogatory word—'bad', 'fat', 'hippy', 'short', 'stumpy', 'frumpy' (you name it, Annie had heard it) 'in this.'

No. With Fern it was always reversed: the garment was to blame.

'Annie! Look how badly they've cut the back,' or 'Oh, these seams don't sit well at all', 'The shoulders are a disaster', 'This colour does nothing for me.'

It was another message Annie tried to impart to her more timid, understated shoppers. 'Blame the clothes! Not yourself! Let's find the right thing, the cut and the colour that does you justice. And if it's still not right, you know what? We'll get it altered.'

Her mother pulled back the curtain and came out onto the shop floor in a beautiful creamy-beige suit. A very simple cut: nipped-in jacket, no lapels, a just-below-the-knee panelled skirt.

She would wear her hat, the inevitable hideous sandals, a pink rose corsage and a ruffle-necked blouse underneath.

'Handbag?' Annie wondered.

'The little brown alligator, you know, the secondhand shop one you gave me. It's a treasure. It goes with everything.'

Annie felt the nice glow of giving the right gift.

'Oh, I met the dentist's wife, you know. Marilyn,' Fern said all of a sudden.

'Oh right, yes . . .' Annie tried to sound as casual as possible, but could not have been more interested. She'd still not even seen a photograph of Marilyn.

'Because you've been out with Gray a few times, haven't you?' Fern was still turning herself carefully before the mirror.

'Aha . . . yeah.' Annie had not exactly kept her mother up to speed with the rapid developments on the Gray front. Her own vacillations and Dinah's strident views ('*You're going to do what?! You're moving to Essex for him?! Are you out of your MIND?!!!!*') were quite enough to be getting on with.

'Well, Marilyn did not have one good thing to say about him.' Fern forged ahead. 'And you have to admit, Annie, he may be charming, but he is a pernickety fusspot. I know I invited him to that party for you, but with hindsight . . . Anyway, Marilyn was terribly upset. She'd always assumed Gray was going to sell their house and split the proceeds with her. In fact she has Ronald on the case—so you can be sure she'll be getting as much as she possibly can.'

Ronald being another family friend. In fact, Fern went to their youngest daughter's wedding just last year.

'So Gray's decided not to sell?' Annie prompted her.

'According to Marilyn, Gray has told Ronald he has a new partner, it's serious, they're getting married just as soon as the divorce is through and he's moving this person into the house as soon as possible. So he's claiming he needs the house. This new person has children . . . It's his asset, he's paid for it, he's keeping it.'

'Well, he has a point.' Annie decided to wade in on behalf of Gray. 'Marilyn has no children and has never worked.'

'Hmmm.' Her mother sniffed just a little, as if this was absolutely no excuse for anyone to be turfed out by their husband.

'He's not exactly planning to leave her destitute . . . I'm sure.'

'No. I'm sure there's a valuable settlement to be made. Gray is a very wealthy man.'

There was a moment's pause and Annie was just about to take that deep breath and tell her mother that she was Gray's new woman, when her mother added, 'Of course Ronald is convinced it's a scam by Gray. Move some poor woman in, keep the house, then ditch her again.'

'I thought you said he was a charming man!' Annie could barely contain her outrage.

'Well, people do get funny about money though, don't they?'

Move some poor woman in . . . keep the house . . . then ditch her . . .

'It's me,' Annie blurted out. 'It's us. We're moving in with Gray.'

'What!' Fern exclaimed, looking astonished at this news. 'Good grief, Annie, isn't this a bit soon? I mean you have to think about the children.' She sat down abruptly on the changing-room stool.

'Of course I've thought about the children. A big part of the reason I'm doing this is for them. But you know, it's a trial period. I'm going to rent our flat out for six months and see how it goes.'

Her mother did not look impressed. 'Is he serious though, love? You don't think he's doing this for the money?' she asked.

'No! Of course I don't. Maybe he's a bit desperate for the company. Maybe he's speeding things along for that reason.'

What Annie didn't add was how much she wanted the company too. The best thing about moving in with Gray was that she would no longer be the only adult in the household. She would no longer, every day, have to cope and battle and try to pretend that everything was just great and she was getting along just fine. If she moved in with Gray, she would have someone else there, to help her through. She would have back-up. A security net. Right now, these reasons were more important to her than anything else.

Back at The Store after shopping with her mother, Annie was hardly pleased to be told on arrival at the Personal Shopping suite that Donna wanted to see her.

One look at Donna's sucking-on-a-sour-plum face and she felt her heart sink. This wasn't going to go well, she knew it.

'You've been taking The Store's customers to other shops,' Donna began. 'Don't even bother trying to deny it. Apparently you were doing a consultation in Jaeger this morning, during time when you're employed by The Store.'

'I had a couple of hours off this morning to meet my mum,' Annie defended herself. 'She's shopped in Jaeger since I was knee-high, I'm not going to stop her now.'

Undeterred, Donna carried on, 'I've seen you leave our shop with customers so you can take them somewhere else.'

For a moment Annie was confused. Then it dawned on her that Donna had seen her with Ed that day.

'But that was . . .' she began. *A special case? An eccentric individual who could find nothing right here?* It was a slightly lunatic defence.

'Although you're in possession of a written warning, you're constantly advising people to shop elsewhere. I heard you telling one woman to buy her Chloé bag on eBay!'

'You can't *sack* me for any of these things,' Annie told her.

'No,' Donna said, eyes locking onto Annie's. 'But I can sack you for theft.'

'Theft?' Annie almost laughed. 'I've never stolen anything in my entire life. Not even an unpaid grape from the greengrocer's.'

'Oh, really?' Donna picked a sheet of paper up from her desk. 'Recognise this?'

It was a printout of a computer page. The image was faint but Annie could still make out a digital photograph of a handbag, a Marc Jacobs handbag, BNWT and serial number. It was the one she'd bought from Lana's website and had sold on the Trading Station for £490 last week.

Annie felt a lurching sensation in her stomach.

'Thanks to the serial number you've displayed so nicely here . . .'—the note of triumph in Donna's voice was unbearable—'I can tell you that this bag was stolen from our Accessories department on the eighteenth of February. Maybe you'd like to explain how you ended up selling it?'

'I did not steal it, Donna.'

Annie's mind raced as she tried to work out what explanation she could offer. The bag had come from Lana. Had one of the Syrup Six dared to come into The Store and walk off with a top designer handbag? That would mean police involvement and instant expulsion. Although Annie was certain Lana would not have stolen the bag, maybe she'd be expelled too for playing a part in the sales team.

The thing that was just so utterly infuriating was that usually Annie checked everything she sold as scrupulously as she could. She'd seen straight away it was genuine, and she'd assumed (Argh! Assume and be damned) that some incredibly rich parent had decided to be generous and offload it on the website. It hadn't crossed her mind for a moment (and she was usually so careful) that the bag could be stolen . . . and from her own shop. Jesus. There was nothing she could tell Donna without landing Lana and her friends in huge trouble. And even then, couldn't Donna imply that she'd somehow put the girls up to it? Then she considered the rumours that would stir up at St Vincent's. Lana's mother had stolen an expensive bag from her shop to put on the charity website . . . It was all horrible.

'I had no idea the bag was stolen. I never, ever knowingly sell stolen items,' Annie told Donna. 'I can't explain to you how I got that bag because someone, who couldn't have known about it, would get into trouble. I did not steal it, Donna. At least show me you believe that!'

Donna just kept her gaze trained on Annie's face.

There was a Roman expression, wasn't there? To fall on your sword. Annie saw that she was going to have to leave. Right now. Without a fuss. Cave in to Donna completely. 'I'll get my things.'

Donna just nodded.

But if she were to leave in disgrace, there'd be no pay-off. She might not even be paid for the rest of the month. 'You have to give me references!' Annie exclaimed, feeling a wave of panic. 'You can't put me down as leaving for theft. I'll never get another job.'

There was almost a smile playing about Donna's lips. Annie would have loved to smack her, right there and then. 'I suppose I could tell HR you left for personal reasons . . . a personality clash, maybe?'

'Well, that wouldn't be a lie, would it?' Annie retorted. Then the enormity of losing her job, when she was the sole provider for her children, began to dawn on her. 'You can't do this, Donna. Are you really going to sack me? I'm your best sales assistant. Couldn't you at least give me time to find something else? I've got my children's—'

'School fees to pay . . . Oh yes, yes, Annie, my heart bleeds,' Donna snapped. 'No. I've had enough of you. Flouncing round here like you own the place, like The Store owes you a living, because we should all feel so, so sorry for you . . . just because your husband . . .' She broke off abruptly and the rest of her words hung in the air.

'Donna,' Annie said, pulling herself up straight, feeling her fight and her fire return, 'I might be many things and wrong in many ways, but at least I'm not a heartless, ruthless bitch like you.'

She should of course have thought to phone Gray first, but instead she phoned the man who'd been her first port of call for several years now.

'You've been *what*?!' was Connor's astonished response. 'OK, sweetheart. Name the drinking establishment of your choice and I can be there within the hour.'

Gray at home:

Pink V-neck golfing sweater (Pringle)
Beige chinos (Gant)
White T-shirt (Gap)
Crested velvet slippers (Jermyn Street)
Total est. cost: £270

'But they're comfortable!'

GRAY'S IMMACULATE HOUSE was not looking quite so good these days. His hotel-tidy master bedroom was lined with the racks and stacks of clothes, accessories and items currently for sale on the new and improved Annie V Trading Station. The guest bedrooms had become home to Owen and all his paraphernalia and Lana and her endless clothes, make-up, CDs, and currently atrocious teen tantrums.

Several things had gone wrong at once for Lana: Seth had finally snipped off their budding romance, plus her allowance had been severely docked for her part in fencing the stolen bag that had cost Annie her job at The Store. *'The bag came from Suzie's dodgy boyfriend?'* Annie had shrieked at her. *'Why didn't you tell me? Why didn't it cross your mind that there might be something not right about it?'*

It was obvious from Lana's long face and even longer sulks that she missed Highgate, especially the regular after-school visits with friends.

'Give it a chance here,' Annie kept urging her. 'You'll meet some people. Maybe you should join the tennis club? You love tennis.'

But suggestions like this were met with slammed doors.

At least Owen seemed fine, playing the guitar a lot, but then he'd always liked the company of his family and himself best.

Gray was finding family life something of a change. He had never experienced noise or mess on a scale like this. Because it was a school holiday, the children were always around, underfoot, when he came back from work. He stumbled about his home, tripping over new piles of stuff in unexpected places. He found his sofa already occupied, his Jacuzzi filled with embarrassingly nubile teen girls, his kitchen utterly void of anything edible, although it was now stacked with Annie's cash-and-carry treasures: industrial-sized boxes of clingfilm and tinfoil, 1,000 bin bags. His new live-in lover was surprisingly unavailable: either on her mobile, at her computer or out again, making another round of house calls, consultations, drop-offs or pick-ups.

Ever since she'd left The Store, Annie had woken up every morning ready to hustle. Within days, her flat had been stripped of everything personal, redecorated, and she and the children had moved to Gray's while tenants paying top dollar had moved in.

With her mortgage payments covered, Annie had turned her attention to earning enough money to keep the children at St Vincent's and provide her with the monthly income she was accustomed to. This meant a rapid expansion of the Trading Station and her own Dress to Express make-over and personal shopping service.

Things weren't looking too bad; she was learning that Gray's corner of Essex was ripe with well-heeled women who hadn't the slightest clue how to accessorise and weren't shy about recommending her services to all their friends. The only downside to drumming up all this business was that Gray didn't seem to like it very much.

'You know, Annie, I don't really want you to work so hard,' he was telling her again one evening, over a glass of red wine out on the garden terrace. Several days ago, he'd suggested she become his PA; now he was bringing the subject up again. 'You could help me with my admin, keep track of all my meetings, appointments . . .' he said. 'It won't keep you as busy as you are now, so you'll be around a lot more, for me and your children. Obviously, I'll keep on my secretary at work . . . and I'll pay you.'

Of course the idea of not working so hard was appealing, but did she want to work for Gray? There were quite enough teething problems: arguments about food on the sofa and using a spoon for the jam, without Annie risking a move into Gray's work life and being told off for not doing things quite the way he wanted there as well.

'I'll have to think about it,' she said. 'What would you pay me? . . . *What?*' was her undisguised surprise at the figure. 'How do you expect me and mine to survive on that?'

'Well . . .' Gray was flustered, taken aback by her reaction. 'I don't expect you to pay anything towards the house; I'm happy to pay the bills and for groceries. This is money just for you.'

'My pin money?' she'd asked with more than a touch of sarcasm.

'Well, that's a bit old-fashioned,' he replied. 'What I mean is . . . Marilyn was my PA, she spent her wages on herself and I paid for everything else—'

'Gray . . .' Annie cut him off. 'Don't misunderstand me; it's lovely that you're well-off and that you want to help us out, but Marilyn did not have two children of her own to keep in school. I have always, *always* supported myself and the children and often Roddy too. Relying on you to pay for us and to give me a tax-deductible little allowance is out of the question.' She gave him the stern look that he was learning meant: no further discussion.

In slight need of a change of subject, he decided to ask, 'Are you doing much tomorrow?'

'I've got a home consultation in the morning, but I'm not too busy after that. I'll just be at my day job, buying and selling. Why?'

'I've invited my parents round. I mean, I said I'd check with you first, obviously . . .'

'For drinks?'

'Well, no. I think I might have said dinner . . .'

Annie had not yet met Gray's parents, although she'd heard plenty about them. They were in their early eighties, but apparently this had not dimmed their sharp opinions, pointed criticism of and interminable stream of advice to their precious one and only son.

'They were very fond of Marilyn,' he had warned her earlier. 'I'm afraid moving you three in has put them in a huff.'

Now, obviously, they had been talked round and were to meet over a civilised dinner—which Annie was to provide, presumably, as Gray had a full day's work ahead of him.

'Why don't we all go out for dinner?' she suggested.

'Well, I just thought for Lana and Owen's sake . . . They can go off and do their own thing . . . won't have to sit and listen to us talk all evening.'

He had a point, but hadn't he noticed that she couldn't cook? Hadn't he realised that most of her meals came in a plastic tray?

'I mean, if it's a problem . . .'

'No, no, it's not a problem,' Annie insisted, wondering in which removals box one of her three barely touched cookbooks might be found—and what kind of simple, but nevertheless impressive, dish could be served up for six.

Annie didn't make it back to Gray's house until after 2 p.m. the next day, later than she'd intended, considering his parents were due at seven. Laid out across the back seat of the jeep, carefully wrapped in many layers of damp newspaper, was a whopping great fish.

In her endless quest for trade suppliers, discount outlets and bargains, she'd made quite a few new friends. One of them, who was a fishmonger, had supplied tonight's centrepiece at a superb price. An enormous line-caught wild Scottish salmon. The beast was so long and so heavy, she'd barely been able to wrestle it into the back seat. The plan was to make new potatoes, a lovely salad, hollandaise sauce—if Dinah was available to talk her through it step by step on the telephone—then strawberries, cream and meringues to follow.

She would start on the meringues just as soon as she got back. She would keep calm. There was plenty of time. What could go wrong?

'Jesus! Owen! Could you have made any more mess? Where's Lana?' was Annie's reaction on surveying the state of the front room.

'In her room, crying,' came Owen's reply. '*Seth, Seth . . . I'll never love anyone as much as you . . . waaaah,*' he mocked.

'Stop it. That's mean. Can you please start clearing up in here? Gray's parents are coming for dinner, remember? I better go and talk to her.'

It took thirty vital minutes to talk Lana from blotchy-faced misery into some sort of useful state:

'*There, there, babes . . . You will start to feel better really soon, I promise. I know everyone says it, but there really are plenty more fish in the sea . . .*'

And in exasperation when that didn't work: '*He was far too old for you . . . and anyway, he was covered in acne . . . even on his back.*'

And finally losing all patience: '*I'm sorry, I don't care any more! You'll just have to blow your nose and come and help me downstairs.*'

At last, Annie had Lana employed in the house along with Owen, hoovering, plumping cushions, cunningly disguising packing boxes with tablecloths and throws.

With a great deal of concentration, Annie managed to separate one dozen eggs, then her mobile rang and she was very surprised to hear Svetlana on the line.

In a few breathless sentences the former Miss Ukraine spelled out the crisis going on in her life. Potato-faced Igor had inevitably met someone much younger, much more beautiful and willing, so he had filed for *divorce*! But the billionaire gas baron, with an eye towards safeguarding every penny of his fortune, had filed in Russia, leaving Svetlana convinced she was going to get nothing.

'I am phoning all my Russian friends, they are putting me into a panic,' Svetlana was blurting into Annie's ear. 'I think: I must phone an English friend and I think of you.'

Annie couldn't help but be flattered. 'Darlin', you've got to calm down, right now. You live in London. Your children were both born here. The boys are English. I'm absolutely certain he can't divorce you in Russia. I'm sure you can make sure it goes through the English courts.'

'But his fortune, his estate is Russian, all in Russia,' Svetlana went on, her voice rising. 'He can hide things, hide everything from the English courts. He's told me this before. Annie, if I don't agree, I'm going to lose everything. He will threaten to take the boys away . . .'

'Svetlana, calm down, calm down, darlin'.' The bowls of separated eggs had been completely forgotten. 'This is not a Dostoyevsky novel . . .' Somewhere up there, her late Francis Holland English teacher was smiling. 'Babes, you live in a sixteen-bedroomed mansion in Mayfair; Igor would have a job hiding that.'

Annie thought hard about what Svetlana needed to do next. Suddenly, it was obvious. 'You know what?' she began. 'I know someone who has been through a very nasty divorce with big money at stake. I'm sure I can ask her which lawyer you need.'

It hadn't occurred to Annie before just how powerful the women who formed her client base at The Store could be . . . and she had all of their mobiles on speed-dial, in order to inform them at the press of a button when something new and perfect for them had come in.

Aha . . . and here was the number of the very glamorous forty-something whose monumental divorce settlement had made headlines.

'Hi! Megan? How are you? Yes, it's Annie Valentine. Not of The Store any more . . .'

When Annie got back to Svetlana, she was in for a surprise. 'Got a pen and paper, babes? His name is Harry Roscoff, of Roscoff, Barry and Mosse . . . *How will you pay for him?*' It had never occurred to Annie that Potato-face would already have cut off Svetlana's allowance precisely so she couldn't go in search of expert legal advice. 'You've no money?' Annie asked incredulously.

'Not one penny.'

Once this had taken its moment or two to sink in, Annie issued the following instructions: 'OK, darlin', here's what you have to do. Fill up a big suitcase with some things in your wardrobe you don't want any more, the more labels the better. Then I'll sell everything for the best possible rates. And absolutely not one penny of commission, babes.'

Now she didn't envy Svetlana her army of staff, her gilded lifestyle and her utter dependency on a total arsehole quite so much.

When she'd hung up, a glance at the clock caused Annie to swear and ram the slightly runny meringue mix into the oven, set the timer and begin to hunt for a pot to cook the fish in.

'Dinah!!!!!! Why haven't I been able to get you on the phone for twenty minutes? Heeeeelp!'

'What's the matter?' Dinah exclaimed, totally panicked.

'I need you here. I can't cope. I can't do this on my own. I have to make dinner for Gray's parents and everything's going wrong.'

'OK.' Dinah breathed a sigh of relief. 'Talk me through it.'

The bloody, blinking hollandaise had curdled . . . Annie was going to have to go out again in the car in search of more eggs . . . oh and the cream she'd forgotten. There was no pot in the entire house big enough for the fish . . . but Dinah was assuring her that salmon could be cooked in the dishwasher.

'The dishwasher?' Annie did not sound convinced.

'Yes—provided you've got enough tinfoil. But you always do. You just put it on the hottest wash for thirty-five minutes and you *must* make sure there's no powder in the dispenser, obviously.'

It sounded simple enough. 'Will you talk me through the sauce on the phone when I get back with the eggs? Where are you? I can hear music.'

'I'm in the Rialto, hiding from the builders.'

Because the strangest things had happened to Dinah and Bryan just as soon as Annie had left London: Dinah had been offered a part-time job and Bryan had landed himself a major contract. Now, believe it or not, Dinah was having a new kitchen installed.

'Oh . . . How's the Rialto?' Suddenly Annie felt a swoop of longing for the bustling Italian café she and Dinah liked best for coffee. 'Café culture has not made it this far east, sadly. Bugger. Damn . . .'

'Charming,' Dinah commented.

'I've just realised that bleeping's the oven. Balls! The meringues!'

'Eton mess, remember, Annie!' were Dinah's parting words. 'If your meringues are crap, scrunch them up with strawbs and cream and call it Eton mess.'

The meringues had merged, moulded . . . She had a baking tray entirely covered in one great big sandy-brown, slightly crispy meringue. 'Never mind . . . Eton mess,' she told herself.

She loaded up the dishwasher, put in the powder and turned it on, so she could empty it out later, all ready for the wrapped fish, then she rushed out to get eggs and cream.

It was already approaching 5.30 as she stepped back into Gray's house to the sound of Connor calling out a hello from the kitchen.

'What the bloody hell are you doing here?'

'Just passing—well, filming—not a million miles away.' He picked up the glass of wine on the table behind him and swilled it down. 'Mmm . . . gorgeous,' he said.

'That's not anything too fancy, is it?' Annie said. She turned the wine bottle and saw what looked like a new-looking Spanish label.

No, fortunately Connor hadn't broken into Gray's vintage French burgundies, all neatly stacked from floor to ceiling in the pantry.

'Yup, Owen's an excellent host.' Connor gave her son a hearty pat on the back. 'So, what's for dinner?'

'You can't stay for dinner,' Annie told him. 'Gray's parents are coming. I'm meeting them for the first time and I'm totally stressed.'

Connor's reaction was to sit down, put his long legs up on the kitchen table, fold his arms behind his head and utter the challenge: 'Just try and make me leave, babes, just try and make me.'

Owen giggled as Annie told Connor, 'You can stay for a bit but by seven p.m., you are out of here. Owen, you do the salad, Connor, scrub the potatoes. I have to phone Dinah about the sauce again.'

The next hour did not go happily. While Annie tried to make the hollandaise again, Connor snuck up behind her and asked her heavy questions.

'How's it working out?'

'It's fine. We're settling in . . . I think it's going to work.'

'Aha . . . *fine* . . .' Then standing close behind her he whispered into her ear, 'And how's it going in the bedroom?' and made several pelvic thrusts against her hip for emphasis. Unfortunately he chose the moment she was carefully pouring a spoonful of vinegar into the sauce.

'Jesus! Connor!' She tried to spoon the vinegar overflow out of the bowl as quickly as she could. 'It's fine, thank you,' she snapped.

'Oooooh tetchy . . . another "fine" from Annie.' Then in a suddenly serious voice, he added, 'He's got to be right, Annie, he's got to be the *Next* One . . . Absolutely no one says you have to settle.'

'Go away, Connor,' she growled. 'I can't have this conversation now. Open the dishwasher and check my fish.'

'What?' Connor opened the machine and let a cloud of scalding steam into the kitchen as Annie pulled back the fridge door to bring out her meringue mess and beaten cream.

'Smells lovely and lemony,' Connor commented.

'*Lemony?*' Just as it was dawning on Annie that maybe she should have double-checked the powder drawer hadn't jammed shut on the last wash only to open and tip soap over her salmon, she also spotted the meringue bowl, totally empty, standing by the kitchen sink. 'CONNOR! Did you and Owen eat the meringues?' she shouted.

'The leftovers; I told Owen those had to be . . .' Connor broke off. He could tell by Annie's face that it hadn't been a bowlful of scrapings they'd wolfed down. 'They were very good,' he said sheepishly.

'Aaaaaaargh!' She ran at him, but at the last minute veered to the dishwasher, which stank of lemony-bleachy dishwasher powder.

'Aaaaaaaargh!' she cried again.

Only for Gray to walk in and ask what was the matter? And hello, Connor, and . . . could he smell fish? Didn't she remember his father was allergic to fish?

Annie ran out of the kitchen and into her bedroom and began to sob noisily. It wasn't just that she was exhausted, or a crappy cook. There was something else. She was frightened. She was beginning to suspect that she didn't like Upper Ploxley, didn't like suburban Essex life.

And then there was Gray. It was only when she'd moved in that she'd got a sense of how set in his ways he was. How—dare she use the word?—old and old-fashioned he seemed to her and the children.

He wore shabby purple velvet slippers round the house ('But they're comfortable!') and wouldn't listen to her protestations about them. Although he looked dapper in a suit and tie, in his preferred golf V-neck and chinos he didn't. He liked to read the paper, undisturbed, from cover to cover, taking a full two hours over it. The children bugged him. They made too much noise for him, too much mess. They required too much of her time and attention. He was used to a wife who fussed over him. Maybe he was sorry too. Maybe he was wondering what the hell he'd got into. Maybe Annie *was* being used as a tactic in the divorce battle.

Had she experienced the same feelings of claustrophobia and uncertainty when she and Roddy had first moved in together? Now, when she thought back to that time, she remembered only delirious happiness: painting their tiny bedroom sexy pink . . . Roddy nursing her through appalling morning sickness when she got pregnant so soon . . .

But maybe she had been just as unsure, she kept telling herself. There must have been some moments of doubt. But she'd been so young. Nothing mattered so much when you were young. Now there was no denying that she'd made a great big important decision far too quickly. But she couldn't just walk away, she had to be a grown-up and give it a real, considered chance.

In the kitchen, Gray made the mistake of telling Lana, Owen and Connor that he'd better go upstairs 'to see if I can calm down this tantrum'.

This caused Lana to jump up and shout: 'How dare you call it a tantrum! Maybe if you hadn't asked your parents round on a day when my mum's working! Just expecting her to cook for you all like some sort of housekeeper! She can't cook! Haven't you noticed that yet? Haven't you worked out the slightest thing about her?'

'Lana,' Connor intervened, 'I think you're being a bit—'

'But look at him,' Lana raged. 'He doesn't do anything for himself, he's the most unreconstructed chauvinist pig I've ever met. He just wants to turn Mum into his housewife!'

'Lana, that is not true,' Gray insisted.

'I'm going up to her,' Lana stormed. 'You can just keep away!'

With that she rushed out of the room.

'Why don't you have a glass of wine?' Connor said amiably. 'Then it's probably best if you cancel your parents for tonight. Don't worry about all this. I'm sure it'll blow over . . . Teenagers! Total nightmare,' he tried to sympathise.

Gray let out a deep sigh and turned the bottle of wine towards him. 'For God's sake!' he exclaimed. 'That's my Dominio de Pingus 1996! Three hundred pounds a bottle!'

'Ah . . . sorry . . .' Connor hung his head apologetically, then, reaching for a fresh glass, he added, 'I think you'd better have some.'

Annie back in town:

Orangey-red linen wrap dress (Joseph sale)
Beige mac (the trusty Valentino)
Large orange leather tote (Coccinelle on eBay)
Caramel heels (the Chanels, for morale)
Orangey red lipstick (Mac)
Total est. cost: £390

'You're not dead yet, woman.'

ANNIE WALKED DOWN the charming flagstoned pavement of one of her favourite Highgate streets. Smartly painted fences enclosed gardens brimming with blossoming lilac bushes, buddleia and honeysuckle.

Almost all the three-storey Georgian houses had been beautifully and expensively renovated: lime mortar pointing restored, old wooden windows and doors repaired, fresh coats of historically appropriate Farrow & Ball paint applied.

To buy a whole house on this street . . . At least £1.5 million, she reckoned, which is why most were carved up into bijou flats. It was still her property dream to own a house in Highgate—but maybe it would have to be something a little smaller than one of these.

She passed a plump woman striding along in navy-blue shorts, a pale floral blouse and black pumps. A black bag was strung diagonally across her chest, bisecting her cleavage to horrible effect. Annie considered stopping her to hand over a business card and urge her with the words, 'C'mon. You're not dead yet, woman, why have you given up?'

Number 39 was not a house that had been renovated. The paint was flaking, the stonework was grubby, parts of the fence had rotted away. Absent landlord, Annie guessed, or maybe landlord down on his luck.

She'd been told to follow the garden path round to the back of the house where the entrance to the basement flat could be found: 39B.

Through the overgrown garden she went. The black door was flaking paint and all the windows needed not just repainting but cleaning too. She pressed hard on the buzzer, and after a few moments Ed appeared at the door, looking—despite her efforts—as much in need of care and attention as his home.

'Hello there, erm, Annie . . . why don't you come on in?' Ed gave her a smile and waved her into the cramped hallway.

A rack stuffed with coats, walking boots, shoes and wellingtons had to be shuffled past before she could follow him into a tiny, low-ceilinged kitchen also crammed to bursting. She took in the overflow of pots, pans, piles of newspaper, small table overwhelmed with a burden of books, pens and papers, as Ed made welcoming but slightly apologetic chat. 'Sorry . . . always such a mess . . . hopeless . . . Can I get you a tea? Hope you don't have to rush off . . . Owen's getting on great . . .'

She was here to collect Owen from his music lesson. Now that Ed could no longer swing round to their address, the new arrangement was that Owen would go home with Ed after school on Thursdays and Annie would pick him up at 7 p.m. But she'd been held up twice and had had to send Dinah, so this was her first visit to Ed's.

'Tea would be great, thanks,' Annie told him and knocked over a dish of cat food on the floor as she tried to get out of his way.

'Come on, I'll take you through,' he offered and she followed gingerly, wondering what housekeeping horrors lay ahead.

The sitting room was reached by way of a tiny corridor lined with packed bookshelves. 'Hi, Owen!' she called to her son, who was sitting cross-legged on the sofa, a guitar cradled between his knees.

'Listen to this,' was his response and he strummed a complicated-sounding chord sequence.

'Brilliant,' she told him, taking in the room around her. It had been painted dark pink and the curtains and sofa were of a faded and threadbare floral pattern. The upright piano, three guitars and a framed collection of concert posters Annie might have expected Ed to have. The breathtaking, voluptuous oil painting of a nude woman was a little more unexpected. The frilly ornaments and porcelain figurines clogging up the mantelpiece and windowsills were also out of keeping and Annie was guessing that Ed was still curating every single item that had once belonged to his mother.

There was no denying the character of the place. The doors all hung at a wonky angle, the floor squeaked, and, if she were to drop a marble, she suspected it would roll right towards the black fireplace at the side of the room.

As Owen played on, Ed came in bearing a little tray with two mugs and a teapot. 'Please, take a seat,' he insisted and as she settled herself into a saggy armchair, her amateur property-developer's eye fell on the buckled skirting board and the peeling sheet of wallpaper working itself away from it.

'Looks like you've got damp,' she told him.

'Oh . . . these old places'—he waved a biscuit in the air—'always have a touch of something.'

'No, Ed.' Annie lifted the flap of wallpaper and saw across the back, as she'd suspected, a plume of black mould. 'You've got damp and a serious mould situation and—'

With perfect timing, Ed gave one of his spectacular sneezes, so she could tell him, convincingly, 'You're allergic to it. Most people would be.'

'You're joking!' he said and he came over to look at the paper she was holding up. He sneezed again as soon as he was up close.

Owen came too and declared the situation 'gross' but nevertheless went on to tell Ed all about the dry rot 'fruiting body' that had been discovered in the basement of their previous home. 'It was orangey-brown and huge and mushroomy, alive! It looked like it had just come down from outer space,' he told them in an excited voice.

'That's just lovely, Owen. Would you like to see if you can find Hoover and Dyson in the garden for me? My cats,' he said in response to Annie's raised eyebrows.

'Erm . . . there's something I need to talk to you about,' Ed began a little awkwardly, once Owen was out of the back door.

He sat forward, elbows resting on his knees, and looked directly at her, terribly seriously. 'How's it going in Upper Ploxley?' he asked.

'It's fine,' she replied. 'Good,' she added quickly. When he made no reply, but kept on looking at her questioningly, she felt compelled to add, 'I suppose we're all having some teething problems . . . but I really think it's going to work out for the best.'

'Do you?' he asked, still very serious. Oh brother, he was about to mention the kissing, she knew it. Neither of them had ever referred to that . . . incident . . . and she'd not given it a thought since it had happened. Well, not really. But now her toes were tightly curled at the thought of him bringing it up.

'Look, Ed,' she jumped in, 'if this is about what I—what we . . . you know, in the stairwell . . .' she mumbled. 'Look, I didn't mean anything by it. I don't want you to get the wrong idea. I'm very happy with Gray.'

Ed's face seemed to cloud over. She'd tried to clear the air, but her words seemed to have had the opposite effect. He looked almost angry.

'No, I wasn't going to talk about that,' he said, making her want to kick herself hard. 'I thought I should tell you, in case you hadn't noticed, that Owen is not happy. He's stopped speaking in class and judging by how well his guitar playing is coming along, he must be in his room practising for hours every day. I don't think that amount of time on his own can be very good for him.'

Annie didn't know what to say. Had she overlooked Owen? He'd seemed to settle into Gray's home quite well, compared with Lana.

'Don't you think it was a bit soon to move them?' Ed asked her. 'Maybe you've rushed into things for your own reasons?'

That was too much. He had totally overstepped the line. 'I don't think that's any of your business, Ed,' she told him angrily, then added in a raised voice, 'Of course I only want what's best for the children. I made the move to give us all some more security. Saying I did it for my own reasons is just completely wrong!'

'I'm sorry,' Ed replied, which took the wind out of her sails a little.

'I'm helping Owen as much as I can,' she added, voice not so angry now. 'I hadn't realised what was going on at school. You were right to tell me about that.'

His head was bowed. 'Well, maybe this isn't my business either,' he began, not looking up at her, 'but I think you should know that there's about two thousand pounds missing from the school's charity fundraising account. I haven't spoken to Lana and her friends about it yet, but obviously I'm going to have to.'

'Two thousand pounds!' Annie repeated in astonishment.

'There's over eight thousand left, but there have been three withdrawals which have added up to two grand. Only Lana and one other girl are signatories entitled to make withdrawals,' he told her gravely.

'Oh, no!' was Annie's stunned reaction. Immediately she wondered what Lana was planning to do with the money. Run away? 'Ed? Can you give me the chance to speak to Lana about this first?' she asked. 'She's being so difficult at the moment. She doesn't like it at Gray's, her boyfriend's dumped her, she's missing her friends . . . It looks like she's done something totally out of order, but can you just give me a couple of days to find out what she knows about it?'

And if she's got £2,000 on her, she could just take off were the words Annie didn't add.

'Right, well . . .' Ed stood up. 'I'll see Owen at the weekend then?' He was referring to the long-planned camping expedition.

Annie got up too and felt awkward. 'I will understand if you don't want to do the trip any more,' she told him.

He looked at her with surprise. 'Why wouldn't I want to do it? Owen would be gutted.'

She gave Ed a smile, grateful that he at least understood this.

Owen was too hot in his sleeping-bag. Also, his right thumb, carefully wrapped in a clean plaster, was starting to throb. Opening a family-sized tin of beans with his penknife had turned out to have been a bad idea. The knife had left a cruelly jagged edge, which had ripped his thumb open as he was tipping the beans out into the pot. For a few moments, Owen hadn't registered the pain and his blood had dripped down onto the beans. But as soon as he'd uttered his first 'Owww!' Ed, on cooking duty at the camp along with two dads and four other boys, had sprung into action.

The cut had quickly been assessed, cleaned with disinfectant wipes and held up high to stem the blood flow. Once the plaster had been expertly applied and soothing words administered, they'd both gone back to the gas stove to check over the beans.

There was a small puddle of blood sitting on top of them.

'Do you think we should throw them out?' Owen had asked.

'No, no, no,' Ed had heartily assured him. 'Of course not—as long as they get a good boil. Extra iron for everyone.'

Ed had sat next to him at supper, chatting with him and some of the other boys, telling jokes. When Owen's yawns had come thick and fast Ed had suggested he head for his sleeping-bag in one of the boys' tents. This is where Owen, overdressed in socks, jogging bottoms and a T-shirt, now wriggled uncomfortably. On one side of his stomach there was a slightly sore patch—too many beans, he suspected. Then he found he couldn't help thinking about his dad, a cheerful and extrovert farter who'd had about fifty different words for the process.

And he was thinking about the other thing and worrying quite a lot more. He'd thought he'd be able to keep it to himself, make it his own little project, but now he wasn't so sure.

Then Ed, in cord trousers and an old stripy pyjama top, came into the tent with one of Owen's books. 'Thought you might want this,' he said. He looked around; there were three other boys in the other corner of the big tent. 'How are you doing? Do you think you'll get any sleep?'

'Don't know,' Owen said.

'You're warm enough, though?' Ed asked.

'Yeah . . . hmmm . . . fine.'

Something about Owen's slightly pained face made Ed ask, 'Sore tummy?' When this got a nod, he suggested, 'Too many beans maybe?'

'Yeah . . . too many beans.'

'I'm sure everyone will understand if you need to release a little'—he raised an eyebrow—'pressure. Just keep your bag pulled tight.'

This made Owen grin and he suddenly found himself telling Ed, 'The maps that I made for this trip—the special walk that I'd planned along Even Ridge—I've forgotten to bring them. I left them on my bed.'

'It's OK,' Ed assured him. 'We'll buy an Ordnance Survey first thing in the morning and plot it out with that.'

'Yeah, well, but the thing is . . .' Owen continued, 'I'm worried my mum or my sister will find them.'

'Now why would you worry about that?' Ed asked, puzzled.

'Well, you see.' Owen made a long pause, but Ed gave him such an encouraging look he began to explain: 'It's about my dad.'

It wasn't nearly as hard to tell someone as he'd expected.

Lana goes outdoors:

Fuchsia rebel girl T-shirt (Camden market)
Pale grey skater trousers (Quicksilver sale)
Silver parka (Topshop)
Fuchsia trainers (Rocket Dog)
Total est. cost: £110

'There's no way I can tell you about it . . .'

'MUM!' There was an unusual note of urgency to Lana's voice as she walked into Gray's kitchen.

'It's eight fifteen! What are you doing up so early?' Annie asked as Lana handed her several sheets of paper covered with Owen's cramped handwriting and intricately detailed pencil drawings.

Annie leafed through the pages, but couldn't see what was exciting her daughter so much. 'These are Owen's little maps and drawings of the campsite he's at with Ed,' she said.

'Did you have any idea where they were going?' Lana asked her.

'Of course. They've gone to the Black Mountains.'

'Yeah . . . the bit otherwise known as the Brecon Beacons.'

Annie could feel her heart rate speed up at these words.

'This map . . .' Lana began accusingly, but Annie's eyes had now picked out the words 'Even Ridge' running along one of the contours.

'Oh my God!' she exclaimed. Even Ridge was known for only one reason in their family. It was Roddy's place.

'Don't you get it?' Lana was almost shouting at her. 'Owen wants to visit Dad's—'

'Why does he want to do that?!' But Annie already knew of this deep-seated wish of Owen's. He had asked her to take him many times before and she had always assured him they would go together as a family, 'when they were all ready'.

What she'd really meant was when *she* was ready. And she was not.

But clearly, Owen was determined to go and had hatched this clever little plan. Annie snatched up the kitchen phone and punched in the number of the mobile Owen had with him. Ed, of course, infuriatingly, did not have a mobile. She heard her own voice coming down the line at her. 'Hi, it's Annie . . .'

'Owen, it's Mum,' she began her message. 'Please phone me, straight away.' As soon as she'd hung up, she told Lana, 'Get dressed. We have to go there. If Owen's going to do this today, he needs us to be there with him.'

And there was a conversation Annie had to have with her daughter.

Gray came downstairs for breakfast just as Annie, fully dressed and all set to head off with Lana, was about to wake him and explain what was happening.

'There's a problem with Owen,' Annie told him. 'Lana and I have to head up there and be with him.'

'Is he OK?' Gray asked.

'He's not hurt, it's nothing medical. Look, we really have to go . . . Do you mind if I explain it to you later?'

'Right, well.' Gray looked grumpy. 'I'll have a quiet little day to myself, will I? Maybe I'll do some tidying up in this pigsty. Perhaps if I search hard enough, *Lana*,' he said pointedly, 'I'll come across the two boxes of medicine currently missing from my supplies.'

'What?' Annie and her daughter chorused together.

'Yes, that's right.' Gray was clearly furious. 'One box of fifty Valium tablets, one box of fifty Temazepams. Both missing from my locked office cabinet. A nice little earner for somebody.'

'Do you know anything about this?' Annie snapped at Lana.

She shook her head emphatically, not taking her eyes from Gray.

'Gray, if there's a problem with my children, you come and talk to me about it first,' Annie told him, now furious too. 'Don't just go about making completely unfounded accusations.'

'But we know Lana's dishonest!' he exclaimed. 'Didn't she cost you your job? It wouldn't surprise me one bit to find out she's on drugs!'

This was too much for Annie. She took Lana by the arm and hustled her out of the front door, giving it a great dramatic slam.

No words passed between mother and daughter until they were miles out of Upper Ploxley and on the motorway heading west, then finally Annie asked first about the drugs, to which she got an emphatic, 'I don't know anything about that, I promise.'

Then she began her enquiry into the missing £2,000.

After a long pause, Lana asked her mother a question in return: 'How do you know about that?'

'Ed told me. He checked the bank account.'

'I didn't think he ever looked!'

Annie let this incriminating remark pass without comment.

'There's no way I can tell you about it . . .' Lana said slowly. 'No way.'

'Of course there is,' Annie said gently. 'I'm your mum. I care about you more than anyone else in the world does.'

Then Lana began to sob. And Annie began to feel very afraid. Lana had obviously done something terrible, or something terrible had happened. Wild thoughts raced through her mind. An abortion? Gambling? Drugs? Guilt that she hadn't paid close enough attention to her stroppy, about-to-turn-fifteen-year-old was coursing through Annie's veins.

'Lana, whatever it is, I'm going to look after you.'

'It was for Suzie . . .' the words began, in between tears and sniffs and fresh sobs. 'She's in such a mess . . . Her parents have split up and her boyfriend's a . . . total . . . He's just a cokehead, Mum.'

Annie was nodding encouragingly, but her grip on the steering wheel was knuckle-white.

'She started bringing it into school. She was a mess! We kept telling her to split up with him and get some help.'

Annie moved the jeep over into the slow lane so she could give Lana's story better attention.

'She persuaded us to lend her money from the fund. She said she needed it to get treatment and she'd get it back from her dad, as soon as he was back in the country. But I think . . . we all think . . . she's taken the money and spent it with her boyfriend. She's never going to ask her dad now and'—her voice raised to a desperate crescendo—'we're all going to get expelled once this comes out.' The sobbing broke out afresh.

Annie couldn't help breathing a sigh of relief that, for Lana at least, it wasn't nearly as awful as Annie had imagined. 'Lana,' she began, 'don't worry. OK? Try not to worry. I wish you'd told me sooner. But we will sort this out. Blimey,' she added several moments later. 'There's never a dull moment with you around, is there?'

'Mum?' Lana asked, wiping her face. 'Are we going to carry on living with Gray?'

Annie let out a deep sigh before confiding, 'No, babes, and I'm so, so sorry. I thought he was going to be really good for all of us. I wouldn't have put you through another move if I hadn't thought it was the best thing to do. I am so sorry.'

'We'll have to move again,' Lana pointed out.

'I know.'

'Where to?' Lana wondered, knowing full well that they couldn't go back to their flat for months.

'I'm working on that,' Annie told her and began to chew her lip. 'We'll go back to town though . . . definitely. I can't stand Upper Ploxley,' she added with feeling. 'Where am I supposed to go for a coffee? Let alone a nice pair of shoes.'

Lana tried and failed to reach Owen on the mobile as the jeep ate up the miles between them. Annie exited the motorway and began to navigate the smaller, twisty roads that led to the campsite. The towns and red-roofed housing estates had fallen away now and they'd entered gentle green countryside; first farms with patchwork fields and then the roll of hills began.

Annie wanted to know if Lana was all right about a visit to Even Ridge.

'If Owen's going to do it—or if he's already done it—then I will too,' came the quiet reply. 'But it's OK to be nervous, isn't it?'

'Yes, of course it's OK to be nervous,' Annie assured her. 'I'm absolutely terrified.'

Soon, the jeep was moving slowing through the high street of the small town closest to the campsite. Suddenly Lana shouted, 'Look, over there! I think that's Owen!'

Sure enough, walking with his back turned to them was her brother and several feet behind him, recognisable by his nest of hair, was Ed.

Annie pulled up ahead of them. Moments later, she and Lana were on the pavement, standing in front of the surprised campers.

'Mum?' Owen spoke first. 'What are you doing here?'

'We came into town to look for a phone box,' Ed began, in no doubt as to why Annie was here. 'But we've not been able to get through to you.'

'Owen has a phone,' was Annie's irritated response. 'Why couldn't he have used that?'

'No reception,' Ed answered, a picture of calm.

'Owen!' She turned all her attention on her son. 'Don't you think it would have been a good idea to tell me about your plan?'

'What plan?' Owen asked, trying to avoid the inevitable showdown he'd been dreading ever since Ed had told him, kindly but firmly, that he couldn't take him up to Even Ridge without his mother's blessing.

Annie took Owen's drawings out of the back pocket of her trousers.

'I knew you'd say no,' Owen burst out. His face was suddenly pale with a bright spot of red in each cheek. Annie knew this meant he was very upset, or very angry, maybe both. 'I should be allowed to see Dad's place!' he added in a surprisingly loud voice.

'I haven't driven all this way to tell you no,' she said, hugely relieved to realise that they hadn't gone up to the ridge yet. 'Lana and I came here because if it's so important to you to go, then we'll go with you.'

Annie saw Owen's shoulders loosen a little.

'I was about to take Owen for a scone,' Ed chipped in, patting Owen on the shoulder. 'It's still too misty to do any serious hill walking. But it looks like it's going to clear up nicely, so in the meantime I think we should hide out at Edna's Tea Corner over there. Great cakes in the window.'

All three Valentines felt deeply grateful for Ed's tension-breaking enthusiasm for home baking.

Annie looked at herself in the mirror in the town's little outward-bound clothing shop with undisguised horror. 'An anorak? *An anorak?*' she repeated. 'I don't do anoraks.' Especially maroon cagoules paired with—*horror of horrors*—maroon waterproof trousers, tucked into—*this can't be happening*—hiking boots.

Her children were giggling. Ed had one arm folded across his woolly-jumpered chest as, chin in hand, blue eyes twinkly, he scrutinised her. 'Oh, now that is sooo you,' he said. 'Brings out the colour in your cheeks. And the trousers, they coordinate so well,' he added.

'Who'd have thought of putting those two together? Very clever.'

Annie couldn't decide whether to laugh at him or hit him.

'Do I have to wear this? All of it?' she pleaded once again.

He nodded his head. 'Oh, yes. Strictly necessary. I'm going to insist you put the hood up and tie it tightly round your face as well.'

Ed had broken the news to her after an impressive amount of Edna's home baking had been consumed. 'If we're going to go up Even Ridge, Annie, then you'll have to get some waterproofs and a pair of boots.'

Although Lana had left the house in an unusually sensible outfit, Annie had dressed for a day's window-shopping in a short belted mac and leather trainers. But obviously that wasn't going to do.

She pulled the maroon hood on and tied the drawstring tight round her face so that she peered out like an owl.

'I can't . . . I just can't.' She made one final protest.

'Twit-to-woo,' Owen teased.

The walk towards Even Ridge began straight after the purchase of the maroon waterproofs, once Ed had satisfied himself that they were all absolutely sure they wanted him to come with them. He had shown them on the map the way the ridged path curved right along the face of the hill, moving slowly up to the summit and then bringing walkers back down by a different route.

'It's about two and a half hours' walk, all in,' he'd told them. 'Do you know roughly where we're aiming for?' he'd asked.

Annie had shaken her head in reply to this, but told him, 'I don't think it's far from the top.'

A gentle grey drizzle was still blanking out both sky and sun and wrapping itself around them. Within fifteen minutes of starting the walk, Annie felt damp everywhere. She watched her feet moving for a while, clumpy in the brand-new hiking boots. She tried to concentrate hard on this rather than think about where they were heading.

Every so often she lifted her head to take in the view, which, as the drizzle began to lift, was much more pleasant than she'd expected. She was also on the lookout for some clue that they were in the right place, although she had no idea what this clue was going to be.

She had expected to feel very anxious up here, panicky even . . . so close to Roddy. About to see the place where . . .

But she was surprised to find that a sense of calm had come over her.

She looked back at Owen and Lana and wondered what they were thinking. Owen broke into a jog; he flashed her a smile before passing.

'Are you going to be first to the top?' she asked him, cheered by the irrepressible fun he was managing to squeeze from this.

'Definitely,' he called back over his shoulder.

They had been walking for about fifty minutes and seemed to be making good time towards the summit when Owen, eighty feet or so ahead of her, called out, 'Muuum! Mum, come and look at this!'

Annie, Lana and Ed hurried up the pathway to reach him and followed his pointing finger to a colourful bundle propped next to a large grey boulder. The side of the hill was much steeper here, so if they wanted to take a closer look they would have to scramble down the grass to get down to the rock about thirty feet below the path.

Owen was already crawling his way down backwards, hands, knees and toecaps in the grass for grip.

'I think he'll be OK,' Ed reassured her, climbing down from the path himself and holding out a hand to Lana, who clearly wanted to join them. 'It's grassy, but I don't think it'll be too slippery.'

So all four of them moved, sliding and crawling, down the steep bank towards the stone. By the time Annie made it down to the boulder, the colourful bundle had come into focus as a weatherbeaten bunch of flowers.

'May I have a look?' Annie asked and Owen put the wet bundle into her hands. It was sodden wet and browning, but these had once been fat pink and orange roses. The smart cellophane was shredded in places, but she could make out a London, WC1, postcode.

About ten days ago, or so, this had clearly been a sensational bunch of flowers and the significance of the date did not pass Annie by. She had done her very, very best to try to forget the anniversary of Roddy's death this year, but still the date had slapped her hard in the face.

She was certain this had something to do with Roddy. At the inquest, it had been stated that no other serious accident had happened on Even Ridge; unless there had been something since, of course.

Lana pointed down into the flower stems. 'Look, there's a card.'

Annie peeled back the wrapper and brought out a small silver envelope. For a moment she didn't know if she dared. What if this was something she didn't know about? Shouldn't know about? What if it was private to Roddy? Or even to do with someone else entirely?

But Owen and Lana were crowding close and urging her on, so she pulled out a white card no more than two inches square. Scribbled over the front and back in a handwriting she recognised were the words: *The third anniversary, my friend . . . three whole years without you. I just hope that, wherever you are, you have some idea how much we all miss you.*

Annie stared at the card. The words were blurring.

'It's from Connor, isn't it?' came from Lana.

Annie just nodded, could feel the tears overflow from the bottom lid of her eye. 'Yes,' she managed.

'Did Daddy fall off the path and hit his head here?' Owen asked.

'Yes.' Her voice was down to a husky whisper. 'He was so unlucky, babes, so very, very unlucky.'

Unlucky . . . this was the way she chose to describe it now, after long and pointless hours raging about how 'unfair' it had been.

Why had Connor never told her he was making this journey? Had he made it the years before as well? She carefully placed the bunch back at the foot of the stone, moved to tears by Connor's gesture.

Now she suspected they were going to have to do the thing she'd been dreading, halfway up a hillside with the odd passer-by to see them. They were going to have to huddle together and cry.

With her nose pressed into the top of Lana's head, with Owen tucked in against her cagoule, they cried together.

She thought at first she would just have a short cry: a let it out, blow nose, then move back to the path sort of thing.

She thought she had to be strong for the children, she had to hold it together. *They're the ones who are really, really upset, they need me to keep it together here.* But she began to feel horrible, big, wrenching sobs bursting out of her lungs. She couldn't do anything to stop them.

Roddy was not away on location as she so often tried to fool herself. He was gone. Taken away for ever. He wasn't ever, ever going to come back to them. She was never, ever going to wake up in the morning and find the nightmare over and him safely back home beside her.

The finality of the situation broke over her and it hurt so much she didn't know if she could stand the pain, she was struggling for breath, struggling to stand.

Roddy had been fatally injured right here on Even Ridge. A 'freak fall', apparently, so everyone involved in the accident had told her at the time. As if the words 'freak fall . . . could have happened to anyone' had made it any easier to bear. In fact, she often thought it made it much harder.

If Roddy had set off that weekend to scale an Alpine glacier, she might have been more prepared for a terrible accident. But he'd left with three of his mates for a beer-drinking and hill-walking weekend. 'It'll be much more about beers than hills, I can tell you that,' he'd joked as he'd flung his overnight bag into the boot of Connor's car.

After a big night out, a little bit hung over, Roddy and his friends had set off for a pick-me-up jaunt up to the top of Even Ridge.

Close to the summit, Roddy had stumbled and fallen. His misfortune had been to hit his head hard enough against this boulder right here to cause a massive brain haemorrhage. A helicopter had been scrambled and he'd been airlifted to the nearest intensive-care unit, but he'd never regained consciousness and after a week on life support had come the devastating news that he was brain dead. His family and his closest friends had all come to visit. They had talked to him and held him and told him things they wished they'd told him so much more often when he could still have heard. They'd cried over him, touched him, kissed him, curled up in bed beside him.

Until finally Annie had signed the forms.

With Lana and Owen in the fiercest embrace of Fern next door, with her own arms tight round the waist of Roddy's mother, Penny, Annie had watched the nurses quietly and sensitively switch off the machines, unhook the drips and remove the needles.

With his wife holding one hand, his mother clinging to the other, it had taken Roddy several excruciatingly long minutes to die. The moment she knew it had happened, Annie had felt a dreadful, physical snap. Something inside her had broken irreparably.

There were hundreds of phone calls to make, flowers, church, relatives to deal with. More flowers, more cards, and still more phone calls to make and the endlessly ringing phone to answer, like a permanent ringing in her ears.

After all that, after all the noise and the bustle and the deadlines and the plans and preparations and the great rush and swell of emotion on the day . . . after that came the most deafening silence.

Annie's days and evenings became totally silent. She could talk to her children, she could hear her children, she could phone her mother, visit her sister. It didn't make any difference. All she could hear, for months on end, was the silence in her life where before there had been Roddy.

Now that she was here on the hillside, she realised how furious she was. How outraged, how totally, totally livid she was about this.

How dare this stupid, innocuous bit of ground, this hard grey useless stone, how dare they take Roddy away from them? How dare they?

She kicked furiously against the stone.

'How dare they? How dare they?' Annie realised she was saying it aloud, over and over again. She was squeezing Lana and Owen too tightly, could feel them both pushing slightly against her.

She let go of them and sat down heavily on the ground. She cried and cried. Didn't care now that Lana and Owen had stopped crying, didn't care whether anyone on the path up there was looking down at them or what Ed, the outsider, was making of it all.

She howled. She keened.

Then there was an arm round her shoulders, a heavy arm, holding her tight. With her eyes shut, she briefly leaned her head on the shoulder the arm was attached to and felt supported enough to cry more. Cry hard, really hard, cry with some intention of crying herself out.

Because she was going to have to cry about something else now too: how much she missed her job.

All day long, she caught herself thinking about little things happening at The Store. Walking past racks of new shoes, inhaling the smell of unbroken leather. The Store's staff: Avril, Delia, Paula, Janie in Accounts. The flow of women in through her suite every day, the transformations in front of the mirror . . . She missed it all so much.

She liked the fact that this solid arm and shoulder didn't come with words. It didn't say: 'There, there', or 'Don't cry'. It was just there. Long enough to catch her breath again, to grope for the sides in this pool of grief and begin to pull herself up, out of the water.

After a long time, she felt able to open her swollen eyes again. Slowly, she released herself from the grip of the arm and stood up.

When she could manage the words, she said, 'I'm really sorry' to Ed, the owner of the arm.

'No need to be, I understand,' he said gently.

'Where are the children?' she asked.

'They've gone on to the top of the hill. Do you feel ready to walk up after them?' When she nodded in reply to this, but looked anxiously at the steep slope, Ed held out his hand and told her, 'Don't worry, I'll help you up.'

Annie took hold of the hand offered and let him pull her up the steep slope. On the summit of the hill, she could see Lana and Owen standing close together. When she finally got up beside them, Owen slipped his hand into hers, and told her, 'Thanks, Mum. I always wanted to finish Daddy's walk for him.'

When Lana heard this, she told her brother in a voice close to a whisper, 'That's really nice, Owen. I never thought of it like that . . . I'm glad you brought us here.'

'Are you OK?' Ed had asked Annie with concern as she'd scrambled to her feet, pained and winded, after a backwards-on-her-bottom skid down a substantial chunk of hill in the torrential rain that had accompanied them all the way down. The force of the slide had split her trousers in two and caused her anorak to ride up, wetting all her clothes underneath.

'I'm fine, but I'm bloody soaked!'

'That's no problem,' Ed had assured her. 'I've got some spare things in my tent.'

Back at the campsite, Ed's tent had collapsed under the weight of the downpour. Nevertheless, Ed managed to fish out his holdall and told Annie to take whatever she needed.

In the dank toilet and shower block, she undid the zip on the ancient sports bag and looked inside. Chaos. She felt in gingerly, but at least it seemed to be a clean sort of chaos. She pulled out a pair of jeans, a white T-shirt, almost threadbare, and a worn-out sweatshirt. She'd need those socks and boxers, too. Should she risk wearing his boxers?

She scrambled out of her wet clothes and into the dry ones as quickly as she could. She used her belt to hitch up the trousers, making the denim bunch and gape. Then her phone, tucked into the wet trousers she'd just peeled off, began to ring.

'Mum! Hi! How are you?'

'Where are you, Annie?'

'I'm with Owen and Lana and their music teacher . . .' she began. 'Owen was at this campsite and it's right beside the hill where Roddy fell.' She talked Fern through the journey they'd just made.

'Oh my God!' was Fern's reaction. 'Are you OK?'

'Yes,' Annie assured her, 'we're fine. It was . . .' She paused. 'I think it was a good thing to do. What are you phoning me for at three p.m. on a Saturday anyway?' Annie wondered.

'I've just seen Gray,' Fern told her. She paused.

'What do you mean?'

'Do you know where he is?' Fern asked her.

'Not really. He said he was having a quiet day at home—but he might go out. Why? Where have you seen him?'

'Well, maybe you should phone him up, sweetheart. See if he tells you that he's in a cosy little booth at Le Pont d'Or having a three-course meal with his *wife*, Marilyn.'

'Really??!' Annie could hardly believe it. 'You've just seen them *there*?'

'Yes. I'd love to be mistaken . . . and maybe there's a completely innocent reason for it . . . but there we are.'

As soon as Annie had hung up on Fern, she dialled Gray's number. She felt slightly caught out when he answered straight away.

'How's it going?' he wanted to know. 'Where did you rush off to? Is everything OK with Owen?'

He sounded so concerned that she thought her mother must have been wrong.

'Everything's fine. Are you still at home?' she asked.

'No. I couldn't face the tidying up so I headed into town. I gave John a call and we met up for lunch.'

'John?'

'You know, yachtie John. We had a bit of a blowout at Le Pont d'Or.'

'Great . . . Sorry, babes, I've got to go . . .' was all Annie could manage in response to this. 'Speak to you later.'

Bloody hell!

It was one thing for her to decide that moving in with Gray had been a mistake. It was something else for him to be sneaking off to see his soon-to-be-ex-wife behind her back. After brushing carefully through her wet hair, she tied it up tightly and took several minutes to apply her lipstick perfectly. Like a soldier in a combat zone, she never let rough times get in the way of a bit of grooming or shoe polishing. That would be bad for morale.

Unfortunately, she had to pull her soggy walking boots back on and the wet cagoule because the stair-rod rain had not eased.

Out on the campsite field she located Ed's tent, which had been pulled back to rights, and guessed that her children were inside with him. She crawled in, trying to avoid putting her hand into the wet mud on the crackling plastic floor of the tent.

Casting a glance round at the quiet, thoughtful faces surrounding her, she raised her voice to be heard above the drumming raindrops to say, 'Well, this is fun, isn't it? I hadn't realised how much fun camping could be.'

Although Lana and Owen giggled, Ed was the first to speak. 'Owen, do you want to do another night under canvas?' he asked. 'Or should we pack up and do this another time when it's not so wet?'

Once the four of them had tossed about the pros and cons of staying or going and decided to go, there came an unexpected offer.

'Can I make you all supper tonight? At my place. Yes.' He waved away Annie's protests, although she was wondering whether she could face going back to Gray tonight . . . having to have the row about his Lana accusations and his expensive lunch, on top of the day she'd already had. 'It's the least I can do. No trouble at all.'

Cross-legged on the floor, Annie was contemplating her row of Scrabble letters with as much concentration as she could manage with a fourth glass of wine in her hand. KLJWKIU. Impossible.

Ed had somehow managed to cram them all into his tiny kitchen and feed them, even though Annie had stood in the cat's bowl this time.

The potatoes baked in the microwave had taken a surprisingly long time. 'I'm just used to making one,' Ed had flustered. 'I forgot it would take four times as long.' When they were finally served up, they were tough, dry and chewy and they came with baked beans, grated bright orange cheddar cheese and, inexplicably, tinned sardines.

But Annie and her children were so starvingly hungry after the walk and the long drive back that they ate everything and scraped their plates, causing Ed to scratch his head, then declare he was going to make scones. Annie had been sceptical, but they came out beautifully and Ed was totally redeemed.

After supper, he'd opened wine and settled them all into his sitting room, stoking up the fire that the chilly May evening seemed to require. Annie glanced at her row of letters again despondently, then looked up to see Owen laying the word 'zenith' down right across the triple letter and triple word score boxes, earning himself about 1,000 points.

'Owen!' she groaned. 'You don't even know what zenith means.'

'Are you trying to argue with my budding Junior Scrabble champion here?' Ed asked, as he coolly placed three tiles down, extending two words and creating a third, collecting about 10,000 points.

'We never play Scrabble,' she said, as if that wasn't obvious from her pathetic three-letter offerings so far. 'How did you learn to play, Owen?'

'Ed's Scrabble club at school,' came the short response.

'Wednesday lunchtimes,' Ed explained. 'He's never mentioned it?'

'I am constantly asking Owen about school,' she explained, 'but I probably only know about fifteen per cent of what goes on there.'

'It's best that way, believe me,' came Lana's comment from the sofa. At Annie's insistence, Lana had had a private, slightly shamefaced conversation in the kitchen with Ed, in which she'd explained enough about the missing funds and what she would do to get them back for Ed to feel relieved that he didn't have to take the matter up officially.

Lana had opted out of the Scrabble and was now rummaging through a pile of heavy books stacked up against the sofa.

'Those are my sister's,' Ed explained.

'Where does your sister live?' Annie asked, curious.

'In London,' came the response, but perhaps because Ed was focused on the Scrabble, no further information was offered.

'But you didn't grow up in London, did you?' she prompted, noticing S and T on the board and putting her new tiles in front to make the word 'resist'. But this only netted her about eight points.

'Mum, that is feeble.' Owen didn't spare her.

'No, no, we grew up all over the place. Dad was in the army,' came

Ed's reply to her question. 'Home sweet home for me was boarding school . . . seriously!' he added when she laughed.

He told them how he was sent to boarding school the week after his seventh birthday. 'That was the norm, all the army kids went. We left on the plane together, went off to our various schools, then met up again on the plane home at the end of term.' When they all looked at him with various shades of surprise, he added, 'I don't really remember being homesick . . . maybe I was too young. But my mum was totally traumatised. She used to say that I'm institutionalised.'

'What do you mean?' Annie was sure he was joking about this.

'I've never really left school. I've been teaching at boarding schools most of my adult life. St Vincent's is a real departure, believe me. I have my own home . . . well, Mum's old home. I have to cook for myself and clean . . . well, in my own way . . . Believe me, these are big steps! I mean,' he went on, 'I have tried to break free before. For a year or two I was in this travelling band . . .'

Owen looked up at him with something approaching awe.

'But I don't know, I think I must have missed the custard and steamed pudding too much. Come September, I feel a real longing for the smell of fresh radiator paint and newly kicked-up rugby pitches.'

'But you're getting over it?' she reminded him.

'Trying to. There's something so appealing about boarding schools though. You don't have to worry about all the things other people have to worry about. Meals are served on the dot. There are cupboards all over the school with everything you need: food, stationery.'

'Clothes?' Annie wondered.

'You can always raid the lost property box—find an old rugby shirt.'

'This is really explaining a lot about you.' Annie was smiling at him over her wineglass. 'What about your dad?' She decided to come out and just ask, because the desire to know was burning.

She heard Owen give a little sigh before Ed began his answer. 'My poor old dad got himself killed. Occupational hazard, obviously.'

'I'm so sorry,' Annie offered.

'I was just about to sit my 'O' levels. My sister and I flew out to my mum, then after a few days we flew back to school again and life carried on as normal. See, that's the thing about boarding schools—these enormous shocks can happen, but you're totally buffered. My daily life was just the same as if nothing had happened.'

'Not very healthy,' Lana informed him.

'No.' He shook his head. 'Maybe that's why Mum dying was such a blow . . . I had some catching up to do.'

With these words, Annie, who'd previously found the mess, clutter and chaos of Ed's home so irritating, suddenly felt some real understanding and sympathy for what he was going through.

When she took herself off to his bathroom, she saw a bar of soap on the sink, worn down to a sliver hardly bigger than a thumbnail. Presumably this was the kind of thing Ed would have found in one of those cupboards at boarding school. Now she felt a pang of protectiveness towards him.

Back in the sitting room, she found that Ed had used his tiles to change her 'resist' into 'irresistible'. He caught her eye and gave such a tiny quirk with his eyebrow that she wasn't sure if she'd seen it or not.

Two more rounds of the game were played, with Owen and Ed in an increasingly vicious and competitive battle, when Annie saw to her surprise that it was close to midnight and announced that they would have to go, although she was tired and too cosy and comfortable here. 'So . . . you're all heading back to Essex now?' Ed asked.

'No. Not after this much wine,' she reminded him. 'We're going to stay with Connor. I spoke to him earlier.' And now she was going to have to turn her attention to the difficult phone call ahead of her. Already there were voicemail messages and five missed calls from Gray's numbers.

Hector in love (with Connor):

Organic cords (Howies)
Eco-slogan T-shirt (Howies)
Two-strap vegan sandals (Birkenstock)
Sheer black net boxers (La Redoute)
Total est. cost: £180

'Darlings, isn't it a wonderful evening!'

ANNIE LEFT HER CHILDREN in Connor's care and drove alone to Essex through quiet Sunday-morning traffic to face Gray.

Gray kissed her gently on the cheek and showed her in. He'd been tidying, that was obvious. He offered coffee and she followed him through into the kitchen, where the taps gleamed and surfaces sparkled in a way they'd never done while she was in residence.

While the coffee was brewing he began with a string of apologies.

He was sorry he'd been so grumpy and difficult to live with . . . he was finding it hard to adjust to having so many people living in his home, but he was enjoying so much about it, '*honestly*', he assured her.

His dazzling chrome Gaggia coffee machine chugged and glugged in the background as he went on.

'I found the Valium and the Temazepam,' Gray told her, shamefaced, 'under a pile of stuff in the sitting room. I owe Lana an apology. I'm going to do much better at all of this, I promise you.'

Now Annie's big bold decision to tell him goodbye, pack up some of their things and leave him didn't feel so clear-cut. He wasn't a bad person. He saw what had gone wrong, didn't he? This was a man who had a lot to offer. She looked out through the windows into the garden, where green branches were swaying in the gentle breeze, and she imagined Lana on a sun-lounger reading, Owen digging up earth to conduct a biological experiment.

Gray set her coffee before her and poured in the right amount of milk without asking, which struck her as a caring action. Then he held out a small leather-covered box to her. No prizes for guessing what was in there, she told herself.

Wordlessly, she took the box from him and carefully opened the lid.

From the dark velvet bed inside, a bright white diamond—oval, marquise cut—shone back at her. At least one carat, she estimated, maybe even 1.2. It was absolutely breathtaking. She'd waited patiently all her adult life for a ring like this.

'Oh . . . my . . . God,' she managed finally in a low and breathy voice.

Gray's eyes were trained on her face, waiting for the smile to break and the overwhelming 'yes' of renewed commitment to come.

Instead, Annie asked, 'What about Marilyn? I know you saw her yesterday.' And with those words she wondered when he had bought the ring. Before seeing his wife? Afterwards? It seemed important to know.

'Marilyn . . . well . . .' Gray stammered, 'she wanted to have a chat about the divorce . . . how things were going with me. And I didn't tell you because I didn't want you to think—'

'There's never any need to lie to me about anything . . . I hope,' Annie told him coolly. 'If you lie and I find out then I'm going to think all sorts of things. Right now, I'm thinking: your ex-wife wanted to talk, so you take her for a cosy lunch at Le Pont d'Or? Hmmm. Then you offer me a big, stunning diamond. Hmmm. This is strange behaviour, Gray. This is a man who's not sure what he wants.'

Something about his flickering look—it went from her to his coffee cup, to the ring box in her hand and back to her—made her decision clear to her once again. Carefully she closed the box on the breathtaking, once-in-a-lifetime diamond and slid it slowly back towards him.

Feeling tears of regret pricking, she told him, 'I'm sorry, Gray. I'm really sorry, but we're not going to work out. You're a very special person'—the tears were slipping freely down her cheeks now—'you'll be really good for someone. But you're not the one for us. I'm sorry.'

He hung his head at these words and may even have been squeezing back some tears of his own. Annie wiped at her cheeks. 'Bloody hell!' she added after a moment's pause. 'Packing again!'

'Where are you going to go?' he asked. 'Your flat's—'

'Rented out for another five months, I know. Well . . .' She'd worked through a plan on the way up the motorway. 'We'll stay at Connor's till I've hustled up a deposit, then I'll mortgage myself to the hilt and buy the place in need of a make-over I was planning to get anyway.'

'You can stay here as long as you need to,' Gray offered, maybe in some last hope that he'd be able to persuade her to stay . . . or maybe just because he felt guilty.

'No, no. It's best we go. I might have to leave some boxes here for bit, just till we get sorted. But I'll load up now with whatever I can.'

'**S**trong drink required,' was Connor's verdict when Annie arrived back, laden down with most of her and her children's possessions.

'Is that your answer to everything?' she wondered.

'In what situations does strong drink not work?' he wondered back.

She, Connor and his boyfriend, Hector, got a little tipsy on fizzy wine and shared giant man-sized pizzas with Lana and Owen. Annie hadn't realised that Hector was now a live-in fixture at Connor's.

Conscious that Annie might not want to have to talk about Gray, Connor and Hector drummed up enthusiasm for a ruthless card game with truth or dare as the consequence of failure.

It involved Connor having to reveal who he'd first kissed (a girl, of course, way back before he'd admitted he was gay), and Hector having to lean out of the window and shout 'Darlings, isn't it a wonderful evening!' Lana had to promise she would go to school in the morning with her shirt tucked in, her cardigan done up all the way and pigtails.

Owen had no problem with imitating five different farmyard animals on the balcony and then finally it was Annie's turn.

'Truth! Truth!' Lana chanted. 'We want to know everything.'

'No way!' was Annie's response. 'Oh . . . it'll all come out in the wash eventually. Cover your ears, Owen.' In a whisper she added, 'Yes, he was rubbish in bed . . . you already know that though, don't you?'

Connor and Lana nodded, while Owen added, 'I heard that!'

'Anyway, dare. I chose dare, go on . . . Bet you can't think of anything I'm scared to do. I ain't scared of anything now, Connor McCabe.'

A slow, cunning smile began to spread across Connor's face. 'Oh-oh! Nothing I like more than a challenge. Right . . . here's your dare.' He paused for a moment, for entirely dramatic effect.

'You have to kiss again the last person you kissed passionately.'

'That's impossible.' Annie laughed. 'I've broken off with Gray, Roddy's . . . unavailable. I haven't got the numbers of any previous dates—'

'No, no, no, my girl,' Connor interrupted. 'I don't mean any of them.'

Annie looked at him blankly. 'No idea what you're talking about,' she insisted. 'Oh, not the One Night Wonder! Just a little snog,' she added quickly, seeing the surprise on Lana's face.

'I heard that!' came from Owen.

'No, no, no, not him. I'm going to tell you a little story, Annie,' Connor began. 'One afternoon, I took the tube up to Highgate to see my friends Annie, Lana and Owen. When I arrived at their lovely little mansion block, the lift was out of action, so I swung open the heavy door at the foot of the stairs and began my climb up . . .' In full dramatic flight, Connor went on, 'I thought I heard your voice high up in the stairwell above me. Yes, it was definitely you, and you were talking to someone . . . Is it starting to come back now?'

Annie made no reply, so he went on. 'Yes, you were talking, then all of a sudden there was silence, and that's when I got a glimpse of you, two flights above me, totally entangled with someone. Remember now?'

Annie was starting to look a little strange.

'I tiptoed as quietly as I could back down the staircase. Imagine my surprise when tripping down the stairs, with a great spring in his step, came—'

'That's enough utter nonsense, Connor!' Annie stopped him.

'Who?!' asked Lana.

'All I'm saying,' Connor looked squarely at Annie, 'is that you better go and kiss *that* man again. That's my dare.'

'Huh!' Annie huffed, looking thunderous. 'I need to go to bed,' and with that, she headed towards the door.

But then she turned and added angrily. 'Here's my dare to you, Connor McCabe. Grow up, and you know what else? Come out properly, for God's sake. Don't fudge it in the interviews any more. In the twenty-first century it's a bad career move to be an actor who isn't gay.'

She slammed the door hard behind her.

'Some people,' said Connor, 'are just stubborn. They have no idea what's good for them and they have to be taken firmly in hand.'

Annie in action:

Pale grey and silver striped trousers (Toast sale)
Crisp white wrap blouse, big collars and
cuffs (last year's MaxMara)
Shiny silver and turquoise neck cuff (Camden Market)
Pale caramel shoes (Chanel)
Light red nail varnish (Chanel)
Light red lipstick (Chanel)
total est. cost: Don't even think about it

'It's a waste of money to economise on yourself.'

IT WAS CLOSE TO 1.30 A.M., but Annie was still hunched over her laptop putting the finishing touches to the introductory paragraphs on her Annie V Trading Station web pages.

This was the largest amount of goods she'd ever tried to sell, but she was hoping to raise money just as quickly as she could. Life with the actor boys could not be tolerated for more than a few more weeks at the most and she wasn't quite ready to accept a family loan.

Hello girls, her website note began, as usual. *Do I have some fabulous, fabulous things in store for you today. It's the online equivalent of Opening Day at the Harrods sale. Today, I'm bringing you the property of:*

One Russian fashion maven (Svetlana's divorce fighting-fund)

Several wealthy young ladies (the Syrup Six's prized personal possessions, rustled up to plug the hole in the charity account)

A footballer's moll (Dannii was ridding her life of bling after another bitching in *heat*)

An unbowed divorcee (Megan had been talked into selling off some of the clothes from her married years)

A Lady of the Arts (These were very special things. The one client she'd asked for a short-term loan: Mrs B-P—recovering nicely and determined to live life to the full—had handed over designer labels, expensive classics, and wouldn't hear of taking a penny for them.)

As well as the treasures unearthed for you this week by me, your very own on-line Personal Shopper.

As I said before, girls . . . do not hang about. Grab yourself a bargain! Remember always that it's a waste of money to economise on yourself.

Annie pressed the return button and posted the words up. Her room at Connor's house was crammed to bursting with boxes of things she still had to photograph and post up before she went to bed.

And she had an early start. Her ring-round of all her former Store clients to tell them she was now freelance and could shop with them anywhere in London had resulted in twelve appointments for the week ahead. Somehow she would also have to squeeze in attendance at Lana and Owen's speech day.

Speech Day was a big event at St Vincent's. It was held two days before the end of the summer term and even the most stressed and frantically busy London parent pulled out all the stops in order to attend.

Annie had persuaded Dinah to come with her despite their little debate: 'I'm not sending Billie there, you know.'

'But you've got enough money now.'

'But it's the principle.'

'Fine, fine . . . and where is the principle in moving out of your flat and into the catchment of the best church school in the city? Just don't tell me you've started going to church too . . .?'

'The church is nice.'

'But you're an atheist!'

Both Dinah and Annie were in knee-length dresses with bold prints and fashionable cuts (Annie: TK Maxx, Dinah: Marc Jacobs full price!).

Settled into the middle of a row, not too far from the front, Annie and her sister watched the prizes being handed out: Athletics, Cricket, French, German, House Cup for this, House Cup for that, Tiddlywinks. It went on for ever, but finally it was time for Lana and the other members of the Syrup Six to cross the stage and hand over a cheque for £11,000 to Mr Ketteringham-Smith.

Two days ago, Annie had written the girls a cheque for £500: the money raised by the sale of their stuff on her website. The other £1,500 had come from Suzie's father. Lana walked shyly across the stage to deafening applause. Despite the hiccups with the fund-raising, Annie still felt a rush of pride in her daughter.

Now it was time for the musical performance. Annie could feel her stomach knot with tension. The school choir filed on stage, a group of musicians in front of them: two violin players, a drummer and finally Owen, clutching his guitar.

Annie could see he was pale with anxiety. Her stomach knots pulled tighter. The music began: verse one, then the chorus, then the strummed solo guitar intro to verse two and then Owen's solo . . . She never breathed once during the entire verse, as his clear voice sailed over the crowd, then his lone guitar chords followed, and finally the choir and other musicians joined in. Owen was still singing but now there was a delighted flush of pink and a smile trying to run away all over his face. Annie let out a great sigh of relief and an irrepressible smile of her own broke out.

'Wasn't he amazing!' She sought Ed out afterwards. 'I don't know if I can ever thank you enough.'

Ed, balancing teacup, saucer and a tiny plate overloaded with three scones and a mountain of cream, gave one of his blushes, then sneezed, spilling tea all over the floor. 'Whooops, I didn't hit you, did I?'

'Not with tea,' she assured him. 'Just snot . . . I'm joking, Ed,' she added quickly, when his blush threatened to go nuclear. 'This is my sister Dinah,' Annie said introducing her. 'Lana and Owen's music teacher, Ed Leon. So when are you heading to Boston?' Annie asked, adding for Dinah's benefit, 'Ed's got a term's placement at Harvard to study American folk music and he's spending the summer travelling round the States.'

'Day after tomorrow,' he told them, but looked more anxious at the prospect than excited. 'First day of the school holidays, I'm away.'

He was looking at Annie in a slightly troubled way, as if there were something he wanted to say to her.

'Well, we should be saying our goodbyes then,' Annie said with a smile. 'I hope you have a great time. Really great.' She met his eyes and held them for a moment. 'You deserve this, Ed, enjoy it.'

She was just about to lean over his full hands and give him a little kiss on the cheek when he said, 'Yeah, well . . . have a good summer holiday all of you,' then, teacup, saucer, scones and all, he turned away from them and headed into the crowd.

'Huh? That was a little cool, considering how friendly he's been with the children,' Annie couldn't help telling her sister.

'Annie!'

Her thoughts were disrupted by the sight of Tor in front of her. Tor in a summer dress and heels, with pink nail varnish and lip gloss. 'Good grief!' was Annie's reaction, quickly followed by, 'Good girl! New job?'

Tor shook her head.

'Greatly improved love life?'

Tor shook her head again and confided, 'Just new scarves, Annie!'

'**A**nnie? Hello, it's Ed.'

'Oh . . .? Hi.' Annie was slightly taken aback to hear from him, especially after his abrupt goodbye yesterday. 'You must be busy packing.'

'Yes . . . yeah . . . look . . . There's something I wanted to ask you.'

Annie put a hand over her left ear, blocking out the noise of traffic on Oxford Street. 'Yup, fire away,' she said. She made a quick check on her watch: 9.50 a.m., just ten minutes before she was due to hook up with a client in Selfridges.

'Well, it's just . . .' Ed began. 'You and the children could do with a temporary home . . . Lana's explained you've moved back to London. Anyway, I really need to get my place redecorated because I'm planning to sell it, so while I'm away in the States I just wondered . . . It would be a hassle for you, but you'd obviously not pay any rent and I'd pay for all the decorating . . . Well, I need help with it and I just thought maybe it would tide you over . . .'

She understood exactly what he was suggesting. 'Brilliant idea, Ed!' she exclaimed. 'We probably won't even be there long, just enough time to sort it out for you and find a place of our own. Fantastic!'

Recently, Annie had begun to think that even a few more nights of living on top of Connor and Hector was going to kill her. Here was this fantastic, unexpected solution coming at her out of the blue, proof that one should always wear lipstick, perfume and nice heels, and stay positive.

'I'd need to see you before I go,' Ed was saying. 'Give you keys, show you round, ask what you think should be done, see what kind of budget is needed.'

She told Ed she would come round to his just after 1 p.m., so she would have an hour or two to talk to him before the children broke up from school for the summer holidays.

'How come you're not at school today, anyway?' she wondered.

'They gave me the day off to get organised. Maybe they had some idea how long it would take me.'

'Aha.'

Then Annie almost dropped her phone at the sight of the woman walking—no, make that sashaying—towards her. Was that . . . ? Could that be . . . ? 'I have to go,' she told Ed. 'See you later.'

'Hey! Nit girl!' Annie shouted once she'd hung up.

Martha Cooper's head turned and when she spotted Annie, she began to laugh. She'd lost weight, her hair was even lighter than the last time Annie had seen her. She looked great.

'Look at you!' Annie said coming up to her. 'You look fabulous. And it's only . . .'—she gave Martha a quick up and down—'only the shoes I can take credit for! Wow, good work! I hope you're going to recommend me to all your friends.'

'They are clamouring for your number!' Martha told her. After a quick chat, Martha thanked Annie sincerely for her help and advice. 'I hadn't realised,' she told her, 'how much money I was spending on the kids and their clothes. Those days are over . . .'

Ed answered his battered door and showed Annie into the kitchen. He was wearing trousers and a shirt from the clothes they'd chosen together, his hair had been trimmed rather than hacked off and she couldn't help thinking how well he looked. Fleetingly she wondered if he might land himself an American girlfriend and maybe not come back to St Vincent's again. That would be so nice for him, she told herself. She wasn't sure what Owen would do but . . .

'What time's your flight tomorrow?' she asked him, stepping well away from the cats' dishes that she'd landed in twice before.

'Four p.m.,' he replied.

There was something of a restlessness to him she hadn't seen before, because usually he was so calm. His hair-rummaging had increased, he spilled water on the kettle's journey from the sink to the hob and couldn't seem to locate a cloth to wipe the puddle away.

'I'm fine for tea,' she assured him. 'Shall we start looking round?'

After a pause he said, 'Yes, yes, no problem.'

They went into the sitting room, where Annie inspected the damp again. 'This will have to be treated first,' she told him. Did he want to put in a chemical damp-proof course, or did he want to go the conservation route and look into lime plasters and porous paint?

'Oh, right . . . well, whatever you think,' was his distracted answer.

'OK, focus, Ed!' she reminded him. 'If you don't want to finalise the damp issue today, we could at least talk about kitchen units and sub-floor insulation and colour schemes. I need to know your budget.'

'I'm going to leave it up to you. I'm selling anyway, so I'll write a cheque and then you just make it look as nice as you can. As nice as you will,' he added. 'I know your flat, it's lovely.'

'Aha, very trusting.' Annie was wondering why someone who hadn't been able to clear out even a bookshelf for years was suddenly planning an entire home renovation and move. The imminent American sabbatical was obviously having a motivating effect on him.

'OK, I've seen your kitchen, your sitting room, your bathroom . . . if it's not too personal, can I see your bedroom?' she asked him.

Ed rummaged with his hair, gave a sneeze. 'It's obviously fairly untidy . . . what with all the packing,' he warned her.

'You're really nervous about the trip, aren't you?' Annie ventured. She stood up from the sofa arm she'd perched on briefly and walked over towards him. 'You're going to have the time of your life,' she reassured him with a smile. 'I promise I'll take care of everything here, including the storage of all your mother's things.'

'Right.' He gave her a tight little smile, then turned. 'My bedroom,' he said and she followed him into the corridor. 'Here we go.'

Then they were both in the dark green room, standing side by side. She looked round, taking in the wooden double bed, piles of books, overflowing drawers. It was messy, just like Ed, but it was also welcoming and comforting . . . just like Ed. A narrow French window led out to a dainty garden in as luscious and unkempt a state as Ed's hair.

'Very nice,' Annie said, 'but a much lighter green . . . maybe?'

'Maybe,' came back, the word sounding as if it had been forced through a dry throat.

'It's OK,' she assured him again. 'You're going to have a great time!' and then, in what she felt was a kind and maternal sort of gesture, she put her arm round Ed's waist and squeezed a little.

The result was that he turned, moved his arms round her and, not for the first time, they *seemed* to be kissing. Mouth against mouth, they touched each other. That definitely counted as kissing, didn't it?

She realised that she had a clear memory of the taste of him. His warm body, pushed against her, was welcomingly familiar. She'd held him before. But this time was better. This time they pulled each other close. 'How are you doing?' she said against his soft, slightly downy ear when they stopped for a moment, to pause for breath.

'I'm extremely, extremely nervous,' he whispered back to her.

'Where's your sense of adventure?' she asked in between landing little licks and kisses against his warm neck. 'It's the trip of a lifetime.'

He pulled her slightly away from him so he could look at her face. 'It's not the trip. It's you . . . I'm in a total state about you.'

'Oh!' This was unexpected . . . to say the least.

Annie didn't know what to say next, so she leaned forward to press her lips against his; her hands moved to the small of his back and held him tightly. His mouth pushed at hers and she felt the hungry tingle start to buzz through her body. 'Does kissing help?' she broke off to ask.

'Uh-huh,' he told her. He was holding her chin in his hands and kissing down her neck. Shivers were travelling over her shoulders and down her arms. Gently, he pushed her shirt and bra strap away so he could kiss the top of her shoulders.

Everywhere he touched or stroked or brushed against was desperate to be felt by him again. Unbuttoning his shirt as quickly as she could, she pulled his warm body against hers.

They were both topless and kissing frantically at mouths, nipples, necks and shoulders, feeling each other over and over at once quickly and yet tenderly. When her hands moved to undo his belt buckle, his hands moved on top of hers, holding them still.

'Annie?' he said into her neck. 'I don't want you to rush into—'

'Well, I do.' She cut him off and gave a vigorous tug at the belt. She began to rub against the swelling underneath the fabric of his trousers, causing him to groan against her ear. 'Ed,' she began. 'Do you have any idea'—she'd found the fly buttons buried in the fabric below the belt buckle—'how much I want you?' True. She hadn't realised until the moment they'd started kissing—well, maybe that last kiss on the stairwell had been an inkling—but now that they were half naked together there was going to be no backing out. She had to have him.

The first button was undone, then the second, but his back was arched away from her.

'Ed,' she said into his hair, 'my husband died when I was thirty-two, I've got to make up for so much lost time . . .'

The third button sprang open. 'I'm not letting you get away . . .'

The back moved in now. His warm, bare arms closed in round her and she was squashed up against him. He'd finally agreed to go with the flow. Then they were busy, stripping off their clothes as quickly as they could.

Before, she'd found him boyish, chaotic, incapable and needy . . . but it turned out he was much more grown up than that. Much more insistent and yet tender, much more practised, and yet still so very, very kind. In his every move against her and with her was the fine balance of intention and question. As if he were asking her over and over again, but without words: I'm going to do this, go here, and move in here . . . but only if it's OK. Is this what you want? Yes? And this too?

They took off every shred of clothing, although she'd thought she didn't want to be so exposed to him. She had to let him keep on moving and touching and moving until she felt the tiny rush build. She'd wanted to keep herself in reserve, hold back from him, but he hadn't let her. He wanted all of her and deep into her mind too.

Afterwards, she lay stretched out on the bed beside him, utterly naked, and remembered how glorious sex could be. He tucked her in under his arm and they lay side by side, not wanting to break the silence. But Annie couldn't resist leaning over to kiss him again and the kiss broke the spell.

He smiled broadly, crinkling the skin round his eyes, and told her, 'Parent–teacher relationship . . . We've really overstepped it this time.'

'Did you know you liked me?' she asked him, feeling with her hand for his and running her fingers across it.

'Did I know I liked you? Let me see . . .' Ed began, eyes fixed on the ceiling, a fresh smile on his face. 'I've considered taking up smoking for the first time in five years, I'm playing Elvis ballads till two in the morning, not to mention "My funny Valentine", I can't think about anything else except your face and the way you flick your ponytail and walk very, very fast and call everyone around you "babes" . . . yes, I think we can safely say I knew I liked you . . . but you'—he put his finger on the tip of her nose—'you didn't know you liked me, did you?'

'I liked you, Ed,' she told him, running her hand across his stomach. 'I just hadn't realised until today that I fancied the pants off you.'

'What about that kiss?' he wanted to know. 'Before, on your stairwell? The one I've been thinking about maybe ten, twenty times an hour ever since?'

She let out a shriek of laughter at this then told him cheekily, 'I was on a detox that week; it can have strange effects.'

They turned, rolled into one another and began to kiss again.

'It's after two,' she told him, raising her arm to catch a glimpse of her watch behind his head.

'You're going to be very late,' he warned her. 'Better phone Lana, tell her to walk over here with Owen very, very slowly.'

After the second time came not a spellbound silence, but tears. Annie curled away from Ed in the bed and couldn't stop herself from crying.

'What's the matter?' He leaned over her, desperately concerned.

'Please don't go away now,' she heard herself say, although she hated how small and sad her voice sounded. 'Don't leave me now. You're going to be away for ages and what if something happens?' She found she was wailing, 'What if I lose you too?' Then general blubbing noises followed. It was horrible. Horrible.

But Ed's arm was round her, holding her together through this, just as it had done before. What was it about this man?

He got to her. Got through to her. Connected. Got past the shell she'd built tightly around herself and saw how she really was. Drew the inner Annie out and made love to her. In a way no one had since Roddy. That's why it felt so breathtaking. So private and close. So real.

'I'm away for four and a half months,' he was telling her gently, kissing her hair. 'I've always wanted to do this trip and I think I should. I think it's good . . . for . . . us.' He said the word as lightly as possible, hardly daring to use it. 'You shouldn't be rushed into anything, Annie.

You should take things very slowly. I'll come back and visit you at half-term,' he added. 'That's not so many weeks away. No time, no time at all. You can come out and see me . . . if you want to.'

'But I'll miss you . . . we'll miss you so much.' She was still crying. Still feeling great confusion about why she suddenly cared so very much about this man. This morning she'd have waved him off happily at the airport; now she felt prepared to lie down in front of the plane.

He brushed her tears carefully away and held her close for several long, quiet minutes. Then he got up from the bed. 'Time to get dressed,' he told her. 'Come on—I want to show you where Owen and Lana can sleep, before they get back here.'

'I've already planned it,' Annie told him as she pulled on her clothes and tried to sound brighter than she felt. 'Owen and I will share your room, Lana can have a sofa bed in the sitting room.'

'No, no,' Ed told her. 'There's some space upstairs.'

'Oh.' This was obviously one of those wonky conversions where neighbours had done deals in the past and a cupboard full of stairs would lead to a stairwell converted into a poky little room.

Once they were in their clothes, Ed led her by the hand to a door in the sitting room. He opened the door and a stone staircase, lit by a window from above, was in front of them.

'This connected the basement kitchen to the dining room, back in ye olde days,' he explained.

She followed him up and they came out into a big, fabulous, pale yellow room, flooded with light from the tall Georgian windows at both ends.

'There's a roof problem,' he began. 'I've had to take loads of stuff downstairs from the other rooms.'

'Other rooms?' Annie repeated.

'Yeah, there's this dining room . . . Well, it was Mum's sitting room. Then there's her kitchen next door, and her bedroom upstairs, and two little attic bedrooms.'

Annie gaped at him, eyes wide, mouth hanging wide open. Finally, when her power of speech had returned she asked him in utter amazement, '*You own the whole house?!*

'I owe my sister a third . . . Mum helped her buy her flat . . . so the arrangement was Hannah would get a third when it was time to sell up.'

'A whole house . . . on my favourite street.' Annie was heading towards the dining-room door, eager to see the rest of the rooms. 'Ed, baby, do you realise? All this time you've been hiding your most attractive feature from me!'

The Preppie returns:

White cotton button-down shirt (Brooks Brothers)
Slim-fit khaki chinos (Banana Republic)
Midnight blue cashmere V-neck (Brooks Brothers)
Hiking boots (some things are harder to change)
Total est. cost: $390

'*Are you sure, Annie? I mean, are you really, really sure?*'

'You look brilliant. Absolutely fantastic! Completely shaggable—and take that as a big compliment because I'm a gay man. Very gay,' Connor added, waving a copy of the *Daily Mail* at them.

Right across the top of page five was a photo of him and Hector attending a film première in matching kilts with the caption: *The Manor's Connor McCabe shows off the new man in his life.*

'Shut up will you!' Annie shot at him. 'You were supposed to stay in the kitchen with Dinah and keep out of our way.'

But Svetlana was laughing. 'Is fine,' she said in her melodious alto. 'I miss a man's opinion of how I look.'

'OK, come and see in the mirror,' Annie instructed. She directed Svetlana towards the three-sided mirror in the corner of her bright white office. The room, which had once been Ed's tatty sitting room, was now transformed. There was a desk with a filing cabinet next to it. The room's centrepiece was a comfortable pink sofa, with several all-important clothes' rails for clients to hang up their many, many clothes: the ones they needed help to part with or help to dare to wear.

'Oh, this is very good,' Svetlana declared. She was in a tight white Chanel suit with black trim on the lapels. Black and white T-bar shoes and a black patent bag completed the look. The gas baron's soon-to-be-ex-wife had her hair pulled back, soberly but softly, and her make-up had been under-applied by Annie to make her look beautiful but vulnerable. This was a dress rehearsal for her day in the divorce court.

'Perfect,' Annie agreed with Svetlana. 'You go kick Igor in the balls tomorrow. Just make sure,' she added with a twinkle, 'that you do it . . .' her voice dropped low, '*sexy but ladylike.*'

This made both Connor and Svetlana laugh. Then the Russian's eye fell on the big black and white framed portrait photograph that dominated one of the white walls. She walked towards it. 'A client?' she asked. 'He is very handsome, no?'

'Oh yes, babes, isn't he?' Annie agreed and felt . . . well . . . She walked over to stand beside Svetlana, so they were both looking at the photo of the roguish man in a black leather jacket suppressing a grin and unmistakably hamming it for the camera. 'That's Roddy,' Annie said and she felt OK. She was even able to smile proudly and add, 'My late husband, Lana and Owen's daddy.' She looked at Svetlana and gave a wink. 'We were very lucky to have had him. Weren't we, Connor?'

That's how Annie thought of it now. She had made peace with the reality that Roddy was no longer with them; now she was able to appreciate all the time they'd had together. She tried to think of his life as completed, rather than tearing herself to pieces with the thought that it was unfinished. Only very recently had she begun to believe that just as much happiness as she'd once had would come her way again.

There was something else Svetlana wanted to ask: 'Are you going to come back to The Store, Ahnnah?'

In all honesty, Annie hadn't decided.

Paula was the one who had phoned first to announce Donna's demise with the words, 'Ding, dong, the wicked witch is dead!'

'Maybe two or three days a week,' Annie told Svetlana. 'I don't know yet . . . I like working for myself. I like taking clients to whatever shop I think will suit them best. And I love bossing them about in my office!'

When Svetlana had left, it was time to see what Dinah and Billie were doing in the kitchen upstairs. The former dining room had been transformed into a modern, glamorous kitchen (but by using only the finest discount suppliers, Annie had come in under Ed's careful budget).

'How's the cake? Oh, Billie, what a brilliant idea! Is it a boat?' Annie asked, looking at the grey, knobbly sausage of mauled icing Billie had plonked into the middle of the iced 'welcome home' cake.

'No, stupid!' came the insulted reply. 'It's a plane.'

'Aren't you changing, Annie?' Dinah asked, expecting Annie to have a whole top-to-toe outfit planned for this big reunion moment.

'Something from your New York trip,' Connor urged. 'It was three weeks ago and you've not shown off a single thing.'

'Ah, New York!' Annie gave a sigh. 'I told you, Connor, it was a total shopping disaster. There I was in the shopping capital of the Western world with three empty credit cards and I never got round to shopping! I . . . we . . .' and all of a sudden she felt slightly shy.

'Shall we take that to mean that you and Ed were a little bit too busy to go shopping?' Connor asked.

'Errm . . . maybe,' was all the answer she made.

'Is that the sound of a taxi engine outside?' She ran over to look out of the window. 'Bloody hell!' she shrieked. 'It is! It's him! Early.'

As Annie flew out of the room and down the stairs, Dinah and Connor looked at each other and grinned. They stayed in the kitchen with Billie and listened to the sound of Annie pulling open the heavy front door. The grand, newly painted one with the polished brass handle and letterbox, which was once again the entrance to the house.

They heard the excited greetings and Ed's gasps of admiration as he saw his transformed home for the first time.

'My God, this looks incredible!' he told her. 'Absolutely incredible.'

'So do you,' she told him, arms tight round his waist. 'Cashmere?' she noticed immediately. 'You bought yourself cashmere? The sales assistants over there must be even better than me.'

'They are,' he teased. 'But you're the one I wanted to rush back to.'

'Come and see the kitchen. Connor and Dinah and Billie are up there waiting to see you. They've baked a cake—and it's a plane on top,' she warned him quietly. 'Just so you know!'

Later that evening, Annie curled up with Ed on the sofa, trying to have a conversation while Owen and Lana seemed to be trampolining to something loud and blasting in their attic bedrooms upstairs.

'Shall I go and tell them to keep it down?' Annie asked.

'No, no,' Ed insisted. 'I like it! They've picked a good song,' he said approvingly. 'And anyway, it makes this old place feel alive again. Like a proper home. I hated it when upstairs was all shut off and empty.'

'You really do like this house, don't you?'

'I love it,' Ed admitted. 'It's going to be such a wrench to sell it.'

'And what if you didn't have to sell?' Annie wondered. 'What if someone bought a third of the house, so you could buy your sister out?'

'Sell off the basement and maybe the garden as a separate flat, you mean?' Ed asked. 'Do you think that would raise enough?'

Annie shook her head and waved a rectangular piece of paper in front of Ed's face. 'I have a plan,' she told him mischievously, as he took the paper from her hand and saw that it was a cheque for a hefty six-figure sum. 'I've sold my flat—to the tenants,' she began. 'And with that money and a mortgage, that's how much I could offer you for a third of your house, which I think is generous,' she added, 'and then all four of us could live here . . . together.'

She realised her heart was beating very fast as she waited for the enormity of this offer and all its implications to settle on Ed.

'Oh . . . goodness!' he managed at last, with the hand-in-hair rummage that she knew meant he was nervous. 'Are you sure, Annie? I mean, are you really, really sure? What about the children? This might be too fast for them.'

Holding his hands tightly, she explained that she was making the offer because of the children. She'd talked it through with them at length. They were the ones who didn't want to leave, who loved their rooms, who felt at home here and, most importantly, who deeply approved of Ed. (Provided he acted like their teacher and absolutely nothing else at school . . . in fact if he could practically ignore Lana at school if possible . . .)

'They are very into the idea,' she assured him. 'Owen told me the other day that Roddy would have really liked you. Lana and I agree.'

There was a pause while Ed took this, their ultimate compliment, on board. 'So you all want to live here with me?' he asked and when Annie nodded at him, she saw that he was moved to tears.

'And definitely you?' he asked, just to make sure.

Annie nodded. 'Definitely, babes.'

'That's great . . .' he said, blinking hard. 'I really love your children. I mean . . . Owen is great, I find him really easy to understand and get along with . . . I'll need your help to get a much better handle on Lana.'

'Good grief, Ed!' Annie smiled at him. 'We all need help to get a handle on Lana. She's a fifteen-year-old, now. No one understands her, not even Lana! Is this what you want?'

Ed pulled her in close. Although he'd wanted to say something, he now found he was too choked to do anything other than nod.

'Excellent! That's all decided then,' Annie said gently against his ear. 'Now, apparently if I make you the children's legal guardian, they get a fifty per cent discount at St Vincent's.'

When he laughed at this, she told him, 'Hey, babes, I never, ever joke about discounts, you should know that about me,' in such a serious voice, he couldn't tell if she was joking or not.

His grip on her grew very tight as he asked her, 'So you're going to stay with me then?'

She nodded slowly in response to this, then told him gently, 'Babes, you are in need of serious modernisation and upgrading, but I think you're an excellent investment with long-term potential.'

'I am so glad you spotted that,' Ed said.

'Yes, well . . . I've always, always had an eye for a bargain, babes.'

Carmen Reid

Where were you born?

In the town of Montrose on the east coast of Scotland. My parents still live in the area, on a farm, so I spend lots of time up there.

When did you start writing?

I've always been a writer, ever since I learned to write. I have volumes and volumes of diaries and notebooks (dating from age eight) to prove it! But when I was twenty-eight, I left my job to have a baby and that's when I started writing my first novel.

What's your routine?

I write best when my children are out of the house (funnily enough!), so I tend to keep school hours, working from Monday to Friday between 9.30 and 2.30. But sometimes, when it's going really well or, more likely, when deadlines are looming, I write at night and through the weekends. I try to take plenty of time off in the school holidays. A novel is thousands of words though—you have to keep going!

What's next?

Lots! I'm just finishing off a book for ten- to thirteen-year-olds, which is due to be published in 2008. And there is more from Annie Valentine to come: a *Personal Shopper* sequel is due out in summer 2008. So, watch this space . . .

What advice would you give to novice authors?

Keep writing and writing and writing! We all get better with practice. Also, keep reading, because you'll learn so much from the writers you love.

Describe yourself in three words.

Very, very tall.

What are the sounds and smells of your childhood?

I grew up on a farm with two sisters, so the sounds are tractors, dogs barking, children laughing. The smells: machine oil, dusty barns, straw bales and my mother's fabulous baking.

What was the first book that you remember?

My mother is German, so we had lots of German storybooks, including the Brothers Grimm fairy tales and *Struwwelpeter*, which used to terrify me. Especially the story of the thumbsucker, whose thumb gets chopped off, because I used to suck my thumb.

Which childhood dream has not yet come true?

Sadly, I have not yet won a gold medal for running in the Olympics! But my biggest dream was to write books, so I am not too disappointed about the medal.

What's the best decision of your life?

Having children. Yes, it's much more exhausting and far more time-consuming than you could ever imagine, but it is absolutely wonderful. Life without my son and daughter is unthinkable. I remember reading this once and it's so true: 'There are two things one never regrets—a baby and a swim'!

What puts you in a bad mood?

Broken nights make me grumpy for days. Also, I'm the most impatient person in the world.

What puts you in a good mood?

Red wine, staying out too late and best quality chocolate.

Tea or coffee?

Good grief, I'm British. It's tea of course. Weak Earl Grey with milk!

Classical music or pop/rock?

Both. Operatic arias make me blub (yes, even during the Mr Bean film). I put Mozart on the iPod when I'm trying to concentrate but I do love to dance, with all the moves (!), to very camp disco.

Cinema or DVD?

Both, I love films. But a night in with the *Seinfeld* or *Father Ted* box set is hard to beat.

Which product could you advertise?

Carrots. The perfect snack. I eat too many and my husband has been known to nickname me 'the horse'.

Which person from your novels would you like to meet and why?

A night out with Bella Browning (*Three in A Bed, Up All Night)* would be un-forgettable. I'd also love to have Annie Valentine (*The Personal Shopper*) in the changing room with me to advise, as I am a rubbish shopper!

Who should play the starring role in the movie about your life . . . and why?

I don't know if there's anyone tall enough, maybe Nicole Kidman in very high heels. A movie about my life would be very boring, by the way. Woman sits at desk and types a lot . . .

Taken from: www.carmenreid.com

Married
to a
Stranger

Patricia MacDonald

Twenty-six-year-old Emma seems to have it all—a fortune inherited from her father, a job she loves as a counsellor at an adolescent crisis centre, good friends, and a boyfriend who, after a whirlwind romance, has asked her to marry him. Emma's life feels like a dream—until her honeymoon begins . . .

1

THE WIZENED GIRL turned her head and stared at Emma Hollis with large, blank eyes. 'Leave me alone. I'm too tired to talk any more.'

Emma gazed worriedly at the frail teenager sitting opposite her. Tasha Clayman had been admitted to the Wrightsman Youth Crisis Centre the day before. Emma could see every one of the sixteen-year-old's bony ribs beneath her thin sweater. Her cheeks were hollow, her blonde ponytail dry and lank. An image of Ivy Devlin rose into Emma's thoughts, and she had to force down a feeling of panic. You did everything you could for Ivy, she reminded herself. It was too late for her. It wasn't your fault. But it was hard to convince herself. Nightmares about Ivy, her large, sunken eyes full of rueful accusation, still woke Emma in the middle of the night.

'Tasha?' Emma asked gently. 'Let me ask you this. Can you tell me what would it take to make you want to live?'

'I didn't say I didn't want to live,' the girl protested in a monotone voice so weak it was hard to hear. 'I just have to watch my food intake because I'm too fat.'

Emma hesitated, choosing her response carefully. At twenty-six she had a PhD in psychology, but this position at the crisis centre was her first full-time job as a clinical psychologist. Working with patients was much more daunting than doing research in the university library and treating clients under the constant supervision of an experienced professional. Sometimes she felt as if she hadn't recovered her equilibrium after Ivy succumbed to her anorexia six months ago. Burke Heisler, the psychiatrist who ran the centre, had supported the decisions she'd made about Ivy's treatment. Even after Ivy's death, he had refused to allow Emma to second-guess herself. You did all you could to help her, he had assured her.

'Tasha, we both know that starvation can lead to death. And death is a way to escape from whatever it is that's hurting you. Something is hurting you, putting you in so much pain.'

A tear rolled down the girl's sunken cheek. She did not bother to wipe it away.

'Talking about it is a better way of escaping,' Emma persisted. 'Once you can say it out loud, we can look for solutions.'

Tasha looked at Emma with haunted eyes. 'I hate myself. How do I escape from myself?' she asked. 'I'm fat. I'm a failure. I have no boyfriend, because no one can ever love me. My grades aren't good enough. I'm not pretty. I'm a disappointment to my parents . . .'

Tasha's parents were educated, attractive and well-to-do. And Tasha was their only child. They had told Emma that they were people with means, who had given their daughter everything.

'OK,' she said, taking a deep breath. 'Tell me about your parents.'

After the session, Emma headed down the cheerfully painted hallway leading to the office of Dr Heisler. She had a few minutes before she had to see her next client. Emma entered the director's reception area. His secretary, Geraldine Clemens, looked up at her over her half-glasses.

'Is he in? Can I see him for a minute?' Emma asked.

'I'll check,' said Geraldine, picking up the phone and buzzing her boss.

'Hello, Dr Hollis,' said a voice behind Emma.

She turned and saw Kieran Foster, one of the members of her Thursday therapy group for drug abusers, sitting in the reception area. It was nearly impossible to look at Kieran without flinching. The troubled seventeen-year-old dressed all in black, had a tuft of magenta hair at the top of his head, and a tattoo of an eye in the middle of his forehead.

'Kieran,' she said. 'Hi. We missed you at group yesterday.'

'I was busy,' Kieran muttered. Abandoned by his alcoholic mother, Kieran was an outpatient who lived with a half-sister and her extremely wealthy husband. His guardians provided him with all the cars, electronics and spending money he could ever want, and then went about their lives as if he weren't there. Kieran had a long history of drug abuse and had dropped out of high school. His only real interest was in playing his electric guitar and writing atonal songs focused on death and decay.

'Is something wrong?' Emma asked.

'No,' he said, looking down at the floor. He rarely made eye contact. 'Dr Heisler asked my sister to come in.'

Emma knew that Burke must have had to threaten the woman to get her in to talk about Kieran. 'Well, I hope you'll join us next Thursday,' Emma said. 'I always like to see you there.'

'Dr Heisler says he'll squeeze you in,' said Geraldine, setting down the receiver and looking up at Emma. 'Go on in.'

Emma opened the door and looked in. 'Hey,' she said.

Burke Heisler looked up at her and smiled. He was young to hold such a responsible position—only in his mid-thirties. His blond hair was cut short and combed back, and he had a broad, rugged-looking face that would have been more appropriate on a boxer. His grey-eyed gaze was keen. Emma had first met Burke Heisler when she was a college freshman and he was a graduate assistant teaching her introductory psych course.

She had had a mad crush on him at the time, although he never paid her any more attention than he did the other hundred students in the class. But then he ended up courting, and ultimately marrying, Emma's beautiful room-mate, Natalie White. A year ago, when Natalie invited Emma to visit their home in Clarenceville, New Jersey, Burke seemed pleased to learn that she had pursued her doctorate in psychology. Before the weekend was over, he had offered her a job at the Wrightsman Centre, part of the huge complex that was Lambert University.

Burke gestured for her to come in and sit down. 'Finding it a little hard to concentrate today?' he asked.

Emma blushed, wondering if it showed on her face. She was trying to remain professional, but it was difficult. Tomorrow was her wedding day. 'That's an understatement,' she admitted.

'Well, it's only natural. Hey, now that you're here, what do you want for a wedding gift? I was thinking of something practical, like a food processor.'

'If you'll come over and show me how to use it,' Emma said, with a smile. Burke was known for his culinary skills. His wealthy father had owned a casino in Atlantic City, and Burke had spent several summers working in the kitchens.

'Done,' he said, making a note. 'Buy Cuisinart and demonstrate.' He set down his pen and gazed at her. 'So, what's up?'

'I'm worried,' said Emma, 'about my new patient, Tasha Clayman.'

'The anorexic,' he said.

'I can't help it . . . after what happened,' she said.

Burke nodded. 'I understand. Ivy Devlin. Look, I'll have Sarita keep close tabs on Tasha.' Sarita Ruiz was a youth counsellor who tended to her teenage charges with skill and kindness. 'You just enjoy your big day, you hear me? Although I don't understand why you two are only taking a weekend for the honeymoon. You could have had the week off if you wanted it.'

'This is fine for now,' Emma said. 'My mother is giving us a trip to Europe as a wedding present, but that will take time to plan. Besides, this has all come together so quickly, and David has an interview in New York next week with some big-shot producer, so we're just going to the Pine Barrens for a couple of days.' Emma was referring to the million-plus acres of sandy, boggy, pine-covered wilderness in the centre of New Jersey called the Pineland National Reserve. It was a nature lover's paradise, crisscrossed by rivers and sparsely populated by a reclusive group of people known as Pineys. 'We're going canoeing and hiking—David and I love that sort of thing.'

'You staying in that fishing cabin his aunt and uncle own?'

'That's the place,' she said.

'His uncle used to take us there when we were boys,' said Burke. Burke and Emma's husband-to-be, David Webster, had been best friends since boyhood. 'We were always afraid the Jersey Devil would get us,' Burke remembered, referring to the reputedly immortal demon-child said to haunt the Pinelands.

'I'm not into folklore and monsters,' said Emma. 'Anyway, it'll be great, just to get away together.'

'Those days when you're first married, being together is all that counts,' said Burke with a sigh. For a moment, his gaze fell on the framed photo of a beautiful, pale-skinned woman with silky red hair, looking pensively out over a Venetian canal. Three months ago, Burke had come home from a business trip to find Natalie missing. The police found her car parked on a bridge over the Smoking River, her bag and keys still on the front seat. Her body did not surface for a month, but the note she'd left behind had clearly stated her intentions.

Emma's brilliant, accomplished former room-mate, a published poet, had been bipolar and often had refused to take her medication, claiming that it dulled her ability to write. Emma remembered Natalie's many bouts of manic highs and depressive lows from college. When Emma arrived in Clarenceville, Natalie had been exuberant. She had just published her latest book of poems to great critical acclaim. When the book won the prestigious Solomon Medal, she was interviewed for national publications and became a popular TV talk-show guest. Despite her success, Natalie's spirits began to plummet. She refused to take her medication and reacted angrily when Emma urged her to seek counselling. Still, despite the warning signs, Natalie's suicide came as a terrible shock to her husband, and to Emma as well.

'I hope this wedding won't be too painful for you,' said Emma.

Burke sighed. 'She's going to be very much on my mind, but I'll be proud to stand up for David. I feel like Natalie and I were the matchmakers for you two.'

'You were,' she said. 'You introduced us.' Burke had invited Emma to a dinner party at their house to celebrate the Solomon award. Burke's friend, David Webster, a freelance writer from New York City, was invited also. The gathering was festive, and Natalie was witty and luminous. Emma would always remember that night because it was the last happy evening she spent with her old friend. And because the sparks between her and David flew instantly.

Emma's pager beeped. She checked it. 'Speak of the devil,' she said.

'The groom?' Burke asked.

Emma nodded and glanced at her watch. She only had a few minutes till her group was due to start. But the thought of seeing David, waiting for her in the lobby, filled her with the same giddy excitement that she'd felt the first time she'd set eyes on him six months ago. 'Thanks, Burke,' she said, standing up.

'Don't worry about a thing,' he said. 'See you tomorrow.'

As she passed through the reception area, Emma heard Geraldine saying to Kieran, 'That was your sister. She has to cancel. I'm sorry, Kieran.' Emma sighed and shook her head.

When she pushed the doors open and scanned the lobby, David was leaning against the front desk, making conversation with the new receptionist. Emma drew in a breath at the sight of him, as she often did. He was, to her eyes, the most attractive man she had ever known.

'David,' she said.

He turned to look at her, his eyes widening. 'Hey, baby.' He was Burke's age, thirty-three, but despite the grey that flecked his long, dark brown hair and the lines around his fine hazel eyes, he looked much younger. He had a strong jaw and perfect white teeth, which he flashed in a boyish smile. Today he was dressed, as usual, in jeans and a leather jacket—an urban cowboy style that suited his maverick image. He admitted to a stubborn resistance to all authority and told her that he had become a freelance writer because he could never stand the constraints of a regular job.

Before they'd met, David had travelled far and wide for a variety of magazines. His steadiest source of assignments was *Slicker*, a glossy men's magazine in the *Esquire* mould, but with a younger slant. When he'd attended the dinner party at Burke and Natalie's, David had been living alone, subletting a New York City rent-controlled apartment. He never talked about old girlfriends, but Emma knew that he was just being chivalrous. Right at this moment, the new receptionist was devouring him with her eyes.

Emma ran to him and kissed his soft, insistent lips. She felt the flush that raced through her whenever they touched. She marvelled anew at her luck, and her happiness. 'Hey,' she whispered. 'What brings you here?'

'I'm here to make you change your mind,' he said. 'About staying at Stephanie's tonight. It's old-fashioned.'

Stephanie Piper, a middle-school teacher who had been Emma's room-mate in Clarenceville since she'd first moved here, was going to be her maid of honour tomorrow. Only a month ago, Emma and David had faced up to the practicalities of their impending marriage, and in deference to Emma's job they had rented a house in Clarenceville and moved in together. But tonight, Emma was returning to her old digs for one last 'girls' night' before the wedding. 'I am old-fashioned,' she said. 'I don't want to see you until I'm walking down the aisle. Have a bachelor party or something.'

'With who?' he said. 'I don't know anyone here any more.' She knew it was true. He hadn't lived in Clarenceville since high school. When she and David met at Burke and Natalie Heisler's house, he was in town from New York City to visit his mother, Helen, who had advanced heart disease. As Emma had left the dinner party that night, she'd thought she might never see the mysterious writer again. But as soon as she got home, her phone was ringing. David was calling from the Clarenceville train station asking her to come back to New York with him that very night. After a moment's hesitation, she had thrown caution to the wind and met him on the platform.

The rest was a whirlwind romance. Because Emma shared her apartment with Stephanie, they'd spent much of their time in David's sparsely furnished apartment in New York, ignoring the outside world altogether and enjoying Chinese food eaten out of cartons, long conversations and helpless laughter. Through their entire six-month courtship, she'd felt as if love made the rules. But tonight was about traditions and transitions.

'So go out with Burke,' Emma suggested.

David grimaced. 'I'm not sure he's in the mood for a bachelor's night. It's asking a lot of him just to be at the wedding.'

Emma sighed. 'You're right. Well, maybe you could run up to the city. Just make sure you're back by ten tomorrow, mister.'

He grinned at her. 'Nothing could keep me away.'

'Dr Hollis,' said the receptionist.

Emma tore herself away from his gaze and tried to look businesslike. 'Yes?'

'This came for you.' She held out a plain white envelope with EMMA HOLLIS printed on it in large letters.

'You're busy. I'll let you go,' David said.

'No, wait,' Emma said, clutching his arm.

David suddenly looked wary. 'Is that one of those letters?'

Emma reached for the envelope. 'I don't know. It looks like the others.' She tore it open with a slight tremble in her fingers and pulled out a sheet of paper. *You could not understand the depth of my love or you would not be making plans to hurt and shame me.*

'Let me see that,' said David, snatching it from her fingers.

Emma turned to the receptionist. Her heart was pounding, but she kept her voice calm. 'Where did this come from?' she asked.

'I found it on the desk when I started my shift,' the receptionist said. 'Is something wrong?'

'No. No. It's all right,' Emma said.

David looked at her gravely. 'This is not all right, Emma.'

'I know,' said Emma. 'This is the fourth one.'

'Baby, we need to call the cops,' he said.

All the notes were on the same plain paper, printed on a computer. Whenever one of them arrived, Emma's heart sank, and she spent the next few days trying to imagine, as she talked to people she saw every day, if any of them were studying her, dreaming of her. After a while, she would relax and begin to think that it was over. And then the next one would come. Emma retrieved the latest letter from David, folded it, and stuffed it into her pocket. 'The police can't do anything. They aren't threats.'

'What do we do? Wait until this guy does something crazy?' David said angrily.

'It is probably one of my patients. They get these crushes that spin out of control. Believe me, it creeps me out too.'

'We can't just let it go,' David insisted. 'He's hounding you.'

'I know. I know. Believe me, I am hoping this will wind down on its own. I hate it too, but I'm afraid it comes with the territory. It's par for the course in a place like this. We've got a lot of troubled kids here with a boatload of problems.'

'I'm not sure it is one of these kids. What if it's some lunatic?'

'Lunatics tend to be a little bit showier,' said Emma wryly. 'So come on. Try and forget about this for now.'

He took a deep breath. 'Some pencil-necked geek probably has his closet walls plastered with your pictures,' he fumed.

'Jealous?' She squeezed his hand, trying to lighten the mood.

He sighed, and one corner of his mouth turned up. 'I'm the only pencil-necked geek who's allowed to do that.'

'You aren't pencil-necked,' she said.

He made a growling sound and pulled her to him. She began to laugh. 'Look, I really do need to get back to work.'

'You won't change your mind about tonight?' he said. 'You're going to leave me all alone?'

'Well, you'd better be all alone,' she teased. Burke had introduced David as his 'playboy' best friend, and when Emma first got involved with him, she had truly expected it to be no more than an exciting fling. Now things had changed, and she hated thinking about his playboy past. But she wasn't really worried. She gave him one more lingering kiss and pulled away from him.

'Tomorrow, babe,' he said. 'You and me.'

'I know,' she said, beaming.

'My wife.'

Emma's heart swelled. 'My husband,' she whispered.

2

THE GENERAL CROSSEN INN was a colonial-era building with a mustard-coloured clapboard façade, crisp white trim, and brick chimneys at either end. It was located in a quiet street and surrounded by gardens. Emma's mother, who lived in Chicago, had rented the whole eight-bedroom inn for the night, even though Emma had told her repeatedly that the wedding was going to be tiny.

As she pulled up in front of the inn, Emma saw that Stephanie's car was already parked there, as well as the florist's van and the caterer's truck. Last night she and Stephanie had had a great girls' night together, eating junk food and dancing to their favourite tunes, and they had parted this morning when Stephanie had gone to the hairdresser.

Emma parked and carefully removed the fat garment bag that she had hung from a hook in the back seat. The obscenely expensive wedding dress, which her mother had insisted on buying for her, was inside the bag, swaddled in tissue. Emma would have been content with a dress off the rack, but Kay had pleaded with her to let her fly into New York and take her to designer showrooms. Now, to be honest with herself, Emma could hardly wait to put the dress on and see how she looked.

She crossed the porch and opened the door to the inn. At the far end of the timber-beamed room, a young guy with glasses and a crew cut was setting up the chairs and music stands for the jazz trio. Stephanie, dressed in jeans, her blonde hair upswept in ringlets, was studying the placement of the floral arrangements.

'There you are,' Stephanie said, and exhaled in relief. 'The caterer is asking for instructions. I'm dealing with the florist. I thought these people knew what to do. Isn't that why you hire them?'

'Don't worry. My mom will whip everything into shape. I spoke to her on her cellphone a few minutes ago. Hey, I like your hair.'

'I look like something out of *Gidget Goes to the Prom*.'

'It's very elegant,' said Emma loyally. Her own hair fell below her shoulders, honey-coloured and wavy. 'David likes mine loose. What do you think?'

'You look gorgeous. You're glowing. But then . . .'

'Pregnant women do,' said Emma wryly.

Stephanie nodded and looked down at Emma's waist. 'I hope that wedding dress has some wiggle room.'

'Come on,' Emma protested. 'I'm only two months along.'

The truth was that when, four months into their commuter romance, Emma found herself unexpectedly pregnant, she secretly, sadly, expected it to be the end of her relationship with David. He had lived out of duffle bags in temporary quarters all of his adult life. Part of her was certain that this news would send him fleeing. To her shock, he'd responded with an abrupt proposal of marriage. He wanted her, and he wanted their baby. When she pressed him, asking him if he was sure this was what he wanted, he could not be dissuaded.

'How can you be so calm?' said Stephanie. 'Don't you have jitters? All brides have jitters.'

Emma was considering the question when she heard a familiar voice behind her. 'Didn't you two leave anything for me to do?'

She turned to see a fit-looking platinum-blonde-haired woman in a turquoise bouclé suit beaming at her. 'Mom!' she cried, rushing to embrace her mother. 'You look great.'

'Well, thank you. I was afraid I'd get all rumpled on the trip.' Emma's mother and stepfather had flown in from Chicago that morning and driven down from the Philadelphia airport. Emma had wanted Kay and Rory to come the night before, but Rory insisted he had a meeting in Chicago that absolutely could not be postponed. Emma did not believe him. She believed that he was avoiding her, with good reason.

'Rory bringing the bags in?'

'No,' said Kay. 'He dropped me off. He said he had to make one more brief stop. Something about business.'

Emma tried to keep her face expressionless. She had adored her father and idealised her parents' marriage, and her childhood in their mansion on the shores of Lake Michigan had been blissfully happy. When her father died during Emma's first year of graduate school, she was devastated for herself but even more for her mother. Ten months later, at her health club, Kay met Rory, a divorced investment banker. Before Emma knew it, her mother was remarried.

Kay and Rory sold the suburban mansion and moved to a fabulous penthouse on the Chicago Loop. Emma had rushed out to Chicago to rescue a trailer full of bric-a-brac and mementos from her childhood home that her mother planned to jettison. At the moment, Emma's trove resided in a storage unit in Clarenceville. One of these days Emma planned to empty that storage unit and distribute her mementos around her and David's new house.

As for Kay, she seemed to slide seamlessly into her new, city lifestyle and gratefully handed over the family's financial reins to Rory, who now managed Emma's trust fund as well as the fortune from Kay's father's shipping business. Rory McLean was fifteen years younger than Emma's mother, and Kay was thrilled to have a second chance at happiness. Emma had tried her best to be happy for her mother's sake until one evening, two months ago, when she was out for dinner with David and saw her stepfather seated at a cosy table in a New York restaurant called Chiara's with his arm round another woman, laughing and whispering in her ear.

Emma froze in horror at the sight. By the time she'd decided to get up and confront him, Rory and his date had left the restaurant. Torn about what to do, she discussed it with David, who warned her against breaking her mother's heart until she knew the whole story. Emma called her mother anyway, and Kay had cheerfully recounted that Rory was in New York on a business trip. Emma then told her mother that she had seen Rory in Chiara's, but that he'd left before she'd had a chance to talk to him.

'Wait until I tell him,' Kay had bubbled. 'He'll be so sorry he missed you.'

Sorry indeed, Emma had thought.

'Well, they seem to have things well in hand,' said Kay, looking around the room. 'I suppose that table is for the gifts.' She pointed to a flower-bedecked table that already had white-and-gold wrapped boxes on it. 'Honestly, what ever happened to the custom of sending them to the house?'

'Oh, Mom, don't get all Emily Post about this,' Emma said.

'I know, I know,' said Kay. 'Don't mind me. Everything will be perfect. Now let's get you two dressed. I want to talk to the caterer for one minute, and then I'll be right up to join you.'

Emma studied herself in the full-length mirror. 'Well, what do you think?'

'Wow,' said Stephanie wistfully. 'That dress is fantastic.'

Gazing at the form-fitting, strapless Duchesse satin gown, Emily had to admit that it was spectacular. The fabric was the colour of Devonshire cream. The dress clung to her in a perfect line, and there was no telltale tightness around the middle. 'It is pretty,' she said.

There was a tap at the door, and Kay stuck her head in. 'Oh, sweetie,' she breathed. 'You are magnificent.'

'Thanks, Mom. How's everything downstairs?'

'The flowers are beautiful, and the fire is going in the fireplace. And there's a divine scent wafting in from the kitchen.'

Emma smiled. 'Great.'

'And, Stephanie, you look lovely too. You two really do look like you could be sisters.'

'I feel like her sister today,' said Stephanie, twirling round in her olive-green gown.

As Emma looked tenderly at Stephanie, she could not help thinking about her friends who would not be here today. Foremost on her mind was Natalie, of course. And her childhood friend, Jessica, who lived in New York with her husband, Chris. Jessie was six months into a very difficult pregnancy, and the doctor had put her on bed rest.

There was a knock on the open door. Rory, wearing an expensive suit and tortoiseshell glasses, his greying auburn hair slicked back off his forehead, said, 'Oh, Emma, you are a vision.'

'Thank you.' Emma turned back to the mirror.

'Done with your business?' said Kay, walking over to her husband and kissing him on the cheek. 'What could possibly be so important, anyway?'

'Well, that's what I came up to talk to our girl about.' Rory looked at Stephanie. 'Young lady, would you excuse us for a minute?'

Stephanie stood up awkwardly. 'Me? Sure. I'll just . . .' She lifted the hem of her gown and edged towards the door.

Emma felt alarmed. Surely Rory couldn't be choosing to explain his secret tryst right now, just minutes before her wedding. 'What's this about?' she asked.

Rory cleared his throat and reached into the pocket of his jacket. 'I was just over at your new home, talking to your husband-to-be.'

Emma stared at him. 'Talking to David?'

'Well, this is why we couldn't come down last night. I was meeting with our attorney to hammer out the details.' He extracted a few folded sheets of paper. 'This is a prenuptial agreement, and I strongly advise you, as I advised him, to sign it before the wedding.'

Emma was momentarily stunned into silence.

'I must say, he was very polite. He said if it was what—'

'You can't be serious!' Emma cried.

'Completely serious,' Rory assured her. 'There's nothing more serious than large sums of money.'

'How dare you?' Emma demanded. 'I can't believe you did this. Mother, did you know he was doing this?'

Kay McLean looked flustered. 'Rory, honestly!'

'Now, Kay, there's a lot of money involved here. As the manager of your trust fund, it is my duty to advise you. I know it's last-minute, but we didn't know about the wedding until—'

'This is insulting!' Emma said.

'Rory,' said Kay. 'Put that thing away. My daughter is a grown woman. If she doesn't want to do this . . .'

'There's a lot of money at stake, Kay,' said Rory.

'My money, not yours!' Emma cried.

Rory tucked the document back in his pocket. 'This is not something to be emotional about. We need to be realistic, the divorce rate being what it is.'

'Rory, go!' said Kay, steering her husband out of the room.

'Emma, I'm only trying to do what's best for you . . .'

Emma was shaking and refused to meet his gaze. She could hardly believe it. Instead of being guilty and ashamed of himself, Rory had marched in here and insulted her. She wanted to blurt out all that she knew. But she couldn't. Rory stepped into the hallway, and Kay closed the door firmly behind him.

'Oh, Em, I'm sorry. I had no idea he was going to spring that on you. His timing can be atrocious.'

'I think this is about more than bad timing,' Emma fumed.

'Don't be angry. He's only thinking about your welfare.'

'My welfare,' Emma scoffed. 'David must be freaking out. I need to call him and explain.' She rummaged in her bag for her cellphone and punched in the number at their house. There was no answer. Then she tried David's cellphone. Still no answer.

'Take it easy, Em,' said Kay. 'Don't let this spoil your day.'

'David is probably furious,' Emma said.

'He knows it wasn't your idea. If he loves you, he'll understand.'

'If?' Emma cried.

Kay took her daughter's hands. 'Of course he loves you. I know that.'

'What if he's so mad he decides not to show up?'

'He'll show up. Have a little faith,' said Kay.

Emma took a deep breath. It was all she could do not to expose Rory's secret. 'Look, Mom, David and I have talked about it. He's just not someone who thinks all that much about money. He says it's my money to do with as I see fit. Let me ask you something. I don't mean to be rude, but do you have a prenup?'

Kay shook her head. 'I'm like you. I'm a romantic. I believe in getting married without hedging your bets. Trust and hope. You need those things in a marriage.'

Emma nodded agreement, but there was a sickening feeling in her gut, and in her mind's eye, an image of Rory nuzzling another woman.

'And I can see that you're happy,' Kay continued. 'And very much in love.' She put her arms round her daughter and rested her cheek softly against Emma's face. 'Stay that way.'

Emma's heart was thudding as she descended the staircase. Stephanie picked up their bouquets from the hall table and handed the bride's bouquet up to her. Emma peeked into the timber-ceilinged room. All the guests fitted into a few short rows of chairs that faced the flower-bedecked mantelpiece and blazing hearth.

Standing in front of the fireplace, in his robes, was Judge Harold Williamson. David had insisted on a civil ceremony. As he carefully explained to Emma, he had no use for organised religion. In her heart of hearts, Emma would have preferred a church wedding, but she deferred to David's strong feelings. Next to Judge Williamson was Burke Heisler, wearing an impeccable grey suit that matched his grey eyes. The space reserved for the groom was empty.

'Where is he?' Emma whispered. Her bouquet of white roses and lily of the valley trembled in her hand.

'Don't worry,' Kay soothed. 'He'll be here.'

David has changed his mind, she thought. She closed her eyes, wishing she could make herself disappear. I should have known. He's always been a free spirit, a guy with no strings attached. What made me think he could change overnight? And he probably thinks I sent Rory to blindside him. But still, it's so cruel.

'Here he is,' said Kay.

Emma opened her eyes, faint with relief.

He was heading towards the front. His dark, wavy hair had been trimmed, and he was wearing a beautiful navy suit with a silk tie. He inserted himself between the judge and his best man and then glanced towards the back of the room. Meeting her gaze, he mimed a wolf whistle. There was a chuckle from the assembled guests.

Emma's face turned pink, and her anxieties melted away.

Kay took her hand. 'OK, sweetie. Are you ready?'

'Yes,' Emma whispered.

The fervent vows pledged, the rings and kisses exchanged, Emma and David turned to face their guests. A waiter came round with a tray of champagne, but Emma asked for a glass of sparkling cider. When he brought it to her, she and David clinked glasses and drank. Silverware tinkled as guests began to visit the buffet table laden with rich pâtés, fresh seafood, and chateaubriand. The jazz combo riffed, and more hors d'oeuvres were passed. People took seats at small tables covered in white linen and anchored with clear bowls of white butterfly orchids and gardenias. The first person whom Emma encountered was Aurelia Martin, Kay's oldest friend and the mother of Emma's closest friend, Jessica. Aurelia stood up to give Emma a kiss.

'Aunt Aurelia,' Emma said. 'I'm so glad to see you. Where's Uncle Frank?'

Aurelia's husband was much older than she and in ill health. 'Darling, he's not really well enough for an occasion like this.'

'Well, give him a hug for me. And how's Jessie doing? She always tells me she's bored staying in bed.'

'Oh, she's bored all right. She hates missing your wedding. I'll tell her how beautiful you look. And what a handsome groom you have there.'

'Thank you.' Emma beamed and followed Aurelia's gaze. David was crouched down beside the chair where his mother sat, offering her a plate with tiny portions of food.

Helen Webster, gaunt in a pink polyester coat dress, was tethered by a pair of long tubes to an oxygen tank on wheels. Helen's sole hope for survival was a heart transplant, but her blood type was rare, and her chances seemed slim. She was in the end stages of heart disease, but she watched the wedding scene with lively eyes.

'He seems like a very nice young man,' said Aurelia.

'He is,' said Emma.

'Has Jessie met him?'

'Not yet,' Emma admitted. David had resisted her efforts to get together with Jessie and Chris in New York City. He had insisted that he didn't want to waste precious time with other people. Emma suspected that he also didn't want her friends judging him. But that was no longer an issue. 'She'll meet him soon.'

'Well, you two be happy together,' Aurelia said, laying a feathery touch on Emma's hand before she resumed her seat.

'Excuse me, may I kiss the bride?'

Emma turned and saw Burke Heisler gazing warmly at her. She put her arms round his neck as he held her tightly for a moment. 'Oh, Burke. I'm so happy.'

'You look happy,' he said. 'And completely ravishing.'

Emma made a little curtsy of gratitude.

'I was worried for a minute,' Burke said, 'about the groom.'

'So was I,' Emma admitted. 'When I saw he wasn't here, I thought he'd changed his mind.'

'I never thought that. He'd have to be insane,' said Burke.

Emma blushed. 'Well, thanks. And thanks for being such a good friend to us.'

'I only wish Natalie were here. She would have approved.'

'I like to think so,' said Emma. She squeezed his hand. 'I think the only real happiness she ever knew was with you.'

Burke shrugged. 'I won't lie to you, Emma. It was difficult at times. But it could be great too. Those are the times I prefer to remember.' He forced himself to smile.

'Thanks for being here for us today. I know how hard it is.' Emma smiled and then said apologetically, 'I should go say hello to my mother-in-law.'

'You go on,' he said.

Emma started across the room towards the table where Helen sat next to a podgy, cheerful-looking woman with short grey hair. Birdie, Helen's first cousin, was a widow. A few years ago she had moved into David's boyhood home in Clarenceville to look after her ailing cousin.

David turned to Emma with relief in his eyes. 'Hey, baby.'

Emma kissed him and then bent over and touched Helen's ice-cold hand. 'How are you feeling today, Helen?'

'Oh, I'm fine,' said Helen. Her voice was faint. 'I just wish Phil could have been here.' A Seattle attorney, David's older brother hadn't been able to rearrange his schedule.

'Me too, Mom,' said David.

Helen had struggled fiercely, working as a waitress, to raise her sons after David's father, a furniture salesman and a chronic gambler, abandoned his family. Alan Webster was a man whom David never mentioned without disgust. He told Emma that his father's abandonment was one reason he was afraid of fatherhood. He didn't want to be that kind of father, despised by his wife and children.

'Hey, mind if we join you, sis?' said a paunchy white-haired man carrying a plate piled high with lobster. He was followed by a little woman with frizzy hair and a weathered face.

'John, Tilly,' said Helen. 'Sit down here.'

'We will. Hey, cuz,' John said, pecking Birdie on the cheek.

'Hi, sweetie,' Birdie said cheerfully, stopping a passing waitress to exchange her empty champagne glass for a full one.

'Emma,' said David. 'I'd like you to meet my aunt and uncle, Tilly and John Zamsky. They're the ones with the cabin.'

'Oh, hello,' said Emma warmly, shaking their hands. She had heard many stories about the good-natured plumber who had tried to include his nephews in his family life. 'Thank you so much for lending us your place.'

John Zamsky waved a meaty hand. 'You're welcome to it. I don't use the place any more. I never get out that way nowadays.'

'Nowadays, you can't get him out of his recliner,' Tilly confided.

'How long since we been there, Till?' John asked.

'A couple of years.'

'Our kids never use it,' said John. 'We ought to sell it.'

'Well, we appreciate your lending it to us,' said Emma. 'It should be lovely there in November.'

'Perfect time of year,' said John. 'You kids enjoy it.'

Emma and David smiled at each other. 'We will,' said David.

'Helen, how are you feeling?' Tilly asked. 'Is this too much excitement for you?'

'I'm enjoying myself,' said Helen.

'Just don't overdo it,' Tilly said.

Helen's bloodless lips turned up in a weak grin. 'Oh, stop fussing. I'm fine. I never thought I'd see this day. This kid always said he'd never get married. Remember that, Davey?'

David looked at her without smiling. 'I don't remember that.'

Helen shook her head. 'This does my heart good. If I collapse, so be it. At least I'll die happy.'

3

'I'M GONNA HAVE TO make you quit driving,' said David.

Emma opened her eyes and yawned. 'Where are we?' she said.

'Almost there. Every time you get into a car these days, you fall asleep. I'm not sure it's safe to let you behind the wheel any more.'

Emma smiled and sat up. 'It's true. It's the pregnancy. I'm always sleepy. Although I usually stay awake when I'm behind the wheel.'

'Usually?' he said with disbelief in his deep, languid voice.

Emma laughed. 'Hey, it's not your average day. I got married a few hours ago. It was a little bit exhausting.'

She revisited the day's events in her mind's eye. After the ceremony, the buffet lunch, the toasts and the wedding cake, Emma had run back upstairs, removed her dress and squeezed into her jeans. She then put on a long-sleeved Henley shirt and a down vest, and pulled her shining honey-blonde hair up under a baseball cap. She and David had escaped to their car in the obligatory shower of rice and good wishes.

'All in all, I'd say it was a success,' she said.

'I think so,' he said. 'You looked incredible. I thought the other men there were going to fall over at the sight of you.'

'The other men? What about you?'

He gave her a sly grin. 'Oh, baby, you know about me.'

Emma grinned, then took a deep breath. 'I'm just so sorry about that business with the prenup.'

'Don't be. Rory was looking out for you.'

'Rory,' Emma said disgustedly, shaking her head.

'I think he does care about you in his own weird way. Anyway, I told him I'd sign it.'

'Well, I told him I wouldn't. We don't need that,' said Emma.

'It's your decision,' said David.

'My mother said we needed to start our marriage with trust and hope. I thought that was kind of nice. Even though her own husband can't be trusted.'

'You didn't mention that to her today, I hope.'

'No, of course not. She was happy today. And so thrilled. Actually, both our mothers seemed happy.'

'Well, you heard my mother,' David said. 'She was sure I was not the marrying kind.' He was silent for a moment, and Emma saw the frown in his eyes.

'I'm glad you decided to become the marrying kind,' she said.

'Me too.' His face broke into a sweet smile; then he abruptly changed the subject. 'Ready for our camping trip?'

'It's not a camping trip,' protested Emma. 'There's a cabin, running water, electricity. And a fireplace. It's gonna be great.'

'A pregnant woman in the wilds of New Jersey,' he teased.

'Oh, come on. "Wilds of New Jersey" is an oxymoron.'

'You look so cute—just like a Piney—in that outfit.'

'Thanks. I guess,' said Emma. Glancing in the sideview mirror, Emma saw herself dressed for the woods, her face burnished by the sun's weakening rays. The perceived wisdom about pregnancy was true. Or was it the glow of being a newlywed? Her skin had never looked better, her blue-grey eyes softer. She held up her left hand and examined her wedding band.

David glanced over. 'You like that?' he asked gently.

They were husband and wife, starting out on their life together. She felt as if she would burst with happiness. 'I like it.'

'Good,' he said.

She gazed out of the window. The November afternoon was golden, shafts of slanted light piercing the surrounding forests. 'It's gorgeous here,' she said.

David nodded. 'It really is remote. You'd never believe you were an hour from Clarenceville.'

'I never thought when I met you that you'd turn out to have this L.L. Bean side to you.'

'I'm full of surprises,' he said.

She sat back in the seat and smiled, remembering. From the first day, he had surprised her. After their impulsive night of passion in his New York apartment, she had fully expected that he would be in a rush to get his privacy back. Instead, he woke her up with fresh bagels and coffee and insisted on taking her to a street fair in Little Italy, where he bought her a cameo ring. After Emma suggested that it was time for her to head for the train station, he had turned to her with a puzzled look. 'No, don't go,' he had said.

She could remember how her whole body had tingled as she'd met his gaze. Their love affair had been a heady, dizzy ride. But was it all too soon, too quick? she wondered. A moment's doubt fell across her happiness like a cloud, and then, just as quickly, it was gone. You are starting out on life's great adventure, she thought. Enjoy it. She began to relax and take in her surroundings again.

The deepening woods filled her with a sense of mystery and excitement. Her favourite vacations had always been camping trips. She and her father would visit national parks and go hiking and swimming by day, making campfires and stargazing at night. It was something special that she was now going to share with David.

'Oh, look! There's the river!' she cried. 'It's gleaming. Is that where we're going to be canoeing?'

'Yeah, I guess so. We're almost to the cabin.'

'How can you remember the way after so many years?'

David hesitated. 'I don't know. I guess I'm a born scout.'

'How many years has it been?' she asked.

David shook his head. 'I can't remember. A long time.'

They rode along in silence for a few minutes. The Jeep Cherokee jounced along on the dirt for about half a mile until they came to a cabin set in a clearing. Built from russet-coloured cedar, it had a fieldstone chimney and a set of steps with wooden railings leading to the front door. A shed and a large woodpile stood some hundred yards away. A canoe was resting upside-down on a pair of sawhorses. The river could be glimpsed from where they parked the car.

Emma opened her door and jumped out. 'Oh, David, this is precious. This is great!' she said.

'You know, for a rich kid, you are so easy to please,' he said.

'Promise me that we can sleep in front of the fireplace.'

'It's our wedding night. We can do whatever your little heart desires,' he said. 'It's just you and me.'

Emma took a deep breath of the pine-scented air. 'Oh, this is fabulous. Talk about getting away from it all. I love it.'

'Well,' David said, going round and opening the trunk. 'Let's go in, and I'll show you the place.'

Emma walked round and tried to pull her bag out of the trunk, but David tugged it away from her. 'I'll carry this stuff. You just take it easy there, pioneer girl.'

Emma giggled and ran up the steps ahead of him. She turned back to her husband. 'Keys?' she said.

'Uncle John always kept the key under the mat.'

Emma lifted the weather-beaten welcome mat. 'Sure enough.' She turned the key in the stiff lock and pushed the door open.

'Wait a minute. Stop.' He set the bags down, lifted her in his arms as if she were no heavier than a doll, and carried her in. 'Allow me, Mrs Webster. It's our first threshold.'

'That is so sweet,' she said. 'I forgot all about that.'

'We don't want any bad karma,' he said, setting her down.

The cabin smelt a little musty. The main room was simply furnished with a braided rug, and a sofa and chair that faced the fieldstone hearth. A pair of canoe paddles rested against the fireplace. Along the opposite wall was a stove and refrigerator and russet-stained cabinets. A gate-leg table and two chairs nestled against a kitchen island, which held the sink and a butcher-block countertop. 'Does it look the same after all these years?' Emma asked.

'Yeah. Pretty much,' he said. 'Let me go get the bags.'

Emma opened a few cupboard doors and found old bottles of spices and some rusty cans of food.

'Good thing we bought supplies,' she said as David hauled in the duffle bags.

'I'll put these in our bedroom,' he said.

'Let me check it out with you,' she said, following him. He set the bags down in the room that had a queen-size bed.

'Do you want to drag the mattress out now?' he asked.

'No. Let's wait until after supper,' she said with a smile. 'But I definitely want a fire going the whole time.'

'As you wish, madam,' said David. 'Uncle John has an axe in the shed. I want to split a little more wood. That stack won't last until morning. I'd better get to work and start chopping before it's too dark.' He made a bicep for her to admire.

Emma squeezed his arm and kissed him. 'You're right,' she said. 'Go do your woodsman thing.'

He kissed her and headed outside.

Emma began unloading the food they had brought into the empty refrigerator. I wonder if there's any ice, she thought absently, opening the door to the freezer. Inside was a can of coffee and a package of lasagne, completely frosted over. Ugh, she thought. How long has this been here? She wiped the frost off the package and, to her surprise, the sell-by date was August of this year. August? she thought. Maybe one of the Zamskys' kids came to visit. She debated throwing the package away, but it didn't belong to her. She filled the empty ice cube trays with water and put them back in the freezer.

When she was done unloading, the fridge was not exactly full, but there was enough to keep them well fed for the weekend. David had brought beer, and she had two bottles of sparkling cider from the wedding. She could hear the sound of cracking from outside as David split the wood. She glanced out and saw him placing logs on a stump and cleaving them deftly with a shiny axe.

I'd better make up the bed, she thought. Even if they did pull the mattress in front of the fire, it would be better if the sheet were already on it. She went into the bedroom and turned on the bedside light. Then she reached for the sheets she had placed in a large shopping bag. As she began to stretch the bottom sheet round the corner of the bed, she realised that the cracking sound of the logs being split had ceased.

That was quick, she thought.

She walked round, pulling on the sheet, and then she sat down on the edge of the bed and looked out of the window. The river gleamed silver like a knife through the pine trees. The whole world seemed to be silent except for the faint rustle of leaves.

I like this, she thought. I need this. She heard a creak, as if the front door had opened.

'David?' she called out.

There was no answer.

Probably the wind, she thought. Or the Jersey Devil. She got up and tossed open the top sheet.

Through the bedroom door, she thought she saw a movement in the outer room. 'David?' she said.

There was no reply. She took a deep breath. You're spooking yourself. You're just not used to silence. She smoothed a blanket over the sheets and put the pillows in their cases.

Typical David, she thought uneasily. He probably took off exploring somewhere. Couldn't wait until tomorrow. She straightened up and patted her belly. Let's go find him, Aloysius, she thought, using her pet name for the baby growing inside her. What do you say?

Turning off the bedside light, she went back out into the main room.

The light was on over the kitchen stove top, but everything else was in a twilight gloom, and the temperature seemed to have plummeted with the fading of the day. She opened the front door and walked outside onto the landing. There was wood, stacked by the piles of logs, but no sign of her husband. Emma could see the light withdrawing from the trees. Don't go out there, she thought. You'll get lost in those woods. He'll be back any minute.

With a sigh, she went back inside the musty room. There were two red pillar candles on the mantelpiece, and a pair of straight candles in ceramic holders on the little gate-leg table. I could light those, she thought. Get the place in the mood. On the mantelpiece was an old box of wooden matches. She lit the candles, and the room instantly felt warmer and cosier. I wonder if I should start the fire, Emma thought. There was a basket of wood and old papers next to the hearth. Your mother can do this, Aloysius, she thought. She learned to make a fire when she was not much bigger than you.

Balling up the papers, Emma set them in the hearth. She placed short branches on the paper for kindling and then arranged the wood in a tepee. She crouched down and lit a match. The flame seemed to hesitate, dancing for a moment, and then it ran down the edge of the paper, leaping to ignite the kindling. All right, she thought. David will be so proud of me.

At that very moment, as she felt the little triumph of having lit the fire, she felt the candlelight from the table disappear as if the flames had gone out. The flames on the pillar candles wavered. Emma's heart seized. Someone was moving up behind her. 'David?' she said. She turned and looked up.

In the twilight gloom, she saw him. Three feet away. A figure in a hooded sweatshirt. A black ski mask covered the face save two ragged eyeholes outlined in red. Emma's limbs were stone. Her heart was bursting. 'Who are you?' she cried.

He did not reply. In his gloved hand he held an axe. Its edge gleamed in the fire as he advanced. She put up her hands to shield herself, her baby. This can't be happening, she thought. As he lifted the axe, she looked around frantically. She screamed, and tried to scramble away. It was no use. He was too close.

She saw a flash of steel descending.

Claude Mathis had not had a good day. Last night he had bet Holly, his ex-wife, that his fourteen-year-old son, Bobby, would want to come hunting today, but when Claude showed up at dawn, in camouflage from head to toe, at her trailer, Holly had told him with satisfaction that Bobby was still asleep and was planning on going to some Japanese animation festival. Whatever that was.

Claude had driven out to the woods in his pick-up, his hound, Major, patiently flopped down on the rear bed. Claude was trying not to feel angry, but why couldn't the kid show an interest? There was a lot he needed to learn, and it was time he started learning it. Claude had fumed about it all day, and it had probably affected his aim, because he had had a few opportunities but no luck.

Finally, it was time to go home. He was tramping through the woods, thinking about the bar he liked to go to, its welcoming glow visible in his mind's eye. Sausage and sauerkraut and a golden brew. He was trying to make up a story he could tell the guys about today that wouldn't be humiliating, that the guys would find funny, when he heard the woman's scream.

Claude, trailed by Major, stopped short. It was a horrible sound that made Claude's thinning brown hair stand on end. Then it came again. At the same moment, Claude smelled wood smoke, and he realised exactly where that scream was coming from. He had passed that little cabin not too far from the river. Cocking his automatic rifle, he began to lope in that direction, Major keeping pace with him.

Emma, screaming, had rolled away from the first blow, which landed with a horrible clang on an andiron. All she could think about was her baby. She had to protect the baby. She tried to scramble to her feet, but the second blow hit her. The down filling of her vest kept the blade from landing on her with full force, but it landed all the same, slicing her side open. Her blood flew through the air as she tried to lunge out of his range. Through her panic, she noticed a canoe paddle by the fireplace and lifted it to ward him off. The axe fell again, splintering her would-be shield into bits.

The pain in her side felt like a hot poker had perforated her lungs. She launched herself towards the door, collapsing as he hit her again, a glancing blow on her thigh. She let out a cry of pain.

'What the hell?'

Emma and her masked assailant looked up in the same instant and saw a man dressed in camouflage coming through the door, holding his rifle. His face was aghast. 'Help me,' Emma cried.

The hunter stared for a moment too long. Spinning away from Emma, the man in the hooded sweatshirt struck the hunter. The axe came down the front of his balding head, cleaving a bloody channel through it. His shocked gaze turned empty, and he crumpled, the gun falling from his hands.

'No!' Emma shrieked in horror. The hunter was on the floor, a bundle of flesh and camouflage, the area around him slick with blood. Emma's assailant pulled the axe from the man's skull and turned on her again.

Now he will kill me, she thought.

She could not see his face, just the wild gleam of his eyes, encircled with red. She thought of her child, who would never see this world, and in the instant that it took to pray for both their souls, she heard a horrible growl, and a brown-and-white setter bounded into the cabin and leapt at the man in the mask, knocking him off-balance and sinking his teeth into his bulky sweatshirt.

'Good boy!' Emma screamed, and scuttled across the floor to the rifle. She'd never shot a rifle. She'd shot tin cans with her father's revolver. That was all. It didn't matter. It was a gun, and she would use it. The assailant jammed the dog's snout with the axe handle, and the dog let go with a wail of pain, stunned. The man lifted the axe, and Emma lifted the rifle. She pulled the trigger.

A deafening roar thundered in the cabin, and the gun bucked in her arms. The empty shell flew from the port, and Emma heard another shell click into the chamber. The assailant staggered back, and for one moment Emma thought she had shot him. Then she saw a black smoking hole beside the doorway where he stood. For one second they all froze, Emma on the floor with the rifle, the setter growling over the body of his dead master, and the man in the mask.

Emma did not hesitate. She held the rifle's sight up to her eye. The barrel wavered slightly and fixed on him.

The assailant tossed the axe in her direction as the angry dog leapt at him again. The axe missed Emma and embedded itself in the pine floor. Emma fired again, but the assailant had bolted out of the door, pulling it shut against the hound, who was barking as if possessed.

Shaking, Emma clutched the rifle and crawled over to the hunter bleeding on the floor. The dog snarled at her.

Help, Emma thought. Help was nearby. In her pocket. She reached inside the vest, pulled out her cellphone, and dialled 911.

Then she began to sob so hard she could barely speak.

Chief Audie Osmund, dressed in a khaki uniform stretched taut over his wide belly, a black down vest, and a black cap over his white hair, was standing beside his patrol car, talking on his radio to the New Jersey State Police, putting out an APB on the suspect. The female victim was weak from loss of blood but had given a sketchy description of the killer. Unfortunately, it wasn't worth too much because of the mask. The male victim, Claude Mathis, was beyond all help. DOA. 'Yeah,' Audie was saying to the commander on duty. 'We gonna need some help on this one.'

The bloody scene had left Audie shaken. He knew that a lot of police chiefs would be reluctant to cede any authority to the state police. But he didn't have the manpower or the technical sophistication to process the evidence on this crime.

The commander promised to send a detective down tonight. 'Don't let anybody mess with the crime scene,' he said.

'We're guarding it,' said Audie. 'Thanks for the help.'

The ambulance bay was standing open. The Emergency Medical Technicans (EMTs) were in the cabin with the woman now. Another black-and-white and three pick-up trucks were crowded into the clearing, their headlights crisscrossing. The search of the woods had already begun. Audie could see bouncing flashlight beams among the trees.

All of a sudden he heard a cry. 'Chief, we got him!'

The chief lumbered towards the sound of the voices at the edge of the clearing. Two men emerged, one a volunteer, the other Sergeant Gene Revere, half dragging a third man out of the woods. He had dark hair flecked with grey and was wearing a canvas barn coat, heavy boots, and filthy soaking-wet blue jeans. He was resisting the men, who had handcuffed him.

'Where's my wife?' the suspect was pleading. 'What happened here? I heard shots. Is my wife all right? Emma!'

'He said he's the husband,' said Gene.

David looked helplessly at the chief. 'Why is there an ambulance? Did someone shoot my wife?'

'David Webster?' asked Audie.

'I'm David Webster. Yes. Where is Emma?'

'Your wife's been attacked,' said Chief Osmund bluntly. 'By a man with an axe. Where have you been, mister?'

'We found him out near the duck hide,' Gene said. 'He says he walked onto a rotten platform and fell through it. He claims it took him a while to get free.'

David Webster stopped struggling and stood very still. His hazel eyes widened and sweat broke out on his forehead. He stared at the chief. 'Emma. Is she . . .?'

Osmund watched the man carefully. 'She's alive,' he said.

David sagged against Gene, the blood draining from his face.

The cabin door opened, and the EMTs emerged, carrying a stretcher. At the ambulance bay, an EMT readied an IV bag.

'Emma!' David cried.

Her white face was barely visible beneath an oxygen mask. She was covered to the neck with a Mylar blanket, but the stretcher mattress, where it was visible, was blotched with huge red stains. Chief Osmund nodded to his sergeant to unlock the handcuffs. David staggered towards the stretcher. He tried to reach her, but the largest of the EMTs blocked him. 'You need to get out of the way, sir,' he said.

'I want to go with her. She needs to know I'm here. Emma.'

'There's no room,' said the EMT. 'We need every inch of space to get her ready for the ER. Please step back and let us work.'

David stumbled back, his eyes wide in disbelief. Chief Osmund and his deputy, Gene Revere, exchanged a glance as the EMTs loaded the stretcher into the ambulance. The siren began to wail.

'Mr Webster,' said Osmund. 'You need to come on down to the station. You hop in my car, and I'll give you a lift.'

'No!' David cried. 'I have to be with her.'

'We'll let you know if there's any news from the docs,' Audie said.

David turned on the chief. 'Are you crazy? I'm not leaving her alone in some strange hospital. Get out of my way.'

Audie looked at the distraught husband, assessing his reaction. 'I can see you're all tore up, Mr Webster. But we need to figure out what happened in that cabin. We got a murder here.'

'Who was murdered?' David cried.

'A hunter, passing by. Tried to help your wife.'

'Oh my God.' David ran his hand through his hair. 'This is my fault. I should have been here. I want to help you, but can it wait?'

'Like I said, we'll get this over with, and then I'll have somebody drive you to the hospital. Now, you go on and get into my car.'

'Wait a minute. Are you arresting me?' David cried.

'Why would I do that?' Audie asked. 'I just want to talk to you. Get some answers that might help us out.'

David glowered and seemed about to protest again. Then, suddenly, he turned away and headed for the squad car.

Gene Revere sighed. 'Well, we'd better get back to looking. We didn't realise that was the husband. That nut is still out there.'

'Maybe,' Audie said. 'Anybody actually see the husband stuck in that duck hide platform?'

'No. We just saw this guy kinda staggering along with no business being out in the woods, and we figured it was the killer.'

'Go on back out to the hide. Get some dogs if need be. I want every inch of ground between here and there looked at.'

'The guy probably got away by now,' said Gene dejectedly.

'Maybe not,' said Audie. 'It'll probably be in a bag.'

'What will?'

'A ski mask with red circles round the eyes, one of them hooded sweatshirts, maybe some pants and sneakers too.'

'You think the killer changed before he got away?'

Audie glanced over at his patrol car. From the back seat David Webster was staring at the cabin with haunted eyes. 'Or maybe he changed out of them,' said Audie grimly, 'and he's still here.'

4

'SWEETHEART,' said a soft voice.

Emma struggled to open her eyes. Every part of her hurt. Even her eyelids felt sore. It took all her will to blink and focus. She saw short platinum-blonde hair and anxious eyes.

'Mom,' she whispered.

'Oh, darling, you're awake,' said Kay. She bent over and kissed her daughter on the forehead.

Emma tried to nod. Her head ached. 'What time is it?'

'It's about midnight. They had to give you a sedative.'

'David,' Emma breathed. And then her eyes opened wide, and she struggled to sit up. 'My baby.'

Kay patted her shoulder, pushing her gently back towards the pillow. 'It's all right. They did a sonogram. The baby is fine,' she said, blinking back tears.

'Thank God.' Emma knew she had lost a lot of blood. Now that she was awake, she remembered bags of blood being carried aloft, blinding lights, people in masks and gowns, urgent murmurs about clamps and sutures. But her baby was still alive. Their baby. David. 'Where's David?'

Kay's gaze travelled across the room, where a man was rising from a chair. Emma followed her gaze, and for a moment her heart lifted. Then she recognised her mother's husband.

'How you doin', slugger?' asked Rory, his expression hidden by the reflection off his tortoiseshell glasses.

Emma did not reply. Her lips were dry and cracked. She tried to moisten them with her tongue. Kay reached for a washcloth and gently pressed it to her parched lips. 'David?' Emma repeated.

Rory cleared his throat. 'David's down at the police station.'

'He's helping the police,' said Kay.

Emma tried to shift her position, but her entire left side felt as if it were on fire. 'Do they know who did this?' she whispered.

Kay hesitated. 'Not yet. But you're safe now, darling. No one's going to hurt you. There's a lieutenant from the state police outside who's been waiting to talk to you. Do you think you're up to it?'

'I'll try,' Emma said, her voice wobbly.

'I'll go,' Rory said. Through the fog of her sedation, Emma knew there was something negative she was thinking about Rory, and then she remembered. The woman in the restaurant. She closed her eyes and thought about her father—with his soothing voice, which she could no longer summon in her memory. A tear leaked out from under her eyelids and down her face.

'Mrs Webster?'

Mrs Webster, Emma thought, visualising David's mother. And then she realised, she was Mrs Webster. She looked up at the woman standing beside her bed, frowning down at her. She looked to be in her thirties and was wearing a fitted charcoal-grey trouser-suit. She was sharp-featured, with keen dark eyes and chin-length brown hair.

'Yes,' Emma whispered.

'I'm Lieutenant Joan Atkins of the state police. Chief Osmund requested the assistance of our bureau with his investigation.' Joan showed Emma her ID and her badge.

'Lieutenant Atkins is here to help you, honey,' said Kay.

'You've been through a horrible ordeal, Mrs Webster,' said Joan. She sat down beside Emma's bed and studied her for a moment. Emma was stiff, her left side heavily bandaged, and the bandages were misted with blood. 'I'm going to try to keep this brief, Emma. Can I call you Emma?'

Emma nodded slightly. 'OK.'

Joan reached for the pad and pen in her black shoulder bag. 'Do you know who did this to you, Emma?' she asked.

Tears spilled down Emma's face, and she began to tremble. 'No. I told the first policeman. No. He was wearing . . .'

'A mask and a hood. But was there anything . . . familiar about him?'

'Familiar?' Emma's brain felt slow and woolly. 'No.'

'Did you recognise his movements? His eyes beneath the mask?'

Emma tried to think back. 'No . . . It was so fast.'

'I understand you were married this morning,' Joan said.

Emma blinked, realising she had forgotten that. The wedding seemed like it took place a year ago. 'Yes. Where is my husband?' Her heart started to race. 'Is he all right?'

'Yes, he's fine,' said Joan gently. 'Weddings can be very stressful, Emma. Did any disagreements arise between you and your husband before or after the wedding?'

Emma shook her head. 'No. Not really. No . . .'

Joan gazed at her grimly. 'Has David Webster ever threatened you or attacked you physically?'

Emma's eyes widened. 'David?' She struggled to sit up, to protest. 'David did not hurt me.'

Joan's face remained expressionless. But years of experience on the job had left her with the conviction that there could be few things more dangerous than an angry husband. 'Emma, we need to determine whether this was a random attack or you were a specific target. Can you think of anyone else who might have had a reason to want to hurt you? Any threats you've received?'

Emma sank back against the pillow. She heard Joan's words, but thinking was difficult. 'No,' Emma said. And then she hesitated. 'Not threatening.' Her mind was foggy.

'Can you review what happened in the cabin for me?'

Emma's eyes filled with fear. 'Why?'

'It might give us something more to go on,' Joan said.

'No, I can't.' The idea of recalling the attack filled her with dread, and her head was aching. She closed her eyes, forcing herself to see it again. That creature without a face looming above her, the axe gleaming. Chasing her, swinging it at her. The hunter with the rifle. The man in the mask turning on him. 'Oh no,' she mumbled. 'The man who tried to save me.'

'No, honey,' Kay crooned. 'Don't think about it.'

'Mrs McLean, please,' said Joan. 'It's important.'

Emma saw the hunter, crumpled on the floor, the axe cleaving his skull, the blood everywhere. She groaned, her pounding headache tightened like a vice, and suddenly, out of nowhere, she began to retch. The spasmodic movement ignited the pain of her wounds. She wailed as her empty stomach heaved.

'Oh no! Her stitches!' Kay exclaimed. 'Call the nurse!' She reached for a basin beside the bed as Joan rushed out of the room.

A moment later a nurse appeared, as did a doctor in scrubs and a lab coat. The doctor checked her chart and ordered a tranquilliser and painkiller. 'What happened?' the doctor demanded.

'She was remembering the attack,' the lieutenant said grimly.

Just then Joan's phone vibrated in her jacket pocket, and she turned away, holding it to her ear. 'Yes,' she said.

It was Chief Osmund. 'The husband clammed up,' he said. 'He called his attorney brother in Seattle who's contacted some hotshot lawyer who just walked in the door.'

'I see,' said Joan.

'We ain't got enough to hold him. We're gonna cut him loose.'

'I understand,' said Joan. 'I'll talk to you tomorrow.' She replaced the phone as Emma fell back against the pillow, her retching having finally subsided but her complexion the colour of clay.

'That's enough,' Kay pleaded. 'Please, leave her alone.'

'Mrs McLean, I won't be long. I understand your concern.'

'Make it quick,' said the nurse. 'She's gonna be out again in just a few minutes.'

Joan nodded and returned to her seat by the bed.

'David,' Emma was moaning. She turned her head and looked at Joan with bleary eyes. 'Where's my husband?'

'He'll be along soon,' Joan said. Too soon, she thought. That meant she did not have much time left before the husband went to work, trying to convince the victim he had nothing to do with this. 'Emma. Earlier, you seemed to hesitate when I asked if someone might have threatened you. Who were you thinking of?'

'It's not threats. I've been getting . . . messages. Anonymous.'

Joan raised an eyebrow. 'What kind of messages?'

'Like . . . love notes. But a little . . . not normal.'

'Do you still have them?' Joan asked. 'How many have you received? For how long? Are you receiving them at home?'

Emma closed her eyes. 'At work. Maybe . . . two months. Four of them. I kept them.'

'Do you have any idea who sent them?'

Emma shook her head. 'Dunno . . . could be a patient.'

A patient? Joan thought. For a moment Joan's certainty about the husband faltered. Kay McLean had told her that her daughter was a psychologist. She worked at some kind of crisis centre.

'Where can I find these notes?' Joan asked.

'Ask Burke. Dr Heisler. He's my boss,' Emma said. 'He knows about them. They're in my office.'

'Thank you, Emma,' said Joan. 'You just concentrate on getting better. I'll leave you my card in case you want to reach me.' As she stood up to leave, the door to the room opened, and a handsome but haggard-looking dark-haired man walked in.

'David!' Kay exclaimed.

Joan turned and eyed him. 'Mr Webster?' she said.

'Could I possibly see my wife now?' said David bitterly.

Emma's eyes opened. 'David.'

Joan stepped out of the man's way. She saw an anxious look in Kay McLean's eyes. 'I'm staying,' Kay said firmly, though no one had asked her to leave.

David walked over to Emma's bedside, looked down worriedly, and leaned over to kiss her. 'Hey, baby,' he whispered.

Emma looked up with eyes full of confusion. 'David. Where were you? I was so afraid . . .'

David sank down in the chair beside her and lifted her hand to his lips. 'Shhh . . . Rest. You're safe now. I won't leave you.'

Joan pulled open the door and glanced back. Tears ran down the sides of Emma's face. David wiped them gently away with his thumb. Joan frowned as she stepped out into the hallway.

A rustling sound registered in her sleep, and Emma's eyes flew open, her heart pounding. A woman wearing a shower cap, polyester trousers and a tunic, was carrying a tray of food. 'Here we go,' she said. 'Breakfast. Better wake up, Prince Charming.'

Emma turned her head on the scratchy hospital pillow, damp from tears she had shed in her sleep, and saw her husband slumped in the visitor's chair, fast asleep. 'David,' she said.

David jerked his head upright. In his hazel eyes she saw confusion and sleepiness. But something else too. His gaze met hers, and his eyes looked as if he had seen a ghost. 'Breakfast is served,' she said gently. She turned to the aide. 'Could you put the tray there?' She pointed to the table on the other side of the bed.

'OK. You be sure and eat now. You need your strength.'

Emma nodded. 'OK,' she said, although the familiar nausea of morning sickness was unsettling her stomach.

David rubbed his unshaven face, then scraped the chair across to her bedside and kissed her on the forehead. 'Baby,' he said. 'How are you feeling?'

Emma put a hand gingerly on her wounded side. 'I've been better. I guess I fell asleep as soon as you got here last night.'

David nodded. 'I was tempted to crawl into bed with you, but I didn't want to jostle all those stitches.' He took her hand. 'Not much of a wedding night.'

Emma nodded sadly. His hand felt like the only warm thing in the whole room. 'I'm glad you were here with me,' she said. 'I would have been afraid if I woke up alone.'

'Emma, I don't know what to say. I should have been with you in that cabin. I never should have left you there.'

Tears began to leak out of her eyes again. 'It was terrible.'

'I know,' he said angrily. 'I know it was.'

'I kept praying for you to come back.'

David sighed. 'I couldn't feel any more guilty. Believe me. If I could do it over . . . I went walking along the riverbank, just wandering. I was kind of filled up with all the events of the day. The sunset was so beautiful. I found this old duck hide my uncle used to take us to. I climbed up on it to look at the water, and I fell through where it was rotted. I could hear the gunshots. I was frantic to get out, but that only made it worse. By the time I got free, the police were searching for your attacker, and instead, they found me.'

'Did you see him?' she asked, agitation in her voice.

'Who?' David frowned at her.

'Him,' she said. 'The man with the axe.'

David hung his head. 'I wish I had. He'd be a dead man now.'

For a moment they were both silent. Then David stood up abruptly and adjusted the table in front of her. 'Here, eat something,' he said. 'You need your strength.'

'I'll try,' she said.

He ripped the paper lid off the cup of apple juice, and Emma had a careful sip. Her stomach started to settle. 'Were you able to help the police?' she said.

David snorted with laughter. 'Help them?'

'They said you were at the station trying to help them.'

David shook his head. 'I was at the station being interrogated. Look, Emma, as your husband, I'm the prime suspect.'

'You?' she cried.

'The husband always is,' David said. 'I was at the scene. My fingerprints were on the murder weapon.'

'The axe? But you were chopping wood,' Emma protested.

'Didn't Atkins ask you about me last night?'

And then it came back to her. That lady lieutenant asking her if they'd argued. If he'd ever hurt her. Emma grimaced. 'She asked me if I could think of anyone who would want to hurt me. I told her about those anonymous letters at work.'

David frowned. 'You shouldn't do that, Em.'

Emma looked at him in surprise. 'Do what?'

'Offer information. My brother told me not to do that.'

'Phil said that? When did you talk to Phil about this?'

'I called him last night.' David hesitated. 'Actually, Phil called a friend of his, an attorney named Yunger. The guy drove down and got me out of there. From now on, Em, all our communication with the police should go through Mr Yunger.'

Emma chewed a piece of toast, avoiding his gaze. 'Why do we need an attorney? We have nothing to hide.'

'Emma, a man was killed. We need to protect ourselves.'

'From who?' she said.

'From the police.'

Emma felt a little chill. 'The police are trying to find the man who attacked me. Why do we need protection from them?'

He gazed at her for a long moment without replying. 'The police are looking for an easy answer. I am that easy answer.'

'That's stupid. We just got married. We love each other.'

'You're rich. We have no prenup, remember?' he said. 'They see your money as a motive.'

'David, no. That's ridiculous. They can't blame you.'

'Emma, you read the paper. Innocent people get railroaded all the time. We have to avoid talking to the cops.'

She was trembling inside. 'But that seems wrong to me.'

'You need to be with me on this,' he said.

The door opened, and a grey-haired man wearing a white lab coat came in. He frowned at Emma. 'How are we doing here? Do you remember me? I'm Dr Bell. I took care of you last night.'

Emma blinked. 'I'm afraid I don't remember too much.'

'That's understandable. You were heavily sedated. I thought you'd like to know you can probably go home tomorrow.'

'Oh, that's great,' said David. 'Honey, that's great.'

'Getting around is going to be difficult for a while,' Dr Bell cautioned. 'You had over two hundred stitches.'

'I appreciate all you did for me. And my baby,' Emma said.

'That's my job,' he said, smiling. 'As for your recovery, the good news is that no ligaments or tendons were cut. I'll give you medication for pain, of course. Perfectly safe with the pregnancy, at the recommended dosage.'

Emma nodded.

'The nurse will show you how to change your dressings. And you have to be careful of the sutures. No heavy lifting. No driving. Restricted activities.' Dr Bell smiled. 'But all things considered, you were very lucky, young lady.'

First thing on Monday morning, Lieutenant Joan Atkins appeared at the Clarenceville police station. She introduced herself to the chief of police and waited while he summoned a young detective named Trey Marbery and assigned him to work with her on the investigation of the assault on Emma Webster.

'What am I taking you away from, Detective?' she asked.

The young man shrugged. 'My biggest case is a hit-and-run. A retired professor from Lambert University who got killed last spring. The perp hit him head-on and left the old guy to die. I haven't made much head-way though. I could use a change of pace.'

'Well, I'll keep you busy,' said Joan. 'I need someone who knows his way around this town.' As she briefed Marbery, she was favourably impressed by the young man's focused attention and intelligent questions. They walked out of the station house together.

'Where are we headed first?' he asked.

'Do you know where the Wrightsman Centre is?'

'Yes, ma'am,' said Marbery.

'Good. You drive,' said Joan.

The building that housed the crisis centre was a large grey-stone colonial house. Marbery parked in the gravel lot, and the two officers went to the front door. As Marbery pressed the bell, he observed, 'I was here a few months ago.'

'Really?' Joan asked. 'What for?'

'Dr Heisler's wife took a header off the bridge into the river.'

'Was it suspicious?'

Marbery shook his head. 'She was a poet. Very artsy and high-strung. She got into a depressive spiral, according to the interviews. Still, she didn't wash up right away, so we were keeping the pressure on the husband. But it was a suicide all right.'

A smiling Hispanic woman answered the bell and said that Dr Heisler was expecting them. 'I'll take you to his office,' she said.

They arrived at Dr Heisler's door, and the woman indicated that they should go in. Burke Heisler was waiting nervously. 'Detective Marbery,' he said grimly. 'We meet again.'

'Nice to see you again, sir,' Trey said politely. 'May I present Lieutenant Atkins of the state police.'

'Good to meet you, Lieutenant,' said Burke, shaking hands. 'Won't you have a seat?' The detectives each took a chair. 'How can I help you?' he asked. 'Anything I can do. Anything.'

'Mrs Webster told us that she was receiving mysterious notes at work,' said Joan. 'She kept them here. We'd like to see them.'

'My secretary can take you to her office,' said Burke.

Joan nodded to Trey. 'Can you take care of that?'

Burke called Geraldine on the intercom, and Marbery left the office to meet her in the reception area.

'Dr Webster told us that she showed you the notes,' Joan said.

Burke nodded. 'She did.'

'Was she concerned about them?'

Burke hesitated. 'They made her anxious, of course.'

'What about you? What did you think?'

Burke frowned. 'I knew there was a possibility of obsession, but generally speaking, the obsessed person doesn't remain hidden. He threatens the love object with harm if they refuse to reciprocate his feelings. These notes didn't fit the profile, because there are no threats in them. It's not the first time I've encountered this sort of acting out in a facility populated by highly emotional adolescents.'

'And there were no other incidents? Someone stalking her, peeping Tom, anything like that?' Joan asked.

'Not that I know of,' said Burke.

'I'll need a complete list of her patients.'

Burke nodded. 'I can get that for you. Lieutenant Atkins, there is one thing I feel I have to mention.'

'What's that?' Joan asked.

'Not long ago Emma was treating an anorexic patient, and the girl's parents took issue with her methods. They pulled the girl from the centre, and she died shortly thereafter of her disease. The girl's father was extremely angry at Emma. He came to me, demanding that she be fired.'

Joan raised an eyebrow. 'Mrs Webster didn't mention this.'

Burke sighed. 'She doesn't know about it. Emma's confidence was shaken by the girl's death as it was. And, in my judgment, she had acted appropriately.'

Joan nodded. 'The man's name?'

'Lyle Devlin. He's a music professor at Lambert. His daughter's name was Ivy. I need to be clear about this. I'm not accusing Mr Devlin of anything. But he was extremely angry at Emma.'

'I'll talk to him,' said Joan.

Marbery tapped on the door. 'Come in,' said Burke.

The young detective, wearing disposable gloves, brought a manila envelope to Joan, who, also donning gloves, pulled out the contents. Joan shuffled through the notes, reading certain phrases aloud.

'"In my dreams your face glows like a distant star. I try to fly to you. The pain is more than I can bear. How can you look through me and not see the secrets of my soul?" She seems to have inspired quite a passion in this guy,' Joan observed, replacing the notes. 'Tell me, Dr Heisler, you said that Mrs Webster is a personal friend.'

'She was my wife's college room-mate. As a matter of fact, I was the best man at Emma's wedding,' said Burke.

'Really? So you're friends with David Webster as well.'

'We're friends from childhood. My family owned a casino, and his mother was a waitress at one of the restaurants. I went away to private school, but when I was home, I used to hang around the restaurant kitchen, and sometimes David's mom would bring him with her to work. We became best buddies.'

'Did you ever have any reason to suspect Webster's motives in marrying Emma Hollis?'

'No, of course not. What are you talking about?'

Joan studied his reaction. 'Mrs Webster is a wealthy woman. If she died, her husband would inherit her money.'

'David? No. David doesn't care about money.'

'Doctor, if his mother worked as a waitress, I suspect he probably does. We haven't ruled out anything yet.'

'Well, you can forget about David,' Burke insisted. 'He would never hurt Emma. David is crazy about her.'

Joan glanced at the envelope in her hand. 'Is that an observation,' she asked, 'or a diagnosis?'

5

EMMA PRESSED HER forehead against the passenger window of David's Jeep Cherokee. It was a gloomy November afternoon, the bare tree branches etched against the smoky grey sky. The air had a restorative tang after the medicinal stuffiness of the hospital.

The two hundred stitches Emma had received had made it impossible to move without pain for the first twenty-four hours. Now, two days later, it was merely very difficult. A physical therapist had visited her room and showed her how to use a cane, to minimise the pressure on her left side. But when David had pulled the car up to the hospital entrance, she had nearly started to cry, wondering how she was going to manage climbing into the high front seat of the SUV. He had gone round to the trunk and pulled out a plastic milk crate, which he kept as a boost for his mother. Still, Emma knew that physical restrictions would be the least of her worries. There would be other woes, more taxing by far.

She was lucky to be alive, lucky to have escaped, lucky that her baby was still safe inside her. She knew she should be grateful. But she was plagued by melancholy. A maniac, who was still on the loose, had attacked her, and a good man had lost his life trying to save her. She had always known that there was random violence in the world, but being its victim was something else altogether.

'Almost home,' said David.

She turned to him and forced herself to smile. 'I'll be glad to get back to our house,' she said. 'To our own bed.'

'Well, you're not going to be able to make those stairs for a few days, maybe longer. You heard the doctor. I'll make up the bed for you downstairs.' They had a guest room off the kitchen. David had his computer and his files in there and had claimed it for his office.

'But I don't want to disrupt your workspace.'

'It's only temporary,' he said. 'I don't mind.'

'All right, as long as you sleep downstairs with me.'

'I'm not sure that's a good idea. I'd be afraid of hurting you. I don't want to take a chance of opening up those stitches.'

'I don't want to be by myself. I'm afraid, all right?'

'No one's going to hurt you, honey. Whoever it was who attacked you is probably still in the Pine Barrens, looking for some other victim. There's nothing to be afraid of. It'll be all right—'

'It's not all right!' Emma cried. 'Aren't I allowed to be afraid? Who wouldn't be after something like this?'

'I'm sorry. Of course you are,' David said. 'Take it easy.'

'I just can't do it by myself,' she insisted.

'I get it, Em. I understand. Maybe I can put up a cot.'

Emma forced herself to take a deep breath. 'I'm sorry,' she said. 'I'm being a baby.'

He reached over and put a reassuring hand on hers. 'Hey, you lived through a nightmare. But once we get home, everything will feel better. Just try to relax.'

Emma looked out of the window at the quiet streets of Clarenceville. She pictured their house in her mind's eye. Alone at the end of a wooded cul-de-sac, it was only a rental, but she had fallen in love with its Arts and Crafts style, its wide mahogany woodwork that contrasted with the ecru stucco-like walls, and its patterned windows of pale stained glass. The William Morris fabrics and leather mission-style antiques they'd bought suited it perfectly.

She closed her eyes and rested her head against the headrest. Home. She would feel better once she got home.

'Oh, hell,' David said.

He had turned the corner onto their street. Emma opened her eyes. 'What?' she asked. They had reached their secluded road and were headed for their house, but instead of seeing their peaceful haven at the end of the street, they saw an assortment of haphazardly parked vehicles on either side of the road and a crowd milling at the edge of their front lawn. Reporters with microphones had assembled, waiting for them.

She felt her anxiety mount. 'What are we going to do?'

Almost as if in answer, the reporters began to surge towards them. David continued driving slowly, not looking at the people who were swarming around the car, shouting questions at them. Emma turned her face from the glass as he inched along.

A TV news van was blocking the driveway. David started to lower the window to call to the driver, but a microphone was instantly shoved into the gap. He raised the window as the reporter protested loudly, then he pressed down on the horn. Emma clapped her hands over her ears.

The driver of the van finally backed up just enough to let David pull in. 'Oh, great, look who's here,' David said, parking and pointing to a car already parked in their driveway. 'That's Rory's rental car from the airport.'

'Oh,' said Emma, trying to sound surprised. But she wasn't really surprised. Her mother had rarely left her hospital room.

David was swearing under his breath. 'Stay right there,' he said. 'I'll come and get you. They can't come onto our property, so just ignore the yelling.' He slammed the door and pressed the remote to lock it. He walked round to her passenger door.

When Emma opened the door and slid out, grabbing his hand, she felt a searing pain in her leg and her side. She set her cane on the ground and leaned against it.

'Emma, how are you feeling?' a woman cried.

'Emma, do you know who the Pine Barrens killer is?' a bespectacled man holding a microphone cried out.

'What about you, Dave?' cried another man. 'You have any comment about who tried to murder your wife?'

Emma glanced at David and saw that he was smouldering.

'Where were you when it happened, Dave?' another called out.

The front door to the house opened, and Rory, dressed in a green golf shirt and khakis, appeared on the doorstep. 'All right. That's enough,' he bellowed at the assembled reporters. 'This woman is injured. You people gather up your junk and get out.'

David steered Emma up the path and into the house. Kay, who was waiting just inside the front door, held out her arms and carefully hugged her daughter.

'Please, Kay, let her sit down,' said David.

Kay's eyes flashed at her son-in-law, but she released her daughter. They went into the living room and David helped Emma to the sofa.

'Dave, you can't let those people walk all over you,' Rory said.

David did not reply. 'I'm getting your bags,' he told Emma.

'Emma, you poor kid,' said Rory. 'You look awful.'

'I'm just sore,' said Emma irritably. 'It'll pass.'

Kay, in a taupe Calvin Klein trouser-suit, sat down beside Emma and massaged her hand between her own.

'Oh, Mom, everything hurts,' said Emma. Stress and weariness had caught up with her. Tears rolled down her cheeks. They seemed to come and go without warning.

'Oh, my poor baby,' said Kay.

'What are you doing here?' Emma asked. That morning at the hospital, David had quickly quashed Kay's plan to stay and take care of her daughter. 'I thought you were going back to Chicago.'

'We were,' said Kay. 'We are. But I wanted to make sure you were safely home. And I remembered that your wedding presents were still at the inn. So we brought them over.' She pointed to the wrapped and beribboned boxes piled in front of the hearth.

'Thanks, Mom. That was thoughtful,' said Emma.

David came back into the house, carrying the bags. Emma gave him a wan smile as he mounted the stairs. Then she put a hand on her stomach and closed her eyes.

'Honey, can I get you a cup of tea?' Kay asked.

'I'm fine,' Emma said.

Rory came over and perched on the edge of the armchair across from

Emma. 'You're not fine,' he said in a low voice. 'From what the doctors told your mother, it's a miracle you're still alive.'

'Actually, I'm alive because Claude Mathis came to my rescue. And got killed for his kindness.' Emma shook her head. 'I want to do something for his family. He has a teenage son. I want you to arrange for some financial support for the boy. Just move it from one of my investment accounts.'

'There will be plenty of time for that when you're feeling better,' said Rory in a placating tone.

'That family is suffering. Please take care of it,' Emma insisted.

'All right,' said Rory. 'All right. Consider it done.'

Kay rubbed her tanned, well-manicured hands together. 'Emma, Rory and I think it might be best if you came home with us, to Chicago, where we can take care of you.'

'This is my home. I'm fine right here, Mom,' Emma said.

Kay and Rory exchanged a glance.

'What?' Emma asked indignantly. 'What's the look for?'

'Nothing. I'd just feel safer if you were with us,' Kay said.

'David will take care of me,' said Emma.

'We don't know David that well,' said Kay.

'He's my husband, Mother,' Emma said in a sharp tone.

'Let me tell you something from a man's perspective,' Rory said. 'A lot of men don't view pregnancy the same way women do. They start thinking about when they were free and irresponsible. Maybe your husband had second thoughts about this marriage.'

Emma's mouth dropped open. 'What are you saying?'

'I'm just telling you what the police are saying,' said Rory.

'How dare you?' said Emma. 'You, of all people.'

Rory stared at her without flinching. Kay did not seem to notice. She reached for Emma's wrist. Emma made a fist. 'Come home, Em,' Kay crooned. 'Stay with us until they've made an arrest. It will give me a chance to fuss over you.'

'We just want to protect you, Emma,' Rory insisted.

'I'm not going anywhere. I don't need your protection.'

'Sweetheart,' Kay protested. 'You were nearly killed.'

'By some maniac in the Pinelands!' Emma cried. 'Not by my husband.'

Kay's eyes glistened. 'Oh, please, honey. Let me help you.'

David came down the stairs and glared at Kay and Rory. 'We don't need your help. Pardon me for eavesdropping, but I don't appreciate being slandered in my own home.'

'David,' said Emma. 'My mother didn't mean any harm.'

'Do you agree with them? Do you want to go with them?' he cried. 'I mean, if you think they're right, then go ahead.'

Rory stood up stiffly. 'Kay, I think we should be going.'

'Sweetie, please,' Kay pleaded. 'At least hire a nurse who can take care of you.'

'I can take care of her,' David insisted.

'That's right, Mom,' said Emma. 'I don't need anyone else.'

Kay's eyes welled with tears, and she reached out, but Emma stiffened. 'I'll be worrying night and day. Darling, please call.'

'I'll be fine,' Emma whispered. 'Go on.'

Emma did not watch them leave. She couldn't bear to see the anguish in her mother's eyes.

David followed them to the door and locked it. He came back into the living room. 'Where are the sheets?' he asked, avoiding her worried gaze. 'I'm going to make the bed down here.'

'I'm sorry about that, David. My mother's just so afraid.'

'Upstairs linen closet?' he asked.

'Yes,' she said. 'Are you mad at me?'

'No!' he barked. Then his face softened. 'No. You rest.'

Emma leaned back against the sofa. David was right. Even if they were worried about her, her mother and Rory had no business coming here and virtually accusing him. Especially Rory. His self-righteousness made her furious. She was clenching her fists so tight that her fingernails were gouging her palms. Stop ruminating about this. Think about something else, she told herself.

She turned her head and looked at the mountain of wedding gifts. She knew she should be thrilled at all the thoughtfulness. These people cared about her. She had been aware of their support in the hospital. The flowers, the cards, the brief visits. She reached for the nearest, smallest box and began to untie the ribbon.

There was no card, but she unfolded the gold-and-white paper and saw that the box came from Kellerman's, an upscale housewares and jewellery store on Main Street. The box wasn't heavy. A silver-plated egg timer, she thought with a hint of amusement. She lifted the lid, and as she did, an odd, unpleasant smell reached her nostrils. As she was pulling out the paper shavings, she realised that she was making a mistake. But it was too late.

Nestled on a cushion of paper shavings was a silver dish in the shape of a scallop shell. Resting in the dish was the matted fur and stiffened body of a mouse, now dead, its tail curved to fit in the box, its beady eyes still open.

The sound of a piano being expertly played drifted through an open window of the white, Gothic-style Victorian cottage. A Mazda convertible sat in the driveway behind a minivan. Lieutenant Joan Atkins knocked on the front door and waited, with Trey Marbery by her side. In a moment a large blonde woman opened the door. Her heavily mascaraed eyes were a dazzling blue, and her lips were full. She was wearing a nearly sheer voile blouse that revealed an impressive décolletage, and tight jeans that were unflattering to her spreading figure.

'Morning,' she said in a sweet, high voice.

'Mrs Devlin?' Lieutenant Atkins asked.

'That's me,' she said. Her voice was slightly slurred, but she did not smell of alcohol. And her eyes were unfocused. Tranquillisers or sleeping pills, Joan thought, not unkindly. A bereaved mother might well need pharmaceuticals to get through the day.

'I'm Lieutenant Atkins of the state police. This is Detective Marbery of the Clarenceville police. We're looking for your husband.'

The woman's eyes widened. 'Why? What's the matter?'

'We have a few routine questions. Is your husband here?'

'Yes. He's working in his study. He's writing music.'

'Before I speak to him,' said Joan, 'can you tell me, Mrs Devlin, where your husband was Saturday night?'

The woman looked confused. 'What?'

'It's a simple question.'

'Saturday night? I don't remember.' Joan could see she was earnestly searching her mind. 'My memory,' she apologised.

The piano music stopped, and the dark figure of a man appeared in the corridor behind her. 'Risa, who's at the door?' he demanded.

The woman frowned. 'Two police officers. They want to know where you were Saturday night.'

The man was in his forties, with stubbly black hair sprinkled with grey, and wire-rimmed glasses. He was wearing a leather vest and a black turtleneck. 'We rented that Italian movie, remember?'

She squinted. 'That's right. You were here.'

'What's this about?' Devlin asked.

'Professor Devlin?' Joan said. 'I'm Lieutenant Atkins of the state police. This is Detective Marbery. May we talk to you?'

'All right,' Lyle Devlin said. 'Follow me. Excuse us, Risa. Come on into the conservatory. I'm composing on the piano.'

Joan and Trey followed the man to a chilly glassed-in room with shabby wicker furniture, shelves of books and sheet music, and a large piano. 'No classes today?' Joan asked.

'The university understands that I need time for my own work,' said Devlin with a thin smile. 'Have a seat.' They sat down, and he faced them on the piano bench. 'Now, what can I do for you? Why in the world would you be concerned about my whereabouts last Saturday?'

'Mr Devlin, you had a daughter named Ivy who died recently?' Joan asked.

Devlin straightened. 'Why are you asking me about Ivy?'

'I'm sorry to bring up a painful subject, but apparently you felt that Ivy's psychologist may have been partly to blame for her death. Dr Webster. She used to be called Dr Hollis.'

'Oh, right. She was the one who was attacked in the Pine Barrens.'

Joan studied Devlin. 'There was an attempt on Dr Webster's life. She narrowly escaped death.'

'What has this got to do with Ivy?' Devlin asked.

'We have information that you were very angry at Dr Webster after your daughter's death. Threats were made.'

The man's expression became stony. 'Who told you that?'

'Is it true?'

Lyle Devlin looked away from the detective. 'I may have vented my anger,' he said. 'I was out of my mind with grief.'

'Why did you blame Dr Webster?' Joan asked.

Devlin stared out at the bare trees in the back yard. Then he looked back at Joan. 'Detective, do you have any children?'

Joan pursed her lips. She did not like Lyle Devlin. It wasn't rational, it was visceral, but this question really peeved her. Suspects who over-estimated their own cunning always tried to get her on their side with a variation of it. You and me, Detective, aren't we both . . . fill in the blank . . . parents, working people, dog-lovers? 'Why did you blame her, Mr Devlin?'

Arms crossed over his chest, Devlin sighed. 'How can I explain this, Lieutenant? Anorexia is a special kind of hell for a parent. A child who refuses to eat. My wife cooked every kind of treat, coaxed and cajoled her. Tried everything. We brought her to Dr Hollis out of desperation. It's true that I did blame her, but I needed someone to blame.'

'But your daughter must have been ill for quite some time. Surely she saw other doctors,' Trey interjected.

Devlin took a deep breath. 'You're right. But Dr Webster was the last doctor. We took Ivy out of the centre because we found Dr Webster's methods unacceptable. My daughter's condition worsened, and she was admitted to the hospital too late.'

'I'm so sorry,' said Trey sincerely.

'But you no longer hold Dr Webster responsible?' said Joan.

Devlin looked at her directly. 'My daughter died of anorexia, and I was not able to prevent it. I blame myself for that.'

Clearly, Devlin had come to terms with his own behaviour and could explain it in a most cogent fashion. But that resentment of Emma Webster was still there, not far below the *mea culpa*. Joan would bet her badge on it.

'So you maintain that you were home here Saturday night between the hours of, say, six and ten o'clock?'

Devlin glowered. 'I was at home. My wife told you that.'

After you told her what to say, Joan thought. She stood up, and Trey followed suit. 'All right, thank you for your time.'

Devlin rose stiffly from the bench. 'My wife takes tranquillisers. Ivy's death nearly destroyed her. Sometimes, because of the medication, she forgets things,' he said.

Joan and Trey walked to the front door. Risa Devlin emerged from one of the rooms and opened it for them.

'Is everything all right?' she asked.

Joan nodded. 'Sorry to bother you.'

'It's no bother. As long as everything's all right.'

Trey followed Joan out of the door, and they crossed the road. 'What did you think?' he asked as he aimed the remote to unlock the doors of his car.

Joan gazed back at the little house. The piano chords had not resumed. 'I think he's hiding something,' she said.

The chime of the doorbell woke Emma from a dream that she was being chased. She groaned as consciousness brought back the pain of her injuries. She had slept little, and badly, during the night. The bed quivered as David got up from the cot he had set up beside her. She reached out a hand to touch him, but he was already out of the room. Emma closed her eyes again. As she lay there, she couldn't help thinking of the box she had opened last night, with its repulsive contents. David had nearly fallen down the stairs rushing to reach her when she'd cried out for him. Grimacing with distaste, he had taken the box, carried the dead creature outside, and thrown it away in the woods behind the house. He had tossed the box and silver dish in the outdoor garbage can. Don't think about it, he told her when he came back into the house. Easier said than done.

David reappeared in the doorway of their makeshift bedroom, barefoot, and wearing only his pyjama pants. He was frowning.

'Who was it?' Emma asked.

'Your nurse,' he said. 'She's waiting in the hall.'

'My nurse? What nurse?'

David glanced behind him. 'The private duty nurse your mother and stepfather hired to take care of you. She's got an ID badge, and all her paperwork, including written orders from Rory for her to show up here and only talk to you.'

Emma pulled her robe around her. 'Let me speak to her.'

David turned and gestured to the nurse to join them. 'I'm going upstairs to throw on some clothes,' he said. 'Send her on her way. We don't need some stranger here, Emma.'

He stepped out of the doorway, and a small woman with short greying hair took his place. She was wearing sneakers, jeans and a sweatshirt, and had a rucksack over her shoulder. 'Good morning, Mrs Webster,' she said, unsmiling. 'I'm Lizette Slocum.'

'Nice to meet you. But I think there's been a misunderstanding,' said Emma. 'I mean, I didn't know you were coming.'

The older woman had a cool, steady gaze. 'I'm a private duty nurse. Your parents hired me to stay with you.'

'Well, I'm not really sick,' Emma said.

'For your protection. I have a black belt in tae kwon do.'

'Protection? My husband is here!'

David returned to the room. 'Have we straightened this out?'

'Mrs Slocum . . .' said Emma.

'It's Lizette. Call me Lizette.'

'Lizette, could you wait in the other room for a minute? I need to talk to my husband.'

Lizette obediently withdrew, but before they could confer, the telephone on the desk rang. David picked it up and barked an irritable 'Hello.' Then his whole demeanour changed.

'Nevin, how's it going?' he said in the false tone he always used when he spoke to Nevin McGoldrick, the editor of *Slicker*. 'The wedding was fine. Everything's fine. What's up?'

Fine? Emma thought.

David hesitated a fraction of a second. 'Oh, right. I was distracted by all the excitement here.' Then he said, 'Sure . . . Great. I'll be there. Bye.'

David punched the OFF button. 'That was Nevin. Giving me details about my interview with Bob Cheatham, that LA producer.'

Emma stared at him anxiously. 'When is it?'

'Actually, it's today. He wants me to run up to New York and meet this guy for lunch, and then I'll be right back.'

'You're going to leave me alone here?' she cried.

'No, of course not. Maybe Birdie can come over. Leave my mother for a little while.' ·

'Birdie? She's a frail old lady. What's she going to do if he comes back?' Emma cried.

'Who? The guy with the ski mask? Honey, look, he's some nut who picked you at random. We can't be afraid to live our lives.'

'You don't know that. I could be a target. What about all those notes I got? And that disgusting wedding present. It could all be the same person. You're not the one who was attacked.'

'You don't have to remind me of that,' he said quietly.

Emma looked at him balefully. 'David, couldn't Nevin get someone else? Doesn't he know what happened?'

David ran his hand over his unruly hair. 'I guess we didn't make the news in New York. If it didn't happen there, it didn't happen.'

'Why didn't you say anything? I was almost killed.'

'I'll tell him about it,' said David. 'But Nevin's not interested in my problems. He's interested in my getting this interview.'

'But today? Does it have to be today?'

'Believe me, I would rather not do it today. But the guy is only going to be in New York for a day or two.'

'Well, fine. You go then,' she said petulantly. 'And I'll tell Lizette Slocum that I need her to stay here after all. At least she knows something about self-defence. It's a good thing my mother was concerned about me.'

David frowned at her. 'What does that mean? That I'm not?'

Emma ignored his protest. 'I think I am going to call Lieutenant Atkins and tell her about the . . . wedding gift. I had nightmares all night about opening that box. The police need to know about this.'

'But, baby, you know what Mr Yunger said. I thought we agreed we were not going to talk to the police.'

Emma stared at him. 'I never agreed. I have to call them.'

'Emma, they're not looking at anybody else but me.'

'Well, this will give them somewhere else to look,' she insisted. Then she hesitated. 'Do you hear water running?'

David looked out of the door. Lizette had found a watering can under the sink and was filling it. He shook his head and turned back to Emma. 'Lizette is watering the plants.'

'They do need it,' Emma said. She extended a hand to him, but he did not reach for it. She pulled it back. 'David, the wedding present may have fingerprints that could help the police.'

'Do what you have to do,' he said. 'I'm going to get ready.'

Stung by his rebuff, Emma pulled herself up and eased her bandaged leg out of the bed. Every movement was torture.

'Just a minute,' said David. 'What are you doing?'

'I need to get my pills,' she said.

'I'll get your pills for you,' he said.

'I don't want to depend on you,' she said stubbornly.

He stared at her for a long minute. 'Thanks, Emma. That's just great.'

6

AUDIE OSMUND'S stiff joints told him what the dark, lowering sky also portended. A storm was on its way. The wind whipped leaves around the desolate clearing where the Zamskys' cabin stood. The crime scene tape was still up, but Audie batted it away like a pesky fly. He climbed the steps, opened the cabin door, and grimaced as he looked around the blood-splattered room.

He kept returning to this place, walking through the crime in his mind. Claude Mathis's funeral was tomorrow, and Audie was no closer to an arrest.

Audie didn't see a lot of killings in his part of the Pine Barrens. Last year a guy got drunk in a bar and shot his cousin. And two domestic disturbances had ended in homicide in the last few years. Well, three, if you counted Shannon O'Brien, the pretty little Irish girl who disappeared one night after working her shift at a local gas station. Her boyfriend, a known drug user, had an alibi, and Audie couldn't disprove it, but he was sure that was not a random killing. It was true that people around here didn't like strangers, and sometimes they'd wave a gun around and holler, but nothing like this.

The floor behind him creaked. Audie reached for his gun.

'Don't shoot!' protested a female voice.

Audie whirled round and stared at the woman in the doorway. She had washed-out skin with no make-up, short black hair, and was dressed in a plaid shirt, jeans and muck boots. Outside the door, Audie saw a large bay horse tied to a tree.

'Excuse me,' she said, 'but I saw the car. Aren't you Chief Osmund?'

Audie frowned at her. 'I'm Chief Osmund. Who are you?'

'My name's Donna Tuttle. My son and I live in the old Fiore house. We're the next house over the rise.' The woman stepped into the cabin. Audie put up a hand to stop her, but he was too late.

'Oh my God!' she cried out. 'Those poor people.'

Audie sighed and looked back into the blood-splattered room. 'Why don't we step outside?' he said grimly, helping her down the steps. 'It isn't pretty.'

Donna Tuttle took a deep breath. 'Usually I got a pretty strong stomach. My husband was a hunter, you know.' Her gaze drifted. 'He always planned to retire here. Butch was a fireman up in Trenton. He got killed fightin' a fire when a roof collapsed on him.'

'I'm very sorry,' said Audie sincerely.

'You know, if he had retired when he was eligible, he wouldn't have even been in that building. He already had twenty-five years on the job when it happened. Of course, he started really young. We were just kids when we got married and he joined the department.'

Audie nodded patiently. 'Mrs Tuttle, you say you're the next house over. Were you there Saturday night?'

Donna Tuttle nodded eagerly. 'I sure was. My boy and I were both home. One of your officers came and questioned us. A nice young man named uh . . . Roberts, maybe?'

'Revere. Gene Revere,' said Audie.

'That's right. He didn't tell us what happened, of course. He just wanted to know if we'd seen or heard anything.'

'And did ya? Anyone lurking around? Strange noises?'

'No, I sure didn't. We didn't even hear the shots. The wind must have been blowing in the other direction. We heard the police, of course. Can't miss all those sirens.'

Audie sighed. 'No, I guess not.'

'But I paid attention to the news about it. That's why I stopped when I saw your car. The radio had a recap this morning because of that hunter's funeral tomorrow, and that got me thinking.'

'About what?' Audie asked.

'Well, the reporter said that the couple had come here for a honeymoon weekend, that the husband hadn't visited this place since boyhood.'

'That's right,' said Audie.

'Well, a few months ago, I can't remember if it was late spring, early summer. There was flies, so it could have been summer—'

'What about it?' Audie interrupted impatiently. This woman could talk a hole through a pot.

'We ride by here all the time. Usually the place is empty.'

'Right,' Audie prodded.

'But this one time there was a guy here. Naturally I didn't want to be rude, so I said "Hey" and remarked about the weather. I asked him if he bought the place. And he said no, that the place belonged to his uncle.'

Audie felt a shiver of interest. 'His uncle? Are you sure?'

'Yeah,' said Donna. 'So when I heard that on the radio this morning about him not being here since he was a kid, I thought . . . that's strange.'

'He told us he hadn't been here in years,' said Audie. 'Of course, this Webster has a brother out west somewhere. Did he introduce himself?'

Donna Tuttle grimaced. 'He did, but I'm not much for names.'

'Would you be willing to come down to the police station and look at some pictures?'

'Sure. I can do that. Sure.'

'Let me speak to this man again. See if he continues to deny being here.'

'Well,' said Donna. 'I didn't know if I should even bother you with this, 'cause it was such a small thing, but when I saw your car going by I thought I'd follow you and tell you. Just in case.'

'Thank you, Mrs Tuttle. Thank you very much.'

'Glad I could help,' she said. She untied the horse and hoisted herself up on its back. 'I hope you get him.'

'Oh, we will,' said Audie, and his heart felt lighter than it had in a while. 'By the way, was he alone when you saw him?'

Donna Tuttle shrugged. 'I didn't see anybody, but now you mention it, I have a feeling there was a somebody with him. I don't know why.'

After David left, Lizette did a careful, thorough job of changing Emma's bandages, all the while recounting the story of her life. She explained that her husband died in a car wreck when she was twenty-five, and she'd never remarried or had kids. She was new to the area. She lived alone, liked her independence, and was hoping someday to retire to the Florida Keys. At Emma's request, she went upstairs and retrieved some clothes for her, in case Emma felt like getting dressed.

Too weary to read, Emma sat up, numbly watching morning talk shows on television while Lizette worked around her, straightening up and dusting the house. The pain medication soon sent Emma back to bed for a nap. When she woke up, Lizette prepared her lunch, then said that she was going to change the beds.

'We only slept on those sheets for one night,' Emma said. 'It's not necessary.'

'Let me be the judge of that,' Lizette said. She disappeared into the guest room and emerged with her arms full of sheets. 'Where's your washer?'

'In the basement. I wish you wouldn't do all this.'

'I don't like to sit idly,' Lizette said.

The energetic Lizette descended the stairs to the laundry area. Emma sighed and began to hobble around the house in her bathrobe. She looked out of every window at the ominous sky, clutching in her hand a slip of paper with the phone number of the police department on it. As soon as David had walked out, she had looked up the number and written it down.

She understood that David felt under siege, unfairly targeted by the police. But he was turning it into a test of her loyalty. And ultimately, she knew she had to put her own safety first. And that of her baby. Still, several times she picked up the phone and then replaced it. She knew how betrayed he would feel if she went to the police behind his back.

But Emma felt sure that the evidence on that gift box could be important. This might help to clear your husband, she reassured herself as she dialled the number, only to learn that Lieutenant Atkins was not at the station. Emma gave the receptionist her information, then hung up the phone. Now I wait, she thought.

Over and over, her thoughts returned to the horrific wedding gift. The longer it sat out in the trash can, the more likely it was that the evidence would be contaminated. It might be destroyed altogether if it rained and the lid was loose. She pushed herself to her feet. Get dressed, she thought. It'll make you feel more in control.

She ran a comb through her hair and looped it into a knot at the nape of her neck. She examined her face in the bathroom mirror, then dabbed some make-up on the dark circles around her eyes and put on some lipstick. Then she put on the black V-necked jersey dress made in a wide A-line style that she had bought for late in her pregnancy. It was voluminous and didn't press on her wounds.

She walked to the back door and opened it. Lizette's voice drifted up the cellar steps. 'Everything all right?'

'Yes. Fine,' Emma said in a cranky tone.

With the aid of her cane, she walked outside to the garbage can, lifted the plastic lid, and removed the Kellerman's box containing the silver shell dish. Just as David had said, the mouse was gone. Then, as she turned to walk back inside, she had an idea. Perhaps, she thought, just perhaps, if they were armed with more information, she could convince David that it was in his best interests for both of them to speak to the police. And there was a way to obtain more information. It would not be easy, but it was possible.

She looked longingly down the driveway at her car. Lizette's brown Toyota had blocked her in. She wasn't allowed to drive anyway, and she really wasn't supposed to leave the house today. A taxi would be a reasonable compromise.

Back inside, she called the cab company. Then she slipped the Kellerman's box into a paper sack and went to the hall closet for her coat. It felt unbearably heavy and constricting over her flayed skin. For a minute she was stymied. Then she remembered the soft blue-green alpaca cape that Rory had given her last Christmas. It hung in the office closet. Emma limped towards the door of the office—now her bedroom—wondering if Lizette was still in the basement.

As she reached for the knob, Lizette pulled it open from inside. Emma let out a little cry.

'I was just making up your beds,' Lizette said. 'Now you can lie down and rest. I'm going to vacuum.'

'Fine,' Emma said. Vacuuming. Good, she thought. The roar of the vacuum would cover up the sounds of her leaving the house. She went across to the closet, found the cape, and put it round her shoulders. She walked over to the desktop and wrote a note that read DO NOT DISTURB. She could hear the loud whine of the vacuum cleaner from the back of the house.

Emma taped the sign to the office door, closed the door behind her, and let herself out of the house. The taxi was idling out front. She slid gingerly into the back seat, resisting the urge to cry out from pain.

'I want to go to Kellerman's. On Main Street,' she said. 'And I'll need you to wait for me while I'm inside.'

The pretty young clerk at Kellerman's wrinkled her nose in distaste. 'What happened to the box?' she asked.

'It got thrown in the garbage by accident,' said Emma.

'It smells like it,' said the clerk, looking down at the stained box, which was sitting on top of the glass display case that served as a counter.

'It was a bit chaotic after the wedding,' Emma said. 'There's no card. I need to know who bought me the gift so I can thank them.'

'The box looks kind of old,' the clerk observed doubtfully. 'I mean, ours are much brighter.' She reached under the counter for a gleaming white box. 'See?'

'You're right,' said Emma. 'This one is a little bit yellowed.' She lifted the lid.

The clerk reached in gingerly and took out the silver scallop-shell dish. She studied it for a minute and then shook her head. 'We don't carry these.'

'Well, it did come from this store,' said Emma.

'Maybe they bought it somewhere else and pretended it came from Kellerman's. People do that, you know. They buy at Wal-Mart and then put it in a Kellerman's box.'

'This dish is silver. It did not come from Wal-Mart.'

'Well, you know what I mean. Some discount place.'

Emma felt suddenly weary. 'You're sure you don't carry a dish like this? Did you ever carry a dish like this?'

The girl called out to a bald man with a bow tie who was dusting crystal with a feather duster. 'Harvey, did we ever carry a silver dish like this?' She held the scallop shell aloft.

'Oh yes,' the man said. 'We carried those for years. We stopped stocking them maybe a year ago. Where did it come from?'

'I received it as a gift,' said Emma. 'There was no card.'

The man sniffed. 'I'm afraid you were . . . regifted, if you know what I mean.'

Emma nodded. 'All right. Thanks for your help.' She put the dish back in the box and deposited the box into her paper sack. Leaning on her cane, she slowly made her way to the front door of the store, then managed to get herself back into the taxi.

On the way home, Emma prepared her excuse. She expected that Lizette would be miffed if she had discovered her charge had left the house. But as the cab pulled up and she paid the driver, she noticed, to her surprise, that Lizette's brown Toyota was not in the driveway.

Emma painfully made her way to the front door and opened it, as the empty cab sped away up the street. 'Lizette,' she called out. 'Lizette?' But there was no answer. The house was silent. All she could hear was the wind whistling outside, whipping the trees. She locked the door behind her, telling herself aloud that there was nothing to be afraid of. She turned on the lights in the living room, wishing David were back.

She looked around for a note from Lizette. There was nothing. Lizette's rucksack was nowhere to be seen. The door to the office was ajar, and Emma's heart leapt unpleasantly. The DO NOT DISTURB sign had been ripped away, its ragged corners still fastened with tape. Lizette must have torn it off in frustration when she realised that Emma had sneaked out of the house. Emma's gaze swept the narrow hallway, and she saw the wadded paper on the floor. She bent slowly and awkwardly to pick it up and smoothed out the handwritten sign. Her face flamed to think of the anger her escape had obviously provoked.

Emma knew she was to blame, and she didn't want to think about it. David, she thought, when will you get back? Part of her felt childishly angry at him for not being there with her. Lizette had departed, and now she was all alone. She could feel her heart thumping and hated the sensation.

How long did she have to wait here by herself? She felt an over-whelming urge to call David. Emma moved to the desk and tried the number of his cellphone, but it was turned off. Of course it was. She knew he would turn it off during the interview. Could they still be at the restaurant at this hour?

Nevin would know how to reach him. But David wouldn't want Nevin involved in their personal business. He had made that clear enough. And then she thought, The hell with Nevin. I need to get in touch with my husband. She knew that David had Nevin's private number in his address book. She scanned the messy desktop but did not see it. It was probably in the desk drawer. She pulled the handle without thinking and met resistance.

Is something stuck? she wondered. She pulled on the drawer from beneath, with both hands. It did not budge. It was locked. What has he got that he needs to lock away? The thought made her feel irritable on top of her anxiety. She rattled the handle impatiently. Forget the drawer. It's none of your business.

The phone rang at her elbow. She jumped at the unexpected ring. Picking it up, she punched the button to receive the call. 'Hello?' she said.

There was silence at the other end. She could hear breathing.

'Hello? Who is this?' she demanded. Emma heard a click, and the call was over.

There was someone there, she thought. Why wouldn't they answer? Suddenly she no longer felt safe in the little bedroom. The ringing phone. The locked drawer. The nurse mysteriously gone. The wind was rising, and branches from the bushes outside flailed at the window-pane. She wondered if all the windows in the house were locked, but the prospect of going round to every window seemed like more than she was physically capable of doing.

I need help, she thought frantically. Her mind raced, thinking of the people she knew. She dialled Stephanie's number and got the machine. Maybe she's still at school, Emma thought. It took her a moment to remember the number of the school. But the secretary there said that Stephanie had left an hour ago.

Emma slammed down the phone in frustration. Part of her wanted to collapse in a sobbing heap. She tried to focus on her sensible side. You have to try to make sure the windows are locked, she thought. Anyone could come in. The thought propelled her from the chair, and she limped out to the kitchen, tears drizzling down her face. David, why aren't you with me? She shuffled over to the sink and leaned up to check the window. Just as she reached for the latch, she heard a loud crack above her head. She whirled round, her heart pounding.

Someone in the house. Upstairs. They got in. She imagined the man in the ski mask starting down the stairs. Emma lurched across to the phone and punched in 911.

The operator put the call out for a patrol car right away, telling Emma the officer was not far from her and to look out of her window. She approached the glass to try to see outside. All of a sudden there was a flashing light in her driveway and, a moment later, a knock at her door.

Emma hobbled to the peephole, still clutching the phone receiver. A young patrolman stood on her front step. She let him in.

'Thank you, officer. Thank you for getting here so quickly.'

'That's all right, ma'am,' he said. 'You think there's someone in the house?'

'Yes, upstairs. Be careful,' Emma said, following him into the living room.

The young man flipped the light switch at the foot of the stairs and began to climb up. Emma's heart was pounding in her chest. The shrill blast of the phone in her hand made her cry out. She pressed the button and barked, 'Who is it?'

'Emma?' said a worried voice. 'It's Burke.'

Emma let out a sigh. 'Burke. Oh, thank God.'

'What's the matter? Are you OK?'

'No. I have the police here. There's someone in the house.'

'Where's David?' he demanded.

'David's not here,' said Emma.

Burke was silent for a moment. 'I'll be there in no time.'

'Thank you,' Emma whispered, but he had already hung up.

'Ma'am?' The officer appeared at the upstairs landing. 'The bathroom window is open, and the door was shut,' he said.

Emma shook her head. 'I don't understand. Did someone come in the window? I heard a loud cracking sound.'

'There's no one here,' he said. 'But there is a lot of wind out there. Sometimes the wind will blow a door shut.'

Emma was silent, but her face flamed. She slumped down into a living-room chair. 'I'm so sorry,' she said. 'I shouldn't have bothered you. I'm sorry.'

7

RAIN BEAT AGAINST the large casement windows in Burke Heisler's kitchen, but Emma did not fear its fury. Seated in a club chair, with her feet up on the ottoman and a glass of sparkling water in her hand, Emma finally began to feel relaxed. When Burke had arrived at her house, he had offered to order some food and wait there with her until David came home. But Emma was overcome by a suffocating feeling of claustrophobia and the desire to be anywhere but in her own house. Burke suggested that they leave a note for David and go to his place, where he could throw some dinner together for them and Emma could rest.

'I'm sorry about all this, Burke,' she said. 'I feel like the girl who cried wolf. My nerves are shot.'

'Don't worry about it. I'm just glad I could help.'

Burke stood facing her at his kitchen island, sipping at a glass of wine as he stirred the pasta on the stove. Fragrant sauce was bubbling on a nearby burner. He was wearing a silly butcher's apron that read KISS THE COOK. The warmth of the kitchen, in combination with her painkillers, was making Emma comfortably drowsy.

'You just don't look like a cook,' she said, smiling.

Burke picked up a shiny spatula and gazed into its surface. 'Why? Because I have the face of a bulldog?' he asked.

'You do not,' she said stoutly. 'I remember when you taught my freshman psych class. I had such a crush on you.'

Burke's eyebrows rose in his furrowed forehead. 'You did?'

'Well, you were kind of a glamorous, mysterious figure. I reckoned you secretly liked me back but didn't want to cross that teacher-student line. At least, that's what I thought until you started dating my room-mate.'

'I did notice you, Emma. I thought you were cute.'

'Oh, don't bother saying that. Natalie was in a whole different league. She was so magnetic.'

'I actually did feel a little guilty about the student-teacher thing, but Natalie always defied the rules,' said Burke. 'When I tried to explain, it was like waving a red flag in front of a bull. She wouldn't take no for an answer.'

Emma felt a prickle of indignation. 'She came on to you?'

'Like a freight train,' Burke said. 'Why? You look surprised.'

'It's just that . . . she knew I liked you. I was always gushing about you,' Emma said.

'Well, if it's any consolation, there were times over the years when I wished I had resisted her,' he admitted with a sigh.

Emma saw a shade of melancholy descend on her host. She wanted to change the subject. 'Look, can't I at least set the table? I feel like a lazy slug sitting here.'

Burke pulled out a tray table from behind the kitchen door and set it down next to her. 'No,' he said. 'Absolutely not. Set the table indeed. You probably shouldn't even be out of the house.'

'Actually, I'm hoping I can come back to work next week.'

'It's too soon, Emma.'

'Burke, I can't sit around thinking about what happened. Besides, my patients' problems will get my mind off my own.'

'Let's discuss it in a day or two,' Burke said firmly.

He set a place for her on the tray table and one at the kitchen island for himself. He dished up the food and brought her a plate.

'I wonder if we should wait for David,' she fretted.

'I'll save him a plate,' said Burke.

The smell of the food made her mouth water. 'Burke, thank you again,' she said as she shook out her napkin.

Burke sat down and raised his glass to her. 'To your speedy recovery,' he said.

Emma lifted her glass and smiled. 'Thank you for rescuing me. I feel much better being here with you.'

'Good,' he said. '*Mangia*.' For a few moments they ate in silence.

'This is great,' Emma said.

Burke smiled. 'Now, Emma, have you heard anything more from the police about the progress of their investigation?'

Emma shook her head. 'Our attorney advised us not to talk to them. Besides, they seem to have blinkers on. David says all their attention is focused on him.'

Burked nodded. 'Before they found Natalie, they kept questioning me. More like harassing me. But you have to talk to them. They need your input.'

Emma's cheeks reddened. 'That's what I think, but David says he's being targeted, for no other reason than that he married a woman with a trust fund.'

'Wads of money is a time-honoured motive for murder.'

'Burke, how can you say that? David is your best friend.'

'I don't mean that I think that. Of course not. And when I gave Lieutenant Atkins the anonymous letters you had received, she seemed very interested. I also told her—I hope you won't mind this—that they ought to talk to Lyle Devlin.'

Emma set down her fork. 'Lyle Devlin? Ivy's father?'

'Well, they asked me if anyone had threatened you. I didn't tell you about this, but when Ivy died, Devlin came to my office ranting and raving.'

'About me?' Emma said.

'I didn't want you to know. You were upset enough as it was.'

Emma blanched. 'You agreed with me about the decision I made.'

'I did. And I told Devlin that. Still, I thought the police ought to know about it.'

Emma nodded and tried to eat some more, but suddenly her appetite was gone. She felt tears rising to her eyes again, and dabbed them away with her napkin.

'Oh, Emma, I'm sorry,' Burke said.

Emma shook her head. 'You didn't do anything. I think it's the pain and the exhaustion.' She looked out at the driving rain. 'I hope David's all right.'

'Was he driving to New York?' Burke asked.

'No. He took the train.'

'I'm surprised he left you alone in this condition.'

'Actually, I wasn't alone. My mother hired a private nurse to stand guard over me. But I sneaked out of the house, and I guess she left in a huff. She wasn't there when I got back.'

'That's kind of odd,' Burke said. 'Is she supposed to come back tomorrow?'

'I have no idea. She'll probably request a transfer,' said Emma.

Burke looked at her with a concerned expression on his face. 'So, you left the house by yourself? Where did you go?'

'Well, this is kind of disgusting, but . . .' Emma gave him a brief account of the ghastly wedding present.

'Oh no,' said Burke, unsmiling. 'Another message from your admirer? Did you find out who sent it?'

Emma shook her head. 'Kellerman's doesn't carry this item. They used to, but they don't any more. It was pretty, actually—a dish in the shape of a shell. Like a scallop shell, made of silver.'

'How big was it?'

'Not too big,' said Emma. 'No bigger than a . . . mouse.'

Burke had a strange expression on his face.

'Burke, what is it?'

'We received one of those when we got married,' he said.

'Really?' Emma asked.

A pounding on the front door made them start. Burke got up from his counter stool, but before he reached it, the door opened.

'David!' Emma cried.

His hair was wet, and his leather jacket was dripping. 'Well, you two look cosy,' he said.

'Your wife wanted to wait for you,' said Burke in a teasing tone, 'but I figured saving you a plate would be enough.'

David waved it away. 'Emma, I got your note. What are you doing here? You shouldn't be out.'

'It's a long story. I had to call nine-one-one . . .'

'Nine-one-one?' he cried. 'For what?'

'I thought there was someone in the house. It turns out it was just the wind slamming a door, but I was really scared. In the middle of it all, Burke called, and came and got me out of there.'

'What happened to Lizette?' David demanded.

'She left. As I said, it's a long story,' said Emma.

'Sit down,' said Burke to his old friend. 'Take that wet coat off.'

'No thanks,' said David. 'I've got the car running outside. Emma, I need to get you home. If you're going to that funeral tomorrow, you have to get some rest.'

'What funeral?' Burke asked.

'Oh, I almost forgot. I guess you're right,' said Emma, struggling to her feet. Burke lifted the alpaca cape off a hook by the kitchen door and laid it gently on her shoulders. 'The funeral is for Claude Mathis,' Emma said. 'The hunter who tried . . . to save me. And yes, I absolutely am going.'

David turned to Burke. 'Thanks for looking out for her,' he said.

'Yes, thank you very much, Burke,' said Emma. 'You really were a lifesaver.'

Burke smiled. 'Anytime,' he said.

'How did the interview go?' Emma asked as David drove.

'Fine,' he said.

'Fine,' she repeated reproachfully. 'That's it?'

'Look, I can't talk and drive in this rain.'

'Fine,' she said.

They rode the rest of the way in silence, David hunched over the wheel, trying to peer through cascades of water the windshield wipers couldn't sweep away quickly enough.

When they arrived in their driveway, David told her to wait for him, but Emma struggled out of the car and put up her umbrella. She made it a few steps up the path before she felt his arm round her, guiding her. She wanted to relax against him, but she couldn't. She felt too irritated with him. When they got inside, she hung her cape and dress in the laundry room and pulled on her robe.

David came out of the bathroom, rubbing his wet head with a towel. 'Can I get you your medication?' he asked.

'I can get it,' she said coldly. It took all her will not to grimace as she limped into the kitchen to find her pills. David entered in his pyjama bottoms, opened the refrigerator, and took out a beer.

'Do you want one?' he asked.

'No,' she said. 'The baby. Remember?'

'Right. Sorry,' he said.

She hobbled to the little ground-floor bedroom, sank down on the bed, and stared at her soggy bandages. They were seeping pink, and the idea of changing them seemed more than she could do.

After a few dreary minutes, David appeared, holding the box of bandages. 'Can I fix you up with some of these?'

Emma sighed with relief and met his gaze briefly. 'That would be good,' she said.

David sat down and began to peel away the old dressings. Emma felt herself relax at his familiar, warm touch.

'Lizette really spruced up the place,' he said.

'I know,' said Emma. 'She was very thorough.'

'So, tell me what happened. She just left? Did she say why?'

'Well, I called a cab and went down to Kellerman's to see if they might know who sent the dish with the mouse in it.'

'Emma, are you crazy? You're in no condition.'

'Look, I don't want to discuss it. I went. All right?'

David shook his head. 'Did they tell you anything?' he asked.

'No. And when I got back, she was gone. Bag and baggage. And then I panicked.'

'And called the cops,' he said.

'Not immediately. I kept waiting for you to arrive.'

'I was late. I'm sorry. So what happened?'

'Well, the storm was howling. Then there was a breather on the phone. Somebody called, but they wouldn't speak to me.'

'I'm sure it's nothing. Probably a wrong number,' he said.

She hesitated, then plunged ahead, goaded by his imperturbability. 'I wanted to find you. I thought I'd call Nevin, so I looked for your phone book. How come your desk drawer's locked?'

David frowned. 'I don't know. Why?'

'It seems odd that you'd lock it,' she said in a challenging tone.

His eyes narrowed, and suddenly she knew she had crossed the line. It was his desk, and she was snooping in it. He was entitled to his privacy.

'Maybe I locked it when we moved so stuff wouldn't fall out.'

She felt relieved at the obvious explanation. 'Of course.'

'If it bothers you so much, I'll hunt up the key.'

'No, no. It's your desk. I shouldn't have even asked.' She felt stupid. Intrusive. 'I'm sorry, David. Really.'

There was a chilly look in his hazel eyes. 'We're not going to make it if you don't trust me.'

'Of course I trust you,' she said.

David picked up the messy wads of gauze. 'I hope so,' he said.

The Chapel in the Pines was packed for the funeral of Claude Mathis. Emma and David arrived early enough to slip in unnoticed, but a whisper rippled through the mourners as Emma took her seat. She had dressed in a knit trouser-suit and paisley shawl, realising that people would, inevitably, be watching her curiously. She had carefully applied her make-up, and David had washed her hair that morning, so that it fell in shiny waves around her pale face.

Emma was moved to tears several times by the stories his friends told about Claude during the service. She tried to imagine him alive, this man who had died coming to her aid. Claude's dog, Major, was allowed into the church and lay by the feet of Claude's teenage son, Bobby, looking bereft.

After the service, Emma approached Claude's son and his ex-wife, who were greeting people in the vestibule. 'Excuse me,' she said. 'I'm Emma Webster. I wanted to tell you how terribly sorry I am.'

Claude's ex-wife, Holly, was a brittle-looking woman wearing high heels, jeans and a red vinyl jacket. 'I know who you are,' she said. 'Your stepfather explained about the money you're giving us. That was nice.

God knows, we're gonna need it. Bobby, this is the woman.'

The teenage boy, dressed in a baggy black sweatshirt, looked warily at Emma. He was holding Major on a leash. The dog was silent and patient, a forlorn look in his eyes.

'Your father was very brave, Bobby,' said Emma. 'He died saving me and my baby from certain death.'

The kid shrugged, but his eyes flickered. David shook the boy's hand as well, murmuring his condolences, then reached down and patted Major. The dog let out a low, menacing growl.

'Major, shut it.' Bobby yanked at the dog's collar. 'He don't like strangers,' he explained.

David straightened up. 'Sorry. Em, we'd better get going.'

'Major,' Emma said, holding up a tentative hand.

The dog began to bark frantically, its loud, anxious barks bouncing off the walls of the chapel. The sound was terrifying, causing Emma to flash back to the night of the attack. She froze in place as the dog jerked madly on his leash.

'Major, quit!' Bobby yelled.

'Get that mutt out of here!' Holly shouted at her son.

Emma clung to David as the boy pulled Major out of the church.

Crowded at the foot of the steps now were as many reporters as there were mourners. They scattered from the path of the snarling dog Bobby Mathis barely held under control.

'Come on,' said David. 'They're distracted. Maybe we can get by.'

As David and Emma descended the steps, the reporters, recognising Emma from her limp and her cane, surged towards her.

'All right, that's enough,' David insisted as one photographer after another shoved a video camera in her face. 'Leave my wife alone.' When the nearest man refused to back off, David pushed him out of the way. The man protested in a loud voice, and Chief Audie Osmund immediately approached.

Ignoring the protests of the newspeople, Chief Osmund shielded Emma and steered her out of the crowd, with David trailing them. Lieutenant Joan Atkins was waiting next to Osmund's patrol car.

'Hello, Lieutenant,' Emma said.

David took her arm. 'Come on, darling,' he said.

Audie Osmund put a beefy hand on David's shoulder. 'Mr Webster, I wonder if you would come with me for a few minutes?'

'What for?' said David.

'I want to take a ride out to the cabin so you can retrace your path to the duck hide for me,' Audie said.

'My attorney has instructed me not to speak to you.'

'Mr Webster, you've just attended Claude Mathis's funeral. I've got his unsolved murder on my hands. Don't you feel the least bit beholden to him?'

'I'm sorry, but I'm within my rights,' David said.

Chief Osmund turned to Lieutenant Atkins, who was watching them with her keen gaze. 'I can't force him to talk,' he said.

'Let's go to the car,' David said to Emma. They walked towards the Jeep Cherokee, trailed by Chief Osmund and Lieutenant Atkins. David opened the front passenger door for Emma and then went round to the trunk and pulled out the milk crate. Emma climbed up on it and slid into the passenger seat. David put the crate back and walked round to the driver's side.

Joan Atkins blocked his path. She smiled, though her eyes remained chilly. 'You may as well go and talk to the chief, Mr Webster. I need to talk to your wife.'

'She doesn't want to talk to you,' said David.

'Actually,' said Joan, 'she left a message saying she did.'

David paled. He bent over and looked into the car at Emma. 'Is that true?' he said.

'I wanted to tell her about the gift.' She reddened at his accusing gaze. 'I told you I was going to.'

'Fine. You talk to her. I'll wait for you.'

'David, please. They're right about Claude Mathis. It's the least we can do. We don't need to hide behind an attorney.'

David shook his head. 'They're double-teaming us, Emma,' he said. 'They knew you would react this way.'

'You coming, Mr Webster?' the chief asked. 'Lieutenant Atkins can follow us in your car.'

David's eyes were leaden. He tossed his car keys to Joan Atkins and walked towards the black-and-white with the portly Chief Osmund trailing him.

Lieutenant Atkins got into the Cherokee and inserted the key in the ignition. 'Your husband seems a bit aggravated,' she said.

'My husband is fine,' Emma said.

'What's this about a wedding gift? I called you back, but no one picked up.'

Emma told her about the shell dish and the dead mouse.

'I'll need to collect that box from your house. Although I imagine it's pretty well contaminated by now,' said Joan.

Emma did not reply. They rode along in silence, following the chief's squad car down the highway lined with tall pine trees. His right blinker flashed, and with a sickening feeling in her heart, Emma began to recognise the area. As they reached the clearing, she said, 'I'm not going in that house again.'

'You don't have to,' said Joan.

Chief Osmund stopped the car, and he and David got out, then disappeared into the woods. Emma leaned back against the seat and sighed. Lieutenant Atkins drummed the tips of her fingernails on the wheel. Then she turned and looked at Emma.

'Emma, can I tell you something? Everyone thinks they know their mate. Believe me. Ask any woman on the street. What he likes. Where he goes. Who he sees. All women think that.'

Emma turned her head and gazed at the river.

'Emma, I used to be married. If you had asked if my husband would ever harm me, I would have said absolutely not. Until one day, in a rage, he raised his hand to me.'

Emma spoke softly. 'That must have been terrible.'

Joan coloured slightly. 'It was. I'm only telling you this because you need to understand the gravity of your situation. I don't know what David told you about his interrogation, but he refused to take a lie detector test. Even before he called the attorney.'

Emma stared out at the cabin. The river glinted through the trees. It looked so peaceful, but Emma knew better. She could picture the assailant, the fury with which he attacked her. It was not David. It was someone who lived here in these woods. Someone who hid out here. They were looking in the wrong place.

'Why would an innocent man refuse a lie detector test?'

Emma turned her head and met Joan's gaze. 'There could be any number of explanations, and you know it. It's a flawed tool. It's not admissible in court. Why are you so determined to blame this on my husband?'

Joan Atkins looked at her squarely. 'Emma, did your husband ever bring you out here before this incident occurred?'

'No. He hadn't been out here in years.'

'That's what he told us too,' said Joan. 'But it wasn't true. He was out here just a short while ago.'

Emma glared at her. 'No, he wasn't.'

'One of these Pineys that lives back here talked to him.'

Emma's heart was thumping. She could remember, in spite of herself, that frozen package of lasagne in the cabin freezer, with its August sell-by date. She saw David come strolling into view from the woods, talking to Chief Osmund, who was frowning.

'So what if he was out here?' she said. 'So what? Maybe he just needed to get away for a day. And forgot to mention it.'

'Or maybe he was formulating his plan,' said Joan. 'Ask him.'

8

DAVID FIXED JOAN ATKINS with an implacable stare. 'We've cooperated with you more than we should have,' he said. 'We're leaving.'

'Go ahead,' Joan said to Emma. 'Ask him.'

'Ask me what?' David said. He peered at Emma.

Joan gazed at him coolly. 'When was the last time you were here, at your uncle's place?'

'You know,' said David. 'My wife doesn't need to go over this again. She doesn't need to relive this experience.'

'Before the day of the attack,' said Joan.

David made a face. 'I don't know. I was what . . . ten years old.'

'That doesn't agree with our information.'

'Maybe I was twelve,' David said. 'So sue me.'

'We have a witness who saw you here recently.'

Emma watched him. His eyes blazed. 'What witness?'

'A reliable witness,' said Chief Osmund. 'Did you forget to tell us about a more recent visit?'

Emma felt her stomach turning over. She put her hand out to steady herself against the car.

'All right. That's it,' said David. 'You're making this crap up, and I have had enough. And my wife has clearly had enough.' Without another word he boosted Emma up in the Jeep. Lieutenant Atkins handed him the keys. Then they headed off down the dirt road, raising a cloud of leaves and dust.

David and Emma didn't speak until they reached the highway. Finally, without looking at her, David said, 'You should never have put me in that situation.'

'Don't tell me what to do,' she snapped.

He did not reply. They were silent the rest of the way home.

Once inside the house, David went directly to his office.

'What are you doing?' Emma said.

'Calling Yunger. He needs to know about this mystery witness.'

She followed him to the door and saw him punch in the number. Yunger was not at his office. David turned his back and left him a message, speaking quietly.

He replaced the phone and turned to look at her. Emma was studying him with a pained gaze. 'All right. What is it?' he said.

'Why did you lie to the police?'

'Lie about what?'

'About being at the cabin,' she said.

'You're beginning to sound like a cop.' David raised his hands in surrender. 'All right. Don't believe me.'

'You heard Detective Atkins. They have a witness.'

'Emma, she's making it up. She's trying to turn you against me, and it's working,' cried David.

'She said it because she thinks you're lying,' she said. 'If you were there before, just say so. Why is that so difficult?'

'Because I wasn't,' he said. 'Why do you believe them? They're trying to frame me, and you're letting them.'

'Now it's my fault?' she cried.

'Why is my word not good enough for you? You're my wife. I love you. I need you to have faith in me. Is that so much to ask?'

Emma heard a car door slam. She craned her neck to see out of the window. 'I think it's Yunger,' she said.

'You didn't answer me,' he said.

'You'd better go talk to your attorney,' she said.

'Thanks a lot,' he said, edging past her out of the door. Emma reddened and did not meet his gaze. She felt guilty about her stubbornness. What he said made sense. In a way. The witness could have been mistaken. She walked over to the desk and looked out of the window. David and a distinguished-looking bald man, holding a briefcase, were standing on the front walk.

She sat down heavily in the desk chair, and her gaze fell on the drawer. She tugged at the handle.

This time the drawer slid open smoothly. Since last night he'd unlocked it. She looked in at the usual assortment of junk—paperclips and rubber bands and pencils. And then she had a disquieting thought. If he *had* locked up something secret in there, he had now disposed of it or put it in a new hiding place.

And then she thought about what she was doing. What is the matter with you? Why must you think the worst of your husband? He loves you. You told him that you trusted him. You're letting the police turn you into a doubting, harping wife who snoops through his things. It was probably just as he said. He'd locked it when they moved.

She went to close the drawer. As she did, her gaze fell on a key ring. She picked it up. There was one key on the ring, which had a plastic photo frame with a label that read GARDEN SHED. Inside was a photo of her that David had taken. She was wearing a baseball cap and overalls, and she was stacking lawn furniture in the shed. It was a cute picture, a sweet idea. He had framed the picture as a special way to remind him what the key was for. She started to smile, and then her smile faded.

The front door opened, and she heard voices in the hall. She closed the drawer and got up.

'Have a seat,' she heard David say. 'You want a beer?'

'No,' Yunger said. 'I'm going back to the office.'

'I want you to meet my wife,' David said. 'Let me see if she's lying down. She had kind of a tough morning.'

Emma walked out of the bedroom.

'Hey, honey, I was just coming to get you,' said David. 'This is Mr Yunger. This is my wife, Emma.'

'Hey, Emma. Call me Cal. Nice to meet you,' said Yunger.

'You too,' said Emma, shaking his hand.

'Listen,' said Cal Yunger, 'I know you've been through an awful lot. Now they're pulling phantom witnesses out of the air. I just told your husband, I don't think you have anything to worry about. If they were so sure about this witness, they could have brought him to the funeral to identify David. Obviously they didn't do that, so my guess is that they're not sure this ID is going to hold up.'

'Will you excuse me?' said Emma. 'I'm very tired.'

'Oh, sure.' Yunger looked slightly taken aback. 'I'm sorry.'

'Are you all right, honey?' David asked.

'I'm fine,' she said. 'Just tired.' She went back into their temporary bedroom, closed the door, and locked it behind her.

Emma sat down on the desk chair. For a few moments she sat there thinking. Then she picked up the phone on the desk.

She dialled Stephanie at the middle school and got one of the secretaries, who said that Stephanie had gone to Trenton for a meeting. Emma thanked her, and hung up.

Where else could she go? she thought.

She thought about calling Burke, but she didn't want to drag him into this. She looked at the phone, thinking of her mother, wishing she could magically transport herself to Chicago and be taken care of, like a child. She thought she could even tolerate Rory's company if it meant being with her mother, but she knew it was too much of a trip to make in her condition.

All of a sudden, the phone rang. Emma picked it up. 'Darling,' said Kay McLean, 'I know you're mad at me, and I don't blame you, but I just had to call you.'

'Mom, I was just thinking about you. Just this minute.'

Kay chuckled. 'Well, we've always had a little mother-daughter telepathy, haven't we?'

Emma smiled, knowing it was true. 'I guess we have.'

'What's the matter?' Kay asked. 'How are you? Did the nurse come? I know you told me not to interfere . . .'

'She was here,' Emma said carefully.

'Was? Isn't she still there? We hired her until further notice.'

'She got a little peeved. I left the house without telling her.'

'Emma! She was supposed to be there to take care of you.'

'I know, Mom. And I appreciate it. Really, I do. I guess I'm just wishing I could come and be with you.'

'Really?' Kay said. 'Emma, why don't you do it? Oh, nothing would make me happier.' Then she hesitated. 'Honey, has something else happened?'

'No. Not really. I'm just feeling stressed out.'

'Then get on the next plane, darling. Are you up to the trip?'

'That's just it,' said Emma. 'I don't think I am. My luggage. The security queues. That long walk to the gate.'

'Oh, Em,' Kay said. 'Then let me come there.'

'No. Better not,' Emma murmured.

'I hate being this far away from you,' said Kay.

Tears filled Emma's eyes, and she couldn't speak.

'Honey, listen to me,' said Kay. 'Why don't you go up to New York and visit Jessie? You can call a car service and have them take you right to her door.'

'Mom, she's on bed rest. She's in no shape for company.'

'Now, Emma, listen to me. I talk to Aurelia all the time. Jessie has all kinds of help. Her mother has made sure of it. And there's lots of room in that apartment. She's bored to death, stuck at home. You just call and tell her you're coming.'

Emma thought of Jessie's cheerful face and the warmth she always saw in her eyes. 'Do you think I should?' Emma asked.

'Yes. Please, honey. It would be good for both of you.'

'OK,' said Emma. 'I will. Thanks, Mom.'

'Call me from Jessie's,' Kay insisted, hanging up.

Before she could change her mind, Emma punched in Jessie's number and asked if she could visit. Jessie reacted like the true friend she was. 'How soon can you be here?'

'I'll be on the next train.'

'Can't wait,' Jessie said. 'We'll lie around together. It'll be like one of our old sleepovers.' Emma did her best to sound enthused, then she hung up the phone and sat staring out of the front window at the drizzling sky. Get up, she thought. Get out of here. Put two or three things in a bag. She couldn't carry anything heavy. She knew her mother was probably right about the car service, but it was an easy trip by train, in those big comfortable seats.

She went over to the closet and pulled out a light microfibre duffle bag. She folded a nightie and a burnt-orange tunic top and stretchy black trousers into the bag. Then she unlocked the door and limped to the bathroom, where she picked up her toothbrush, a box of bandages and her medication.

When she walked back, David was standing by the bed, staring down at her open duffle bag. He looked at her. 'What's this?'

'Is your lawyer gone?' she asked.

'*Our* lawyer. Yes. What is going on with you?'

Emma did not reply. She put her toiletries into the duffle bag.

'Emma,' he said.

'You lied to me,' she said.

'Here we go again. How many ways can I tell you? I was not at the cabin.'

'This is not about the cabin,' she said. 'You lied to me about your desk drawer. You said you locked it when we moved.'

'I did,' he said.

'No, you didn't.' She walked over to the drawer and pulled out the key ring. 'You see this?' she said. 'It's a picture of me you took the day we moved in.'

'So what?' he cried.

'So, if the drawer had been locked since we moved, how could you possibly have put that photo on the key ring?'

David stared at her. 'I don't believe this. Are you building a case against me? Are you working for the cops?'

Emma blushed, but she zipped up her bag. 'That's the second time today you've compared me to a cop.'

'Well, excuse me, but I feel a little beleaguered. It's a drawer. You're walking out because of a drawer? That's my crime?'

She started for the door, but he blocked her way.

'Move,' she said.

He hesitated, then stepped aside. Emma walked past him.

'All right, wait,' he said. 'Will you listen?'

She stopped, but she did not reply or look at him.

'All right, look.' He sat down on the edge of the bed. 'There is something I probably should have told you. It's embarrassing.'

Emma stood trembling. 'What is?' she asked.

'Emma, I was seeing another woman when we met.' He heaved a sigh. 'Her name is Connie. She's a flight attendant. She had the idea that we were serious. I guess I let her think that. Anyway, when I met you, I realised that I'd met the woman for me, and I dropped her. I tried to do it gently, but she hounded me for a while. She wrote me a lot of letters that made no sense. In fact, they were kind of crazy. Very intense.'

Emma peered at him. 'And that's what was in the drawer? This woman's letters?'

David nodded. 'I don't know why I kept them. After you mentioned the drawer, I realised how stupid it was. I mean, if the police saw those letters . . . between that and their so-called witness, they might jump to the wrong conclusion.'

Emma nodded. 'So you got rid of them.'

'Last night. Nobody wants to hear about their husband's old girl-friends. And it seemed like adding insult to injury to have the cops tracking her down. I mean, she wrote me some crazy letters. Didn't you ever do anything like that in the throes of a broken heart? I didn't think it was fair to drag her into this.'

Emma felt as if her head would explode. 'My life and the life of our baby is in danger, and you want to protect this woman? Did it ever occur to you that she might be the person who was trying to kill me?' she said.

David shook his head. 'Emma, it wasn't Connie. I haven't heard from her in months. She doesn't even know I got married.'

'How can I believe you? You have too many secrets.'

He looked stunned. 'I have secrets? What about you?'

She stared at him. 'What is that supposed to mean?'

He met her gaze defiantly. 'Nothing,' he said. 'Forget it.'

Emma set the bag down on the bed. 'No. You brought it up. Let's hear it. What are you talking about?'

'All right. I'm talking about you and Burke.'

'Me and Burke?' She looked at him in disbelief.

'You knew him in college.'

'That's no secret. I knew him in college. So what?'

'You had an affair with him, didn't you?' David demanded.

'An affair? No,' she said. But Emma blushed, thinking about her confession to Burke the other night. 'He wasn't interested in me. He married my room-mate, remember?'

'And yet, after a weekend visit, he asked you to work for him.'

'Because . . .' she said.

'Because what? Because of your vast experience?'

Emma blushed furiously. It was a simple question, but she found herself fumbling to answer it.

David looked triumphant. 'I think it's because he had a crazy wife who made him miserable, and he wanted to resume his affair with you. And then I got in the way.'

Emma gaped at him. 'David, you're just imagining something that didn't happen. I'm telling you the truth,' she said.

'Well, I don't believe you,' he said. 'How do you like it?'

For a moment Emma was stunned. And then she glared at him. 'Oh. Oh, I see. This is a game meant to enlighten me.'

'Games are supposed to be fun,' he said bitterly.

Emma picked up her bag again. 'Well, we're agreed on one thing. There is nothing fun about this.'

'All right, stop,' he said. 'I was trying to make a point. Of course I believe you. Now where are you going?'

'I'm leaving, David. I'm going to see Jessie for a few days.'

'Emma, you can't,' he said, but before he could protest further, the phone rang. He picked it up and barked, 'Hello!' He listened for a moment, his jaw working, then he held it out to Emma. 'You'll never guess who.'

She took the phone from him as he stalked out of the room.

'Hello?' she said.

'Emma, it's Burke. Am I calling at a bad time?'

Emma pushed open the door of Tasha Clayman's room at the Wrightsman Youth Crisis Centre. Tasha's mother, Nell, was beside the bed, stroking Tasha's arm, while her father, Wade, hovered in a corner, his eyes filled with worry. Burke had called to tell Emma that Tasha had begun slipping and refused to see anyone but her. Apologising profusely, he had asked if Emma could possibly find a way to come and talk to her.

Wade greeted Emma with a cry of relief. His relief turned to dismay as she limped in on her cane. 'My God!' he exclaimed. 'You poor girl.'

Tasha lifted her head, oversize on her skeletal frame, and stared. 'Dr Hollis! What happened to you?'

'I was the victim of a crime,' said Emma. 'I wasn't planning to come in yet, Tasha, but I am so concerned about you.'

Tasha's bulging eyes widened, and a rare smile wrinkled her skin into accordion folds. 'Thanks,' she said.

'I need you to work for me today,' Emma cautioned.

Tasha nodded tentatively. 'I'll try,' she said.

Nell, who could not tear her anxious gaze from her daughter's gaunt face, let out a sound between a laugh and a sob. 'Please try, Tasha,' she pleaded.

Wade pulled up a chair for Emma, and she sat down.

'Let's talk about disappointment,' she said.

Audie Osmund pulled into the clearing where the old Fiore house stood. It was a run-down farmhouse with asbestos shingles and a roof that desperately needed replacing. A tin-roof lean-to was probably used now as the barn. Audie got out of his patrol car, climbed up the front step, and knocked at the door. There was no car around.

No one answered his knock, and when he tried to peep through the windows, the panes were too grimy to be transparent. They haven't done much for this place, Audie thought. It would probably be different if the husband was still alive.

He looked around the clearing impatiently. She could be out with the horse, he thought. It was worth a try. He began to walk towards the broken-down old lean-to, which was overgrown with vines. He heard a whinny as he approached.

'Mrs Tuttle?' he called out.

'Who is it?' a deep voice asked.

'Police,' Audie announced. 'Who are you?'

A teenage kid wearing a grey sweatshirt and a pulled-down Philadelphia Eagles cap emerged from the lean-to, holding a currycomb. He looked warily at Audie.

'I live here,' said the kid.

'You're Mrs Tuttle's son?'

The boy nodded.

'What's your name, kid?'

'Sam,' the boy said.

'Well, Sam, I'm looking for your mother.'

'She ain't here. She had to go up to Trenton. Some insurance thing about my dad. Why do you want her?'

'She's helping me with a case,' Audie said. 'Do you have a number where I can reach her?'

The boy frowned. 'No. We had a cellphone, but we had to get rid of it. My mom said we couldn't afford it.'

Audie sighed. 'All right, son. When do you expect her back?'

'Tomorrow, I guess. Maybe late tonight.'

'Well, I'm the police chief. Chief Osmund,' said Audie. 'You have her call me.'

Emma led the Claymans through a good session. At the end of it, Wade admitted that he regretted wasting time on late-night business meetings, time that he could have spent with his daughter, and Tasha looked at him in amazement.

On her way out of the centre, Emma kept her gaze lowered so she would not have to explain her life to everyone she encountered. But she had to speak to Burke before she left. She tried not to make eye contact with the person coming out of his reception area.

'Hey,' said an angry voice. 'Wait a minute.'

Emma looked up and found herself face to face with a glowering man in a black leather vest, engineer's boots, and wire-rimmed glasses. 'Mr Devlin,' she said.

'Well, isn't this a surprise. I'll tell you what I just told him,' Lyle Devlin said, gesturing towards Burke's office. 'You have a lot of nerve, after what you did, sending the police to hound me.'

'I didn't . . .' Emma protested.

'What's going on out here?' Geraldine called out anxiously.

'You will be sorry,' Devlin said, pointing a finger at Emma's chest. 'You'll pay dearly for this. The worst thing I ever did was to let you get your hands on my daughter.'

'I'll call security,' Emma said faintly.

Burke, alerted by Geraldine, opened his door and looked out. When he saw Emma up against the door frame, he began to shout and rush towards the man. 'Hey. I told you to get out of here.'

Devlin's face was close to Emma's. 'Security's not gonna help you, honey.' Before Burke could reach him, Devlin turned his back on Emma and stormed towards the exit.

Burke arrived at Emma's side in a moment, studying her worriedly. 'Emma, are you OK?' he asked. 'Come in and sit down.'

Emma shook her head. 'I'm all right. What set him off?'

'The police questioned him about what happened to you. About his threats against you. Now he's all bent out of shape. He doesn't want this whole thing to come out in the open.' Burke shook his head. 'How did it go with Tasha Clayman?'

Emma said that the session had gone well, and she had promised to see Tasha again the minute she got back from New York.

'You're going to New York? Is that a good idea?'

'It's just for a few days. I need to get away from all the publicity. I have a close friend there.'

'You're not driving, I hope.'

'I've got a cab waiting to take me to the train.'

'You take care of yourself. Rest and recuperate.' Burke kissed her cheek. 'Be careful, Emma. You're very important to us.'

The Clarenceville train station was located adjacent to the sprawling Lambert University campus. The taxi dropped Emma off in front of the station house, and she went inside. There was a college kid in a parka sound asleep on one of the benches, snoring lightly. Through the window Emma could see a couple of young teenagers, knitted caps pulled down to their eyebrows, sailing down the cement platform on skateboards.

As she approached the ticket window, the man behind it, wearing a blue uniform, was muttering, 'Those kids! Excuse me, miss.' He let himself out of the office, opened the door to the outside, and hollered, 'Hey, get those skateboards out of here.'

The teenagers laughed derisively, but began to roll towards the parking lot. 'Get off and carry 'em,' the agent yelled.

He came back inside, scowling, and climbed onto his stool again. 'Where you going?' he asked.

'New York. Penn Station.' Emma hesitated. 'Round trip.'

'The express doesn't stop here. The local's at five o'clock.'

'That's fine,' she said. Emma paid for her ticket and thanked him. Then she went outside to wait. The platform was deserted. Emma was the only traveller. The day was growing dark, and the halogen lights were beginning to come on.

Emma thought about sitting on one of the benches attached to the station house, but she was too anxious to just sit. She walked slowly down to the end of the platform, away from the station house. Standing there on the lonely platform, she started to wonder why she had even decided to go. Now that she was away from David, she missed him and began to think she had been too hasty in walking out. They were coping as best they could, between the police, the reporters, her injuries. If she left now, was she playing into the hands of all the doom mongers? A marriage took time and trust. She shivered, glad she had worn the alpaca cape.

A bright white light appeared in the distance, along with the noisy clatter of the approaching express. The shrill whistle sounded, warning that the train would not stop. Emma stiffened against the harsh scream of the whistle and stared at the white light growing larger as the train barrelled down the tracks.

It's not too late, Emma thought. You can rip this ticket up and go back home. She put a protective hand on her stomach. Aloysius, what do you think? You'd probably vote for me to return to your daddy. Kids always vote for that, she thought wistfully.

The clatter of the approaching train was deafening. Emma took a step back from the yellow safety line on the platform. As she did, she noticed a swift movement out of the corner of her eye. One of the skateboarders was sailing down the ramp in his black knitted cap and baggy sweats. The ticket agent's going to be furious, she thought, smiling. The skateboarder was zooming towards her, gesturing wildly, yelling something she could not hear.

'What?' she said. Seeing him speeding her way, she wasn't taking any chances. She took another step back and suddenly, from behind, felt a vicious thud. Hands shoved up her shoulder blades. She stumbled and screamed but was drowned out by the whistle. She saw the white light as she pitched forward, into the path of the oncoming train.

9

OH GOD, NO, she thought desperately. My baby!

Suddenly Emma was jerked back, nearly strangled by the fastened neck of her cape. Her head snapped forward. Her arms flailed, and she fell, landing on one hip. The train was screaming by, and she saw the lights from inside the carriages careening past.

The skateboarder bent down. 'You OK?' he asked.

The boy had swept behind her and yanked her cape. His young

reflexes had saved her. Emma, stunned to be alive and safe, tried to speak but couldn't. She nodded.

A man in a Burberry trench coat who had just stepped out of the station house with a middle-aged woman, rushed up to them. 'What did you do to this woman?'

'I didn't do nothin' to her,' the kid snarled.

The man crouched down and put an arm under Emma's shoulders. 'Let me help you. And, young man, I want to talk to you.'

The skateboarder, resuming his swift, illegal cruise, leapt off the platform and into the parking lot.

'Delinquent,' muttered the man. 'Did he hurt you?'

The train had passed, and the station was silent again. 'It wasn't him,' Emma managed to croak. 'Someone . . . tried to push me in front of the train.'

The man frowned at her. 'They pushed you deliberately?'

'My baby,' Emma cried. 'What about my baby?' She began to weep. 'I'm pregnant,' she said.

'Linda,' the man said to his wife. 'Get your cell. Call nine-one-one.'

Joan Atkins careened into the station parking lot. An ambulance was there, as well as black-and-whites everywhere, flashing red lights. The news media were being held outside the station by a policeman. Joan flashed her badge and hurried into the station house.

There were at least ten cops in the building, two of them talking to the stationmaster. Another was escorting the man in the trench coat and his wife onto the platform. Joan saw Trey Marbery talking on his cellphone and signalled to him. Marbery nodded grimly.

Emma was lying on a gurney while EMTs worked to staunch the blood flow from the reopened wound in her side. Her face was dead white. When she looked up, a spark of recognition came to her eyes. 'Lieutenant Atkins,' she said.

Joan squeezed her hand briefly. 'Emma. What happened?'

Emma's eyes filled with tears. 'Sorry,' she said, waving a hand impatiently. 'I'm just so freaked out.'

Joan looked up at Trey Marbery, who had finished his phone call and was approaching the gurney.

'What do we know?' she asked.

Trey cleared his throat. 'The couple who came upon the scene thought she had collided with a skateboarder, but the young lady tells us otherwise. Apparently, somebody pushed her from behind, and the skateboarder pulled her back.'

Joan winced. 'Where's the skateboarder now?'

'There's a half-dozen guys out looking for him.'

'Good,' said Joan. She looked down at Emma. 'Tell me about it. What were you doing here?'

Joan's piercing eyes were focused on Emma's face, and her calm, no-nonsense presence was comforting. 'I was waiting for the New York train. Going to visit an old friend. I saw the express train coming, and then the skateboarder. He was trying to warn me. I had no idea.' Emma let out a sob, then tried to compose herself.

'OK,' said Joan. 'Take it easy.'

Emma closed her eyes. She could hear Joan Atkins and the young detective conferring.

'Any other witnesses? Anyone at all?' Joan was asking.

'The platform was deserted. The stationmaster was inside. We were able to contact the train driver by phone, but he was moving too fast to see anything.'

Joan walked to the window. 'What about those buildings?' she said.

'That's the Lambert campus,' said Marbery.

'Maybe somebody was looking out and saw something.'

'I'll get a couple of patrolmen on it right away.'

'Thanks, Detective.' Joan returned to Emma's side. 'Where's your husband? The police have not been able to contact him.'

Emma opened her eyes. 'I don't know,' she whispered.

'Did he know you were coming here to take the train?'

Emma remembered her accusations, and David pleading with her not to leave. She nodded.

'Anyone else know?' said Joan sharply.

'A few people.'

'Can we continue this at the hospital?' asked an EMT. 'We need to get her over there now.'

'Sure,' said Joan, stepping back.

Emma felt the gurney rattling beneath her. Back to the hospital, she thought, and woolly-headed though she was from the painkiller they had given her, she felt unutterably depressed at the thought.

Suddenly, there was a commotion at the door to the station house. Lieutenant Atkins appeared beside Emma's stretcher, grasping the arm of a young man in a knitted cap and a baggy sweatshirt.

'Don't push me, lady,' the kid said. 'I didn't do nothing.'

'Emma,' said Joan, 'is this the young man you talked about?'

Emma took a look at the skateboarder's angry features. 'Yes.' She nodded to the boy. 'You saved me.'

'Whatever,' said the kid.

'His name's Josh,' said Joan. 'Josh, that was a fine, brave thing you did. Now this is really important. Did you see the person who tried to push Dr Webster onto the tracks?'

'She's a doctor?' the kid said.

'Answer the question.'

'I saw him come up behind her, getting ready to push her.'

'What did he look like?' Joan asked.

Josh shrugged. 'I don't know. He was wearing a hooded sweatshirt, and a ski mask. Red around the eyes.'

Emma gasped. She felt as if something heavy had just landed in the middle of her chest.

'What else?' Joan asked. 'Tall? Short?'

'I don't know anything else. It all happened so fast.'

'OK. Well, give your name and number to this officer here. We may need to talk to you again.'

'Thank you, Josh,' Emma whispered to the boy, who was turning away.

Joan frowned at Emma. 'You know this eliminates any possibility that the attack in the Pine Barrens was random?'

Emma did not reply, but she knew.

The EMT said, 'Lieutenant, we really have to go.'

'OK,' Joan said. 'Emma, I'll get some patrolmen to escort you out. They'll stay with you at the hospital.'

'Thank you,' said Emma in a small voice.

A pair of officers appeared at the head of the gurney. Emma lay back against the pillow and allowed herself to be moved out of the train station.

As she was being lifted down the steps, she saw the large lighted windows of the campus building opposite. In one window were two students. A boy propped up a large bass fiddle, and the girl beside him placed a violin under her chin. They had music to practise.

The music building, Emma thought. It looked out over the station platform.

'This will be cold,' said the technician as she smeared gel onto Emma's belly and attached the wires that led to the monitor beside her bed. A tall, bespectacled resident in a white coat entered the emergency-room cubicle.

'All ready for you, Doctor,' said the technician.

'OK,' said the young man. 'I'm Dr Weiss, from obstetrics and gynae-cology. I think everything is fine here, Mrs Webster. But just to be on the safe side, we'll have a look.' He switched on the monitor and positioned the scanner on her abdomen. An upside-down fan-shaped image appeared on the screen, covered by blotches and streaks. The doctor nodded, then said, 'Do you hear it?'

'I hear it,' said Emma. The thump of her baby's heart brought tears to her eyes. Dr Weiss watched for another moment and then switched off the ultrasound machine. 'The littlest patient is doing fine. How are you feeling?'

'Better now,' she said. 'I'm OK. Can I go home?'

He looked doubtfully at her newly resutured and bandaged wounds. 'As long as you have someone to look after you,' he said. 'By the way, there is somebody outside to see you. Are you up to some company?'

'Who is it?' Emma said, but Dr Weiss had already disappeared from the cubicle. Could it be David? she thought. And then she thought, No. If David somehow found out she was here and tried to see her, the police guarding her would hustle their prime suspect directly down to the police station. And according to Lieutenant Atkins, the police had still not been able to find him. Emma looked up as the doctor held the white curtain back, gesturing for the visitor to come in.

Stephanie, looking pretty in a navy-blue knit suit, edged past the open curtain. 'Oh Lord, Em, are you all right?' she asked, kissing Emma gently on the forehead. 'I heard about it on the radio driving back from Trenton. I tried to call David, but there was no answer, so I rushed over here.'

'Somebody tried to push me in front of the express train.'

Stephanie clutched her chest. 'I know.' She sat down in the moulded plastic chair. 'Do they think it was the same guy as in the Pine Barrens?'

Emma nodded. 'Yes. He was wearing the ski mask and the hoody. There's no doubt now. Someone wants me gone.' She shuddered. 'Detective Atkins thinks it's my husband.'

Stephanie absently rubbed the back of Emma's hand.

'You're awfully quiet,' said Emma. 'Is that what you think?'

'I'm just trying to take this all in. I don't think anything.'

'Yes, you do. Tell me what you think. Let's hear it.'

Stephanie's expression was pained. 'Look, I like David. He's a nice guy. And you two seem pretty happy . . .'

'We just got married, for God's sake. Why would he marry me and try to kill me on the same day?'

'I don't know. Maybe he decided it was a mistake. Maybe he's got a girlfriend. Men are cheaters.'

'Steph, come on. We're talking about murder here.'

'Emma, I'm not trying to be mean, but you do have a lot of money. And only one person stands to profit by your death.'

'He doesn't care about money,' Emma insisted.

'Everybody cares about money,' Stephanie said.

'I know what you say makes sense in a way. But it's so hard for me to imagine. I married less than a week ago. Promised to love and cherish till death. Now people want me to believe that the man I entrusted my life to is my own would-be killer.'

'But you hardly know him, Em. It was all so quick.'

'That doesn't mean it was wrong. David loves me.'

'Yeah. Well, if he loves you so much, why isn't he here?'

Emma's eyes filled with tears. 'I don't know.'

Stephanie immediately looked guilty. 'Oh, Em. All right, then, who would do it? You don't have any enemies.'

Emma was silent for a moment. 'Obviously, I do. There may be someone . . . I had a patient at the centre who died, an anorexic. Her father blamed me and threatened revenge.'

'I don't get it. Why would the guy blame you? By the time you get to the end stage of an eating disorder . . .'

Emma hesitated. 'While I was treating her, I began to suspect that he might be sexually abusing her. When I first met the parents, I noticed that the mother was very fleshy, very provocative in a way. I first thought the anorexia might be a reaction to her mother, but I began to think it might be the result of her avoiding having to take on her mother's role, so to speak.'

'So what did you do?'

'Well, I spoke to Burke, my boss. He agreed with me that we needed to have a doctor examine her. A gynaecologist who specialises in sexual abuse cases agreed to do it. When the father found out, he was furious.'

'So she never had the exam?'

'No. She did have it. Her mother gave us permission. The doctor couldn't find any physical evidence,' Emma admitted. 'The father took her out of treatment, and she died several weeks later.'

'So you think you were wrong about the father?'

'I may have been. But there are different kinds of molestation.' She shook her head. 'Now the police have gone and questioned him. The guy is more furious than ever. He confronted me at the centre today. And then, as I was being carried out to the ambulance, I noticed that the music building, where he works, is across from the train station.'

'What's that got to do with what happened to you?'

'He could have seen me waiting there and come after me.'

Stephanie nodded. 'I guess it's possible.'

'But Lieutenant Atkins is fixated on David,' said Emma. 'In her eyes, it's David or no one.'

Stephanie frowned. 'Was your patient named Ivy Devlin?'

Emma looked up sharply. 'Why do you say that?'

'Oh, come on, Em. I teach middle school. There aren't many kids who die from anorexia. Ivy's sister is in one of my classes.'

'Oh Lord, now I feel guilty. I shouldn't have told you.'

'Why? You didn't tell me what she said to you.'

'Still, I was wrong to even discuss it.'

'Alida—that's the sister—used to be really shy. Not long after Ivy died, she started coming to school in full glittery make-up, bare midriff. Very junior sexpot.'

'Uh-oh,' said Emma.

'Why uh-oh? Lots of girls dress like that in seventh grade.'

'I know. But it's the timing that sets off alarm bells.'

'You think he might be messing with her now? The father?'

'Steph, I really cannot talk about this.'

Stephanie looked at her thoughtfully. 'He can't be allowed to just get away with this. As one of her teachers, I could talk to Alida. She might confide in me.'

'Please, Stephanie, don't get involved in this. I mean it. I should never have opened my mouth. I was really out of line.'

'But the kid could still be suffering!' Stephanie cried.

'Look, let me be blunt,' said Emma. 'Alida might tell her parents if you started asking questions. And I think Lyle Devlin could be dangerous. Promise me you won't—'

Dr Weiss pulled back the curtain. He was holding a clipboard. 'Emma, if you sign your release form, you can be on your way.'

'Great,' said Emma, reaching for the clipboard.

'Is there someone who can pick you up and stay with you?'

'She's coming to my house,' Stephanie said.

Emma looked at her friend gratefully. 'Thanks, Steph.'

'You have to leave in a wheelchair,' said Dr Weiss. 'And you need to speak to your attending physician before you go.'

'Thanks,' Emma said.

Once Dr Weiss was gone, Stephanie helped Emma off the bed and into her dress, which was bloodstained and dirty. 'We'll wash this when we get home,' she said. She brushed out Emma's heavy, honey-coloured hair and dabbed some blusher on her pale cheeks.

The attending physician came in and gave Emma instructions on the care of her wounds, and an orderly arrived with the wheelchair. 'All right,' said Stephanie, gathering up Emma's handbag and her blue-green cape. 'Let's get you out of here.'

Emma obediently eased herself into the wheelchair and allowed Stephanie to push her out of the door. The young police officer stationed outside the cubicle in the ER jumped to his feet at the sight of them. Stephanie handed him the release form, and he examined it.

'I need to call my CO for instructions,' he said. He spoke on his radio, and then turned back to them. 'I'll escort you to where you're going. Then a patrol will come by the house once an hour.'

'Fine,' said Emma. 'Thank you, officer.'

Following the signs, they wended their way out of the ER, past the admitting and lab areas. As they turned the corner into the lobby, Emma glanced at the elevators and let out a cry. 'David!'

He was holding a cardboard tray of coffee cups and waiting for the elevator.

David looked in her direction. His eyes widened in alarm. The elevator doors opened, but he dropped the tray on a table and rushed to her. He knelt by the wheelchair and gathered her in his arms. 'Baby, what are you doing here? I thought you went to New York. Are you all right?'

The cop drew out his truncheon and pointed it at David. 'Excuse me. Do you know this man?' he asked Emma.

Every bit of anger she had felt vanished with the relief of seeing David's face. 'This is my husband,' she said. 'David, what are you doing here? The police are looking for you.'

David rocked back on his heels. 'Why? What's happened?'

Emma looked baleful. 'I got pushed in front of a train.'

'What?' he cried. 'Oh, Emma.' He grabbed her hands and squeezed them so tightly she winced.

Emma nodded. 'The same guy. In the ski mask. I was on the train platform, and he pushed me from behind. A skateboarder saved me. I tried to call you. There was no answer.'

The officer pulled out his radio and began to speak into it.

'Are you all right? Is the baby all right?'

'They're both all right,' said Stephanie coolly. 'I'm taking Emma home with me.'

'This is all my fault,' David said. 'I should never have let you leave that way. I shouldn't have let you out of my sight.' His gaze looked tortured. 'Why would anyone hurt you?'

'I don't know. What are you doing at the hospital?' Emma asked.

He ran a hand through his unruly hair. 'Oh, I've been here for hours.'

My mother took a turn for the worse. Birdie called me in a panic and said she couldn't breathe at all.'

'Oh no.' Emma looked at him worriedly. 'How is she doing?'

He sighed. 'She's stabilised. They had to do some kind of procedure. Anyway, I just went out to get Birdie a cup of coffee.'

The officer prodded David with his truncheon. 'Sir, stand up. I've been instructed to bring you to the police station. Right now.'

'Officer, I think this is a misunderstanding,' Emma protested. 'My husband has been at the hospital all afternoon.'

'We'll sort this out at the station. Sir, please stand up.'

David's eyes narrowed. 'Are you arresting me?'

'If necessary,' said the cop. 'Now let's go.'

David looked at Emma with a stricken gaze. 'I'm sorry, Em.' He reached out a hand to her. She hesitated. The officer gripped David's arm and forced him along, towards the door.

'Oh, Steph,' said Emma. 'This is all a mistake.'

'Come on,' said Stephanie. 'The police will take care of it. Let's get out of here.'

10

'I WANT TO GO HOME,' Emma said.

'Home?' Stephanie asked, taking her eyes off the road for a second to stare at Emma. 'As in, your house?'

'Yes. I want to be there when David gets back.'

'Honey, you don't know he's even going to get back tonight.'

'He was with his mother, Steph. You heard him.'

Stephanie sighed. 'If you want to go, I'll take you home.'

'Will you stay with me?' Emma asked.

'Of course.'

When they arrived at Emma's house and got out of the car, cameras and microphones were thrust in their faces. Emma's house, glowing warmly from lights inside, seemed as distant as Shangri-la.

'Emma, what happened?' a reporter cried.

'Did he try it again?' asked another.

'Are you all right? What happened?'

'Leave her alone!' Stephanie cried. The officer who had been following them held the reporters back with outstretched arms.

As they entered the house, Stephanie closed the door and leaned against it. 'God, Emma, they are brutal,' she said.

'Yeah, but you were great,' Emma said. 'I thought you were going to punch one of those guys.'

'I should have,' said Stephanie.

They smiled at each other, and then, suddenly, they began to laugh. It wasn't exactly mirth, but it still felt like a relief.

'Mind sharing the joke?'

Emma jumped, and Stephanie cried out. Emma turned and saw her stepfather standing in the doorway to the living room. 'How did you get in here?'

Rory's expression was placid. 'Your mother gave me her key.'

'So you just waltz in here without asking?' Emma cried.

Rory did not reply. He turned and went back into the living room, settling himself comfortably in an armchair. Emma turned to Stephanie and shook her head in disbelief.

'I'll go and make us a cup of tea,' said Stephanie.

Emma had no choice but to follow Rory into the living room. 'Rory,' she demanded, 'why are you here?'

'I was in New York on business, and your mother called from Chicago. She was terribly worried about you after she spoke to you today. Something about the nurse leaving. And then, when you didn't show up in New York, Jessie called her.'

'Oh no. I called Jessie to tell her I wasn't coming.'

'Not until you were at the hospital,' said Rory.

Emma reddened. 'How do you know about that?'

'I called the police, of course. And no, I haven't told your mother yet. You'd better let her know that everything is all right. It is all right, isn't it? The baby and all?'

'Yes. Fine,' said Emma.

'And I take it they have your husband in custody?'

'You'd like that, wouldn't you, Rory?'

'Well, don't they?' he asked.

'David was at the hospital when I was attacked. With his mother. Sorry to disappoint you, but he did not do this.'

Rory adjusted his tie. 'I know you don't like me, Emma. But your mother adores you, and her happiness is important to me.'

'Is it really?' Emma asked. Her anger at him boiled up inside, and suddenly it seemed the ideal opportunity to confront him. 'Is that why you date other women?'

'Please sit down, dear. You're injured. You're pregnant.'

'Don't change the subject,' she said. But she edged round the sofa and sank down onto a cushion, huddled against the arm furthest from Rory.

'What is the subject?' he said.

'I saw you in Chiara's in New York. You were nuzzling up to some woman, not my mother.'

'I'm sorry I didn't see you. You should have spoken to me.'

'I didn't want to interrupt,' she said.

'Not at all. I would have enjoyed introducing you. You'd like Charlotte. She was my first wife, actually.'

'Your wife?' said Emma.

'First wife. Yes. I loved her dearly, but she left me.'

'So, what now? She's changed her mind?' Emma asked.

'She left me for a lady veterinarian down in Florida.'

Emma blanched.

'Oh, don't look so embarrassed. I survived and went on to have a much better marriage with your mother. Charlotte happened to be in New York when I was. I know you were hoping it would be something sordid that you could report to your mother—'

'I only mentioned I saw you from a distance,' Emma said.

Rory waved his hand dismissively. 'Kay knows all about Charlotte. Emma, your mother and I are very fortunate to have found each other.'

Emma blushed. 'Sorry,' she mumbled. 'No offence.'

'None taken,' said Rory. Then he frowned. 'So your mother said the nurse we hired for you left and didn't come back?'

'That's right. She got mad and walked out.'

'I called the health-care agency. The supervisor didn't know anything about Miss Slocum's leaving.'

'They didn't know?' Emma asked. 'Were they concerned?'

'Yes. They were going to call her home to check on her.'

'What if she's not there? Maybe they should call the police.'

Rory shook his head. 'I think your own experiences have you a little jumpy here. Adults are not considered missing until several days pass. Still, it seems a little strange.'

'It is,' said Emma.

Stephanie came into the room, carrying a tray with three teacups on it. 'Anyone for a pick-me-up?' she asked.

Rory pushed himself out of the chair. 'I'd love to stay with you ladies, but I need to conclude my business in New York. Emma, what are we doing about protecting you now?'

'Stephanie is staying until David gets back. And the police are coming by every hour. Checking on the house.'

'I don't think that's adequate. There have been two attempts on your life. The police should be stationed outside, not just driving around. If they refuse to do that, you should have a bodyguard.'

Emma sighed. 'You're probably right. I'll look into it.'

'Your mother and I will check in with you tomorrow. By the way, I have the papers for the Mathis boy's trust.' Rory reached into a calfskin folder and handed them to Emma. 'If you want to sign them, I'll take them along and set things in motion.'

'OK.' Emma glanced at the sheaf of papers, signing everywhere he had put an X. 'Thanks for arranging this.'

'Glad I could help.' Just then David opened the front door and walked into the hallway.

'David!' Emma cried.

She started to rise from her seat, but he was beside her before she had stepped away from the sofa. He wrapped his arms around her and held her. Emma felt all the tension inside of her give way in his embrace. She looked up at him.

'What happened?' she asked.

'Nothing. Yunger read them the riot act, and they let me go. I had an alibi for the entire afternoon. I didn't want to dignify their questions with answers, but that's why you have a lawyer. To keep you from acting stupid.' He turned. 'Hello, Rory. This is a surprise.'

'I'm just leaving,' said Rory.

David turned to Stephanie. 'Thanks for taking care of Emma.'

Stephanie nodded. 'No problem.'

Rory put the papers back into his briefcase. 'Keep Emma and my grandchild safe,' he said in a warning tone.

'I'll do my best,' said David.

'Your best has been a little short of the mark,' Rory said.

Emma felt resentment start to rise in her throat, but David smiled and shook Rory's hand. 'I promise you,' he said.

'Goodbye, Emma.' Rory patted her shoulder awkwardly.

'I guess I'll go too,' said Stephanie. 'Are you sure you don't want to come home with me?'

'I'm fine right here,' said Emma. She and Stephanie embraced.

'I'll call you tomorrow,' said Stephanie. 'Get some sleep.'

'I need to hang my coat up. I'll see you out,' David said.

After they walked out of the room, Emma sank back down into the sofa. She felt light-headed and drained, and relieved to have her husband home again.

David came back into the room. 'Are you sure you're OK?' he said, flopping down on the sofa beside her.

Emma nodded. Then she glanced at him. 'Now I am.'

'Are you still angry at me? I was such a jerk. Trying to excuse my own missteps by implying that you and Burke—'

'It's all right. That seems like a million years ago,' she said.

Headlights flashed outside as a car slowed. David got up and walked over to the window. 'The police are out there.'

'They're going to check on the house regularly tonight.'

'I'm glad. This nightmare won't quit. We need to talk about taking serious measures for keeping you safe.'

'Rory said the same thing. But not now. I'm exhausted.'

'I know you are,' David said, looking at her closely. 'We'd better get you to bed.'

'I wish we could sleep upstairs in our bed. The two of us.'

He stood gazing at her for a moment. Then he bent over and lifted her into his arms. 'We can,' he said.

Despite her exhaustion, Emma felt irresistibly drawn to her husband, and they managed cautiously to make love. Then she fell into a deep sleep. But sometime into the third or fourth hour, something caused her to wake up. She turned over to fold herself against David and fall asleep again, lulled by his warmth. His covers were pulled back, his side of the bed empty.

Immediately, she was wide awake, feeling a rush of panic. Calm down, she thought. He probably went to the bathroom. She listened for the sound of running water, but the house was silent.

'David,' she whispered. There was no answer.

Her heart was thudding now, and she felt sick to her stomach. Stop it, she thought. Maybe he couldn't sleep and didn't want to disturb her. Maybe he was downstairs, watching TV with the sound muted. But none of it made her feel better. Maybe he had disappeared too, like the nurse. Vanished from the house.

She knew she could get up and go and find out. But she was too frightened to budge.

Then she remembered the knife. David had gone down to the kitchen for a cold drink after they had made love. He'd brought back the knife and tucked it under the mattress, just in case.

Emma stuck one arm out from under the covers and wrested the knife from its hiding place. Reluctantly, she swung her legs out over the floor and pulled on her robe. She thought about snapping on the light, but if the worst had happened, if her enemy was here and had somehow subdued her husband, she was better off in darkness.

She tiptoed out to the hallway. Knife in hand, she looked over the railing into the living room. Where are you, David? she thought. You promised not to leave me alone. For one moment she regretted that she had not stayed with Stephanie.

Stop it, she thought. You're letting your imagination run away with you. David is here, in the house. Just go down and look. But the thought of descending those stairs was terrifying. As she hesitated, her eye caught a movement in the unfinished nursery across the hall.

Only a corner of the room was visible, but she saw something move across the patch of moonlight on the floor. Gripping the knife, she took a few steps closer. The curved rockers on the chair had moved slightly as the barefoot man sitting in it shifted his weight. Though his back was to her, she recognised her husband right away. Wearing a T-shirt and his pyjama bottoms, he was bent forward, the palms of his hands pressed against his eye sockets. He looked as if he was trying to keep his head from exploding.

Emma slipped the knife into her pocket. 'David?' she said.

He uttered a strangled cry and turned to her, dropping his hands.

'Honey, what's the matter?' she asked. She approached the chair and sank down carefully, aware of the knife in her pocket, laying her forearm across his knees. 'You look terrible.'

'Nothing,' he said. 'I couldn't sleep.'

'You looked like you were in pain,' she said.

He patted her arm in the soft bathrobe. 'I'm fine.'

'Why are you sitting in this room?'

'I didn't want to go downstairs and leave you alone up here.'

Emma nodded, but her mind was racing. He had obviously been in terrible distress. 'So much has happened,' she said. 'I've been so focused on myself, I haven't been thinking about you. Are you worried about your mother?'

For a moment, he looked at her blankly. Then he shrugged. 'Well, sure. But unless she gets that transplant, this kind of thing is inevitable. Look, I don't want to think about her.'

'OK,' she said. 'It's just that you looked so . . . despairing.'

'Well, you weren't meant to see me,' he said in a mild, placating tone. 'You were supposed to be sleeping.'

'Don't do that,' she pleaded. 'Don't shut me out like that. It scares me to see you looking so hopeless. We need to say what we feel. Whatever it is.'

David stared at her, half illuminated by moonlight. In the dark room, his eyes were glittering. 'You don't want to know.'

'Yes,' she said as her stomach did a sickening flip. 'I do.'

He sighed, reached out, and took her hands. 'You're such a good person,' he said. 'The kind of woman any man would be proud to call his wife.'

The compliments alarmed her. They sounded strangely impersonal. She withdrew her hands. 'What's this all about?'

He shook his head. 'Emma, you should never have married me. I'm not meant to be a husband. Or a parent,' he said.

She felt as if he had slammed her in her heart. 'Don't say that,' she protested. 'Why would you say that?'

'You asked me to tell you what I was thinking,' he said.

'It's not true!' she cried. 'You're a wonderful husband. It's just all this horrible stuff that's happened. Anybody would feel overwhelmed.' But even to her own ears her words sounded panicky. 'When did you start to feel this way?' she asked.

'Always,' David said. 'Having kids was too much for my father. He walked out on us when I was two. And my mother never seemed to be there. She had no choice, of course. She did the best she could, but she had to work, and my brother hated having to take care of me. He used to play this game where he would throw lighted matches at me. Or take me places like the movies and then just leave me behind.'

'Oh, David,' she said.

'I'm not fishing for sympathy. It's just that I saw myself as a burden to people. Maybe I would treat a child the same way.'

She felt a terror in her heart that equalled the fear she had felt earlier in the day, teetering over the abyss of the train tracks. He was threatening not her life but her happiness. Her hopes, her dreams.

'David, once this mess is behind us, once they catch whoever is doing these horrible things, you're going to start to feel better. You and I are going to have a wonderful life together. As for kids, lots of people with unhappy childhoods are excellent with their children. They try harder. It matters more to them.'

He regarded her silently.

Please, God, she thought. Don't let him desert me. Help him to see how much I need him. 'Come back to bed,' she said. 'What you need is rest. We both do.'

She leaned up to embrace him and felt the point of the knife pierce her robe pocket and nick her in the thigh. She stifled a yelp. She didn't want him to know that she had the knife in her pocket. Didn't want him to know she was afraid.

Long after David was breathing peacefully, Emma lay awake, thinking about her husband. He seemed to have changed in the short time they had been married. Of course their experience had been nightmarish, she thought, but maybe it was her very vulnerability that was alarming him. Maybe all her injuries, her feebleness, her fears, were reminding him of the difficult role that he was taking on. After all, as a father, he would be responsible for a small, vulnerable human being. The idea of having a wife who was also weak and dependent might be overwhelming to him.

Although there was nothing Emma could do about his anxieties about fatherhood, she could try to face her own fear. Yes, someone was trying to kill her. But she was not a weak person. She would prove it to David. If she lived through all this turmoil and lost her marriage, she would be completely miserable. She had to try. This determination, however fleeting, calmed her turbulent heart, and she was finally able to sleep.

The next morning, when she woke and looked at her husband, she saw that he was propped up on one elbow, gazing at her.

'Hi,' she whispered. 'How are you feeling?'

'Better. Sorry about last night,' he said.

'It's all right. I'm glad you're feeling better.'

'I am. Except that I'm worried sick about you. I'm supposed to go to New York again today. Another assignment. But I'm going to cancel. We can do it on the telephone.'

'Maybe you should go. It might get your mind off all this.'

'No. I can't leave you here alone,' he said.

'What are you going to do?' she teased. 'Go to work with me?'

'You can't go to work,' he said.

'David, I want to. I can't just sit around here, waiting for . . . I don't know what. Especially after what happened yesterday.'

'You need to rest,' he insisted.

Emma smiled. 'Being occupied will be the best medicine.'

He frowned at her. 'I might as well be talking to the wall.'

Emma pressed her lips together. 'David, now that we know I am the target of this maniac, I have to live in a different way. I can't rely on others to take care of me all the time. I can't be looking over my shoulder every minute. I'm going to get a gun,' she said.

'A gun?' he cried. 'That's crazy. I thought we were talking about a bodyguard.'

'Well, maybe the police will provide one,' Emma said.

David shook his head. 'Nothing doing. I asked about protection for you last night, but the police chief said that there was no money in his budget for private bodyguards. Do you believe that? Anyway, I'm going to call a few places and enquire.'

'That's fine. But meanwhile, I want to carry a gun.'

'Do you even know how to use a gun?'

'My dad taught me how to use a gun when I was a kid and we'd go camping together. We used to shoot our empty cans.'

'Emma, I don't like it,' he said.

'David, there's a man trying to kill me. What's to prevent him from trying again?'

'Don't even say it,' he insisted. 'Besides, it takes time to get a gun. You can't just walk into a store and plunk down your money.'

'I own one,' she said.

David looked around the walls of their bedroom as if seeing them for the first time. 'You have a gun here?'

'No. You know that storage space I have? It's still half-full of stuff from home. Stuff of my father's that my mother cleaned out when she and Rory were moving to the city.'

'The gun is in there?' he said.

'I'm pretty sure it is. It's a pistol that belonged to my dad.'

'Emma, I just don't know.'

Emma swung her legs over the side of the bed. 'I do,' she said.

'What are you doing?' he asked.

'I told you,' she said. 'I can't sit and wait for this maniac to find me. I'm going to work. And then I'm going to get my gun.'

David drove her to the Wrightsman Centre and accompanied her up to her office, helping her take off the blue-green alpaca cape. Beneath it she wore a long, camel-coloured skirt and a matching high-necked sweater. Her shiny hair hung in a French braid. David kissed her. 'You look beautiful,' he said. 'Now listen. Do not leave these premises alone. Not for anything. Call me when you need me to come and get you. I'll pick you up and we'll head over to the . . . you know . . . storage place.'

'OK,' she assured him.

'On my way out I'll ask Burke to have somebody from security follow you wherever you go today.'

'All right,' she said. 'Go ahead.' She gave him a last kiss goodbye.

David turned to leave her office, and let out a sudden cry.

'What is it?' she said.

She heard a deep voice say, 'Is Dr Webster here?'

David stood back, and Kieran Foster, clad in black, with his magenta-topped hair and three eyes, appeared in the doorway, wielding a guitar.

'Kieran,' said Emma. 'Good to see you.'

David frowned and waved as the boy edged past him and seated himself next to Emma's desk. Emma blew her husband a kiss as he disappeared from view. 'I wanted you to hear a song I wrote,' Kieran said.

Emma smiled. She knew that Natalie, at Burke's behest, sometimes used to critique the creative writings of the centre's patients. Natalie had said that Kieran's lyrics showed promise, and Kieran had been on top of the world for a short time. But then again, Natalie was a published poet, so her opinion had a certain amount of heft. 'I'm not much of a judge,' said Emma. 'But I'd love to hear it.'

The shrill bell rang just as Stephanie was yelling out the pages for homework. 'And leave your composition books on your desks so I can grade your essays tonight.'

There was the usual flurry of shouts and good-natured shoving that always accompanied the changing of classes. Stephanie walked over to a slight, blonde-haired girl who was gathering up her books. 'Alida?' she said. 'Can I talk to you for a minute?'

Alida Devlin looked at Stephanie warily. Her lips and cheeks were painted in shades of pink that matched a gauzy shirt. Her blonde hair was twisted into a coil, and long bangs curved across mascaraed eyes.

'I have to go to health,' the girl said.

'I'll give you a pass,' said Stephanie. 'Sit down a minute.'

Alida sighed, sat down at her desk, and took a purple marking pen from her bag. She began to doodle on the brown cover of her composition notebook. 'What'd I do?' she asked.

'Nothing,' said Stephanie, sitting at the desk in front of her.

'So why do I have to stay?'

Stephanie hesitated. 'Look, I know this year has been very tough for you. I know about your sister. I don't mean to bring up a painful subject, but I was wondering if you were seeing anybody. You know, a psychologist or a counsellor.'

Alida's heart-shaped face hardened, and she continued to doodle. 'My dad says that shrinks are full of it.'

'When something happens in a family, sometimes the adults are too upset to help the kids. It can help to go outside.'

'For what?' Alida said.

'Well, for someone to talk to,' said Stephanie. 'Especially if things are out of hand at home. In any way.'

'What do you mean?' the girl asked, keeping her eyes focused on the scribblings of the purple pen.

'Sometimes, losing a child, parents can blame each other. Sometimes when parents . . . depend on their children for comfort, it can become . . . an unhealthy situation.'

Alida stopped doodling and stared at Stephanie, as if she did not understand one word of what Stephanie was suggesting.

'Look, Alida, all I'm trying to say is, you can talk to me. About anything. Just so you know that.'

'Can I go now?' Alida said

'Sure,' said Stephanie, feeling defeated, even foolish.

'I need that pass,' said Alida. 'For health.'

'Oh, of course.' Stephanie scribbled out the pass and handed it to her.

'Thanks,' said Alida softly. She hurried out of the room.

Stephanie sighed and looked at her watch. She had just enough time in this free period to mark a few essays. She began collecting the composition books Alida's class had left. When she picked up Alida's book, something purple caught her eye.

On the front was a small purple drawing of a girl's face. A ponytail stood straight up from an inverted triangle with round vacant eyes and two dots for a nose. The mouth was a tiny bow. A balloon hovered cloudlike above the head, with tiny circular puffs, indicating thoughts, leading from the ponytail to the balloon.

Stephanie frowned and bent lower, looking closely at the words. Inside the balloon Alida had written: HELP ME.

11

EMMA LISTENED TO Kieran's ballad of teenage angst, of death and destruction, as sincerely as she could. Then she left him to keep her appointment with Tasha Clayman and her parents. Wade and Nell surprised Emma with their willingness to make the changes she had suggested. Emma felt hopeful. As if to confirm her hope, Sarita Ruiz entered with a lunch tray and whispered, 'Yesterday she ate a bite of her sandwich.' Emma's heart lifted.

Trailed by the security guard Burke had provided, Emma returned to the cubbyhole that was her office. As she unlocked the door, the phone was ringing. She picked it up.

'Emma,' Burke said. 'We've got a situation here. Can I see you in my office right away?'

Emma's heart skipped a beat. 'Sure.' She hung up and turned to the guard. 'We're being summoned,' she said to him.

Geraldine rolled her eyes in warning as Emma entered Burke's reception area. The guard settled himself on a chair, and Emma walked into Burke's office. He was behind his desk, and Stephanie sat facing him.

'Steph,' Emma said. 'What are you doing here?'

Burke answered for Stephanie. 'Based on information you provided, Miss Piper decided to investigate the Devlin family.'

Emma grimaced. 'Steph, I told you not to.'

'Now wait a minute,' said Stephanie. 'I did not mention you or this place. I simply had a talk with one of my students. I told her I was concerned about her and offered to be available if she needed to talk.'

Burke picked up the composition book on his desk and handed it to Emma. 'Take a look at that.'

Emma frowned, then noticed the purple face. '"Help me"? Alida Devlin wrote that? Did you ask her what it meant?'

Stephanie grimaced. 'I wasn't sure what I'd do if she told me. So I decided to talk to a couple of experts. What do I do now?'

There were two women in the hospital room: a thin, pale old woman asleep on the bed with an oxygen tube in her nose and an IV in her arm, and another elderly woman, this one red-faced and healthy-looking, slumped in a chair, snoring loudly.

'Excuse me,' said Joan Atkins, touching the woman in the chair.

Birdie started and instinctively clutched her pocketbook, as if to hide its contents. She blinked at Joan and Trey Marbery. Her grey hair was in disarray, and she smelt of alcohol.

'Is this Mrs Webster?' Joan asked, pointing to the sleeping woman.

Birdie nodded. 'Yes. Who are you?'

'I'm Lieutenant Joan Atkins of the state police. This is Detective Marbery. You must be Mrs Theobald.'

'That's right. I'm her cousin. I take care of her.' Birdie straightened up in her chair. 'I'd ask you to sit, but . . .'

'That's not necessary,' said Joan. 'I wanted to ask you about yesterday afternoon.'

'Is this about David? Because they already asked about this last night. Some detective called me at the hospital.'

'That was me,' said Trey.

'I want to go over a few things, if you don't mind.' Joan had been called away on a case in Newark when David Webster was brought in. 'Mrs Theobald, were you here with Mrs Webster all afternoon yesterday?'

'Oh yes,' said Birdie. 'I never left her.'

'What about her son? David Webster?'

'Yes. I told this fellow here. I called David because I couldn't wake her up. He helped me get her here.'

'What time was that?' Joan asked.

'Oh, it was around three thirty. Maybe four at the latest.'

'And did Mr Webster stay at the hospital after that?'

'Oh yes,' said Birdie. 'He was in this room until nine.'

'And you were awake that whole time?' Joan asked.

'Awake? Of course. Why wouldn't I be awake?'

'Hospitals can be stressful, especially when you're tired.'

'I wasn't tired,' said Birdie.

'Maybe you take medications that make you drowsy?'

'Not me,' Birdie insisted.

'Mrs Theobald, you were asleep when we walked in just now. And I have to say there's a strong smell of alcohol in this room.'

Birdie stuck out her chin. 'I may have nodded off for a minute. But if I did, it was just for a minute or two.'

Joan looked at her intently. 'Is it possible you could have been asleep here yesterday?'

'Not asleep,' Birdie corrected her indignantly. Then her bravado wilted. 'I might have just . . . catnapped.'

Joan raised her eyebrows. Trey Marbery sighed.

'So,' said Joan, 'you can't say for sure that Mr Webster was here from three thirty to nine o'clock yesterday. He may have left the hospital while you were sleeping.'

'I didn't say that. As far as I know, he was here. Why don't you people leave him alone?' said Birdie. 'He's a good boy.'

Burke unlocked his silver Lexus and tossed his mail onto a pile of papers on the front seat. 'Just shove those on the floor,' he said.

Emma looked on in disbelief. He was so orderly in his office and in the house. But she could see at a glance that there were unopened bills and bank statements in the car. 'You look like you're getting a little bit behind on things,' she said.

Burke sighed. 'I've had a hard time concentrating lately.'

Emma started to place the papers on the back seat, but it was too painful to twist her torso. She got in. 'I'll just hold them,' she said. She settled herself on the front seat, the pile of papers on her lap.

'I must be crazy to do this,' said Burke as he pulled out of the centre's parking lot and onto the main street.

'You're not crazy. You're just not the typical administrator.'

Burke shook his head. 'I could lose my job for this.' Then he glanced at Emma. 'Don't worry. I'm not changing my mind. It's too important.'

Emma nodded. 'Do you know where we're going?'

'It's not too far.'

Emma settled back in the seat. She glanced down at the manila envelope on the top of the mail pile and lifted her eyebrows at the return address. 'The coroner's office?' she said.

Burke glanced over at the envelope. 'Oh, did that come?'

Emma lifted it from the stack. 'Yeah. Who died?'

'Natalie,' he said grimly.

Emma felt chastened. 'I thought it might be about a patient.'

'I wanted to see the final autopsy report. I've wondered if maybe, in light of what happened to you . . .'

Emma frowned at him. 'You think she might have been killed?'

Burke shrugged. 'It didn't seem possible, but I don't know. I guess I'm not sure of anything any more.'

'Burke, the note was pretty clear about her intentions.'

'That's true,' he said. 'But I keep thinking there was something I overlooked. The change in her was so abrupt. Usually, there was some kind of trigger . . .'

'Oh, Burke, don't do this to yourself,' said Emma. 'She'd made other attempts. There is very little you can do when a person is truly committed to the idea of suicide.'

Burke did not reply. 'There it is,' he said, pointing to a white cottage with arched windows. They knew from Stephanie that Alida had drama club that afternoon, so this was the perfect opportunity to speak to Alida's mother without the girl—or her father—knowing about it. There was one car in the driveway—a minivan. Devlin drove a sports car, which meant he was probably at the university.

'OK,' said Emma. 'This looks good.'

Together they walked to the front door. The shades were all drawn, giving the house a gloomy, deserted look. Emma knocked and waited.

From inside she could hear the television blaring. She knocked harder and called out, 'Hello?' Risa Devlin did not come to the door.

'Let's walk round back,' Burke said. 'Maybe she's in the yard.'

Emma scuffed through the leaves around the side of the house. As she passed a pair of casement windows, she looked in. The windows gave onto the kitchen, and Emma was startled to see a large blonde-haired woman wearing jeans and a satiny low-cut blouse seated at a table littered with dirty dishes, an open half-gallon container of ice cream in front of her. The woman was slowly spooning the ice cream into her mouth.

Emma tapped on the window, and the woman jumped and turned to look, her eyes wide with alarm. Emma waved a hand and grimaced apologetically. The woman rose and cranked open the window. Emma thought what a pretty face she had, even though it was somewhat swollen, and there were dark circles under her large cornflower-blue eyes.

'Mrs Devlin, I'm so sorry to startle you. I tried knocking at the front door, but no one answered.'

Risa Devlin blinked. 'I didn't hear you. The TV, I guess.'

'Dr Heisler and I were wondering if we could talk to you.'

Anxiety rose instantly to the woman's glassy eyes. 'If my husband comes . . .'

'It's just for a minute. Alida's teacher came to see us.'

'Alida!' the woman cried. 'Is Alida all right?'

'Alida is OK,' said Emma.

'You scared me,' Risa said. 'Come on in.' She pointed vaguely in the direction of the front door.

Emma and Burke entered the house and followed the woman down the hall, assuming they were heading to the living room. Instead, Risa Devlin led them to a bedroom that was, unmistakably, the lair of a teenage girl. The walls were papered with posters of rappers, athletes and movie actors. There was a bed with a flowered quilt, a desk with a chair, and a white bureau. Risa indicated the chair, and Emma sat down. Risa lay on the bed. 'I hope you don't mind,' she said, her voice slightly slurred. 'I'm very tired.'

'No. It's all right,' said Emma.

'This was Ivy's room. I spend a lot of time in here.'

'I'm sure it's a comfort,' said Emma, although she could tell that this woman was anything but comforted. She was clearly trying to medicate her problems away.

'Why are you here? Why didn't the teacher come?'

Emma looked at Burke. 'Mrs Devlin,' he said. 'Thank you for talking to us. I realise we put you in an awkward position when Ivy was at the centre. I know your husband is still very angry.'

Tears rose to the woman's large blue eyes. 'You were trying to help Ivy. Even if you were wrong about what you thought.'

'Alida's teacher talked to her at school today,' Emma began.

'Her grades are good,' said Risa.

Emma nodded. 'She hasn't done anything wrong. It's just that her teacher was thinking that this was a difficult time for her.'

Risa's eyes glistened. 'Of course it is. She lost her sister.'

'Her teacher has noticed changes in Alida,' Emma continued. 'She seems old for her age. She suggested she might want to go to counselling, but Alida indicated that her father wouldn't approve of that. Miss Piper came to us, to see if there was any way we could straighten out the problem.'

Risa stared impassively at Emma, her head resting on Ivy's pillow. She appeared to be drifting away. 'What is the problem?'

Burke frowned. 'Mrs Devlin, we came to you once before, to ask for your help, and you were ready to move heaven and earth for your daughter's sake.'

Tears began to trickle down Risa Devlin's face. 'It didn't work,' she said. 'Nothing worked.'

Burke held up Alida's notebook, which he had brought with him. 'While she was talking to Miss Piper, Alida was drawing something. We thought you might want to see it.'

Risa struggled to a sitting position and reached for the notebook. Her gaze travelled over the drawing as if Burke had handed her the photo of the corpse of a loved one, long missing. In her eyes was a combination of horror, sorrow and recognition.

'Obviously she has been doing her best to hide her distress,' Emma said. 'Can you think why she would write that?'

Risa began to shake her head. Her hands trembled.

'Mrs Devlin?'

Risa Devlin's face had changed. She looked up and lifted the notebook in her trembling hands. 'I can't do this again. I won't,' Risa said. Her sweet voice had an edge, and her fuzzy blue gaze had begun to clear.

Burke poured a glass of mineral water and handed it to Emma, who was sunk into the comfort of a deep-cushioned sofa in his living room.

'I couldn't believe the way she reacted,' Emma said.

Burke nodded and sat down in a buttery leather club chair. 'I know what you mean. I didn't know what to expect. Risa Devlin seems so . . .'

'Passive. But she's not. She's actually got quite a stiff spine. Although she's nearly broken by Ivy's death.'

'I hated to lay this on her, but it was the right decision.'

'I wish she had called the police,' said Emma. 'I'm worried about leaving her alone to face him. If it was Lyle Devlin who attacked me, he is a horribly dangerous man.'

'I plan to call her at regular intervals tonight,' said Burke.

'Good,' said Emma. All of a sudden she straightened up. 'Burke, do you hear someone. Footsteps?'

Burke frowned and then gestured towards the back deck. Emma nodded. He got up and threw on the outdoor floodlights. David stood staring through the sliding glass doors.

'David,' said Burke. He opened one of the doors.

'Honey, what are you doing out there?' Emma asked.

'I thought I'd have a look. Wondered what I'd see.'

'What does that mean?' Burke asked.

David ignored the question and stepped into the room. His wife was curled up on the sofa, her camel-coloured skirt tucked beneath her, her discarded boots on the carpet. 'Well, you look comfortable,' he said. 'I went over to the centre to pick you up. No one knew where you were. Didn't you realise I'd be worried? You knew I was going to come and get you after work.'

'Oh, David, I'm so sorry,' said Emma. 'I forgot to call you. We went to see Lyle Devlin's wife.'

'What for? You should stay as far away from that guy as you can.' David turned on his friend. 'Why would you take her there?'

Burke grimaced. 'It was unfinished business, David. I think you'll agree it was worth while when we tell you about it. Can I get you something? A glass of wine?'

'I don't want any wine. I want to take my wife home.'

'This is my fault, David,' Burke said. 'I should have realised you'd think something terrible had happened.'

Emma set her glass down on the table. 'Burke, this was my mistake. David, I promise you it was an important meeting.' She stuck her stockinged feet into the boots and straightened her clothes. 'I'll tell you all about it on the way to the storage unit.'

'The storage unit?' David cried. 'It's almost dark.'

'You said you'd take me there after work. It won't take long.'

David shook his head.

'Please. You know I can't drive there myself.'

'Is there anything I can do?' Burke asked.

'Stay out of it,' said David. Then he turned to Emma. 'Do you have the key?'

'Right here in my bag.'

'All right. Let's get this over with.'

Emma reached up and kissed him. 'Thanks,' she said. 'Burke, I'll see you at work tomorrow.'

The U-Kan-Keep-It Storage Facility was located along the Smoking River, where there were warehouses and a recycling centre and the offices of the water company. All were deserted now, and halogen lights illuminated row upon row of locked garage-size units surrounded by a chain-link fence. There was a trailer, which served as an office during business hours, and a parking lot.

David parked and came round to help Emma out of the car. 'We're only going to be in there for a minute, right?' he asked.

'Right,' she said. 'Let's go.'

A letter was clearly painted at the end of each row of units. Emma and David walked to row G. There was not another soul around, but that didn't stop Emma from feeling apprehensive as she limped, with David right beside her, down to unit 14.

'This is the one,' she said, stopping in front of a corrugated metal door. She stuck the key in the lock and turned it. David grabbed the handle, and the door clanked as it rose. Emma flipped the switch, and a weak bulb illuminated the storage area. For a moment her heart sank. Why did I save all this stuff? she thought.

At the time of her mother's remarriage, it had seemed sensible to hang on to the things of her childhood. But now, looking at all the boxes bursting with toys, a broken rocking horse, mouldy camping equipment and childhood videos, she wondered.

'Look at all this junk,' David said.

'It's not junk,' she said, bristling.

'Did I say junk?' he asked teasingly. 'I meant treasures. Look at all these treasures.'

'That's better,' she said, smiling.

'How are you going to find anything in this?'

'I know where everything is. Just stay out of my way.' With a sigh, she climbed over rolled-up rugs and tennis rackets until she reached the back of the unit. She had to shift a couple of boxes, even then, to find the one she was seeking. She started to lift a carton marked LINENS.

'Don't you pick that up. You'll break your stitches.' David walked towards her. 'Give it to me. I'll move the stuff so we can get out of here.'

Standing among the shabby mementos, she felt crowded by his impatience. 'David, stop. I want to do this at my own speed. I won't lift anything heavy. I promise.'

He looked at her sceptically. 'All right. I'll wait by the door.'

Moving one box at a time, being sure to test their weights, she found the box she was looking for at the bottom of a pile. She began to lift out the familiar, long-forgotten effects. Her father's old wristwatch that no longer ran. A canvas fishing hat. A book of essays by H. L. Mencken. A small retractable telescope. A framed photo of the two of them, holding up a string of fish. She studied their jubilant, innocent smiles.

She heard David let out a groan. 'What's the matter?' she asked.

'Stubbed my toe on one of these valuable andirons you have hidden in here,' he grumbled.

Emma smiled. 'Sorry,' she said. 'Is it bad?'

'Bad enough. Now we'll both be limping,' he said.

'Well, if it makes you feel any better, those andirons are valuable,' she said.

'Oh, I do feel better. Let me kick it with the other foot and see if I can break that toe too,' he said.

Emma laughed. 'You're a baby. Go and sit down,' she said. 'I found the box. It won't take me long.'

She pushed aside the remaining contents of the box, and there on the bottom, snapped into a mouldy suede shoulder holster, was her father's old Smith & Wesson double-action revolver. In an equally mouldy pouch were the bullets.

From outside the unit, she heard David groan again. Then there was a thud, as if he had flopped down on the concrete. I hope he didn't really break that toe, she thought. Emma opened the pouch and shook out some bullets. Then she unsnapped the holster and pulled the gun out. She moved the latch and shook the cylinder open. One by one she fed the cartridges into the chambers.

'David, I'm all set!' she cried triumphantly, turning round.

Standing at the open door, staring at her, was Lyle Devlin.

Emma let out a cry.

The halogen lights glinted off his wire-rimmed glasses. His fists bulged in his jacket pockets.

'Mr Devlin. What are you doing here? Where's my husband?' she said. She tried to sound calm and collected, but she could hear the panic in her own voice.

'I thought I told you to stay out of my business,' he said.

She kept the gun hidden. 'I have nothing to say to you.'

'First you set the police on me. They came round, suggesting that I was to blame for what happened to you.'

Emma met his glaring gaze but remained silent, her stomach churning. Where was David?

'But that wasn't enough, was it?' he asked. 'When you didn't get your way with the cops, you came to see my wife. Based on some drawing, you accuse me of being a monster, not a father.'

Emma's heart was thudding. 'David!' she called out.

'You persecute me. You hound me. And then you ask why I'm here?'

'I didn't—' Emma started to protest.

Devlin suddenly pulled his fists from his pockets, raised them up, and grasped the door handle above his head.

'What are you . . . what?' Emma heard the clank of the door as it began to descend. 'No, stop that!' she cried, stumbling across boxes and objects that blocked her path.

Devlin was jerking the door down. It was at his waist. In a moment it would slam shut, trapping her inside. 'Enjoy your stay.'

Emma could see only the lower half of his legs. With trembling hands, she pulled her father's gun to eye level, squinted down the barrel and fired at his shins.

There was a horrible scream. Devlin crumpled, shrieking in pain. Emma clambered across the space and jammed her wooden rocking horse beneath the sinking door.

Devlin was screaming, grasping his shattered shin.

Emma pocketed the gun, grabbed the door handle, and with a cry of pain began to lift. The door rolled back up, and she staggered out. Devlin was rolling on the asphalt walkway.

She heard a groan, turned, and saw David sprawled on the cement. 'David!' She fell to her knees, and he struggled to sit, gripping his head. 'You're bleeding!'

He looked at his hand. 'What happened?' he said.

'Devlin. He was trying to lock me in the storage room.'

'Oh God, I never saw him coming. I got sucker punched.' He looked searchingly at Emma. 'Are you all right? Did he hurt you?'

She shook her head. 'I shot him!' she cried.

'You did?' He grabbed her, his eyes wide.

'He's over there. I shot him in the knee.'

David looked at the figure on the ground, writhing in pain and hollering. His expression changed from horror to glee. He pulled her close. 'That's my girl. Serves the bastard right. Way to go.'

12

THE DEVLIN HOUSE was dark, except for one light behind a shaded window. A blue minivan was parked in the driveway. Joan Atkins rapped loudly on the door. 'Mrs Devlin,' she called out. 'It's Lieutenant Atkins and Detective Marbery.'

There was silence from inside the house, and she rapped again. 'Are you in there, Mrs Devlin? Are you all right?'

After a few more moments, Risa Devlin opened the door.

Joan could hardly believe it was the same woman that she had met during her earlier visit. She was wearing a dark jacket that was buttoned up and belted round her ample waist. Her eyes were flinty. 'What do you want?' she said.

'We need to talk to you. Your husband's been shot. He is at the hospital. In police custody.'

Risa's eyes widened. 'He was shot?'

'He was shot in the knee. He's in surgery right now, having the bullet removed. Could we come in and talk to you?'

Risa shrugged. 'You can come in. But I'm busy packing. We need to get to the airport.' She turned away, leaving the door ajar. Joan and Trey Marbery followed her into the house. Sure enough, right in the front hallway were three suitcases, sitting side by side.

'Where are you going?' Joan asked.

'Back to Wisconsin. My father and brothers live there.' She walked to the foot of the stairs. 'Alida? Are you ready?'

The muffled voice sounded tearful. 'Almost. I'm coming.'

'You and your husband had an argument?' Joan asked.

Risa turned and frowned. 'How did you know?'

'Your husband was shot by Dr Webster. He was very angry about her coming to see you. He accosted her, and she shot him.'

Risa stared at Joan. 'Did he hurt Dr Webster?'

Joan watched Risa's face. 'No. Luckily. But we want to talk to him about the other attempts on Dr Webster's life.'

Risa's blue eyes widened in horror. She sat down on the stairs with a thud. 'You think he's the one who tried to kill her?'

'We don't know. Dr Webster pointed out that your husband works across from the station where someone tried to push her onto the tracks, and so far we haven't located the student he claimed he was tutoring at the time. As for the first attempt, you agreed he was here watching some Italian movie. Was that true?'

Risa Devlin sighed. 'I vaguely remember watching the movie. I couldn't swear to you it was that night.'

'Where do you rent your movies?' Trey interjected. 'They'll have a record of when you rented it.'

Risa Devlin frowned. 'Blockbuster. The one on Shelby.'

'Mrs Devlin,' said Joan. 'Why did Dr Webster come and see you earlier?'

Risa looked at her warily. 'Didn't she tell you?'

'Not without your permission,' she said. 'Privileged.'

Risa seemed to consider it, and then she shook her head. 'I'm not saying anything else. My daughter doesn't need to have this all over the newspapers. No. We're getting away from here. Alida,' she called. 'Come down. We have to go.'

'Mrs Devlin. You can't run away from this. If you know why your husband went after Dr Webster, you're going to have to testify in court.'

'What did Daddy do?' cried a soft voice from the staircase.

They all looked up. Alida, in a baggy sweatshirt, her eyes red-rimmed, was standing stock-still on the stairs.

'Come on, honey,' said Risa. 'Never mind about it. We have to go.'

Alida did not budge. 'What happened?'

'Your dad is in the hospital,' said Risa. 'He's been shot.'

Alida blanched. 'Is this because of me?'

'No, baby, of course not,' her mother insisted.

'Why would you think that, Alida?' Joan asked.

'My parents had a huge fight about me after those two doctors left. My father was screaming.'

'That's enough,' said Risa. 'Don't say anything else.'

The girl looked at her mother. 'You said it wasn't my fault.'

Risa took a deep breath. 'No, baby, it wasn't your fault.'

'What happened, Alida?' Joan asked gently.

Alida's small voice trembled. 'My dad did stuff. He said he wanted me to know what to do when I had a real boyfriend.'

Risa Devlin's shoulders slumped. 'Both my babies. He did it to both my babies. My Ivy was starving herself. Trying to disappear, to escape from him. That's what Dr Webster said, but I wouldn't believe it.' She began to sob. 'They showed me the picture from school, and it finally dawned on me. How could I have been so blind? He'd moved on. To Alida.'

Alida rushed down the stairs. She put her arms round her mother and buried her face in the dark jacket. 'Don't cry, Mom. Let's go to Grandpa's. Let's go before he gets back.'

Risa held her daughter close and looked pleadingly at Joan. 'Let me get her away from here. Please.'

Joan looked at her thoughtfully. 'I need a written statement from you. It won't take long. Then you can go. This is not the end of it, you understand. I'll need to talk to you again.'

'I understand,' Risa said.

'All right. We'll knock out your statement as quickly as possible, and then I'll have an officer take you to the airport. Do you mind if my officers search your house and your computers?'

Risa looked around at the home she had tried to make. 'It's all yours,' she said.

Reporters called so persistently that David ended up turning off the ringer on the phone. It was all anyone could talk about on television. Lambert University professor Lyle Devlin had been shot and was in surgery. Police were waiting to question him in connection with the attack on Emma Webster and the murder of Claude Mathis in the Pine Barrens, as well as to question him about accusations of sexual abuse of his daughters. Emma stared at the TV until David switched it off.

'How could he?' she asked, shaking her head.

'He's sick,' he said. 'But you know that. You tried to warn them. The guy is evil.'

She reached up and touched the bandage on his head. 'How are you feeling?' she asked.

'Well, on the one hand, I've got a hell of a headache,' he admitted. 'But,' he said, smiling, 'I forgot all about my toe.'

She lifted his hand and kissed it. They sat together in their bathrobes, the remains of the pizza they had ordered in a box on the table. 'How 'bout you? Feel better?' he asked.

'Starting to.'

A pounding on the front door made Emma shrink into a corner of the sofa. David stood up. 'They never quit. I'll get rid of them,' he said wearily, and walked to the door.

Emma heard voices, then Lieutenant Atkins stepped into the living room, wearing a grey microfibre trench coat over her suit. 'Emma,' she said. 'How are you feeling?'

'Better, thanks.'

'I'm sure you've heard the news. We'll be placing Devlin under arrest once he's out of recovery. We have enough evidence to hold him. His computers reveal numerous contacts with underage girls. And his daughter signed a sworn statement.'

'What about the attacks on Emma?' David demanded.

'Well, we're going to question him, of course,' Joan said.

'Do you have any doubt?' David asked.

Joan gazed at him thoughtfully. She found his eagerness to blame Devlin a bit convenient. 'Technically,' she said, 'Devlin didn't lay a hand on your wife tonight.'

'I don't believe this,' said David. 'He tried to lock her away. And he certainly whacked me.'

'I know. But so far we haven't tied him to the other attacks.'

'I told you about the music building,' Emma reminded her.

'I haven't forgotten. It's possible he will become our prime suspect.' Joan took a deep breath. 'But regardless of how much Devlin may have deserved it, Emma, you assaulted him with a deadly weapon. An illegal firearm to boot. I think this can safely be classified as self-defence, but you will have to appear in court on a misdemeanour charge. Right now I'm here to confiscate the weapon.'

'But I need that gun,' Emma protested.

'You're not licensed to use it,' Joan reminded her.

'It was my father's. I don't want to part with it,' Emma said.

'You'll get it back eventually.'

Emma sighed. 'All right, Lieutenant.' She got up from the sofa and went to the cabinet in the dining room. She pulled out the unloaded gun and handed it over.

'Thank you,' Joan said. 'Now, try and get some rest.'

Emma walked the lieutenant to the door. When she turned round, David was cleaning up pizza crusts and folding paper plates into the box. 'It's not fair,' she said.

'I'm relieved in a way,' he said. 'I wasn't comfortable with you carrying that gun. Although I admit, you did a great job with it tonight.'

'Thanks,' she said, smiling. Together they carried the remains of their dinner into the kitchen and tossed it into the trash.

'I'm going to have a shower,' David said. 'And you'— he pointed a finger at her—'no more news on TV.'

Emma followed him through to the living room and flicked on the TV with the remote. 'No news,' she promised. 'I'm watching the Discovery channel.' She sat back down and stared as sharks glided across the Great Barrier Reef. 'Don't get your bandage wet,' she called after him.

In a few moments Emma could hear the water running. She hesitated, and then got up and went over to the phone. She dialled Burke's number, but his machine picked up. 'Burke, call when you get back. They've arrested Devlin.'

She pushed up the volume on the ringer before she hung up and returned to the sofa and the programme she had been watching. Even the brightest of tropical fish looked dull on the small blue screen, as if they were trapped in a ghoulish aquarium. She switched the TV off and began to think about making the long trek up the stairs to their bedroom. She had made it down that morning, although it had taken her a while.

She was on the fourth step when the phone began to ring. She could hear David's shower still running. She couldn't very well call out to him to answer it. If it's Burke, she thought, I'll hobble down and pick up when I hear his voice on the machine. She waited for several rings and then heard a man's voice recording his message.

'David, this is Bob Cheatham. Look, I feel terrible about missing our interview the other day. There were postproduction problems on the film, and they needed me in California, but I owe you one. I'll make good next time I'm in town.'

He hung up. Emma stood on the stairs, staring at the phone. Then, slowly, she started back down.

In a short while David reappeared in the living room gingerly blotting his hair with a towel. 'I am beat,' he said to Emma, who was sitting on the couch with the TV off. 'Hey, are we sleeping up or down tonight? I'll be glad to carry you again.'

Emma did not reply or meet his gaze.

'Honey, what's the matter?' he said. He frowned at her. 'What is it? You look sick.'

Emma looked up at his ruddy, freshly shaven face. He looked guileless and innocent. Looks could be deceiving, she thought. 'We got a phone call while you were in the shower,' she said. 'It was Bob Cheatham.'

David's face fell. He pressed his lips together and sat down in a chair opposite the sofa. 'Oh.'

'He said how sorry he was to cancel your interview.'

David sighed.

'Where were you,' she said coldly, 'if you didn't go to New York?'

'I did go to New York. I didn't know he was going to cancel. I found out when I got to the restaurant.'

She thought about how frightened she had been when she returned from Kellerman's. When the wind was howling, and the nurse was gone. 'So you did what? Stayed for lunch?'

'No, of course not. Nevin called the restaurant. Told me that Cheatham had cancelled, and asked me to pick up another interview instead. The guy was a French novelist, very elusive, who was leaving the country the next day. I had to jump in a cab and go meet him in the Village.'

Emma just stared at him.

'Em, I was right there in the city. I couldn't turn him down. I had to take the job. Nevin needed me to cover it for him.'

Emma stood up and pulled her bathrobe tight around the waist. 'Why didn't you just tell me that? Why lie about it?'

'Because I knew you would react like this. You didn't want me to go in the first place. If I told you I accepted another assignment instead of rushing home . . .'

She made her way slowly to the downstairs bedroom, where she took off her robe and got under the covers. She could hear David double-check the locks and turn off the lights.

In a few minutes he came in, turned off the light, and sat down carefully on the bed beside her. She turned on her side, with her back to him. Their breathing was audible in the dark.

'I should have told you,' he said. He placed a hand on her shoulder, but she shook it off. 'Emma, listen. I know this sounds stupid, but I thought I was sparing your feelings.'

'You were lying, David. Please get off my bed. It hurts when your weight pulls it down.'

David sighed and stood up. He looked at her for a moment. Then he went round to the bed. 'Emma, I intended to tell you the truth when I got home. I figured you were safe with the nurse, and I would just explain how the plans had changed. You're not the kind of woman who goes crazy over a change in plans. I wouldn't have married you if you were.'

Emma said nothing.

'But then I got back and found out you were at Burke's and that the nurse had walked out. I didn't want to make it worse.'

'Excuses.'

David flopped down on the bed and stared up at the ceiling.

After a few silent minutes Emma turned over and looked at him. 'What?' she demanded. 'What are you thinking about?'

'I'm thinking that you're right. That is what I do. I make excuses. Anything but tell the truth. I'm afraid that's who I am,' he said, his voice hollow. 'I tried to tell you it was a mistake for you to marry me. I knew you would regret it.'

Emma lay down again with her back to him. 'I didn't say I regretted marrying you,' she said.

They lay tensely side by side in their separate beds, and then, after a few moments, he propped himself up on one elbow, put his hand out, and touched her arm. 'You don't know how much I need you,' he whispered. 'I'm going to try to be the husband you hoped for. At least they've arrested the man who tried to hurt you.'

'Lieutenant Atkins didn't say that,' she said.

'It is Devlin. It has to be. And now I know you are safe.'

'Maybe,' she said.

'You are.' He lay down again. 'It's over now. You'll see.'

A few minutes later he was breathing evenly. As if all was well in their world. His complacency made her angry. His lies forgotten, he slept peacefully. But why shouldn't he? The police have Lyle Devlin. There is nothing more to fear.

Still, she lay beside her sleeping husband, wide awake.

The next morning Joan Atkins arrived at the Clarenceville police station at about ten o'clock and stopped at the coffee machine to pour herself a mug. As she looked around the busy squad room she noticed that Trey was at his desk. Perched on the chair beside him was a girl wearing glasses and a turquoise cardigan.

'Morning, Lieutenant,' said a passing patrolman.

'Morning,' said Joan.

Hearing her voice, Trey looked up. Then he rose and walked over to the coffee machine, holding a sheet of paper.

'Morning, ma'am. You'd better look at this.'

'What is it, Detective?' Joan asked, sipping her coffee.

'It says Lyle Devlin rented the video of that Italian flick the night of the attack on Emma Webster. He returned it the next day.'

'OK,' said Joan slowly, feeling a pinprick of apprehension.

'Plus, you see that girl by my desk? That's Olive Provo.'

'Devlin's tutorial student.' Joan set down her mug and walked over to the girl. 'Miss Provo? I'm Lieutenant Atkins of the state police. We've been trying to reach you. Where have you been?'

'I didn't know you were looking for me,' the girl said.

'We checked with your room-mate and your adviser. Nobody knew where you were.'

Olive rolled her eyes. 'I spent the night with a guy, OK?'

'Oh,' said Joan. 'Well, we just need you to answer a simple question. Where were you Tuesday afternoon between four thirty and six thirty?'

'I was at my music tutorial with Professor Devlin.'

'And during this tutorial, did Professor Devlin leave the room at any time?'

Olive considered this. 'No. Not at all. I'm working on a solo piece for the winter concert. I play the cello, and he was giving me an extremely hard time about the eighth notes.'

'Would you sign a sworn statement to that effect?'

Olive's eyebrows rose above her glasses. 'Yeah. Sure.'

Trey Marbery spoke into Joan's ear. 'There's something else,' he said. 'The desk sergeant got a call from an agency that's been missing a private nurse. They said the last place she was seen was Emma Webster's house.'

Emma had not fallen asleep until dawn, and she was not ready to be woken when the phone rang. When she opened her eyes, she saw David sitting on the edge of his bed, murmuring into the phone. Then he hung up and turned to look at her. 'Did that wake you up? I'm sorry.'

'It's all right. Who was it?' she asked.

'Birdie, calling from the hospital. They're letting my mother go this afternoon around one, and she needs my help to take her home.' He frowned. 'But you can't stay here alone,' he said.

'I'll be all right. They've got Devlin now,' she said.

'I did look into getting a bodyguard for you yesterday. I talked to a guy who used to play in the National Football League who does this for a living. He gave me references, and I checked them out. He's got a good rep.'

'You did all that?' she asked.

'Sure. I said I would.'

'Thanks.' In the morning light Emma wondered why she had been so angry at him last night. His lie about the interview might have been unnecessary, but it wasn't some unforgivable deception.

'So why don't I give him a call?' David said.

'Actually,' Emma said, 'I think I'm going to go into work today. I have my group this afternoon. By the time that's over, you can come and get me.'

'You have to have the security guard with you. Just in case.'

'All right. Just in case.'

Joan Atkins stood on the front porch of the brick-front duplex where Lizette Slocum lived and pounded on the door for the tenth time. Lizette's mailbox, beside the door, was stuffed full of mail. A short, pleasant-looking woman stepped out onto the adjacent porch. 'There hasn't been a peep from over there in the last few days,' she offered.

'Do you know Ms Slocum?' Joan asked.

The woman shook her head. 'She only moved in a few months ago. My husband and I say hello when we see her.'

'When is the last time you saw her?'

The woman frowned. 'I saw her leaving Wednesday morning.'

'Who's the landlord here?'

'His name is Jarvis. I'll get his number.' She disappeared into her house just as Trey Marbery came up the sidewalk to the foot of the porch steps.

'What is it?' said Joan.

'I heard it on the two-way radio,' he said. 'A couple of officers just located her car. It's parked at the bus station.'

Joan leaned against Lizette's porch. 'The bus station? We'd better see if anyone remembers selling Ms Slocum a ticket.'

The woman emerged from her house and gave Joan a slip of paper. 'This is the landlord's number,' she said.

'Thanks,' said Joan. 'When you saw Ms Slocum on Wednesday, did she mention she might be leaving town?'

The woman shook her head. 'We just waved. Do you think she went away on a trip?'

'I hope so,' said Joan.

Emma turned down the corridor to Burke's office. Geraldine was not at her desk, and Burke's office door was open. 'Burke?' Emma called out.

There was no answer. Emma went up to the door and looked inside. The room was empty. There was no overcoat on the coat rack. The banker's lamp on his desk was not lit.

She saw Geraldine carrying a coffee mug into the reception area. 'Geraldine,' she said. 'Is Burke here today?'

'No. He called and said he wouldn't be in. Said he was involved in some kind of urgent business. Any message for him?'

Emma shook her head and walked down to her group session.

She was seated in the circle of chairs when a new patient named Rachel, who was missing her eyebrows and eyelashes, took a seat. Emma felt her energy for work coming back to her, her desire to root out the psychic pain that caused a pretty girl to pluck every hair from her face.

The group consisted of six that day—four boys and two girls. One of the boys was Kieran, who slumped in his chair and refused to meet her gaze. Emma began by deflecting questions about her injuries and turning the talk to her patients' lives. 'I'd like to hear about the future that each of you imagines for yourself. The dreams you have that you tell yourself will never come true. But still, you secretly hope for them. Finish this thought. In five years I'd like to be . . .'

The group members avoided each other's gaze, all too timid to put their dreams out where they could be publicly trashed.

Then the eyelashless Rachel meekly raised her hand.

'Rachel?' Emma said.

'Sometimes I think about becoming an aromatherapist.'

All the boys sniffed the air. And we're off, Emma thought.

Once the session was over, Emma fell into step with Kieran on the way to the front door.

'Glad you came today, Kieran,' she said.

He stopped. 'Uh, yeah,' he said. 'You leaving, Dr Webster?'

'Yeah,' said Emma. 'I'm still taking it a little bit easy.'

'You need a lift?' he asked, reddening slightly.

'You drove?' she asked, surprised. Most of the kids at the centre had lost their licences due to drug or alcohol problems.

'Oh yeah,' he said. 'I got my own car.'

'Well, thanks, Kieran, but my husband's coming for me.' Emma glanced at the magenta hair and the third eye. 'Don't speed,' she said.

13

DONNA TUTTLE, her black hair spiky, wearing a brown Henley shirt beneath a camouflage jacket, edged into Audie Osmund's tiny office. 'Chief, my son gave me your message. I was going to call, but then I figured I would just come on in.'

Audie sat up. 'Mrs Tuttle. So good of you to come. Sit right down. I want to show you a picture. How's your memory today?'

'Sharp as a tack,' she said, nodding her head.

'Be right back,' Audie muttered. He went out into the main room of the station house and rummaged on Gene Revere's desk for a manila folder. It held six photos—one of David Webster, the others of men somewhat similar in appearance. None of them was as square-jawed or good-looking, but they all had longish dark hair. That was the best Audie could do.

He carried the folder back into his office and set the six photos out in two rows on his desk, facing Mrs Tuttle. 'Now,' he said. 'I want you to look at these and tell me which man you spoke to at Zamsky's cabin that day you told me about.'

Donna Tuttle nodded solemnly, a citizen ready to do her part for truth and justice. She stood up and leaned over the desk, frowning as she picked up each of the photos and muttering to herself. Audie saw her pick up the photo of David Webster and stare at it. She tilted the photo back and forth, and then looked at Audie. 'He's a looker, isn't he?' she said. 'Looks like a movie star.'

'Is that the man you saw that day?' Audie asked.

Donna sighed and chuckled. 'Oh yeah. You don't forget a face like that.' She glanced again at the rogues' gallery, then shook her head. 'And, you know, I was thinking about it. You asked if he was alone, and I said I didn't see anybody.'

'Yeah?'

'Well, for some reason it bothered me. Like I hadn't exactly told the truth about it. But then I remembered. I did see a bra and a pair of women's panties on the porch railing. Like they'd been washed and hung out there to dry.'

Audie exhaled and sat back heavily in his chair.

David reached out a hand to help Emma down the steps of the Wrightsman Centre. He led her to the car and helped her in.

'How did it go with your mother?' she asked as he pulled out into the road.

'I got her home.' David sighed. 'She thinks I'm Phil.'

'Really?' Emma asked. 'A little confused?'

'Birdie was already pouring rum into her coffee when I left.'

'Into your mother's coffee?' Emma exclaimed.

'No. Her own. Although it might not hurt. My mother's heart needs a jump-start. This is a temporary respite.'

'Oh, honey, I'm sorry.'

David shrugged. 'Maybe a heart will come along.'

Emma glanced at him as he drove. She knew it had to bother him that his mother mistook him for his brother, even as he was trying to care for her, and her failing health had to be frightening. Emma admired his stoic attitude, but now she wondered. Was it more deception on his part? He admitted last night that he had trouble with the truth. Would she ever really know how he felt?

She shook her head. 'Let's go now and visit her,' she said.

It had not been difficult to locate the ticket sellers on duty Wednesday afternoon at the Clarenceville bus station. It was exactly the same crew that was working this Thursday afternoon. Earlier, Trey and Joan had entered Lizette Slocum's apartment with the aid of the landlord and picked up a photo of a smiling Lizette that they took with them to the bus station.

As one clerk after another asserted that they did not remember selling a ticket to Lizette Slocum, Joan got on the phone and asked the manager of the Toyota dealership to bring down skeleton keys for the year and model of Lizette's car. Eager to cooperate, the manager said he would be there shortly. Now Joan stood looking out at the brown Toyota in the parking lot as she waited for the results of Trey's last interview. He was meeting with the supervisor, going through surveillance tapes of Tuesday afternoon to see if Lizette Slocum appeared anywhere on them. The side door to the station opened, and a man with a moustache came in wearing a sports jacket and tie. 'I'm looking for Lieutenant Atkins,' he said.

Joan walked over to him. 'Are you Mr Vetri?'

'I am,' he said.

'I'm Lieutenant Atkins.' They shook hands.

Just then, Trey emerged from the supervisor's office. Joan looked at him questioningly. Trey shook his head.

Joan took a deep breath. 'All right. Let's open the car up.'

The three of them walked across the parking lot to the brown Toyota. The early twilight of November was beginning to descend. The manager tried several keys, and then they heard the locks click. He opened the driver's door and they looked inside. The car was not new, but it was extremely clean. Lizette Slocum was a person of tidy habits. Joan straightened up and looked across the roof at Trey.

'Mr Vetri, can you pop the trunk for us?' she said.

'Sure thing.' The manager found the key and put it into the lock, then pressed the lever and pulled it open. His eyes widened, and a look of anguish came over his face. 'Oh no,' he cried, as if he'd been deceived. 'Did you know she was in here?'

Lizette was curled up in the trunk, her rucksack thrown on top of her. Her eyes were open, and her skin was a splotchy grey.

Joan Atkins sighed. 'I was afraid she might be,' she said.

It was nearly five and the sky was charcoal grey when David and Emma returned to their cul-de-sac and headed down the street towards their house. Emma let out a groan of dismay as she recognised the unmarked police car parked in front of her home.

Lieutenant Atkins and Detective Marbery got out, slamming the doors. David sighed, pulled in the driveway, and came round to help Emma out of the front seat.

'We need to talk to you both,' Joan said. 'Let's go inside.'

'Of course,' said Emma.

David said nothing but led the way to the living room. 'What is it now, Detective?' he said as Emma took a seat.

'Several things. Number one, Mr Devlin's alibi checked out. He is no longer a suspect for the attack on your wife in the Pine Barrens or at the train station,' said Joan bluntly.

'What?' David cried. 'You let him go? You saw what he did to me and what he tried to do to Emma.'

'He's still under arrest for the sexual assault of his daughter.'

'Is there any question about his alibi?' Emma asked.

'None at all,' said Joan. 'It wasn't Devlin.'

Emma looked up at David from where she sat. David was raking his hand through his hair.

'That's not everything. Acting on a missing persons report, we began a search for Lizette Slocum, the nurse whom—'

'I know,' said Emma. 'Have you found her?'

'Yes, we found her,' said Joan grimly. 'We found her dead, stuffed in the trunk of her car, which was left at the bus station.'

'Oh no,' Emma said, as she felt her stomach start to churn. David came and sat down close to her.

'We're not yet sure how she died. We're waiting for the coroner's report. But Lizette Slocum was last seen alive in this house, taking care of you, Dr Webster. We are theorising now that the person who tried to kill you came here to attack you and found Lizette instead. Where were you at the time she disappeared?'

'I went downtown,' Emma said. 'When I came back, she was gone. I thought she left because I sneaked out without telling her.'

'We wasted precious time because we didn't know her disappearance was linked to you,' Joan said.

'It's not my wife's fault,' David protested.

'And what about you, Mr Webster? Where were you that day?' Joan asked.

'I was in New York. Doing an interview,' David said.

'We'll need to get in touch with that person,' said Trey.

'Well, I don't have a number for him. He's in Europe.'

'How inconvenient,' said Joan Atkins.

'You can call my editor. He'll tell you. I was with a French author named Bernard Weber.'

'I need dates, times and places,' Joan said loudly, 'and I need them right now.'

'If you talk to me in that tone of voice,' David said, 'I'm going to call my attorney.'

'Stop, David. Forget the attorney,' Emma cried. 'Just give her the information. That poor woman is dead.' She could see the fury on his face, but she didn't care. 'Why make this difficult?'

David went into his office. In a few minutes, he came back and handed the detective a sheet of paper. 'Here. Talk to everybody. Knock yourself out.'

Joan pocketed the paper. 'This investigation is ongoing, Mr Webster. Do not leave the state under any circumstances. Dr Webster, your life is in danger. I would recommend that you hire someone to protect you. Round the clock.'

'My husband found a bodyguard. We will call him.'

Joan Atkins looked at Emma with narrowed eyes. 'I'm not sure that's the wisest course of action. Why don't you let the local police advise you on who would be competent?'

'We don't need your advice, OK?' said David.

Joan turned and glared at him. 'I was talking to your wife. Call the station. The desk sergeant can help you.' She nodded to Trey, and the two of them headed for the door.

David sat on the sofa and clapped his head in his hands.

'I can't win,' he said. 'I'm back to being the prime suspect. They're determined to make a case against me.'

Emma sat back against the sofa cushions, stunned. 'That poor woman,' she said. 'She came here to take care of me and ended up dead. Who would want to kill me that badly?'

'I figured it was Devlin,' David said. 'Or maybe whoever sent you those notes. I don't know. But I have a sinking feeling that the cops are not going to believe Nevin, or even Mr Weber, if they get hold of him.'

Emma frowned at him. 'Now you're sounding paranoid, David. Your alibi is solid as far as Ms Slocum's death is concerned. Besides, they may find traces of DNA that lead to another suspect. Try not to worry.'

'Try not to worry,' he scoffed. 'The police are busy trying to work up a case against me while your life is in danger.'

'I know. But I still feel safe, as long as I'm with you.'

All of a sudden, the phone rang, and they both jumped. David hurried across the room and picked it up. 'Chief Osmund, yeah,' he said in a surly tone. 'You want to talk to my wife?'

He was listening intently. Then he looked at Emma, his eyes wide with astonishment. 'Really? Tonight? Where should we meet you? . . . Yes, we'll be there . . . OK.'

Emma stared at him as he hung up. 'What happened?'

David sat down beside her. 'Chief Osmund said there's been another attack in the Pine Barrens. Same everything. Ski mask. The works.'

Emma gasped and covered her mouth.

David nodded. 'This time, they think they've got him.'

'Can't it wait? We're almost there, honey,' David said.

'Obviously, you have never been pregnant,' Emma said.

'All right. All right. There's a gas station up ahead. They'll have a rest room. I'll get us some gas,' he said.

'Thanks, honey. Oh, David, I feel hopeful. If this is the guy, then this nightmare will finally be over.'

'I'd like to believe that,' David said, frowning. 'But you were a specific target. You haven't forgotten the attack at the train station?'

Emma shuddered. 'Hardly. But at least there's a chance.'

'We're going to be all right,' David said. He flashed her his sad-eyed smile, which always made her heart turn over.

'God, I can't wait until we have our lives back,' she said.

'Me neither,' he said. 'Here. We'll pull in here.'

Evening had come to the Pine Barrens, and Emma hoped it would be the last evening she would ever spend here. Chief Osmund wanted her to view their suspect in a hooded line-up to see if she could pick him out by his size and body language. Emma understood all too well how important this was to Chief Osmund. It was even more important to her. She looked around as David pulled into the service station. The jagged outlines of pines surrounded them, looming black against the moonlit sky.

There was a missing persons poster with a picture of a pretty girl on the pumps, as well as a sign that read THE ATTENDANT CARRIES NO MONEY. The man who came to the car window had hooded eyes and was lacking several teeth. 'What can I do for you?' he asked.

'Fill it,' said David.

Emma leaned across the seat. 'Excuse me. Do you need a key for the rest room?'

The man breathed through his mouth and studied her with a faintly hungry look. 'No, ma'am,' he said. 'Help yourself.'

Emma forced herself to smile. 'Thanks.' She grabbed her bag and climbed out of the Jeep.

'Want me to go with you?' David asked. 'I'll stand guard.'

Emma smiled, relieved. 'OK. It's so creepy around here.'

Together they walked to the side of the service station, and Emma turned the knob on the door marked LADIES. She steeled herself, but when she turned on the light, the rest room was neat and clean. She poked her head out.

'Civilised,' she said to her husband.

David smiled and jammed his hands into his pockets. His hair shone in the halogen lamplight, and Emma felt her love for him well up in her heart as he waited for her like a sentry. She locked the door. On the wall in front of her was the same missing persons poster that she had seen on the pumps outside. This time she was close enough to read it. It announced the disappearance of Shannon O'Brien from this very station several months ago, after finishing her shift. There was a blurry photo of the auburn-haired girl and a statement that anyone with information should contact Chief Audie Osmund at the police phone number shown.

Emma glanced at her watch. It had taken them a while to get going, and seeing the chief's number on the poster gave her an idea. I'll call him, she thought, to tell him we're almost there. She quickly relieved herself, washed her hands, and then fished in her bag for her phone and punched in the number.

'Police,' said a female voice.

'Yes. I want to talk to Chief Osmund. This is Emma Webster.'

'Can someone else help you? Chief Osmund isn't here.'

Emma frowned. 'Oh, there must be some mistake. We're meeting him there tonight. I just wanted to let him know we'd be arriving very soon. Would you just check in his office?'

'I'm telling you he's not here,' the woman said. 'And he's not coming back. His grandson has an awards dinner tonight. Audie was talking about it all afternoon.'

'But I was supposed to view a line-up tonight.'

'A line-up? Oh. Well, maybe Gene Revere is in charge of that. Hang on a minute.' Emma's heart was pounding. She heard the phone muffled. Then the woman got back on the line.

'Honey, Gene says there's no line-up tonight. He don't know what you're talking about.'

Emma's face was burning. 'Look. This is Emma Webster. I was attacked the night Claude Mathis was killed.'

'Oh,' said the woman. 'How are you doing now, honey?'

'I'm doing fine,' said Emma. 'Chief Osmund called and told my husband about the latest attack. He said they were holding the guy. There was going to be a line-up.'

'No,' said the woman. 'We didn't have no attack. Look, Mrs Webster, there's been some kind of mistake.'

Emma punched the OFF button on her phone and stood staring, unseeing, at the poster on the wall.

The rest room doorknob rattled. 'Emma, are you OK in there?' David asked. 'What's taking you so long?'

14

EMMA STARED at the rattling knob as if it were a hissing snake.

'Are you OK?' David called out. 'Emma, answer me.'

Emma's mouth was dry. 'I'm OK,' she managed to say.

'Hurry up, honey. Chief Osmund's waiting for us.'

Emma's knees felt like they were about to give way. 'Right there.' She groped for the basin and turned on the taps.

She tried to make sense of what she had just heard on the phone. Chief Osmund was not waiting for her. No one was waiting for her. It was all a lie. That phone call was not from Chief Osmund. David had said it was, but it wasn't.

'Who were you talking to in there?' David asked.

'No one,' she said. 'I'll be right out.'

She didn't know whether to cry or scream. The conclusion was obvious. Inescapable. Her husband was waiting on the other side of that door. Waiting to betray her. Or worse. Kill her. Her and their baby. David? Could it be David? The David she loved, and had promised her life to? Why would he do such a thing? It couldn't be. But a swirl of stern faces and warning voices warred for dominance in her head. No, she thought. He loves me. He couldn't. She leaned against the basin, clutching her stomach. No!

And then, in the midst of her terror and abject misery, she suddenly found another way to explain it. There was another possibility. Remote, but possible. Maybe David was a victim of this hoax, just as she was. Maybe whoever wanted to kill her had lured them both down here. After all, how many times had David talked to Chief Osmund? How well did he know his voice?

Yes, that had to be it. She was not alone, not betrayed, not her husband's intended victim. For a moment her heart sailed. And then it plummeted.

That's right, she thought. Be stupid all over again. Be trusting. Insist that you know better than the police because you are in love and believe in your husband no matter what.

The doorknob twisted again. 'Emma. What's going on? Is it the baby?' he asked.

Emma looked down at her stomach. Yes, she thought. It is the baby. The only one who is completely and utterly innocent in all this. And in mortal danger. Aloysius, I have to protect you. Your life depends on me. I can't trust anyone but myself.

Somehow, that thought, however horrifying, was also calming.

Call for help, she thought. Lieutenant Atkins. She fumbled in her bag, found the lieutenant's card, and punched in the number with trembling fingers. After two rings the voicemail answered. Oh hell, she thought. 'Lieutenant, it's Emma Webster. I'm in the Pine Barrens. I'm in trouble,' she whispered, hoping to be heard over the sound of the running water. She punched off the number and called 911. When the operator answered, she whispered, 'Help. I think my husband wants to kill me.'

'Where are you, ma'am?' the operator asked.

'At a gas station.'

'Where is the gas station?'

'I don't know,' Emma said helplessly.

'I can't hear you, ma'am . . . and I'm not getting any address. You're on a cellphone?'

'Yes. He's right outside,' whispered Emma.

'Emma, I don't believe you're all right,' David shouted. 'I'm gonna force open this door.'

Emma pushed the OFF button and dropped her phone in her bag. 'I'm fine,' she said, turning off the taps. 'Here I come.'

She opened the door. David was standing just outside.

'Are you OK? You look sick.'

She stared into his eyes, which were now, perhaps had always been, the eyes of a stranger. She had thought she knew that face, knew those eyes. Hadn't those hazel eyes mirrored her deepest feelings, shared them, sworn undying love and loyalty? She wavered in her heart, but her gut reminded her of all that was at stake. Only trust yourself. 'I'm fine,' she said. 'Just my nerves.'

'Well, I have to pay for the gas inside the mini-mart, and then we'll be on our way.'

'OK,' she said. He had to pay for the gas. He probably left the keys in the ignition. She could drive, whether she was supposed to or not. This was a matter of life or death.

David slipped his hand beneath her arm. 'Come with me,' he said. 'I don't want you out here by yourself.'

'I'm just going to the car to sit. I feel a little woozy.'

'Probably the smell from the pumps,' he said. 'Here, come inside. You know you hate the smell of gas, especially now that you're pregnant.' He knows me, she thought. He knows I like milk, no sugar, in my coffee, and he knows that I sleep on my side and that I love lily of the valley and hate the smell of gasoline. How could you know and indulge a person's every little habit and tic, and all the time be planning to kill them? How could it be?

He was steering her towards the lighted door, even though she was dragging her feet. She could yell at him, or try to run. But who would help her? Inside the mini-mart she could see a woman at the cash register. Maybe the woman would help her, she thought.

'Come on,' he said. 'What's the problem, Emma?'

'Nothing,' she said. 'No problem.'

His hand firmly gripping her elbow, he led her up to the counter. The woman was shouldering a phone, muttering into the receiver, and did not even look up as she checked the price of David's gas. Emma's heart sank. She looked around the little store and suddenly noticed a lighted EXIT sign in the back.

She withdrew her arm. 'I'll get a soda to settle my stomach.'

'I'll get it for you,' he said.

'Is this going to be credit or cash?' the woman snapped.

David turned to look at the cashier.

'I'll go grab something. I'll be right back,' said Emma.

Before he could reply, she started down the aisle, passing bags of crisps, cookies and Kleenex. She headed to the refrigerated cases at the back and pretended to look inside. Instead, she looked towards the EXIT sign. A hand-lettered sign posted beneath it at the entrance to the corridor read EMPLOYEES ONLY.

Emma took a deep breath. You have to do this, she thought. She bolted across the store, ducked into the corridor, and hurried past a rest room on the left. Then she saw the door leading outside.

Don't be locked, she thought. Please, God. She pressed on the waist-level bar, and the door opened with a clank. The gas station attendant came out of the rest room and saw her.

'Hey, you're not allowed back here,' he said indignantly as she stumbled out into the night.

Emma plunged through dry grass and weeds, stumbling over the empty plastic bottles and soda cans littering the overgrown lot behind the mini-mart. She headed towards the nearest bank of trees, grateful for the moonlight.

She knew she only had a few moments to get away, a few moments before her husband came after her. Why, David? her soul cried out, but immediately she stopped herself. Make a plan. Go into those trees. Once you're hidden, call the police again.

Panting, she reached the copse of fir trees. Her breathing was ragged from fear and the unaccustomed effort of running. She could feel the stitches pull in her side. Her skin felt fiery. She kept going, hiding herself in the cover of the trees.

From the direction of the service station, she heard a shout. It was her name. David had discovered she was gone. He was after her. Don't panic, she thought. He can't hear you from where he is. With trembling fingers she punched in the numbers on her cellphone, praying that Atkins would answer this time.

'Hello?'

Emma's heart leaped. 'Lieutenant Atkins?' she whispered.

'Speak up. I can't hear you. Who is this?'

She spoke aloud. 'It's Emma Webster. I'm in danger.'

'I got your message. Where are you?' Joan demanded.

'I'm hiding in a grove of trees. In the Pine Barrens.'

'What the . . . Where in the Pine Barrens are you?'

She wished she had paid more attention to the signs as they drove. 'I'm not sure. There's a service station right nearby.'

'What exit did you get off at? What kind of service station?'

Emma craned her neck, but she could not see the mini-mart sign. 'I don't know—' She gasped. David had walked round to the back and was calling her name.

'Ask them for help in the station,' Joan said in an agitated tone. 'Go in and tell them you're in danger.'

'I can't,' she said. 'He's there.'

'Who is it, Emma? It's your husband, isn't it?'

Emma was silent.

'Chief Osmund's witness picked your husband's photo out of a line-up, said he was in that cabin several months ago with a woman. Wasn't you, was it?'

Emma had to force back tears. 'No,' she whispered. As she clutched the phone, quivering, she watched David pick his way across the littered lot. Why did you do this to me? she thought.

'Emma, you have to give us some idea of where to find you.'

'I can't,' Emma croaked. And then, suddenly, she remembered. 'Lieutenant, there's a missing persons poster. A girl used to work at this station. Shannon O'Brien.'

'That's great, Emma!' Joan exclaimed. 'It'll take a few minutes, but stay on the line. We're coming to get you.'

'Thank you,' Emma whispered, her gaze fixed on David, who had stopped and looked towards the trees where she was hiding. He can't see you, she told herself. All he can see is darkness. But it was no use. He was starting to walk her way.

Emma dropped the phone in her bag and fled, crashing through the low branches and beginning to bleed from her broken sutures. She had no idea where she was running. She zigzagged through the trees, turning one way and then another, seeing only darkness all around. How would Lieutenant Atkins ever find her?

And then, up ahead, flickering through the pine needles, Emma saw something that made her feel faint with relief. The lights of a house. Someone was there. Someone to let her in until the police came. Please, God, she thought. Let me get there.

Ignoring the pain that seared her side, Emma pitched herself through the dense tangle of branches, using her arms to clear a pathway. As she made her way towards the light, she noticed that she no longer heard David's voice calling to her. Either he was in silent pursuit, a thought that filled her with dread, or he had given up chasing her. But she didn't have the time or the will to try to figure out his plan. She had her plan. That was all she could do. Once she got inside that lit-up house, she would find her phone and speak to Joan Atkins, tell her exactly where she was cached. Wait for rescue. The lights were closer, ever closer. She called on all her strength and thought of her baby.

Finally, she emerged at the edge of a clearing. The sight of the house up close, however, was not reassuring. Even in the moonlight it appeared dingy.

Emma hesitated. Suddenly, from a dark tin-roof shed, she heard a faint whinny. A horse. Something about a horse was comforting. Animals were gentle and could not betray you. Rather than knock at the door, maybe she should hide in the makeshift barn.

You're just being paranoid, she chided herself. So the people in this house aren't rich. That doesn't mean that they won't help you. Besides, they're nature lovers. That's usually a good sign. She had just about changed her mind, decided to knock at the door, when she suddenly heard the sound of wheels slowly coming up the gravel drive. She saw the flash of headlights, and her mind was made up. She bolted to the shed and dived inside, behind a bale of hay.

The horse tied up in the shed looked at her with its gentle eyes and made a snorting sound. 'Shhh . . .' Emma said. She rummaged in her bag for the phone and held it to her ear. 'Lieutenant Atkins?' she whispered.

There was no sound on the line. It was as if it had died somewhere along the way. Emma pushed every button, then shook the phone in frustration. All of a sudden she heard the sound of a car approaching. She looked out and realised that she had hidden herself just in time. The car that pulled into the clearing was their Jeep. Emma's heart hammered as David jumped out, walked to the front door of the house, and knocked. He peered around, as if suspecting her presence. Emma pulled herself back behind the hay bale.

In another minute she heard two male voices talking. She lifted herself up just far enough to glimpse David on the step, talking to a young guy wearing a baseball cap. He was silhouetted in the doorway by the light behind him, the brim of the cap pulled low on his head. David's voice was urgent as he gestured around the clearing, and Emma abruptly lowered her head. He's asking that kid if he's seen me. She heard the kid bawl, 'Mom,' into the house, but didn't hear if there was any reply.

The voices ceased, and then she heard the crunch of David's footsteps on pine needles. Was he coming to search the barn? Emma's heart was pounding so hard that she couldn't breathe. All of a sudden she heard the car door slam and the engine roar. The Jeep rolled back down the drive through the woods, towards the road.

Oh, thank God, Emma thought. He's gone. We're safe. She placed her hand on her belly and blessed her baby. Now that we know there's a woman in the house, we'll go up and ask for help.

Creeping out of the barn, Emma stayed in the shadows. She edged her way round the clearing, then rushed up to the front door and knocked.

The lock snapped back, and Donna Tuttle opened the door.

'Thank goodness,' Emma said. 'I'm sorry to bother you, but I'm desperate. I need your help,' she implored. Then she froze.

The woman's eyes were glacial. 'What a surprise,' she said.

Emma stared and shook her head, as if she did not trust what her eyes registered. She clutched the door frame to keep herself from sinking to the ground. 'You're alive?'

'I must be dreaming,' Emma said. Tears sprang to her eyes. 'Natalie, is it you?' Emma tried to take it in. It was Natalie, but not Natalie. Her red hair was dyed black, and she wore a shapeless plaid shirt. But she was alive, and Emma reached out to hug her friend. Natalie was wooden in her embrace, and Emma quickly released her.

She shook her head. 'I can't believe my eyes. And to find you here, in this godforsaken place.'

Natalie did not smile. 'It's not a coincidence. David's uncle's place is up the road. I assume that's where you were going.'

It crossed Emma's mind to wonder how Natalie knew where David's uncle lived, but it seemed unimportant. Emma stared at her friend, enjoying for a moment the unimaginable pleasure of seeing a loved one return from the grave. 'Do you realise that everyone thinks you're dead, Nat?' she asked.

A defiant look flickered across Natalie's beautiful face. 'I know.'

'What happened? Did you survive the fall?'

Natalie looked anxiously around the clearing. 'Come inside,' she said. She pulled Emma in and shut the door.

Emma studied her old friend: the lithe, strong body hidden by baggy clothes, the fine features and translucent skin, which glowed pearly even in the yellowy shaded lights of the dingy, unkempt house. 'Nat, why are you hiding out like this? Look, you shouldn't feel ashamed if you changed your mind about the suicide. It's wonderful. It's a miracle that you're still alive. Come home. Burke has been in mourning for you. We all have.'

'Oh, Emma,' said Natalie. 'I'd forgotten what you were like. Always the rock. No problem is too great for Emma.'

Emma felt the sting of Natalie's sarcasm, but her compassion welled up. 'Look, let me take you home. I'll help you.'

'You've got your own problems,' said Natalie.

Emma's heart constricted. 'What do you know about that?'

'Well, that attack on the night of your wedding happened just beyond those trees,' Natalie said.

For one moment, the shock of seeing Natalie had made Emma forget all about the fact that her life was in danger. 'It's true,' she said. 'David was just here. Did you see him? If you did, he must not have recognised you. He's . . . trying to find me.'

'Are you hiding from him?' Natalie asked.

'Yes. I think he's the one who's been trying to kill me. It's a long story. A nightmare. Who was it that answered the door to him, anyway?'

'A friend,' said Natalie.

'He called you "Mom",' said Emma.

'I'm not his mother,' Natalie said.

'So why . . .?'

'It's just easier this way,' Natalie snapped. 'But tell me more, Emma. If you need to escape from your husband, why don't you just disappear, like I did?'

'Why should I disappear?' Emma cried. 'No way. I'm not going to live on the run and hide. The police will get him for what he's done to me.'

Natalie gazed at her impassively. 'You're like a little policeman yourself,' she mused. 'Trying to maintain law and order.'

This time there was no mistaking the insult. 'At least I know right from wrong,' said Emma. 'What you're doing here is wrong. Letting Burke suffer, thinking you're dead.' A disquieting thought occurred to her. 'Wait a minute. Burke identified your body.'

'The great psychologist,' Natalie scoffed. 'He believed exactly what he was supposed to believe. He read my note, saw my car. When they found a decomposed body in the water with red hair, wearing my clothes, he made a positive ID.'

'Well, if it wasn't you, who was it?' Emma demanded.

'What does it matter? You don't know her,' Natalie said irritably. 'She worked in a gas station around here.'

Emma thought of the poster she had seen at the service station. The pale-skinned redheaded girl who had disappeared after her shift. 'Shannon O'Brien?' Emma cried.

Natalie looked at her warily. 'Well, very good, Emma.'

'You mean you put her in the river? Oh, Natalie, you didn't . . .'

Natalie's gaze was cool and blank. 'She was a drug addict. She was lying by the side of the road when I found her. Actually, when I found her, it gave me the idea. If everyone believed I was dead, it would be better. After all, the life of Natalie White, the poet, was over. My life was ruined. I figured that suicide would at least make my work more interesting.'

'Over? Ruined? What are you talking about? You were riding high. You just won the Solomon Medal.'

Natalie shook her head impatiently. 'They would have taken it away from me. My reputation would have been destroyed. I certainly wasn't about to go to jail. There was no other choice.'

'You're not making any sense,' Emma said.

'Oh, forgive me,' said Natalie sarcastically. 'I thought your husband might have told you how all that publicity backfired. You see, there was an accident last spring. An old man got run over. Some retired professor from the college.'

'Oh yes. I remember. It was a hit-and-run, wasn't it?'

Natalie shrugged. 'There was a witness. Some guy who was videotaping his girlfriend's comings and goings on that block. He videotaped the accident, but he never told the cops, because he didn't want his wife to find out. Anyway, he saw me on TV, and he recognised me from the videotape. He was blackmailing me.'

Emma stared at her. 'It was you? You were the driver?'

'He was old,' Natalie protested.

'You are so selfish,' Emma cried. 'It really doesn't matter to you, does it? None of it.'

Natalie glared at her. 'I'm selfish? You can say that? You, the girl with the perfect family. You don't know what I suffered in my life.'

'Oh, sure I do, Nat,' said Emma in disgust. 'Your terrible childhood. Everybody knew what you suffered. I listened to it a million times. Not know what you suffered? You never would let anyone forget.'

'Emma, you bitch!' Natalie pushed Emma with all her might. Emma fell to the grimy floor, and Natalie reached into a leather sheath under her flannel shirt and pulled out a hunting knife. Before Emma could rise, Natalie kicked her in the side. Emma felt the stitches split and the sticky spread of blood beneath her shirt.

'Now, get up,' Natalie commanded. Gasping for breath, Emma grabbed her throbbing side, astonished at the turn this bizarre reunion had taken. She thought of resisting, but the look in Natalie's eyes was terrible. It was a good bet that Natalie would use that knife on her at any moment. She had to cooperate. For a minute she thought of the other person, the man she had seen at the door in the baseball cap. Who was he, and where had he gone? Was he still here? Maybe she could appeal to him, whoever he was, to help her.

'Get up!' Natalie shrieked, poking Emma in the shoulder with the knife. Emma scrambled to her feet. Natalie pressed the knife's tip to Emma's throat. 'Go,' she said. They passed from the garbage-littered kitchen to a small bedroom with nothing in it but a rumpled, unmade bed, a straight-backed chair and a bureau.

'Sit,' Natalie commanded, banging the chair down in the middle of the room. Emma sat down, and Natalie opened a drawer, grabbed a length of rope, and looped it around her, making knots as she went.

Emma tried to keep her arms as far from her torso as possible as Natalie trussed her to the chair. 'Why are you doing this to me, Natalie?' she demanded. 'I never hurt you. I've been your friend through all of it, all these years. Even on my wedding day, I wished you were with me.'

Natalie's eyes blazed. 'Oh yeah. I really hated to miss that. Your wedding.'

Emma looked at Natalie and suddenly felt a new fear, blooming like a black rose in the middle of her chest. 'Wait a minute. You said earlier you thought David might have told me about the hit-and-run.'

'But he didn't, did he?' said Natalie.

'How could he have known about that?'

A sly grin spread across Natalie's face. 'You really don't know, do you? He kept our secret.'

'What secret?'

'Well, think about it. Who do you think I would call for help?'

'Your husband,' Emma said. 'Burke.'

Natalie rolled her eyes. 'Burke. Oh, sure. Mr Pure-as-the-driven-snow? He'd be all sympathy.'

'Burke adored you.'

'His wife, the poet. I was a prop in his perfect little universe. The brilliant, beautiful wife who required a bit of psychological fine-tuning. He couldn't have coped with the thought of his precious bride as a killer. No. I told a friend. A friend who I used to meet for afternoon delights at your little honeymoon cabin.'

'You and David.'

'Oh yes,' said Natalie.

'He wouldn't have kept that from me,' Emma protested weakly.

'But he did. Didn't he.'

'Yes,' she whispered.

Emma felt as if she couldn't breathe, couldn't catch her breath. It was as if no air would enter her body. She pictured David there, with Natalie, in that honeymoon hideaway, adulterous lovers trysting in the very cabin where he had carried Emma over the threshold to their new life. The cabin where she'd been slashed by an axe. The place where he had tried to kill her.

The cruel thought pierced her, and she let out a moan. She knew what it was to wish to die.

15

NATALIE'S EYES WERE ALIGHT. 'You didn't know, did you? He kept our secret. You didn't know he was mine. That he loved me.'

The door to the bedroom banged back, and a young man stood framed there, his eyes black with rage. He had taken off his Eagles cap. Emma saw the shock of magenta, the third eye. 'Stop it!' he cried. 'Stop talking about him like that. He's not here to help you. He's gone. I'm the one who loves you. What about me?'

'Kieran!' Emma stared at him.

'Get out of here,' Natalie said.

'You're mine. You said so. Why do you talk about him all the time?'

'Calm down. Let's talk out there,' Natalie said.

Kieran's eyes were frantic. 'I've done everything you wanted. Why do you have to torture me? I thought we were going to get away from here. Why did you let her in? Why did you tell her?'

'She needs to know. She thinks I'm lying, Kieran.'

Kieran shook his head. 'You said you were through talking about him. You promised.' He flung himself into the other room.

'Kieran,' Natalie cried, rushing after him. 'Baby, don't.'

Emma could hear the sound of their voices rising and falling from the living room. She did her best to make out the words. 'Of course I do, baby,' Natalie crooned. Emma strained to hear David's name. To punish herself by catching every reference to him, to imagine him with Natalie, betraying her.

'I've had enough,' Kieran wailed. 'When will it be over?'

Suddenly it was quiet in the other room. What's going on? Emma thought. Kieran, that misguided, messed-up kid—had he known all along that Natalie was alive? Emma remembered his tortured lyrics, his loneliness. She remembered that he showed his lyrics to Natalie.

How had they got from there to here? From cookies and gentle criticism to this godforsaken hovel in the woods? Emma's head was reeling from the unexpected, but one thing she knew for sure. This situation was volatile and dangerous. The first order of business was to get away from them.

There was no way to get to the phone. It was in her bag, in the room where Natalie had pushed her over. Besides, there had been no reception. She tried to figure out a means of escape. There was one multi-paned window, which looked as if it had not been opened in years. First things first, she thought. You have to get out of these ropes.

She thought of her baby, not yet born, who needed to live. I will not let them kill us, Aloysius. She contracted every muscle, pulled her arms close, and felt the ropes loosen, but not by much. She did the same with her legs. How long will this take? she thought. How long do I have?

She began to work the bonds as best she could, expanding and contracting her muscles to create wiggle room. It was slow and painful, and she kept one ear on the murmurs and shouts that were coming from the other room. And all of sudden, she had an idea. Maybe if she looped the rope on her wrists around one of the knobs on the low bedposts, she could prise the rope loose. Hunching her shoulders, she leaned forward and lifted the chair off the floor. Balancing it on her back, she scuffled over to the bed and was able to lean back and set it down.

She glanced at the door, but there was no sign that anyone had heard her. Now, she thought. She raised herself up, chair and all, lifting her tethered hands to swing them over the knob. But because she could not see behind her, she missed and toppled to the floor. She lay there on her side, every muscle aching from the fall.

She could hear the door open, though she could not see it.

'She fell over,' she heard Kieran say.

'Leave her like that,' Natalie said.

Emma felt tears spring to her eyes, both from pain and from hopelessness. Clumps of dust from under the bed tickled her face and seemed to suffocate her. She stared, unseeing, at a mound of dark clothing stuffed under the bed. A fleece hood and sleeves, and something else. It took Emma a moment to recognise it. A knitted ski mask. Black. With red rims around the eyeholes.

Emma jerked back and stifled her own scream.

The clothes of her attacker, both here, in the Pinelands, and at the station.

I've done everything you wanted, Kieran had said.

What did you do, Kieran? Was it you who tried to kill me? Or Natalie? What about David? she thought, confused. One of them wore those clothes.

She thought of the two people conspiring in the other room. One she had called a patient, the other a friend. Emma felt weak at the thought of that much hatred aimed at her from people she had cared for. You did nothing to deserve it, she reminded herself. Don't let them defeat you. Think of your baby.

Using her feet, she pushed herself away from the bed, scuttling backwards. When her chair hit the wall, she was jarred from head to toe. She began to rock backwards carefully until the chair felt anchored, then slowly she worked the chair upright. When at last she was seated, she was gasping for breath.

From outside the house, she heard a faint, familiar sound. A whinny. Not once. But several times. Could the horse possibly be alert to someone else in the area? Could the police have found their way to her? Hoping against hope, she looked out of the window.

She almost screamed. A man looked back at her, his face pressed to the grimy pane, his sad hazel eyes filled with horror at the sight of her.

'**S**top,' Joan Atkins cried. 'What's that?'

Audie Osmund, summoned by his dispatcher from the awards dinner, had joined the search. Gathering up a half a dozen men, he had met Joan and Trey Marbery at the service station that Emma had described. 'She sure was in a hurry,' the attendant had said, pointing out the back door to them. And so they began to hunt for Emma.

Audie felt sure she must have left a trail. How far could she get in her condition—an injured, pregnant woman? Several officers started out on foot, but Audie, who knew the dirt roads around there, offered to drive.

Now Joan sat tensely beside him in his truck, while Trey had folded himself into the narrow space behind the front seat. With the headlights on bright, they began to drive through the woods. Every ten seconds, Joan would try Emma's cellphone again but to no avail.

All at once Joan saw something. 'Over there!' she cried.

Audie frowned. 'That's the road to the uncle's place,' he said, peering towards Zamskys'. Through the darkness of the trees, he did think he saw something.

'A light?' Joan asked. 'Is that from the house?'

Audie shook his head. 'Too faint for that.'

'You're right,' said Joan. It was even fainter than the glow of a flashlight in the night. And unlike a flashlight, it was fixed. It had about the intensity of a single weak bulb. 'Let's go see about it,' she said. 'It will only take a minute to check.'

Pulling the truck off the road, Audie hopped out, gripping his long-handled flashlight like a weapon. Joan and Trey jumped out of the cab and began to walk up the rutted dirt path. 'Emma!' Joan cried out. 'Can you hear us?'

The light source was just past a curve in the drive. They rounded the curve, and then they saw it.

A car was stopped in a clump of pines, tipped nearly on its side off the dirt shoulder. The front passenger door hung open, and the inside light had come on. The car looked empty.

Joan approached cautiously, drawing her gun. There was definitely something ominous about this abandoned car with an open door. Who would leave it there? All of a sudden she heard a faint sound. A human voice, groaning.

Emma, she thought.

Wielding his flashlight, Audie began to run.

'Who's there?' Trey cried. 'Mrs Webster, is that you?'

The car was a silver late-model Lexus. In the back window was a parking sticker for the Wrightsman Centre. As they reached the vehicle, they realised that the car door was propped open by a human body that had fallen halfway out, and was wedged against the low-lying branches of the pines that crowded the edge of the road.

Joan climbed in, lifting the man's upper body. Burke Heisler's face was barely recognisable for the blood, and his half-closed eyes had a milky gleam.

'Dr Heisler!' she cried. 'What happened to you?' It looked as if the man had been beaten savagely and propped up in the driver's seat. The weight of his slumped body must have pushed open the door. Or he had somehow managed to open it himself in an effort to escape.

Audie unhooked his radio from his belt and called for help.

'Dr Heisler, hang in there. Help is on the way,' said Joan.

There was no response. The psychiatrist's breathing was extremely shallow. 'What happened?' Joan said softly, not expecting an answer.

Burke's eyelids fluttered. 'Natalie,' he whispered.

'That's his wife,' said Trey, who was on the other side of Burke, propping him up. 'The one who killed herself.'

'Alive,' Burke whispered. 'In these woods. Help Emma.'

Emma swallowed the cry that rose to her throat. David, she thought. He brought a finger to his lips, warning her to be silent. She pleaded with him with her eyes, and he nodded slightly. He had come back. Why? What could have made him come back? She nodded to him and then turned her head quickly, looking to the bedroom door, which had begun to scrape against the floor.

Her heart hammered as she saw them enter.

'How did you get over there?' said Natalie with a frown.

Emma glared at this woman whom she had loved and then mourned. 'I saw the clothes under the bed.'

Natalie did not try to pretend that she did not understand. 'I should really throw them away. I won't need them again.'

'It was you who tried to kill me. Why?' Emma said.

'So he'd go to jail for it. My parting shot for the traitors.'

'You and David were the traitors,' Emma said.

Natalie shrugged. 'You weren't satisfied with being a little rich girl. You had to take what was mine. David was mine.'

'Don't say that,' Kieran muttered.

'And the nurse? Why did you kill her?' Emma cried.

'Kieran killed the nurse,' Natalie said.

'Don't tell her,' Kieran cried.

'Why not? She won't be alive to tell. Kieran was supposed to kidnap you, but she answered the door. He panicked and hit her. Not very smooth, but—'

'You were glad I did it,' he protested.

'Kieran, why do this to me?' Emma pleaded. 'We've talked so many times at the centre. In the group.'

Natalie laughed. 'He killed Burke too. He does whatever I say.'

'Burke!' Emma felt as if her heart was being shredded.

'Somehow Burke suspected I wasn't dead. I don't know how.'

Immediately, Emma thought of the autopsy report lying on the front seat of Burke's car.

'Burke was poking around up at the Zamsky house when I stumbled across him. Luckily, Kieran was there to help.'

'You don't care what happens, do you, Natalie?' Emma asked.

'She cares. She cares about me. She and I are going away together,' Kieran said. 'And never be apart.'

Emma looked at him sadly. 'Oh, Kieran, you don't believe that, do you? She's just using you, and then she'll throw you away.'

He was holding the knife, and Natalie was behind him, an excited smile in her eyes and on her lips. He turned and looked at Natalie, his young eyes full of pain. 'That's not true,' he retorted.

'She's just stalling,' Natalie said. 'She knows she's going to die.'

'It's not too late for you, Kieran. Don't do what she says,' Emma pleaded. 'The police are coming. You won't get out of this.'

He turned back to Emma, and she saw his eyes. There was a flicker of fear there. Just a flicker, but it gave her a moment's hope.

'She doesn't love you, Kieran. She doesn't love anyone,' Emma insisted.

'She does love me. From the first time I showed her my songs, she realised I was a genius.'

What Emma had to do was cruel, but she had no choice. Divide and conquer. 'Kieran, I hate to tell you this, but she made fun of your songs. She said they were simple and pathetic.'

Kieran's eyes widened, and when he turned them on Natalie, his face seemed ragged with doubt. 'You told me I was a genius.'

'She's making it up,' Natalie said. 'Don't listen to her.'

Kieran turned and slapped Emma's face. Her head jerked back. 'You're a liar,' he said.

Emma's face burned. 'I'm not lying,' she insisted.

'What are you waiting for?' Natalie cried. She snatched the knife from his hand, jabbing it in the air.

'Natalie, for God's sake,' Kieran said. 'Give that to me.'

'If you can't do it, I will. You can't do it, can you?'

'I can, and I will. Give me the knife,' he said.

Natalie raised the knife with both hands. 'Are you too weak, Kieran?'

'Of course not,' he said, trying to reach for her, to embrace her.

Natalie held him off, jabbing the air around him with the knife.

Kieran ignored the blows she was trying to inflict on him and grabbed at her wrists. 'I love you. I have no life without you, Natalie. Of course I'll kill her for you.'

Natalie lowered the knife warily. His back to the door, Kieran pulled her close. Natalie encircled his ungainly body with her arms, the knife still in her hand. Kieran pressed his defaced forehead into her shoulder.

Natalie looked past him to the door. 'David!' she exclaimed.

Kieran stepped back, eyes blazing, and threw off her embrace. The knife fell to the floor. Kieran grabbed her by the neck and began to throttle her. 'No!' he cried. 'Stop it! Stop wishing I was him.'

David sprang across the room, wielding a tyre iron, and whacked it across Kieran's back. The boy's grip on Natalie loosened. He staggered and cried out.

David did not hesitate. He struck a blow at Kieran's shoulder that glanced off the side of his head. Kieran crumpled to the floor.

Natalie was staring at David.

David crouched down and picked up the knife. Kieran was unconscious, a bruise blackening the side of his face. David stood up. Emma watched him, her heart in her throat. He looked at Natalie. Then he turned and cut Emma's bonds and handed her the knife. In that instant,

Natalie understood. She threw herself at him, clawing at his face, pummelling him with her fists.

David lifted the tyre iron. 'Natalie, don't make me kill you. I promise you, if I hit you with this thing, I will kill you.'

Natalie stopped for a moment and stepped back, eyes wide. Emma raised the knife, ready to plunge it into Natalie if she came one step closer, but Natalie did not notice. She was gazing at Emma's husband.

'How did you know I was here?' Natalie asked.

David returned her gaze coldly. 'I was searching for Emma. When I came to the door, I knew there was something familiar about the boy. I was driving away, and I kept thinking I had seen his face. It was the hat that threw me off. Hiding his pink hair and tattoo. And then I remembered. The boy with the three eyes. From the Wrightsman Centre.'

'I told Emma about us, David. She didn't know.'

David's face reddened. 'There's nothing to tell,' he said dully. 'It was a meaningless affair.'

'Meaningless? You loved me!' she cried.

'I never loved you,' David said.

'You did!' Natalie cried. 'You did, and you know it.' She looked at Emma with loathing. 'He couldn't get enough of me.'

'I don't want to know,' Emma said.

Natalie glared at David. 'Did you mourn for me?' she cried. 'Did you weep over my grave?'

David shook his head. 'Weep for you? Hardly. I thought it was justice, although you took the coward's way out. You ran over that old man. You got out of the car to make sure he was dead, and then kept on going.'

'Were you with her when it happened?' Emma cried, horrified.

David shook his head. 'No. I didn't even know about it until the guy with the videotape contacted her. I had already met you, and broken it off with her, but she called me and pleaded with me. Said she had a horrible problem and only I could help.'

'And you helped her?' Emma asked.

'I told her to turn herself in,' he said. 'Or I would.'

'You didn't give a damn about helping me,' Natalie said.

'You killed a man, Natalie,' said David.

Natalie shook her head. 'You make it sound so righteous. Tell the truth, David. You wanted me to turn myself in so I'd be out of the way and you could marry this heiress for her money. Did you think I would just go away quietly and let you get away with that? I asked you for help and you betrayed me. Whose crimes are worse?'

Outside the house, cars were roaring into the clearing and doors were slamming. Emma could hear Chief Osmund yelling for his men. She knew she should feel elated, but all she could feel was numb. 'The police are here,' she said.

David looked sadly at Emma, who turned away from his gaze. Then he looked back at Natalie. 'Your crimes are worse. But tell that to my wife, who will not look at me. And to my best friend, whom I did betray.'

'Burke is dead,' Emma said. 'They killed him.'

'No!' David protested.

'That's what they said,' said Emma.

David blanched and seemed to sway. 'He was never anything but good to you, Natalie. He did everything to help you.'

'He kept me prisoner in his little well-ordered world, with his theories and medications and his KISS THE COOK aprons. I was dying living with him. I told you that the first time we were together. Remember?'

'David,' Emma said, recoiling. 'My God.'

'I remember,' said David. 'I remember thinking at that moment that my friend Burke was too good for you. That I should walk away from you and never look back.'

'But you didn't!' she cried triumphantly. 'Did you?'

David shook his head. 'No, I didn't.'

There was a pounding on the door. 'Police!' yelled Audie Osmund.

'Come in!' Emma cried, gripping the knife tighter and holding it high, ready to strike if she had to. 'We're in here.'

'Save me,' Natalie whispered to David, stepping over Kieran's limp body on the floor. Her cheeks were flushed, her alabaster skin beaded in sweat.

Emma looked at him, wondering what he felt, wondering how she could have known him so little. His face was expressionless.

'Never,' David said. 'Not even if I could.'

It was after midnight when they were finished, for the time being, with the police, the hospital and the press. Natalie was in jail, held without bail. Kieran was treated at the hospital, and then he too was arrested and held in jail. Burke was in intensive care, but conscious. He told the police he began to suspect that Natalie was not dead when Emma received the shell dish as a wedding present. The autopsy results confirmed that he had identified the wrong body. And he had gone in search of his wife. With dire results.

David and Emma had given their statements, advised by Mr Yunger.

They had run the gauntlet of reporters. Now, finally, they were home. David unlocked their front door and held it open as Emma slowly and painfully made her way inside.

Emma walked to the door of the living room and leaned against the door frame as David went around switching on the amber glass table lamps. The room was relatively tidy, thanks to the late Lizette. Once, Emma and David had imagined themselves on cold nights like this cuddled in front of their fireplace, the room illuminated by the colour of the glass. But now, even in the warm amber glow, the room did not beckon her.

'Come and sit down,' David said.

Emma felt too exhausted to protest. She went over to the sofa and sat down in the corner, against a tapestry cushion.

'Can I get you anything?' he asked.

She shook her head. 'I feel like we've been gone for years.'

'I know,' he said.

She studied him for a moment. 'Did you ever suspect?' she asked.

'Never,' he said. 'I'm ashamed to admit this, but I had really begun to think that it might be Burke.'

'Burke?' she cried.

'I didn't know what to think. The notes at your job. I thought he might have found out about my affair with his wife. I was becoming pretty paranoid.'

'Poor Burke,' Emma said.

'I know. But they think he'll be OK.'

Emma shook her head. 'How is he supposed to ever recover from this? The shock. The betrayal . . .'

They were silent for a moment. 'I don't know,' David said. 'We all have to recover.'

'Somehow,' she said.

'Tomorrow we'll start over again. Start fresh.'

'I've been thinking,' she said. 'I think I'll go to Chicago and stay with my mother for a while.'

'Why?' he said, staring straight ahead.

'Because I feel like I need to get away.'

'From me,' he said.

'Just get away. David, I don't want to argue. I'm too tired.'

'From our marriage,' he said accusingly.

'What marriage?' she snapped.

For one second she looked at him balefully, directly in the eye. She saw that she had wounded him. In a way, she was glad. In a hollow way.

She looked down at her hands, flexing them in her lap. 'Look, I am grateful to you for coming after me. And I don't blame you for what Natalie tried to do. She's mentally ill, and she's cruel. I owe you my life, David. I'll never forget that.'

'Well, that's really touching,' he said bitterly. 'Considering that you assumed I was trying to kill you.'

Emma straightened up. 'What would you have thought if you were me?' she demanded. 'I couldn't take a chance with my baby's life. If you're insulted, well, I'm sorry. I didn't see myself as having a lot of choices.'

'I know,' he said.

They sat tensely side by side. Emma was aware of her heart aching. A little part of her wanted to say so, but David might interpret that to mean everything was all right. And it wasn't.

'Tell me what you're thinking,' he said at last.

Emma did not reply.

'We're not going to make it if you don't tell me,' he pleaded.

'I can't understand how you justified it, taking the wife of your closest friend for a lover.'

David flinched but did not look away. 'I wanted to,' he said.

Tears sprang to her eyes. 'That's great, David,' she said.

David drew in a deep breath. 'I could say she seduced me, but I'm not a teenager. I wanted her, and I thought . . . I don't know.' He exhaled. 'I wish I could tell you how I agonised over it. But in the end, I did it.'

'He was your dearest friend.'

'He was more like a brother. Complete with rivalry. As a kid, I always envied him. That's not an excuse, by the way.'

Emma was silent.

'What else are you thinking?' he asked.

'Isn't that enough?' she cried.

'Yeah,' he said. 'But it's not all.'

She didn't want to say it, because deep in her heart, she suspected that Natalie must have been lying. But even a lie can fester. 'She said you still loved her. Even though you married me.'

David stared at her, silently insisting that she meet his gaze. Finally, she acquiesced. 'Do you believe that?' he asked.

She said nothing.

'Look. I'm not going to tell you all about my affair with Natalie, Emma. Neither one of us is a masochist. But she killed a man. How can you think I ever loved her?'

'But you wanted her enough to betray your friend.'

'I acted like a pig,' he said.

'And with me? What was it with me?'

'Emma. You know what it was. What it is. Surely you haven't forgotten us. Emma, I am just not that good an actor. You know?'

Emma thought of all their days and nights together. The way their bodies met, heart and soul. 'I know. I'm just so mad at you. For not being what I thought you were.'

'Honourable?' he asked.

Tears came to her eyes again, and she let them fall.

David sighed. 'You know, when you started to get those crazy letters, I actually thought for a moment that they sounded like something Natalie would write. But then I thought, Natalie is dead. I wasn't even capable of imagining what she did.'

'Were those her letters in the locked drawer?'

David nodded. 'Yes. After I broke it off, she kept sending them to me. They were . . . fascinating. In a repulsive sort of way.'

'I can imagine,' Emma said glumly.

'Emma, it's over now. You don't need to go to your mother's.' He slid right beside her on the sofa and carefully put his arm round her. 'We need to start our marriage over. Get ready for our baby. We need to prove that Natalie did not destroy our dream.'

Emma shook her head helplessly.

'Look, I'm not any good at this,' he said. 'All my life I despised my father, and I acted just like him. I've always been good at leaving, not staying. But when I made those wedding vows to you, I said them from the heart. They were for you, and our baby too. You're the smart one, Em. Help me figure out how to do this.'

His face was near hers, and his eyes searched hers. She looked away, at the blackness outside the windows, and thought of spring, when the baby would be born. How she longed for those endless pale blue evenings. 'Did you sleep with her again, after we met?'

'No,' he said.

Yes. No. What did it really prove? she wondered. How could you ever really know?

'I did not betray you, Emma. I will never betray you.'

'How can I believe you?' She looked at him, wondering.

'I can't tell you that,' he said.

'Swear it,' she said. 'Swear it on our baby's life.'

David hesitated. Then he shook his head. 'No. I won't. Leave our baby out of it. This is between you and me.'

To her surprise, his words filled her with relief. She realised that she had posed him an impossible condition. After all, it was the nature of lovers to promise to be true. But a parent, a father, did not barter his child's life to get his way. In denying her request, he had actually convinced her it might be possible to try again. There was no going back to the innocent bliss of her wedding day. She would have to mourn that loss for a while.

Emma sighed. 'I think maybe if I just spend some time away from you, go to my mother's, it might help. I need time to think.'

'No, Em. Think here. I'll give you all the room you want. But this is no time to be apart.' He picked up her left hand, where her gold band glinted. 'For better or for worse.'

She looked at her hand in his. 'That is what we promised.'

'We're due for some "better",' he said. 'Can we start over?'

She frowned, wondering if they could. He was not the prince she had imagined him to be. She knew that it was foolish to imagine any man a prince. But all the same, she had.

He lifted her fingers to his lips. 'We can make it, Em,' he said. 'If you can forgive me and let us try again, we can make it. The three of us. You, me and our baby.'

'The three of us,' she said, imagining her baby safely sleeping inside of her. She did want to believe they would be a family. That was why she married him in the first place. He was no prince, but a man, like any other. Their life would not be perfect, but it was the life she wanted. Forgiveness was a good place to start. She hesitated, and then made her choice. She reached out and ran her fingertips down the side of his face. And in her heart, she prayed for grace.

RD Exclusive with Patricia MacDonald

What triggered the idea for *Married to a Stranger*?

Like most Americans, I watched the unfolding of the Laci Peterson case with fascination. [Laci Peterson was the subject of one of the most discussed missing-person cases in United States history, after she went missing while eight months pregnant with her first child. Laci was last seen alive on December 23, 2002. Her husband, Scott Peterson was eventually convicted of her murder and is currently on death row at San Quentin Prison.] It was impossible to see the photos of the beaming, pregnant Laci and her handsome husband and not wonder about that relationship. How could she have been so deceived? What role did self-delusion and denial play in her terrible fate? How could appearances veer so far from reality? As an author, I wanted to think about these questions.

Much of the action in *Married to a Stranger* takes place in the Pine Barrens. Why did you set it there?

It has always seemed wonderful and strange to me that a wilderness like the Pine Barrens should exist in New Jersey, the most densely populated state in the union. I visit the Pinelands from time to time and always feel as if there are hostile eyes watching me from the woods. Then again, my imagination tends to run away with me!

***Married to a Stranger* falls into the 'woman in peril' genre of mystery story. Is there anything that particularly draws you to this genre or to mysteries in general?**

I am always drawn to stories of an ordinary life turned upside down by a violent event. I don't think of my heroines as victims, but as people who struggle to take charge of their lives after some horror befalls them.

How did you get started in your career as a writer?

Before I became a writer, I worked as an editor of a magazine about television soap operas. It was a job I loved, and I would probably be there still, but our parent company closed the magazine down. One of my freelance writers suggested that we collaborate on a *roman-à-clef* about the soap opera world.

I had never written fiction before, but it seemed like something fun to do while I was unemployed. Together we wrote fifty pages and then showed it to several literary agents. No one found our story of interest, but those fifty pages did eventually lead me to the literary agent who still represents me to this day. You never know!

You're a best-selling author in France as well as in the United States. Why do you think the French are such enthusiastic fans of your work?

Go to any French movie and you'll notice that the French like their fiction low-tech and grounded in everyday life. That describes my books to a T. They also eschew violence and share my interest in the psychology of crime. But there is still that indefinable *je ne sais quoi* that makes it a love match between us. I can't really explain it. I always say that I must gain something in translation.

Can you tell us a little about your family?

My husband is the author of seven books and also owns a bookstore in Philadelphia. He is my first reader and best critic. We've been married for twenty-three years, and I still find him the wisest, most insightful and funniest person I know. Our daughter is an avid reader, dancer, musician and actress. Being her mother has been the greatest delight of my life.

What goals do you have for the future?

For a suspense writer, there is always the dream of the perfect story—an utterly surprising and satisfying plot that needs scarcely any explanation. I'll keep on trying!

The Hoodle-Doodle Bird

When **Married to a Stranger**'s heroine, Emma, sees the candlelight flicker in her isolated cabin in the New Jersey Pine Barrens, she wonders whether the disturbance could be caused by the legendary Jersey Devil. This creepy creature, said to haunt the bogs and forests of the Pinelands, is often described as roughly four feet long and having the head of a horse, the wings of a bat and the tail of a rat. Eyewitnesses say that, from a distance, it resembles a crane, with its curved back and awkward two-footed gait, and that it emits a high, humanlike scream. But despite its whimsical nicknames—including the Hoodle-Doodle Bird and the Wozzle Bug—its appearance is no laughing matter to the people who claim to have seen it.

Legend traces the creature's origins to the mid-1700s, when one Mrs Leeds, a resident of southern New Jersey, became pregnant with her thirteenth child. In despair, she cried, 'I don't want any more children! Let it be a devil!' At that point the baby, horribly deformed, supposedly crawled from the womb and into the woods, feeding on children and animals and terrorising the populace.

Sightings continued sporadically until 1909, when, incredibly, more than a thousand people claimed to have seen the monster in one week in January. There was another flurry of sightings in 1951; after that, the last recorded sighting occurred in 1966.

But the legend lives on—in films, books, music, television, and on the Internet. Everyone, it seems, loves a good scary story!

The right to be identified as authors has been asserted by the following in accordance with sections 77 and 78 of the Copyright, Designs and Patents Act, 1988: Jane Green, Carmen Reid and Patricia MacDonald.

PICTURE CREDITS: COVER: © Getty/Image Bank. Jane Green photograph and page 164 © Ian Philpott. Carmen Reid photograph and page 334 © Martin Hunter. Patricia MacDonald photograph and page 478 © Steve Oliva. SECOND CHANCE: pages 6 & 7: © Corbis. THE PERSONAL SHOPPER: pages 166 & 167 cover illustration © Masaki/CWC International. Hand lettering © Ruth Rowland. MARRIED TO A STRANGER: pages 336 & 337 © Stanislaw Fernandes.

ACKNOWLEDGMENTS: SECOND CHANCE: 'Goodbye My Friend' on page 44 © 1988 Seagrape Music.

Printed and bound by GGP Media GmbH, Pössneck, Germany

601-043 UP0000-1